I0592382

Andrew Richard Scoble, Philippe de Commines

The Memoirs of Philip de Commines, Lord of Argenton...

Vol. I

Andrew Richard Scoble, Philippe de Commines

The Memoirs of Philip de Commines, Lord of Argenton...
Vol. I

ISBN/EAN: 9783337047948

Printed in Europe, USA, Canada, Australia, Japan

Cover: Foto ©Raphael Reischuk / pixelio.de

More available books at **www.hansebooks.com**

PUBLISHED BY

DICTIONARY

LANGUAGE.

...ions of the above celebrated
*Dictionary are those here described : no other Editions
published in England contain the Derivations and Etymological Notes of Dr. Mahn, who devoted several years to this
portion of the Work.* See Notice on page 4.

WEBSTER'S GUINEA DICTIONARY

OF THE ENGLISH LANGUAGE. Thoroughly revised and improved
by CHAUNCEY A. GOODRICH, D.D., LL.D., and NOAH PORTER, D.D.,
of Yale College.

The peculiar features of this volume, which render it perhaps the most useful
Dictionary for general reference extant, as it is undoubtedly one of the cheapest
books ever published, are as follows:—

1. **Completeness.**—It contains 114,000 words—more by 10,000 than any other Dictionary; and these are, for the most part, unusual or technical terms, for the explanation of which a Dictionary is most wanted.

2. **Accuracy of Definition.**—In this department the labours of Dr. Webster were most valuable, in correcting the faulty and redundant definitions of Dr. Johnson, which had previously been almost universally adopted. In the present edition all the definitions have been carefully and methodically analysed by W. G. Webster, Esq., the Rev. Chauncey Goodrich, Prof. Lyman, Prof. Whitney, and Prof. Gilman, with the assistance and under the superintendence of Prof. Goodrich.

3. **Scientific and Technical Terms.**—In order to secure the utmost completeness and accuracy of definition, this department has been subdivided among eminent Scholars and Experts, including Prof. Dana, Prof. Lyman, &c.

4. **Etymology.**—The eminent philologist, Dr. C. F. MAHN, has devoted five years to perfecting this department.

5. **The Orthography** is based as far as possible on Fixed Principles. *In all cases of doubt an alternative spelling is given.*

6. **Pronunciation.**—This has been entrusted to Mr. W. G. WEBSTER and Mr. WHEELER, assisted by other scholars. The pronunciation of each word is indicated by typographical signs, which are explained by reference to a KEY *printed at the bottom of each page.*

7. **The Illustrative Citations.**—No labour has been spared to embody such quotations from standard authors as may throw light on the definitions, or possess any special interest of thought or language.

8. **The Synonyms.**—These are subjoined to the words to which they belong, and are very complete.

9. **The Illustrations,** which exceed 3000, are inserted, not for the sake of ornament, but to elucidate the meaning of words which cannot be satisfactorily explained without pictorial aid.

The Volume contains 1576 pages, more than 3000 Illustrations, and is sold
for One Guinea. It will be found, on comparison, to be one of the cheapest
Volumes ever issued. Cloth, 21s.; half-bound in calf, 30s.; calf or half-russia,
31s. 6d.; russia, £2.

To be obtained through all Booksellers. Published by

GEORGE BELL & SONS, YORK STREET, COVENT GARDEN, LONDON.

2

WEBSTER'S DICTIONARY.

From the QUARTERLY REVIEW, *Oct.* 1873.

" Seventy years passed before JOHNSON was followed by Webster, an American writer, who faced the task of the English Dictionary with a full appreciation of its requirements, leading to better practical results."
. . . .

" His laborious comparison of twenty languages, though never published, bore fruit in his own mind, and his training placed him both in knowledge and judgment far in advance of Johnson as a philologist. Webster's 'American Dictionary of the English Language' was published in 1828, and of course appeared at once in England, where successive re-editing *has as yet kept it in the highest place as a practical Dictionary.*"

" The acceptance of an American Dictionary in England has itself had immense effect in keeping up the community of speech, to break which would be a grievous harm, not to English-speaking nations alone, but to mankind. The result of this has been that the common Dictionary must suit both sides of the Atlantic." . . . .

" The good average business-like character of Webster's Dictionary, both in style and matter, made it as distinctly suited as Johnson's was distinctly unsuited to be expanded and re-edited by other hands. Professor Goodrich's edition of 1847 is not much more than enlarged and amended, but other revisions since have so much novelty of plan as to be described as distinct works." . . . .

" The American revised Webster's Dictionary of 1864, published in America and England, is of an altogether higher order than these last [The London Imperial and Student's]. It bears on its title-page the names of Drs. Goodrich and Porter, but inasmuch as its especial improvement is in the etymological department, the care of which was committed to Dr. MAHN, of Berlin, we prefer to describe it in short as the Webster-Mahn Dictionary. Many other literary men, among them Professors Whitney and Dana, aided in the task of compilation and revision. On consideration it seems that the editors and contributors have gone far toward improving Webster to the utmost that he will bear improvement. The *vocabulary has become almost complete,* as regards usual words, *while the definitions keep throughout to Webster's simple careful style,* and the derivations are assigned with the aid of good modern authorities."

" On the whole, the Webster-Mahn Dictionary as it stands, is most respectable, and CERTAINLY THE BEST PRACTICAL ENGLISH DICTIONARY EXTANT."

LONDON: GEORGE BELL & SONS, YORK STREET, COVENT GARDEN.
4

SPECIAL DICTIONARIES AND WORKS OF REFERENCE.

Dr. Richardson's Philological Dictionary of the ENGLISH LANGUAGE. Combining Explanation with Etymology, and copiously illustrated by Quotations from the Best Authorities. *New Edition*, with a Supplement containing additional Words and further Illustrations. In 2 vols. 4to. £4 14s. 6d. Half-bound in Russia, £5 15s. 6d. Russia, £6 12s.

The *Words*, with those of the same family, are traced to their origin. The *Explanations* are deduced from the primitive meaning through the various usages. The *Quotations* are arranged chronologically, from the earliest period to the present time.

The Supplement separately. 4to. 12s.

An 8vo. edition, without the Quotations, 15s. Half-russia, 20s. Russia, 24s.

Synonyms and Antonyms of the English Language. Collected and Contrasted. By the late Ven. C. J. SMITH, M.A. Post 8vo. 5s.

Synonyms Discriminated. A Catalogue of Synonymous Words in the English Language, with their various Shades of Meaning, &c. Illustrated by Quotations from Standard Writers. By the late Ven. C. J. SMITH, M.A. Demy 8vo. 16s.

A New Biographical Dictionary. By THOMPSON COOPER, F.S.A., Editor of "Men of the Time," and Joint Editor of "Athenæ Cantabrigienses." 1 vol. 8vo. 12s.

This volume is not a mere repetition of the contents of previous works, but embodies the results of many years' laborious research in rare publications and unpublished documents. Any note of omission which may be sent to the Publishers will be duly considered.

"It is an important original contribution to the literature of its class by a painstaking scholar. . . . . It seems in every way admirable, and fully to justify the claims on its behalf put forth by its editor."—*British Quarterly Review.*

"The mass of information which it contains, especially as regards a number of authors more or less obscure, is simply astonishing." — *Spectator.*

"Comprises in 1210 pages, printed very closely in double columns, an enormous amount of information."—*Examiner.*

"Mr Cooper takes credit to himself, and is, we think, justified in doing so, for the great care bestowed upon the work to insure accuracy as to facts and dates; and he is right perhaps in saying that his dictionary is the most comprehensive work of its kind in the English language."—*Pall Mall Gazette.*

A Biographical and Critical Dictionary of Painters and Engravers. With a List of Ciphers, Monograms, and Marks. By MICHAEL BRYAN. *Enlarged Edition, with numerous additions*, by GEORGE STANLEY. Imperial 8vo. £2 2s.

A Supplement of Recent and Living Painters. By HENRY OTTLEY. 12s.

The Cottage Gardener's Dictionary. With a Supplement, containing all the new plants and varieties to the year 1869. Edited by GEORGE W. JOHNSON. Post 8vo. Cloth. 6s. 6d.

THE ALDINE SERIES OF THE BRITISH POETS.

CHEAP EDITION.

In Fifty-two Volumes, Bound in Cloth, at Eighteenpence each Volume.

Akenside, with Memoir by the Rev. A. DYCE, and additional Letters. 1s. 6d.

Beattie, with Memoir by the Rev. A. DYCE. 1s. 6d.

Burns, with Memoir by Sir Harris NICOLAS, and additional Copyright Pieces. 3 vols. 4s. 6d.

Butler, with Memoir by the Rev. J. MITFORD. 2 vols. 3s.

Chaucer, edited by R. Morris, with Memoir by Sir HARRIS NICOLAS. 6 vols. 9s.

Churchill, Tooke's Edition, revised, with Memoir, by JAMES HANNAY. 2 vols. 3s.

Collins, edited, with Memoir, by W. MOY THOMAS. 1s. 6d.

Cowper, including his Translations. Edited, with Memoir, and Additional Copyright Pieces, by JOHN BRUCE, F.S.A. 3 vols. 4s. 6d.

Dryden, with Memoir by the Rev. R. HOOPER, F.S.A. Carefully revised, 5 vols. 7s. 6d.

Falconer, with Memoir by the Rev. J. MITFORD. 1s. 6d.

Goldsmith, with Memoir by the Rev. J. MITFORD. Revised. 1s. 6d.

Gray, with Notes and Memoir by the Rev. JOHN MITFORD. 1s. 6d.

Kirke White, with Memoir by Sir H. NICOLAS, and additional Notes. Carefully revised. 1s. 6d.

Milton, with Memoir by the Rev. J. MITFORD. 3 vols. 4s. 6d.

Parnell, with Memoir by the Rev. J. MITFORD. 1s. 6d.

Pope, with Memoir by the Rev. A. DYCE. 3 vols. 4s. 6d.

Prior, with Memoir by the Rev. J. MITFORD. 2 vols. 3s.

Shakespeare, with Memoir by the Rev. A. DYCE. 1s. 6d.

Spenser, edited, with Memoir, by J. PAYNE COLLIER. 5 vols. 7s. 6d.

Surrey, edited, with Memoir, by JAMES YEOWELL. 1s. 6d.

Swift, with Memoir by the Rev. J. MITFORD. 3 vols. 4s. 6d.

Thomson, with Memoir by Sir H. NICOLAS. Annotated by PETER CUNNINGHAM, F.S.A., and additional Poems, carefully revised. 2 vols. 3s.

Wyatt, edited, with Memoir, by JAMES YEOWELL. 1s. 6d.

Young, with Memoir by the Rev. J. MITFORD, and additional Poems. 2 vols. 3s.

Complete sets may be obtained, bound in half-morocco.

N.B.—Copies of the Fine Paper Edition, with portraits, may still be had, price 5s. per volume (except Collins, 3s. 6d.).

LONDON: GEORGE BELL & SONS, YORK STREET, COVENT GARDEN.

6

THE ALDINE EDITION OF THE BRITISH POETS.

SUPPLEMENTARY SERIES.

The fifty-two volumes which have hitherto formed the well-known Aldine Series, embody the works of nearly all the more popular English poetical writers, whether lyric, epic, or satiric, up to the end of the eighteenth century. But since that time the wonderful fertility of English literature has produced many writers equal, and in some cases far superior, to the majority of their predecessors; and the widely augmented roll of acknowledged English poets now contains many names not represented in the series of " Aldine Poets."

With a view of providing for this want, and of making a series which has long held a high place in public estimation a more adequate representation of the whole body of English poetry, the Publishers have determined to issue a second series, which will contain some of the older poets, and the works of recent writers, so far as may be practicable by arrangement with the representatives of the poets whose works are still copyright.

One volume, or more, at a time will be issued at short intervals; they will be uniform in binding and style with the last fine-paper edition of the Aldine Poets, in fcap. 8vo. size, printed at the Chiswick Press. Price 5s. per volume.

Each volume will be edited with notes where necessary for elucidation of the text; a memoir will be prefixed, and a portrait, where an authentic one is accessible.

The following are ready, or in preparation.

THE POEMS OF WILLIAM BLAKE. With Memoir by W. M. Rossetti, and portrait by Jeens.

THE POEMS OF SAMUEL ROGERS. With Memoir by Edward Bell, and portrait by Jeens.

THE POEMS OF THOMAS CHATTERTON. 2 vols. Edited by the Rev. W. Skeat, with Memoir by Edward Bell.

THE POEMS OF SIR WALTER RALEIGH, SIR HUGH COTTON, and Selections from other Courtly Poets. With Introduction by the Rev. Dr. Hannah, and portrait of Sir W. Raleigh.

THE POEMS OF THOMAS CAMPBELL. With Memoir by W. Allingham, and portrait by Jeens.

THE POEMS OF GEORGE HERBERT. (Complete Edition.) With Memoir by the Rev. A. B. Grosart, and portrait.

THE POEMS OF JOHN KEATS. With Memoir by Lord Houghton, and portrait by Jeens.

LONDON: GEORGE BELL & SONS, YORK STREET, COVENT GARDEN.

7

In Ten Volumes, price 2s. 6d. each; in half-morocco, £2 10s. the set.

CHEAP ALDINE EDITION OF
SHAKESPEARE'S DRAMATIC WORKS.

EDITED BY S. W. SINGER.

Uniform with the Cheap Edition of the Aldine Poets.

THE formation of numerous Shakespeare Reading Societies has created a demand for a cheap portable edition, with LEGIBLE TYPE, that shall provide a sound text with such notes as may help to elucidate the meaning and assist in the better understanding of the author. The Publishers therefore determined to reprint Mr. Singer's well-known Edition, published in 10 vols., small 8vo., for some time out of print, and issue it in a cheap form, uniform with the well-known Aldine Edition of British Poets.

CONTENTS.

Uniform with the above, price 2s. 6d; in half-morocco, 5s.

CRITICAL ESSAYS ON THE PLAYS OF SHAKESPEARE,

BY WILLIAM WATKISS LLOYD;

Giving a succinct account of the origin and source of each play, where ascertainable, and careful criticisms on the subject-matter of each.

A few copies of this Work have been printed to range with the fine-paper Edition of the Aldine Poets. The price for the Eleven Volumes (not sold separately) is £2 15s.

LONDON: GEORGE BELL & SONS, YORK STREET, COVENT GARDEN.
8

POCKET VOLUMES.

A SERIES of Select Works of Favourite Authors, adapted for general reading, moderate in price, compact and elegant in form, and executed in a style fitting them to be permanently preserved. Imperial 32mo., cloth, gilt top.

Bacon's Essays. 2s. 6d.

Burns's Poems. 3s.

———— Songs. 3s.

Coleridge's Poems. 3s.

C. Dibdin's Sea Songs and Ballads. And others. 3s.

Midshipman, The. Autobiographical Sketches of his own early Career, by Captain BASIL HALL, R.N., F.R.S. 3s. 6d.

Lieutenant and Commander. By Captain BASIL HALL, R.N., F.R.S. 3s. 6d.

George Herbert's Poems. 2s. 6d.

———— Remains. 2s.

———— Works. 3s. 6d.

The Sketch Book. By WASHINGTON IRVING. 3s. 6d.

Tales of a Traveller. By WASHINGTON IRVING. 3s. 6d.

Charles Lamb's Tales from Shakspeare. 3s.

Longfellow's Evangeline and Voices, Sea-side, and Poems on Slavery. 3s.

Milton's Paradise Lost. 3s.

———— Regained, & other Poems. 3s.

Robin Hood Ballads. 3s.

Southey's Life of Nelson. 3s.

Walton's Complete Angler. Portraits and Illustrations. 3s.

———— Lives of Donne, Wotton, Hooker, &c. 3s. 6d.

White's Natural History of Selborne. 3s. 6d.

Shakspeare's Plays. KEIGHTLEY's Edition. Thirteen Volumes in cloth case, 21s.

ELZEVIR SERIES.

Small fcap. 8vo.

THESE Volumes are issued under the general title of "ELZEVIR SERIES," to distinguish them from other collections. This general title has been adopted to indicate the spirit in which they are prepared; that is to say, with the greatest possible accuracy as regards text, and the highest degree of beauty that can be attained in the workmanship.

They are printed at the Chiswick Press, on fine paper, with wide margins, and issued in a neat cloth binding.

Longfellow's Evangeline, Voices, Sea-side and Fire-side. 4s. 6d. With Portrait.

———— Hiawatha, and The Golden Legend. 4s. 6d.

———— Wayside Inn, Miles Standish, Spanish Student. 4s. 6d.

Burns's Poetical Works. 4s. 6d. With Portrait.

———— Songs and Ballads. 4s. 6d.

These Editions contain all the copyright pieces published in the Aldine Edition.

Cowper's Poetical Works. 2 vols., each 4s. 6d. With Portrait.

Coleridge's Poems. 4s. 6d. With Portrait.

Irving's Sketch Book. 5s. With Portrait.

———— Tales of a Traveller. 5s.

Milton's Paradise Lost. 5s. With Portrait.

———— Regained. 5s.

Shakspeare's Plays and Poems. Carefully edited by THOMAS KEIGHTLEY. In seven volumes. 5s. each.

Southey's Life of Nelson. 4s. 6d. With Portrait of NELSON.

Walton's Angler. 4s. 6d. With a Frontispiece.

———— Lives of Donne, Hooker, Herbert, &c. 5s. With Portrait.

HISTORY AND TRAVELS.

Rome and the Campagna. A Historical and Topo-
graphical Description of the Site, Buildings, and Neighbourhood of ancient Rome. By the Rev. Robert Burn, late Fellow and Tutor of Trinity College, Cambridge. With eighty engravings by Jewitt, and numerous Maps and Plans. Demy 4to. £3 3s.

An additional Plan and an Appendix, bringing this Work down to 1876, has been added.

Ancient Athens; its History, Topography, and Re-
MAINS. By Thomas Henry Dyer, LL.D., Author of "The History of the Kings of Rome." Super-royal 8vo. Illustrated, cloth. £1 5s.

The History of the Kings of Rome. By Dr. T. H.
Dyer, Author of the "History of the City of Rome;" "Pompeii: its History, Antiquities," &c., with a Prefatory Dissertation on the Sources and Evidence of Early Roman History. 8vo. 16s.

The Decline of the Roman Republic. By George Long,
M.A., Editor of "Caesar's Commentaries," "Cicero's Orations," &c. 8vo.

Vol. I. From the Destruction of Carthage to the End of the Jugurthine War. 14s.

Vol. II. To the Death of Sertorius. 14s.

Vol III. Including the third Mithridatic War, the Catiline Conspiracy, and the Consulship of C. Julius Caesar. 14s.

Vol. IV. History of Caesar's Gallic Campaigns and of contemporaneous events. 14s.

Vol. V. From the Invasion of Italy by Julius Caesar to his Death. 14s.

A History of England during the Early and Middle
AGES. By C. H. Pearson, M.A., Fellow of Oriel College, Oxford, and late Lecturer in History at Trinity College, Cambridge. Second Edition, revised and enlarged. 8vo. Vol. I. to the Death of Coeur de Lion. 16s. Vol. II. to the Death of Edward I. 14s.

Historical Maps of England. By C. H. Pearson, M.A.
Folio. Second Edition, revised. 31s. 6d.

An Atlas containing Five Maps of England at different periods during the Early and Middle Ages.

The Footsteps of our Lord and His Apostles in
PALESTINE, SYRIA, GREECE, AND ITALY. By W. H. Bartlett. Seventh Edition, with numerous Engravings. In one 4to. volume. Handsomely bound in walnut, 18s. Cloth gilt, 10s. 6d.

Forty Days in the Desert on the Track of the
ISRAELITES; or, a Journey from Cairo to Mount Sinai and Petra. By W. H. Bartlett. 4to. With 25 Steel Engravings. Handsome walnut binding, 18s. Cloth gilt, 10s. 6d.

The Nile Boat; or, Glimpses in the Land of Egypt.
By W. H. Bartlett. New Edition, with 33 Steel Engravings. 4to. Walnut, 18s. Cloth gilt, 10s. 6d.

The Desert of the Exodus. Journeys on Foot in the
Wilderness of the Forty Years' Wanderings, undertaken in connection with the Ordnance Survey of Sinai and the Palestine Exploration Fund. By E. H. Palmer, M.A., Lord Almoner's Professor of Arabic and Fellow of St. John's College, Cambridge, Member of the Asiatic Society, and of the Société de Paris. With Maps, and numerous Illustrations from Photographs and Drawings taken on the spot by the Sinai Survey Expedition and C. F. Tyrwhitt Drake. 2 vols. 8vo. 28s.

The History of Egypt. From the Earliest Times till its
Conquest by the Arabs, A.D. 640. By Samuel Sharpe. New Edition, revised. 2 vols. Small post 8vo. With numerous Illustrations, Maps, &c. Cloth, 10s.

LONDON: GEORGE BELL & SONS, YORK STREET, COVENT GARDEN.

STANDARD WORKS.

Corpus Poetarum Latinorum. Edited by E. WALKER.
One thick vol. 8vo. Cloth, 18s.

'Containing:—Catullus, Lucretius, Virgilius, Tibullus, Propertius, Ovidius, Horatius,
Phaedrus, Lucanus, Persius, Juvenalis, Martialis, Sulpicia, Statius, Silius Italicus, Valerius
Flaccus, Calpurnius Siculus, Ausonius, and Claudianus.

Cruden's Concordance to the Old and New Testament,
or an Alphabetical and Classified Index to the Holy Bible, specially adapted for Sunday
School Teachers, containing nearly 54,000 references. Thoroughly revised and con-
densed by G. H. HANNAY. Fcap. 2s.

Perowne (Canon). The Book of Psalms. A New
Translation, with Introductions and Notes, Critical and Explanatory. By the Rev.
J. J. STEWART PEROWNE, B.D., Canon Residentiary of Llandaff, and Fellow of Trinity
College, Cambridge. 8vo. Vol. I., Third Edition. 18s.; Vol. II., Third Edition, 16s.

Adams (Dr. E.). The Elements of the English Lan-
GUAGE. By ERNEST ADAMS, Ph.D. Fifteenth Edition. Post 8vo. 4s. 6d.

Whewell (Dr.). Elements of Morality, including Polity.
By W. WHEWELL, D.D., formerly Master of Trinity College, Cambridge. Fourth
Edition. In 1 vol. 8vo. 15s.

Gilbart (J. W.). The Principles and Practice of
BANKING. By the late J. W. GILBART. New Edition, revised (1871). 8vo. 16s.

BIOGRAPHIES BY THE LATE SIR ARTHUR HELPS, K.C.B.

The Life of Hernando Cortes, and the Conquest of
MEXICO. Dedicated to Thomas Carlyle. 2 vols. Crown 8vo. 15s.

The Life of Christopher Columbus, the Discoverer of
AMERICA. Fourth Edition. Crown 8vo. 6s.

The Life of Pizarro. With Some Account of his Asso-
ciates in the Conquest of Peru. Second Edition. Crown 8vo. 6s.

The Life of Las Casas, the Apostle of the Indies.
Second Edition. Crown 8vo. 6s.

The Life and Epistles of St. Paul. By THOMAS LEWIN,
Esq., M.A., F.S.A., Trinity College, Oxford, Barrister-at-Law, Author of "Fasti
Sacri," "Siege of Jerusalem," "Cæsar's Invasion," "Treatise on Trusts," &c. Third
Edition, revised. With upwards of 350 Illustrations finely engraved on Wood, Maps,
Plans, &c. In 2 vols., demy 4to. £2 2s.

"This is one of those works which demand from critics and from the public, before
attempting to estimate its merits in detail, an unqualified tribute of admiration. The first
glance tells us that the book is one on which the leisure of a busy lifetime and the whole
resources of an enthusiastic author have been lavished without stint. . . . This work is a
kind of British Museum for this period and subject in small compass. It is a series of
galleries of statues, gems, coins, documents, letters, books, and relics, through which the
reader may wander at leisure, and which he may animate with his own musings and reflections. It must be remembered throughout that this delightful and instructive collection is
the result of the devotion of a lifetime, and deserves as much honour and recognition as
many a museum or picture-gallery which has preserved its donor's name for generations."
—*Times.*

LONDON : GEORGE BELL & SONS, YORK STREET, COVENT GARDEN.

ILLUSTRATED OR POPULAR EDITIONS OF STANDARD WORKS.

Dante's Divine Comedy. Translated by the Rev. HENRY FRANCIS CARY. With all the Author's Copyright Emendations. Post 8vo. 3s. 6d.

Shakespeare. Shakespeare's Plays and Poems. With Notes and Life by CHARLES KNIGHT, and 40 engravings on wood by HARVEY. Royal 8vo. Cloth. 10s. 6d.

Fielding. Works of Henry Fielding, complete. With Memoir of the Author by THOMAS ROSCOE, and 20 Plates by GEORGE CRUIKSHANK. Medium 8vo. 14s.

Fielding. The Novels separately. With Memoir by THOMAS ROSCOE, and Plates by GEORGE CRUIKSHANK. Medium 8vo. 7s. 6d.

Swift. Works of Jonathan Swift, D.D. Containing interesting and valuable passages not hitherto published. With Memoir of the Author by THOMAS ROSCOE. 2 vols. Medium 8vo. 24s.

Smollett. Miscellaneous Works of Tobias Smollett. Complete in 1 vol. With Memoir of the Author by THOMAS ROSCOE. 21 Plates by GEORGE CRUIKSHANK. Medium 8vo. 14s.

Lamb. The Works of Charles Lamb. With a Memoir by Sir THOMAS NOON TALFOURD. Imp. 8vo. 10s. 6d.

Goldsmith's Poems. Illustrated. 16mo. 2s. 6d.

Wordsworth's White Doe of Rylstone; or, the Fate of THE NORTONS. Illustrated. 16mo. 3s. 6d.

Longfellow's Poetical Works. With nearly 250 Illustrations by BIRKET FOSTER, TENNIEL, GODWIN, THOMAS, &c. In 1 vol. 21s.

Longfellow's Evangeline. Illustrated. 16mo. 3s. 6d.

Longfellow's Wayside Inn. Illustrated. 16mo. 3s. 6d.

Washington Irving's Sketch-Book. (The Artist's Edition.) Illustrated with a Portrait of the Author on Steel, and 200 Exquisite Wood-Engravings from the Pencils of the most celebrated American Artists. Crown 4to. 21s.

Adelaide Anne Procter's Legends and Lyrics. The Illustrated Edition. With Additional Poems, and an Introduction by CHARLES DICKENS, a Portrait by JEENS, and 20 Illustrations by Eminent Artists. Fcap. 4to. Ornamental cloth. 21s.

Mrs. Gatty's Parables from Nature. A Handsomely Illustrated Edition; with Notes on the Natural History, and numerous Full-page Illustrations by the most eminent Artists of the present day. Fcap. 4to. 21s. Also 2 volumes, 10s. 6d. each.

The Book of Gems. Selections from the British POETS. Illustrated with upwards of 150 Steel Engravings. Edited by S. C. HALL. 3 vols. Handsomely bound in walnut. 21s. each.

> FIRST SERIES—CHAUCER TO DRYDEN.
> SECOND SERIES—SWIFT TO BURNS.
> THIRD SERIES—WORDSWORTH TO TENNYSON.

LONDON : GEORGE BELL & SONS, YORK STREET, COVENT GARDEN.

BOOKS FOR THE YOUNG.

CAPTAIN MARRYAT'S BOOKS FOR BOYS.

Poor Jack. With Sixteen Illustrations after Designs by CLARKSON STANFIELD, R.A. Twenty-second Edition. Post 8vo., 3*s.* 6*d.* Gilt, 4*s.* 6*d.*

The Mission; or, Scenes in Africa. With Illustrations by JOHN GILBERT. Post 8vo., 3*s.* 6*d.* Gilt, 4*s.* 6*d.*

The Settlers in Canada. With Illustrations by GILBERT and DALZIEL. Post 8vo., 3*s.* 6*d.* Gilt, 4*s.* 6*d.*

The Privateers Man. Adventures by Sea and Land IN CIVIL AND SAVAGE LIFE, ONE HUNDRED YEARS AGO. Illustrated with Eight Steel Engravings. Post 8vo., 3*s.* 6*d.* Gilt, 4*s.* 6*d.*

Masterman Ready; or, the Wreck of the Pacific. Embellished with Ninety-three Engravings on Wood. Post 8vo., 3*s.* 6*d.* Gilt, 4*s.* 6*d.*

The Pirate and Three Cutters. Illustrated with Eight Steel Engravings from Drawings by CLARKSON STANFIELD, R.A. With a Memoir of the Author. Post 8vo., 3*s.* 6*d.* Gilt, 4*s.* 6*d.*

A Boy's Locker. A Smaller Edition of the above Tales, in 12 volumes, enclosed in a compact cloth box. 21*s.*

Hans Christian Andersen's Tales for Children. With Forty-eight Full-page Illustrations by Wehnert, and Fifty-seven Small Engravings on Wood by W. THOMAS. A new Edition. Very handsomely bound. 6*s.*

Hans Christian Andersen's Fairy Tales and Sketches. Translated by C. C. PEACHEY, H. WARD, A. PLESNER, &c. With 104 Illustrations by OTTO SPECKTER and others. 6*s.*
   This volume contains several tales that are in no other Edition published in this country, and with the above volume it forms the most complete English Edition.

Mrs. Alfred Gatty's Presentation Box for Young PEOPLE. Containing "Parables from Nature," "Aunt Judy's Tales," and other Popular Books, 9 volumes in all, beautifully printed, neatly bound, and enclosed in a cloth box. 31*s.* 6*d.* Any single volume at 3*s.* 6*d.*

Anecdotes of Dogs. By EDWARD JESSE. With Illustrations. Post 8vo. Cloth. 6*s.* With Thirty-four Steel Engravings after COOPER, LANDSEER, &c. 7*s.* 6*d.*

The Natural History of Selborne. By GILBERT WHITE. Edited by JESSE. Illustrated with Forty Engravings. Post 8vo. 5*s.*; or with the Plates Coloured, 7*s.* 6*d.*

A Poetry Book for Schools. Illustrated with Thirty-seven highly-finished Engravings by C. W. COPE, R.A., HEMSLEY, PALMER, SKILL, THOMAS, and H. WEIR. Crown 8vo. 1*s.*

Select Parables from Nature. By Mrs. GATTY. For the Use of Schools. Fcap. 1*s.*
   Besides being reprinted in America, selections from Mrs. Gatty's Parables have been translated and published in the German, French, Italian, Russian, Danish, and Swedish languages.

SOWERBY'S ENGLISH BOTANY:

Containing a Description and Life-size coloured Drawing of every British Plant. Edited and brought up to the Present Standard of Scientific Knowledge by T. BOSWELL (formerly SYME), LL.D. F.L.S., &c. With Popular Descriptions of the Uses, History, and Traditions of each Plant, by Mrs. LANKESTER, Author of "Wild Flowers Worth Notice," "The British Ferns," &c. The Figures by J. E. SOWERBY, JAMES SOWERBY, F.L.S., J. DE C. SOWERBY, F.L.S., and J. W. SALTER, A.L.S. In Eleven Volumes, super-royal 8vo.

"Under the editorship of T. Boswell Syme, F.L.S., assisted by Mrs. Lankester, 'Sowerby's English Botany,' when finished, will be exhaustive of the subject, and worthy of the branch of science it illustrates. . . . In turning over the charmingly executed hand-coloured plates of British plants which encumber these volumes with riches, the reader cannot help being struck with the beauty of many of the humblest flowering weeds we tread on with careless step. We cannot dwell upon many of the individuals grouped in the splendid bouquet of flowers presented in these pages, and it will be sufficient to state that the work is pledged to contain a figure of every wild flower indigenous to these isles."— *Times.*

"Will be the most complete Flora of Great Britain ever brought out. This great work will find a place wherever botanical science is cultivated, and the study of our native lants, with all their fascinating associations, held dear."—*Athenæum.*

"A clear, bold, distinctive type enables the reader to take in at a glance the arrangement and divisions of every page. And Mrs. Lankester has added to the technical description by the editor an extremely interesting popular sketch, which follows in smaller type. The English, French, and German popular names are given, and, wherever that delicate and difficult step is at all practicable, their derivation also. Medical properties, superstitions, and fancies, and poetic tributes and illusions, follow. In short there is nothing more left to be desired."—*Guardian.*

"Without question, this is the standard work on Botany, and indispensable to every botanist. . . . The plates are most accurate and beautiful, and the entire work cannot be too strongly recommended to all who are interested in botany."—*Illustrated News.*

Sold separately, prices as follows:—

	Bound cloth.			Half morocco.			Morocco elegant.		
	£	s.	d.	£	s.	d.	£	s.	d.
Vol. I. (Seven Parts)	1	18	0	2	2	0	2	8	6
II. ditto	1	18	0	2	2	0	2	8	6
III. (Eight Parts)	2	3	0	2	7	0	2	13	6
IV. (Nine Parts)	2	8	0	2	12	0	2	18	6
V. (Eight Parts)	2	3	0	2	7	0	2	13	6
VI. (Seven Parts)	1	18	0	2	2	0	2	8	6
VII. ditto	1	18	0	2	2	0	2	8	6
VIII. (Ten Parts)	2	13	0	2	17	0	3	3	6
IX. (Seven Parts)	1	18	0	2	2	0	2	8	6
X. ditto	1	18	0	2	2	0	2	8	6
XI. (Six Parts)	1	13	0	1	17	0	2	3	6

Or, the Eleven Volumes, 22*l.* 8*s.* in cloth; 24*l.* 12*s.* in half-morocco; and 28*l.* 3*s.* 6*d.* whole morocco.

A Supplementary Volume, containing ferns and other cryptogami, in preparation by Professor BOSWELL (formerly SYME).

LONDON: GEORGE BELL & SONS, YORK STREET, COVENT GARDEN.

14

LIBRARY OF NATURAL HISTORY.

"Each volume is elegantly printed in royal 8vo., and illustrated with a very large number of well-executed engravings, printed in colours. . . . . They form a complete library of reference on the several subjects to which they are devoted, and nothing more complete in their way has lately appeared."—*The Bookseller.*

BREE'S BIRDS OF EUROPE AND THEIR EGGS, not observed in the British Isles. With 238 beautifully coloured Plates. Five vols. 5*l.* 5*s.*

COUCH'S HISTORY OF THE FISHES OF THE BRITISH ISLANDS. With 256 carefully coloured Plates. Four vols.

GATTY'S (MRS. ALFRED) BRITISH SEAWEEDS. Numerous coloured Illustrations. Two vols. 2*l.* 10*s.*

HIBBERD'S (SHIRLEY) NEW AND RARE BEAUTIFUL-LEAVED PLANTS. With 64 coloured Full-page Illustrations. Executed expressly for this work. One vol. 1*l.* 5*s.*

LOWE'S NATURAL HISTORY OF BRITISH AND EXOTIC FERNS. With 479 finely coloured Plates. Eight vols. 6*l.* 6*s.*

LOWE'S OUR NATIVE FERNS. Illustrated with 79 coloured Plates and 900 Wood Engravings. Two vols. 2*l.* 2*s.*

LOWE'S NATURAL HISTORY OF NEW AND RARE FERNS. Containing Species and Varieties not included in "Ferns, British and Exotic." 72 coloured Plates and Woodcuts. One vol. 1*l.* 1*s.*

LOWE'S NATURAL HISTORY OF BRITISH GRASSES. With 74 finely coloured Plates. One vol. 1*l.* 1*s.*

LOWE'S BEAUTIFUL-LEAVED PLANTS: being a description of the most beautiful-leaved Plants in cultivation in this country. With 60 coloured Illustrations. One vol. 1*l.* 1*s.*

MORRIS' HISTORY OF BRITISH BIRDS. With 360 finely coloured Engravings. Six vols. 6*l.* 6*s.*

MORRIS' NESTS AND EGGS OF BRITISH BIRDS. With 223 beautifully coloured Engravings. Three vols. 3*l.* 3*s.*

MORRIS' BRITISH BUTTERFLIES. With 71 beautifully coloured Plates. One vol. 1*l.* 1*s.*

MORRIS' BRITISH MOTHS. With coloured Illustrations of nearly 2000 specimens. Four vols. 6*l.* 6*s.*

TRIPP'S BRITISH MOSSES. With 39 coloured Plates, containing a figure of each species. Two vols. 2*l.* 10*s.*

WOOSTER'S ALPINE PLANTS. First Series. With 54 coloured Plates. 25*s.*

WOOSTER'S ALPINE PLANTS. Second Series. With 54 coloured Plates. 25*s.*

LONDON: GEORGE BELL & SONS, YORK STREET, COVENT GARDEN.

STANDARD WORKS

PUBLISHED BY

GEORGE BELL & SONS.

** For List of Bohn's Libraries see the end of the Volume.

FRENCH MEMOIRS.

PHILIP DE COMMINES.

VOL. I.

SIR WALTER SCOTT, who founded one of his best novels [Quentin Durward] upon the MEMOIRS OF PHILIP DE COMMINES, calls him "one of the most profound statesmen, and certainly the best historian of his age;" and quoting Ronsard, the poet, adds, "that he was the first to show the lustre which valour and noble blood derived from being united with learning."— *See a Note to Quentin Durward.*

"Above all men," says Dryden, "in this kind of writing, may be accounted the plain, sincere, unaffected, and most instructive PHILIP DE COMMINES. I am sorry I cannot find in our own nation (though it has produced some commendable historians) any worthy to be ranked with him."

Charles the Bold.

THE MEMOIRS

OF

PHILIPPE DE COMMINES,

LORD OF ARGENTON:

CONTAINING THE

HISTORIES OF LOUIS XI. AND CHARLES VIII. KINGS OF FRANCE

AND OF

CHARLES THE BOLD, DUKE OF BURGUNDY.

TO WHICH IS ADDED,

THE SCANDALOUS CHRONICLE,

OR

SECRET HISTORY OF LOUIS XI.,

BY JEAN DE TROYES.

EDITED WITH LIFE AND NOTES,

BY ANDREW R. SCOBLE, ESQ.

IN TWO VOLUMES.

VOL. I.

LONDON: GEORGE BELL AND SONS, YORK STREET,
COVENT GARDEN.
1877.

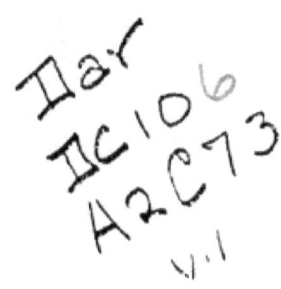

INTRODUCTION.

PHILIP DE COMMINES has been called the Father of Modern History. "His Memoirs," says Mr. Hallam, "almost make an epoch in historical literature. He is the first modern writer who in any degree has displayed sagacity in reasoning on the characters of men and the consequences of their actions, or who has been able to generalise his observations by comparison and reflection." This ability to discuss motives as well as events renders him far superior to Froissart, who, on the other hand, greatly exceeds him in picturesqueness of style and fertility of invention. Froissart merely described notable occurrences ; Commines delineated great men. "The one," says Sir James Stephen, "had contemplated the strife of kings and kingdoms as a spectator of the Isthmian Games may have gazed at that heart-stirring spectacle. The other had watched the schemes of statesmen and the conflict of nations, with some approach to that judicial serenity which we ascribe to a member of the Amphictyonic Council." If Froissart may be termed the Livy of France, she had her Tacitus in Commines.

The Memoirs of Philip de Commines relate to one of the most interesting periods of history. In the words of the Preface to the old English translation of 1723: "He gives us a prospect of all the most memorable occurrences in the reigns of Louis XI., his son Charles VIII., Charles the last Duke of Burgundy, and Mary his only daughter and heir; as likewise a description of the most remarkable passages in England, Flanders, Germany, Italy, Spain, and other neighbouring countries, which happened in the space of thirty-four years, from 1464 to 1498. He teaches with as much verity as plainness and simplicity of style, such fair lessons as will show princes the way of governing their people with gentleness and order. There it is to be seen how kings can never be at peace with their subjects, whilst they are at variance with the King of kings, to whom all mankind, of what dignity or qualification soever, must give an account. There it is to be seen how justice, equity, moderation, and uprightness in all things, is that which gives them a quiet and happy dominion over the hearts of their subjects, without employing either menaces or force. In short, his book is a pleasant and profitable field, full of infinite good fruits, useful for all conditions, in good fortune as well as bad, —for him that commands as well as him that obeys; and all enforced with such Christian-like persuasions, and fortified with such important and excellent precepts, that it is impossible to read them without being affected."

On the peculiar interest attaching to the Memoirs of Commines, Dr. Arnold has the following remarks: "The Memoirs of Philip de Commines terminate about twenty years before the Reformation, six years after the first voyage of Columbus. They relate, then, to a tranquil period immediately preceding a period of extraordinary movement; to the last stage of an old state of things, now on the point of passing away. Such periods, the lull before the burst of the hurricane, the almost oppressive stillness which announces the eruption, or, to use Campbell's beautiful image,

'The torrent's smoothness ere it dash below,'

are always, I think, full of a very deep interest. But it is not from the mere force of contrast with the times that follow, nor yet from the solemnity which all things wear when their dissolution is fast approaching— the interest has yet another source : our knowledge, namely, that in that tranquil period lay the germs of the great changes following, taking their shape for good or for evil, and sometimes irreversibly, while all wore an outside of unconsciousness. We, enlightened by experience, are impatient of this deadly slumber ; we wish in vain that the age could have been awakened to a sense of its condition, and taught the infinite preciousness of the passing hour. And as, when a man has been cut off by sudden death, we are curious to know whether his previous words or behaviour indicated any sense of his coming fate, so we examine the records of a state of things just expiring, anxious to observe whether in any point there may be discerned an anticipation of the great future, or whether all was blindness and insensibility. In this respect, Commines' Memoirs are striking from their perfect unconsciousness : the knell of the middle ages had been already sounded, yet Commines has no other notions than such as they had tended to foster; he describes their events, their characters, their relations, as if they were to continue for centuries. His remarks are such as the simplest form of human affairs gives birth to ; he laments the instability of earthly fortune, as Homer notes our common mortality, or in the tone of that beautiful dialogue between Solon and Crœsus, when the philosopher assured the king that to be rich was not necessarily to be happy. But resembling Herodotus in his simple morality, he is utterly unlike him in another point; for whilst Herodotus speaks freely and honestly of all men without respect of persons, Philip de Commines praises his master Louis the Eleventh as one of the best of princes, although he witnessed not only the crimes of his life, but the miserable fears and suspicions of his latter end, and has even faithfully recorded

4 4

them. In this respect, Philip de Commines is in no degree superior to Froissart, with whom the crimes committed by his knights and great lords never interfere with his general eulogies of them: the habit of deference and respect was too strong to be broken, and the facts which he himself relates to their discredit, appear to have produced on his mind no impression."*

This tendency on the part of Commines to praise the princes who successively enjoyed his aid and allegiance, is thus noticed by Sir James Stephen:—" He regards Charles the Rash with that affectionate interest which the heroism even of the unwise will excite in the bosoms of the wisest. He contemplates Louis XI. with that combination of curiosity, attachment, and awe, which minds of more than ordinary power so often cherish for each other. The images of the fiery duke and of the crafty king were projected in bold relief on the imagination of this acute and vigilant observer; and the truth and distinctness of those images forms the great charm of his retrospect of his own eventful life. The higher charm of a just sensibility, whether to moral beauty or to the absence of it, is, however, wanting in his pages. He is the unqualified admirer, if not the unscrupulous apologist, of his royal master, and seems insensible alike to the injustice of the ends at which he aimed, and to the baseness of the means by which he pursued them. Yet man is not less inconsistent in his faults and errors than in his virtues, and thus, even the utilitarian Commines is unable to survey the revolutions in which he so largely participated without an occasional, and apparently heartfelt acknowledgment that, in bringing to pass the disastrous catastrophes of the world's history, the will and agency of man are but instruments by which the Divine will accomplishes its immutable purposes

* Lectures on Modern History, pp. 117- 119.

of wisdom and of justice. In the subtlety of his analysis of the great characters of his generation— in the force and discrimination of his portraits of them — in the sagacity with which he explores, and the perspicuity with which he interprets, the hidden causes of the events in which they acted,— and in the vigorous dispersion of the mists with which ignorance or passion obscures the true aspect of human affairs, Commines is emphatically a Frenchman. In the reverence with which, on reaching the impassable limits of human investigation, he ceases to inquire, and pauses to adore, he rises higher still, and becomes not only a citizen, but a teacher of the great Christian Commonwealth."*

The composition of his Memoirs was the occupation of the last years of the life of Commines, when circumstances had, sorely against his will, condemned him to retirement and repose. He wrote the first six books in the years 1488—1494, and the last-two, probably, in 1497—1501. They remained in manuscript until 1524, when the first edition was published by Galliot du Pré. This contained only so much of the work as related to the reign of Louis XI.; but as the book immediately became popular, the remainder was put to press and published in 1528. In 1552, Denys Sauvage republished the whole work, under the title which it now bears, and divided into books and chapters. This was the standard edition of Commines until 1649, when Denys Godefroy, historiographer of France, brought out a new one, in which he corrected numerous errors into which Sauvage had fallen. This edition was printed at the Royal Press in the Louvre, and Louis XIV. assisted with his own hands in pulling some of the copies of the first sheet. In 1747, another and still more accurate edition, with a copious appendix, was brought out by the celebrated Lenglet Dufresnoy. This has recently

* Stephen's Lectures on the History of France, vol. ii., pp. 221—223.

been superseded by the edition published by Mdlle. Dupont, who has carefully collated the various manuscripts and editions of the text, and added biographical, genealogical, and historical notes, of great value and accuracy.

The present translation has been made from the text as restored by Mdlle. Dupont, and the notes are mostly taken from her edition. The various treaties mentioned in the Memoirs are given at large in their proper places; and with a view to render the work more complete as a history of Louis XI., the "Chronique Scandaleuse" of Jean de Troyes is printed at the end of the second volume.

A R. S.

LIFE OF PHILIP DE COMMINES.

THE town of Commines, on the confines of France and Belgium, is situated on the River Lys, by which it is divided into two parts; the right bank belongs to France, and the left to Belgium. It possesses no great importance at the present day; but formerly, and until the end of the seventeenth century, it could boast of strong fortifications and a castle, which were destroyed by the French in 1672. The lordship of the town had been enjoyed by several noble families in succession; but for our present purpose it will be sufficient to state that about the year 1373, Jeanne de Waziers, Lady of Commines and Halewin, brought it in marriage to Nicholas, surnamed Colart de la Clite. The name of Commines, which had been honourably mentioned at the time of the first Crusades, was still so imposing that the new lord, or at least his descendants, did not hesitate to substitute it for that of their original race. This nobiliary lustre, however, would not have sufficed to have rescued it any more than other mediæval names, from the obscurity of genealogical archives, if a distinction of a higher character had not secured it immortal renown.

In the Castle of Commines, in the year 1447, was born that celebrated historian whose works have saved from oblivion the meaner glories of his ancestral line. His father, the sovereign-bailiff of Flanders, had been dubbed a knight by the Duke of Burgundy on the day of the battle of St. Riquier, the 31st of August, 1421, on which day that prince had also received the honour of knighthood from the hands of John of Luxembourg; and perhaps this circumstance, adroitly called to mind by the father, induced Philip the Good to do the new-born babe the honour of holding him at the font, and presenting his god-son to baptism under the invocation of his own patron saint. A most hopeful future seemed thus to open before young Commines, who was placed, from his very birth, under the protection of a most powerful monarch; but he was ere long destined to suffer cruel losses. His mother, Marguerite d'Armuyden, died soon after giving him birth, and a few years later, the death of his father left him completely an orphan, with an estate greatly impoverished by bad management and reckless expenditure.

The young orphan and his property were placed by the king under the guardianship of his cousin-german, Jean de la Clite, Lord of Commines, who succeeded, not without great difficulty, in preserving to his ward a small part of his patrimony — so small, indeed, that its value amounted only to the sum of 2424 livres 16 sols 6 deniers tournois. The development of the mind of young Commines was almost as utterly neglected as the management of his property; for his guardian was too much absorbed by more personal business to attend to either. His ward received the same education as, with but few exceptions, was then given to all the children of the nobility. Greek and Latin formed no part of his instruction, and bodily exercises were cultivated with far greater assiduity than mental discipline. Perhaps, however, we ought to congratulate ourselves that this was the case. Intellects like that of Commines form themselves, and advance all the faster and farther because they have no useless acquirements to forget, and no false instruction to unlearn. The sagacious and meditative mind of the future historian was likely to learn far more from the great book of the world than from all the writings of the schoolmen; and that book soon opened before him.

The brilliant and splendid court of Philip the Good then rivalled those of more powerful monarchs in magnificence and lustre. Commines was summoned to this sphere of action by his godfather, who attached him to his person as one of his esquires, probably in the year 1463, and soon transferred him, in the same capacity, to the service of his son, the Count of Charolois. He was then about seventeen years of age, and his youthful inexperience was easily dazzled by two dominant qualities of his new master, self confidence and courage, which were fated so soon to involve him in acts of presumption and temerity. Under such a prince, the opportunity of winning his spurs was not long delayed. Commines accompanied him into France at the time of the war of the Public Good (1465), fought by his side at the battle of Montlhery, and did not leave him during the whole of that eventful day —feeling less alarmed at his own danger, than astonished at the audacity of the French in resisting his master. Two years later, he entered Liege with the victorious duke, and there is every reason to believe that at this period he was dubbed a knight.

Soon after his return from this expedition, and a short time before the marriage of Charles the Bold, which took place on the 16th of February, 1468, Commines was appointed chamberlain and councillor of that prince. The privileges of this double office secured him, though he was only about twenty years of age, the right of entrance into the Burgundian council, and a sort of respectful intimacy with his master. Doubtless the duties of a councillor could not have been easy to fulfil in the household of a prince of such unmanageable disposition, and " who despised all other advice in the world, except only his own;" but the chamberlain, at all events, might make himself agreeable, and succeed in obtaining a considerable degree of familiar intimacy with his sovereign. Commines soon obtained this, either from trying some indirect, but certain means of acquiring influence over the mind of the duke, or because daily communications between two persons not separated by any great difference of age naturally led to this result. The influence to which we refer, and which we have no wish to exaggerate, was ere long to be subjected to a decisive test, under very memorable circumstances.

In the month of October, 1468, Louis XI. came to Péronne, and imprudently placed himself at the mercy of Charles the Bold, against whom he was then secretly instigating the Liegeois to revolt. This step involved him in great peril, and his danger was increased by the fact that the duke, irritated at so audacious a piece of perfidy, was surrounded by scarcely any persons who were not animated by powerful motives of hatred against the king. The most violent counsels were given, and favourably received by a prince who was naturally inclined to extreme courses.

Commines, aided by some other servants of the duke, few in number, but more sensible, more jealous of the honour of their master, and, in a word, more politic than his other advisers, succeeded in partially allaying the storm; but it soon burst out afresh with still greater vehemence. The king alone could avert its direful consequences. In his first alarm he had recourse to means of safety whose efficacy was well known to him: now, gold was of no further avail; he must bow his royal head.

Numerous propositions of a humiliating character were about to be made to him; he would have to accept them all, and that at once and unreservedly; otherwise all would be lost. The duke had dishonoured himself by breaking his plighted word; he was detaining his guest in captivity; and certain members of his council seemed to hope that he would venture still further. A happy inspiration of Commines saved France and her king, Burgundy and her duke, from the incalculable misfortunes which would have resulted from so fatal an event. He secretly informed Louis XI. of all that had been resolved upon regarding him, and of the risk he would incur by the slightest resistance to the demands of the duke. Two important results, equally desirable to every loyal servant of Charles the Bold, might be produced by this hazardous proceeding. It might compel the duke to respect the safe-conduct which he had given to Louis XI., and at the same time secure him as great, if not greater, advantages than those which he might hope to obtain by violating his promised word. The event proved that Commines had calculated rightly. Louis, it is well known, submitted, with the best grace in the world, to all that the gaoler chose to exact from his captive; so that the duke, who, on approaching him had used angry gestures and language, left him in high contentment.

On leaving Péronne, in order to perform one of the conditions which had been imposed upon him, the king had to march with the Duke of Burgundy against the Liegeois. He had encouraged their rebellion, and he was obliged to suffer the disgrace of contributing to punish it. Commines accompanied the two princes on this expedition, and had his share in the imminent danger to which they were exposed. He was sleeping with three others in his master's bed-chamber, when

a band of Liegeois, favoured by the darkness, fell suddenly on
the lodgings of Charles the Bold and Louis XI. This sortie
was ably conducted, and nearly met with all the success
which the besieged hoped for ; the two princes, with their
servants, narrowly escaped finding defeat and death where
they had imagined their triumph would be certain and easy.
It was most fortunate for the duke that he had not followed
the advice of some of his councillors, who recommended him
" to dismiss a part of his army, seeing that the city of Liege
had had its gates and walls demolished during the previous
years, and that it could hope for succour from no quarter."
The king, who had his reasons for it, was inclined to adopt
this suggestion ; but Commines and other prudent councillors remonstrated against so imprudent a step, and their
advice was followed, less perhaps because of its wisdom than
because the duke greatly suspected the king.

The alarm was so sudden and unforeseen that Commines
and his two fellow-chamberlains had scarcely time "to arm
the duke with his cuirass, and put a helmet on his head."
The enemy were pouring in on all sides, and, in order to
get out into the street, it was necessary to drive back the
Liegeois, who were resolutely attacking the doors and windows. Numbers at length obtained the advantage over desperate courage ; the Liegeois, hemmed in on all sides, were cut
to pieces. They met with a similar fate at the king's quarters, which were valiantly defended by the Scottish archers
of his guard. We may note, *en passant*, that these brave
Scottish archers, renowned above all others for their skill,
were on this occasion so awkward that, with their numerous
arrows, " they wounded more Burgundians than Liegeois."

On the following day, the town, attacked on both sides,
was captured, set on fire, and given up to pillage. The
devastation and massacre lasted for five or six days longer,
after which the king began to negotiate for leave to return
home : and, in a short time, he departed, leaving the Duke
of Burgundy to pursue his work of destruction alone.

To return, however, to Commines. His father had not
been an irreproachable administrator of the public funds,
and had died, owing the duke enormous sums, for the recovery of which the agents of that prince sold one of the estates
of the defaulter, named Renescure. The proceeds of this

sale, however, did not amount to a sufficient sum to liquidate
the entire debt.   On the 1st of October, 1469, Commines
obtained, in reward for his services, a receipt in full for all
that might still be due from his family to the ducal treasury.
In the following year, he was sent on a mission to the
Governor of Calais, which, though very simple at first, was
eventually rendered by circumstances very delicate, and even
dangerous.   At one moment the danger became so great,
that he thought it prudent to apply for a safe-conduct, and
inform his master of his position.   He soon received an
answer : the duke sent him his signet ring, ordering him to
continue his negotiation, and promising that if he were made
prisoner, he would ransom him.   Commines had acted wisely
in obtaining sureties, for the duke " never hesitated to
expose one of his servants to danger, when he had need of
his assistance."   The negotiation, however, was ably conducted, and brought to a successful issue, to the satisfaction
of all the parties concerned.

The skilful agent of this treaty was entrusted with a new
mission about the month of July or August, 1471.   We are
not acquainted with the object he had in view, but it is certain that he had an interview with Louis XI., by permission
of the Duke of Burgundy.   It was a very great mistake on
the part of the duke to have allowed this; for, as Molinet
says, the king's speech " was so gentle and virtuous, that,
like the voice of the siren, it lulled to sleep all who listened."
To this remarkable suavity of language Louis XI. added,
according to the testimony of Commines himself, another no
less powerful means of attraction; of all contemporary
princes, he was the one " who most laboured to gain any
man who was able to serve or injure him.   And he was
never diverted from his purpose by being once refused by any
man whom he was endeavouring to gain ; but steadfastly
continued making him large promises, and actually giving
him money and estates which he knew would please him."

Commines, who was moreover allured by many great and
truly royal qualities of Louis XI., allowed himself to be
seduced, as many others had been, by promises and gifts.   For
we do not hesitate to believe that it was during this journey into France, that he deposited in the hands of Jean
de Beaune, a merchant of Tours, a sum of 6000 livres

tournois, to which we shall presently have occasion to refer
again, and which he had probably received from the king.

The interested liberality of the monarch required some
return, and Commines, in exchange for the favours he accepted, doubtless had to contract one of those engagements
which are seldom evidenced by written agreements, but
proved only by subsequent facts. What was the nature of
this convention? We cannot say with certainty, but it appears extremely probable that the conditions of the treaty
were these: Louis XI. assured to Commines, if he would
consent to leave Charles the Bold and enter his service, the
same position of councillor and chamberlain at the Court of
France that he had held at the Court of Burgundy, together
with numerous estates and lordships, offices and dignities
of great value, and an annual pension of 6000 livres
tournois. He further engaged to give him in marriage one
of the rich heiresses of the kingdom. Of a truth there was
in these offers enough to dazzle a young and ambitious man;
the siren had lulled many consciences to sleep at less cost.

Commines accepted the conditions of the treaty; but on his
return to his native land, a very natural feeling of hesitation
made him recoil from the final accomplishment of the transaction. Louis XI., however, daily pressed him more urgently;
the wily monarch could not consent to have tried his powers
of seduction in vain. If Commines escaped his grasp, he
determined at least to make sure of his money. A councillor
of the great council, Master Pierre Clutin, was ordered to
proceed to the residence of Jean de Beaune, and, in the
king's name, to seize the 6000 livres which had been entrusted to him by Commines. This was an able and decisive measure. The publicity of this seizure placed Commines in the unpleasant alternative of seeing his practices
divulged, without gaining any profit by them, or of securing
their advantages only by setting aside the scruples which delayed him. He took the latter and safer course, and during
the night of the 7th of August, 1472, he abandoned Burgundy for ever. The king was then at Pont-de-Cè, and
there his new servant joined him.

Very different opinions have been passed on this act in the
life of Commines; some are too severe, and others too indulgent, to be adopted without qualification. Some writers,

LIFE OF PHILIP DE COMMINES.

among whom we may instance Voltaire, seem to have forgotten that in weighing the actions of men, regard should be had to the times in which they lived, and to the daily examples which they had before their eyes; while others appear to have fallen into the opposite error of forgetting that, although equity requires us to take all the circumstances of the case into consideration, there are nevertheless certain acts which a healthy morality cannot wholly absolve. Let us award to Commines all the blame that he merits for his defection, but let us neither exaggerate his fault beyond due measure, nor extenuate it with blind and unreasoning partiality. Would that it were the gravest reproach to be addressed to his memory!

The confiscation of all the property, moveable and immoveable, which Commines left behind him, was an inevitable and expected consequence of the resolution he had taken. On the very day of his departure, at six o'clock in the morning, the Duke of Burgundy bestowed on the Lord of Quiévrain all the rights and properties reverting to the fugitive from the Lord of Trazegnies and his estate, in virtue of a decree of the Court of Mons. But whatever Commines lost on the one side, he regained a hundredfold on the other. No sooner had he arrived at the court of Louis XI., than he received in the first place, the title of councillor and chamberlain of the king; soon after, a pension of 6000 livres was bestowed on him, "that he might have the means of honourably maintaining his rank;" he was also rewarded with the office of captain of the castle and donjon of the town of Chinon; and, finally, he was presented with the rich principality of Talmont, the importance of which was greatly increased by its numerous dependencies, Olonne, Curzon, and Chateau-Gaultier, and which was soon after still further augmented by the chastellanies, lands, and lordships of Bran and Brandois. To impart additional value to these gifts, the town of Sables, in the lordship of Olonne, was exempted from all taxes, on condition that the inhabitants should enclose and fortify it.

Before pursuing our narrative any further, it will be expedient at once to acquaint the reader with certain details necessary to the proper understanding of our subsequent statements. The letters of Louis XI., conferring on Commines the principality of Talmont and its dependencies, although dated in the month of October, 1472, were not registered by the Parliament until the 13th of December, 1473, or by the Cour des Comptes until the 2nd of May, 1474. The proverbial slowness of judicial procedure was not the only cause of this delay. Opposition, which was only too well founded, as we shall presently see, had prevented Commines from entering upon the enjoyment of his royal master's liberalities at an earlier period. The king's title to the estates and lordships with which he had enriched his new chamberlain, was very doubtful and disputable. It was by a series of violent and arbitrary acts that the royal domain had been increased by these spoils of the house of Amboise. The last male representative of that illustrious family, Louis d'Amboise, Vicomte de Thouars, was the father of three daughters, of whom the eldest, Frances, was sought in marriage by George de la Tremoille, the all-powerful minister of Charles VII., who intended her for his eldest son. But a more advantageous match had previously presented itself, and Mademoiselle d'Amboise was already betrothed to Pierre de Bretagne, second son of the reigning duke. The minister could not see so rich an heiress escape from his grasp without feeling the utmost disappointment and displeasure. As his pride had, moreover, been wounded by the haughty manner in which his proposals had been rejected, he conceived a project of revenge which he carried, ere long, into execution. Under the pretext that the Vicomte de Thouars had made an attempt to deprive him of his liberty, he ordered him to be arrested and imprisoned in the Castle of Poitiers. The parliament was then sitting in that town. George de la Tremoille obtained a decree from that assembly, dated May 8. 1431, which declared the Lord of Amboise guilty of high treason for having attempted to seize upon the person of the king, by arresting the Lord de la Tremoille his minister, and by this means to obtain the direction of state affairs; and condemned him, as a traitor, to the punishment of death, and the confiscation of all his property. The latter part of this sentence was alone executed, as the king commuted the punishment of death into perpetual imprisonment. But even his captivity came to an end after three years, in consequence of the intervention of the Queen,

Marie of Anjou. With his liberty, Louis d'Amboise recovered in September, 1434, the viscounty of Thouars, and
his other estates, with the exception of the principality of
Talmont, and the lordships of Amboise, Chateau-Gaultier,
Olonne, Bran, and Brandois. At a later period, in
January, 1438, Charles VII. declared that malevolence
alone had stimulated the persecutors of the Lord of Amboise,
who had been condemned without any form of trial, and he
therefore restored him to the possession of all his estates of
which he was still deprived. This restitution, however,
was coupled with this, among other conditions, that he should
not marry his eldest daughter without the king's permission.
Was this permission ever obtained? Apparently it was;
for a short time after he had recovered his property, the
Vicomte de Thouars celebrated the marriage of his eldest
daughter with Duke Pierre of Bretagne. His third daughter, Marguerite d'Amboise, married the rejected suitor of
Frances, that very Louis de la Tremoille, who had so
recently been the involuntary cause of his father-in-law's
misfortunes; and this alliance, as we shall presently see,
occasioned the transfer of all the property of the house of
Amboise to the family of La Tremoille. On ratifying the contract of this second marriage, by an act dated August 22. 1446,
Louis d'Amboise assigned to Marguerite, as her future
share in his possessions, the estates of Talmont, Bran, Olonne,
Curzon, Chateau-Gaultier, La Chaume, Les Sables, and
Marans; reserving to himself, however, the enjoyment of
them during his lifetime. In his old age, the Vicomte de
Thouars gave himself up to the most foolish prodigalities,
and to such disorderly conduct that his children were obliged
to sue for the appointment of trustees to his estate.

He did not surrender his rights without a contest, but
alleged that the Duke and Duchess of Bretagne were moved
solely by discontent at not having been able to persuade him
to give them the estate of Thouars, and that, furthermore,
the proceedings instituted against him were irregular, inasmuch as, from his rank and relationship to the royal
family of France, he must be tried by the king and "the
duly assembled court of peers." The parliament, disre-
garding his protest, made a provisional order that the
vicomte should not alienate his property, or make any

conveyance thereof without the advice and consent of Master
Robert Thiboust, then president of that court. This decree
was dated on the 16th of January, 1457. The suit was
still in progress when Louis XI. ascended the throne ; and
it seemed to him that it would be easy to take advantage at
once of the weakness and irritation of the vicomte. At a
summons from the king, the vicomte proceeded to Tours,
and Louis proposed to him to marry the Duchess of Bretagne,
who had become a widow, to the Duke of Savoy, and appointed him to negotiate the alliance. The duchess gave a
distinct and formal refusal to these overtures ; and in order
to destroy all chance of gaining her compliance, she pronounced a vow at the altar never to marry again. Louis
XI. gave a very ungracious reception to the luckless nego-
tiator, and frightened him so by his threats and the violence
of his reproaches, that Louis d'Amboise, duped by this
simulated anger, readily listened to the counsels of certain
courtiers, who advised him to propitiate the king by giving
him the viscounty of Thouars. But in order that this donation
might be valid, it was necessary to get rid of the decree
pronounced by the court in January, 1457. This obstacle
did not long stand in the way of Louis XI. The affair was
referred to the council, which, by a decree of the 5th of
September, 1462, reversed the order of the parliament. Thus
restored to the uncontrolled management of his property,
Louis d'Amboise sold to the king the viscounty of Thouars
for 100,000 crowns, to be paid within a week : but the king
was not to take possession of the estate until the death of
the vicomte. 10,000 crowns were paid to him a few days
after the signature of the contract, and Louis XI. received
in return a general receipt for the entire sum. The
Duchess of Bretagne hastened to protest against this ill-
disguised act of spoliation ; but ere long, having taken the
veil, she transferred all her rights to her nephew, Louis
de la Tremoille, the eldest son of her sister Marguerite.
Louis d'Amboise, after having spent the last years of his
life in disgraceful disorders, died at length on the 28th of
February, 1470. While he was on his death-bed, Jacques
de Beaumont, Lord of Bressuyre, came, in pursuance of the
king's command, at the head of some thirty gentlemen, to invest
the Castle of Thouars, from whence he had orders to remove

a 3

the children, the wife, the relatives, and even the friends of the dying man.   He executed these commands to the letter ; and it was among strangers, and under the care of physicians selected by the Lord of Bressuyre, that Louis d'Amboise breathed his last.   Some notable inhabitants of the town attended his funeral, which was arranged by Jacques de Beaumont, who caused an inventory to be taken immediately of the furniture and title-deeds, and seized in the king's name on the viscounty of Thouars, and all the other pro-perty of the deceased.   Such was the title of Louis XI. to the estate with which he had just enriched Commines.   The head of the despoiled family opposed the registration of the king's letters, both in the parliament and in the Cour des Comptes ; but after some slight resistance, both the sovereign courts were constrained to yield.   Commines took possession of the gifts of Louis XI., which were destined to prove to him the source of great anxiety and the cause of painful and scandalous lawsuits.

These honours and emoluments certainly recompensed Commines very amply for any loss he had sustained by leaving his native country.   Louis XI., however, did not rest satisfied with these proofs of his gratitude.   An ad-vantageous marriage which he had long had in view, soon secured an increase of fortune to the Prince de Talmont, for that was the title assumed by Commines on the 27th of January, 1473, when he signed his contract of marriage with Hélène de Chambes, eldest daughter of the Lord and Lady of Montsoreau.   The dowry of the bride amounted to 20,000 golden crowns, as an equivalent for which Commines received from her parents the castle, town, barony, estate, and lordship of Argenton, in Poitou, with all its rich and numerous dependencies.

To all these benefits, Louis XI. added a gift of which he was not lavish—his confidence.   Commines apparently proved himself worthy of it, for the favours of the king continued to shower down upon him.   It would be tedious to enumerate them here ; we will only mention that he was invested with the office of Seneschal of Poitou, in November, 1476, and with the captaincy of the Castle of Poitiers in February, 1477. Such continued favour could not fail to arouse the jealousy and even the hatred of less fortunate courtiers, especially of those who found it difficult to obtain their share of influence, which they were incapable of earning by services of so high an order as those rendered by Commines. Envy, when brooding in the heart of such a man as Tristan l'Ermite, might produce the most fatal results ; and the more so, as the new favourite was not naturally inclined to pause of his own accord in the career of honour which opened before him, and scarcely attempted to dissemble his disdain for the unworthy rival who endeavoured to stand in his way. The court was soon divided, as it were, into two camps, each of which maintained the pretensions of its chosen leader; and the prudence of Louis XI. had frequently to interfere to restore peace between two servants who, on different grounds, were equally necessary to him.

The first person who brought this prince any important news was sure to be rewarded by him with favour and gifts; skilful courtiers knew this, and lost no opportunity of profiting by this means of pleasing their master. Commines was one of the first to announce to him the result of the battle of Morat on the 22nd of June, 1476; and he received as his share of the recompense 200 marks of gold. No message could have been more agreeable to the king, excepting, perhaps, that which announced to him, a few months afterwards, the total defeat of the Duke of Burgundy, after the disastrous battle of Nancy on the 5th of January, 1477. The duke had been found dead on the field. At this news, even before it was known whether Charles the Bold had survived his defeat, Louis XI. "felt such exceeding joy that he almost lost countenance." The Bastard of Bourbon and Commines were immediately sent into Picardy, with full power to receive and establish in the king's allegiance all who were willing to surrender. The plan of Louis XI. was to march an army into Burgundy, and to take possession of the country in the name of the duke, after expelling the *Germans*, who had occupied it since their victory. Commines seems to have believed in the sincerity of these intentions, which, whether real or feigned, were not long entertained ; for the positive news of the duke's death soon reached the king's ear, and altogether changed his plans.

Meanwhile, Commines and the Bastard of Bourbon proceeded towards Abbeville, whither they had taken the

precaution of sending an emissary before them, to pave the
way for an accommodation. But notwithstanding all their
diligence, they had been anticipated, and when they reached
the town, the people had already delivered up the gates to
the Seigneur de Torcy. The two plenipotentiaries next
went to Doullens, whence they sent to summon Arras to
submit to the authority of the king. Commines set out
alone to conduct this negotiation ; but all his address failed
to corrupt the loyalty of the people of Arras, who formally
refused to acknowledge any other sovereign than their
young duchess. He therefore contented himself with labouring secretly to gain the greatest possible number of partizans
for his master ; and this was, after all, the principal object
of his mission. He had acted, moreover, on the mere an-
nouncement of the defeat of Charles the Bold ; but the
certain news of the death of that prince had, as we have
already stated, totally changed the king's intentions. It was
no longer his object to preserve Burgundy from the invasion
of the Germans ; he wished to take possession of the country, and distribute its lordships among his servants. This
failure at Arras was all the more displeasing to him because
other negotiators had met with better success : Guillaume
de Bische, for instance, had secured Peronne. His valet de
chambre, Oliver, boasted that he would reduce to his allegiance the city of Ghent ; and Robinet d'Odenfort answered
for the submission of St. Omer. The king, flattered by
these promises, and believing himself already in possession
of these places, compared the meagre result of the mission
entrusted to Commines with the happy issue promised him
by the zeal of his faithful servants. The Lord du Lude and
others, on being questioned by the king, concurred in his
opinion ; and all that Commines could do was to suggest
doubts as to the facility with which such strong towns would
be induced to surrender.

He was better acquainted with the country than any
other member of the council ; and his advice was to secure
to the crown of France the possession of the rich domains
which it coveted, rather by some valid title, as marriage or
friendly cession, than by the means which it was intended
to adopt. Louis XI. doubtless thoroughly understood the
wisdom of this advice, and had once approved it ; but the

facility with which he had just succeeded almost everywhere in getting possession of important places had intoxi-
cated him. Commines persisted in thinking that the wise
slowness of negotiations and alliances was preferable to the
dangerous risks which would otherwise be incurred, because
by maintaining the kingdom in peace, it would hold more
secure possession of its pacific conquests. These prudent
suggestions, meliciously interpreted, were obnoxious to the
king, who had made up his mind to pursue a different
course. Under the pretext of a mission into Poitou, on the
frontiers of Bretagne, he dismissed his unwelcome adviser.
This was a real disgrace. All the courtiers saw this, and
amused themselves at Commines' expense ; but, as he tells
us himself, he had no mind to laugh at their jokes, as he
feared that the king might be at the bottom of the sport.
Another circumstance added the climax to his anxieties.
He had written into Hainault to enlist partizans for his
master ; and one of his relatives came to him, bearing promises of adherence from a number of notable persons, who
undertook to deliver into his hands the principal towns and
fortresses in the country. Before his departure, Commines
communicated these offers of service to Louis XI., who flatly
refused them, thinking he would be able to dispense with the
assistance of these noblemen ; but he afterwards had reason
to repent his refusal; "for," says Commines, "I saw he
would have highly esteemed them, if he could have renewed
his dealings with them."

The king's ill-humour, however, was not of long duration,
and his liberalities to others did not prevent his remember-
ing Commines, who received his fair share of the confiscated
property of Jacques d'Armagnac, which Louis XI. distributed among his favourites.

Towards the end of the year 1477, or perhaps at the
beginning of the year following, Commines was sent into
Burgundy at the head of the pensioners of the king's household : but he does not explain the object of his mission.
New annoyances awaited him in that country, and his stay
therein was short. That rich province was unfortunate in
its governors. The Lord of Craon, who had been recalled
on account of his extortionate rapine, had been lately succeeded by Charles d'Amboise, Lord of Chaumont, "a very

valiant and prudent man," but no less avaricious than his predecessor, and who treated the province which he ruled "as if it were his own estate." In relating these facts, Commines registers rather than censures them. If he blames the conduct of the Lord of Craon, it is with prudent reserve, and because "his pillagings, in truth, were too excessive." The spirit of tolerance in which his narrative is composed lends some probability to the accusations which were, ere long, brought against himself. He was denounced to the king as having spared "certain burghers of Dijon concerning the quarters of men-at-arms." This peccadillo alone would doubtless have been insufficient to necessitate his recall; but, "with some other slight suspicion," about which the discreet historian makes no revelation, it combined to induce Louis XI. to send him "very suddenly" to Florence.

As soon as he had received his credentials, Commines set out on his journey, travelling very rapidly, and halting at as few places as possible. He remained for two or three days only at Turin, to pay his respects to the Duchess of Savoy; and about the same time at Milan. In this latter town, he had instructions to demand, in his master's name, the execution of a treaty of offensive and defensive alliance which pledged the Milanese government to support the Florentines. The assistance which he solicited was liberally and readily granted. He then continued his journey to Florence, where he arrived towards the end of April, 1478. A formidable plot, which had been sternly repressed, had just deluged that city with blood: and Commines has given a graphic account of it in his Memoirs. If the sole object of his mission had reference to this event, it also tended to prove the interest felt by France in the cause of the Florentines (or, to speak more correctly, of the Medici family), who were then menaced by a powerful league, headed by Pope Sixtus V. and the King of Naples. The favour thus openly avowed was not injurious to the *protégés* of Louis XI., but a good army would have served them far more effectually. Commines brought with him no troops, and wielded no weapons but those of diplomacy. Of these, he made the best use he could, and, as it would appear, to the entire satisfaction of the parties interested.

After a stay of some months in Florence and the towns in its territory, he began to think of returning to France; but, before his departure, he renewed with the ambassadors of the Duke of Milan, the ancient treaties of alliance between France and that duchy. This act of renewal was executed at Florence on the 18th of August, 1478, and was signed by Commines and Lorenzo de Medici, as representatives of the King of France. In the same capacity, on the 7th of September following, our historian received from Giovanni Galeazzo-Maria, Duke of Milan, the fealty and homage due by that prince for the duchies of Genoa and Savona, of which Louis XI. was suzerain lord.

A considerable period had now elapsed since Commines had left the court in order to discharge these various missions. On his return, he was struck by the change which had taken place in the appearance of his royal master, whom he found "somewhat aged," and "beginning to have a tendency to illness." He met with a most flattering reception from the king, who consulted him more than ever about his affairs, and, as a mark of signal favour, allowed him to sleep with him. This favour continued until the monarch's death; but before we proceed any further, we must go back a little to relate the most painful part of Commines' personal history.

We have already described the iniquitous and violent proceedings by which Louis XI. had seized upon the property of Louis d'Amboise; and we have related how the Lord de la Tremoille, in the name of his children, gave all the opposition in his power to the putting Commines into possession of that part of the spoils which had fallen to his share. It will be remembered that the parliament, after an honourable resistance, had finally yielded; but on the very day after its submission to the orders of the king, it entered a protest on its records, declaring that its conduct had been under compulsion, and could not therefore be prejudicial to the rights of the family of La Tremoille, in whose favour it renewed its reservations. That family was in no degree disposed to abdicate its rights, but pursued its claims with courageous perseverance. Commines was in possession, it is true; but, finding himself disturbed in his possession by ceaseless lawsuits, he requested the Procureur du Roi, in conformity with the terms of the letters-patent granting him the property in question, to secure him from all future hindrances to his peaceable enjoyment of the same. The Procureur du Roi consequently interfered; and thenceforward the parties to the suit, in appearance at least, were Louis XI. and those whom he had spoiled. The parliament, with an independence which does it honour, availed itself of every pretext for securing to the oppressed family some remnant of their ancient domains. A great deal of the property had been sold to the king by the last possessor, but the conveyance had been illegally made, and of this the La Tremoilles furnished abundant proof. Louis XI. then adduced the letters of confiscation issued by his father against Louis d'Amboise: and if this property had been subsequently restored to that nobleman, it was, urged the king's advocates, on conditions which had not been accomplished — among others, on condition that Jeanne d'Amboise should not marry without the consent of Charles VII. That permission, replied La Tremoille, had been obtained; but where was the proof? doubtless in the archives of the Chateau de Thouars, the ancient residence of their ancestors.

Louis XI., it will be remembered, had ordered the Seigneur de Bressuyre to take possession of this chateau at the beginning of the last illness of Louis d'Amboise. After his decease, no member of his family, not even his widow, was allowed to enter it. A very summary inventory of the furniture was hastily prepared, and great care was taken not to particularise the contents of the charter chests. In order to sustain his pretended rights against the persistent opposition of the La Tremoille family, and to cloak the most revolting iniquity with a show of justice, the king appointed a commission of inquiry to search the archives of Thouars for letters likely to serve his case. Two documents of great importance were found, under the hand and seal of Charles VII.; one granting the Vicomte de Thouars the restitution of all his confiscated properly, and the other giving him permission to marry his daughter to the Prince of Bretagne, or any other husband he might select. Commines, who was one of the commissioners, saw at once that these papers would destroy all his chances of success, and he threw them into the fire. Jean Chambon, another commissioner, took them out again immediately, expressing his indignation at such culpable conduct ; and the papers were transmitted to the king, whom Commines had informed of their character. On receiving them from the Seigneur de Bressuyre, the wily monarch threw them into the fire, saying, "It is not I who burn them, but the fire:" and he required all present to swear never to divulge what they had seen.

Thus were destroyed the only deeds which could establish the right of the La Tremoilles to protest against the spoliation of which they were the victims. This was done in October, 1476; but it was not until many months later that the king determined to avail himself of the advantage he had thus iniquitously obtained. On the 21st of July, 1479, a decree was issued, terminating the suit in favour of the king and his servant Commines. This decree, however, as it often happens in such cases, satisfied none of the parties, and least of all, the Lord of Argenton. He certainly found himself maintained in the possession of Talmont, Chateau-Gaultier, and Berrye; but Olonne, Curzon, and La Chaume, which Louis d'Amboise had given to his daughter as her dowry, were adjudged to the La Tremoille family, as appertaining to their maternal inheritance. By this sentence of the parliament, therefore, Commines found all his plans frustrated. "That sort of maritime sovereignty," says M. de Vaudoré, "which he was anxious to create for himself in Lower Poitou, and which he had delighted in representing to his master as likely to prove a second Flanders, as far as commerce and productiveness were concerned, was now greatly diminished. To lose Olonne and La Chaume was to be deprived of a port to which he expected to attract the ships of all countries, and whither, in fact, they afterwards came by hundreds: to give up Bran and Brandois was to renounce the drainage of fertile marshes: to restore Curzon was to resign a position which combined both these advantages." And yet, how was he to avoid compliance with the orders of justice ? His genius, ever fertile in expedients, suggested to him the means of doing so. At his instigation, Louis XI. offered to Louis de la Tremoille certain other lands and lordships in exchange for those of which the parliament had acknowledged his children to be proprietors. This offer was indignantly

rejected as an insult to misfortune; for of the estates thus
offered, two only did not proceed from the spoils of the house
of Amboise.   But Commines was not discouraged by this
refusal.   What the father had rejected might probably, he
thought, be accepted by the children.   These young persons,
though still minors, were drawing near the age when the
young nobility usually aspired to rank among men of war;
and their forced idleness was irksome to them.   Louis XI.
would not admit them into his service, notwithstanding the
urgent solicitations of their brother-in-law, the Bastard of
Maine; but it was intimated to them that they might over-
come the monarch's resistance, and even obtain his favour,
by condescension to his wishes.   This implied acquiescence
in all the past, as they well understood; but they resigned
themselves to their fate, in appearance at least.   At the
same time that they consented to the transfer, they executed,
in the presence of a notary, a deed claiming the rights which
they were about to renounce, in which they stated that,
being compelled to yield to the moral violence exercised
over them, they protested beforehand against anything they
might be forced to do.   A few days after the estates had
thus passed once more into the hands of the king, he
renewed his gift of them to Commines, by letters patent,
which, thanks to the show of legality by which the agreement between the two parties was surrounded, were registered without obstacle by both the parliament and the Cour
des Comptes.

Commines' high favour had now reached its climax; it
seemed impossible for it to increase.   A terrible accident
however, which threatened to deprive him of his royal
protector, served to make it still more evident.   In the
month of March, 1481, Louis XI. was attacked by a fit of
apoplexy, which temporarily deprived him of speech, memory, and sense.   As soon as he came to himself, he sent
for his confessor and for Commines, who was at the time at
Argenton.   Commines hastened to rejoin the king, and by
his order (expressed by signs, for he had not yet sufficiently
recovered his speech), he slept in his room, and served him
at table and in other respects, for fifteen days, as a valet de
chambre.   After two or three days, Louis XI. recovered
sense and speech, but not so perfectly as to render Com-

mines' constant attentions unnecessary : for he alone was able accurately to understand him. He was even obliged to act as his interpreter to the official of Tours, and to acquaint him with the state of mind of his royal penitent, "for otherwise they would not have understood each other." Public affairs remained for a time in suspense, although Commines read most of the despatches which arrived to the king, who either by word or sign indicated the answer he wished to have made; but no one was willing to execute these doubtful orders. "We did little business," says Commines, "awaiting the termination of his illness; for he was not a master to be trifled with."

Towards the middle of the year, the king became sufficiently convalescent to be able to inspect the troops which had been collected by his orders near Pont-de-l'Arche. Thence he proceeded to Tours, where he had a relapse; "again he lost his speech, and for two hours we thought he was dead; he lay in a gallery, on a mattrass." The servants who attended him, Du Bouchage, Commines and others, vowed him to St. Claude; "immediately his speech returned to him, and within the hour he went about the house again." He soon resumed his old habits, and made an excursion to one of the estates he had given to Commines. He remained for a month at the Château of Argenton; a longer time, probably, than he had intended, but he was detained by illness. Such royal visits are usually an expensive honour to those who receive them; but the chamberlain of Louis XI. did not suffer by his hospitality, for his master contributed handsomely to the embellishment of his residence. From Argenton the king went to Thouars, where he made some stay, on account of ill-health; and on leaving that town, he repaired to St. Claude, doubtless to perform the vow made by his faithful servants. Before he left Thouars, he confided to the Lord of Argenton a difficult and delicate mission, of which Commines gives us only a confused idea; we will, therefore, briefly state its object.

Yolande of France, Duchess of Savoy, had died on the 29th of August, 1478, leaving as her successor a son under thirteen years of age. The appointment of a regent devolved on Louis XI., the uncle of the young duke, who conferred that office on the Count de la Chambre, who, he believed, would prove a pliant instrument in his hands. In this expectation he was deceived, and the object of Commines' mission was to assist the Count of Bresse, one of the paternal uncles of the Duke of Savoy, in deposing the obnoxious regent, and taking possession of the government.

In the meanwhile, Louis XI. daily grew more infirm ; his moral energy alone sustained him, and, as in past times, he continued to travel about the country. Commines, on his return from his embassy, joined him at Beaujeu : and he was struck by the ravages which disease had wrought in the person of the prince, whose last hour, he felt, was at hand. We shall not attempt to describe the final scene ; in his Memoirs, Commines has given a wonderful picture of the dying agonies of his sovereign. Louis XI. breathed his last on the 30th of August, 1483, and from that moment, a new era began in the life of Commines, as fatal to his honour and fortune, as the preceding period had been propitious to his ambition and interests.

No sooner had the deceased monarch been laid in his grave than, in virtue of letters patent granted by the new king, at the solicitation of the La Tremoille family, Jean Douhalle, lieutenant-general of the Governor of Touraine, proceeded to make inquiries to substantiate the fact that, in his last moments, Louis XI., stung by remorse, had declared to the Bailiff of Meaux that he had wrongfully and illegally seized on the inheritance of La Tremoille, and had enjoined the bailiff to request the dauphin to restore Talmont to its legitimate owners, and to compensate Commines for its loss by the gift of a pension of 2000 livres. Ten witnesses deposed unanimously to the truth of this statement : and in consequence, on the 29th of September, 1483, Charles VIII. directed his chancellor to reinstate the family of La Tremoille in the possession of the property of which they had been so unjustly deprived.

Commines resisted this order on the ground that there were no title-deeds to justify the restitution of the estates. But though these documents had been destroyed, they had once existed ; and numerous witnesses were ready to reveal the manner in which they had been made away with. Inquiries were instituted as to the result of the examination of the papers in the Château de Thouars, and Commines himself was interrogated. At first he could remember nothing, but on being compelled to speak, he strove hard to make no confession which his enemies might afterwards turn against him; but though his answers were carefully weighed, and coupled with endless restrictions and explanations, he was unable to invalidate the testimony of the other witnesses. Fully conscious of the weakness of his cause, his only object was to gain time, and to this end, he put in requisition all the thousand subtleties of legal chicanery. At length, on the 9th of March, 1486, the parliament pronounced sentence against him. Commines appealed, but in vain; and he was finally condemned to restore to the La Tremoille family the estates of which they had been unjustly deprived, to disgorge the revenues he had derived from them during his unlawful possession, and to pay the expenses of the suit, amounting altogether to 7811 livres 4 sous parisis. Thus, after having lasted nineteen years, this affair was terminated, and Commines was enabled to satisfy the demands of his opponents by means of an indemnity of 30,000 livres granted him by Charles VIII.

We must now take up our history at the death of Louis XI. One of the first acts of Madame de Beaujeu, the eldest sister of Charles VIII., was to confirm in their governments, positions and offices, all those who had held them at the accession of the new king. This was a wise measure, and Louis XI. had more than once repented that he had acted otherwise towards the servants of his father. Commines was maintained on the list of royal councillors, and continued in the office of Seneschal of Poitou. Shortly afterwards, he was sent on an embassy to the Duke of Bretagne, with the Lords of Châtillon and Richebourg. Finally, he had the honour to be one of the fifteen notable persons whom the princess suggested to the States-general for admission into the council of the young king. In that council, at which the most important affairs of the realm were decided, Commines one day had to defend the rights of Charles VIII. over the county of Provence against the pretensions of a prince, Duke René II. of Lorraine, whom all the courtiers treated with the greatest consideration. He maintained the interests of the crown with so much heat that the duke, in anger, addressed him "in rough and foolish words;" and even succeeded in obtaining his banishment from court. The disgraced courtier easily found a refuge with one of those princes who, dissatisfied with the narrow share allotted to their ambition by the States-general of the kingdom, held themselves aloof from Madame de Beaujeu, and openly fomented rebellion against her administration. It was to Moulins, where the Duke of Bourbon then resided, that the Lord of Argenton betook himself. He met with a gracious reception, and his counsels were listened to with favour: but the duke was a man of notoriously feeble character, and Commines had to employ all his ingenuity to keep him faithful to the opposition party. In this he so far succeeded as to induce the duke to go to the king for the purpose of complaining of the evil administration of his government; but one of the consequences of this interview between Charles VIII. and his uncle was, that Commines was dismissed from the Duke of Bourbon's service. Upon this, he transferred his allegiance to the Duke of Orleans, whose intrigues were secretly favoured by the king himself, who, as he grew in years, became impatient of the wise, but imperious control of Madame de Beaujeu. In concert with some other nobles, Commines made an attempt to carry off the young king, and place him under the care of the Duke of Orleans; but although Charles was a party to their design, they failed, and he punished them for their failure. Commines was arrested at Amboise, and conducted to Loches, where he was confined for eight months in an iron cage, which had been constructed by order of Louis XI. By decree of the Parliament of Paris, his property was confiscated, and on the 17th of July, 1487, he was brought to Paris, and imprisoned in the Conciergerie. There he remained for twenty months, until, on the 24th of March, 1489, he was condemned to be banished for ten years to one of his estates, and to give bail to the amount of 10,000 golden crowns for his good behaviour.

Long before the expiration of this sentence, in December, 1492, Commines had been recalled to his seat in the council of Charles VIII. He now gave most evident proof of his sagacity and devotedness by joining, with other enlightened servants of the crown, in a vain attempt to dissuade the young monarch from engaging in an expedition into Italy. Interested advice, however, prevailed over their wise counsels.

and the conquest of Naples was undertaken without funds, and almost without an army. Notwithstanding his opposition to the projected expedition, Commines was one of the first on horseback. He attended his master as far as Asti, whence he was despatched on a mission to Venice, for the purpose of aiding by diplomacy the progress of the king's arms. He remained in Venice for eight months, using every effort to prevent the formation of a league of the States of Italy against Charles VIII. In this he might have succeeded, had not the affairs of France and the position of the invading army been so unfavourable as to frustrate all his efforts. The league was formed, and when Commines received orders to rejoin the king at Sienna, the French army was in retreat. He at once advised the king to hasten his return to France; but his prudent counsel, far from being favourably received, was greeted with incredulous laughter and boastful jeers. Much precious time was wasted in frivolous amusements; and when at length, Charles VIII. began his homeward march, he foolishly left garrisons in many of the towns through which he passed, thus seriously diminishing his own army without opposing any effectual barrier to the progress of his enemies.

The presentiments of Commines were soon realised. On the 5th of July, 1495, the French king, on arriving at the village of Fornova, found 40,000 Italians drawn up in an excellent position, to bar his further advance. The chances of success were not on the side of the French, and at the suggestion of Commines, it was resolved to parley with the enemy. The negotiation was entrusted to our historian, but before it could be commenced, the two armies came to blows. Victory at first seemed to incline to the Italians, but French impetuosity and discipline eventually carried the day. Notwithstanding this unexpected victory, however, Commines received orders to continue his negotiations; and mainly by his exertions, the treaty of Verceil was signed, which restored the Duke of Orleans to liberty, by raising the siege of Novara, and enabled Charles VIII. and his army to return into France with all the honours of war.

Commines was next sent to Venice to obtain the ratification of this treaty by the senate of that powerful republic. But after a fortnight's deliberation, the signiory refused to

accede to the treaty, and offered, in its stead, propositions
which Commines undertook to submit to the king.   From
Venice, he proceeded to Milan, to require the duke to execute
certain clauses in the treaty which he had signed.   But
that prince evaded giving a categorical answer, and forced
the envoy to take his leave before he had obtained anything
more than a false promise that the duke would speedily fulfil
all his engagements.

This was the end of Commines' active career.   On his
return to France, he continued his attendance on Charles
VIII., but took no part in the management of affairs beyond
speaking and voting in the council.   During a temporary
visit to his Chateau of Argenton, he received the news of the
king's unhappy death.   He hastened with all speed to Amboise, and passed five or six hours in prayer by the body of
his deceased sovereign.   On the following day, he went to
pay his homage to the new king, from whom he anticipated
a favourable reception.   But on ascending the throne, the
Duke of Orleans had forgotten past services as well as past injuries; and Commines merely remained a member of the grand
council, as during the previous reign.   He soon ceased even
to attend the meetings of this body, for his name appears on
its registers for the last time on the 26th of July, 1498.
After this date he seems to have retired into private life,
and although he made a great effort in 1505 to obtain public
employment, through the influence of the queen, he was
obliged to remain, for the rest of his days, a mere spectator
of the scenes and conflicts of political life.

His activity meanwhile displayed itself in the conduct of
his private affairs.   On the 13th of August, 1504, his daughter
Jeanne de Commines was contracted in marriage to René de
Brosse, Count of Penthièvre, and heir to the duchy of Bretagne; by which union the blood of Commines has passed
into the veins of more than one sovereign of the royal lines
of France, Spain, Portugal, and Savoy.

The last years of Commines were occupied and embit-
tered by vexatious lawsuits relating to the property of his
wife, and to other matters, into which it would be tedious to
enter.   He died at his Chateau of Argenton on the 18th of
October, 1511, at the age of about 64 years.   In other times,
his death would have constituted almost a political event;

but times had changed.   It was, however, sufficiently noticed to induce one writer, whose name is unknown to us, to compose a sort of poem, deploring his decease.

The mortal remains of Commines were conveyed to Paris, and interred in the chapel which he had built in the Convent des Grands Augustins.   Those of the Countess de Penthièvre were soon laid by his side; and ere long Helène de Chambes joined her husband and daughter in their last resting-place. A splendid monument was erected by René de Bretagne to the memory of his wife's parents.   The chapel has long since been destroyed, but the statues of its founder and his wife, which formed part of their monument, are still preserved in the Gallery of the Louvre.

To conclude this sketch in the words of his old biographer, Sleidan: " Commines was tall, fair, well shaped, and of a comely personage.   He spoke Italian, Dutch, and Spanish incomparably well; but his excellence consisted chiefly in the French, and he had read all the histories that were extant in that language, especially that of the Romans.   As he grew in years, he extremely lamented his deficiency in the Latin tongue, and complained of the little care that had been taken of his education in that respect.   He had a prodigious memory, and such a wonderful facility in expressing his thoughts, that he would at the same time dictate to four secretaries different things, all of them of great importance, and with the same ease and dexterity as if there had been but one.   His conversation was chiefly among foreigners, as he was desirous to inform himself of all things and places, and very careful of employing his time well; so that he was never known to be idle."

CONTENTS.

BOOK THE FIRST.

BOOK THE SECOND.

BOOK THE THIRD.

BOOK THE FOURTH.

BOOK THE FIFTH.

Dedication.

TO

THE ARCHBISHOP OF VIENNE.

IT was your request, my Lord Archbishop of Vienne*, that I should give you in writing an account of what I knew and had heard of the transactions of the late King Louis XI.†, our master and benefactor — a prince, indeed, whose actions well deserve to be remembered. In compliance with your Lordship's desire I have done it, as near the truth as my memory would permit me.

Of the occurrences that happened in his youth I can say little besides what I have heard his Majesty state in conver-

---

* Angelo Cato, born at Sopino, in the diocese of Benevento, was "a person of exemplary life, great learning, extreme modesty, and wonderful knowledge of mathematics." In his youth, he entered the service of the princes of Anjou; but, being sent by them on a mission to the Duke of Burgundy, he transferred his allegiance to that prince, at whose court he began his life-long friendship with Commines. Cato was a skilful astrologer, and predicted to Charles the Bold that he would lose the battles of Granson and Morat. After the fulfilment of his predictions, he took leave of the duke, and was immediately taken into the service of Louis XI., who appointed him his physician and almoner, and made him Archbishop of Vienne in 1482.

† Louis XI., son of Charles VII. and Mary of Anjou, was born on the 3rd of July, 1423; consecrated and crowned on the 15th of August, 1461; he was married, first, to Margaret of Scotland, and, secondly, to Charlotte of Savoy; and he died on the 30th of August, 1483.

sation ; but, from the time of my first being entertained in
his service to his death, at which I was present, I was more constantly in attendance on him than any one about the court,
being always one of his chamberlains, and employed in the most
important affairs of the kingdom. In him, and in all the rest of
the princes that I have either served or known, I perceived
ever a mixture of good and bad ; for they are but men like
us, and perfection belongs only to God Himself. But when in
a prince virtues and good qualities outweigh vices, he is certainly worthy of more than ordinary commendation and applause ; because persons of such rank are more inclinable to
excess in their actions than other people, by reason that
their education in their younger years is less strict ; and
when they are grown up to man's age, the generality of
those who are about them make it their endeavour to con-
form themselves to their caprices and humours.

As I have been unwilling to dissemble the matter, I may,
perhaps, in several places have said something that seems to
lessen the character of my master ; but I hope the reader
will consider the reasons that have induced me to do so.
This I dare affirm in his praise, that I never knew any
prince less faulty in the main, though I have been as conversant among great princes as any man in my time in
France ; and not only with those who have reigned in this
kingdom, but in Bretagne, Flanders, Germany, England,
Spain, Portugal, and Italy, princes spiritual as well as temporal ; besides several whom I never saw, but knew by their
letters and instructions, and by my conferences with their
ambassadors, which gave me a sufficient character of their
natures and conditions. However, it is not my intention
in the least to detract from the honour and renown of the
rest, by praising my master. I send you only what has
readily occurred to my mind, hoping you have asked for it in
order to write it in some work which it is your design to

publish in Latin (a language which your Lordship understands to perfection), by which will be shown the learning and abilities of the author, as well as the magnificence and grandeur of the prince of whom I speak. Where I am defective, you have the Lord du Bouchage * and others to apply to, who can give you a better account, and in better language; though, considering the honour King Louis XI. did me, the possessions he gave me, the privacies he admitted me to, and his never discontinuing any of his favours to me to his dying day, no person ought to remember him better than myself; and if I could forget his good actions, my misfortunes and sufferings since his decease would be sufficient to remind me of them; though it is not unusual upon the death of such great and powerful princes to see confusion among their officers, some of them being advanced, whilst others are laid aside; for honours and preferments are not always distributed according to the inclination of those who desire them.

Though your Lordship seems only to demand of me an account of such occurrences as happened during the time that I was near the king's person, I am obliged to begin a little earlier; and, having deduced them from the time of my being first entertained in his service, I shall continue them in a regular method to his death.

* Imbert de Batornay, knight, Count du Bouchage, and Lord of Ornacieux, was one of the councillors and chamberlains of Louis XI. He died on the 12th of May, 1523.

THE MEMOIRS

OF

PHILIP DE COMMINES

LORD OF ARGENTON.

BOOK THE FIRST.

CHAPTER I.

The Occasion of the Wars between Louis XI. and the Count of Charolois, afterwards Duke of Burgundy. — 1464.

As soon as my childhood was over, and I was old enough* to mount on horseback, I was presented at Lisle to Charles, Duke of Burgundy†, at that time called the Count of Charolois, who took me into his service: this was in the year 1464.

About three days after my arrival at Lisle, the Count d'Eu‡, the Chancellor of France, called Morvillier§, and the

---

* Commines died in 1511, at the age of sixty-four; so that he was about seventeen years old when he entered the service of the Duke of Burgundy.

† Charles, Count of Charolois, and afterwards Duke of Burgundy, was the son of Philip the Good and Isabella of Portugal. He was born on the 10th of November, 1433, and married 1. Catherine, the daughter of King Charles VII. of France; 2. Isabella of Bourbon; and 3. Margaret of York, sister of Edward IV., King of England. He was killed at the battle of Nancy, on the 5th of January, 1477.

‡ Charles of Artois, Count d'Eu, was the son of Philip of Artois and Mary of Berry. He was taken prisoner at the battle of Agincourt, and remained for twenty-three years in captivity in England. He died on the 25th of July, 1472, at about seventy-eight years of age.

§ Pierre de Morvilliers, knight, Lord of Clary, was the son of Philip

B

Archbishop of Narbonne*, as ambassadors from the King of France†, arrived there also ; and, in the presence of Philip, Duke of Burgundy‡, the Count of Charolois, and their privy council, were admitted to a public audience in open court§. Morvillier's speech was exceedingly arrogant, accusing the Count of Charolois of having (during his late visit to Holland) caused a small man-of-war belonging to Dieppe to be seized, in which was the Bastard of Rubempré ‖, whom he had also caused to be imprisoned, upon pretence that his design was to have surprised and carried him into France; which report he had had published wherever he went, and especially at Bruges (a town of great resort for strangers of all nations), by Sir Oliver de la Marche ¶, a Burgundian knight; for which cause the French king, finding himself, as he said, unjustly traduced, demanded of Duke Philip that Sir Oliver de la Marche might be sent prisoner to Paris, to receive such punishment as his offence deserved. To which Duke Philip made answer, that Sir Oliver de la Marche, being a native of Burgundy, and steward of his household, was in no respect subject to the crown of France; but if, however, it could be fairly proved that he

de Morvilliers and Jeanne du Drac. Though created Chancellor of France on the 3rd of September, 1461, he did not begin to discharge the duties of his office until November, 1465. He died on the 15th of December, 1476.

* Antoine du Bec Crespin was appointed Bishop of Laon on the 3rd of March, 1449, and translated to the Archbishopric of Narbonne on the 18th of January, 1460. He died at Rouen on the 15th of October, 1472.

† According to documents discovered by Mdlle. Dupont, the Seigneur de Rambures was also a member of this embassy.

‡ Philip the Good, Duke of Burgundy, son of John the Fearless and Margaret of Bavaria, was born on the 30th of June, 1396. He married 1. Michelle, daughter of Charles VII. of France ; 2. Bona of Artois ; and 3. Isabella of Portugal. He died on the 15th of June, 1467.

§ This took place on the 6th of November, 1464.

‖ The natural son of Antony, Lord of Rubempré, in Picardy.

¶ Oliver de la Marche, councillor, chamberlain, and captain of the guard of Charles, Duke of Burgundy, and chief steward of the household of the Archduke of Austria, was the son of Philip de la Marche and Jeanne Bouton. He was born in 1426, married Isabeau Machefrin, and made his will at Brussels, on the 8th of October, 1501. He is the author of some valuable memoirs relating to the times in which he lived, and also of several poetical works.

had either done or spoken anything that reflected on the king's honour, he would take care to see him punished according to the nature of the crime. That as to the Bastard of Rubempré, he had been taken prisoner upon information of intelligence which he and his confederates held in the Hague, where his son Charles, the Count of Charolois, had his residence at that time. That if his son were more suspicious than he ought to be, he had not learned it from him (for he never was of a jealous temper), but rather from his mother *, who, he must confess, was the most fearful and apprehensive lady he had ever known. But yet, though he was not timorous himself, had he been in his son's place, when the Bastard of Rubempré was hovering about that coast, he should have caused him to be apprehended, as his son had done. However, if, upon inquiry, the said bastard should not be found to have conspired against his son, as was reported, he would cause him to be released immediately, and sent back to the king, as the ambassadors demanded.

No sooner had Duke Philip ended his speech, but Morvillier began again with great and dishonourable complaints against Francis, Duke of Bretagne†; affirming that the said Duke of Bretagne and the Count of Charolois, at the time when the Count of Charolois paid his majesty a visit at Tours‡, had interchangeably set their hands and seals to an instrument of amity, whereby they had become brothers-in-arms; which instrument was delivered by Messire Tanneguy du Chastel§, who has since been made Governor of Rous-

---

* Isabella, daughter of John I., King of Portugal, and Philippa of Lancaster, married the Duke of Burgundy on the 10th of January, 1430. She died on the 17th of December, 1472, and was buried in the Carthusian convent of Gosnay-les-Béthunes.

† Francis, son of Richard, Count d'Estampes, and Margaret of Orleans, succeeded his uncle Arthur, Duke of Bretagne, in 1458. He married, 1. Margaret of Bretagne, and 2. Margaret de Foix. He died on the 9th of September, 1488.

‡ The Count of Charolois paid Louis XI. a visit at Tours in 1461. He arrived there on the 22nd of October, and left the king on the 11th of December following.

§ Tanneguy du Chastel, Viscount de la Bellière, filled the office of Grand Ecuyer of France until the death of Charles VII., on the 21st of July, 1461; upon which he withdrew to the Duke of Bretagne, who had him appointed Governor of Roussillon, in 1472. He afterwards entered the service of Louis XI. He was the son of Oliver, Seigneur du Chastel,

sillon, and borne great authority in this kingdom; and this action Morvillier heightened and exaggerated in such a manner, that he omitted nothing that could possibly be said on the subject, which might tend to the shame and dishonour of a prince. The Count of Charolois, being nettled at the severe reflections he had cast upon his friend and ally, often attempted to answer him; but Morvillier always interrupted him, saying, " My lord, I was not sent hither on an embassy to you, but to the prince your father." The count, however, repeatedly entreated his father to give him leave to speak, who at last replied, " I have answered for you as, in my judgment, a father ought to answer for his son. Nevertheless, since your desire is so great, think over it to-day, and to-morrow you shall have liberty to say what you please." Morvillier still urged the matter farther, and declared, that he could not imagine what could have induced the Count of Charolois to enter into that association with the Duke of Bretagne, unless it were a pension the king had given him *, together with the government of Normandy, but which, for some reasons, his majesty had since taken from him.

The next morning, before the same audience, the Count of Charolois, kneeling upon a velvet cushion, addressed himself first to his father, and began his discourse about the Bastard of Rubempré, alleging that the causes of his apprehension and imprisonment were just and reasonable, as would appear upon his trial. Yet I am of opinion that nothing was ever proved against him, though the presumptions were great; and I afterwards saw him discharged out of prison, where he had been kept five years. Having cleared this point, his next business was to vindicate the Duke of Bretagne and himself. He confessed that the Duke of Bretagne and he had entered into an alliance and friendship together, and had sworn to be brothers-in-arms; but that the said alliance was not intended in any way to prejudice the king

and Jeanne de Ploeuc; he married Jeanne de Raguenal, Viscountess de la Bellière, in 1462; and he died in consequence of a wound received at the siege of Bouchain in 1477.

* Chastellain relates that when the Count of Charolois visited Louis XI. at Tours, "the king, after having treated him handsomely, appointed and constituted him Governor of Normandy, with a pension of thirty-six thousand francs."

or his kingdom, but rather to serve and support him when occasion required. And lastly, as concerning the pension that had been taken from him, he said, he had only enjoyed it for one quarter, and that amounted to nine thousand francs ; and that, for his part, he never was solicitous either for that pension, or for the government of Normandy; for as long as he was so happy as to be in favour with his father, he could afford to dispense with the bounty of other people. I really believe that, if it had not been for the respect he bore his father, who was there present, and to whom he directed his speech, he would have answered in much sharper terms than he did. However, Duke Philip concluded his discourse* with great modesty and wisdom, beseeching his majesty to continue to regard him with favour, and not easily to entertain an ill opinion of him or his son. After which, he called for wine and sweetmeats; and then the ambassadors took their leave of them both. When the Count d'Eu and the Chancellor had taken their leave of the Count of Charolois, who stood at some distance from his father, the Archbishop of Narbonne coming last, the count said to him, " Present my most humble respects to the king, and tell him that he has handled me very roughly by his chancellor; but before the year is at an end, his majesty may have reason to repent it." The archbishop delivered his message punctually to the king at his return, as you will find hereafter; and these words bred a mortal hatred between his majesty and the count, which was augmented by the king's late redemption of certain towns upon the Somme— namely, Amiens, Abbeville, St. Quentin, and others; delivered formerly to Duke Philip by King Charles VII.†, in pursuance of the treaty of Arras‡, to be enjoyed by the said duke and his heirs male, till the sum of 400,000 crowns should be paid.§ How this affair was managed, I can give

* The duke's answer is given in full by Monstrelet, vol. ii. pp. 303— 304 (Bohn's edition.)

† Charles VII., King of France, son of Charles VI. and Isabel of Bavaria, was born on the 22nd of February, 1402, married Mary of Anjou in 1422, and died on the 22nd of July, 1461.

‡ The treaty of Arras was concluded on the 21st of September, 1435. It is given in full in Monstrelet, vol. ii. pp. 9—17.

§ The sum was paid in two instalments ; the first receipt of Philip the

no certain account; only this I can say, that the affairs of
the duke in his declining years, were so entirely governed by
two brothers, the Lords of Croy* and Chimay†, and others
of their family, that he consented to take the king's money,
and restore the towns that were mortgaged to him, to the
great concern and disadvantage of the Count of Charolois;
for they were the frontiers and limits of their dominions, and
they lost, in parting with them, several thousands of brave
soldiers and good subjects. The count charged the whole
matter upon the house of Croy; and when his father was
grown decrepit and superannuated, which at that time he
was very near, he drove all the said Lords of Croy from his
father's palace, took away all their employments, and confiscated their estates.

*A Treaty of Alliance between Francis, Duke of Bretagne,
on the one part, and Charles, Count of Charolois, on the
other. Made at Nantes, the 22nd of March, 1464.*

" FRANCIS, by the Grace of God, Duke of Bretagne, Earl of
Montfort, Richemond, Estampes, and Vertus, to all who
shall see or hear of these Presents, Greeting.

"Whereas love, unity, and agreement between princes,
are a means to preserve them and their dominions, in due
obedience towards God, in a flourishing state, virtue, magnificence, and tranquillity, and even to improve and augment
them; in order to which, all princes and lords ought to be very
intent and watchful, so as to repress the contentious, and all
such as would invade or form any enterprises against them :
and seeing there has been, from time immemorial, a firm
friendship and alliance made, cultivated, and maintained, as
well in respect to consanguinity, affinity and natural affection,
as otherwise, between the late most high and potent princes

Good is dated at Hesdin, on the 12th of September, 1463, and the
second on the 8th of October following.
* Antony, Lord of Croy, Count of Porcean, first chamberlain to
Philip the Good, and Knight of the Golden Fleece, became lord steward
to Louis XI., on the accession of that prince to the throne. He was the
son of John of Croy and Margaret of Craon ; and he died in 1475.
† John of Croy, Lord of La Tour-sur-Marne, Count of Chimay,
Knight of the Golden Fleece, and High Bailiff of Hainault, married
Marie de Lallain, Lady of Quiévrain, and died at Valenciennes in 1472.

the Dukes of Burgundy, and the late Dukes of Bretagne,
our predecessors (may they rest together in glory!)—and
seeing we are and have for some time been assured that
certain people in authority and near the person of the King
f France, excited thereto by an evil and accursed disposition,
have, and do daily move him to entertain enmity, indignation, displeasure, and ill-will towards several princes of his
own blood, and by false and wicked reports set him at
division and variance with them, to the detriment of the
whole kingdom; advising and exciting him to invade and
divest them of their countries and signiories; and among
others, the most high and potent princes, our most dear and
well-beloved uncle and cousin, the Duke of Burgundy, and
the Count of Charolois his son, and especially us, upon the
account of them, their territories and subjects, so as to do us
and ours all the damage and displeasure they can; for the
prevention whereof, being desirous to make use of all just
and reasonable means, we have—in conformity to the rules of
right reason, and the most just and laudable actions of our
predecessors; and to prevent any sudden, unexpected, and
injurious enterprises, which the said king, by the persuasions,
counsels, and earnest solicitations of those our ill-willers,
may form against us; and the better to enable us to withstand and resist the same, and to defend our territories,
subjects, and signiories, as we are in duty bound — entered
and do by these presents enter into an alliance, confederacy,
and agreement with our said most dear and well-beloved
cousin, the Count of Charolois, son and only heir of our said
most dear and well-beloved uncle of Burgundy, in the following manner and form, that is to say : — That we are and
shall continue a true friend and ally to him, will assist him,
take his part, advise, comfort, and succour him, and with all
our power protect, save, and defend his person, and those of
his children born or to be born, and his estates, countries,
territories, signiories, and subjects, as well those dominions
which he now holds and possesses, as those which he may
or shall possess, for the future, in the same manner as we do
our own, without any distinction, against all and every
person and persons who shall molest, lessen, make war upon,
or usurp anything from him, and his said children, their
countries, territories, signiories, and subjects, in any

manner whatsoever, without any reservation or exception
of the said lord the king; and in case he shall, by the
advice and enticements of our said enemies, or otherwise,
invade or make war upon our said cousin of Charolois, we
do promise our aid and assistance to him, our said cousin,
against the king, and all others whomsoever, that would
invade, or make war against him.   And to this end we will,
for and in favour of him, and for his assistance, engage ourselves, our territories, countries, and signiories, in possession
or reversion, our whole power, in making war against such
invaders or assailants; and we will signify and impart to
him whatever shall come to our knowledge, that may
be said, done, projected, or contrived to his prejudice, and
will defend him to the utmost of our power : And we do
comprehend in this alliance, convention, and confederacy,
our most honoured lord the Duke of Berry, and our most
dear and well-beloved cousins the Dukes of Calabria and
Bourbon; and in regard to the engagements we have
already entered into, and may do hereafter, we do comprehend therein our said cousin of Charolois, his countries,
subjects, and signiories, with his friends and allies, present
and to come, and their countries and subjects, as much as we
do ourselves and our own dominions, so far forth as they are
willing to be received and comprehended therein ; and we
shall not enter into any other alliances or confederacies, that
are prejudicial to this treaty; and we do by these presents
promise and swear by our faith, and upon corporal oath, on
the word of a prince, and upon our honour, firmly to observe
these alliances and confederacies, without doing anything to
the contrary whatsoever ; upon condition and so far forth as
our said cousin of Charolois gives us the same assurance
and promises, and observes the same.   In witness whereof,
we have signed these presents with our own hand, and sealed
them with our seal."

　　Done at Nantes, March the 22nd, in the year of our Lord
　　　1464.   Signed FRANCIS, with a flourish.   Upon the
　　　fold was written, "By the Duke's Command," and
　　　signed MILET, with a flourish.

How the Count of Charolois and several great Lords of France raised an Army against King Louis XI., under pretence of the Public Good.—1464.

A VERY few days after the departure of the king's ambassadors, John, late Duke of Bourbon*, came to Lisle, pretending a visit to his uncle Philip, Duke of Burgundy, who loved the family of Bourbon most of all the families in the world. This Duke of Bourbon was the son of Duke Philip's sister† : she was a widow, and was at that time with him, with several of her children — three daughters and one son.‡ However, this was not the true cause of the Duke of Bourbon's visit ; but his coming thither was to persuade the Duke of Burgundy to consent to the raising of an army in his dominions, as the rest of the princes of France had agreed to do; in order to demonstrate to the king the injustice and ill-management of his kingdom, and to put themselves into a condition to compel him to reform the State, if fair application could not prevail. This war was afterwards called the Public Good, it being undertaken upon that pretence. Duke Philip, who since his death has been called the Good, consented to the raising of men ; but the real object of the business was never made known to him, nor did he ever think they would ever have proceeded to blows. Immediately they began to enlist forces in his countries ; and the Count of St. Paul§ (afterwards Constable of France), being

* John II., Duke of Bourbon and Auvergne, Count of Clermont, peer, constable, and chamberlain of France, was the son of Charles I., Duke of Bourbon, and Agnes of Burgundy ; he married Jeanne, daughter of Charles VII. of France, and died on the 1st of April, 1488. He arrived at Lisle on the 14th of October, 1464.

† Agnes of Burgundy, married on the 17th of September, 1425, to Charles I., Duke of Bourbon. She became a widow on the 4th of December, 1456, and died on the 1st of December, 1476.

‡ These princesses were, 1. Catherine, who married Adolphus of Egmont, Duke of Guelders, on the 18th of December, 1463 ; 2. Margaret, who married Philip II., Duke of Savoy, on the 6th of April, 1472. The third was probably Isabella, Countess of Charolois. The son was John, Duke of Bourbon, named above.

§ Louis de Luxembourg, Count of St. Paul, was created Constable of France on the 5th of October, 1465, and took the oaths on the 12th of the same month. He was the son of Pierre de Luxembourg, Count of Couversan, and Margaret de Baux. He married, 1. Jeanne de Bar, on

come with the Marshal of Burgundy* (who was of the house
of Neufchâtel) to wait upon the Count of Charolois at
Cambray, where Duke Philip then was, the count assembled
the council, and others of his father's chief subjects, in the
palace of the Bishop of Cambray†, and there declared all the
members of the house of Croy mortal enemies both to his
father and himself‡, though the Count of St. Paul had long
before married one of his daughters to a son § of the Lord of
Croy, and alleged it would be much to his prejudice. In
short, the whole family were forced to fly out of the Duke of
Burgundy's territories, and lost great part of their estates.
These proceedings were highly displeasing to the Duke of
Burgundy, whose chief chamberlain was one of them, called
afterwards Lord of Chimay ‖; a young gentleman of good
parts, and nephew to the said Lord of Croy. This gentleman,
for the security of his person, went away without taking
leave of his master, otherwise (as he was informed) he
would have been made prisoner, or killed.¶ The old age of

the 16th of July, 1435; and 2. Mary of Savoy, on the 1st of August,
1466. He was beheaded on the 19th of December, 1475.

* Thibault IX., Lord of Neufchâtel and Blamont, and Marshal of
Burgundy, was the son of Thibault, Lord of Neufchâtel, and Agnes de
Montbeliard. In reward for his services, the king bestowed the town of
Espinal upon him in 1463. He died about 1470.

† John, Bastard of Burgundy, Bishop of Cambray in 1440, was a natural son of John, Duke of Burgundy, and Agnes de Croy. He died in 1479.

‡ The manifesto of the Count of Charolois against the Lords of Croy
will be found in M. Gachard's *Collection de Documents Inédits*, vol. i.
p. 132. It is dated Brussels, March 12th, 1464, (O. S.).

§ Philip of Croy, son of Antony, Lord of Croy, and Margaret of Lorraine, was first Hereditary Chamberlain of Brabant. Having joined the
Duke of Burgundy, who created him a Knight of the Golden Fleece, his
estates were confiscated by Louis XI. in 1476. He married Jacqueline
de Luxembourg, daughter of the Count of St. Paul, in 1455; and he
died in 1511.

‖ Philip of Croy, Count of Chimay, Baron of Quiévrain, and Knight
of the Golden Fleece, was son of John of Croy, Lord of La Tour-sur-
Marne, and Mary de Lalain, Lady of Quiévrain. He married Walpurge
de Mœurs; and died on the 8th of September, 1482. Du Clercq says,
" He was reputed to be a very wise young man, and a great *historian*."

¶ According to Du Clercq, he threw himself at the duke's feet,
" thanking him for the favours he had bestowed upon him, and begging
him to think with favour of his services; beseeching him to give him
leave to quit his court, and in great terror telling him that his life was in
danger. . . . When the duke had heard this, he was greatly troubled,

Duke Philip forced him to endure this patiently; but the
true reason of this declaration against his favourites, was the
restitution of the towns upon the River Somme, which the
duke had restored to King Louis for 400,000 crowns, and the
Count of Charolois charged the house of Croy with having
persuaded him to do it.

The Count of Charolois having made up this business, and
reconciled himself to his father as well as he could, immediately took the field with his army, being attended by
the Count of St. Paul, as chief manager of his affairs, and
general of his forces under him. His troops consisted of
about 300 men-at-arms, and 4000 archers, besides a large
number of good knights and squires from Artois, Hainault,
and Flanders, all under his command, by the appointment of
the Count of Charolois. There were other brigades as great
and considerable, under the command of the Lord of Ravestain*, brother to the Duke of Cleves†, and Lord Anthony‡,
the Bastard of Burgundy; besides several other eminent
officers, whose names, for brevity sake, I shall omit. But
above all the rest, there were two officers in more than ordinary reputation with the Count of Charolois. One of
them was called the Lord of Haultbourdin§, an old soldier,

and forbade him to depart, and very angrily took a truncheon or spear
in his hand, and went out of his chamber, saying that he would see
whether his son would kill his servants."

* Adolphus of Cleves, Lord of Ravestain, was the son of Adolphus,
Duke of Cleves, and Mary of Burgundy, sister of Philip the Good. He
married, 1. Beatrice of Portugal; and 2. Anne of Burgundy, bastard
daughter of Duke Philip. He died on the 18th of September, 1493.

† John I., Duke of Cleves, was born on the 10th of January, 1419;
married Elizabeth, daughter of John of Burgundy, Count of Nevers; and
died on the 5th of September, 1481.

‡ Anthony, Bastard of Burgundy, surnamed the Great Bastard, Lord
of Beures, in Flanders, Count of La Roche, in Ardennes, and knight of
the orders of the Golden Fleece and of St. Michael, was the son of Philip
the Good and Jeanne de Prelle. He was legitimated in January, 1485.
He died in 1504, at the age of eighty-three. He was for some time first
chamberlain to his half-brother, Duke Charles.

§ John, surnamed Hennequin, Bastard of St. Paul, Lord of Haut-
Bourdin, Knight of the Golden Fleece, councillor and chamberlain of
Charles, Duke of Burgundy, was the son of Waleran de Luxembourg,
Count of St. Paul, and Agnes de Brie. He was legitimated on the 19th
of February, 1436; and he died on the 28th of July, 1466, at about
sixty-six years of age. He was the second cousin, and not the brother
of Louis, Constable of St. Paul.

bastard brother to the Count of St. Paul, and trained up in the wars between France and England, when Henry V.* King of England, reigned in France, and Duke Philip was joined with him as his confederate and ally. The other was the Lord of Contay†, much about the age of the first: both of them were wise and valiant commanders, and of high rank in the army. There were also abundance of young gentlemen, and among them one more particularly famous, who was called Philip de Lallain‡, of a family very remarkable for their courage and loyalty, most of them having lost their lives in the service of their princes. The whole army consisted of about 1400 men-at-arms, neither well armed nor well exercised, by reason of the long peace which these princes had enjoyed; for since the treaty of Arras they had had little or no wars; only some small differences with the citizens of Ghent, which lasted not long; so that (if I am not mistaken) they had been at peace for more than thirty-six years.§ However, the men-at-arms were well mounted, and well attended; for few or none were to be seen without five or six lusty horses in his equipage. The archers might be about 8000 or 9000; out of whom, at the general muster, they selected the best; but more of them were disbanded than retained.

The subjects of the house of Burgundy were at that time very wealthy, by reason of the long peace they had enjoyed, and the goodness of their prince, who laid but few taxes upon them; so that in my judgment, if any country might then be called the land of promise, it was his country, which enjoyed great wealth and repose; more than ever it has

* Henry V., son of Henry IV. and Mary of Hereford, was born in 1388; crowned on the 9th of April, 1413; married Catherine, daughter of Charles VI., on the 2nd of June, 1420; and died at Vincennes on the 31st of August, 1422.

† William le Jeune, Lord of Contay, Governor of Arras, was the son of Robert le Jeune and Jeanne de Beauvoir, Lady of Laignicourt. He married Margaret de Sully; and died in 1468. He was a councillor, chamberlain, and chief steward of Duke Philip the Good.

‡ Philip de Lallain, knight, chamberlain of Philip, Duke of Burgundy, was the son of William de Lallain and Jeanne de Créqui. He was killed in the battle of Montlhery, on the 16th of July, 1465.

§ As the treaty of Arras was concluded on the 21st of September, 1435, peace had lasted only twenty-nine years.

since ; and it is now probably three and twenty years since their miseries began. The expenses and dresses both of women and men were great and extravagant : and their entertainments and banquets more profuse and splendid than in any other place that I ever saw. Their baths and other amusements with women, lavish and disorderly, and many times immodest: I speak of women of inferior degree. In short, the subjects of that house were then of opinion that no prince was able to cope with them, at least to impoverish them : and now in the whole world I do not know any people so desolate and miserable as they are : and I question not but the sins they committed in their prosperity are, in some measure, the occasion of their present adversity, and have brought down this heavy judgment upon them; especially since they did not own and acknowledge that all good things proceed from God, who distributes and disposes of them according to his pleasure.

The Count of Charolois having got his army in readiness as it were in an instant, and being furnished with all things necessary for a campaign, marched forward with all his troops, which were all on horseback, except those who were attached to the train of artillery, which was large and fine for those times, and accompanied by such a vast number of waggons, that, with his own only, he could enclose the greatest part of his army. At first he marched towards Noyon, and besieged a small castle called Nesle (in which there was a garrison), and took it in a few days.* Joachim, a Marshal of France†, having drawn what forces he could out of the garrison of Peronne, observed his motions, but was too weak to attempt anything against him ; and, therefore, when the Count of Charolois drew near Paris, he threw himself into that town. The Count of Charolois, during the whole of the march, would not suffer the least act of hostility to be committed, but made his soldiers pay wherever they came ; so that the towns upon the Somme, and all the others by which he marched, received his troops, in small bodies, within their

* The attack began on the 7th of June, 1465.

† Joachim Rouault, Lord of Boismenart, a councillor and chamberlain of Louis XI., and created Marshal of France in 1461, was the son of John de Rouault and Jeanne du Bellay. He died on the 7th of August, 1478.

walls, and furnished them with what they wanted for their
money; being desirous (as it seemed) to watch whether the
king or the princes would be master of the field. The count
advanced so far, that he came to St. Denis*, about a league
from Paris, where all the lords of that kingdom had promised
to meet him, but none of them came. The Duke of Bretagne,
however, sent, as his ambassador to the count, the Vice-
chancellor of Bretagne†, who had blanks with him signed by
his master, of which he made use to send news and letters,
as occasion required. He was by birth a Norman, a wise
and clever man; and so it behoved him to be, for many murmured against him. The Count of Charolois presented
himself before Paris‡, and had a smart skirmish with the
Parisians at their very gates, which was much to their
disadvantage. In the town there were no men-at-arms, but
those under the command of Marshal Joachim, and the
squadron of the Lord of Nantouillet §, who was afterwards
grand-master of the household, and who did the king as much
service in this war as any subject who ever served King of
France in his hour of need. Yet after all he was ill-requited;
but it was more the malice of his enemies, than the king's fault;
though, to speak impartially, neither of them was altogether
excusable. The common people in the city (as I have since
been informed) were in so great a consternation that day
that they cried out, "The enemy have entered;" but without
any grounds. However, the Lord Haultbourdin (whom I
mentioned before, and who had formerly lived in that town,
when it was nothing near so strongly fortified as it is now)
was entirely for storming it; and the soldiers, despising the citizens, whom they had beaten up to their very gates, were also
eager for it. Yet, probably, after all, it was found impracticable,
and so the Count of Charolois marched back to St. Denis.

* On Friday, the 5th of July: he remained there until the 10th.
† John de Rouville, doctor of laws, Vice-chancellor of Bretagne, was
the son of Pierre Gougeul, Lord of Rouville, and Aldonce de Braque-
mont. He was still living in February, 1476.
‡ On the 8th of July.
§ Charles de Melun, knight, Lord of Nantouillet and Normanville,
and Grand Master of France, was the son of Philip de Melun and Jeanne
de Nantouillet. After having for some time enjoyed the favour of King
Louis XI., he fell into disgrace, was accused of treason, and beheaded on
Saturday, the 20th of August, 1468.

The next day, in the morning, a council of war was held, in which it was debated whether or no they should march forward to meet the Dukes of Berry * and Bretagne, who were not far off, as the Chancellor of Bretagne affirmed, and produced letters to that effect; but the truth is, he had written them upon his master's blanks, and knew nothing of them besides. The decision was, that they should pass the River Seine with their army. The greatest part of the officers opposed this; and were of opinion, it was best to return home, since the rest of the princes had not been punctual to their day; saying, it was enough for them to have passed the Somme and the Marne, without endeavouring to pass the Seine too. Some even began to start great difficulties in this undertaking, upon the account of not having any places behind us to retreat to in case of necessity; yet, notwithstanding all this, the Count of Charolois passed the river with his whole army, and posted himself at Pont Saint Cloud, which made the whole army murmur extremely against the Count of St. Paul and the Vice-chancellor of Bretagne.

The next day after his arrival, news was brought (from a certain lady of that kingdom, written with her own hand) that the king was come out of the county of Bourbon, and advancing against him with forced marches. But, before I proceed, it will be necessary to say something of the occasion of the king's march into Bourbonnois.

The king, understanding that all the great lords of his kingdom had declared against him, or at least against his government, resolved first of all to invade the Duke of Bourbon's dominions, who seemed to have most openly declared himself against him; and because his country was in an ill posture of defence, he believed he might easily conquer it. Accordingly he made himself master of several places, and would have entirely subdued the whole province, had he not been prevented by succours from Burgundy under the

* Charles of France, Duke of Berry, and brother of Louis XI., was born on the 28th of December, 1446. He died Duke of Guienne, most probably on the 28th of May, 1472; having made his will on the 24th. He had taken advantage of the king's absence to leave Poitiers, and join the disaffected nobles in Bretagne.

command of the Lord of Coulches*, the Marquis of Rottelin†, the Lord of Montagu‡, and others; with whom there was also in arms William de Rochefort §, Chancellor of France, a person at this day in very good esteem. These forces were raised in Burgundy by the Count of Beaujeu‖ and the Cardinal of Bourbon ¶ (who was brother to John, Duke of Bourbon), and by them thrown into Moulins. On the other side also, reinforcements were sent to the Duke of Bourbon, by the Duke of Nemours**, the Count of Armagnac ††, and the Lord of Albret ‡‡, with a strong party of men, some of whom were very good soldiers, who had deserted the king's side, and had retired to them; yet the greatest number of them

* Claude de Montagu, Lord of Coulches, councillor and chamberlain of Dukes Philip and Charles of Burgundy, Knight of the Golden Fleece, was killed in the battle of Bussy in 1470.

† Philip, Marquis of Hochberg, Count of Neufchâtel, in Switzerland, Lord of Rottelin, and Marshal of Burgundy, was the son of Rodolph of Hochberg, and Margaret, the daughter of William de Vienne, Lord of Saint-George. He married Mary of Savoy in 1480; and died in 1503.

‡ John de Neufchâtel, Lord of Montagu and Resnel, councillor and chamberlain of the King of France and of the Duke of Burgundy, and Knight of the Golden Fleece, was the son of Thibault VIII., Lord of Neufchâtel, and Agnes de Montbéliard. He was still living in August, 1486.

§ William, Lord of Rochefort and Pleuvant, knight, chamberlain of Philip the Good, was created Chancellor of France on the 12th of May, 1483. He was the son of James, Lord of Rochefort, and Agnes de Cléron. He died on the 12th of August, 1492.

‖ Pierre II., Duke of Bourbon and Auvergne, Count of Clermont, and Lord of Beaujeu, was born in November, 1439. He was the son of Charles I., Duke of Bourbon, and Agnes of Burgundy. He was betrothed on the 22nd of March, 1463, to Mary of Orleans; but this alliance was broken off by Louis XI., who gave him his daughter Anne in marriage. He married her in 1474; and died on the 8th of October, 1503.

¶ Charles II., Duke of Bourbon, brother of the Count of Beaujeu, Cardinal of the Holy See, Archbishop and Count of Lyons. He died on the 13th of September, 1488.

** Jacques d'Armagnac, Duke of Nemours, Count of La Marche, son of Bernard d'Armagnac and Eleanor of Bourbon; married Louisa, daughter of Charles of Anjou, Count of Maine; beheaded on the 4th of August, 1477.

†† John V., Count of Armagnac, son of John IV. and Isabella of Navarre; assassinated on the 5th of March, 1473.

‡‡ Charles II., Lord of Albret, son of Charles I., Lord of Albret, and Mary de Sully; died in 1471, at the age of seventy.

were very ill provided, and having no pay, they were forced
to live upon free quarters.   But the king, for all their great
numbers, found them employment enough; so that by degrees they came to a treaty; especially the Duke of Nemours,
who swore fealty to the king *, and engaged to continue firm
and loyal to his cause : however, he afterwards revolted,
which was the occasion (as the king often told me) of the
displeasure he retained against him so long.   But when the
king found he could not finish the war in the Bourbonnois
so soon as he expected, and that the Count of Charolois was
advancing on Paris, apprehending lest the Parisians should
give admission to him, and to the Dukes of Berry and Bretagne (who were marching from Bretagne, and all of them
pretending the good of the kingdom), and fearing likewise
that if the Parisians should receive them, all the other towns
would do the like — he resolved by great marches to throw
himself and what forces he had with him into Paris, and (if
possible) hinder the conjunction of those two mighty armies ;
but he had no intention of fighting, as he has since told me
many times in our discourse about these affairs.

* * *

Chap. III.

How the Count of Charolois encamped with his Army near Montlhery, and
of the Battle fought in that place between him and the King of France.—
1465.

As I said before, as soon as the Count of Charolois was informed of the king's departure, that he had left Bourbonnois,
and (as he at least supposed) was marching directly to fight
him, he resolved also to advance forward and meet the king.
Then, communicating the contents of the letter he had received from the above-mentioned lady (still concealing her
name), he declared his resolution of venturing a battle, and
encouraged his soldiers to behave themselves like men.
Upon this, he immediately advanced with his army, and took
up his quarters at Longjumeau, a village not far from Paris;
but the Count of St. Paul, with the whole vanguard, marched

* This oath, dated November 5. 1465, is quoted by Lenglet, vol. ii.,
p. 561.

c

forward to Montlhery, which is about two leagues beyond; from whence several scouts and spies were immediately sent out, to discover which way the king took, and to give notice of his approach. After some deliberation, Longjumeau was chosen for the place of battle, in the presence of the Count of St. Paul, the Lord Haultbourdin, and the Lord of Contay; and thither, by agreement amongst themselves, the Count of St. Paul was to retire, upon the first notice of the king's arrival.

Now you must know, that the Count of Maine*, with 700 or 800 men-at-arms, was marching against the Dukes of Berry and Bretagne, who had in their army several wise and experienced officers, who had been cashiered by king Louis at his first accession to the crown, though they had done his father eminent service in the recovery and pacification of his kingdom; which treatment the king afterwards acknowledged to be an error, and frequently repented. Among others, there was the Count of Dunois†, a person considerable in all things; the Marshal de Loheac‡, the Count of Dammartin§, the Lord of Bueil‖, and many others, besides fully five hundred men-at-arms, who, having deserted his majesty's service, had retired to the Duke of Bretagne, as they were all his subjects, born in his country, and at that time in his army. The Count of Maine, who, as I said before, was marching against them, finding himself too weak to engage them, retired before them as they advanced, and

* Charles of Anjou, first of the name, Count of Maine, son of Louis II., Duke of Anjou, and Yolande of Arragon. He was born on the 14th of October, 1414, and died on the 10th of April, 1472.

† John, Bastard of Orleans, Count of Dunois, and Grand Chamberlain of France, was the son of Louis of Orleans and Mariette d'Enghien, the wife of Aubert Le Flamenc, Lord of Cany. He died on the 24th of Nov., 1468.

‡ André de Laval, Lord of Loheac, Admiral and Marshal of France, died in 1486, at the age of seventy-five.

§ Antoine de Chabannes, Count of Dammartin, Lord of Saint-Fargeau, and grand-master of the king's household, was born in 1411. He was the son of Robert de Chabannes, and Alix de Bort. He married, by contract signed on the 20th of September, 1439, Margaret de Nanteuil, Countess of Dammartin; and he died on the 25th of December, 1488.

‖ John, fifth of the name, Lord of Bueil, Count of Sancerre, knight, councillor and chamberlain of the king, and Admiral of France, was the son of John, Lord of Bueil, and Margaret Dauphine, Lady of Mermande. He commanded ninety-five lances in 1474.

retreated towards the king ; whilst the Dukes of Berry and
Bretagne were endeavouring to join with the Burgundians.
Some would have it, that the Count of Maine held intelligence with them ; but I could never discover this, and
therefore do not believe it.*

The Count of Charolois being posted, as I said before, at
Longjumeau, and his van at Montlhery, was informed by
a prisoner that was brought to him, that the Count of Maine
had joined with the king†, who had then in his army all the
standing forces in the kingdom, amounting to about 2200
men-at-arms, besides the arrier-ban of Dauphiny, and about
forty or fifty gentlemen of Savoy, all very good soldiers.

. In the meantime the king had called a council of war, at
which the Count of Maine, Monsieur de Brezey‡, the Grand
Seneschal of Normandy, the Admiral of France§, who was
of the house of Montauban, and several other officers, assisted : and in conclusion, whatever had been said either for
or against it, his majesty resolved not to fight, but only to
throw himself into Paris, without coming near the place
where the Burgundians were encamped ; and in my judg-

* Oliver de la Marche, who is generally well informed, mentions the
Count of Maine among the princes and lords who were in league with the
Count of Charolois.

† "The Count of Maine was with the king, to whom he brought about
five hundred lances, and blamed him for having determined to fight ; and
as he could not divert the king from his purpose, he said to him, 'My lord,
I had come to you to serve you and accompany you, and endeavour to
effect a friendly arrangement between you and your cousin of Charolois,
and the other princes of your blood, and not to fight against them ; and
as it pleases you to do so, and not otherwise, I shall depart ; so farewell.'
And so he departed with all his company, many of whom murmured
greatly against him ; for they thought he should have taken leave earlier,
and without coming so far.   And when the king heard that he had really
departed, and abandoned him in this peril, he said that he was betrayed.
Nevertheless, he remained unmoved, and kept his army together ; and,
having exhorted his men, determined to fight Charolois before the arrival
of his brother, the Duke of Berry, and the Duke of Bretagne."—*Hennin*,
p. 430.

‡ Pierre de Brezé, Lord of Varenne, Count of Maulevrier, Grand
Seneschal of Anjou, Poitou, and Normandy, was the son of Pierre de
Brezé and Clemence Carbonnel.   He married Jeanne Crespin, and was
killed in the battle of Montlhery, on the 16th of July, 1465.

§ John, Lord of Montauban and Romilly, Marshal of Bretagne, and
Admiral of France, was the son of William of Montauban and Bona
Visconti.   He died in May, 1466.

ment, his resolution was good. He had no great confidence
in the Grand Seneschal of Normandy, and therefore asked
him one day very seriously, whether or no he had given
anything in writing under his hand and seal to the princes
who were confederate against him; to which the grand
seneschal replied that he had, and they might keep it, but
his body should be the king's: and he said this jocularly, as
his custom was to speak. The king was satisfied, and gave
him the command of his vanguard, and the charge of his
guides, because, as is said before, he wished to avoid a battle.
But the seneschal being resolved to have his own way, privately told some of his confidants: "I will bring the armies
so close together this day, that he must be a very experienced
general who will part them without fighting:" and, indeed,
he was as good as his word, and the first men killed were
himself and his troops. This expression of his the king
afterwards told me himself; for at that time I was in the
service of the Count of Charolois.

In short, on the 27th of July, 1465*, the king's vanguard
was advanced near Montlhery, where the Count of St. Paul
was posted, who immediately informed the Count of Charolois (who was encamped at Longjumeau, about two leagues
off, at the place marked out for the field of battle) of their
arrival; desiring him to send him a reinforcement with all
speed, for all his men-at-arms and archers were dismounted
and on foot, and so encumbered with their waggons, that
they could not possibly retreat to Longjumeau, according to
the orders he had received, without seeming to run away,
which would involve the whole army in great danger.
Upon receiving this message, the Count of Charolois immediately sent a large detachment of troops under the command
of the Lord Anthony, Bastard of Burgundy, to reinforce the
Count of St. Paul with all diligence; and was himself in sus
pense whether he should follow him or no; but at length he
marched after the rest of the army, and arrived about seven
in the morning. Five or six of the king's standards were,
however, already planted along the side of a great ditch,
which separated the two armies.

There was still in the host of the Count of Charolois the

* The battle of Montlhery was fought on Tuesday, the 16th of July,
see the *Chronique Scandaleuse*, and Lenglet, vol. ii. p. 27.

Vice-chancellor of Bretagne, called Rouville, and with him
an old soldier, called Maderey*, who had surrendered Pont
Saint Maxence to the Burgundians. These two were in no
little fear, in respect that the whole army murmured against
them, seeing the battle was ready to begin, and the forces
they had so much boasted of were not yet arrived to join
the army. Whereupon, before the fight began, they both
betook themselves to their heels, and fled that way by which
they presumed they would find the Bretons. The Count of
Charolois found the Count of St. Paul on foot, and his
troops ranged themselves in order of battle as they marched
up; and we found all the archers dismounted, and every man
with a stake planted before him; several pipes of wine had
been broached, and were set for them to drink; and from
the little I saw, never men had more desire to fight, which
I took to be a good omen, and which comforted me extremely. Our first orders were, that every man should
alight, without any exception: but that was countermanded
afterwards, and nearly all the men-at-arms mounted again.
However, several good knights and squires were ordered to
remain on foot; and among the rest, the Lord des Cordes†
and his brother.‡ The Lord Philip de Lalain was likewise
on foot (for at that time, among the Burgundians, it
was most honourable to fight in that manner among the
archers), and there was always a large number of these
volunteers among them, to encourage the infantry, and make
them fight the better; which custom they had learnt from
the English, when Duke Philip made war upon France,
during his youth, for two-and-thirty years together without

---

* The *Chronique Scandaleuse* names him Madre, and says that he was
captain of Pont Saint Maxence, "for Master Pierre L'Orfèvre, Lord of
Ermenonville."

† Philip of Crèvecœur, Lord des Cordes or Desquerdes, Governor of
Artois and Picardy, and Knight of the Golden Fleece, passed over to the
service of Louis XI. after the death of Charles the Rash, and was named
Marshal and Grand Chamberlain of France. He was the son of James
of Crèvecœur, and Margaret de la Trémoille, Lady of Desquerdes. He
died on the 22nd of April, 1494, at the age of seventy-six.

‡ Antony, Lord of Crèvecœur and Thiennes, councillor and chamberlain of Duke Philip the Good, Knight of the order of St. Michael, councillor and chamberlain of Louis XI., and Grand Louvetier of France,
was the son of James de Crèvecœur and Bonne de la Viefville. He died
about 1493.

any truce. But the greatest part of the burden of the war
lay upon the English, who were powerful and rich, and
governed at that time by that wise, graceful, and valiant
prince, King Henry V., who had many wise and brave men
under him, and very great commanders, such as the Earl of
Salisbury *, Talbot †, and others whom I pass by, as being
before my time, though I have seen some few of them who
survived; for when God was, as it were, weary of doing
them good, that wise king died at the Bois de Vincennes, and
his son ‡, a weak prince, was crowned King of France and
England at Paris: after which factions began to stir, and
civil wars arose in England, which have almost lasted till
this present time, by reason of the usurpation of the crown
by the house of York. §   But whether their title was good or
not, I cannot determine, for the disposal of those things is
from heaven.

But to return to my subject. The dismounting and
mounting again of the Burgundians took up a great deal of
time, and occasioned the loss of abundance of men ; and by
this means, that valiant gentleman, Philip de Lalain, was
slain, being but slightly armed. The king's troops defiled
through the forest of Torfou, and were not, at their first appearance, above four hundred men-at-arms; so that, if they
had been charged at once, in all probability there had been
but little or no resistance ; because, as I have said, they were

* Thomas Montague, Earl of Salisbury, was the son of John Montague, and Maude, the daughter of Sir Adam Francis. He married
Eleanor, daughter of Thomas, Earl of Kent ; and was killed at the siege
of Orleans, on the 3rd of November, 1428. In his will he assumes the
titles of Earl of Salisbury and Perch, and Lord Monthermer.

† John Talbot, Earl of Shrewsbury and Weysford, was the son of
Richard Talbot, and Ankaret, daughter of John Strange, of Blackmere.
He married, 1. Maude, daughter of Sir Thomas Neville, knight ; and 2.
Margaret, daughter of Richard Beauchamp, Earl of Warwick. He was
killed at the siege of Châtillon, on the 20th of July, 1453.

‡ Henry VI., son of Henry V. and Catherine of France, was born on
the 6th of December, 1421 ; crowned at London on the 6th of November,
1429 ; and consecrated King of France, at Paris, on the 17th of December,
1431. He married Margaret of Anjou in November, 1444 ; and died on
the 23rd of May, 1471.

§ Edward IV., Earl of March, was the son of Richard, Duke of York ;
he dispossessed Henry VI. of the throne, on the ground of being descended from an elder son of Edward III.

forced to march one abreast; but their numbers still increasing, the Lord of Contay, who was an experienced officer,
rode up to the Count of Charolois, and told him, that if he
had a mind to win the battle, it was high time to charge the
enemy; giving his reasons for it, and telling him, that if
he had attacked them sooner, he would have routed them
already, for then they were but few, but now they increased
visibly; and indeed, this was true. Upon which the whole
order and disposition of the battle was altered, every man
throwing in his advice; whilst, in the meantime, a great
and smart skirmish was begun at the end of the village of
Montlhery, between the archers on both sides.

The king's troops, consisting of all the archers of his
guard glittering in their liveries, and very well disciplined,
were commanded by Poncet de Riviere*; those of the
count's party, being volunteers, were in no regular order, and
under no command. However, in this manner they began
the engagement, in which the Lord Philip de Lalain, and
James du Mas † (an excellent officer, afterwards master of
the horse to Charles, Duke of Burgundy), fought on foot
among the archers. The Burgundians, who were superior
in numbers, possessed themselves of a house, and unhinging
two or three of the doors, made use of them, instead of
shields; after which they advanced into the street, and set
fire to one of the houses. The wind did them service, driving
the fire upon the king's forces, who began to give ground,
retire to their horses, and fly. Upon which the noise and
shouting was so great, that the Count of Charolois marched
forward, and abandoned the whole order which he had first
adopted.

By the count's first orders, his troops were to halt twice
by the way, because of the great distance between the vanguard and the main battle. The king's forces were drawn
up towards the castle of Montlhery, with a large hedge and
ditch in their front; and besides, the fields that lay behind

* He was then the captain of a hundred lances, of which office he
was deprived by the king soon after, and in exchange for which he
received the title of Bailiff of Montferrant. He subsequently left the
service of Louis XI., and entered that of the Duke of Bretagne, who
appointed him one of his councillors and chamberlains.
† He was killed in the battle of Morat, on the 22nd of June, 1476.

c 4

them were full of corn and beans, and such kind of grain, the soil being very rich and good. All the count's archers marched on foot before him in very ill order; though I am of opinion, that the chiefest strength of an army in the day of battle consists in the archers; but they must be strong and very numerous, for few are of no avail. I would have them also but indifferently mounted, that they may not be afraid of losing their horses, or rather that they had none at all; and for one day it is better to have raw soldiers that have never been in any action, than those that have been trained up in the wars; and in this I am of the same opinion with the English, who, without dispute, are the best archers in the world. It was said, that orders had been given that the army should halt twice by the way, to give the infantry time to breathe, because it was a great distance which they had to march, and the stiffness and stubbornness of the corn hindered their progress extremely. However, all things were done as perfectly contrary, as if they designed to lose the battle on purpose; whereby God did plainly manifest to all the world, that all battles are in his hands, and that he disposes of victory as he pleases. And indeed I cannot be persuaded, that the abilities of any one man are sufficient to manage and command so great a number, nor that things can be executed in the field in the same manner as they have been concerted in the council; and I am of opinion, that any man possessed of natural reason, who is so arrogant as to think himself able to effect this, assumes much of the honour that is due only to God. For though every man is obliged to perform his duty, and to endeavour to do what lies in his power, yet at the same time he ought to acknowledge, that war is one of God's means of accomplishing his will which he often begins upon small and trivial occasions, and gives the victory sometimes to one and sometimes to another; and this is a mystery so great, that from it all the kingdoms and governments of the world do take their rise and increase as well as their end and dissolution.

But to return from this digression; the Count of Charolois advanced, without giving any breath either to his archers or foot soldiers. The king's troops (being all men-at-arms) marched out at both ends of the hedge, and when they came near enough to make use of their lances, the Burgundian men-at-arms broke through the ranks of their own archers (who were the flower and hope of their army), without giving them leisure to discharge one arrow. The whole number of our horse was, I believe, not above 1200, and of them scarce fifty understood how to lay a lance in rest; there were not 400 of them armed with cuirasses, and very few of their servants had any arms at all; and the reason of it was, because of the long peace, and because, for the ease of their subjects, the house of Burgundy had not been used to keep any standing forces in pay: but since that time that country has not enjoyed any repose, but is rather grown worse than better at this very day. However, though the strength and flower of their army was thus broken and thrown into disorder by themselves, God (who disposes of these mysteries as he pleases) ordered things so, that on the right wing towards the castle, where the Count of Charolois commanded, victory declared on his side without any considerable opposition. It was my fortune to be with him all that day, during the whole action, in less fear than in any engagement I have ever been in since, which I impute to my youth, as not having a just sense and apprehension of the danger, but I rather wondered at the presumption of any man that durst venture to oppose the prince I served, whom I believed to be, without comparison, the greatest monarch in the world. Such vain notions inexperienced people frame to themselves; whence it arises that they often maintain strange and irrational arguments, without any ground or foundation at all; for which reason it is good to make use of the advice of him who says, that "A man never repents of speaking little, but often of speaking too much."

The left wing was commanded by the Lord Ravestain, the Lord Jacques de St. Paul*, and several other men of quality, who plainly perceived that their body of men-at-arms was too weak to encounter the enemy; but they were too near to alter the order of battle. To be short, this wing was entirely broken, and driven, some of them to their waggons; but the greatest part of them made towards a forest, which was nearly half a league from the field of

---

* James of Luxembourg, Lord of Richebourg, councillor and chamberlain of the King of France, and Knight of the Golden Fleece. He was brother of the Constable of St. Paul. He died on the 20th of Aug., 1487.

battle. At their waggons some of the Burgundian infantry rallied and stood to their arms. The chief of those who pursued us, were the nobles of Dauphiny and Savoy, with a great party of men-at-arms, who verily believed they had won the victory; and not without reason, for the Burgundians on that wing, among whom were several persons of note and distinction*, fled in great numbers; and most of them fled upon the spur towards Pont St. Maxence, which they supposed still held out for the Count of Charolois. However, a good number still maintained their ground in the forest, amongst whom was the Count of St. Paul, who had retreated thither with a good body of forces; for he was pretty near to the forest, and he plainly showed afterwards that he did not think the battle utterly lost.

CHAP. IV.

Of the imminent Danger to which the Count of Charolois was exposed, and the manner of his being rescued. — 1465.

THE Count of Charolois pursued the enemy on the side where he commanded, about half a league beyond Montlhery, and with a very small body of forces; for though the enemy were numerous, yet they made no resistance, and therefore he concluded the victory was his own; but it was not long before one Monsieur Anthony le Breton, an ancient gentleman of Luxembourg, came up to him and told him the French had rallied their forces on the field of battle, and if he followed the pursuit any further he would certainly be lost; yet, though he repeated his opinion over and over, the count would not stop for him; but presently the Lord of Contay (whom I have mentioned before) came in also, brought him the same intelligence as the old gentleman had done, and delivered it with such eagerness, that he began to hearken to his counsel, and quickly faced about; and it was well he did; for had he advanced but two bow-shots further, in my judgment he had been taken prisoner, as

* Among them were the Lords of Happlaincourt, Ameries, Inchy, and Robodenghes; the last of whom returned on learning that Charles had gained the victory.

several were that had got before him. In his return, near
the village of Montlhery, he discovered a flying body of
foot, whom he pursued (though he had scarce a hundred
horse with him); and of that whole brigade, but one single
footman made any opposition, who gave the count such a
blow on the stomach with a spear, that the mark of it was
to be seen at night. Most of the rest saved themselves in
the gardens, but he who struck the count was killed upon
the spot. As we marched by the castle, we discovered the
archers of the king's guard drawn up before the gate, who
did not stir upon our coming up to them, at which the count
was extremely surprised; as he imagined there was not a
man left to oppose him. As he wheeled about to march into
the field (part of his men had already become separated
from him), he was so furiously attacked on a sudden by
about fifteen or sixteen men-at-arms, that at the very first
charge they slew Philip D'Oignies *, his esquire-carver, who
bore his guidon. The Count of Charolois himself was in
imminent danger † in this encounter, and received several
wounds, but especially one in the neck with a sword (the
mark of which remained to his dying day), for want of his
beaver, which, being slightly fastened on in the morning,
dropped from his head in the battle, and I myself saw it fall.
The enemy immediately laid hands on him, crying out,
"My lord, surrender yourself; we know you well; do not
obstinately throw away your life." However, he still made
a gallant defence, and at that very instant one John
Cadet ‡, a physician's son of Paris, who was in his service (a
tall, stout, lusty person), mounted on a horse as large as
himself, broke in, and parted them by riding between them ;
upon which the French party wheeled, and marched off to

* Philip D'Oignies, Lord of Bruay and Chaulnes, son of Antony, Lord
of Bruay, and Jeanne de Brimeu, Lady of Chaulnes. He was Bailiff of
Courtray ; and married Antoinette de Beaufort.

† "The Count of Charolois," says the *Chronique Scandaleuse*, " was so
hotly pursued that he was twice taken prisoner by Geoffroy de Saint-Belin
and Gilbert de Grassay, and afterwards rescued again." See Lenglet,
vol. ii. p. 28.

‡ Oliver de la Marche names him Robert Cotereau, and adds that
"the Count immediately dubbed the said Master Robert Cotereau a
knight, and bestowed on him the office of lieutenant of the fiefs in Brabant." La Marche, vol. ii. p. 237.

the ditch, where they had been drawn up in the morning ;
for they were afraid of another party which they perceived
advancing towards them. The count, covered with blood,
marched out to them into the field. They were the colours
of the Bastard of Burgundy, which were so torn when they
came, there was scarce a foot of them left ; and under the
banner of the count's archers, there were not above forty
left in all, to whom we joined ourselves (being about thirty)
in no little fear. The Count of Charolois changed his horse
immediately, and had another given him which belonged to
Simon de Quingy *, who was at that time his page, but has
since been very well known. The count, as I said before,
drew out into the field to rally his men, but for the half
hour we stayed there, we thought of nothing but running
away, provided we had seen a hundred of the enemy
advancing to attack us. There came to us about ten or
twenty men, both horse and foot. Most of our infantry
were either wounded or extremely fatigued with the battle
and their long march in the morning; and for an hour together
our whole body did not exceed a hundred, but by degrees
it increased. The corn was very high and thick, and the
dust was most terrible ; the whole field was scattered with
dead horses and men, yet none of the dead men could be
recognised on account of the dust.

Immediately afterwards, we discovered the Count of St.
Paul marching out of the forest, at the head of about forty
men-at-arms, under his own colours, and advancing directly
towards us, still increasing in numbers as he moved on ; but
they still seemed very far from us. We sent to him three
or four times to pray him to hasten his march; but he kept
his own pace, marching on very slowly and in good order,
and causing his men to gather up the lances that lay scattered
on the ground, which sight greatly rejoiced and animated our
troops. With him a great number rallied again, and at last
came and joined us, so that we found ourselves to be a complete body of about eight hundred men-at-arms ; but we

* Simon de Quingy was, in 1471, cup-bearer, and in 1472 gentleman
of the bedchamber, to the Duke of Burgundy. Molinet speaks of him
as " Lord of Montbaillon." According to Commines, he became Bailiff
of Troyes ; and perhaps it is he who figures, with the title of " knight of
the court of Parliament," among the plenipotentiaries sent to Saint-Jean-de
Lône, in the year 1515, by the Archduchess Philiberte of Luxembourg

had few or no foot, which prevented the count from gaining
a complete victory, for there was a ditch and a thick hedge
between the two armies.

On the king's side there fled the Count of Maine with
several other persons of quality *, and not fewer than
eight hundred men-at-arms. Some will have it, that the
Count of Maine held correspondence with the Burgundians;
but to speak truth, I think there was no such thing. Never
was there a greater rout on both sides; but (which is
remarkable) the two princes themselves kept the field. On
the king's side there was a person of note who fled as far as
Lusignan without stopping, and on the count's there was
another ran as far as Quesnoy-le-Comte ; which two gentlemen certainly had no intention or desire to encounter one
another.

While both armies stood thus drawn up in order of battle
facing one another, the cannon began to play on both sides,
which killed abundance of men, but neither party desired to
venture a second engagement. Our army was more
numerous than the king's: yet so powerful was his royal
presence, and so efficacious the obliging language he used to
his soldiers, that I verily believe had it not been for him,
they would certainly have all fled ; as indeed I have since
learned was the case. Some few there were on our side
who were for fighting again, and particularly the Lord
Haultbourdin, who affirmed he saw the enemy filing off, and
preparing to run : and doubtless had we had but a hundred
archers to have shot through the hedge, the victory had
been entirely ours.

Whilst both armies were in this posture and suspense,
without offering to engage, the night came upon us, and the
king retired to Corbeil†, though we supposed he had encamped in the field. A barrel of their powder was accidentally blown up where the king had been, which set fire
to several waggons that were placed along the hedge ; and

* In addition to the Count of Maine, the *Chronique Scandaleuse*
mentions " the Admiral de Montauban, the Lord of La Barbe, and other
captains, who had fully seven or eight hundred lances." See Lenglet,
vol. ii. p. 28.

† The king arrived at Corbeil, " on the day of the battle, at about
eleven o'clock at night ; and sojourned in that place until the 18th of
July." Du Clercq, vol. xv. p. 26.

we imagined the blaze to be fires in their quarters. The
Count of St. Paul, who seemed to be a great man among us,
and the Lord Haultbourdin, who was a greater, commanded
our carriages to be brought to us where we lay, and our
whole body to be enclosed with them, which was presently
done. As we stood thus rallied, and drawn up in order of
battle, several of the king's soldiers, who had been following the pursuit, returned, believing the victory was their
own; and being obliged to pass through our camp, were
slain, and very few of them escaped. The men of note that
fell on the king's side were the Lord Geoffroy de St. Belin*,
the Grand Seneschal of Normandy, and one Flocquet, a
captain.† On the Burgundian side there was slain Philip
de Lalain. Of infantry and common soldiers we lost more
than the king: but of horsemen the greatest loss was on the
king's side. The king's forces took most of those who fled
prisoners. On both sides there were at least two thousand
men slain; however, the battle was well fought, for both
sides had brave men, and both were thoroughly tired of it.
But in my opinion, it was an extraordinary action to rally
in the field, and to face one another for three or four hours
together; and certainly both princes had great reason highly
to esteem those subjects that stood so firmly by them in
this pinch: but in short they acted like men, and not like
angels. One man lost his places and estates for running
away, and they were given to others, who had fled ten
leagues beyond him. One of our great men lost his employment, and was banished his master's presence, yet in a
month's time he was restored again, and in greater authority
than ever.

When we had thus surrounded ourselves with our waggons, every man reposed as well as he could: we had a
great number of wounded men, and most of us were much
dispirited and alarmed, fearing lest the Parisians, under the

* Geoffroy de Saint-Belin, knight, Baron of Saxefontaine, was the son
of Pierre de Saint-Belin, Lord of Blaisy, and Simonne de Nogent. He
married Margaret de Baudricourt; and is mentioned, with the title of
Bailiff of Chaumont, as one of the chamberlains of the King of France, in
the years 1463 and 1464.

† Robert de Flocques, or Flocquet, son of Robert and brother of
James, both of them Bailiffs of Evreux. He also filled that office; and
was buried in the Abbey of St. Catherine-du-Mont, at Rouen.

command of Marshal Joachim (who was the king's lieutenant in that city), should sally out upon us with two hundred
men-at-arms, who were there in garrison; and we should be
attacked on both sides.   As soon as it was quite dark, fifty
lances were commanded out, to get intelligence where the
king was quartered; of which number about twenty only
went forth.   The place where we believed the king lay, was
not above three bow-shots from our camp. In the meantime,
the Count of Charolois ate and drank a little, and all the
rest of the army did the same; after which the wound in his
neck was carefully dressed. To make room for him, before he
could sit down to eat, four or five dead bodies had to be
removed, and two trusses of straw were brought for him to
sit on.   As we were removing the dead men, one of the
poor stark naked creatures called out for some drink, and
on putting a little of the ptisan (of which the count had
drank) into his mouth, he came to himself, and proved to
be one Pierre Savarot, an archer of the count's guard, and
a very brave fellow; upon which his wounds were dressed,
and he was cured.

It was then debated in council what measures were best
to be taken.   The Count of St. Paul, who was the first that
gave his opinion, said, that we were posted in a very dangerous place, and advised that we should retreat towards
Burgundy by break of day; that we should burn part of our
waggons, preserving only such as belonged to the artillery;
and that no man should carry off his waggon unless he had
above ten lances under his command; and that it was impossible for us to remain without provisions in the camp we
were in, between Paris and the king's army. Next to him
the Lord Haultbourdin made a speech much to the same
purpose, without waiting to hear what intelligence the
scouts we had sent out would bring us. After him three or
four more spoke, and all of them concurred. The last who
gave his opinion was the Lord of Contay, who said, that,
as soon as these resolutions should be spread abroad in the
army, the soldiers would immediately prepare for flight,
and would be taken prisoners before they could get twenty
leagues: which opinion he strengthened with several substantial reasons; and therefore his advice was to rest themselves that night as well as they could, and that in the

morning, by break of day, they should attack the king's army, with a full resolution either to conquer, or die upon the spot; which he conceived a much safer way than to take to flight. The result of all was that the Count of Charolois took the Lord of Contay's advice, and gave orders that every man should repose himself for two hours, and be ready at sound of trumpet; and at the same time he desired several officers that were about him to go and encourage his men.

About midnight the scouting party returned, and you may believe they went not far; for they brought word the king was encamped where the fires were seen: immediately, others were sent out, and about an hour after, every man put himself into a condition to fight, but the greatest part had more inclination to retreat. About break of day, the party that had been sent out last met a waggoner of ours (whom the enemy had taken that morning) as he was bringing a pitcher of wine from the village, who told them the enemy were all fled; whereupon they sent us back the news, and went on themselves to the place, and finding all true as he had said, they posted back to acquaint us with it; which greatly rejoiced the whole army; and abundance of them were then very eager for the pursuit, who but an hour before had been very doleful. I had an extremely old and tired horse, which drank up a whole pailful of wine, into which he accidentally thrust his head; I let him finish it, and I never found him better or fresher.

As soon as it was broad day, we all mounted on horseback, and our troops made a rather thin appearance; however, a great number of them that had lain concealed in the woods, soon rejoined us. The Count of Charolois caused a friar to come in, and pretend he came from the Duke of Bretagne's army, and that they would be with us that day; which news comforted the whole army, though not a man of them gave any credit to it. However, about ten o'clock in the morning, the Vice-Chancellor of Bretagne, called Rouville, and Maderey with him (of both of whom I have spoken before), arrived in our camp, attended by two of the Duke of Bretagne's archers of the guard in their regimental clothes, which was a very welcome sight to us all. They were asked where they had been, and were highly praised for absenting themselves (considering the murmurs against them), but more for their return, and every one entertained and treated them kindly.

All that day the Count of Charolois kept the field *, rejoicing extremely, and imputing the whole glory of this action to himself; which has cost him dear since, for after that he was governed by no counsel but his own; and whereas before he was altogether unfit for war, and took delight in nothing that belonged to it, his thoughts became so strangely altered upon this point, that he spent the remainder of his life in wars, in which he died, and which were the occasion, if not quite of the ruin of his family, at least, of the misery and desolation of it. Three illustrious and wise princes (his predecessors) had advanced it to a great height, so that few monarchs, except the King of France, were more powerful than he, and, in large and fair towns, none exceeded him. No man ought, but especially a great prince, to presume too much upon himself; but ought freely to acknowledge, that it is God alone that grants us favours and success. Two things more I will say of him; the one is, that I believe no man ever endured more fatigues than he in all sorts of bodily labour and exercise, when the occasion required it; and the other is, that, in my opinion, I never knew a person of greater valour and intrepidity; I never heard him complain of being weary, nor betray the least signs of fear, during the whole seven years I was in his service in the wars, though he was constantly every summer in the field, and sometimes winter and summer. His designs and enterprises were great; but no man could ever accomplish them, unless God added the assistance of his power.

CHAP. V.

The King's Brother the Duke of Berry, and the Duke of Bretagne, join with the Count of Charolois against the King. — 1465.

THE next day, which was the third after the battle, we took up our quarters in the village of Montlhery. The inhabitants had all fled, some to the church-tower, and others into

* In the place "anciently called the Champ de Plours." Oliver de la Marche, vol. ii. p. 240.

D

the castle ; but the Count of Charolois caused them all to
return to their houses, and they lost not the value of a far-
thing, for every soldier paid his scot exactly as if he had
been in Flanders.   The castle held out for the king, and was
never attacked.   After we had refreshed ourselves there for
three days, the Count of Charolois, by the Lord of Contay's
advice, marched from thence to possess himself of Estampes*
(which was good and convenient quarters, and situated in
a plentiful country), that he might be there before the
Bretons (who were marching that way), and lodge his sick
and wounded men in the town, and encamp with the remainder of his forces in the fields round about the town ;
and these good quarters, and that little time which they staid
there, saved the lives of abundance of his men.   At Estampes
arrived also the Lord Charles of France, at that time Duke
of Berry, the king's only brother; the Duke of Bretagne,
the Count of Dunois, the Count of Dammartin, the Marshal
of Loheac, the Lord of Bueil, the Lord of Chaumont†, and
the Lord Charles of Amboise‡ his son (who since that time
has been a great man in this kingdom) ; all which lords, the
king, upon his first accession to the crown, had disappointed
and dispossessed of their places, though they had done his
father and the kingdom eminent service in his conquests in
Normandy, and in several other of his wars.   The Count of
Charolois, attended by all the officers of his army, went out
to meet and greet them, and conducted them to their quarters
that were prepared for them in the town, but their army
encamped in the fields.   In their train were 800 men-
at-arms, very good soldiers, the greatest part of whom
were Bretons, who had lately deserted the king's service (as
I have stated elsewhere), and were a great improvement to
their army ; besides, they had a great number of archers

* "On Friday, the 19th of July, the count marched to Estampes,
where the Dukes of Berry and Bretagne, and the other princes of their
alliance, arrived soon after ; and they remained there until Wednesday,
the 31st of July." Lenglet, vol. ii. p. 183.

† Peter of Amboise, Lord of Chaumont, knight, councillor and
chamberlain of Kings Charles VII. and Louis XI., was the son of Hugh
of Amboise and Jeanne Guenand ; he died on the 28th of June, 1473.

‡ Charles of Amboise, Count of Brienne, Lord of Chaumont, Governor
of the Isle of France, Champagne and Burgundy ; he died on the 16th
of March, 1481.

and other soldiers, armed with good brigandines* ; so that one might compute them at about 6000 men on horse-back, all very well accoutred ; and, to behold them drawn up was enough to convince a man that the Duke of Bretagne was a very great lord, for all of them were paid out of his treasury.

The king, who (as I have already said) was retired to Corbeil, did not forget what he had to do, but hastened into Normandy to raise men; and, to secure the country from any commotion, put some of his guards into the towns near Paris, where he conceived there was any necessity.

The princes spent the first night of their arrival at Estampes in relating their several adventures. The Bretons had taken some of the king's party that fled, and, had they been but a little forwarder in their march, they would either have taken or cut in pieces the third part of the army. At first, indeed, they had thought of sending a party out, judging that the two armies must be near, but those orders were afterwards countermanded; however, the Lord Charles of Amboise and several other officers, with a small detachment, advanced before the army, to see what they could meet with, and they took several prisoners, and some pieces of the king's artillery. The prisoners told them that for certain the king was dead, and they believed what they said ; for they had fled as soon as the battle began. The Lord of Amboise and his party brought this news to the army of the Bretons, where it was exceedingly welcome ; every man fancying that the news was true, and hoping for mighty rewards when the Lord Charles of Berry should come to the crown ; and a council was immediately called (as I have been told since by a person of honour and credit that assisted at it), in which it was debated how they might rid themselves of the Burgundians, and send them packing ; and the general opinion was, if nothing else would do, to do it by force. But their joy was not long-lived, from whence it may naturally be collected to what changes and revolutions this kingdom is exposed.

But to return to my subject, and the army at Estampes. When all had supped, and many people were walking with

---

* The brigandine was a species of corslet, made of plates of iron, riveted to one another longitudinally, by nails or hooks.

great liberty in the street, the Lord Charles of France and the Count of Charolois withdrew to a window and were discoursing of their affairs in a very friendly manner. It happened that among the Bretons there was a poor man who took great delight in throwing squibs into the air, and seeing them break and blaze among the people when they had fallen ; and he was called Master John Boutefeu, or Master John of the Serpents, I know not which. This idle fellow, having hid himself in some house that he might not be perceived by anybody, from a garret where he was, cast two or three into the air, one of which, by accident, happened to strike against the bar of the window where the two princes were standing with their heads very near together. Both of them started in great surprise, and stared upon one another, suspecting it a design, and done on purpose to injure them. The Lord of Contay came up to the count, and having whispered a word in his ear, went down, and ordered all the guards of his household, and what other soldiers were at hand, to stand immediately to their arms. And the Count of Charolois persuaded the Duke of Berry to do the same ; so that in a moment there were 200 or 300 men-at-arms drawn up before the gate, and a great number of archers, who were employed to search everywhere, to find out from whence the fire had come. At last the poor fellow who had caused all this uproar came and threw himself at their feet, confessed the whole matter, and, by throwing two or three more of them into the air, entirely took away the suspicion several persons had conceived of one another. Thus was this surprising accident turned into a jest, and all laid down their arms and returned to their quarters.

The next day, early in the morning, the Count of Charolois called a great and splendid council of war, at which all the princes and their chief officers assisted, to consult what measures were best to be taken; and as they were of different parties and not all obeying the same lord (which is very much to be desired in such assemblies), their sentiments were also different ; but of all that was said, nothing was so much taken notice of as some expressions of the Duke of Berry, who was but young, and had seen nothing of the war. By his words he seemed to be weary already, taking occasion to mention the great number of wounded men whom he had observed in the count's army, and by way of compassion he declared he had rather the war had never been begun, than that so much mischief should be occasioned through his means and on his account. Which language was very unpleasing to the count and his party, as I shall show afterwards. Nevertheless, the result of this council was, that they should march towards Paris, to try if they could bring that city to join with them for the good of the kingdom, for which (as they pretended) they had taken up arms; and they were all of them fully persuaded, that if the capital would listen to them, all the rest of the towns in the kingdom would follow its example. As I said before, the speech in council of the Duke of Berry so startled the Count of Charolois and his party, that they asked one another, "Did you hear this young duke? He is astonished at the sight of 700 or 800 wounded men in the town, who are nothing to him, nor does he know them; he would certainly be more troubled where he was concerned; and he would be a likely man to make his peace upon small invitation, and leave us in the lurch." And the Count of Charolois further said, "that on account of the ancient wars which had long continued in time past between King Charles (the Duke of Berry's father) and the Duke of Burgundy (his own father), it was to be feared they would easily unite, and turn all their forces against us; for which reason it would be necessary to look out for allies in time." And it was purely on this suspicion that Messire William of Cluny *, the prothonotary (who died afterwards Bishop of Poictiers) was despatched into England to the court of King Edward IV.†, who then reigned; and who had been always the mortal enemy of the Count of Charolois, who had supported against him the house of Lancaster, from which, by the mother's side, he was descended.‡

* William de Cluny, born about 1423, was the son of Henry de Cluny, Lord of Conforgieu, and Perrette Collot, Lady of Sagy. He was a councillor of the Duke of Burgundy, and prothonotary of the Holy See. He was appointed to the bishopric of Poitiers in 1479, and died about a year afterwards.

† Edward IV., son of Richard, Duke of York, and Cicely Neville, daughter of the Earl of Westmoreland; he married Lady Elizabeth Woodville in 1464, and died on the 9th of April, 1483.

‡ Isabella of Portugal, the mother of the Count of Charolois, was the

In his private instruction, he had orders to propose a marriage with Margaret*, the King of England's sister; but to treat only and negotiate, without coming to any conclusion: for the Count of Charolois, who knew how desirous the King of England was of this match, believed by this means, either to bring him over to his side, if he should have any occasion for his assistance, or at least to hinder him from attempting anything against him. However, though he had no real intention at first to consummate the marriage, upon account of his inveterate hatred to the house of York, yet affairs were so managed, that several years after, the match was concluded; and he moreover accepted the order of the garter†, and wore it to his death.

Many such like actions as this have happened in the world upon suspicion only, especially among great princes, who are always much more suspicious than other men, by reason of the many false stories and groundless reports that are brought them often merely by court flatterers, without any manner of occasion.

A Renewing of the Treaty of Alliance between Francis, Duke of Bretagne, and Charles, Count of Charolois, made at Estampes, July 24, 1465.

1. WE, Francis, Duke of Bretagne, are, and will be, the good brother, perfect friend, ally, and confederate of Charles, Count of Charolois: we will aid and assist, counsel, succour, and support, and, with all our power, guard and defend his person, and his children born or to be born, their honour, estates, countries, territories, lordships, and subjects, as much

daughter of John, King of Portugal, by Philippa, daughter of John, Duke of Lancaster.

* Margaret of York married Charles of Burgundy, in pursuance of a treaty signed at Brussels on the 16th of February, 1467 (O. S.); and the marriage was celebrated at Dan, on the 3rd of July, 1468. She died on the 28th of November, 1503. Unless Commines is in error with regard to the time at which William of Cluny was despatched on his mission, the Count of Charolois contemplated this new alliance whilst his second wife was still living; for Isabella of Bourbon did not die until the 26th of September, 1465, two months after the battle of Montlhery.

† In Rymer, vol. v. part ii. p. 173., is a letter from Duke Charles, acknowledging the receipt of the garter from the English ambassadors.

as we would do our own, without any manner of distinction, against all and every person and persons (without excepting our lord the king) whoever they are, that would injure, make war upon, or usurp anything from our said cousin and his children, their countries, subjects, lands, and territories, in possession or reversion, in any manner or upon any account whatsoever.   And we also promise, in all the other good and laudable quarrels and enterprises of our said cousin of Charolois, to succour and assist him and his children, as well against our lord the king, as all other persons whatsoever ; and to employ in their behalf and in their favour our own person, subjects, countries, territories, and lordships against all invaders, or such as make war upon them ; and to defend them in person, and with all our power, in such a way and manner as our good cousin shall require ; and, moreover, we will impart to him whatever shall come to our knowledge to be done, said, or intended to his prejudice, and defend him to the best of our power ; and we shall use our lawful endeavours to have him comprehended in the alliances already made, or to be made hereafter by us, so far as he has a mind to it ; and we will make no alliance in prejudice to these presents.   And, in regard of the great love to, and sincere confidence we have in, our said dear cousin of Charolois, above all others, and also for his greater assurance that we shall, on our part, perform as aforesaid, we have been desirous to make, and we do actually make him our brother-in-arms ; and, forasmuch as we do desire with all our heart, that the said alliances may be inviolably maintained, kept, and observed, and to the end, lest for want of a declaration and good understanding, there may arise any difficulty or doubt, even in respect to the general clause above written, importing, that we will aid and assist our said cousin of Charolois in all his quarrels and enterprises, as well against our lord the king as all others as aforesaid ; we do declare, and our meaning is, that whatever dispute or war by sea shall happen between the English, or any other nation whatsoever, and our subjects, or the subjects of our cousin of Charolois, the subjects of either of us both, who are not engaged in a contest or naval war against the English, shall not be obliged, notwithstanding the said alliances, to quarrel with, nor make war upon them, nor to do anything upon that account against the truces, treaties, or alliances which, for the benefit of trade, have been made between the countries and subjects of our uncle the Duke of Burgundy, and our said cousin of Charolois, his son ; but they shall, as to this particular, remain in force according to ancient usage and custom : and, if it should so happen, that any of our subjects, under pretence of their own war, or otherwise, should come into the countries, ports, and harbours of our said cousin of Charolois, and, by sea or land, rob, pillage, and carry off any merchandise belonging to them, or other people who have the freedom of the said countries, ports, and havens, or shall be at truce and not in war, or have the protection of our said cousin of Charolois, or his officers ; in that case, such of our subjects as shall do so may be taken and seized in the said countries, ports, and havens of our said cousin of Charolois, wherever they may be found, and such punishment, correction, and justice inflicted on them, which in reason ought to be done, according to the customs and usages of the said countries, ports, and havens where they shall be taken.   Moreover, if any of our subjects should by sea rob or destroy any goods and merchandises belonging to the merchants of the countries and territories of our said cousin of Charolois, residing or dwelling therein, or to others who are in a truce or peace with, or under the protection of, our said cousin or his officers as aforesaid, and should afterwards bring the said goods and merchandises, or cause them to be brought into any of the towns, ports, or havens of the said countries belonging to our cousin of Charolois, in order to sell or barter them there ; those who bring them thither may, in that case, be taken and seized, and the said goods and merchandises put into the hands of our said cousin, as being forfeited to him, to dispose of them at his pleasure, either by restoring them to the right owners, or otherwise as he thinks fit ; and, as for the offenders, they shall be punished for what they have done, as he, our said cousin, or his officers, shall judge most convenient.

2. Seeing we are desirous to provide for the security of our dominions and territories for the time to come, and to preserve them for the future from the inconveniences which they have been liable to ; if it should so happen, that any of our successors should hereafter contravene any of these

present alliances (which God forbid), we do, in such a case, give unto our said cousin of Charolois, or his successors, the countries, lands, and lordships of Montfort, Estampes, and Vertus, with their appurtenances and dependencies; and we do divest and dispossess ourselves of the said countries, lands, and lordships, and do yield and transfer them from thenceforward, for ourselves, our heirs, successors, &c., to our said cousin of Charolois, to occupy and enjoy them, with all their rights, profits, and emoluments, by way of inheritance for ever, for himself, his heirs, &c., as fully and in the same manner and form as we do now enjoy them, and as our predecessors have done before us, without reserving any right to ourselves, our heirs, successors, &c., of suing for or laying claim to any right therein, for any reason or upon any account whatsoever.

3. And to the end that the said alliances may be the more strictly observed, we have again and anew chosen, named, and commissioned, and we do on our part choose, name, and commission for the conservators of them, the same persons formerly chosen and nominated in our letters patent mentioning the same, preceding these in date, and also by these presents: conferring on them new authority and the like power to maintain, support, favour, and secure them, as well in the execution of their commission, or otherwise, as our said letters patent of alliance or conservation do import or contain.

4. If it should come to pass that the said conservators, or any of them, should hereafter falter, and be justly accused of a failure in the discharge of the trust reposed in them, in that case, we, and our said cousin of Charolois, and our successors, &c., and every one of us in his own right, may appoint one or more trustees in the room of him or them, who shall transgress, or be justly accused as aforesaid.

5. That the said alliances between us and our said cousin of Charolois may be the better kept, and the more firmly maintained, we have been willing, and we do actually make the same alliances between our territories and subjects as we do between our own persons; promising upon our faith and corporal oath, on the word of a prince, and upon our honour, firmly to keep and maintain the said alliance and brotherhood in all their circumstances and dependencies, without contravening the same in any manner whatsoever,

and to make out unto our said cousin of Charolois good and
authentic instruments of consent and ratification in the presence of the Estates of our said countries and territories, to
last during our life and the lives of our heirs, successors, &c.,
for ever.   In witness whereof we have affixed our seal to
these presents.

Done at Estampes, July the 24th, in the year of our Lord
    1465.   Signed Francis, with a flourish.   Upon the fold
    was written, "by the Duke's command," and signed
    Milet, with a flourish.

CHAP. VI.

The Count of Charolois and his Allies with their Army pass the Seine upon
  a Bridge of Boats; after which, being joined by the Forces of John, Duke
  of Calabria, they invest Paris. — 1465.

THESE great lords, according to the resolution that had been
taken in the council of war, left Estampes, where they had
remained a few days, and marched to St. Mathurin de Lar-
chant and Moret in Gastinois*, in which two villages the
Duke of Berry and his Bretons were quartered : but the
Count of Charolois and his men encamped in a large meadow
on the banks of the Seine, and had proclaimed in his army
that every horseman should bring a hook with him to fasten
his horse; he also caused seven or eight small boats to be
brought upon carts, with several pipe-staves, in order to lay
a bridge over the Seine, there being no other way of passing
it.   The Count of Dunois (who was unable to get on horseback by reason of the gout) attended him in his litter, and
had his colours carried after him.   When they came to the
river, they placed the boats which they had brought together,
and got over into a little island in the midst of the river,
and some of our archers landed and attacked a party of
horse on the other side, who were posted there to secure
that pass, under the command of the Marshal Joachim and
Sallezard†.   They were posted in a place very disadvan-

---

* "On Thursday, the 1st of August, the Count of Charolois encamped
at Saint-Mathurin de l'Archamp, where he remained till the 5th, when
he transferred his quarters to Moret." Lenglet, vol. ii. p. 184.

† John de Salazar, a native of Spain, knight, chamberlain and coun-

tageous for their horse, for it was steep and thick-set with
vines; and the Burgundians had a fine train of artillery,
under the command of one Monsieur Gerault, a very famous
engineer, who had been previously on the king's side, but
was taken prisoner at the battle of Montlhery. In short,
the enemy were obliged to abandon their post, and retire to
Paris. The very same night, a bridge was laid quite to the
island, where the Count of Charolois immediately ordered
his own tent to be pitched, in which he lay that night, under a
guard of fifty men-at-arms of his household troops. At
break of day, a large number of coopers were set to work to
make pipe-staves of clap-boards, which had been brought
over into the island; and before noon the bridge from the
island to the other side of the river being finished, the count
passed over it immediately, ordered his tents to be pitched
(of which he had abundance), and then passing over all his
army and artillery, he encamped with it on the brow of a
hill towards the river, from whence his host made a fine
appearance to those who still remained behind.

The passing over of the count's forces took up all that
day; but the next morning, by break of day, the Dukes of
Berry and Bretagne advanced with their army to the
bridge, which they thought very speedily and commodiously
built; and having passed over it, they encamped also upon
the hill.* As soon as it grew dark, we began to perceive a
number of fires at as far a distance as we could well discern.
Some were of opinion that it was the king; but before midnight we were assured it was John, Duke of Calabria† (only
son of René, King of Sicily) with about 900 men-at-
arms from the duchy and county of Burgundy. He had
a good body of horse, but of foot he had few or none. How-

cillor of the king, captain of a hundred lances of his own raising, and
Lord of Montagne, Saint-Just, Marcilly, Laz, Lonsac, and Issodun,
married Margaret de la Tremoille, Lady of Saint-Fargeau, on the 31st
of October, 1441; became a widower, by her death, on the 18th of
December, 1457; and died at Troyes on the 12th of November, 1479.

* "The Dukes of Berry and Bretagne and most of the lords lodged
at Nemours." Oliver de la Marche, vol. ii. p. 243.

† John of Anjou, Duke of Calabria, son of René, King of Sicily, and
Isabella of Lorraine, was born on the 2nd of August, 1424; married
Mary, daughter of Charles I., Duke of Bourbon; died at Barcelona, on
Sunday, the 16th of December, 1470, and was buried in the cathedral
church of that city.

ever, though their number was small, I never saw a finer
company, or men who seemed better inured to the exercises
of war.   He had with him about six score men in complete
armour, Italians and others, brought up in the wars in Italy,
among whom were James Galiot*, the Count of Campo-
bache †, the Lord of Baudricourt ‡ (now Governor of
Burgundy), and several others.   These men-at-arms were
all very dexterous and ready, and, to speak impartially, the
very flower of our army, at least compared with an equal
number of the others.   He had also, besides these troops,
400 cross-bow men (whom the Count Palatine § had
furnished), all well mounted, and brave soldiers, and with
them 500 Swiss infantry, the first that were ever seen
in this kingdom, who behaved themselves with so much
courage and bravery in all the actions they were employed
in, as have gained reputation for all their countrymen that
have succeeded them.   The next morning this gallant army
drew nearer, and passed over our bridge ; so that one might
venture to say, the whole power of France (except what was
with the king) passed over that bridge.   This I can affirm,
the number of persons of quality and officers was so great,
and the whole army was in such complete order, and made
such a fine appearance, that I could have wished that both
the friends and enemies of the kingdom had been there to

* Jacques Galiot died on the 28th of July, 1488, at the battle of Saint-
Aubin du Cormier, according to Molinet, who calls him "a Neapolitan."
Previous editors have erroneously confounded him with Jacques Ricard
de Genouillac, surnamed Galiot.

† Nicolas de Montfort, Count of Campobasso, leader of Italian men-
of-war, as he signs himself in a document quoted by Godefroy.   He was
also one of the chamberlains of Charles, Duke of Burgundy; and claimed
kindred with the Duke of Bretagne.

‡ John, Lord of Baudricourt, councillor and chamberlain of Louis XI.,
King of France, and Marshal of France under Charles VIII., was the
son of Robert, Lord of Baudricourt, and Alcarde de Chambley.   He
sided with the Duke of Burgundy in the war of the Public Good ; but
the king, having gained him over to his party, made him Governor of
Burgundy by letters patent, dated the 18th of March, 1480 : he died on
the 11th of May, 1499.

§ Frederic I., surnamed the Victorious, Governor of the Electorate
during the minority of his nephew Philip, obtained from the Estates of
the Palatinate permission to retain the electorate during his lifetime.
He was the son of Louis III. and Matilda of Savoy.   He was born on
the 1st of August, 1425 ; and died on the 12th of December, 1476.

1465.] THE CONFEDERATES MARCH TO PARIS. 45

have seen us: for, by that means, the former would have
had a just value and esteem for the kingdom, and the latter
would for ever after have more dreaded its power. The
chief of the Burgundian officers were the Lord of Neufchastel, Marshal of Burgundy, with his brother the Lord of
Montagu, the Marquis of Rottelin, and a great number of
knights and squires, some of whom had been in Bourbonnois, as I said before ; and, to come to us with more
security, all had joined with the Duke of Calabria, who
appeared to be a brave prince, and as great a commander as
any in the army, upon which account a great friendship
arose between the Count of Charolois and him.

When the whole army had passed (which, in my judgment, was little less than 100,000 horse, one with
another) the princes resolved to present themselves before
Paris, and joined all their vanguards together. The Burgundian van was led by the Count of St. Paul ; the
Duke of Berry's and the Duke of Bretagne's by Oudet de
Rye*, and (as I think) the Marshal of Loheac : in this order
they marched. The princes themselves were all in the
main battle ; the Count of Charolois and the Duke of Calabria rode up and down in full armour, and took abundance
of pains to keep their battalions in order, and showed great
readiness to do their duties ; but the Dukes of Berry and
Bretagne were at their ease, mounted on little hackneys,
armed only with very light brigandines, or, as some said,
with gilt nails sewn upon satin, that they might weigh the
less; but I cannot positively affirm this. In this order the
whole army marched to the bridge of Charenton, within two
short leagues of Paris, where we attacked and routed an inconsiderable body of frank-archers that were posted on the
bridge ; after which the whole army marched over it, and
the Count of Charolois encamped (between that bridge and

* Odet d'Aydie, Lord of Lescun, was the son of John d'Aydie, a
gentleman of Gascony. He married Marie de Béarn, daughter of
Mathieu de Béarn, Lord of Lescun. Louis XI., having gained him over
to his side, made him his councillor and chamberlain, gave him the office
of Admiral of France, and created him Count of Comminges in 1472.
After the death of Louis, Odet d'Aydie joined the party of the Duke of
Orleans, in consequence of which he was deprived of his admiralty. He
died before the 25th of August, 1498, at more than seventy years of age.

a house at Conflans*) all along the river, enclosing a large
compass of ground with his waggons and train of artillery,
and drawing his whole army into it; and with him the
Duke of Calabria took up his quarters. The Dukes of
Berry and Bretagne were posted with a strong party of
their men at St. Maur-des-Fossez; the rest of the army was
sent to St. Denis, also about two leagues from Paris, in
which quarters the whole army lay for eleven weeks, during
which time those things occurred of which I shall speak
hereafter.

The next morning a little skirmishing began at the very
gates of Paris; in which place were the Lord of Nantoillet,
High Steward of France (who, as I have elsewhere observed,
did good service to the king), and the Marshal Joachim.
The people were in a great consternation, but many of the
citizens seemed inclinable to admit the Burgundians and
the other lords into Paris; believing (in their judgments)
that their enterprise was for the benefit and advantage of the
kingdom. There were others who declared openly for the
Burgundians, hoping, by advancing their interest, to arrive
at some good office or preferment, which, in that city, are
more coveted than in any other part of the world besides;
for every man makes his employment worth as much as he
can, and not as much as he ought; so that there are some
offices, with no salary at all belonging to them, which are
sold for 800 crowns; and others, whose wages are very
small, are sold for more than the salary could amount
to in fifteen years; from whence it happens that seldom any
man is put out of his place, and the court of parliament main-
tains this privilege, and rightly; but it interferes with almost
all things else. Among the counsellors there is always a
great number of honest and able persons, as well as some
very ill-conditioned individuals; but it is so in all conditions
of society.

---

* "On Tuesday, 20th August, he encamped at Conflans, where he
remained until the end of the month of October." Lenglet, vol. ii.
p. 184.

CHAP. VII.

A Digression concerning Salaries, Offices, and Ambition, illustrated by
the Example of the English. — 1465.

I MENTION these offices and authorities, because they lead
men to desire changes and revolutions, and are thus the
occasion of them ; which evidently appears, not only by
what we have seen in our own days, but also in the time of
King Charles VI. *, in whose reign the wars, which lasted
till the peace of Arras, began ; during which wars, the
English had conquered so great a part of France, that at the
time of that treaty (which lasted two months) the Duke of
Bedford†, brother to Henry V., King of England, and
husband to the Duke of Burgundy's sister, was Regent of
France for the English there, and resided at Paris, and
had 20,000 crowns a month at least, to support the
grandeur and dignity of his office.   At this treaty of Arras,
the King of France sent four or five dukes and counts, five
or six prelates, and ten or twelve councillors of parliament
to take care of his interests.   On the Duke of Burgundy's
side there were more, and those very great persons ; and no
fewer from the King of England ‡ : besides two cardinals from
the Pope §, to act as mediators.   The Duke of Burgundy
being desirous to acquit himself handsomely towards the
English before they parted, on account of the old leagues
and alliances which had been between them, offered the

* Charles VI., King of France, born on the 3rd of December, 1368,
was the son of Charles V. and Jeanne de Bourbon; he married Isabel
of Bavaria on the 17th of July, 1385 ; and died on the 22nd of October,
1422.

† John of Lancaster, Count of Kendal and Duke of Bedford, was the
third son of King Henry IV. and Mary, daughter of Humphrey de
Bohun.   He married 1. Anne, sister of Philip, Duke of Burgundy ; and
2. Jacqueline, daughter of Pierre de Luxembourg, Count of Saint Paul.
He was appointed Regent of the Kingdom of France on the death of his
brother Henry V.; and he died at Rouen, on the 14th of Sept., 1435.

‡ The commissioners for England were Henry Beaufort, Cardinal and
Bishop of Winchester ; John Kemp, Archbishop of York ; William de
la Pole, Earl of Suffolk ; John Holland, Earl of Huntingdon ; the
Bishops of Norwich, St. David's, and Lisieux, with divers knights and
gentlemen.

§ Eugenius IV. (Gabriel Condolinieri), elected in 1431; he died on
the 23rd of February, 1447.

duchies of Normandy and Guienne to the King of England, for himself and his lords, upon condition that he would do homage for them to the King of France, as his predecessors had done before him; and that he would restore whatever else he held in that kingdom except the said duchies. But the English absolutely refused to do any homage, and they suffered extremely by it afterwards; for, being forsaken by the house of Burgundy, they soon lost their time, and their influence in that kingdom daily declined, and dwindled at last to nothing. Soon afterwards they lost Paris, and by little and little all they were possessed of in France. Upon their return into England not one of the English lords thought of lessening his estate; and the whole revenue of the kingdom was not sufficient to satisfy them all. Wars arose among them for command and authority, which lasted a long time, and in which Henry VI. (who had been crowned King of England and France at Paris) was declared a traitor and imprisoned in the Tower of London*, where he continued the greatest part of his life, and was at last put to death. The Duke of York†, father of Edward IV., lately dead, proclaimed himself king‡, but in a few days he was beaten and slain; and the heads of all that were killed in the battle were cut off; and, among the slain, was the father § of the late Earl of Warwick, who was so famous in England. This last Earl of Warwick ‖ conveyed the Earl of March (since called King Edward) to Calais by sea, with some few

* In August, 1465; he was liberated again in October, 1470, and re-imprisoned in the following year.

† Richard of Coningsburgh, Duke of York, was the son of Richard, Earl of Cambridge, and Anne, daughter of Roger Mortimer, Earl of March. He married Cicely, daughter of Ralph Neville, Earl of Westmoreland, and was killed on the 24th of December, 1460, at the battle of Wakefield.

‡ The Duke of York never assumed the title of king, which was retained by Henry VI. until his death, though the parliament had declared the Duke of York his successor on the throne.

§ The Earl of Salisbury, father of the great Earl of Warwick, was not slain in the battle of Wakefield, but taken prisoner to Pontefract Castle, and soon after beheaded.

‖ Richard Neville, Earl of Warwick, was the son of Richard Neville, Earl of Westmoreland and Salisbury, and Alice, daughter of Thomas Montague, Earl of Salisbury. He married Anne, daughter of Richard Beauchamp, Earl of Warwick; and he was killed in the battle of Barnet, on Easter Day, the 14th of April, 1471.

forces which remained of that battle*: the Earl of Warwick
espoused the interest of the House of York, and the Duke of
Somerset † that of Lancaster; but the civil wars lasted so
long, that all those of the houses of Warwick and Somerset
were either slain in battle or lost their heads. King Edward
caused his brother the Duke of Clarence‡, to be drowned
in a pipe of malmsey, charging him with a design of endeavouring to dethrone him; but after King Edward's death,
his second brother, the Duke of Gloucester§, caused his two
sons to be murdered, declared his daughters to be illegitimate,
and had himself crowned king.

Immediately after this, the Earl of Richmond‖, the present
king (who had been many years a prisoner in Bretagne) returned into England, and in a set battle defeated and slew
this bloody King Richard, who had so barbarously murdered
his two nephews. Thus have there been slain in these civil
wars of England, within my remembrance, near fourscore
persons of the blood royal, some of whom I was acquainted
with myself, and the rest I have heard of, by the report of
several English gentlemen that resided at the Duke of Bur-

---

* It was after the defeat at Ludlow, in October, 1459, that the Earl
of Warwick retired to Calais with the Earl of March, and not, as Commines' narrative would lead us to suppose, after the battle of Wakefield.

† Edmund Beaufort, Duke of Somerset, was the son of Edmund
Beaufort, Duke of Somerset, and Eleanor, daughter of Richard Beauchamp, Earl of Warwick. He was slain in the battle of Tewkesbury on
the 4th of May, 1471.

‡ George of York, Duke of Clarence, brother of King Edward IV.,
died on the 18th of February, 1478. He married Isabel, the eldest
daughter of Richard Neville, Earl of Warwick, by whom he had two
children : Edward, Earl of Warwick, who was three years old when his
father died; and Margaret, who afterwards married Richard de la Pole.

§ Richard of York, Duke of Gloucester, afterwards King of England,
under the name of Richard III. He was killed at the battle of Bosworth
Field on the 22nd of August, 1485.

‖ Henry, Earl of Richmond, was the son of Edmund of Hadham, Earl
of Richmond, and Margaret, daughter of John Beaufort, Duke of
Somerset. He was proclaimed King of England under the name of
Henry VII., on the 22nd of August, 1485. He married Elizabeth,
eldest daughter of King Edward IV. ; and he died on the 21st of April,
1509. When escaping from England in 1471, he fell into the hands of
the Duke of Bretagne, who detained him prisoner for thirteen years,
after which he escaped, hearing that the duke was negotiating to deliver
him up to King Richard III.

E

gundy's court, during the time of my being in his service. So that it is not at Paris only, nor in France alone, that the riches and honours of this world occasion quarrels and disputes. Yet all monarchs and great princes ought to be very careful and circumspect, and not permit any faction or party to spring up in their courts, for from thence the fire spreads, and runs over the whole kingdom. However, I am of opinion that all these revolutions happen by the divine permission and appointment; for when kings and kingdoms have enjoyed a long series of riches and prosperity, and forgotten the fountain from whence those blessings and advantages proceed, God raises up enemies against them, of whom they never had the least suspicion, which appears evidently by the history of the kings mentioned in the Bible, and by the surprising events that have happened of late years, and do daily happen, both in England, Burgundy, and other places.

CHAP. VIII.

How King Louis entered Paris, whilst the Lords of France were tampering with the Citizens.— 1465.

I HAVE dwelt too long upon this subject, and therefore it is now time to return to my history.

As soon as the princes were arrived before Paris, they all began to tamper with the citizens, promising them great places and rewards, and everything that might any ways contribute towards advancing their design. By that time we had lain three days before the town, there was held a grand assembly in the Hotel de Ville of Paris, in which, after many and long harangues, upon hearing the princes' summons and propositions, which (as was pretended) were for no other end than the good of the public; it was unanimously resolved to send commissioners to them to treat of a peace. Whereupon a great number of substantial citizens went to wait on the princes at St. Maur; and Maître Guillaume Chartier* (a person of great parts and eloquence, and at that time Bishop of Paris) was their speaker; and the lords appointed the Count of Dunois to be theirs. The

---

* Born at Bayeux ; he was Bishop of Paris from 1447 until May 1, 1472, when he died : he was a brother of the celebrated Alain Chartier.

Duke of Berry, the king's brother, was president of the
council, and sat in a chair of state, and all the rest of the
princes stood round him : on one hand the Dukes of Bretagne
and Calabria; and on the other the Count of Charolois, completely armed (all but his head-piece and gauntlets), with a
very rich mantle thrown over his cuirass; for he had come
from Conflans, and the Bois-de-Vincennes had in it a strong
garrison for the king, so that it was necessary for him to
come with a strong guard.   The request and object of the
princes were to be admitted into Paris, to hold friendly consultation with the citizens about reformation of the government, of which they sadly complained, and charged the king
with numerous acts of injustice and mal-administration.   The
answer of the citizens was full of respect and modesty, yet
not without some hesitation and demur.   However, notwithstanding that, the king was afterwards displeased with
the bishop, and with all that went with him.   In this
manner the commissioners returned, and great practices
and intrigues were still carried on; for every one of the
princes had a private conference with the citizens ; and I
believe it was secretly agreed by some of them, that the lords
in their own persons might enter the town, and their army
pass through it in small bodies at a time, if they desired it.
This admission of the princes would not only have been the
means of gaining the town, but of finishing the whole enterprise ; for the whole people would, for several reasons, have
easily gone over, in imitation of their example, to their side,
and by consequence the whole kingdom would have revolted.   But God gave the king wise counsel, and he executed it vigorously : being informed of all their secret
practices and cabals, before the commissioners, who had
been to wait on the princes, had made their report, the king
arrived in Paris*, in the condition of a prince that came
to relieve and animate his subjects; for he came with a
very great company, and brought above 2000 men-at-
arms into the city, all the nobility of Normandy, a great
number of volunteers, his household retainers, his pensioners, and other persons of quality that were accustomed
to attend so great a king upon such occasions.   Thus was

* August 28, 1465.

the whole design quashed, and the minds of the people entirely changed; so that not a man, how active soever he had been formerly for us, durst now speak one word in our behalf.   Some of the commissioners, who had been with us, fared but very ill; some lost their places, and others were banished; but the king used no farther cruelty or revenge; for which I think he is highly to be commended, considering that, if this intended design had succeeded, the best he could have expected had been to have escaped out of the kingdom; for he has told me many times since, that if the town had revolted, and refused to admit him, his resolutions were to have retired, either to the Swiss, or to Francis, Duke of Milan *, whom he thought his great friend, and so indeed he afterwards showed himself to be, by the supplies which he sent him, which consisted of 500 men-at-arms, and 3000 foot, under the command of his eldest son Galeas † (afterwards duke); who came as far as Forest, in Auvergne, and made war upon the Duke of Bourbon; but, upon the death of Duke Francis, they were recalled.   His affection to the king appeared, likewise, by the advice which he gave him at the treaty of Conflans ‡, which was to make a peace with the princes upon any terms whatsoever, in order to break the confederacy, and separate their forces; but yet still to keep his own army on foot.

As far as I can remember, we had scarce been three days before Paris, when the king entered with his troops.   Upon whose arrival the war began very briskly, and they often fell upon us; especially upon our foragers, whom we were forced to send under a strong guard on account of their

* Francisco Sforza, Duke of Milan, born at San Miniato de Cotignola on the 23rd of July, 1401, was the natural son of Muzio Attendolo, surnamed *Sforza*, on account of the vigour of his character.   This surname was adopted by his descendants, in preference to that of Attendolo.   The mother of Francisco Sforza was Lucia de Torsciano.   He died at Milan on the 8th of March, 1466.

† Galeazzo Maria Sforza, born on the 14th of January, 1444; married successively Dorothea de Gonzagua, and Bona of Savoy; and was assassinated on the 26th of December, 1476.

‡ The treaty of Conflans was made between Louis XI. and the Count of Charolois on the 5th of October, 1465.   On the 29th of the same month the king made a separate treaty with the confederate princes, which is dated at St. Maur des Fossés.

foraging at a great distance from our camp. But it must needs be owned, that the city of Paris is admirably well placed in the Isle of France, to be able to supply two such powerful hosts with provisions. As for our part, we never found a scarcity of anything in the camp; neither did the inhabitants that were in the town suffer any privation on our account. Nothing grew dearer except bread, which was sold for only a penny more than the usual price; and the reason was, because we had not blocked up the rivers above it, which were three, the Marne, the Yonne, and the Seine, besides several little rivers which fell into them. To say all in a word, Paris is surrounded by the finest and the most plentiful country I ever yet beheld, and it is almost incredible what vast quantities of provisions are brought to it. Since that time, I have been there with King Louis, for six months together, and never stirred, lodging in the Tournelles, eating and sleeping with him very frequently; and besides, since his death (much to my sorrow) I was a prisoner twenty months in the Louvre, from whence I could see, out of my window, whatever came out of Normandy up the River Seine; and on the other side there came in incomparably much more, which I could never have believed, had I not been an eye-witness of it.

The Parisians made frequent sallies every day, which occasioned warm skirmishes on both sides. Our guards, consisting of fifty lances, were posted near the Grange-aux-Merciers *; but our scouts went as near the town as they could, and were often attacked and beaten back to our main guard, sometimes retreating gravely step by step, sometimes at full trot, with the enemy at their heels, who sometimes drove them to our very waggons; upon which we used to send a fresh body of troops to reinforce the beaten party, who very often repulsed the enemy, and drove them back to the gates of Paris. And this happened daily and hourly, for there were in the town more than 2500 men-at-arms, well armed and in complete order, besides a great number of the nobility of Normandy, and volunteers; whom the sight of the ladies of Paris, who were constant spectators

* "Not very far from Conflans," says Oliver de la Marche. It was on the site now occupied by Bercy, where there still exists a street called the Rue de la Grange-aux-Merciers.

of their actions, inspired with an emulation of signalising themselves. On our side we had a very great number of men, but not so strong a body of horse as the enemy; for we had none but the Burgundian cavalry, consisting of about 2000 lances, good and bad, who were not so well disciplined as those in Paris, by reason of the long peace they had had, as I said before.* Besides, 200 of these were with the Duke of Calabria, at Laigny; but our infantry was numerous, and generally very good. The Bretons were posted at St. Denis, and ravaged all the country on that side Paris; the rest of the lords were dispersed, some here, some there, for better convenience of their provision. At length the Duke of Nemours, the Count of Armagnac, and the Lord of Albret, came to our camp, but their forces were left at a good distance behind, because they had no pay, and it would have starved our army if they had taken anything without paying. To my knowledge the Count of Charolois gave them money for their subsistence, to the amount of 5000 or 6000 francs; and it was resolved that they should come no nearer us; for they were full 6000 horse, and did a marvellous amount of mischief in the country where they lay.

CHAP. IX.

How the Count of Charolois and the King cannonaded each other near Charenton; after which Action, the Count of Charolois laid a second Bridge of Boats over the River Seine. — 1465.

BUT to return to the army before Paris. It will not be doubted that scarce a day passed without some loss or gain on both sides, but nothing considerable on either. For the king would not suffer his forces to sally out in great bodies, nor would he bring his affairs to the hazard of a battle; his only desire being for peace, in order to break and divide our forces as wisely as he could. However, one day early in the morning, 4000 of his frank-archers came and posted themselves along the bank of the river, over against the Hôtel de Conflans. The nobles of Normandy, and some few of the household troops, were disposed in a village about a quarter of a league off, with only a fair plain between them and their infantry, and the River Seine between us and them.

* See p. 12.

The king's troops began to throw up a trench over against
Charenton, and made a bulwark there of wood and of
earth, all along the front of our army. This ditch or trench
was thrown up (as has been said already) before Conflans,
with the river between us and them, and upon that trench
and bastion they planted a great number of pieces of cannon,
which played briskly upon the Duke of Calabria's quarters,
and at the first firing drove his men out of Charenton, ar.d
forced them to retire in great haste to our camp, with the
loss of some few horses and men. So the Duke of Calabria
took up his quarters in a little house, between the river and
the place where the Count of Charolois lay.

The enemy immediately began to cannonade our camp,
which threw the whole army into consternation; for, upon
the first firing, they killed us abundance of men, and two
cannon shots coming through the room where the Count of
Charolois was sitting at dinner, killed a trumpeter on the
stairs, as he was bringing up a dish of meat.

After dinner, the count removed to the ground-floor, but
resolved not to decamp, and had it furnished as best he
could. The next morning the princes called a council of
war, which was always held in the Count of Charolois'
quarters, after which they always dined together. The
Dukes of Berry and Bretagne sat next the wall upon a bench,
and the Count of Charolois and the Duke of Calabria over
against them, the count giving all of them the preference as
to matter of place; as indeed was but right, as he was in
his own quarters. Here they resolved to make use of all
the artillery in the army, of which both the Count of
Charolois and the Dukes of Bretagne and Calabria had a
very fine and numerous train, in order to dislodge the king's
troops and dismount his cannon. Accordingly, we made
great holes in the walls, which were along the river, behind
the Hôtel de Conflans, and mounted all our best guns, except
the bombards and other large pieces which could not conveniently be drawn, and so were left in a place where they
might do more service; so that on the princes' side we had
many more than there were on the king's. The trench
which the king's forces had thrown up was of great length,
and carried a great way towards the city of Paris; yet still
they were working at it, throwing up the earth on the side

E 4

next us, to shelter themselves from our cannon, for they
wrought still in the ditch, and none of them durst venture
so much as to put out their heads, for the place where they
lay was in a large meadow, as bare as a man's hand.

I never heard such terrible cannonading for the short
time it lasted, for our design was to dislodge them by flint of
cannon ; and they daily received from Paris fresh supplies,
both of cannon and ammunition, neither were they sparing
of their powder or pains, but fired upon us briskly day and
night. Several of our soldiers dug pits before their tents to
cover themselves, others had them provided to their hands,
their quarters being in a great stone-quarry, so that all got
some shelter or other ; and in this posture we passed three
or four days ; but the fright was much greater on both
sides than the loss, for no officer of any note was killed.

When the princes found they could not dislodge the
enemy, their failure seemed to them not only dangerous and
disgraceful to themselves, but also likely to give fresh
courage to the Parisians, who were already grown so confident, that upon a single day's truce the people flocked out
in such numbers to see us, that one would have thought
there had been none left in the town. It was therefore concluded in council, that a large bridge of boats should be
made, the ends to be coupled together, and the body of them
to be covered with planks, with great anchors behind, to
fasten them into the ground ; upon which several flat-
bottomed boats were brought down the Seine in order that
we might pass that river, and attack the king's forces.

Master Girault, an engineer, had the management and
direction of this affair, who was of opinion, that the trench
which the enemy had thrown up to defend themselves,
would be of great advantage to the Burgundians when once
they had passed the river ; for the king's forces would find
themselves as it were under us in their trenches, and
would not dare to march out for fear of our cannon ; which
opinion greatly encouraged and animated our soldiers, and
made them impatient to begin the attack. Thus the bridge
was finished and made ready, all but the last two boats,
which were there ready to complete it, and all the other
boats for transportation brought together, and when it was
ready, one of the king's heralds came to tell us we had

broken the truce, which was made for that day and the day
before, and that he was come to see the meaning of these
preparations. By accident he met Monsieur de Bueil and
some others on the bridge, to whom he delivered his
message. That night the truce ended.

Our bridge was so large that three of our men-at-arms,
with their lances in rest, might pass easily abreast; besides
we had got six great vessels, each of which would carry
over a thousand men at a time, and several smaller for the
artillery, which we were to make use of in that expedition.
The draught of such troops as were to be employed in this
enterprise was already made; and the Count of St. Paul and
the Lord Haultbourdin were appointed to command them.
Those who were of the party began to prepare themselves
about midnight, and before day all of them were ready, some
of them hearing mass till day appeared, or employing themselves as good Christians ought to do, upon such an
occasion. I was that night in a great tent in the middle of
our army, where the guard was posted, and to speak truth,
I was one of the guard (for nobody was exempted), which
was commanded by Monsieur de Chastel Guyon* (slain
afterwards at the battle of Granson). And as we stood
there, expecting when the attack would begin, on a sudden
we heard those who were in the French trenches, cry out as
loud as they could, "Farewell, neighbours, farewell;" and
immediately they set fire to their tents, and drew off their
artillery. About day-break the detachment that was to
make this attack had already gained the banks of the river
on the other side, at least in part, and they could descry the
French at a good distance, retiring towards Paris; upon
which all of our men disarmed, and were extremely glad of
their retreat. Without dispute the king had sent that body of
troops thither, only to disturb and cannonade us in our
camp, without the least intention of a battle; for, as I said
before, it was not his way to risk anything on a hazard,
though otherwise his army was strong enough to have engaged the united forces of all the princes together: but his pur-

---

* Louis de Chalon, Lord of Chasteauguion, was son of Louis de
Chalon, Prince of Orange, and Eleanor of Armagnac. He was a Knight
of the Golden Fleece, and fell at the battle of Granson on the 3rd of
March, 1476.

pose, as he plainly showed, was still to make peace, and divide the forces of the confederates, without being willing to expose so important and valuable a concern, as the crown of the great and obedient realm of France, to the uncertainty of a battle.

There was scarce a day passed, but some artifice or other was made use of to bring over people from one side to the other; and several times there were truces, and conferences between both parties in order to an accommodation, which conferences were held at the Grange-aux-Merciers, not far from our army. As commissioners from the king, there were the Count of Maine and several others. For the princes, the Count of St. Paul, and as many with him. The commissioners met often, but came to no conclusion. Yet the cessation of arms was continued, and several persons on both sides, who were acquainted, saw and conversed with one another, but with a great ditch between them, as it were in the mid-way between the two armies, which ditch, by the articles of the truce, no person was to pass.* There was not a day passed but, by means of these interviews, some ten or twelve would come over to us; and some days as many of ours went away to them, for which reason that place was afterwards called the Market, because of the bargains driven there. To speak truth, such liberty of communication is, in my judgment, very dangerous at such times, especially for that party which is most visibly declining: for naturally most people are intent, if not upon their advancement, at least upon their safety, which inclines them more easily to the strongest side. There are some, indeed, who are above temptations of this kind, but they are very few, and rarely to be met with. But if ever such communications are dangerous, it is when a prince himself makes it his business to oblige and cajole people; which is an excellent qualification in a prince who knows how to do it well, and renders him clear from that foolish vice and sin of pride and haughtiness, which all persons abhor. For which reason, when any treaty of peace is on foot, it is safest to commit it to the wisest and faithfulest persons about the prince, and those of competent years; lest other-

---

* Oliver de la Marche, however, says, " During these truces, we went to Paris to indulge in good cheer, paying with our own money : and we were very welcome." La Marche, ii. 246.

wise, their want of experience betray them to some dishonourable compact, or they alarm their master with groundless fears at their return. If it be possible, such persons ought to be employed who have received honours or advantages from their princes, rather than any others; but above all, they ought to be men of great wisdom and experience, for nothing ever prospered that was managed by a fool. This kind of treaties ought likewise to be managed at a distance, and not near his camp; and when his plenipotentiaries return, he ought to hear them alone, or in as little company as he can, that if their news should be apt to dishearten the people, he may instruct and dictate what account they shall give to such as are inquisitive; for everybody is desirous to hear news from those that come from a treaty, and many are so conceited as to boast, " Such an one will hide nothing from me;" but if the plenipotentiaries be such as I have described, and know their masters to be wise, they will discover nothing to any man.

CHAP. X.

A Digression concerning some of the Virtues and Vices of King Louis XI.

THE chief reason that has induced me to enter upon this subject, is because I have seen many deceptions in this world, especially in servants towards their masters; and I have always found that proud and stately princes who will hear but few, are more liable to be imposed on than those who are open and accessible: but of all the princes that I ever knew, the wisest and most dexterous to extricate himself out of any danger or difficulty in time of adversity, was our master King Louis XI. He was the humblest in his conversation and habit, and the most painful and indefatigable to win over any man to his side that he thought capable of doing him either mischief or service: though he was often refused, he would never give over a man that he wished to gain, but still pressed and continued his insinuations, promising him largely, and presenting him with such sums and honours as he knew would gratify his ambition; and for such as he had discarded in time of peace and prosperity, he paid dear (when he had occasion for them) to recover them again; but when he had once reconciled them, he retained no enmity towards them for what had passed, but employed them freely for the future.   He was naturally kind and indulgent to persons of mean estate, and hostile to all great men who had no need of him.   Never prince was so conversable, nor so inquisitive as he, for his desire was to know everybody he could; and indeed he knew all persons of any authority or worth in England, Spain, Portugal, and Italy, in the territories of the Dukes of Burgundy and Bretagne, and among his own subjects; and by those qualities he preserved the crown upon his head, which was in much danger by the enemies he had created to himself upon his accession to the throne.   But above all, his great bounty and liberality did him the greatest service: and yet, as he behaved himself wisely in time of distress, so when he thought himself a little out of danger, though it were but by a truce, he would disoblige the servants and officers of his court by mean and petty ways, which were little to his advantage; and as for peace, he could hardly endure the thoughts of it.   He spoke slightingly of most people, and rather before their faces, than behind their backs, unless he was afraid of them, and of that sort there were a great many, for he was naturally somewhat timorous.   When he had done himself any prejudice by his talk, or was apprehensive he should do so, and wished to make amends, he would say to the person whom he had disobliged, " I am sensible my tongue has done me a great deal of mischief; but, on the other hand, it has sometimes done me much good; however, it is but reason I should make some reparation for the injury."   And he never used this kind of apologies to any person, but he granted some favour to the person to whom he made it, and it was always of considerable amount.

It is certainly a great blessing from God upon any prince to have experienced adversity as well as prosperity, good as well as evil, and especially if the good outweighs the evil, as it did in the king our master.   I am of opinion that the troubles he was involved in, in his youth, when he fled from his father, and resided six years * together with Philip

* Louis XI., when Dauphin, fled in 1456 from Dauphiny, whither he had retired ten years previously on account of a misunderstanding with

Duke of Burgundy, were of great service to him; for there he learned to be complaisant to such as he had occasion to use, which was no slight advantage of adversity. As soon as he found himself a powerful and crowned king, his mind was wholly bent upon revenge; but he quickly found the inconvenience of this, repented by degrees of his indiscretion, and made sufficient reparation for his folly and error, by regaining those he had injured, as shall be related hereafter. Besides, I am very confident that if his education had not been different from the usual education of such nobles as I have seen in France, he could not so easily have worked himself out of his troubles; for they are brought up to nothing but to make themselves ridiculous, both in their clothes and discourse; they have no knowledge of letters; no wise man is suffered to come near them, to improve their understandings; they have governors who manage their business, but they do nothing themselves: nay, there are some nobles who, though they have an income of thirteen livres, will take pride to bid you, "Go to my servants, and let them answer you;" thinking by such speeches to imitate the state and grandeur of a prince; and I have seen their servants take great advantage of them, giving them to understand they were fools; and if afterwards they came to apply their minds to business, and attempted to manage their own affairs, they began so late, they could make nothing of it. And it is certain that all those who have performed any great or memorable action, worthy to be recorded in history, began always in their youth; and this is to be attributed to the method of their education, or some particular blessing from God.

CHAP. XI.

How the Burgundians, being drawn up near Paris, and in Expectation of a Battle, mistook high Thistles for a Body of Lances. — 1465.

I HAVE dwelt long upon this subject, but indeed it is of such a nature I could not easily leave off when I would. However, to return to the war.

his father. He sought refuge in Burgundy from the authority of Charles VIII., who wished to force him to return to Court, and remained with his uncle Philip until 1461, when his father died.

You have been informed how the forces that the king had entrenched along the River Seine abandoned their post, and retreated to Paris, the very hour we had designed to attack them. The truces never lasted above one day, or two at the most; at other times the war was pushed on with all possible vigour, the skirmishes continuing from morning to night; and though they often beat our scouts home to our guards, yet they never sallied out of Paris in any considerable body. I do not remember to have seen one day pass without some small action or other; and I believe the king would have been contented they should have been greater, but he was suspicious of many persons, though without any cause: he told me once, that he found the gate of the Bastille of St. Antoine, towards the fields, open one night, which made him entertain a great suspicion of Charles de Melun, whose father * was then governor of that place. I shall say no more than I have done of the said Charles; but certainly never prince had a better servant than he showed himself all that year.

It was one day resolved in Paris that they would sally out and venture a battle with us (I believe it was only a design of the great officers, and that the king was not privy to it). The project they had concerted, was to attack us in three several places at once; in one with a considerable body of forces that were to sally out of Paris; the other by the bridge of Charenton (but that party could have done us no great mischief): and the third, by a brigade of 200 men-at-arms from the wood of Vincennes. About midnight we were informed of this design by a page, who called to us over the river, by directions from some friends of the princes who were in the town, whose names he told us, and immediately returned. Just at break of day, the Lord Poncet de Rivière appeared before the bridge of Charenton; and the Lord du Lau † on the other side, towards the wood

---

* Philip de Melun held the office of Captain of the Bastille Saint Antoine from 1462, until his death, which occurred in 1466. See p. 14. note §.

† Antoine de Castelnau or Chasteauneuf, Lord and Baron of Lau, in Armagnac, Grand Chamberlain and Grand Butler of France, and Seneschal of Guienne. Having incurred the king's displeasure, he was arrested and taken to the castle of Usson, in Auvergne, whence he escaped in

of Vincennes, charged up as far as our artillery, and killed
one of our cannoneers : the alarm was very great, and everybody concluded it was the same design of which the page
had given us notice in the night.   The Count of Charolois
was immediately in arms, but not so soon as Duke John
of Calabria, who, in all alarms, was always the first mounted,
his horse barbed, and himself completely armed : he wore
such a dress as the condottieri usually do in Italy, and
indeed he had the air of a prince and a great general. Whenever he came forth upon any alarm, his first course was to
ride up to the barriers of our camp, to keep our men from
sallying out ; and they obeyed his orders as readily as if the
Count of Charolois had been there himself, and, to speak
truth, he deserved it.   In a moment our whole army was in
arms, and drawn up within our waggons, all except 200
horse, who were abroad upon the guard : and, unless it
were that day, I never knew any great likelihood of a
battle, but then everybody expected it.   By this time the
Dukes of Berry and Bretagne were come in, whom before
that time I never saw in arms : the Duke of Berry was
armed at all points, but neither of them had any great body
of troops with them, only they passed through the camp, and
went to the Count of Charolois and the Duke of Calabria, with
whom they had a conference.   Our scouts, being reinforced,
marched up as near Paris as they could, and were able to discover several of the king's party, who were sent out to learn
what was the matter in our army.   When the Lord du Lau
approached us, our cannon played briskly upon him ; and
the king, having a large train of artillery mounted on the
walls of Paris, fired as briskly into our camp, notwithstanding it was two good leagues off ; but I suppose they mounted
their muzzles very high, and shot amongst us at random.

  This prodigious cannonading made both sides believe some
great design was in agitation : and, to be sure, we sent out
our scouts, and the weather being cloudy and duskish, those
who got nearest the town discovered a party of horse upon

1468, and sought refuge with the Duke of Burgundy, under whom he
fought at the siege of Liege. He afterwards regained the favour of
Louis XI., who appointed him Lieutenant-General and Governor of the
county of Roussillon, of Cerdagne, and of the town of Perpignan. He
was still living in 1483.

the patrol, and beyond them (as they fancied) they perceived a great number of lances standing upright, which they imagined to be the king's battalions drawn up in the field, and all the people of Paris with them : which fancy proceeded merely from the darkness of the day ; upon which they retired immediately to the princes (who were then riding before our camp), acquainted them with what they had seen, and assured them of a battle. The Parisian scouts seeing ours retreat, advanced continually upon them, which made their relation seem more probable. The Duke of Calabria came then where the standard of the Count of Charolois was pitched, and most of the officers of his household stood ready to accompany it : his banner was ready to be displayed likewise, and the guidon, with his arms, which was the custom of that family ; and being come up to us, Duke John said, " Well, gentlemen, we are now where we desired to be ; the king and all his army (as our scouts inform us) are drawn out of Paris, and marching to engage us ; so let each behave with courage and good will, and as they march out, we will march in, and measure out their commodities for them by the pike." And after this manner he rode from rank to rank, encouraging and animating the soldiers. By this time our scouts, perceiving the enemy were weak, began to assume a little more courage, ventured something nearer the town, but still found the battalions in the same place and posture in which they had left them, which put them into a new quandary : however, they stole up to them as near as they could, but could make nothing of them ; till at length the day cleared, and they discovered them to be tall thistles. From thence they marched up to the very gates, but found no troops posted there, of which word was despatched to the princes, and they went immediately to mass, and from thence to dinner. Those who brought the first news were much out of countenance ; but the page's intelligence in the night, and the duskishness of the day, did in some measure excuse them.

CHAP. XII.

How the King visited the Count of Charolois, and talked with him concerning their Quarrel; and of the Importance of wise Councillors to a
Prince.—1465.

HOWEVER, the treaty of peace between the king and the
Count of Charolois still went on, and with greater vigour
than ever; because the principal strength of both parties
consisted in those two. The princes' demands ran very high:
the Duke of Berry demanded all Normandy for his share,
which the king positively refused. The Count of Charolois
would have all the towns restored to him which were
situated on the River Somme, and had been delivered up by
Duke Philip to the king, about three months before *,
for 400,000 crowns; which towns had been surrendered to him upon the treaty of Arras, in the time of
Charles VII. These towns were Amiens, Abbeville, St.
Quentin, Peronne, and others. The Count of Charolois
pretended, that during his life they ought not to have been
ransomed, and put the king in mind of the great favours and
obligations he had received from their family; how he had
been entertained and protected by them for six years together, when he was in rebellion against his father King Charles
VII., supplied with money for his subsistence, attended to
Rheims to be inaugurated, and to Paris for his coronation;
wherefore the Count of Charolois took it very ill that he
should offer to redeem the said towns. However, the negotiation went on so prosperously, that the king came one
morning†, by water, right over against our camp, having
drawn up a good body of horse upon the bank of the river,
but, in the boat with him there were not above four or five
persons besides the boatmen. Among those in the boat,
were the Lord du Lau, the Lord of Montauban (at that
time Admiral of France), the Lord of Nantouillet, and others.
The Count of Charolois and the Count of St. Paul were at
the same time upon the bank of the river on our side,
awaiting his majesty. The king saluted the Count of
Charolois in these words, — " Brother [for his first wife

* This is a mistake : two years had elapsed since their repurchase.
See p. 5., note §.
† On Monday, September 9. 1465.

F

was the king's sister*], do you assure me ?" The count replied, " Yes, my lord, as a brother." I heard him, and so did many others. Then the king came on shore, and the lords with him. The Count of Charolois and the Count of St. Paul received him with great honour (as reason was they should), and he being not sparing, began in this manner : "Brother, I know now you are a·gentleman, and of the family of France." "Why so, my lord ? " replied the Count of Charolois. " Because (said the king) when I sent my ambassadors lately to Lisle, to wait on my uncle your father, and yourself, and that fool Morvillier talked so saucily to you, you sent me word. by the Archbishop of Narbonne (who is a gentleman, and, indeed, he has shown himself so, for every one is pleased with him) that before the year was at an end, I should repent of what Morvillier had said to you. You have been as good as your word, and much before your time was expired." The king spoke these words smilingly, and in a very pleasant manner, as knowing the humour of the person to whom he spoke to be such, that he would be delighted with an expression of that nature ; and, indeed, he was wonderfully pleased with it. Then the king proceeded, " It is with such persons that I would deal, who are punctual to their promise ; " and, afterwards, his majesty disavowed whatever Morvillier had said, and denied that he had ever given him any such commission. In short, the king walked a long time between the two counts, the Count of Charolois's guards standing by in great numbers, under arms, and observing their motions. At this interview the Count of Charolois demanded the duchy of Normandy, the towns situated upon the Somme, and several other favours for his friends. Some proposals were made likewise for the good of the commonwealth, but those were least insisted upon, for the common was now turned into the private wealth. The king would not consent to part with Normandy upon any terms; but, as for the towns upon the Somme, his majesty was willing to gratify the Count of Charolois with them, and, for his sake, to make the Count of St. Paul Constable of France. After which they took their leave of each other very kindly. The king went into

* Catherine of France, who was married in June, 1439, and died in 1446.

his boat, and in that to Paris, and the counts returned to Conflans.

After this manner the time was spent, one day in peace, and another in war: but, though the negotiation between the commissioners, at the Grange-aux-Merciers, was broken off, and absolutely discontinued, yet the private transaction between the king and the Count of Charolois went on still, and several persons passed daily between them notwithstanding the war; among the rest there was one William Bische *, and another called Guillot Duisie †, both of them servants to the Count of Charolois, and both persons who had been obliged formerly to the king; for Duke Philip having banished them ‡, at the request of the Count of Charolois, the king had entertained them. But these messages and correspondences were not pleasing to everybody; the princes began to be jealous, and to grow weary; and, had it not been for an accident, which happened a few days after, they would all have marched shamefully home. I myself saw three several councils held in one chamber, where they were all assembled; and I saw one day, that the Count of Charolois was highly displeased with it, for it was done twice in his presence, which was a thing not fit to be done, to consult of anything when he was by in the chamber, and not communicate it to him, as he had the greatest force in the host: he complained of it to the Lord of Contay, who, being a person of great wisdom and experience (as I said before),

---

* Guillaume Bische, a native of Molins Engilbert, in the Nivernois, was, according to Philip the Good, "the worst and subtlest fellow under the sun." This subtlety was not injurious to him in the opinion of Louis XI., who made him Bailiff of St. Pierre-le-Moustier and Governor of Soissonnois, and honoured him with his confidence and friendship. In 1472, he was Lord of Clery, and chief steward of Duke Charles of Burgundy: and in 1478, he received the additional titles of " knight, councillor and chamberlain of the king, Governor of Peronne, Montdidier and Roye."

† Guillot or Guyon Dusye figures, as an equerry of the stable, in a list of the household of Charles, Duke of Burgundy. He was afterwards created a knight.

‡ After his reconciliation with the Count of Charolois, in February, 1456, the Duke of Burgundy "banished from his dominions two of the principal servants of his son; the first named Guillaume Visse (Bische) was master of his chamber, who not long before had come as a poor valet from Champagne to Burgundy; the second was an esquire, named Guyot Duisy, a native of Burgundy." Du Clercq, xiii. 205.

advised him to bear it patiently for the present ; for, if he should anger them, they would make their peace better than he : and, as he was the strongest, so he persuaded him to be the wisest, to prevent them from separating and breaking the confederacy, to keep them together with all possible industry, and smother his resentment, whatever he thought. However, he told him that, indeed it raised the wonder of several people (and of some even about his person) that such inconsiderable persons as those two before mentioned, should be employed in managing so important an affair ; and he said that it could not but be very dangerous, in respect of the bounty and liberality of the king. It is true the Lord of Contay hated Bische ; however, he said no more than what others had said before him ; and I am of opinion it was not his passion so much as the necessity of the matter, that made him speak as he did ; however, the Count of Charolois was well pleased with his counsel, and applied himself to treat and be more merry with the princes than formerly, and to converse more freely both with them and their creatures, than he had been used ; and, in my judg- ment, there was a necessity for this, in respect of the great danger, lest they should have forsaken him, and the whole confederacy have been dissolved.

In matters of this moment, a wise man is of great import- ance (but he must be believed), and then he is not to be purchased at too dear a rate. But I could never meet with any prince that would distinguish the difference between men, till his necessity instructed him ; and if he did, it was to no purpose, for they generally distribute their authority to such as are most agreeable to them, and suitable to their years, or complying with their humours; and sometimes they are managed by such as are only subservient to their pleasures. However, those princes who have any understanding, do quickly recollect themselves when they are in distress, and find their mistake ; and so I observed our king did, as did also the Count of Charolois at that time, Edward IV., King of England, and several other princes ; but these three especially I have seen in such exigence, that they have been glad of those very persons whom before they had despised. As for the Count of Charolois, when he was Duke of Bur- gundy, and fortune had exalted him to a greater height of glory and honour than ever any of his family had arrived at, and made him so great, that he thought no prince in Christendom equal to him, God was pleased to put a stop to his glory, and to infatuate him so, that, despising all counsel but his own, he lost his own life unhappily, sacrificed the lives of many thousands of his subjects, and brought his family to desolation, as is now visible to all the world.

CHAP. XIII.

How Rouen was delivered into the hands of the Duke of Bourbon to be kept for the Duke of Berry; and the Conclusion of the Treaty of Conflans. — 1465.

HAVING in the preceding chapters enlarged upon the dangers which occur in treaties, and the necessity that princes should prudently, and with circumspection, make choice of such persons as are fit to be employed in the negotiation of such important affairs, especially if they have the worst of the game; I shall now give an account of what it was that induced me to insist upon them so long. Whilst these treaties were managed by way of meetings and conferences, and liberty allowed to converse freely one with another, instead of treating of a general peace, it was proposed privately by some persons, that the duchy of Normandy should be put into the hands of the king's only brother, the Duke of Berry, out of which he should take an equivalent for his patrimony, and deliver up Berry to the king *; and so cunningly was this bargain transacted, that the widow of the Grand Seneschal of Normandy†, with some of her relations and servants who were about her, received John, Duke of Bourbon, into the Castle of Rouen‡, from whence he entered into the town, and the town quickly consented to the change (being desirous to have a prince who would keep his residence in that province), and most of the towns and places in Normandy followed the example §; for the Normans have always thought,

* This treaty is dated October 2. 1465. See Lenglet, ii. 499.
† Jeanne Crespin, daughter of Guillaume Crespin, Lord of Mauny, and of Jacqueline d'Auvricher. Letters of absolution from the treason here recorded were granted her by Louis XI. in January, 1466.
‡ He entered on Friday, September 27. 1465.
§ "At which the king was marvellously vexed, and said one day to

and do still think it reasonable, that so great a duchy as theirs is, should have a duke constantly resident among them ; and, to speak truth, it is very considerable in respect of the vast sums of money which are raised in it, for I myself . have known it pay 950,000 francs in one year, and some say more.

As soon as the town of Rouen had revolted, all the inhabitants swore to the Duke of Bourbon to be true and faithful to the Duke of Berry; except the bailiff named Houaste* (who had served the king as his valet de chambre when he was in Flanders, and had been in great favour with him), and one Monsieur William Piquart† (afterwards General of Normandy); and also he that is at present Grand Seneschal of Normandy‡ would not take the oath, but returned to the king, contrary to the persuasion of his mother, who, as is said before, had the greatest hand in the revolt.

The king no sooner heard the news of the change which had taken place in Normandy, but finding it was not in his power to remedy what was already done, he resolved to conclude a peace, and immediately signified to the Count of Charolois (who was then with his army) that he desired to have a conference with him, and appointed an hour when he would meet him in the fields near his camp, which was then about Conflans. Exactly at the appointed time§ the king marched out of Paris with about a hundred horse, most of them his Scottish guards, and very few besides. The Count of Charolois, attended but by a very few, went to the place

the Count of St. Pol, half between jest and earnest : "Fair cousin of St. Pol, you have said and still say such fine words to me that I have lost Rouen and Pontoise by them."—*Hennin*, 438.

* Jean de Montespedon, surnamed Houaste, Lord of Basoches, Beauvoir, &c., chamberlain to the king, and Bailiff of Rouen. His wife was Drouette de Bar. He was still alive in 1479, and is mentioned as bailiff in public documents of that year.

† Guillaume Picart, Knight, Lord of Estelau, councillor and chamberlain of the king. He was made Bailiff of Rouen, and chief commander of all the artillery, on the 3rd of October, 1479. He was still living in April, 1484.

‡ Jacques de Brézé, Count de Maulevrier, son of Pierre de Brézé and Jeanne Crespin, became Grand Seneschal of Normandy after the death of his father. He married Charlotte, a natural daughter of Louis XI.; and died on the 4th of August, 1494.

§ On Thursday, October 3. 1465.

without further ceremony; yet so many followed after him, that by degrees their number was much superior to the king's; but the count caused them to keep at a distance, while the king and he walked alone together a while. The king told him the peace was concluded, and gave him an account of what had happened at Rouen (of which the count was utterly ignorant till then) adding, that by his good-will he would never have given his brother so large a portion: but since the Normans of themselves had made that change, he was contented, and would sign the treaty * in the same form as had been insisted upon several days before; and there were few other things to grant.   The Count of Charolois was extremely pleased to hear it, for his army was in great want of provisions, but more so of money; and had not this unexpected accident happened, all the princes would have been forced to break up, and march away with dishonour. However, either that day or not many days after †, the Count of Charolois was reinforced by a supply sent by his father, Philip, Duke of Burgundy, consisting of sixscore men-at-arms, 1500 archers, and 120,000, crowns upon ten sumpter horses, under the command of the Lord de Saveuses ‡; besides a great quantity of bows and arrows; which recruited the Burgundian army pretty well, they being fearful before, that the other princes would have patched up a peace, and deserted them.

This discourse of peace was so pleasing both to the king and the Count of Charolois, that (as I have heard him say since), as they were talking friendly together how the remaining difficulties might be adjusted (not regarding their way), they walked on towards Paris; and so far they proceeded, that they were entered into a great bulwark of earth and wood, which the king had caused to be made at a good distance from the town, at the further end of a trench, whose other end led into the city.   The count was attended

---

* The treaty was concluded on the 5th of October, and peace proclaimed on the 29th of the same month.

† On the following Thursday, October 10th, 1465. See Lenglet, ii. 49.

‡ Philip de Saveuses, long Captain of Amiens and Artois, was deposed in 1463 by Louis XI. In 1465, the Duke of Burgundy appointed him Captain general of Artois. His wife was Marie de Lully : and he died at Amiens, on the 28th of March, 1467, at the age of seventy-seven.

by only four or five persons, who were all of them extremely
surprised when they found where they were. However,
the count put the best face on it that he could; but it is
probable that at that time neither of those two princes had
any design in it, for neither the one nor the other received
any prejudice. When the news of the count's being got
into one of the enemy's works was brought to the army, there
was a great murmur in the camp, and immediately the
Count of St. Paul, the Marshal of Burgundy, the Lords
of Contay and Haultbourdin, and several other of the chief
officers, met together about it, and unanimously agreed that
both the Count of Charolois and those that were with him
had been guilty of a great piece of indiscretion, especially
after the misfortune which had happened to his grandfather *
at Montereau-Fault-Yonne, in the presence of Charles VII.
Hereupon they commanded the soldiers that were strolling
up and down in the fields to stand to their arms ; and the
Marshal of Burgundy (whose surname was Neufchastel),
spoke to this effect : " If this mad hair-brained young prince
has cast away himself, let us not ruin his family, his father's
interest, or our own. My opinion therefore is, that every
man should retire to his quarters, and be ready, without
alarming ourselves, for anything that may happen ; for,
keeping together, we are enough to make our retreat to the
frontiers of Hainault, Picardy, or Burgundy, as we please."
   After he had given his opinion in this manner, he and the
Count of St. Paul mounted on horseback, and rode out of
the camp, to see if they could descry anybody coming from
Paris. After they had waited some time, they perceived
a body of forty or fifty horse marching towards them ; who
were the Count of Charolois, and an escort that the king
had sent to guard him to his camp. When the count saw
them coming towards him, he dismissed his escort, and
addressed himself to the Marshal de Neufchastel, of whom
he was most afraid ; for, being a true old soldier, and firm
to his interest, he took the liberty sometimes of repri-

---

* John, surnamed Sans-Peur, Duke of Burgundy, was the son of
Philippe le-Hardi and Margaret of Flanders. He was born on the 28th
of May, 1371 ; married to Margaret of Bavaria on the 9th of April,
1385 ; and assassinated on the bridge of Montereau, on the 10th of
September, 1419.

manding him severely, and ventured to tell him, "Whilst your father lives, I am your servant only by loan." The first thing the count said to him was, "I pray be not angry, I am sensible of my great folly, but I perceived it not till I was too near the bulwark to get off." The marshal replied, "that it was done in his absence." The count bowed his head, and gave him no answer, but returned presently to the camp, where he was joyfully received by the whole army, and every one highly extolled the king's honour and generosity; but, for all that, the count never afterwards would trust himself in his power.

—— ✦ ——

The Treaty of Peace, called the Treaty of Conflans, between King Louis XI., on the one part, and Charles, Count of Charolois, on the other.   Paris, October 5. 1465.

Louis, by the grace of God, King of France, &c.

We being desirous, of our own certain knowledge and good-will, to reconcile to us our dearly beloved cousin and brother, Charles, Count of Charolois, having regard to the great and good services, aids, and succours, he can and is willing to give unto us and our crown, so that our kingdom may be guarded and preserved on all sides from its ancient enemies and our other adversaries; peace, union, and tranquillity being cultivated between us, our said brother and cousin, and other lords of our blood; all hostilities cease, and justice be preserved and administered in our said kingdom: and also in consideration, and for a recompense of the great services and expenses our uncle the Duke of Burgundy has borne and performed for us in the lifetime of our late most dear lord and father, whom God pardon, to whom and into whose country we had withdrawn ourselves, in order to avoid the dangers that were likely to threaten our person; and as well for the support of our own state, and that of our most dear and well-beloved queen, as also upon the account of several notable embassies to our said lord and father, to the Pope and to other potentates, in reference to our coming to the crown; as well as other great charges and expenses our said uncle and our said brother and cousin have been at to accompany us to our coronation at Rheims, and at our public entry into Paris, with a great number of armed

men, for fear we might meet with any opposition in our
kingdom : for all which charges, disbursements, and expenses
we have often agreed and promised to satisfy our said uncle,
and our said cousin and brother ; besides a pension of
30,000 francs, which we had given and granted by way
of recompense to our said brother and cousin, the payment of which, some time before our divisions, had been
interrupted and stopped ; we have by the advice and deliberation of our brother the Duke of Normandy, and of
our well-beloved cousins the Dukes of Bretagne, Calabria,
Bourbon, and Nemours, the Counts of Maine, Perche, Eu,
and Armagnac, of the members of our privy-council and
of our parliament, and other great men of our kingdom,
given and transferred, and we do by these presents give and
transfer to our said cousin the Count of Charolois,—in consideration and for a recompense as aforesaid ; as also upon the
account that our said brother and cousin has frankly and
freely, so far as in him lay, been very instrumental, with our
said brother and other lords of our blood, in appeasing of the
said troubles and obtaining the good of peace,—to himself,
his heirs, whether male or female, descending from him in
a direct line, and the heirs of his said heirs, also descending
from them in a direct line, for ever, the cities, towns,
territories, fortresses, and signiories, appertaining to us
at and upon the Somme, both on the one side and the other—
viz. Amiens, St. Quentin, Corbin, Abbeville, together with all
the county of Ponthieu, on both sides the said river, Doullens, St. Riquier, Crevecœur, Arleux, Montreuil, Le Crotoy,
Mortagne, with all their appurtenances and dependencies,
and whatever else may belong to us upon the account
of our said crown from the said River Somme, inclusively on
the side of Artois, Flanders, and Hainault, which our said
uncle of Burgundy had and possessed lately, by virtue
of the treaty of Arras, and before the re-purchase we had
made of them ; comprehending also, in reference to the
towns situate upon the said river, the bailiwicks and
shrievalties of the said cities, in the same manner as our
said uncle held and possessed them, to be enjoyed by our
said brother and cousin and his said heirs, and the heirs
of his heirs, male or female, with all their profits and
revenues, as well the domain as the aids destined for war,

and also the taillages and all other profits whatsoever, as our said uncle enjoyed them, without any exception whatsoever, save the fealty, homage, and sovereignty; which transfer we have made, and do make, at the re-purchase of 200,000 crowns of gold, current money: neither can we nor our successors buy the same again of our said brother and cousin during his life; but only we and our successors may do it of the heirs of our said brother and cousin, descending from him in a direct line, and the heirs of the said heirs, descending also from them in a direct line, who shall be possessed of these territories, upon securing and paying to them once the said sum of 200,000 crowns current money; for the securing of which re-purchase, our said brother and cousin shall grant unto us his letters patent in due form. And our will and meaning is, that our said brother and cousin and his heirs descending from him, that shall be possessed of those territories, may have such power, and at their pleasure constitute and appoint all such officers, as shall be necessary to be constituted and appointed, in reference to the demand of the said cities, towns, fortresses, lands, and signiories; and that the other officers, which shall be necessary on account of royal privileges, aids, and taxes, be made by our successor's appointment, at the nomination of our said brother and cousin, and his heirs, to impose and levy those aids and taxes, as it was in the time that our said uncle the Duke of Burgundy held and possessed them. Moreover, as by the treaty of Arras, it was agreed, among other things, that the county of Boulogne should be and continue in the possession of our uncle the Duke of Burgundy, and the heirs male of his body, and that our late lord and father was obliged to make reparation to those who pretended a right to it; we, from the above said causes and considerations, and without derogating from the treaty of Arras, have agreed and declared, and we do agree and declare to our said brother and cousin, that he and his male or female children, begot by him in wedlock, during their lives only, do and may hold and possess the said county of Boulogne in the same manner and form as our said brother and cousin by the treaty of Arras might hold and possess and make benefit thereof as their inheritance; and we hold ourselves obliged to make compensation to those who pretend a right

in the said county, and to let our said brother and cousin
and his children enjoy it. And we have also promised and
agreed, and we do agree and promise to our said brother and
cousin, that we will transfer and make over, fully, frankly,
and freely to him, and we do from henceforward transfer
and make over the castles, towns, chatellanies, and provostships of Peronne, Montdidier, and Roye, with all their
appurtenances and appendages whatsoever, discharged of
all mortgages and re-purchases, with the same rights as they
were transferred and made over to our said uncle his father,
by the treaty of Arras, to hold and enjoy them in the same
manner as is contained and declared in the said treaty ; and
we will cause, and effectually procure, our most dear and
well-beloved cousin, the Count of Nevers, to transfer and
make over to our said cousin and brother, the Count of
Charolois, all that right which he hath, or pretends to have,
to those castles, towns, provostships, and chatellanies, and
he shall surrender all that he possesses therein, and give
possession thereof to our said brother and cousin the Count
of Charolois, or those commissioned by him : and herewith
we have made over and transferred to our said brother and
cousin, for himself, his heirs and successors, in inheritance
for ever, the county of Guisnes, with all its appurtenances
and dependencies, to be enjoyed by our said brother and
cousin, and his heirs and successors, with all rights, profits,
and emoluments whatsoever, as well of the domain, as the
aids, taxes, and incomes whatsoever, without retaining
or reserving anything for ourselves, except the fealty,
homage, and sovereignty thereof: and we hold ourselves
obliged to make compensation to the Sieur de Croy and
others in respect to any right they have, or pretend to have,
in the said county, and to keep our said brother and
cousin and his heirs in the quiet and peaceable possession
of the said county against the said De Croy and all others.
All which things we have and do promise, *bonâ fide*, on the
word of a king, upon our oath, and upon the penalty of
all the estates that we are now or shall be possessed of,
for ourselves, our heirs and successors, to hold, keep, maintain, and execute every particular in the same manner
and form aforegoing, inviolably, so as never to contravene
the same, either by ourselves or any other ; neither shall we

suffer any other, directly or indirectly, to contravene the
same, openly or covertly, and all without any fraud, deceit,
or evil design; and for the accomplishment and execution
of the things above mentioned, and every of them, we do and
shall submit to the coercion and power of our holy father
the Pope: and we do and will consent, for ourselves
and successors, in all courts, as well ecclesiastical as civil,
to be constrained to observe all and every of the things
above mentioned, by renouncing all rights, privileges, ordinances, royal edicts, exceptions, and all things whatsoever,
whereby anything, either in part or in the whole, shall
be done contrary to the premises, as fully as if all the said
rights, ordinances, edicts, exceptions, and other renunciations,
were expressly declared and specified by these presents.
Besides which, we will charge, and expressly command
our well-beloved and faithful chancellor, our councillors
in our council of state, treasurers, superintendents of our
finances, bailiffs, seneschals, and other justiciaries and officers,
or their lieutenants, and every of them, so far as it relates
to them, that they strictly observe, and in every particular
fulfil, these presents and the contents of them; and that they
neither do nor suffer anything to be done to the contrary;
and when anything shall be done to the contrary hereof,
they shall immediately make reparation, and, without any
delay, restore matters to their former state and condition;
and especially these presents shall be verified in parliament,
in the chambers of accounts and finances, which shall cause
the same to be published and registered everywhere they
ought to be; notwithstanding any edicts made against
alienating and putting out of our power the demesnes of
our said crown, and all the restrictions, promises, and oaths,
which we or any of our said officers might have made
in general or particular, under any form of words whatsoever, whereby they might or would prevent the effecting,
fulfilling and accomplishing all that is contained in these
presents; which ordinances, restrictions, promises, obligations and oaths we will not, for the sake of peace, as to
the present case, have to be in derogation or prejudice
of the transfers and the other things above mentioned, and of
the said promises, oaths, or other restrictions, which our
officers are subject to, in contradiction to these particulars; but

we do, by these presents, and in fulfilling the contents thereof, hold and esteem them acquitted and fully discharged of them.

CHAP. XIV.

Of the Peace that was concluded at Conflans between the King and the Count of Charolois and his Allies.— 1465.

At length all things were accommodated, and the next day* the Count of Charolois made a general muster of his whole army, to see what men he had left, and what he had lost. On a sudden, without any warning, the king came thither, attended only by thirty or forty horse, and went from regiment to regiment to take a view of them all, except the Marshal of Burgundy's squadron, who was no friend of the king's; because, having given him the goverment of Espinal †, in Lorraine, he took it from him afterwards, and gave it to John, Duke of Calabria, to the great disgust and mortification of the said marshal. The king at last grew sensible of his error, and acknowledged he had been wrong in discarding, upon his first accession to the crown, those worthy and eminent knights that had faithfully served his father, and who, resenting the injury, had joined with the princes against him. The king used his utmost endeavours to retrieve the false step he had made, and by little and little reconciled himself to them. It was resolved, that the next day all the lords should repair to the Castle of Vincennes to do homage to the king, and for their security the Castle of Vincennes should be put into the hands of the Count of Charolois.

The next day, according to agreement, the king came thither, and not one of the princes failed to attend him: the porch and gate were lined and strongly guarded, by a good number of the Burgundian soldiers, in their arms. The treaty of peace was read, and the Lord Charles of France did homage to the king for the duchy of Normandy ‡; the Count of Charolois for the towns he held in Picardy § ;

* On Friday, October 11. 1465.
† This town was given to the marshal in 1463, and taken from him by royal letters dated August 6. 1466.
‡ On the 30th of October. See Lenglet, ii. 532
§ On the 31st of October. See Lenglet, ii. 540

others for what they held in other places : and the Count of
St. Paul took his oath as Constable of France. But there
never was so plentiful an entertainment, but somebody rose
hungry : some had their utmost ambition gratified, and others
got nothing at all : some honest but inferior persons the king
took to himself, but the greatest part remained with the Duke
of Bretagne and the new Duke of Normandy, who took their
leave, and went to Rouen, to take possession of that town.
At their departure from the Castle of Vincennes, they all took
leave of one another, every man retired to his lodgings, and
the letters and pardons, and whatever else was agreed upon
by the peace, were signed and despatched. All the princes
departed upon the same day ; the Dukes of Normandy and
Bretagne went first to Normandy, and the Duke of Bretagne
afterwards into his own country : the Count of Charolois
retired towards Flanders, and, as he was upon his way, the
king made him a visit, and conducted him to Villiers-le-Bel *
(a village some four leagues from Paris), expressing a great
desire to maintain a friendship with him; and that night
they lay together in the village. The king had but a very
small party with him, but he had commanded 200 men-
at-arms to attend him back again, which being told to
the Count of Charolois as he was going to bed, he immediately entertained great jealousy and suspicion, and ordered all
his guards that were with him to arm. From whence one
may observe, that it is almost impossible for two great
princes to agree long, by reason of the reports and suspicions
which hourly arise : and indeed two great princes, who are
desirous to preserve a more than ordinary friendship, ought
never to see one another; but rather employ such honest
and wise men between them, as may cultivate their amity
and palliate their faults.

The next morning the two princes took their leave one of
another, and with very kind and obliging language they
parted. The king returned to Paris under the guard of
the 200 men-at-arms that he had ordered for that purpose; which removed the suspicion the count had conceived
of their coming. The count took the road towards Com-

* The Count of Charolois left Conflans on Thursday, the 31st of
October, and proceeded to Villiers-le-Bel, whither the king accompanied
him. They remained there together until the 3rd of November.

piegne and Noyon, and as he went, all the towns were opened
to him by the king's particular command. From thence he
marched to Amiens, and received homage from that and all
the towns upon the Somme, and what formerly belonged to
him in Picardy was restored to him by virtue of the peace;
for which places the king (as I said before) had paid
400,000 crowns of gold not quite nine months before. *
Having despatched his business there, he marched towards
the country of Liege †, for that state had made war for
five or six months upon his father (during his absence) in
the counties of Namur and Brabant, and had done some
mischief in those parts; but, being in winter, he could not
make any considerable progress: yet he burnt several villages,
and made some small incursions into the territories of the
Liegeois: but a peace ‡ was concluded between them, and
the Liegeois were obliged, upon the penalty of a great sum of
money, to observe it; after which the Count of Charolois
returned into Brabant. §

———◆———

*A Treaty of Peace concluded at St. Maur-des-Fossés be-
tween the Dukes of Normandy, Bretagne, Calabria, and
Lorraine, Charles of Burgundy, the Count of Charolois,
the Dukes of Bourbonnois and Auvergne, the Duke of
Nemours, the Counts of Armagnac, St. Paul, Albret, and
Dunois, and Louis XI. of France.   October 29. 1465.*

1. All hostilities are to cease entirely between the parties,
their subjects, and vassals, and a firm peace and tranquillity
to be restored.

2. No reparation shall be required, upon the account of
these divisions, from the said lords, their subjects, vassals,
and adherents, or prosecutions made by law against them,
but they shall live peaceably both within and without the
kingdom, without molestation from the king or the said lords.

* Two years before, Commines should say. He has made the same
mistake already : see p. 65.

† He encamped at Cleyngelm, in the territory of Liege, where he
remained until the 22nd of January, 1466.

‡ This treaty was concluded on the 22nd of December, 1465 ; Huy
and Dinant were excluded from its provisions. It was ratified by the
Count of Charolois on the 24th of January, 1466.

§ He arrived at Brussels on the evening of Friday, the 31st January.

3. The said lords·shall not, upon the account of what is past, renew the war, either by themselves or others, but continue faithful to the king.

4. The king on his part shall be under the same obligations.

5. The subjects, vassals, and adherents of both parties shall return to the peaceable possession of their houses and inheritances, whether within or without the kingdom, and so remain without any cessions or donations to the contrary.

6. All moveable goods shall be restored to those they belonged to before the said troubles; as also all such as have been taken away during the truce.

7. The cities and communities which took part with either side shall no ways be molested and damaged in their privileges, or otherwise, on that account.

8. The places, taken during the troubles on either side, shall be restored.

9. The king shall not oblige the said lords to come to him in person, but yet they are not exempted from the services they owe him, when there is occasion for the defence and manifest good of the kingdom.

10. And when the king shall please to go to the houses and habitations of the said lords, where they shall be in person, he is to give them three days' notice; neither shall the said lords wait on the king before they first send to know his pleasure.

11. If any crime shall be laid to the charge of the said lords or their adherents, the king shall not proceed against them, or detain their persons, without the utmost deliberation, and very sufficient cause shown ; neither shall the said lords proceed against the king's servants or adherents for any crime alleged, without the maturest deliberation.

12. In order to redress all grievances and disorders on the part of the said lords, and divers of the king's subjects of all conditions, in reference to church and state, and for the public good, the king shall give a commission to thirty-six eminent men of his kingdom, to meet at a place appointed, to inquire into all such grievances and disorders, to hear and determine all remonstrances, and apply suitable remedies for the preservation of justice, the rights and franchises both of the church and all the people.

13. And whatever edicts, ordinances, declarations, and the

G

like, shall be made by the thirty-six persons, or the major part of them, they shall within fifteen days after they are brought before the king, be verified in form in the courts of parliament and chambers of accounts, and all the officers sworn to observe them; and no instruments of the king from the chancery or elsewhere shall disannul or make them void.

14. The commission of the said thirty-six persons shall last two months, and they shall have power to adjourn once for forty-two days : and if any of their number shall be sick, or incapacitated any way to act, the rest shall substitute others in their room.

15. The king and the said lords shall entirely maintain all the pacts and agreements made between them, as well in relation to the appanage of the Duke of Normandy, as other things granted to the said lords and their adherents, as fully as if expressly set down in this treaty.

16. And seeing the king, during the said troubles, seized into his hands the lands and lordships of Parthenay, Vouvent, Mirebeau, Secondigny, Coudray, Salvart, and Chastellerault, and conferred the same upon his uncle, the Count of Maine, in prejudice to and to the dispossessing of the Count of Dunois of the said territories ; it is agreed, for the public tranquillity, towards which the Count of Dunois does much contribute, that the Count of Maine shall surrender up all those lands to the king, in due form, who shall effectually reconvey them to the Count of Dunois, who shall enjoy them peaceably, and without any molestation whatsoever.

17. And the king shall, by way of compensation to the Count du Maine, confer upon him the land and signiory of Taillebourg.

18. The king restores Anthony de Chabannes, Count of Dammartin, to all his honours, castles, territories, &c., as he and his wife, Margaret de Nanteuil, enjoyed them in the time of the late king. All his personal estate shall also be restored, notwithstanding any decree of parliament to the contrary.

19. Both parties shall mutually swear to the exact observation of all these articles, and enjoin them to be observed by all their officers, parliaments, prelates, &c.; and if the king would contravene any of them, they shall no manner of way assist him therein.

20. Both parties shall swear and promise they will not

seek for a dispensation of their said oaths and promises, on any occasion whatsoever.

Lastly. If any of the said lords shall attempt anything against the king, in prejudice of the said treaty, the others shall be obliged to assist the king against them.

Chap. XV.

How the King recovered into his hands whatever had been given to his Brother, by the Division between the Dukes of Normandy and Bretagne.—1465.

But to return to the Dukes of Normandy and Bretagne, who had marched to take possession of the Duchy of Normandy. It was not long after they had made their entry into Rouen, before they began to fall out and differ about the division of the spoil; for the persons of quality and officers whom I have mentioned were still with them, and having been used to great honours and preferments in the reign of Charles VII., perceiving the war was at an end, and the king was not to be depended upon, they thought it hard not to be advanced to some considerable post, and every man expected the best place for himself.

The Duke of Bretagne pretended to a share of them, and thought it very reasonable that part of them should be wholly at his disposal, since he had brought the greatest number of troops into the field, and had been at the greatest expense in the war; which the Duke of Normandy refusing, the dispute grew so high, that, for the safety of his person, the Duke of Bretagne was forced to retire to Mount St. Catherine, near Rouen; and the debate continued so strong, that the Duke of Normandy, by the assistance of the citizens of the town, had resolved to have besieged him, had he not marched away directly for Bretagne. As soon as the king had received the news of this division, he drew down with his forces towards that country, and one may easily imagine he knew what he had to do, for he was a perfect master in that science, and knew how to improve everything to his own advantage. Some of those who had the command of the principal towns began to deliver them up, and make their peace with him. I speak not of these affairs upon my own knowledge, for I was not there present, but as the king has since been pleased to inform me. He treated privately with the Duke of Bretagne (who was in possession of some towns in Lower Normandy), in hopes to persuade him altogether to abandon his brother's interest: they had several conferences together at Caen, where they came to an accommodation *, by which the said town of Caen and several others were to remain in the hands of the Lord de Lescut, with a certain number of paid troops; but this treaty was so intricate and perplexed, I believe neither of them understood it very well. Immediately after this, the Duke of Bretagne returned into his own country, and the king went back towards his brother.

The Duke of Normandy, finding himself unable to hold out against the king, who had taken Pont de l'Arche, and other places about him, resolved to fly, and take sanctuary in Flanders. The Count of Charolois was still at St. Tron † (a small town in the diocese of Liege), but much troubled and disturbed, his army having been defeated and broken, and part of it employed (though in the winter time) against the Liegeois; which division vexed him at the heart, for the only thing which he most ambitiously desired, was to see a duke in Normandy, because by that means the king would be much weakened, and be deprived of almost the third part of his kingdom. He ordered some forces immediately to be raised in Picardy, to reinforce the garrison of Dieppe; but before they could be assembled, the governor had made his peace, and the king became master of all the duchy of Normandy, except such places as were left in the custody of the Lord de Lescut by the treaty at Caen.

CHAP. XVI.

The new Duke of Normandy retires into Bretagne very poor and disconsolate, upon account of his having miscarried in his Design.— 1465.

THE Duke of Normandy (as I said before) had once a design to have retired into· Flanders, but on a sudden, a reconcilia-

* This treaty, dated at Caen on the 22nd of December, 1465, was ratified on the following day by Louis XI. The article mentioned by Commines does not occur in it.

† The Count of Charolois was at Saint-Tron from December 21. 1465, to January 12. 1466; and again from the 25th to the 30th of Jan. 1466.

tion was made between the Duke of Bretagne and him,* when it was too late; for both of them found their errors, and soon grew sensible that there was nothing in this world so firm and stable, but that division is able to destroy it at last. And, indeed, it is next kin to an impossibility, that many great lords of equal quality and power sh uld continue long in a confederacy, unless one of them be invested with a supreme command and authority over the rest; and it is absolutely necessary, that that person should be a man of great wisdom and highly beloved, to keep them all in obedience. With my own eyes I have seen many examples of this nature, and therefore I speak not by report: besides, we are all but too much inclined to divide thus to our own prejudice, without any regard to the consequences which may follow ; and, in my opinion, one wise prince with the command of 10,000 men, and money to pay them, is more to be feared and esteemed than ten, who every one of them has 6000, and all of them allied and confederate together; and the reason is, because they have always so many cere-monies and punctilios of honour to be adjusted and accom-modated between them, that half their opportunity is lost before they can agree or decide among themselves.

In this manner the Duke of Normandy retired into Bretagne, poor and disconsolate, being forsaken by all those officers that had served his father, Charles VII., who had made their peace with the king, and were advanced to places of higher trust and honour than they ever enjoyed under his father. These two dukes were wise, as the pro-verb says of the Bretons, when it was too late, and kept themselves close in Bretagne with the Lord de Lescut, their chief servant; during which time, several ambassadors were still going and coming, sometimes from them to the king, sometimes from the king to them ; now from them to the Count of Charolois, then from the count to them ; sometimes from the king to the Duke of Burgundy, and then again from the Duke of Burgundy to him: some for intelligence, and some to debauch their respective subjects, and make

* They made a treaty of perpetual alliance, which was signed by the Duke of Bretagne on the 10th of August, 1467, and by the Duke of Normandy on the 22nd of the same month.

what pernicious bargains they could, and all under the specious pretence of amity and friendship.

However, some were honest, and went with a true zeal to accommodate matters between them; but they were not a little conceited, to presume so far upon their own wisdom as to think that their presence could prevail anything upon such powerful princes as they, who were cunning and penetrating, and understood their own interest too well. I saw the proposals myself, and truly, in my judgment, neither the one nor the other were reasonable. But there is a sort of people so vain and self-conceited as to believe they can perform things which they do not understand; for very often their masters will not tell them their secret thoughts. People of such a kidney are sent only in formality, and to fill up a table, and many times to their own cost; for always they have some hanger-on or other who has some secret designs, as I have observed at all times, and in all places, wherever I have been concerned; so that (as I said before) great princes ought to be very careful into whose hands they commit the management of their affairs; and it also concerns those who are employed in negotiations abroad, to be very cautious how they undertake them; and he that can excuse himself and get off (unless he knows himself capable of performing it, and finds his master to be well affected to the business) is, in my judgment, the wisest man; for I have known many an honest man much puzzled and troubled in managing such an affair. I have seen princes of two quite contrary, or, at least, very different, dispositions; some are of so subtle and jealous a temper, that no man knows how to live with them, and they think everybody betrays them. Others are as confident on the other side, and commit too much to their ministers, but then they are so dull and so unskilful in state affairs, they cannot distinguish when a man does well or ill; and these princes are very wavering and inconstant, and their love changes suddenly into hatred, and their hatred into love; and though neither with the one nor the other, are there many good ministers to be found (and where they are, they do not continue long in favour, and are never safe), yet I had rather live with a wise than with a weak prince, for there a man may have an opportunity of excusing himself and recovering his favour;

but with the ignorant, there is no reconciliation, for he does nothing of himself, but refers all to his ministers, who have the sole administration of affairs, and then he changes his mind upon every trifling occasion.   However, their subjects are obliged to obey them in the countries where they reign. But the result of all this is, that we should place our confidence only in God, for in him (and in none else) all our virtue, goodness, and safety, consist.   It is our misery that few people understand this, till it is too late, and they have been taught by their misfortunes : yet it is better to be wise late, than never.

BOOK THE SECOND.

CHAPTER I.

Of the Wars between the Duke of Burgundy and the Liegeois; and of the taking, plundering, and razing the town of Dinant.—1466.

Soon after the pacification of the troubles of France, the Duke of Burgundy began a war against the Liegeois, which lasted for several years; and whenever the King of France had a mind to interrupt him, he attempted some new action against the Bretons, and, in the meantime, supported the Liegeois underhand; upon which the Duke of Burgundy turned against him to succour his allies, or else they came to some treaty or truce among themselves. In the year 1466*, Dinant was taken by the Duke of Burgundy, which is a town situated in the territory of Liege, very strong for its size, and very rich by reason of the works which they make in copper, commonly called Dinanderie — namely, pots, skillets, and frying-pans, and such like ware. The Duke of Burgundy (who died in June, 1467†) had so great an animosity to them, that he was carried in his old age to that siege in a litter. The reasons of his displeasure were, the great cruelty which they had exercised upon his subjects in the county of Namur, and especially at a little town called Bouvines, about a quarter of a league from Dinant, there being only the River Maes between them. Not long before that, the inhabitants of Dinant had besieged the town of Bouvines, on the other side of the river, for the space of eight months, committing numerous acts of hostilities, and bombarding it continually with two brass cannon and other great pieces of artillery, battering the houses about their ears, and forcing the inhabitants to shelter themselves in their cellars, where they continued during the whole siege. It is impossible to imagine the deadly hatred that these two

* On Monday, August 25. 1466.
† On the 15th of June, 1467.

towns had conceived one against the other*: yet their children married frequently together, there being no other towns of any consideration in that neighbourhood.

The year before the destruction of Dinant (which was the summer in which the Count of Charolois arrived before Paris, and joined with the French lords who were in confederacy with him) the town made an agreement and peace with the count, by which they were obliged to pay to him a certain sum of money, and had separated from the city of Liege and managed their affairs apart. When people (whose interest binds them together in an alliance) divide and forsake one another, it is a certain sign of destruction, not only for towns and little states, but for princes and great potentates: but because I suppose everybody may have read or observed examples enough of this nature, I forbear to say any more than this, that King Louis our master understood breaking and dividing of leagues better than any prince that I ever knew, for he spared neither money nor pains, and that as well with the servants as the masters. But to return; by degrees the Dinanters began to repent heartily of the above-mentioned treaty, and caused four of their chief citizens, who had been instrumental in concluding the peace, to be most barbarously executed, and began the war afresh in the county of Namur. For these reasons, and upon the earnest solicitation of the inhabitants of Bouvines, this siege was undertaken by Duke Philip; but the command of the army was given to his son, to whom the Count of St. Paul, Constable of France, repaired, but, coming in a private capacity, and acting without any authority from the king, he could not bring any of the standing forces of the kingdom to the assistance of the Duke of Burgundy, but was forced to content himself with what forces he could assemble on the frontiers of Picardy.

The Dinanters made a bold sally one day; but it proved much to their disadvantage, for they were beaten so cruelly, that eight days after (their friends having no time to consider of their relief) the town was taken by storm and set

---

* For the first causes of this hostility, see several documents published in M. Gachard's *Collection de Documents Inédits*, vol. ii. pp. 205, 218, 343, in which the Dinantais charge the people of Bouvines with the same acts of violence and cruelty with which Commines charges the Dinantais.

on fire, and the prisoners (about 800) drowned before
Bouvines at the earnest request of the men of Bouvines.
Whether God permitted it as a judgment upon them for
their malice, I cannot determine, but certainly it was a
dreadful revenge.

The next day after the taking of the town, the Liegeois
(contrary to their agreement *) arrived in great numbers to
have relieved it ; for by that treaty they also had obliged
themselves not to meddle with the affairs of the Dinanters, as
the Dinanters had separated from them.

Duke Philip, on account of his great age, returned home† ;
but his son with the whole army advanced against the Liegeois,
whom we met with sooner than we expected, for, by accident
and the fault of our guides, our vanguard lost their way,
and our main body (in which most of the chief commanders
were) encountered the enemy.   It was already late when we
met, and yet we prepared to engage them, when immediately
certain deputies arrived from them, with a message to the
Count of Charolois, beseeching him, that in honour to the
blessed Virgin Mary (whose eve that was ‡), he would commi-
serate their condition ; and who also made the best excuse they
could for breaking the treaty that was lately concluded
between them.   However, the Liegeois did not seem so
submissive as the deputies represented them to be, but
set a good face on the matter, and made a show as if
they intended to venture a battle.   However, after the
deputies had gone, and returned three or four times,
the peace made the year before was confirmed§, and a certain
sum of money was to be paid‖ ; and that the peace might be
better observed than it had been before, they promised to
deliver 300 hostages¶, who were to be named, and set

* See p. 80, note ‡ .

† " On the first day of September, the duke departed from Bouvines,
and lay that night at Namur."   Du Clercq, xv. 125.

‡ It was Sunday, September 7., the eve of the nativity of the Virgin.

§ The letters of the burgomasters are dated September 10. 1466.
Gachard, ii. 402.

‖ They had promised, by the treaty of December 22. 1465, to " pay
600,000 Rhenish florins in six years, 100,000 each year."   Du Clercq, xv.
129.

¶ This number of 300 hostages was to be furnished by annuity, as
it were ; that is to say, fifty every year, until the full payment of the

down in a roll by the Bishop of Liege* and some of his
officers who were then in the army, and to be sent to
the Count of Charolois by eight o'clock the next morning.
During the whole night the Burgundian army was in great
dread, for they were neither regularly encamped, nor enclosed within their waggons, but scattered up and down
in separate bodies, and in a place very advantageous for the
enemy, who were all foot, and much better acquainted with
the country than we. Some of them had a desire to
have attacked us, and if they had, in my opinion we must
have been defeated; but those who transacted the peace,
opposed and hindered that enterprise.

As soon as it was break of day, our army drew together in
one body immediately; our battalions appeared drawn up in
very good order, and our number was great, consisting of
3000 men-at-arms, good and bad, and 12,000 or 14,000
archers: besides a good body of foot out of the neighbouring country. We marched directly towards them, to receive
our hostages, or fight them if they failed. We found
them separated, and marching off in small bodies, and in
disorder, as people wholly ignorant of order and martial
conduct. It was by this time almost twelve o'clock, and
no hostages delivered; the Count of Charolois asked advice of the Marshal of Burgundy, whether he should fall
upon them or not; the marshal replied, Yes, he might do it
without any danger, and they could not complain, for they
themselves were in the fault. Then he asked the Lord of
Contay (who has been often named), and he was entirely of
the same opinion, affirming we should never have such an
opportunity, showing us how they were divided and in disorder, and pressed hard for attacking them. The next he
asked was the Count of St. Paul, Constable of France, who
was absolutely against it, alleging that it would be inconsistent both with his honour and engagement to fall upon them,
and that it was impossible for so many people to come to a

600,000 florins. The fifty were to be made up "of thirty-two men for
the city of Liege, six for the town of Tongres, six for the town of Saint-
Tron, and six for the town of Hasselt." Du Clercq, xv. 129.

* Louis de Bourbon, Bishop of Liege, son of Charles I, Duke of
Bourbon, and Agnes of Burgundy. He was assassinated on the 30th of
August, 1482.

final resolution and be agreed so soon, especially in a business
of such a nature as choosing of hostages; and he advised the
Count of Charolois rather to send to them, and see what they
intended.   The argument between these three great officers
before the Count of Charolois took up a considerable time,
and he was much divided how to determine the matter.   On
the one hand, he saw his great and inveterate enemies defeated, and in his power, and that without any dangerous resistance; on the other, he found his honour was at stake, and
it would interfere with his promise.   At last he concluded to
send a trumpet towards them, who met them bringing the
hostages, upon which all were hush, and every man returned
to his post.   But the soldiers were highly displeased with the
constable's advice; for they saw good plunder before their
eyes.   An embassy was sent immediately to Liege to ratify
and confirm the treaty of peace; but the people (being inconstant) said that the count was afraid to engage them, fired
their guns upon him, and committed many insolences.   The
count after this returned into Flanders; and, his father dying
that summer, he celebrated his obsequies with great pomp and
solemnity at Bruges; and notified* his death to the king.

CHAP. II.

How the Liegeois broke the Peace with the Duke of Burgundy, before
    called Count of Charolois, upon which he engages and defeats them in
    a set Battle. — 1467.

DURING these wars, and ever since, secret and fresh intrigues were carried on by the princes.   The king was so
exceedingly exasperated against the Dukes of Bretagne and
Burgundy that it was wonderful; they could not correspond,
or hear from one another without great difficulty; sometimes
their couriers were stopped, and, in time of war, they were
forced to send their letters by sea, or, at least, the Duke of
Bretagne was obliged to send his messengers into England,
who, going by land to Dover, embarked there for Calais; for,
when they went the direct way by land, they were often in
very great danger.

* By letter dated from Bruges, June 19. 1467. It will be found in
Lenglet, ii. 620.

During all these years of dissension, and in others which succeeded for, at least, twenty years or more (some in wars, and others in truces and circumventions, every one of the princes comprehending his allies in his truces,) it pleased God to favour the realm of France so far, that the wars and divisions in England were not ended, though they had begun fifteen years before, and had been continued with many memorable and bloody battles, in which several brave men had been slain. In those wars both sides were accounted traitors, by reason that there were two families which pretended to the crown ; one was the house of Lancaster, the other the house of York: and it is not to be doubted but that if England had been in the same condition it was in formerly, the kingdom of France would have been in great danger. The King of France's aim, in the meantime, was chiefly to carry his design against the province of Bretagne, and he looked upon it as a more feasible attempt, and likelier to give him less resistance than the house of Burgundy. Besides, the Bretons were the people who protected and entertained all his malcontents ; as his brother, and others, whose interest and intelligence were great in his kingdom; for this cause he endeavoured very earnestly with Charles, Duke of Burgundy, by several advantageous offers and proposals, to prevail with him to desert them, promising that upon those terms he also would abandon the Liegeois, and give no further protection to his malcontents. The Duke of Burgundy would by no means consent to it, but again made preparations for war against the Liegeois, who had broken the peace, and possessed themselves of a town called Huy*, driven out his garrison, and afterwards plundered it, notwithstanding the hostages which they had given the year before were to be put to death, and a great sum of money to be paid besides, in case the treaty was violated on their part. He assembled his army about Louvain†, which is a town in Brabant and on the marches of Liege. The Constable of France (who was now

---

* "It was far advanced in the month of September," says Chastellain, "when the town of Huy was taken by the Liegeois." Jealousy led the Liegeois to attack it, for "it had always sided with the bishop against the city, and for that cause, Duke Philip had granted it great immunities." Chastellain, 426.

† The duke left Brussels for Louvain on the 13th of October, 1467.

wholly devoted to the French interest, and had his residence
in that kingdom) came to the duke with Cardinal Balue *
and others, to let him know that the Liegeois being in an
alliance with the King of France, and comprehended in his
truce, he should be obliged to relieve them in case the Duke
of Burgundy thought fit to invade them. However, they
offered that in case the duke would consent that their master
might make war upon the Bretons, he would connive at his
designs against the Liegeois. Their audience was short and
in public, and they continued there but one day. The duke,
to justify his proceedings against the Liegeois, replied, "That
they had invaded him; that it was they themselves, and not
he, who had broken the truce, and, therefore, he was resolved
to be revenged of his enemies, without being obliged to
abandon his confederates after a base and dishonourable
manner." The next day, as the duke took horse, he gave
them their despatch, and told them aloud, "That he desired
the king not to attempt anything against the Bretons."
The constable pressed him very hard, and told him, "Sir,
you do not choose, but take all; you will make war at your
pleasure upon our allies, and oblige us to sit still, and not
meddle with yours: it is not to be expected, and the king
will never suffer it." The duke took his leave of them, and
replied, "The Liegeois are now in arms, and within three
days I believe we shall have a battle; if I lose it, I do not
doubt but you will do as you think fit; but if I conquer, you
will leave the Bretons in peace." And, having said so, he
mounted on horseback, and the ambassadors prepared to be
gone. The duke marched in his arms from Louvain to besiege St. Tron †, with a very great army, for all the forces
which could be got together in Burgundy had joined him;
and, to speak truth, his army was far more numerous than
any I had ever yet seen in my life.

Before his departure from Louvain, it was debated in

* Jean Balue was born at Poitiers in 1422, and died in October, 1491.
He was appointed Bishop of Evreux in 1464, translated to the see of
Angers soon afterwards, and raised to the cardinalate in 1467.

† On the 27th of October, 1467, the count "came to the siege of the
town of Saint Tron, and on the 28th he gained a battle over the Liegeois
at the village of Brusten. On the 2nd of November, the town of Saint-
Tron surrendered at discretion, and the duke demolished its gates, towers,
and walls." Lenglet, ii. 190.

council what was to be done with the hostages, and whether
or no they should be put to death. Some were of opinion
that they should all of them die, and particularly the Lord
of Contay was of that judgment; and, indeed, I never
heard him speak so ill and so unmercifully as at that time;
for which reason it is necessary that princes should have several privy councillors; since the wisest men are sometimes,
nay, too often, partial and prejudiced, either out of love,
hatred, contradiction, or indisposition of their bodies, for the
counsel that is given after dinner is not always the best.
But some may object, that persons guilty of any of those
faults are not fit to be admitted into council at all. To
which I answer, That we are all of us but men, and he who
would find out such as should never fail to speak wisely,
nor show more passion at one time than another, must seek
them in heaven, for upon earth we cannot find them: but,
in recompense for this, sometimes he who has never been
used to do so before, will speak wisely in council, which
makes amends for the others.

But to return to the debate : two or three, in deference to
the authority and judgment of the Lord of Contay, were also of
his opinion; for in such councils there are many present, who
(not well understanding the affair that is in debate) give their
sentiments as they hear others before them, being extremely
desirous to please and ingratiate themselves with some person
or other of great power and authority. After him, the
question was put to the Lord of Humbercourt *, who was
born near Amiens, and was one of the wisest and gravest
gentlemen I ever was acquainted with. His opinion was, by
all means, to keep God on their side, and to let the world see
that he was neither cruel nor revengeful; he thought it the
most prudent way to release the 300 hostages, because
they delivered themselves up with a good intention, and
in confidence that the peace would have been inviolably
kept. However, he judged it proper, that at their dismis-
sion they should be put in mind of the duke's mercy towards
them, and exhorted to employ their utmost endeavour to

* Guy de Brimeu, Count of Mehem, and Lord of Humbercourt, was
crea'.d a Knight of the Golden Fleece in 1473. He was a son of Jean
de Brimeu and Marie de Mailly : he married Antoinette de Rambures ;
and he was beheaded at Ghent on the 3rd of April, 1477.

persuade the people to consent to an honourable peace; and
that if they should not be able to prevail, that, at least, in
acknowledgment of the duke's generosity, they should engage
never to bear arms against him, nor against their bishop, who
was then with him.   This opinion was followed, and when
the hostages were dismissed, they consented to what had been
proposed to them; and they were told, that if they engaged
(any of them) actually in the war, and were taken prisoners,
they must expect to suffer death; and so they departed.

It will not be altogether impertinent to add, that after the
Lord of Contay had given his judgment in so cruel a manner
against the poor hostages (part of whom came in with the
rest voluntarily), a gentleman who was then in the council,
whispered me in the ear, and said, "Do you observe that
man? Though he be old, he is in good health and well; yet I
dare lay a wager he dies within the year, in punishment for
the inhumanity of his advice." And so it fell out, for he lived
not long after; however, he did his master good service in
one battle before his death, of which I shall speak hereafter.

But to return to my history. You have heard how the
Duke of Burgundy, upon his departure from Louvain, laid
siege to St. Tron, and erected his batteries.   In the town
there was a garrison of 3000 Liegeois, commanded by a very
good officer*, who was the same person that had managed
the treaty of peace, when we met them, drawn up in order
of battle, the year before.   The third day after our investing
the town, the Liegeois, to the number of about 30,000 or
upwards†, one with another (but all foot except 500), and a
large train of artillery, came to raise the siege, at about ten
o'clock in the morning. Our first discovery of them was in
a strong village called Brustan, about half a league from
our camp, encompassed partly with a great morass; and in
their army was Francis Rayer‡, Bailiff of Lyons, and ambassador from the king to the Liegeois at that time.   The

___

* Renard de Rouvroy.

† It appears from a letter written on the 29th of October by Louis
Van den Rive, pensionary of the town of Ypres, that the Liegeois numbered
17,000 or 18,000 with 400 or 500 horse; whilst Jean de Halewyn,
writing on the 31st of the same month, says they had 1400 men-at-arms.

‡ François Rayer, Esquire, was Bailiff of Mâcon, and Seneschal and
Captain of Lyons, in 1462.

alarm was brought immediately to our army; yet, I must needs say, our discipline was not exact, for we had no scouts abroad to bring us any intelligence of their approach, and the first news we had of them was from our foragers, who fled from them. I was never in any place with the Duke of Burgundy, where I observed him give good orders of himself, but only then. Immediately he drew all his battalions out into the field, except some few which were left to carry on the siege; and among the rest he left 500 English. Upon both sides of the village he placed 1200 men-at-arms, and posted himself with 800 more just before the town, but at a little farther distance. With the archers there were several persons of note and distinction on foot, besides a great many of the men-at-arms. The Lord of Ravestein commanded the duke's van, consisting only of foot, part men-at-arms, and part archers, who marched up with some pieces of cannon to the very trenches, which were broad and deep, and full of water; yet, with our arrows and our artillery together, we forced their intrenchments, and turned their cannon upon them. However, when our arrows failed us, the Liegeois took heart again, and with their long pikes, which are advantageous weapons, charging briskly upon our archers and those who commanded them, they killed 400 or 500 of us immediately; so that all our troops on that side began to give ground, as if the battle had been lost. Upon this, the duke commanded the archers of his main battle to march under the command of Philip de Crevecœur, Lord of Cordes (a wise man), and several other good officers, who falling upon the Liegeois with a great shout, they were immediately discomfited.* Neither the horse, which (as I said before) were drawn up on both sides of the village, nor the duke himself, where he was posted, could come at the Liegeois to attack them, by reason of the morass, only they were posted there to charge them in case our vanguard should have been repulsed, and the enemy thereby encouraged to march out into the plain. But the Liegeois, as soon as ever they were broken, fled along by the morass, and were not pursued by any but the foot; some horse the duke sent to follow the chase, but they were forced to go

---

* On the 28th of October.

H

two leagues about to find a pass, and the night drawing on, several of the Liegeois made their escape, who otherwise would have been slain. Other troops he despatched towards the town, where he heard a great noise, and suspected a sally; and indeed he was in the right, for they made three vigorous sallies, but were always repulsed; and the English, whom the duke had posted in a certain place ready to charge them, behaved themselves very bravely. The Liegeois, who were broken, rallied a little about their waggons, and stood their ground for some time, but were at last entirely defeated. There were slain in this battle about 6000 men *, which, to people that are unwilling to lie, may seem very much; but in my time I have been in several actions, where for one man that was really slain, they have reported a hundred, thinking by such an account to please their masters; and they sometimes deceive them with their lies. Yet, if night had not come on, the Liegeois would certainly have lost near 15,000. The battle being over, as it was very late, the Duke of Burgundy, with his whole army, marched back to his camp, only a thousand or 1200 of his horse were sent two leagues about to a pass to pursue the enemy, there being no other way of coming at them, by reason of a little river which was between them and us. But the night hindered them from doing any great execution; yet some they killed, and others they took prisoners, though the greatest part of them escaped to the town. The Lord of Contay did great service that day in ordering the battle, but a few days after, he died in the town of Huy, and made a very good end. He was a person of great courage and wisdom, but he lived not many days after the cruel sentence which he had given against the hostages, as you heard before. As soon as the Duke of Burgundy had pulled off his armour, he called for his secretary, and wrote a letter to the constable, and the rest of the ambassadors who had left him at Louvain but four days before, to give them an account of the victory, and to desire that nothing might be attempted against the Bretons.

Two days after this defeat (though their loss was not very great) the pride and insolence of this silly people were strangely abated. However indeed, be it who it may, it is

* Jean de Halewyn estimated their loss at " 4000 men and more." Louis Van den Rive says, 2000 or 3000.

an act of imprudence and rashness for any to expose their
fortunes to the hazard of a battle if they can possibly avoid
it; for the loss of a small number of men oftentimes occasions an incredible change and alteration in the courage of
the army that has been defeated, not only in possessing their
minds with a dread of the enemy, but by infusing a dis-
respect and contempt of their commander and his privy
councillors. It also makes them inclinable to mutiny and
rebel, and emboldens them to demand with more confidence
than they were wont, and to resent with more insolence when
they are denied; and three crowns would not satisfy them
so well as one would have done before. Wherefore that
general who has lost one battle, if he be wise, ought to be
cautious how he engages suddenly again with those men who
have been lately beaten; but he should rather act defensively,
or, at least, enter upon some trifling action, in which there is a
probability of succeeding, in order to revive their courage
by dispelling their fears. In all cases, the loss of a battle is
always attended with ill consequences, especially to him that
is beaten. However, those who are conquerors, and those
whose infantry is better than their neighbours' (as may be
said of the English and Swiss), may fight as they please to
put an end to the war. I name not those nations with any
design to reflect upon the rest, but only because they have
gained extraordinary victories, and are not to be kept long
in the field without action, as the French and the Italians,
who are either more grave and sober, or more easily commanded. On the other hand, that prince who is so fortunate
as to gain the victory, acquires greater esteem and reputation
in his army than he had before, and the obedience of his
subjects increasing in proportion, they give him whatever he
desires, and his soldiers become more daring and courageous.
Sometimes also princes are so immoderately vain-glorious,
and puffed up with their victories, that they turn afterwards
to their prejudice, as I have seen; but moderation, and a
just use of success, is a blessing which proceeds only from
God.

The garrison of Saint Tron seeing that the army, which had
been sent to their relief, was routed, and finding themselves
hemmed in on all sides, supposing the defeat much greater

H 2

than it really was, surrendered the town*, went away without their arms, and left ten † men (whomever the Duke of
Burgundy should choose) to be disposed of at his pleasure;
which ten were beheaded, and six of them were of the
hostages who had been released not many days before, upon
the conditions above mentioned. Having taken the town,
he broke up his camp, and marched towards Tongres, which
was apprehensive of a siege : but, being unable to defend
itself, without putting the duke to the trouble of erecting
batteries against it, it surrendered upon the same terms ‡,
and left ten men likewise to his mercy, five of whom were
hostages ; but all ten were put to death, as the others had
been at Saint Tron.

CHAP. III.

How the Liegeois quarrelled among themselves about surrendering their
Town, some agreeing, others refusing to do it ; while, in the meantime,
the Lord of Humbercourt found a way to enter and take possession of
it for the Duke of Burgundy. — 1467.

FROM Tongres the Duke of Burgundy marched directly
against the city of Liege §, which, at that time, was in great
confusion, and strangely divided. Some were for standing
a siege, positively affirming that the garrison was strong
enough to hold out ; and of this opinion was a certain knight,
called the Lord Rasse de Lintre.‖ Others, on the contrary,
who saw and considered the inevitable ruin and desolation
of the whole country, if they persisted in that resolution,
would needs have peace upon any terms ; whereupon, as

* The conditions of the surrender are stated in letters patent of the
Duke of Burgundy, dated November 1. 1467, and ratified on the 7th of
the same month by the mayor and notable inhabitants of Saint-Tron.
Gachard, ii. 420.

† Twelve. See Gachard, ii. 424.

‡ On the 6th of November. Lenglet, ii. 190.

§ The duke arrived before Liege on St. Martin's day, November 11.
1467.

‖ Raes de la Rivière, Lord of Lintre, Heers, &c., and Knight-master
of the city of Liege in 1463, died on the 8th of December, 1477. In
September, 1475, he appears in the list of chamberlains and councillors
of the King of France.

soon as the duke approached the city, some few overtures of peace were made by certain mean and inconsiderable persons, such as fishmongers. But it was promoted much more by some of the hostages, who acted not as those I mentioned before, but acknowledged the favour they had received, and brought along with them 300 of the chief citizens in their shirts, bare-foot, and bare-headed, who presented the duke with the keys of the city, and delivered themselves, without any capitulation *; only they begged the town might be neither plundered nor burnt. At this time the Duke of Burgundy was attended by the Lord of Moüy †, and one Monsieur Jehan Prevost, one of the king's secretaries, who were the king's ambassadors to the duke, and came upon the same affair, and with the same request, as the constable had done not many days before. The same day that things were in this manner accommodated, supposing all things concluded, and that there was nothing remaining but to enter the city, the duke sent the Lord of Humbercourt before him, as a person who had great acquaintance and interest in that city, as having had a share in the administration of their affairs for several years together, whilst they continued in peace. But the citizens denied him entrance at first, and he was forced to take up his quarters in a little abbey not far from one of the gates, with about fifty men-at-arms (of which number I myself was one), and perhaps 200 soldiers in all. The Duke of Burgundy sent him word to continue in that post, if he thought himself secure : but if not, that he should retire to him, for the difficulty of the way would not permit him to send a re-inforcement easily, because all that side of the country was full of rocks. The Lord of Humbercourt resolved not to abandon the abbey where he was posted, it being sufficiently strong, but he detained five or six of the citizens who came to present the duke with the keys, to assist him, as you shall hear. When the clock struck nine at night, we heard their bells

---

* "On the 12th of November, the men of Liege, ten of each trade, came in their shirts to a place half a mile from the town, where my lord was lodged, and prostrated themselves at his feet." Gachard, i. 181.

† Collard, Lord of Moy, Knight, Bailiff of Cotentin. He was son of Nicholas surnamed Colard, Lord of Moy, and Marguerite de la Heuse. He married Marguerite d'Ailli. He was still living in 1493.

ring, at which the people assembled in the town, and the
Lord of Humbercourt was afraid it might be a signal to fall
upon us; for he had certain intelligence that the Lord Rasse
de Lintre and several others had openly declared against
the peace; and his apprehension was just and true, for they
met to that purpose, and were ready to attack us.   The Lord
of Humbercourt told those who were with him, "If we can
but amuse the enemy till midnight, we are safe enough; for
they will be weary, and impatient to sleep, and then those
who are our adversaries will leave the town, since they have
miscarried in their design."   In order to effect that, he
despatched two of the citizens, whom (as I said) he had detained, with certain articles very friendly and amicable, that
he had caused to be drawn up for no other purpose, but only to
give them an occasion of assembling the people, and to gain
time; for they always had a custom, and they retain it to this
very day, upon any news of importance, to flock together to
the bishop's palace upon the sounding of a bell that is within it.

When these two citizens came to the gate (which was not
above two bow-shots from our post), they found the people
in great bodies, and in arms: some were for assaulting
them, but others prevented it.   Whereupon they called out
aloud to the mayor of the city, and told him they had
brought certain fair and honourable proposals in writing
from the Lord of Humbercourt, the Duke of Burgundy's
lieutenant in those parts, and that it would be well to repair
to the palace and peruse them.   The people did so accordingly; and immediately we heard the palace-bell ring
again, by which we understood what they were about.   Our
two citizens returned not; but about an hour after we heard
a greater noise at the gate than before, more of the people
running down thither, crying out, and railing at us over the
walls with most villanous invectives.   By this manner of
proceeding the Lord of Humbercourt knew the danger was
worse than ever, and therefore he despatched the other four
citizens who were with him, with a letter to them in
writing, importing, that he being appointed governor of that
city by the Duke of Burgundy, had treated them civilly, and
would never consent to their destruction; for it was not
long since he had been made free of one of their companies
(which was the locksmiths'), and had worn their livery, for

which reason they might repose the more confidence in what
he said. In short, he told them, that if they would enjoy
the benefit of peace, and preserve their country from ruin,
they must admit the duke into the town according to their
promise, and submit to such terms as were contained in
a certain schedule, which he also sent them. When he
had thoroughly instructed his four citizens, they passed on
directly to the gate as the others had done, and found it
wide open : some of the people threatened them, and gave them
very ill language ; others were willing to hear what they had
to say, and returned to the palace ; and the bell ringing again
immediately, we were extremely pleased, and the noise at
the gate began to decrease. In short, they were then a long
time in the palace, and their conference lasted till two in
the morning, and it was agreed that their promise should
be kept, and that in the morning one of the gates should
be delivered up to the Lord of Humbercourt ; upon which
resolution the Lord Rasse de Lintre and his party abandoned the town.

I should not have dwelt so long upon so inconsiderable a
matter, had it not been to show that sometimes by such artifices and expedients as these (which proceed from great
judgment and penetration in state affairs) great dangers and
inconveniences are prevented.   The next morning by break
of day, several of the hostages came to wait on the Lord of
Humbercourt, and entreated him to go along with them to the
palace, where all the people were assembled, and swear to
the two articles against firing and plundering the city (of
which the people could not be otherwise secure), telling him
that after that they would give him possession of one of the
gates.   He sent an account of all that had happened to the
Duke of Burgundy, went himself into the city, and having
taken the oath, he returned to the gate, caused those who
were there upon the guard to come down, and having put
in a dozen of his own men-at-arms and some archers
in their place, he set up the Duke of Burgundy's standard
upon the gate. From thence he went to another gate (which
was walled up), and put it into the hands of the Bastard of
Burgundy, whose quarters were close by. The third he
delivered to the Marshal of Burgundy, and the fourth to
some gentlemen volunteers that accompanied him. Thus

were the four gates of the city possessed by the Duke of Burgundy's forces, and his banners erected upon them.

To give you a better insight into these affairs, it is necessary to acquaint you, that at that time Liege was (excepting only five or six) one of the strongest and most populous cities in those parts; besides which, great numbers of people being retired thither out of the adjacent country, the loss they had sustained in the late battle was not at all to be perceived; and they were in no want or necessity of anything; it was also in the depth of winter, and prodigious rains had fallen, which had strangely increased the natural softness and miriness of the country. On our side, we were in great want both of provisions and money, and our army was ready to break up; for which reason the Duke of Burgundy had no inclination to have besieged the town; and even if he had been willing to have undertaken the siege, he was not in a capacity of doing it; so that if they had delayed the time but two days longer, he must have marched away as he came, without attempting anything. All these things being considered, it must be owned that the Lord of Humbercourt gained great honour and reputation by the nice management of this important affair, which proceeded wholly from the grace of God towards him; for in human probability such wonderful success was not to be expected, nor could he ever have presumed to have wished for such a surprising turn of affairs as happened; and all the honours that were conferred on him, and the unparalleled success he met with in this expedition, the generality of the world looked upon as a just reward for his tenderness and compassion towards the poor hostages, whom we have mentioned before; and this I write the more willingly, because princes and others do many times complain and repine at such mercy and indulgence as they have granted to other people, esteeming themselves unfortunate, and imputing all their following disasters to that tenderness of soul, and resolving for the future never to be guilty of any such acts of piety or generosity, which are two virtues that ought to be inseparable from their offices.

In my judgment this is a wrong way of arguing, and proceeds from a base and degenerate mind wherever it is found; for a prince or any man else, who has never been deceived, is no better than a beast, nor can he know any just difference between good and evil. Besides, men are not all of the same mould, and for the wickedness and ingratitude of one or two, we ought not to forbear doing good to many, when time and opportunity present themselves; however, at the same time, I would have all mankind so wise as to distinguish between persons, for all people are not equally meritorious; and indeed it is surprising to me how a wise man can be ungrateful to any one that has done anything extraordinary to serve him; yet in this princes too often err, for he that advances a fool never advantages himself long; and I think one of the greatest indications of wisdom that a prince can show, is to converse with and have about him virtuous and wise men, for he will always be esteemed of the same humour and inclination as they are with whom he most intimately converses. So that, to conclude this chapter, methinks the ingratitude of one person ought not to deter us from doing good to the rest; for perhaps the meanest of those whom you have once obliged, may some time or another render you such service, and return you such thanks, as may recompense the ingratitude and unthankfulness of the rest; as may be observed in these hostages, of whom the greatest number were base and ungrateful; for of the whole number there were not above five or six who were honest and grateful, and yet those five or six managed the business so dexterously, that all was concluded to the Duke of Burgundy's satisfaction.

Chap. IV.

Of the Duke of Burgundy's triumphal Entry into the City of Liege; and the Submission of the Gantois, who not long before had treated him disrespectfully. — 1467.

THE next day after the delivering up of the gates to the Lord of Humbercourt, the Duke of Burgundy made his triumphal entry into Liege *, the citizens having broken down the wall for twenty fathoms together, and filled up the ditch in front of the great breach. The duke himself

* On Tuesday, November 17. 1467.

made his entry on horseback, in the midst of his own guards and chief officers of the army, dressed in splendid and sumptuous habits, and riding in great pomp and solemnity to the great church, where he alighted; with him there also entered on foot about 2000 men-at-arms in complete armour, and 10,000 archers; the rest of his forces remained in the camp without the town. To be short, he staid there some few days*, during which time he caused five or six of those who had been his hostages to be put to death, and among the rest, the messenger of the town, for whom he had a more than ordinary hatred. He prescribed new laws † and customs; and exacted great sums from them, which he pretended were due to him upon the breach of the peace and agreement with him some years before. He carried away with him all their arms and artillery, and caused all the walls and fortifications belonging to the town to be demolished.

When he had seen all these orders performed, he returned into his own country, where he was received with great honour and obedience, and particularly by the citizens of Ghent, who before his expedition against the Liegeois were in a kind of rebellion against him, with some other towns; but now they entertained him as a conqueror, the chief citizens marching on foot as far as Brussels to meet him, and carrying all the town banners along with them‡; which they did upon the account, that immediately upon the death of his father he chose to make his entry into Ghent§ before any town besides, out of an opinion that he was better beloved there than in any other town in his whole dominions, and that according to their example all the rest would behave themselves towards him; and in that point he was right. The next day after his entry, the citizens put themselves in arms, and drew up in the market-place, whither they brought the image of one of their saints

---

* Until the 28th of November, 1467.

† In M. Gachard's *Collection de Documents Inédits*, ii. 437, will be found a copy of the sentence pronounced upon Liege by Duke Charles, on the 18th of November, 1467.

‡ Commines is here guilty of an anachronism. The submission of the Gantois was not made until the 15th of January, 1469. See Gachard, i. 204.

§ On Sunday, June 28th, 1467.

called Saint Lievin; and knocking the image against a little
house, called La Maison de la Cueillette (where they collected certain gabels upon corn, raised for the payment of
certain debts which the city had contracted when they paid
the sum of money which was required by Duke Philip
of Burgundy upon the peace of Gavre, after two years'
war with him), they pretended the saint had a mind to
pass through that house erect, and without any distortion;
upon which in a moment it was pulled down. The duke
having notice of this tumult, repaired immediately to the
market-place, and got up into a house to speak to them the
better. Several persons of quality, that were then attending
on him in arms, offered to go along with him, but he ordered
them to stay before the Town-Hall, and wait till he returned;
however, the mob forced them by degrees into the market-
place. The duke being got thither, commanded the image
to be taken away, and carried back again into the church:
some in obedience endeavoured to take it up, but others
threw it down again where it was.

The next insolence was, to demand justice against certain
persons in the city, who had embezzled part of the public
stock; to which the duke answered, that he would take care
and see them satisfied as to that particular: but finding they
would not disperse. he returned to his palace, and they
continued in the market-place for eight days together.* The
next morning they brought him certain articles, by which
they demanded restitution of whatever Duke Philip had
taken from them by the peace of Gavre; and among the
rest this was one, that every company might have its banner
according to former custom, which guilds are in all seventy-
two. To avoid the danger he was in, he granted their
demands †, gave them whatever privileges they asked, and
the word was no sooner spoken but the banners were set up
and displayed in the market-place, having been made ready
for that purpose; from whence one may probably conjecture
they would have done the same thing if the duke had denied

---

* The duke remained only three days in Ghent: he left on the 1st of
July. Lenglet, ii. 190.

† The letters, dated Brussels, July 28th, 1467, by which the duke
granted the demands of the Gantois, will be found in Lenglet, ii. 628—
630.

their requests.*   His opinion was right, that, if he made his
first entry into Ghent, all the rest of the towns would follow its
example, for several of them mutinied as it had done, killed
their officers, and committed many other excesses.   If he
had believed his father's character of that people (which
was, "That the inhabitants of Ghent loved the son of their
prince very well, but for their prince himself they never had
any kindness"), he would not have been so much mistaken ;
for, to speak impartially, next to the city of Liege, Ghent
is the most fickle and inconstant town in the whole world.
But among so many ill qualities, they have one good,
and that is, that they never offer violence to the person
of their prince; and, indeed, the chief citizens and better
sort of the town are generally honest men, and much
dissatisfied with the folly and inconstancy of the common
people.

The duke was forced to wink at these insolences, lest he
should have been engaged in a war with his own subjects
and the Liegeois at the same time; but he resolved, if he
succeeded in the enterprise he had undertaken, to call them
afterwards to a severe account †; and so it happened, for (as
is said before) they brought all their banners on foot as far
as Brussels to meet him, and all their privileges and charters
which they had forced him to sign at his departure from
Ghent; when, in a grand assembly ‡ at the great hall at
Brussels, and in the presence of several ambassadors, they
presented him with the said banners and privileges, to dispose of as he pleased, he commanded his heralds to strip the
banners from the staves to which they were fastened, and to
send them to Boulogne (a town about ten leagues from
Calais) upon the sea, where the rest were then kept, which
his father Duke Philip had taken from them in his wars, in
which he had vanquished and subdued them.   The duke's
chancellor§ also took their charter and all their privileges,

<hr/>

* Chastellain devotes twelve chapters of his *Chronique* to details of this
sedition.

† The Gantois did not receive the duke's full pardon until 1469.

‡ An interesting account of this assembly will be found in M. Gachard's
Collection de Documents Inédits, i. 204.

§ Pierre de Goux, Lord of Goux, Contrecœur, and Wedargate, knight,
chamberlain of Philip, Duke of Burgundy, was created Chancellor of

and cancelled one of them, relating to the magistracy of their city, before their faces : for in all the other towns of Flanders the duke renews the magistrates every year, and receives their accounts ; but at Ghent, by virtue of this privilege, he could elect but four, though the whole number was six and twenty, the remaining two and twenty being left to the nomination of the city. When these magistrates are well affected to the Earl of Flanders, that year they are at peace, and they grant him whatever he desires; but when, on the contrary, they are disaffected, seditions arise, and all goes to wreck. Besides this, they were fined, and paid 30,000 florins to the duke, and 6000 to his courtiers, and some of their townsmen were banished, and then all the rest of their privileges were restored. The rest of the towns, following their example, ransomed their crimes, and made their peace with money*; for they had attempted nothing against his person. By all which it evidently appears what advantages follow the conqueror, and what losses the conquered ; for which reason we ought to be very cautious of coming to a battle before there be a necessity for it, and if any such necessity happens, all things are to be seriously weighed and considered before we engage ; and commonly those who are wary, and go to it with fear, are most circumspect, and by consequence more frequently successful than those who are arrogant and presumptuous. But when God interposes, man's wisdom signifies nothing.

The Liegeois, of whom we were speaking, were excommunicated five years together† for some difference between them and their bishop ; but they despised his excommunication, and continued in their folly and obstinacy, without any

Burgundy by letters dated October 26. 1465.   He married Dame Mathie de Rye, and died on the 5th of April, 1470.

* The Flemings had to pay 1,200,000 crowns, within sixteen years ; the Brabanters 300,000 lions ; and Valenciennes 100,000 livres tournois, within fifteen years.

† The Liegeois, in 1462, put themselves under the protection of Louis XI. and refused to obey their bishop, a nephew of the Duke of Burgundy ; upon which the duke solicited and obtained from the Pope a bull of excommunication against them, by which he was ordered "to crusade against them as against the infidels, and against a people disobedient to the holy apostolical see." The sentence of excommunication is dated December 23. 1465.

other reason besides their excessive riches and pride.   And
to this purpose King Louis had a saying, and in my judgment
a wise one, "That when pride rode before, shame and destruction would follow;" but he had not the least tincture
of that sin in him.

CHAP. V.

How the King of France made War in Bretagne upon the Duke of
   Burgundy's Allies, upon Intelligence of what had happened to the
   Liegeois; and the Interview and Conference of these two Princes at
   Peronne. — 1468

THESE commotions being over, the Duke of Burgundy
retired to Ghent, where he was honourably and magnificently received. He entered the city in arms, and the
citizens made a postern into the fields, that he might bring
in or keep out what company he pleased. Several ambassadors
were sent to him from the king, and others went from him to
the king; the Duke of Burgundy also sent several embassies
to the Duke of Bretagne, and in this manner all that winter
was spent.   The king was very solicitous and pressing with
the Duke of Burgundy to abandon the Duke of Bretagne's
interest, and made him several advantageous proposals to
that purpose; but the duke would not consent, which was
much to his majesty's dissatisfaction, especially when he
considered what had happened to the Liegeois, his allies.
As soon as summer was come, the king could refrain no
longer, but himself or his forces entered Bretagne, and made
themselves masters of two small castles, one of them called
Chantocé, and the other Ancenis.   The Duke of Burgundy
had notice immediately of the taking of these places; and at
the earnest solicitation and importunity of the Dukes of
Normandy and Bretagne, he raised an army with all expedition, and wrote to the king, entreating him to desist from
that enterprise, for they were his allies, and comprehended
in his truce*; but not being pleased with the king's answer,

* On the 26th of May, 1468, there had been a prolongation of the
truce between the king and the three dukes : it was to last from the 1st of
June to the 15th of July.   Morice, iii. 172.

the duke took the field, and rendezvoused near Peronne
with a considerable force. The king himself was at Compiegne, but his army was in Bretagne. The duke staid at
Peronne but three or four days, during which time the Cardinal Balue, who made but a short stay, arrived as ambassador from the king. He made some overtures to the duke,
and told him, that the Bretons could make their peace without his interposition; but the king's design was to separate
them and break the confederacy. The cardinal was received
very honourably, and despatched with this answer, That the
duke had not taken the field to invade his majesty, nor to
make war upon him, but only to relieve his allies; and so
they parted with fair words on both sides.

No sooner was the cardinal departed, but a herald arrived
from the Dukes of Normandy and Bretagne with letters,
importing that they had made their peace with the king*,
and renounced all their alliances, and particularly his; and
that, in satisfaction of all his demands, the Duke of Normandy was to receive a pension of 60,000 livres per
annum, for which he was to relinquish the interest which
had been lately conferred upon him in Normandy. The Lord
Charles of France was not at all pleased with his terms; but
he was forced to dissemble his resentment. The Duke of
Burgundy was extremely surprised at the news; for he had
raised this army on purpose to relieve them; the herald also
was in no little danger; for as he had passed through the king's
quarters, the duke had a suspicion the king had forged the
letters; but it was not long before they were confirmed from
several places. The king thought he had now done his
business, and that it would be no hard matter to persuade the

* By the treaty of Ancenis, made on the 10th of September, 1468, by
the envoys of the contracting parties. It was ratified by the king and
the Duke of Bretagne on the 18th of September following; but the
adhesion of the Duke of Normandy was not obtained to it until the 21st
of June, 1470. No article in this treaty stipulates that the dukes shall
renounce their alliance with the Duke of Burgundy. This was probably
made the subject of a special treaty; for the king alludes to it in his
instructions to his envoys to the Duke of Bretagne on the 1st of December,
1470. "Item, by the treaties and promises which the Duke of Bretagne has made with the king, he has promised and sworn to serve the
king formally against the said Duke of Burgundy, at any time that he
may undertake any war against him." Salazard, iv. Preuves, ccxcv.

duke to abandon them.   Several messengers passed privately
between them; and at length the king paid the Duke of
Burgundy six score thousand crowns of gold in consideration
of the expense which he had been at in raising his army;
half of which sum was paid down before he broke up from
his camp.   The duke sent to the king one John Bosuse *, a
gentleman of his bed-chamber (a person with whom he was
more than ordinarily intimate); which the king taking very
kindly, he took the confidence to propose an interview,
hoping he might gain him entirely over to his party, considering how badly the two above-mentioned dukes had
served him, and what a sum of money he had paid him himself; of which he gave him some hint and intimation by the
said Bosuse, with whom he despatched the Cardinal Balue a
second time, and the Lord Tanneguy du Chastel, Governor of
Roussillon, who represented to the duke the great desire his
majesty had to give him a meeting.   They found the duke
at Peronne: but he had no fancy to the interview; for the
Liegeois seemed inclinable to rebel again at the instigation
of two ambassadors whom the king had sent to them for that
purpose before the truce, which was made for certain days
between the king, the Duke of Burgundy, and their allies.†
The cardinal and his friends replied, that the Liegeois durst
not attempt any such thing, since the duke had not only dis-
mantled their fortifications the year before, but also demolished their walls; and if they had any such design in
view, the news of this accommodation would be sufficient to
prevent it.   In this manner it was concluded, that the king
should repair to Peronne (which was the place he had recommended); and the duke having written to him with his own
hand‡, and delivered a passport (for his better security) to
the ambassadors, they took their leave, and departed towards
the king, who was at that time at Noyon.   But to make all
sure at Liege, the duke sent the bishop thither, upon whose

* Jehan de Boschuise, first butler to the Duke of Burgundy.   Etat de
la Maison du Duc Charles.
† On the 21st of August, 1468, the Duke of Bretagne had, in his own
name and in that of his allies, granted a truce of twelve days to the
Marquis du Pont, who commanded the French army at the siege of
Ancenis.
‡ Dated Peronne, October 8. 1468.

score those tumults had happened, and with him the Lord of
Humbercourt, his lieutenant * in that country, with a considerable body of forces.

You have heard how it was agreed the king should come
to Peronne. Thither he came †, without any guard, more than
the passport and parole of the Duke of Burgundy; only he
desired that the duke's archers, under the command of the
Lord des Cordes (who was then in the duke's service), might
meet and conduct him; and so it was done, very few of his
own train coming along with him. However, his majesty
was attended by several persons of great quality and distinction, and among the rest by the Duke of Bourbon, the
Cardinal his brother, and the Count of St. Paul, Constable of
France, who had no hand in this interview, but was highly
displeased at it; for he was now grown haughty, and
disdained to pay that respect to the duke which he had
formerly done; for which cause there was no love between
them. Besides these, there came the Cardinal Balue, the
Governor of Roussillon, and several others. When the king
came near, the duke went out (very well attended) to meet
him, conducted him into the town, and lodged him at the
receiver's, who had a fine house not far from the castle; for
the lodgings in the castle were but small, and no way convenient.

War between two great princes is easily begun, but very
hard to be composed, by reason of the accidents and consequences which often follow; for many secret practices
are used, and orders given out on both sides to make the
greatest efforts possible against the enemy, which cannot
be easily countermanded; as evidently appears by these
two princes, whose interview was so suddenly determined,
that neither having time to notify it to their ministers in
remote parts, they went on performing the commands
which their respective masters had given them before.
The Duke of Burgundy had sent for his army out of Burgundy, in which at that time there was abundance of the nobility; and among the rest the Count of Bresse ‡, the Bishop

* Appointed by letters patent of November 28. 1467.
† On Sunday, October 9. Lenglet, ii. 192.
‡ Philip of Savoy, Count of Baugé, and Lord of Bresse, was the son
of Louis, Duke of Savoy, and Anne of Cyprus. He was born at

I

of Geneva*, and the Count of Romont†, all three brothers
of the house of Savoy (for between the Savoyards and Burgundians there was always a firm amity), and some
Germans, who were borderers upon both their territories.
And you must know that the king had formerly imprisoned
the Count of Bresse, upon the account of two gentlemen
whom he had put to death in Savoy, so that there was no
right understanding between him and the king.

In this army there were likewise one Monsieur du Lau
(who had been a favourite of the king's, but upon some disgust had been kept afterwards a prisoner by him a long
time, till at length he made his escape, and fled into Burgundy), the Lord d'Urfé‡, since master of the horse to the
King of France, and the Lord Poncet de Rivière; all which
company arrived before Peronne as the king came into the
town. Bresse and the three last entered the town with St.
Andrew's cross upon their clothes (supposing they should
have been in time enough to have paid their respects to the
Duke of Burgundy, and to have attended him when he went
out to receive the king), but they came a little too late: however, they went directly to the duke's chamber to pay their
duty, and in the name of the rest, the Count of Bresse
humbly besought his highness that himself and his three companions might have his protection (notwithstanding the
king was in the town), according to the promise he was
pleased to make them in Burgundy; and at the same time
assured him they were at his service, when and against

Chambery on the 3rd of February, 1438. At the request of his father,
Louis XI. arrested this prince in April, 1463, and imprisoned him in the
Castle of Loches, where he remained until 1466. On the death of his
grand-nephew in 1496, Philip ascended the ducal throne: but he did not
long enjoy his power, for he died at Chambery on the 7th of November,
1497.

* Jean Louis of Savoy, Bishop of Geneva, brother of the preceding.
He died at Turin on the 11th of June, 1482.

† Jacques of Savoy, Count of Romont, Baron of Vaud, brother of the
preceding, was created a Knight of the Golden Fleece in 1478. He died
at the Castle of Ham on the 30th of January, 1486. In 1460, he had
married Marie de Luxembourg, Countess of St. Paul.

‡ Pierre, Lord of Urfé and La Bastie, councillor and chamberlain of
the king, was created Grand Ecuyer of France by Charles VIII. in 1483.
He was the son of Pierre d'Urfé and Isabeau de Chovigny. He died on
the 10th of October, 1508.

whomsoever he might command them.   The duke returned them thanks, and promised them protection.   The rest of this army, under the command of the Marshal of Burgundy, encamped by the duke's orders in the fields.   The marshal had no more affection for the king than the above-mentioned gentlemen had; for the king had given him the government of Espinal in Lorraine, and taken it from him afterwards to give it to John, Duke of Calabria (who has often been mentioned before).   The king had notice presently of all these persons being in the town, and of the habits in which they arrived, which put him into a great consternation; so that he sent to the Duke of Burgundy to desire he might be lodged in the castle, for he knew those gentlemen were his mortal enemies; the duke was extremely glad to hear it, appointed him his own lodgings, and sent to him to bid him fear nothing.

CHAP. VI.

A Digression concerning the Advantage which the Knowledge of Letters, and more especially of History, is to Princes and great Lords.

IT is the highest act of imprudence for any prince to put himself into the power of another, especially if they be at war; and it is no less advantageous to them to be well acquainted in their youth with the passages and surprising accidents of former times; for history shows them at large the success of such assemblies, the frauds, artifices, and perjuries wherewith they have inveigled, imprisoned, and killed such as, relying upon the honour of their enemies, have put themselves into their hands.   I do not say that everybody has met with such treacherous dealings, but one example *

* History furnishes us with abundance of examples of the treachery and perfidiousness that have been practised at such interviews. The first we meet with in Roman history, is that of Jugurtha, who was taken by his father-in-law, Bocchus, and delivered up to the Romans; to which we may add that of Sertorius, who was slain at a banquet by Perpenna. In England, the treason of Hengist to Vortigern is well known to all that have read anything of history. The Scottish chronicles mention the assassination of one William, Earl of Douglas, who

is sufficient to make many people more wise; and teach them to be careful of themselves. It appears to me upon the experience of eighteen years' business (in which I have not only been conversant with great princes, but privy to all the greatest affairs which have been transacted in France, or the neighbouring states), that one of the greatest means to make a man wise is to have studied the histories of ancient times, and to have learned to frame and proportion our councils and undertakings according to the model and example of our ancestors: for our life is but of short duration, and not sufficient to give us experience of so many things; besides our age is impaired, and the life of man is not so long, nor his body so strong and robust as formerly; and as our bodies are degenerated and grown weaker, so is our faith and fidelity one towards another, especially among princes, who are altogether wedded to their own humours, without regard to any reason that can be offered; and (which is still worse) they are commonly surrounded by persons whose only aim is to please their masters, and applaud whatever they do or say, whether it be good or bad; and if any wise man interposes, and endeavours to set things in a better light, the whole court is presently in an uproar.

Again, I cannot forbear blaming and discommending illiterate princes, who generally are led by the nose by certain lawyers and priests, whom they keep commonly about them, and indeed not without reason (for as they are very serviceable to a prince, and an ornament to his court, when

was killed at a treaty by James, King of Scotland. In Germany, one Albrecht, Earl of Franconia, was betrayed by Otho, Bishop of Mentz. John of Anjou was slain by Albertus Bavarus, Earl of Hainault and Flanders, notwithstanding he had given him a passport, and engaged his honour as a security for his person. In France, John, Duke of Burgundy, slain by Charles VII. William, Duke of Normandy, by Arnulph, Earl of Flanders. Louis, King of France, taken prisoner by the Normans and Danes at Rouen. John, Duke of Bretagne, taken at a banquet, and imprisoned by Margaret, Countess of Pontibera. Guido, Earl of Flanders, twice taken prisoner, notwithstanding the promise of safe-conduct, by Philip the Fair, King of France. Charles the Simple slain by the Earl of Vermandois. In short, it would be endless to reckon up all the villanous and barbarous murders that have been committed at these interviews between great princes, and which are recorded in history, as our author here very well observes.

they are persons of honour and probity, so they are as
dangerous if they prove otherwise), who have always some
law or precedent in their mouths, which they wrest and
pervert as they please : but a wise prince, and one that has
read history, will never be deluded; nor will any courtier be so
audacious as to tell a lie in his presence. Believe me, God
never designed the office of a king to be executed by beasts,
or such as glory and pride themselves in giving such answers
as these, "I am no scholar, I refer business wholly to my
council, and commit all things to their management," and
then devote themselves entirely to their pleasures, without
further reason or expostulation. Had they been better
educated in their youth, they would have been wiser, and
have earnestly desired that their person and their virtues
might have been valued and esteemed by all good men. I
do not say all princes employ such ill-conditioned people,
but most of those whom I had ever the honour to converse
with, had always abundance of them. I have known indeed,
upon an exigence of affairs, some wise princes that understood how to cull and select their ministers, and employ
them frankly and without complaint; but of this sort I
knew none comparable to the king my master, than whom no
prince better understood the merit of brave and learned
persons, nor more readily advanced such to the highest posts
of honour and advantage. He was not unlearned himself;
he delighted much in asking questions; and would know a
little of everything : his judgment and natural parts were
excellent, which is better and more preferable than all that
we can learn in this world; for all the books that ever were
written, are only so many helps and assistances to our
memory by the recapitulation of passages of old. For this
reason a man has a greater insight into affairs by reading
one single book in three months' time, than can be observed
or understood by the age or experience of twenty men living
successively one after another. So that, to finish this digression, I am of opinion that God cannot send a greater curse
or affliction upon any nation than an unlearned and inconsiderate prince; for from hence all other misfortunes and
miseries arise, and in the first place wars and division, by
his committing to other persons his own peculiar authority
(of which he ought to be more tender than of anything

I 3

besides); and from this division famine and mortality arise, and all the dreadful consequences attending upon war ; by which one may perceive how much all good subjects have reason to lament when they see the education of their young princes so miserably neglected, and left wholly in the power and management of persons of no qualifications nor desert.

CHAP. VII.

The Occasion of the King's being seized and secured in the Castle of Peronne by the Duke of Burgundy. — 1468.

I HAVE already given an account of the arrival of this Burgundian army at Peronne, almost at the same instant with the king ; for being in Champagne long before this interview was determined, the Duke of Burgundy had no time to countermand the orders he had given them, and their coming was a great check and impediment, by reason of certain jealousies and suspicions which were entertained on both sides.   However, these two princes deputed some of their ministers of state to meet and negotiate their affairs in the most amicable way that could be thought on.   But whilst the treaty was in a fair way of accommodation, and three or four days had been already spent in bringing it to a conclusion, news arrived of a strange turn of affairs at Liege, of which I shall give the following relation.

The king at his coming to Peronne had quite forgot his sending of two ambassadors to Liege to stir them up to a rebellion against the duke, and they had managed the affair with such diligence, that they had got together such a considerable number, that the Liegeois went privately to Tongres (where the Bishop of Liege and the Lord of Humbercourt were quartered with more than 2000 men) with a design to surprise them.   The bishop, the Lord of Humbercourt, and some of the bishop's servants, were taken, but the rest fled and left whatever they had behind them, as despairing to defend themselves.   After which action the Liegeois marched back again to Liege, which is not far from Tongres ; and the Lord of Humbercourt made an agreement for his ransom with one Monsieur William de Ville *, called by the French Le Sauvage, a knight, who, suspecting the Liegeois would kill him in their fury, suffered the Lord of Humbercourt to escape, but was slain himself not long after. The people were exceedingly overjoyed at the taking of their bishop. There were also taken with him that day several canons of the church, whom the people equally hated, and killed five or six of them for their first repast; among the rest there was one Monsieur Robert †, an intimate friend of the bishop's, and a person I have often seen attending him armed at all points, for in Germany this is the custom of the prelates. They slew this Robert in the bishop's presence, cut him into small pieces, and in sport threw them at one another's heads. Before they had marched seven or eight leagues, which was their full journey, they killed about sixteen canons and other persons, the majority of whom were the bishop's servants; but they released some of the Burgundians, for they had been privately informed, that some overtures of peace had already been made, and they were forced to pretend that what they had done was only against their bishop, whom they brought prisoner along with them into their city. Those who fled (as I said before) gave the alarm to the whole country, and it was not long before the duke had the news of it. Some said all of them were put to the sword; others affirmed the contrary (for in things of that nature, one messenger seldom comes alone); but there were some who had seen the habits of the canons who were slain, and supposing the bishop and the Lord of Humbercourt had been of the number, they positively averred that all that had not escaped were killed, and that they had seen the king's ambassadors among the Liegeois, and they mentioned their very names. All this being related to the duke, he gave credit to it immediately; and falling into a violent passion against the king, he charged him with a design of deluding him by his coming thither; ordered the gates both of the town and castle to be suddenly shut up, and gave out, by way of pretence, that it was done for the

* Or rather, Jehan de Wilde. Oliver de la Marche says that he was killed at the assault of Liege by the Burgundians. He is said by some authorities to have been Provost of Liege and Lord of Hautpeene.
† Robert de Morialmé, Archdeacon of the Cathedral of Liege.

I 4

discovery of a certain casket which was lost, and in which there were money and jewels to a very considerable value. When the king saw himself shut up in the castle, and guards posted at the gates, and especially when he found himself lodged near a certain tower * in which a Count of Vermandois † had caused his predecessor, one of the Kings of France, to be put to death, he was in great apprehension. I was at that time waiting upon the Duke of Burgundy in the quality of chamberlain, and (when I pleased) I lay in his chamber, as was the custom of that family. When he saw the gates were shut, he ordered the room to be cleared, and told us who remained, that the king was come thither to circumvent him; that he himself had never approved of the interview, but had complied purely to gratify the king; then he gave us a relation of the passages at Liege, how the king had behaved himself by his ambassadors, and that all his forces were killed. He was much incensed, and threatened his majesty exceedingly; and I am of opinion, that if he had then had such persons about him as would have fomented his passion, and encouraged him to any violence upon the king's person, he would certainly have done it, or at least committed him to the tower. None were present at the speaking of these words but myself and two grooms of his chamber, one of whom was called Charles de Visen ‡, born at Dijon, a man of honour, and highly esteemed by his master. We did not exasperate, but soothed his temper as much as possibly we could. Some time after he used the same expressions to other people; and the news being carried about the town, it came at last to the king's ear, who was in great consternation; and indeed so was everybody else, foreseeing a great deal of mischief, and reflecting on the variety of things which were to be managed for the reconciling of a difference

---

* A portion of this tower still remains incorporated in the existing Castle of Peronne.

† Herbert II., Count of Vermandois, having traitorously seized upon the person of Charles the Simple, imprisoned him in the Castle of Peronne, where the unfortunate king terminated his life in 929, after six years' captivity. Herbert died in 943, and was buried at Saint-Quentin.

‡ Esquire, valet de chambre, and keeper of the jewels to Duke Charles of Burgundy. He was appointed Captain of the Castle of Châtillon, by letters patent granted by the duke at Lille, on the 15th of April, 1470.

between two such puissant princes, and the errors of which both of them were guilty, in not giving timely notice to their ministers employed in their remote affairs, which must of necessity produce some extraordinary and surprising result.

Chap. VIII.

A Digression, demonstrating that when two great Princes meet in order to adjust their Differences, such Interviews are generally more prejudicial than profitable.

It is the highest act of imprudence for two great princes, provided there is any equality in their power, to admit of an interview, unless it be in their youth, when their minds are wholly engaged and taken up with entertainments of mirth and pleasure; but when they are come to years of emulation, though their persons should be in no danger (which is almost impossible), yet their heart-burnings and animosities will certainly augment. It were better, therefore, that they accommodated their differences by the mediation of wise and faithful ministers, as I have sufficiently instanced already in these my Memoirs; however, I will give some examples of the like nature, which I have seen and known myself in my own time.

Not many years after the coronation of our king, and just before the confederacy called the Public Good, there was an interview between the Kings of France and Castile*, princes of the nearest alliance in Christendom, for the kings are akin, their kingdoms almost contiguous, and their subjects bound by oaths and execrations to preserve it inviolable. To this interview Henry, King of Castile, came to Fontarabia, very splendidly attended, and the King of France came to St. Jean de Luz (about four leagues' distance), and each of them was upon the very borders of his kingdom. I was not present myself, but I had my relation from the

* Henry IV., King of Castile, son of John II. and Marie of Arragon, was born on the 6th of January, 1425, and died on the 12th of December, 1474. He married 1. in 1440, Blanche of Navarre, from whom he was divorced in 1453; and 2. Juana, Infanta of Portugal. The interview between Louis XI. and Henry took place at Andaia, near Fuentarabia, in April, 1463.

king, and from Monsieur du Lau, and it was confirmed
to me afterwards by several persons in Castile, who were
then present with their king, and particularly by the
Grand Master of St. James*, and the Archbishop of To
ledo†, the two greatest persons in that kingdom at that
time.   There were present also the Count of Lodesma‡ (that
king's favourite) in great splendour, with his guards, consisting of 300 horse, all Moors of Granada, or Negroes.   It
is true, indeed, that King Henry was a person of no great
sense, for he had either given away all his patrimony,
or suffered it to be taken or embezzled by anybody that had
a mind to it.   Our king was also well attended, according to
his custom, and his guards made a glorious appearance.
The Queen of Arragon§ was present at that treaty, upon
occasion of a difference between her and the King of
Castile about Estella, and some other places in Navarre,
of which difference the King of France was made umpire.||
   To continue our proposition, that interviews of great
princes are not necessary, you must know, these two kings had
never had any quarrels, neither was there the least difference
between them; they saw one another not above once or
twice, upon the bank of a river ¶ (which parts the two

---

* The Grand Master of the order of Santiago, in April, 1463, was
Bertrand de la Cueva, Count of Lodesma, in whose favour the Infante
Don Alphonso, the king's brother, had resigned the grand-mastership in
1462.   The knights of the order complained bitterly of being thus
deprived of their right to elect their chief, and to appease their murmurs,
the king persuaded the Count of Lodesma to resign his new dignity of his
own accord, in return for which he bestowed on him several estates and
lordships, including the dukedom of Albuquerque.   A bull of Pope Paul
II. restored the Infante Don Alphonso to the head of the order.   On
the death of this prince, on July 5. 1468, the knights elected as their
grand master Juan Pacheco, Marquis de Villena, who died in 1474.
This nobleman was present at the interview between Louis XI. and the
King of Castile : and it is to him that Commines refers in the text.
   † Alonzo Carrillo d'Acunha was appointed Archbishop of Toledo in
1447, and died on the 1st of June, 1482.
   ‡ He died on the 1st of November, 1492.   See the first note.
   § Juana, daughter of Frederick Henriquez, Amirante of Castile, and
Maria de Cordova, married John II., King of Arragon and Navarre, in
1447.   She died on the 13th of February, 1468.
   || Sentence was pronounced by Louis XI. on the 23rd of April, 1463.
See Lenglet, ii. 378.
   ¶ The Bidassoa.

kingdoms), near a little castle called Heurtebise, where the
King of Castile passed over to the other side ; but they staid
no longer together than the Grand Master of St. James and
the Archbishop of Toledo thought good; which being
observed by the King of France, he desired their acquaintance, and they went to wait on him at St. Jean de Luz.
His majesty received them very honourably, and a mighty
friendship and intelligence was settled between them and the
King of France, who immediately began to dislike the
King of Castile, and had but little value and esteem for him.
The greatest part of their attendants were quartered at
Bayonne, between whom several quarrels immediately arose
(notwithstanding the alliance); their languages also being
different. The Count of Lodesma passed the river in a
boat, whose sail was of cloth of gold; he was himself
in a pair of buskins set thick with precious stones, in which
he went to wait upon the king; though he was not really a
count, yet he was very rich, and I saw him afterwards made
Duke of Albourg, and invested with great possessions
in Castile. Several jests and scoffs happened between these
two nations, notwithstanding their alliance. The King
of Castile's person was homely, and his dress did not please
the French, who laughed at and derided both. Our king
wore a short coat, as ill made as was possible ; sometimes he
wore very coarse cloth, and particularly then ; his hat was
old and differing from everybody's else, with an image of lead
upon it. The Castilians laughed as heartily at his dress,
supposing it his stinginess. In short, the convention broke
up, and they parted, but with such scorn and contempt
on both sides, that the two kings never loved one another
heartily afterwards ; and such quarrels and animosities arose
in the court of Castile among the courtiers, as continued to
the king's death, and a long time after. I saw the king
afterwards forsaken by all his servants, and the poorest and
most pitiable prince in the world. The Queen of Arragon
was also much dissatisfied with the sentence which the King
of France had given in favour of the King of Castile,
and both she and the King of Arragon* hated him for it ever

* John II., son of Ferdinand, King of Arragon, and Leonora of
Albuquerque. He died on the 19th of January, 1479. He was a
Knight of the Golden Fleece.

after. It is true they made use of him against the town
of Barcelona afterwards in their extremity; but that friendship lasted not long, for a war broke out between our king
and the King of Arragon, which lasted sixteen years and
remains yet undetermined*: but to give other examples.

Since that time Charles, Duke of Burgundy, with great
labour and solicitation, obtained an interview with the Emperor Frederick † (who is still living), and spent vast sums
of money to show his grandeur and magnificence: the place
of meeting was at Treves ‡, where several things were discoursed of, and among the rest a marriage between their
children, which was afterwards accomplished.§ After they
had been several days together, on a sudden the emperor departed without so much as taking his leave, which the Duke
of Burgundy looked upon as so great an affront, and it was so
generally resented, that there was never afterwards any true
love between either themselves or their subjects: the Duke's
pompous and lofty manner of speaking (which they imputed
to his pride) offended the Germans; and the Emperor's
meanness, both in his train and dress, appeared as contemptible to the Burgundians; and so far was this accident
extended, that from it alone the wars of Nuz ‖ had their
origin.

I was also present at an interview ¶, at the town of St. Paul
in Artois, between the Duke of Burgundy and Edward IV.,
King of England, whose sister he had married; and, besides,
they were brethren of the same order.* * They were but two
days together, and yet in that small time there was great

* It was terminated by a peace between the two powers, on the 9th of
November, 1478.
† Frederick III., son of Ernest, Duke of Austria, and Zimpurgis of
Mazovia, was born on the 23rd of December, 1415, and died on the 19th
of August, 1493. He married Eleanor, daughter of Edward, King of
Portugal.
‡ On the 30th of September, 1473.
§ Maximilian of Austria married in August, 1477, Mary of Burgundy,
the sole heiress of Duke Charles.
‖ Neuss, a town in the province of Dusseldorf, Prussia.
¶ On the 7th of January, 1471.
** The King of England was elected a Knight of the Golden Fleece,
of which order the Duke of Burgundy was sovereign, on the 13th of
May, 1468, and notified his acceptance of the honour on the 28th of
October, 1469.

difference between the king's servants, and both parties recommending their quarrel to the duke, and he deciding it for one of them, their hatred increased. However, he assisted the king in the recovery of his kingdom with men, money, and ships, for he had been driven out by the Earl of Warwick. Yet, notwithstanding that good office, they never loved nor spoke well of one another after this interview.

I was present likewise when the Count Palatine of the Rhine made a visit * to the Duke of Burgundy at Brussels, where he staid several days. He was honourably received, nobly entertained, and lodged in an apartment richly furnished. The duke's servants upbraided the Germans for their nastiness and incivility, in laying their dirty clothes and their boots upon those rich beds, and accused them of want of neatness and consideration, and they never liked them afterwards so well as they had done before. The Germans, being as much dissatisfied on the other side, reproached them for their pomp and extravagance ; so that, in effect, they never loved nor did any good office for one another afterwards.

I saw also the meeting between the Duke of Burgundy, and Sigismund, Duke of Austria†, when the latter sold to the Duke of Burgundy the county of Ferrette (which lies not far from the county of Burgundy) for 100,000 florins of gold, as he was unable himself to defend it against the Swiss. These princes also were not well pleased with one another. Afterwards Sigismund made peace with the Swiss, possessed himself again of the county, but never returned his money, from whence great mischiefs resulted to the Duke of Burgundy. At the same time also the Earl of Warwick‡ came to visit the Duke of Burgundy, and ever afterwards a mortal hatred continued between them.

On Tuesday, February 10. 1466.
† Sigismund, son of Frederick IV., Duke of Austria, and Count of Tyrol, by Anne of Brunswick. He was born on the 26th of October, 1424, and married 1. Eleanor, daughter of James II., King of Scotland ; and 2. Catherine, daughter of Albert the Courageous, Duke of Saxony. He died on the 4th of March, 1496. Sigismund visited the Duke of Burgundy at Arras, on the 21st of March, 1468 (O. S.), accompanied him in several journeys, and was with him at St. Omer, on the 1st of May following.
‡ The Earl of Warwick came to the Duke of Burgundy at St. Omer, the 26th of April, 1469.

I was also at the interview * at Picquigny (not far from Amiens) between our king and Edward IV., King of England, and shall give a larger account of it in another place; but must observe by-the-bye that scarce anything was performed that was promised there, but all their whole business was hypocrisy and dissimulation. It is true, they had no wars, because the sea divided them; but there never was any real friendship or good correspondence between them afterwards. To conclude, if great princes have a desire to continue friends, in my judgment they ought never to meet; and my reasons are these: courtiers cannot forbear reflecting upon past actions, and one or other will be sure to take exception†; neither is it possible to hinder the train and equipage of the one from being finer and more magnificent than the other, which produces mockery, and nothing touches any person more sensibly than to be laughed at. The princes being of different nations, their language and habits are commonly different, and that which pleases one will not please the other; besides, among the princes themselves it often happens, that the presence of the one is more obliging and acceptable, which gains him honour and reputation, and everybody extols him, which cannot be done without reflecting on the other. For some few days after they are parted, all their fine stories and observations are whispered and told privately up and down, but afterwards having told them often, they become less cautious, and by degrees their tales grow to be table-talk, and are at length carried to both parties; for few things (especially of that nature) can be concealed in this world. And these are part of the reasons which I have known and observed touching this matter.

* On the 29th of August, 1475. See book iv. chap. x.
† As it happened at Venice, when Henry III., King of France, made, his public entry into that city. The French laughed at the Venetians dress, upon which they were like to have come to blows.

CHAP. IX.

How the King renounced his League with the Liegeois, to be released
out of the Castle of Peronne. — 1468.

HAVING thus fairly represented my judgment of such interviews, I shall now return from my long digression, to speak
of the king, who thought himself (as I said before) a prisoner
in the Castle of Peronne, as he had good reason to do ; for all
the gates were shut and guarded by such as were deputed to
that office, and continued so for two or three days ; during
which time the Duke of Burgundy saw not the king, neither
would he suffer but very few of his majesty's servants to be
admitted into the castle, and those only by the wicket ; yet
none of them were forbidden ; but of the duke's none were
permitted to speak with the king, or come into his chamber,
at least such as had any authority with their master. The
first day there was great murmuring and consternation all
over the town. The second, the duke's passion began to
cool a little, and a council was called, which sate the greater
part of that day and night too. The king made private
applications to all such as he thought qualified to relieve
him, making them large promises, and ordering 15,000
crowns to be distributed among them ; but the agent who
was employed in this affair acquitted himself very ill, and
kept a good part of the money for his own use, as the king
was informed afterwards. The king was very fearful of
those who had been formerly in his service, who, as I said
before, were in the Burgundian army, and had openly declared themselves for his brother, the Duke of Normandy.
The Duke of Burgundy's council were strangely divided in
their opinions ; the greatest part advised that the passport
which the duke had given to the king should be kept, provided his majesty consented to sign the peace as it was drawn
up in writing. Some would have him prisoner as he was,
without farther ceremony. Others were for sending with
all speed to the Duke of Normandy, and forcing the king to
make such a peace as should be for the advantage of all the
princes of France. Those who proposed this advised that
the king should be restrained, and a strong guard set upon

him, because a great prince is never, without great caution, to be set at liberty after so notorious an affront. This opinion was so near prevailing, that I saw a person booted and ready to depart, having already several packets directed to the Duke of Normandy in Bretagne, and he waited only for the duke's letters; and yet this advice was not followed. At last the king caused overtures to be made, and offered the Duke of Bourbon, the Cardinal his brother, the Constable of France, and several others, as hostages, upon condition, that after the peace was concluded, he might return to Compiegne, and that then he would either cause the Liegeois to make sufficient reparation for the injury they had done, or declare war against them. Those whom the king had proposed for his hostages proffered themselves very earnestly, at least in public; I know not whether they said as much in private; I expect they did not: and, if I may speak my thoughts, I believe that the king would have left them there, and that he would never have returned.

The third night after this had happened, the Duke of Burgundy did not pull off his clothes, but only threw himself twice or thrice upon the bed, and then got up again and walked about, as his custom was when anything vexed him. I lay that night in his chamber, and walked several turns with him. The next morning he was in a greater passion than ever, threatening exceedingly, and ready to put some great thing in execution; but, at last, he recollected himself, and it came to this result: that if the king would swear to the peace, and accompany him to Liege, and assist him to revenge the injuries which they had done him and the Bishop of Liege, his kinsman, he would be contented. Having resolved on this, he went immediately to the king's chamber, to acquaint him with his resolutions himself. The king had some friend* or other who had given him notice of it before, and assured him that his person would be in no manner of danger, provided he would consent to those points; but that if he refused, he would run himself into so great danger, that nothing in the world could be greater.

When the duke came into his presence, his voice trembled, by the violence of his passion, so inclinable

* There can be no doubt that this friend was Commines himself. See Lenglet, iv. 133; and Dupont, i. 173.

was he to be angry again.*   However, he made a low reverence with his body, but his gesture and words were sharp,
demanding of the king if he would sign the peace† as it
was agreed and written, and swear to it when he had done.
The king replied he would; and, indeed, there was nothing
added to what had been granted in the treaty at Paris‡,
which was to the advantage of the Dukes of Burgundy or Normandy, but very much to his own; for it was
agreed that the Lord Charles of France should renounce the
duchy of Normandy, and have Champagne and Brie, and
some other places adjacent, as an equivalent.§   Then the
duke asked him if he would go along with him to Liege,
to revenge the treachery they had practised by his instigation, and by means of that interview.   Then he put him in
mind of the nearness of blood between the king and the
Bishop of Liege, who was of the house of Bourbon.   The
king answered, that when the peace was sworn, which
he desired exceedingly, he would go with him to Liege, and
carry with him as many or as few forces as he pleased.   The
duke was extremely pleased at his answer, and the articles
being immediately produced and read, and the true cross
which St. Charlemagne was wont to use, called the Cross of
Victory, taken out of the king's casket, the peace was sworn,
to the great joy and satisfaction of all people; and all the
bells in the town were rung.   The Duke of Burgundy

* " As soon as the king saw the duke enter his chamber, he could not
conceal his fear, and said to the duke, 'My brother, am I not safe in
your house and in your country?' and the duke answered, 'Yes, sir;
and so safe that if I saw an arrow coming towards you, I would put myself in front to shield you?'   And the king said to him, 'I thank you for
your good will, and will go whither I have promised you; but I pray
you that peace may be from this time sworn between us.'"   Oliver de la
Marche, ii. 287.

† Concluded at Peronne, on the 14th of October, 1468.   See end of
chapter.

‡ See above, book i. chap. 13.

§ As we have already seen, by the treaty of Ancenis, Louis XI.
granted his brother an appanage of 60,000 livres a year, in exchange
for the duchy of Normandy.   If it be true, as Commines and Oliver de
la Marche both state, that the treaty of Peronne secured to that prince
Champagne and Brie, instead of Normandy, the clause concerning this
new exchange must have been contained in some secret article; for it
does not occur in the original draft of the treaty, or in any subsequent
edition of it.

K

immediately despatched a courier with the news of this
conclusion of peace into Bretagne, and with it he sent a
duplicate of the articles, that they might see he had not
deserted them, nor disengaged himself from their alliance ;
and, indeed, Duke Charles, the king's brother, had a good
bargain, in respect of what he had made for himself in
the late treaty in Bretagne, by which there was nothing left
him but a bare pension, as you have heard before.   Afterwards the king did me the honour to tell me, that I had done
him some service in that pacification.

—— ✦ ——

*A Treaty of Peace between Louis XI., on the one part, and
Charles, the last Duke of Burgundy, on the other.   Concluded at Peronne, October 14. 1468.*

The Duke of Burgundy having complained of infractions
made on the treaty of Conflans between us and him, and
also on the treaty of peace made at Arras between our late
lord and father and the late Philip, Duke of Burgundy,
insomuch, that we were ready to have recourse to arms
on both sides, and that the subjects of neither party durst
converse with those of the other ; to prevent, therefore,
an open rupture, we thought fit to send our ambassadors
first to them in Vermandois ; and afterwards the treaty
being transferred to Peronne, here, to prevent all the mischiefs and inconveniences that might ensue, we do, in
the most solemn manner, make, conclude, and promise a
firm, solemn peace, friendship, and amity, and we will always
observe the treaty of Arras, with the contents thereof,
as also the said treaty, and all that is contained therein
in reference to our cousin and brother the Duke of Burgundy, and all the donations and transfers we have then
and since made to him.   And we also promise and swear
to observe all the provisions and answers made to his
grievances, complaints, and requests hereafter specified.
And notwithstanding this present treaty of peace, and
the things contained in those of Arras and Conflans, we
do freely consent that our said brother and cousin shall
observe all the alliances, and also the treaty of truce and in-
tercourse of trade with Edward our enemy and the
kingdom of England ; but yet so as that our said brother

shall give no assistance to the English in invading our kingdom and dominions. And by this peace we do declare that no satisfaction shall be demanded and insisted for any damages, hostilities, &c., on either side; but that whatever places, lordships, heritages and possessions, have been seized and occupied, shall be fully restored, and the owners may re-enter without any form or process of law. More particularly, we do, at the request of our said brother and cousin, consent that the places, castles, towns, and territories taken by us in the counties of Beaugé, the country of Bresse, and other lands and signiories appertaining to him and his subjects, shall be surrendered to him; and his subjects that are captive shall be freely set at liberty; and the said Duke of Savoy, our dear sister the Duchess of Savoy, the Bishop of Geneva, the said Philip of Savoy, the Lord of Romont, and other allies of the Duke of Burgundy, their subjects and adherents, shall be comprehended in this treaty, if they are minded, within a year's notification; and if they are not, the present treaty shall be valid; and, with those of Arras and Conflans, so far as this last concerns us and our said brother of Burgundy, shall neither be directly nor indirectly contravened by us, but we shall put our said brother into the peaceable possession and enjoyment of the things declared and contained in the said treaty, and execute, on our part, instruments of the gifts and transfers specified therein, according to the form and tenor of these presents. And we do consent and agree to acquit the subjects and vassals of their homage and services to us, by reason of the duchy, counties, countries, lands, and signiories which the said duke, his heirs, &c., held or shall hereafter hold of us, by reason of our crown and kingdom; and we shall not only faithfully and religiously observe and maintain the peace, and fulfil it in every particular, but we do consent that the princes of our blood shall promise and swear to preserve it, and that each and every of them shall assist our said brother against us, if we infringe the same, &c.

Here follow the grievances, remonstrances, and requests of the Duke of Burgundy, with the concessions and answers of the king to them.

1. As to the fiefs and homages of the county of Ponthieu, and others on both sides of the Somme, and of the three provost-ships of Vimeux, Beauvoisis, and Toullois, transferred to the king ; these fiefs and homages have been made to appear to belong to the duke for several reasons ; and, therefore it is desired the king would leave him in the peaceable enjoyment of the said rights, and that he may have power to force those to it who are refractory.

" It is answered on the king's part, that he declares the said fiefs and homages to appertain to the duke, in the same manner as the other things contained in the said transfer ; and that the vassals, who have not yet taken the oath of allegiance and done homage, shall do it in the usual manner, pursuant to the nature of the fief, still reserving the king's rights, who shall grant his letters patent to discharge the vassals of their oaths and homages, upon the account of the said lands ; and all his officers shall be commanded to do nothing that may hinder the same."

2. As to the taxes and aids of the said provostships, wherein some of the king's officers have caused some interruptions ; and that withal William Lamoureux has been made assessor-general of these provostships by the king, and thereby disappointed the assessor of Amiens, contrary to the form of these transfers ; it is remonstrated to the king, that he would be pleased to remove those lets and hindrances occasioned by the lances, gens d'armes, and free-archers in the same provost-ships, and that the said assessor be restored to his office.

" The duke shall enjoy the said provostships and all the profits of them, and also the royal rights, in the same manner and form as he ought to enjoy the royal provostships upon the said river on the side of Amiens. Those taxes also for lances, free-archers, and other soldiers, shall cease, and none demanded on the king's part ; and the assessor-general of Amiens shall be nominated by the duke, and approved of by the king ; and hereafter the king shall grant his letters patent in due form, that the said aids be given without delay or difficulty."

3. As to the business of the granary of Grand-Villiers depending on the said transfers, it is remonstrated, that all violences, impediments, and troubles, done and given in respect to them, by the king's officers, as well upon the soli-

citation of the people of Beauvais or otherwise, may be removed and cease for the future.

" Agreed to on the king's part."

4. As to the lands and signiories of Mortagne, transferred to the duke, his ambassadors remonstrate against the troubles and vexations given the duke's officers by the Bailiff of Tournay, of the Tournesis, and others, and desire they may be commanded to deport themselves peaceably, according to the treaty of Arras, and the king's letters patent granted in that behalf.

" The duke shall enjoy those lands, and nominate his officers, who shall be approved of by the king; and the Bailiff of Tournay, &c., shall behave himself according to the treaty of Arras, and the letters patent."

5. The king and the Duke of Burgundy being at Villiers-le-Bel, it was desired that the salt of Salins should be vended in Mâconnois, to which the king consented, upon condition the damage did not exceed 4000 francs: it was remonstrated upon this, that in pursuance of the said gift, and with regard to ancient usage, the salt of Salins had been always vended in Mâconnois, and that there the gabel of salt ought to belong to the duke by the treaty of Arras, &c.; therefore, it was desired that the king would allow of the vending of the said salt in Mâconnois, and to prevent that of the salt of Pequeis, for which toll shall be received at Pont St. Esprit, or elsewhere, to the king's use; and that reparation might be made to the duke for the damage he had sustained since the treaty of Arras, in the not receiving the said toll, amounting to above 100,000 francs.

" The king allows the duke salt granaries in the county of Mâcon and the country of Mâconnois, and in the places and royal towns included therein, for him, his heirs, &c."

6. As for the foreign imposition which ought to be raised on the frontiers of the king, and by the treaty of Arras should appertain to the duke in his own territories: first, the duke is disturbed in receiving the said duty; secondly, they would have him levy it in unusual places, and the merchants are obliged to give securities in an unusual form, and even the king's officers, which is very strange, take upon them to receive the said impositions from the goods and merchandises which are carried into the country of Burgundy,

Bar-sur-Seine, Auxerrois, Artois, and those territories
transferred to the duke, as if they were the territories
of the empire; or where the tolls were not levied, especially
in Auxerrois, upon goods belonging to those of the said
county, and brought thither from the neighbouring countries;
wherefore the said innovation is desired to be laid aside, and
that the duke may enjoy his right pursuant to the said
treaty, and that merchants be not obliged to give security
any otherwise than according to ancient usage.

  " The king is content that merchants give security, as to
foreign duty, according to ancient usage; that is, to vend
their goods in any part of the kingdom, where the aids have
their course on the king's part.   Suppose, then, that
the duke, by the king's grant, takes those aids to his own
use, without giving security that the said goods shall be sold,
and vended in the provinces of the kingdom, where the said
aids have their course, as in the country of Artois, and also
in others belonging, and made over by the treaty of Arras,
or otherwise, to the said duke, without any fraud; yet if
hereafter it should appear, that that was not the ancient way
of giving security, the whole will be reduced to the manner
and form prescribed by the ancient royal ordinances, or
other usages.   In like manner as to the duchy of Burgundy,
wherein the duke pretends the like innovations have been
practised, the king and duke shall depute each a commissioner
to inquire into the state of those ordinances, and the truth
of the fact; and shall regulate the differences as seems most
consonant to reason, and that within a year : upon which all
troubles and innovations shall cease, and the duke enjoy his
rights as to the said foreign imposition in those parts of the
kingdom transferred to him by the treaty of Arras.   And
all demands from the subjects of the said duke in his towns
of Arras, St. Omer, Hesdin, Terouenne, Auxerre, and
others, in reference to their giving the said security, shall
cease, and be no manner of charge to them.   Moreover,
all law proceedings shall cease upon the said account above
mentioned, till the commissioners have decided the said
differences, and wholly without prejudice to the king and
the duke's right; and as to the rights of highways, which are
of another nature, the commissioners hereafter named shall
have power to order things in favour of the duke, pursuant

to the treaty of Arras, in and throughout all the royal
territories, and also in the lands on both sides the Somme
transferred to the duke by the king."

7. As to the limits of the duchy of Burgundy, and also
the other towns and villages of the counties of Mâconnois,
Auxerrois, and Bar-sur-Seine, which the duke does not
entirely enjoy, nor in the manner he ought, according to the
form of the said treaty, the said ambassadors insist he may be
put into the peaceable possession of the said towns, villages,
and other rights conveyed to him by the said treaty, that he
may enjoy the profits of them, and that satisfaction be made
to him in reference to the profits received by the king's
officers, since the time they were transferred, and stoppage
had been made of them ; and to this end the said ambassadors
require that four commissioners be appointed — viz., two
on either side, who shall be empowered to go to such places
on the duke's account, in order to inform themselves fully
concerning his pretensions, if information has not already
been given, and thereupon make a declaration of the rights
of the said duke, that he may really, and out of hand, enjoy
the same, according to the form of the said treaty of Arras,
without any farther process or law-suit, on remitting the
same to the cognizance of the king, or any of his officers.

" The king is content, on his part, to appoint four commissioners to decide the matters in dispute, with as many
nominated by the duke ; and if these eight cannot do it,
it shall be left to three on each side ; and if these cannot
effect the matter, each party shall appoint two, who shall
determine the differences, according to the form prescribed
in the said article."

8. As to the troubles and molestations given about the
granaries belonging to the duke by the said treaty of Arras,
and the restraint put upon several of his subjects in the
country of Burgundy, Mâconnois, Charolois, Bar-sur-Seine,
and Auxerrois, to take salt elsewhere than from the said granaries, contrary to the form of the said treaty of Arras, to
his great detriment, the ambassadors desire these grievances
may likewise be effectually redressed.

" The king fully agrees to this, and commissioners may be
appointed to inquire into the defaults, and redress them as
in the preceding article."

9. The ambassadors farther remonstrate about some lands, places, and villages, situate in the bailiwicks and jurisdictions of Mâconnois and St. Gengon, and some others in the county of Auxerrois, and others of Bar-sur-Seine, belonging to the said duke by the treaty of Arras, the enjoyment of which has been denied him.

"The king from henceforward declares, that the duke shall enjoy the villages and jurisdictions in the bailiwicks of Mâcon and St. Gengon, and also the jurisdictions and villages of Auxerre and Bar-sur-Seine, according to the contents of the treaty of Arras, notwithstanding any obstructions to the contrary : and to this end the said eight commissioners, the six, or the four, in the manner above declared, shall be empowered by the king and duke to hear, examine, and determine things equitably, according to the treaty of Arras, and in the same manner and form as is set down in the eighth article aforegoing, and the answer made thereunto."

10. Item, the said Duke of Burgundy is also opposed and molested in the enjoyment of several fiefs and homages belonging to him, by virtue of the said treaty, in the said counties and bailiwicks of Mâcon, St. Gengon, and Auxerre, and their jurisdictions, especially of the counties of Beauvillois, which ought to belong to the bailiwick of Mâcon, of all which the said ambassadors demand redress.

"The king is willing to grant it, and it is left to commissioners to determine it, pursuant to the eighth article, and the answer to it."

11. And as to other points or articles contained and declared in the said treaty of Arras, the ambassadors demand, in the duke's name, that those which shall be found unaccomplished or impeded, and such as the duke has had no cognizance of, shall be decided by the said commissioners as aforesaid, without any farther contradictions or appeals.

"It is answered, that, to put an end, as soon as possible, to all differences concerning the said treaty of Arras and its dependencies, the eight, six, or four commissioners as aforesaid, shall have full power to examine strictly into the same, and by viewing the places, and without any process or form of law, to decide, determine, and execute what they think most just, by putting the said duke into the possession of whatever they find to belong to him, by virtue of the said

treaty, notwithstanding any contradictions or appeals whatsoever; and shall promise from thenceforward to acquiesce
with the same."

12. The third chief point concerns things appertaining to
the said duke, upon the account of his lordships, both within
and without the kingdom.

And, in the first place, as to the limits of the kingdom,
the county of Burgundy, and the territories under the jurisdiction of St. Laurence, the said ambassadors remonstrate
for a determination of the same, and that such an equal
number of commissioners be appointed on both sides to judge
and determine the said differences without any farther review of the same ; and notwithstanding any contradiction or
appeal whatsoever.

" The king agrees, that eight commissioners be appointed—
viz., four on each side—finally to adjudge and determine the
said differences."

13. As for the limits of the countries and territories appertaining to the duke, which adjoin to the counties of Flanders
and Artois, and other territories of the kingdom, concerning
any law-suit that has been commenced by any private persons
in the court of parliament ; the said ambassadors move, that
the king would please to suspend the same for the space of
twelve years, that so a way may be found for deciding it
without the form of a process, and with the least expense.

"The king is content to suspend such proceedings for
eight years ; but yet without prejudicing or derogating from
the right of jurisdiction, which may or ought to belong to
him ; or that the said suspension should give any possession,
or other advantage, contrary to the rights of the king or the
said duke ; and the matter shall be left to the decision of
commissioners."

14. The said ambassadors complain of the grievances occasioned by appeals lodged against the determinations and
judgments of the four principal laws of Flanders, against
the laws and privileges of the said country, and thereby
manifestly disturbing the said duke in his rights. Redress
is also required in matters of traffic, upon which the country
of Flanders principally depends.

"The first part of this article the king fully agrees to —
nothing is said of the last clause."

15. It is remonstrated, that, pursuant to the rights of the country of Flanders, the court of parliament ought to receive no appeals from other laws and judges of Flanders, *omisso medio* ; for the resort ought first to belong to the duke, and he ought not to be obliged to have recourse for a review to the said court, as they do in other countries of the kingdom ; for relief ought not to be given the subjects of Flanders in case of an appeal, if the appeal does not immediately precede the sentence of the count, or his council in Flanders ; and to this end the king is desired to grant him his letters patent in due form.

" The contents of this article he agrees to, pursuant to the custom of the country."

16. They farther remonstrate against the troubles and impediments met with in appeals made in causes within the jurisdiction, lands and chastellanies of Lille, Douay, and Orchies, in the council-chamber of Flanders, against all reason, and of which the duke has been in peaceable possession for a long time, except that short space wherein any contradiction has been made ; and that the said impediments may cease, seeing the said chastellanies continually belonged to the county of Flanders ; and since the king held them upon the contract of the marriage of the great Duke Philip, great grandfather of the present duke, they were re-united to the county of Flanders ; so that the duke may hold them alone in fief with the said county.

" Agreed to by the king."

17. Seeing that neither the king nor his court of parliament have any right, but the duke and his grand council, to take cognizance of the causes of his subjects within the kingdom in the empire ; and that, on the contrary, considering that appeals are not thereby hindered, the ambassadors desire there may be no trouble given therein, either by the king or his officers ; and that the jurisdiction, sovereignty and other rights, both of the king and duke, may be preserved.

" The king is content, that the duke or his great council take cognizance of the causes of his countries and subjects within the kingdom, in the empire ; saving the exception of the parties, and of those of the empire or kingdom, and the whole done without prejudice to the sovereignty and jurisdiction of the king, in relation to the kingdom, and the right

and sovereignties belonging to the duke in reference to the
empire; and this agreement shall last as long as the king and
duke live."

18. As to the 4000 livres yearly rent, belonging to the duke
upon the account of his predecessors the Earls of Hainault
and Ostervant, upon the revenue of Vermandois, appertaining to the king, and of which there are great arrears, the
ambassadors demand both the rent and the arrears.

"The said commissioners shall settle that matter, and do
the duke justice."

19. The ambassadors also complain of the restraint put upon
the duke's subjects and servants—some of them being natives
of his county of Burgundy, in his territories without the
kingdom; others of the duchy of Burgundy, and other territories of the duke's — by obliging them to take new and unusual oaths to serve the king against all persons whatsoever,
and especially against the said duke, without any regard had
to their being his vassals; and upon their delaying to do it,
though they were ready to take the oath of allegiance in the
usual form, and to serve according to the nature and quality
of their fiefs; yet Monsieur de Chastillon and other of the
king's officers have proceeded against them very irregularly
and unjustly, as well by seizing their lands and lordships, and
receiving the profits thereof, and committing outrages in
some of the said lands as in an enemy's country, as by confiscation of body and goods, and the said profits they have
applied to their own use : nay, which is still more, the said
Chastillon has proceeded against the duke himself, upon
account of the signiory of Fouvants, which belongs to him.

"The contents of this and the following 21st, 22nd, 23rd,
and 24th articles, the king is willing to redress fully for the
future; restitution shall be made of the profits aforesaid,
and the king will appoint a commissioner to see reparation
duly made. All prisoners shall be freely released, and free
egress and ingress given to the duke's subjects. The king
also consents that the vassals and subjects of the said duke
living and residing in his dominions, as also his domestic
servants, who have lands, fiefs, and lordships in his kingdom,
upon the account of which they are bound to certain military
services when the king issues out his general mandate for the
defence of his person, shall not be obliged to serve in person,

but find others, more or less in number, as the tenure requires, in their stead."

20. Again, M. de Chastillon and others have driven some ecclesiastics out of Langres, that have livings there, by reason of their being natives of the duke's dominions; and publicly enjoined them and other natives not to reside on those benefices, nor elsewhere in the kingdom.

" The king agrees fully to redress this grievance. "

21. The said M. de Chastillon and others of the king's officers have seized the goods of the inhabitants of Valenciennes at the fairs of Rheims, and of other considerable merchants, subjects and servants of the said duke; namely, M. de Ternant, William de Villiers, M. Jean Jacqueling, the receiver of Auxerrois, Jean Gormont, and others, who have had no reparation made them for their losses.   In like manner with them the king's officers without any cause have seized M. Jean de Janly, the duke's envoy to the Duke of Calabria and the King of Arragon.

" The same answer given to this as to the 20th article aforegoing."

22. The ambassadors demand that such novel and unreasonable constraints may be no more practised ; that the seizing of the lands of the duke's subjects may be entirely discontinued, so as that they may peaceably enjoy the same as formerly, and have restitution made them for the profits, and also that the ecclesiastics of Langres may be satisfied.

" Agreed to as the last."

23. In like manner an entire restitution is required of the goods taken from the duke's subjects in Holland, Zealand, Brabant, and Flanders, of which the said subjects have lately made grievous complaints for redress, and the liberty of those who are imprisoned ; and withal, that letters patent might be granted, that disorders and hostilities may not be practised for the future; the subjects of the said duke having been interrupted in their herring fishery, as well those of Holland, Zealand, and Brabant, as those of Flanders and Boulogne, to their great damage; and therefore they desire the king's passes to secure them for the future, upon producing of which they may proceed unmolested.

" Answered as the last article."

24. The ambassadors set forth, that the gifts made the duke

by the king of the revenue of Chastel-Chinon for six years, and which he did not enjoy above a year or two, may be restored to him for that term.

"This the king fully agrees to."

25. The king, for very good causes and considerations, is desired to cancel those causes that are depending in his court of parliament between Jean Boutilhac, and Christian and Jean de Digonne, both brothers, which were commenced in the time of the troubles, and by the duke's order, M. Jacques de la Galce, Messieurs de Lalain, and de Montigny, Gerard le Febvre, and the people of Bruges, and the king's proctor, joined in the said causes to bring them before him; and afterwards pursuant to the abo'ition made at Conflans, and the contents of the letters patent formerly granted by the king thereupon, to maintain the said letters of abolition.

"The king is willing to cancel the causes above said before himself and council, or the commissioners appointed for the universal reformation of justice through the kingdom, of whom the Chancellor of France is one. And as to the affair of Boutilhac and the king's proctor against the Digonnes, Boutilhac and the proctor shall be silenced; then for Lalain, seeing the said causes have a relation to the business of the limits above mentioned, in respect to which a stop had been made to the re-delivery of their goods seized and detained upon that occasion, these goods which are in the hands of commissioners or others deputed by them, they shall peaceably enjoy, till the dispute about the limits shall be decided by the said commissioners in the form aforesaid, provided that they and all their goods shall be liable to the making good, on their part, the sentence given by the said commissioners in that behalf. And as for the interposition of appeals by Gerard Febvre, and others, from the judgments and sentences of the said court of Bruges, they shall be of no effect."

26. The king is desired to inhibit De Torcy, his heirs, &c., for ever to prosecute a certain decree obtained by him against the late M. de Saveuse, contrary to the tenor of the treaty of Arras; which decree after it was made, had a stop put to it till the death of the late king, and by the king now being, for fifteen years, commencing from that of sixty.

"The said suspension of fifteen years the king is willing shall be observed, and that after the expiration of the said term, the execution of the said decree shall be suspended for twenty years longer, still with a salvo to the king and the duke's rights from thenceforwards, and for the twenty years past."

27. The ambassadors cannot also but remonstrate against the denial of mandates in case of appeal and other points of justice to the duke's officers and subjects, and even when his officers have appealed and demanded security for the preservation of his right and signiory.

"The king will command speedy and strict justice to be done, and all mandates in cases of appeal or otherwise shall be granted without hesitation; so that it may be evident to all men that he is desirous to do right to the duke's subjects."

28. The ambassadors desire the king would let the duke enjoy the lands, signiories and rights made over to him, and to let him have instruments of ratification, by which all impediments to the contrary shall be declared null and of no effect.

"This the king assents to in the full extent of it."

29. The ambassadors demand reparation of damages for himself and subjects during the troubles, which by a moderate computation amount to above 200,000 crowns in gold.

"The king is willing to make reparation, but expects the same on the part of the duke."

30. The king is desired to prohibit the Bailiff of Gens for the future to receive appeals, and to grant relief in cases of appeals by the subjects of the duchy of Burgundy; forasmuch as that duchy is the first peerage of France, and therefore the duke and his subjects ought to appeal nowhere but to the parliament, if they think fit.

"The king agrees to this article."

31. The bailiff, judges and officers of the said duke in that duchy, ought not for the future to be hindered from taking cognizance of the subjects of the said duchy, under pretence that they are burghers of Ville-neuve-le-Roy; and the Bailiff of Gens and all others should be forbidden to grant protections to the subjects of the said duke in his duchy, under pretence of that burghership.

"The king agrees also to this."

32. The king is desired to grant letters patent, and in them to declare that all executions made by virtue of the seal of the said duchy, shall take place according and pursuant to the

privileges of the said seal, and notwithstanding any appeals, and without prejudicing the same.

" The king agrees to this article."

33. All complaints made in respect to innovations, which shall be exhibited by the said duke in his said duchy and his other territories, or by the judges of those countries who may and are wont to offer those complaints, ought really to be redressed, notwithstanding any appeals, &c.

" This the king allows of."

34. Though the villages of Desgrandes, Mallay St. Guillain, Ducray, and other adjacent ones, are directly in the duchy of Burgundy, appertaining to the said duke, and belonging to the bailiwick of Destun; yet the king's officers have attempted to make them to belong to Lyons, as well in point of jurisdiction as in the matter of taxes, to the prejudice of the said duke, and also contrary to the treaty of Arras, by which all the profits and royal rights in the bailiwicks of Mâcon and St. Gengon ought to belong to the said duke; for if the king had any right to the said villages, it must be upon the account of the said bailiwicks of Mâcon and St. Gengon only; and for the late duke, he complained of it to the late King Charles, and since to the present king; and was informed that M. Guichard Bastier, Chief-judge of Lyons, should inquire into the matter of fact, and there determine it. Nevertheless, the said ambassadors require that the said information may be reviewed and examined by the said commissioners, who shall be appointed to transact the other matters above mentioned, and so as to re-instate the said duke in the possession of the said villages whereof he has been deprived wrongfully and without any just cause; in case that information be sufficient to do it, or otherwise the commissioners shall decide it in the manner aforesaid.

" The king agrees to this article in all the parts of it."

35. And in case there are any articles that cannot presently be executed, but that it shall be necessary that they should be examined and determined by commissioners, whom the king and the duke shall appoint, and that in order to this a convenient time be also assigned; and that it may so happen that though the said commissioners have not full power from the king and the duke to determine the things left to their cognizance: insomuch that the said matters may be delayed

through the difficulties which may occur, as well in respect
to the knowing, as making a declaration of the rights
of the parties; let the king and the duke, if they are so
pleased, expedite their powers, by which both sides shall
agree, that, in case the said commissioners cannot accord, they
may choose an umpire, an able man, who cannot be suspected
of partiality, to whom they shall declare and impart their
difficulties and differences; and when he shall be fully
instructed in the whole affair, he shall declare his opinion
according to his conscience, and without any favour or
affection. And so the matter shall be adjudged and determined, according to the advice of those the said commissioners
who shall be of the umpire's opinion, notwithstanding
the opposition of the rest, with a salvo always to the greatest
and soundest part in number of persons and opinions of
the said commissioners, by whose advice the matter shall
be determined as effectually as if all the commissioners had
agreed to it. And in case the said commissioners shall
not be able to agree among themselves about the choice
of an umpire, those on the king's side shall be obliged to
name two worthy persons, and the duke's commissioners
as many, neither of whom shall be natives, or the subjects of
either of them, nor suspected of partiality; out of which
four, one shall be chosen by lot, who shall be the umpire, to
decide the matter as aforesaid; and if the commissioners who
shall be appointed by the king do not agree in the choice of
an umpire as aforesaid, in that case the duke's commissioners
may do it without them. And, on the contrary, if the said
commissioners of the duke do not agree to it, those of the
king's may in like manner do it without them. And that
choice, together with the king's which, by virtue thereof, shall
be made, shall be as valid as if done by the commissioners
on both sides by common consent; and the said commissioners on one side may proceed in the said affair, by
default, and upon the refusal of the commissioners on the
other side, and act with the said umpire, in the same
manner as if all the commissioners were together. And all
that shall be determined, done, and executed, in the things
aforesaid, shall remain firm and valid for ever; and that the
said commissioners and every of them shall swear solemnly
that they will take care of, attend, and manage the said

affairs as aforesaid, and have a very strict regard to the right
of each part, and proceed therein without interruption
or delay, and without alleging any excuse, unless in case
of death or sickness.   And in case of an excuse as aforesaid,
the commissioner, whose business it is, shall appoint one
to act in his stead, who shall proceed with the rest in the
same form and manner as above directed.

"The king agrees to the contents of this article."

[The conclusion and ratification of this treaty being
matters of form, we omit them.]

CHAP. X.

How the King accompanied the Duke of Burgundy in his Expedition
against the Liegeois, who were formerly his Allies. — 1468.

AFTER the conclusion of the peace, the King and the Duke
of Burgundy set out the next morning for Cambray*, and
from thence towards the country of Liege : it was the
beginning of winter, and the weather very bad.   The king
had with him only his Scotch guards and a small body
of his standing forces ; but he ordered 300 of his men-at-
arms to join him.   The duke's army marched in two columns ;
one was commanded by the Marshal of Burgundy (of whom
I have spoken before), and with him were all the Burgundians,
the above-mentioned nobility of Savoy, and a great number
of forces out of Hainault, Luxembourg, Namur, and Lim-
burg ; the other body was led by the duke himself.   When
they came near the city of Liege, a council of war was held
in the duke's presence, in which it was the opinion of some of
the officers, that part of the army should march back, since the
gates and walls of that city had been demolished the year
before, and no hopes were left them of being relieved ; for the
king was with us in person, and had made some overtures for
them, which was almost as much as was demanded of them :
but the duke was not at all pleased with this proposition, and

---

* They left Peronne on the 15th of October, and slept at Cambray on
the 17th.   Lenglet, ii. 192.

it was well he was not, for never prince was nearer his ruin, and it was only his suspicion of the king which was the occasion of his rejecting it. Certainly they who proposed it, out of an opinion of their too great strength, were very ill-advised; it was a great instance of their folly or pride, and I have often heard of such counsel having been given, but it was always by such officers as were either ignorant of what was fit to be done, or such as had a mind to be esteemed for their courage; but our king (whom God pardon!) understood an affair of this nature excellently well. He was slow and timorous in undertaking any action of importance, but when once he had begun, he provided so well, that it was hardly possible for his designs to miscarry.

The Marshal of Burgundy was ordered with the brigade under his command, to advance before us, and possess himself of the city; if he was refused entrance, he was ordered to force it if he could, for there were already several deputies from the city coming and going about an accommodation. The marshal advanced as far as Namur, and the king and duke arriving the next day*, he removed and marched on. As soon as he approached the city, the poor inconsiderate citizens made a sally, but were easily defeated (at least a good part of them), and the rest retired. During this confusion in the town, the bishop made his escape, and came to our army. There was at that time a legate† sent from the Pope‡ to pacify their disputes, and to inquire into the difference between the bishop and the people; for they remained still under excommunication for the above-mentioned reasons and offences. This legate exceeding his commission, and hoping to make himself bishop of that city, favoured the people, advised them to take arms, and to stand upon their defence, and other foolish counsels he gave them besides: but finding what danger the town was in, he endeavoured to make his escape, and got away with his whole train (con-

---

* They arrived at Namur in the morning of the 21st of October, and remained there until the 24th. Lenglet, ii. 192.

† Onofrio de Santa Croce, Bishop of Tricaria, in the kingdom of Naples. He was a native of Rome, where he died on October 20. 1471.

‡ Pietro Barbo, a Venetian, Cardinal of San Marco, was elected Pope under the name of Paul II., on the 31st of August, 1464. He died on the 28th of July, 1471.

sisting of five and twenty persons very well mounted); but they were all retaken. The duke having notice of it, sent word to those who had taken him, that they should carry him somewhere out of the way (without acquainting him with it), and make him pay as great a ransom for his liberty as they could get; because if it came publicly to his knowledge, the honour he was obliged to pay to the apostolic see would not suffer him to detain him a prisoner. They could not take his advice, but fell out among themselves, and some who pretended to a share, coming to the duke with their complaints, as he was sitting publicly at dinner, he sent to have the legate delivered into his hands, took him from them, showed him abundance of respect, and treated him very honourably. The great body of forces which were in the vanguard, under the command of the Marshal of Burgundy and the Lord of Humbercourt, presuming they should carry their point, marched directly to the city, and (moved by their avarice), they thought it better to plunder it, than to accept of a treaty which was offered: supposing there was no necessity of staying for the king (who was seven or eight leagues behind), they advanced until just about night they arrived at the suburbs, into which they entered in a part that led directly to one of the gates which had been lately repaired by the citizens; some parley there passed between them, but nothing was concluded on. Night came upon them, and it grew very dark before they had taken up their quarters; so that not knowing where to dispose themselves, they were in great disorder; some walked up and down, others called out for their masters, their comrades, and their captains. Monsieur Jehan de Vilde and other officers in the town, perceiving their folly and confusion, took courage, and (the inconvenience of having had their walls thrown down being now of great advantage to them), they sallied through the ruins and out of the breaches in the walls as they pleased upon those who were in the front ; but they attacked the pages and servants (who were left with the horses at the farther end of the suburbs, where they entered) by the way of the vineyards and hillocks, and slew many of them, but a greater number fled (for the night knows no shame): in short, they attacked us so vigorously, that in this action they slew above 800 men, of whom 100 were men-at-arms. But the wiser and more courageous of that vanguard kept themselves together in a body (the greatest part of them being men-at-arms and persons of good family), and marched up with their colours directly to the gate, imagining if there was a sally, it would be that way. A continued rain had made the ways prodigiously miry, and the men-at-arms being dismounted, stood up to their ancles in mud and dirt. All the inhabitants that remained in the town resolved to make a general sally at once, and with great shouts and a vast number of torches, they were marching through the gate, when our men (who were not far off, and had four good pieces of cannon with them), fired up the street among them two or three times, and made such a slaughter that they retired out of the suburbs, and shut up their gates. Whilst this dispute lasted in the suburbs, those who had sallied by the walls, being near the town, had got together some few carts and waggons, with which they fortified themselves, and reposed (though but indifferently, for they continued out of the town from two o'clock in the morning till six): but as soon as the day began to break, and we were able to discover where they lay, we immediately repulsed them. In this action, Monsieur Jehan de Vilde was wounded, and died in the town two days after, and two or three officers of note besides.

CHAP. XI.

Of the King's Arrival in person with the Duke of Burgundy before the City of Liege. — 1468.

THOUGH sallies out of a town are sometimes necessary, yet they are very dangerous, and of ill consequence to the besieged; since ten men are a greater loss to them than a hundred to the besiegers, because their number is less, and they cannot be recruited as they please; besides they may happen to lose their governor, or some other considerable officer, for want of whose conduct, not being able to make any longer defence, they may be forced to surrender the town immediately. The news of this action was presently brought to the duke, who was in his quarters about four or five leagues from the city. At first the whole body was reported to be cut off; however, the duke mounted, and ordered all the forces that were with him to march immediately, commanding that the news of this action should be kept secret from the king. In our approach to another part of the town, we had intelligence that all was well, that there were not so many slain as was at first supposed, and that among them there was not any person of note but one Monsieur de Sergine, a Flemish knight. At the same time we were informed, that the gentlemen and officers that were left of the vanguard were in great distress and want of provisions, having been upon very hard duty all night long and upon their feet in the dirt and mire at the very gates of the town; that some of the infantry who had fled, and were returned, were so dispirited and out of heart, that no great exploit could be expected from them; and therefore they desired the duke, for God's sake, to march up with all diligence to their post, which would oblige the enemy to divide their forces, and not lie with their whole garrison upon them. They pressed in like manner for supplies of provisions, for they had not one morsel left to subsist on. The duke immediately sent them what provisions could be got, under a convoy of 300 horse, to comfort and encourage them; and it was time, for none of them, except a few that had brought some wine with them, had either eaten or drunk anything for two or three days and a night, and to mend the matter, they had the hardest weather in the world. On their side it was impossible to enter, unless the duke gave the garrison a diversion. They had abundance of men wounded, and among the rest the Prince of Orange * (whom I had forgotten to name), who gave signal proofs of his courage and conduct, and would not stir from his post during the whole time. The Lords du Lau and d'Urfé behaved themselves very gallantly also, though above 2000 men deserted and ran away from them in the night.

It was almost night when the duke received this last intelligence, and having despatched the above-mentioned supplies, he returned to his standard to give a full relation to the king,

* William VII., son of Louis the Good, Prince of Orange, by Jeanne de Montbelliard, succeeded his father in December, 1463. He died on the 27th October, 1475.

who seemed to be extremely pleased, for the contrary would
have proved much to his prejudice.   It was not long before
we arrived at the suburbs, and then a strong party of volunteers
(men-at-arms and archers) were detached to possess the
suburbs, which was easily done; and the Bastard of Burgundy (who had a great command under the duke at that
time), the Lord of Ravestein, the Count of Roucy* (the constable's son), and several other persons of quality, took up their
quarters in the suburb, and some of them just by the gate
which the townsmen had repaired, as they had done the other.
The duke had his quarters in the middle of the suburbs, but
for that night the king remained in a good, large and well-
furnished farm about a quarter of a league from the town, with
a strong party both of our and his own men for his guard.
   The city of Liege is seated in a very fruitful country, full
of mountains and valleys, with the River Maes running through
the middle of it, and is much about the same size as Rouen,
and was at that time very populous.   It was no great distance
from that gate where we had our quarter, to the other, where
our vanguard were posted, provided we could have gone
straight through the town; but being obliged to go round on
the outside of it, it was full three leagues about by reason of
the holes and little sloughs which (it being mid-winter, and
very foul) the weather had filled up.   The walls likewise were
all demolished, and the citizens might attack our men in what
quarter they pleased : besides the foundation being stony and
a hard rock, they could never make a ditch, and at that time
had nothing but a small trench, which they had thrown up

* Antoine de Luxembourg, Count of Brienne, Ligny and Roussy,
councillor and chamberlain of the king, was the son of the Constable of
St. Paul and Jeanne de Bar.   He was originally attached to the household of Charles the Bold, and on the 18th of February, 1472, received
the provisions of Lieutenant-general of Burgundy.   He was taken
prisoner by the king's troops at the battle of Guipy, near Chateau Chinon,
on the 20th of June, 1475, and confined in the great tower of Bourges,
whence he was transferred to the Plessis-du-Parc.   Louis XI. bitterly
reproached him with his perfidy and treason, and would only consent to
grant him his life on condition of his paying a ransom of 40,000 golden
crowns within two months.   This was probably done, for Antoine de
Luxembourg, Count of Brienne, figured on the 12th of June, 1493,
among the nobles whom the King of France appointed to take back
Margaret of Austria to her father, the Emperor Maximilian.   The count
died in 1515.

not long before to defend them. Our vanguard were extremely overjoyed and animated at our approach on the first
night of our coming; for already the force of the garrison
was divided into two parts. About midnight we had a terrible alarm, and the Duke of Burgundy was immediately in
the street; not long after the king and constable came to him,
and had made great haste to get thither so soon. The darkness and horror of the night contributed much to the terror
of our soldiers, some of them crying out, " They sally out of
this gate, and some of them out of the other." The Duke of
Burgundy never wanted courage, but his conduct often failed
him; and to speak impartially, he did not behave himself at
this very time so prudently as he ought to have done, considering the king was there present. In this confusion, the
king took upon him to command, and said to the constable,
" March you with your men to such a place, for if the enemy
falls upon us anywhere, it must necessarily be there." He
who had seen his countenance, and heard him speak, would
have acknowledged him to be a prince of great courage and
prudence; but this was not the first action in which he had
given demonstration of it; however this was only a false alarm,
and the king and the duke returned both to their quarters.

The next morning the king removed into the suburbs, and
took up his quarters in a little house next door to the duke's;
his guards consisted of 100 Scots, and his household troops
were posted in a village near him. The Duke of Burgundy
was extremely jealous, lest either the king should find means
to get into the city, or return home before he could take it;
or else (being so near), make some attempt upon his person.
To prevent the worst, he made a draught out of his guards
of 300 of the stoutest men-at-arms that he could depend on,
and posted them in a great barn that lay between their two
quarters. The walls of the barn were broken down, to
render their sallies the more easy, if there should be occasion,
and these troops were placed there to watch and observe the
king's motions, who was quartered just by them. In this
manner we spent eight days; during which (for on the last
day the town was taken) neither the duke nor anybody else
pulled off their arms. The night before the surrender, at
a council of war, it was concluded to storm the town the next
morning, which was Sunday, the 30th of October, 1468; and

accordingly orders were given out that at a certain signal
(which was the firing of one great gun alone, then of two serpentines presently after, and then discontinuing), without farther
orders they should begin the assault on one side, as the duke
designed to attack them on the other by eight in the morning.
That night (as was concluded) the duke disarmed himself,
and ordered all his army to do the same, and to refresh themselves, especially those in the barn.   At that instant (having
been informed of our design) the Liegeois resolved to make
a sally upon our quarters, as they had done before upon the
other side.

CHAP. XII.

How the Liegeois made a desperate Sally upon the Duke of Burgundy's
Quarter, where both he and the King were in very great Danger.—
1468.

IN this chapter I shall show you an example, by which you
may observe, that the greatest prince or potentate may suddenly fall into dangerous inconveniences, occasioned by
a small number of their enemies; from whence it may
reasonably be inferred that all enterprises ought to be well
weighed and considered, before they are put in execution.
This city had not one soldier in their garrison, but men of their
own territories, nor one man of quality or good officer among
them; for those few whom they had were all killed and
wounded two or three days before.   They had neither gate,
nor wall, nor fortification, nor one piece of cannon, which
was good for anything.   Their garrison consisted only of
their own townsmen, and 700 or 800 foot from a small
mountain at the back of the town called the country
of Franchemont, but they had always had the reputation of
being valiant and stout soldiers.   They were now arrived
at the height of desperation, and having no hopes of
relief, since the king had come in person against them,
they resolved to make a general sally, and put all to a
venture, for they looked upon themselves as lost.   It

was concluded, that by the ruins of the walls which were behind the Duke of Burgundy's quarters, all their choicest troops should sally, which were 600 of those from the country of Franchemont, led and conducted by the masters of the two houses where the King and the Duke of Burgundy were quartered; near to which houses, by a crack in a great rock, they might march securely before they were perceived, unless they discovered themselves by any noise. Though there were several scouts by the way, they were not discouraged, imagining they should either kill them, or be at the king's or duke's quarters as soon as they should give the alarm. Besides, they presumed their two guides would conduct them directly to their own houses, where (as is said before) the king and the duke were quartered; and not halting anywhere by the way, they hoped they might be able to surprise them, and either kill or take them, before their guards could come in to their assistance. Having not far to march, they supposed they should be able to make their retreat, or if the worst came to the worst, they could but die, and they were contented to lose their lives in such an undertaking; for without it, as is said before, they found themselves utterly ruined. It was also ordered that all the people of the city should sally out of the gate which opened into the great street of our suburbs, with loud shouts and cries, hoping by that means to defeat that body of forces that were posted in the suburbs, and to obtain a complete victory, or a glorious death. Had they had 1000 men-at-arms, all regular forces, their attempt would have been great, and I question not but they would have succeeded in it, since with those few which they had, they were very near effecting their designs.

According to the resolution that had been taken, at about ten o'clock at night, the 600 men from Franchemont sallied forth by the breaches of the walls, seized upon the most of our outguards and put them to the sword (among whom there were three gentlemen of the household of the Duke of Burgundy), and certainly if they had marched on directly, and made no noise till they had arrived at the place where they designed, they had slain both those princes in their beds, without any great opposition. Behind the Duke of Burgundy's quarters there was a tent in which the

present Duke of Alençon* lay, and with him the Lord
of Craon†; they stopped there for some time, thrust their
pikes through the tent, and killed some of the servants.
This giving an alarm to the whole army, some few ran
to their arms, several got up, and leaving their tents, ran
immediately to the two houses, where the king and the duke
were quartered.   The barn I mentioned before, where
the duke had posted 300 men-at-arms, being close to
both houses, they gave them some thrusts with their pikes
out of the holes which had been made for the convenience
of their sallies.   Not full two hours before this attack,
these gentlemen had pulled off their arms to refresh and
prepare themselves for the assault the next day, so that most
of them were unarmed, though some few had clapped on their
cuirasses upon the uproar at the Duke of Alençon's tent, and
attacked the invaders through the doors and the holes which
they had made, and were the only body of troops that preserved those two great princes; for by this delay, several
others had time enough to arm, and make head against them.
I and two gentlemen more of his bed-chamber lay that night
in the Duke of Burgundy's chamber (which was very small),
and above us there were twelve archers upon the guard, all
of them in their clothes, and playing at dice.   His main
guard was at a good distance, and towards the gate of the
town.   In short, the master of the house where the duke
was quartered, having drawn out a good party of the
Liegeois, came so suddenly upon the duke, that we had scarce
time to put on his cuirass and breast-plate and clap a steel
cap upon his head: as soon as we had done it, we ran down
the stairs into the street, but we found our archers engaged
with the enemy, and much ado they had to defend the doors
and the windows against them.   In the street there was
a terrible noise and uproar, some crying out, "Vive le Roi!"
others, "Vive Bourgogne!" and others, "Vive le Roi, et
tuez!"   It was some time before our archers and we could

* René, Count du Perche, son of Jean-le-Beau and Marie d'Armagnac, succeeded his father in the dukedom of Alençon in 1476: and
died on the 1st of November, 1492.

† George de la Tremoille, Lord of Craon, Lieutenant-General of
Champagne and Brie, was the son of George, Lord of La Tremoille, and
Catherine, Lady of L'Isle Bouchard.   He died in 1481.

beat the enemy from the doors, and get out of the house: we knew not in what condition the king was, nor whether he was for or against us, which put us into a great consternation. As soon as we were got into the street, by the help of two or three torches we discovered some few of our men, and could perceive people fighting round about us, but the action there lasted not long, for the soldiers from all parts came in thronging to the duke's quarter : the duke's landlord was the first man of the enemy's side that was killed (who died not presently, for I heard him speak), and with him his whole party (at least the greatest part of them) were cut in pieces.

The king was also assaulted after the same manner by his landlord, who entered his house, but was slain by the Scotch guards. These Scotch troops behaved themselves valiantly, maintained their ground, would not stir one step from the king, and were very nimble with their bows and arrows, with which it is said they wounded and killed more of the Burgundians than of the enemy. Those who were appointed, made their sally at the gate, but they found a strong guard to oppose them, who gave them a warm reception, and presently repulsed them; they not being so good soldiers as the others. As soon as these people were repulsed, the king and duke met, and had a conference together; seeing several lie dead about them, they were afraid their loss had been greater than really it proved to be; for upon examination, they found they had not lost many men, though several were wounded ; and without dispute, if they had not stopped at those two places, and especially at the barn (where they met with considerable opposition), but had followed their guides, they had killed both the king and the Duke of Burgundy, and in all probability would have defeated the rest of the army. Each of these princes retired to his quarters greatly astonished at the boldness of the attempt; and immediately a council of war was called, to consult what measures were to be taken the next morning in relation to the assault, which had been resolved upon before. The king was in great perplexity, as fearing that if the duke took not the town by storm, the inconvenience would fall upon him, and he would either be kept still in restraint, or made an absolute prisoner; for the duke could not think himself secure against a war with France, if he should suffer him to depart.   By this mutual distrust of each other, one may clearly observe the miserable condition of these two princes, who could not by any means confide in one another, though they had made a firm peace, not a fortnight before, and had sworn solemnly to preserve it.

CHAP. XIII.

Of the storming, taking, and plundering the City of Liege; together with the Ruin and Destruction of the very Churches. — 1468.

THE king, to free himself from these doubts, about an hour after his return from the sally (which I mentioned before) to his quarters, sent for some of the duke's officers that had assisted at the council of war, to know the result of it; they told him it was resolved that the town should be stormed next morning in the manner that was concerted before.   The king made several grave and judicious objections, and such as the duke's officers approved of very well; for they were all apprehensive of the assault, in respect of the great numbers of people in the town, and the signal proofs they had given of their courage not two hours before; so that the officers seemed inclinable rather to defer it for some days longer, and to endeavour to have taken it by composition.   They came immediately to the duke's quarters, and made a report of all the king had said unto them, and it was my fortune to be present.   They represented all the king's fears, and their own too, but supposing the duke would not take it so well from them, they fathered it all upon his majesty.   The duke took it extremely ill, and replied, that the king raised those difficulties only to preserve the town: besides, he told them, that it was impossible his design should miscarry, because they had no artillery within, nor walls without, to defend them; that their fortifications and their gates were demolished, and therefore he was resolved to delay no longer, but to storm the town, as had been concluded before.   However, if the king pleased, he might retire to Namur, and stay there till the town was taken; but for his own part he would not

stir till he saw what would be the event of this enterprise.
The whole army dreaded this assault, and therefore none of
the officers were pleased with this resolution, which was
communicated to the king, not bluntly but in the mildest
terms imaginable. The king knew what the duke would be
at, but dissembled it, and declared he would not go to
Namur, but take his fortune the next morning with the rest.
My opinion is, that if he had been willing to make his
escape, he might have done it that night, for he had with
him 100 archers of his guards, several gentlemen of his
retinue, and not much fewer than 300 men-at-arms; but
when his honour lay at stake, he scorned to do it, lest the
world should have upbraided him with want of courage.

In expectation of day, the whole army reposed themselves
in their arms for some time, and several went to their
devotions, for it was looked upon as a very dangerous enterprise. As soon as it was broad day, and the hour had come for
the assault (which as I said before was eight in the
morning), the duke ordered the signal to be given, and the
great guns to be fired successively as was agreed on, to give
them notice who were in our vanguard on the other side of
the town (at a great distance to go about, though through
the town it was but a little way). The vanguard heard the
signal, and immediately prepared to storm the town; the
duke's trumpets began to sound, the colours advanced to the
walls, and the soldiers marched after in very good order.
The king was at that time in the middle of the street, well
attended with his 300 men-at-arms, his guards, and some
lords and officers of his household. When we came so
near that we expected to be immediately at push of pike,
we found no resistance at all, and not above two or three men
upon the guard; for supposing, because it was Sunday, that
we would not have attacked them, they were all gone to
dinner, and we found the cloth laid in every house that we
entered. A multitude is seldom formidable, unless commanded by some officer whom they hold in reverence and
fear; yet there are certain hours and seasons in which their
fury is terrible.

Before this assault the Liegeois were much fatigued and
dispirited, as well for the loss they had sustained in their two
sallies (in which all their chief officers were slain), as for the

great pains and hard service which they had endured for eight
days successively ; for nobody was exempted from being upon
the guard.   They being blocked up on both sides (as I stated
before), I suppose they thought that Sunday might have been
a day of rest to them (but they were mightily mistaken),
for they did not make the least defence, either on our side,
or on the other, where the Burgundians of our vanguard
made their attack, and entered before us * ; they killed but
few, for the people fled over the Maes into the forest of Ardennes, and from thence into such places of refuge as they
thought most proper to secure themselves in.   On that side
of the town where I was, I saw but three men and one woman
dead ; and I believe there were not above 200 killed
altogether, the rest having all fled, and got into the houses
or churches for sanctuary.   The king marched at his own
leisure (for he saw there was no opposition), and the army
(consisting by my computation of about 40,000 men), entered
at both ends of the town.   The duke, having advanced
a good way into the city, turned back to meet the king, con-
ducting him as far as the palace, and then returned to the
great church of St. Lambert, into which his soldiers were
forcing their way for the sake both of the prisoners and the
plunder ; for though he had posted a battalion of his guards
there to secure the church, yet the soldiers could not be
restrained, but fell upon them, and attempted to break open
the doors. I saw the Duke of Burgundy kill one man himself
at his arrival, upon which the soldiers retreated, and the church
was preserved for that time ; but at length all the men that
had fled thither for sanctuary were made prisoners, and all
the furniture was taken away. The rest of the churches, which
were very numerous (for I have heard the Lord of Humbercourt, who knew the town very well, say, that there were as
many masses said in it every day as in Rome), were most of
them plundered under pretence of searching for prisoners.   I
myself was in none but the great church, but I was told so,
and saw the marks of it, for which a long time after the Pope
excommunicated all such as had any goods belonging to the
churches in that city, unless they restored them ; and the
duke appointed certain officers to go up and down his country,

* On Sunday, October 30. 1468.

to see the Pope's sentence put in execution. After the taking and plundering the city, about noon the duke returned to the palace; the king had dined before he came, but expressed much joy at his good fortune, and highly applauded his magnanimity and conduct; for he knew well enough it would be carried to the duke, and he had in his heart a longing desire to be at home in his own kingdom. After dinner the king and the duke were very merry together, and if the king had been lavish in his commendations behind his back, he extolled his actions much more to his face, and the duke was not a little pleased to hear it.

But I am obliged to make a small digression, and give an account of the calamities of those miserable people who fled out of the town, that I may confirm what I said in the beginning of these Memoirs, when I spoke of the misfortunes and dreadful consequences which I have observed to follow those who are defeated in battle, whether king or prince, or any other potentate whatever.

These miserable creatures fled through the country of Ardennes with their wives and children. A gentleman in those parts (who till that time had been of their side), fell upon, and cut off a great party of them; and to ingratiate himself with the duke, he wrote him an account of what he had done, and represented the number both of the prisoners and slain to be much greater than in reality it was, though indeed it was very great; but, however, he made his own peace with the duke by that action. Others fled to Mezieres, which is a French town upon the Maes. Two or three of their ringleaders were taken and presented to the duke (one of whom was named Madoulet), whom he ordered immediately to be put to death; and several of the rest died with hunger, or cold, or watching.

CHAP. XIV.

How King Louis returned into France by the Consent of the Duke of Burgundy; and how the Duke treated the Liegeois and the People of Franchemont afterwards. — 1468.

ABOUT four or five days after the taking of the town, the king began to employ his friends about the duke, to propose his return into France; and he himself broke the matter to him very discreetly, telling him, that if he had still any occasion of his assistance, he should freely let him know it and he would willingly stay longer, but that if his presence could be of no farther importance, he desired to be dismissed, that he might return to Paris, and see the peace published in the court of parliament. *   (For in France it is a custom that all treaties of peace should be published in that court, or otherwise they are void, though indeed the king's power is very great.)   Besides, he desired of the duke that they might have another interview next summer in Burgundy, and enjoy the conversation of one another for a month together.   At length the duke consented he should go, yet not without murmuring a little.   The duke ordered the articles of peace to be read to the king, that, if he repented of anything, it might be altered.   He offered it likewise to his choice, whether he would stand to it or not, and some little apology he made for his bringing him thither.   He desired one thing more, which was, that the king would permit a new article to be added in favour of the Lord du Lau, the Lord d'Urfé, and Poncet de Rivière †, and that he would promise that the lands and preferments, which they had enjoyed before the war, should be restored to them again.   This proposition did not please the king at all, for he thought it very unreasonable that those who were not of his party should be comprehended in the peace.   Besides, they were servants to the Lord Charles, the king's brother, and not to the king.   However, the king replied that he would consent to it, upon condition that the duke would do the same for the Count of Nevers ‡ and the Lord

* The treaty of Peronne was registered by the Parliament of Paris on the 18th of May, 1469.

† The Duke of Burgundy, as we shall presently see, did not insist on this demand, which the king craftily induced him to abandon. Two years later, by letters granted at Angers in August, 1470, Louis granted forgiveness to Pierre d'Urfé and Poncet de Rivière " of all the charges, crimes, offences, and malefactions" of which they had been guilty in contravention of his authority.

‡ John of Burgundy, Count of Nevers, Baron of Douzy, Peer of France, Knight of the Golden Fleece, and Governor of Picardy, was born on the 25th of October, 1415.   He was the son of Philip II., Count of Nevers, and Bona of Artois.   He died on the 25th of September, 1491.   Having abandoned the house of Burgundy to enter the service

of Croy; upon which answer the duke pressed it no farther. This answer of the king's was looked upon to be a very wise one, for the duke hated those two gentlemen, so that he would never consent to their restoration.   In all the rest, the king told the duke he would alter nothing, but confirm whatever had been sworn at Peronne.   In this manner his departure was agreed on, and the king took his leave of the duke *, who conducted him about half a league, but at their last departure the king said to him, "If my brother, who is in Bretagne, should not be satisfied with the appanage, which for your sake I have given him, what would you have me do?"   The duke hastily replied, without considering what he said, "If he should not, it is your part to see him satisfied, but I shall leave that to yourselves."   From which question and answer important actions did afterwards proceed, as you shall hear in the proper place.

The king departed extremely well pleased, and was conducted by the Lords des Cordes, and d'Aimeries † (Grand Bailiff of Hainault) out of the Duke of Burgundy's territories, who himself continued at Liege. ‡   That city indeed was barbarously treated, but they had used his subjects with the same cruelty ever since his grandfather's time, never keeping any promise, nor observing any peace that they made; and it was now the fifth year that the duke had been there in person, and made peace with them every time, and the next year they would be sure to break it.   Besides they had stood excommunicated a long time for their insolence to their bishop; yet they could never be restrained, nor brought to receive the commands of the Church with either reverence or obedience.

As soon as the king was gone, the duke resolved (with a small detachment of his forces), to march into the country of

of Louis XI., he obtained pardon from his uncle Duke Philip, after the peace of Conflans, by the cession of various estates and lordships which he held in his dominions.

* On Wednesday, November 2. 1468.

† Antoine Rolin, Lord of Emeris, and Governor of Hainault, was the son of Nicholas, Lord of Emeris, and Marie de Landes.   His wife was a sister of the Count d'Estampes.   He was one of the conservators of the peace of Senlis for the marches of Hainault.

‡ Until the 9th of November.

M

Franchemont, which is steep, hilly, full of woods, and lies a little beyond Liege, from whence the best soldiers which they had, came, and particularly those who made that desperate sally which I mentioned before. Before the duke left the city, a great number of those poor creatures, who had hid themselves in the houses when the town was taken, and were afterwards made prisoners, were drowned. He also resolved to burn the city, which had always been very populous; and orders were given for firing it in three different places, and 3000 or 4000 foot of the country of Limbourg (who were their neighbours, and used the same habit and language), were commanded to effect this desolation, but to secure the churches. The first thing they did was to demolish a great bridge over the River Maes; then a strong body was appointed to protect such houses of the canons as were near the great church, that they might have lodging and convenience for the performing of divine service. Other parties were likewise ordered for the preservation of the rest of the churches. All things being thus ordered, the duke began his march into the country of Franchemont: he was no sooner out of the town, but immediately we saw a great number of houses on fire beyond the river; the duke lay that night four leagues from the city, yet we could hear the noise as distinctly as if we had been upon the spot; but whether it was the wind which lay that way, or our quartering upon the river that was the cause of it, I know not. The next day the duke marched on, and those who were left in the town continued the conflagration according to their orders*: but all the churches (except some few) were preserved, and above 300 houses belonging to the priests and officers of the churches, which was the reason it was so soon re-inhabited, for many flocked thither to live with the priests.

The cold and frost were so violent, that the greatest part of the duke's detachment was forced to march on foot into the country of Franchemont, which has no walled towns, but consists wholly in villages. The duke lay still five or six days in a

---

* When the duke left Liege, "he established there a captain named Messire Frederic de Withem, who remained there about fourteen days, and destroyed the city entirely by fire, after it had been pillaged." Gachard, i. 203.

little village called Pulleur*(which stands in a small valley); he divided his forces into two bodies for the speedier destruction of the country: his orders were to burn all the houses, break down all their iron mills (which were the greatest part of their livelihood), and search about among the woods for such of the poor people as had with their goods run thither to hide themselves, of whom many were killed, and made prisoners; and the soldiers got good store of plunder. In this march I saw incredible effects of the severity of the cold: one gentleman lost the use of his foot, and never recovered it again. A page had two of his fingers drop off with extremity of cold. I saw a woman and her new-born child starved to death with it. For three days together the duke's attendants could get no wine but what they cut out with a hatchet; for it was frozen in the pipes, and the ice being thick and entire, they were forced to cut it out in pieces, which they carried away in their hats and baskets as they thought fit. I could tell other strange stories of this nature, which would be tedious to write; but we, in short, were starved out of that country, and forced (after we had been there eight days) to march back with all expedition to Namur, and from thence into Brabant †, where the duke was received with joy.

CHAP. XV.

Of the King of France's Subtilty, by which he prevailed with his Brother Duke Charles, to accept of the Duchy of Guienne, in lieu of Brie and Champagne, and contrary to the Duke of Burgundy's Intention. — 1468-69.

THE king, having taken his leave of the Duke of Burgundy, returned with great joy into his own kingdom, not in the least complaining of his usage either at Peronne or Liege, but bearing all things patiently, at least, in appearance; yet, for all that,

* He arrived there on the 14th of October, and resumed his journey on the 17th.
† On the 20th of November, he slept at Landen, in Brabant. Lenglet, ii. 193.

great wars arose afterwards between them, but not presently,
nor was that the cause which I mentioned before (though it
might have contributed towards it); for the conditions of peace
were much the same as if the king had freely signed it at
Paris.   But, by the advice of his officers, the Duke of Burgundy was encouraged to extend the bounds of his dominions,
and great artifice was used to have it done secretly — of
which I shall speak in due time.

Lord Charles of France, the king's only brother, and lately
Duke of Normandy, being informed of the treaty of Peronne,
and of the proportion which he was to have thereby, sent presently to the king to desire his majesty would accomplish the
treaty, and grant him the investiture of those countries he had
promised to give him.   The king sent to him again, and
several messages passed between them.   The Duke of Burgundy sent also an ambassador to the Lord Charles, to desire
him not to accept of any other appanage but Champagne and
Brie, since they were granted upon his interposition.   He also
reminded him of the friendship which he had always shown
him, and that even when he had deserted the Duke of Burgundy, the duke could not be tempted to retaliate as he had
observed others had done, but had comprehended the Duke
of Bretagne in the treaty of peace as his ally*; besides, he
ordered his agents to acquaint him, that the situation of
Champagne and Brie was very commodious for them both, and
if the king should ever attempt to resume his gift, in a day's
time he might have succours out of Burgundy, for those countries were contiguous; besides, all the taxes, subsidies, and
revenues, would accrue wholly to him, and nothing to the
king, but the bare homage and sovereignty.

This Lord Charles of France was a person who did little
or nothing of himself, but in all things was governed and
managed by other people, though he was then above twenty-
five years of age.   In this manner that winter passed, being
half spent before the king left us.   Messengers were passing
continually about this appanage.   The king resolved upon no
terms to suffer his brother to enjoy what he had promised,

---

* The Duke of Bretagne is not mentioned by name in any of the
articles of the treaty of Peronne; but perhaps he must be considered as
implicitly included in the clause which concerns the allies of the Duke
of Burgundy.

for he did not like that the Duke of Burgundy and he should be such near neighbours.   Whereupon the king proposed to the Lord Charles to accept of Guienne and La Rochelle (which is almost all Aquitaine, and more valuable than Brie and Champagne).   Charles was afraid of disobliging the Duke of Burgundy; he feared also that if he should comply, and the king afterwards not stand to his word, he should lose friend and fortune both, and leave himself nothing to depend upon.

The king (who in such affairs was the wisest prince of that age), perceiving that he would lose time, unless he could make interest with some of those who were in credit with his brother, addressed himself to Odet de Rye, Lord of Lescut, and since * Count of Comminges (who was born and married in the country of Guienne), desiring him that he would be pleased to use his interest with his master to persuade him to accept of that for his appanage; it being much larger and of a greater revenue than what he demanded ; which would be the only means to make them live in perfect peace and harmony together like good friends and brothers, and for which all his servants would reap no inconsiderable advantage, but more particularly himself ; and, as to the investiture, he was ready to grant it him presently.   The Lord Charles being wheedled and cajoled in this way, was easily persuaded to accept of Guienne †, to the great dissatisfaction of the Duke of Burgundy and his ambassadors in France.   Cardinal Balue, Bishop of Angers, and the Bishop of Verdun ‡, were arrested and imprisoned, because the cardinal had written to the Duke of Guienne not to accept of any other share

---

* In 1472. See note, book i. chap. 6.

† The treaty of exchange is dated in April, 1469.

‡ Guillaume de Haraucourt, son of Gerard de Haraucourt, Seneschal of Barrois, was elected Bishop of Verdun on the 14th of October, 1456, and took possession of his see on the 10th of August following.   Possessed of the most brilliant qualities, and supported by the credit of Cardinal Balue, he met with a favourable reception from Louis XI., to whom he rendered important services.   Subsequently becoming involved in the cardinal's disgrace, Guillaume de Haraucourt was arrested, and confined in that iron cage, the invention of which is ascribed to him by Commines, book vi. chap. 12.   He was kept a prisoner for fifteen years, and died on February 20. 1500.

than that which was assigned to him by the treaty at Peronne, which the king had promised and sworn to observe. Besides, he added several other arguments to induce him to it, which were directly contrary to the king's designs. So the Lord Charles of France was created Duke of Guienne in the year 1469, and put into peaceable possession of that country, with the government of La Rochelle; after which the king and he had a meeting*, and conversed together a long time.

* On the 8th of September, 1469.

BOOK THE THIRD.

Ch. I.—How the King took an occasion of making a new War upon the Duke of Burgundy ; and of his sending as far as Ghent to summon him to appear, by a Serjeant of the Parliament. — 1470.

In the year 1470, the king, having a fair opportunity, as he thought, resolved to be revenged of the Duke of Burgundy, and secretly endeavoured to persuade the towns upon the River Somme, as Amiens, St. Quentin, and Abbeville, to forsake the duke, and admit some of his troops into their garrisons; for it is always the custom of great princes (especially if they be wise), to seek out some fair pretence or other to cover their designs. In order to your better understanding the intrigues and artifices of the French court in this kind of transactions, I will give a relation of the whole management of this affair; for the king and duke were both of them deceived, and a very bloody and cruel war commenced upon it, which lasted thirteen or fourteen years. The king indeed had a great desire to excite those towns to rebel, and set up his standard, upon pretence that the Duke of Burgundy had extended the bounds of his dominions farther than the treaty would bear. Upon this account several envoys and ambassadors were sent from one court to the other, backward and forward, who passed and re-passed through these towns, and proposed and drove on their several bargains very securely, there being no garrisons in these towns ; for the whole kingdom of France, as well on that side towards the Duke of Burgundy's dominions, as on the other towards the Duke of Bretagne's, was in perfect peace, and the Duke of Guienne was to all appearance in great friendship with the king.

M 4

However, the king had no design to commence a war purely
to repossess himself of one or two of those towns, and no
more; but his intention was to raise a universal rebellion in
the Duke of Burgundy's dominions, hoping, by that means,
to make himself master of all his country.

Many persons, to ingratiate themselves with the king,
undertook the management of these secret negotiations, and
reported them much forwarder than he really found them;
one promised him one town, and another another town, and
that they had bargained for them all; but had the king's
designs reached no farther than the events which succeeded
(though indeed he had cause to complain of his treatment at
Peronne), he would not have violated the peace, nor involved
himself in a new war; for he had published the peace at
Paris* three months after his return into his kingdom; and
he began his enterprise not without some fear and caution;
but the violent desires he had to it, at last prevailed over his
timorousness, and he was spurred on to it by some of his
courtiers.

The Count of St. Paul, a very wise man, and Constable of
France, with several of the Duke of Guienne's servants and
others, earnestly desired a war between those two great
princes, rather than peace, and that for two reasons:—The
first was, that they were afraid their great revenues would be
lessened, if the peace should continue; for the constable had
400 men-at-arms or lances, paid every muster, without any
comptroller, and above 30,000 francs a-year, besides the
salary of his office, and the profits of several good places
which he had in his possession. The other was, because they
had observed and talked among themselves, that the nature
of the king was such, that unless he was at war with some
foreign prince, he would certainly find some quarrel or other
at home with his servants, domestics, and officers; for his
mind must always be working. Prompted by these specious
arguments, they endeavoured to persuade the king to commence the war; and the constable promised to take St. Quentin
whenever he pleased, for his lands lay near it; and he boasted
much of his great intelligence in Brabant and Flanders, and

* The peace was published at Paris on Saturday, November 19, 1468.
See Lenglet, ii. 78.

that he could induce several of those towns to revolt against the Duke of Burgundy.

The Duke of Guienne being of the same opinion, all his principal governors offered the king their services, and promised him to bring along with them 400 or 500 men-at-arms, whom the Duke of Guienne kept constantly in pay ; but their design was not as the king took it, but quite contrary, as you will see hereafter.

The king was always wont to proceed gravely and solemnly in all actions of importance, and therefore he convoked the three Estates at Tours in the months of March and April, 1470 * (a thing which he had never done before†, nor ever did afterwards), but he summoned only such persons as he thought would not oppose his designs.   In this assembly he complained of several of the Duke of Burgundy's enterprises and practices against his crown; he ordered the Count d'Eu to bring in a complaint against the duke for detaining from him St. Vallery and other towns belonging to the jurisdiction of Abbeville and the county of Ponthieu, without giving the Count d'Eu any reason or satisfaction; pretending only he did it by way of reprisals for a merchant-man of Flanders, which had been taken by a small man-of-war belonging to Eu; for which the Count d'Eu offered to make reparation. Besides, the Duke of Burgundy wished to oblige the Count d'Eu to do him homage, and swear fealty to him against all persons whatever; which he would never consent to do, it being against the honour and authority of the king.   In this assembly there were present several lawyers, as well of the parliament as elsewhere; by all of whom it was concluded, ac-

* The declaration of Louis XI. against the Duke of Burgundy, dated December 3. 1470, was the result of all the deliberations of this assembly. After enumerating all his grievances against the duke, and declaring that he would no longer tolerate his outrageous conduct, " we have," he says, " in order to proceed in so great a matter with mature and due deliberation, assembled in our city of Tours, certain of the princes and lords of our blood, prelates, counts, barons, and other nobles, and notable members of our council."   The opinion of this assembly was, that the king was free and discharged from the promises he had made to the Duke of Burgundy by the treaty of Peronne and other treaties, and that the lands and lordships of the duke should be confiscated to him. Lenglet, iii. 68.

† Commines is in error on this point. The Estates had met at Tours in 1467, from the 6th to the 14th of April.   See Lenglet, ii. 71.

cording to the intention of the king, that a day should be appointed, and the Duke of Burgundy summoned to appear in person before the Parliament at Paris. The king knew very well his answer would be insolent, or that he would do something or other against the authority of that court, which would give him a more plausible pretence of declaring war against him.

The Duke of Burgundy received his summons in Ghent from the hands of one of the officers of the Parliament, as he was going to mass; he was much surprised, and highly offended at it, and ordered the officer to be taken into custody, where he remained several days, but at length he was dismissed.

You see the measures that were concerted for the invasion of the Duke of Burgundy's territories; who, having intelligence of it, immediately enlisted great numbers of men, but at half-pay (as they called it), who were to be ready in arms at their houses upon the first summons. However, they were mustered constantly once a month, and received their pay.

In this posture affairs continued for three or four months; but the duke growing weary of the expense, disbanded his soldiers; for the king having sent several embassies to him, he began to think the storm was blown over, and retired into Holland. He had now no soldiers in pay, ready to be employed upon any occasion, nor garrisons in his frontier towns, which was greatly to his disadvantage, by reason of the designs on foot for bringing over Amiens, Abbeville, and St. Quentin to the king. While the Duke of Burgundy was in Holland, John, late Duke of Bourbon[*], gave him notice, that in a short time a war would break out against him, as well in Burgundy as Picardy, for the king had great intelligence both in those provinces and in his household. The Duke of Burgundy being wholly unprovided with troops (having disbanded his army, as I said before), was much alarmed at this news; upon which he passed immediately into Artois by sea, and went straight to Hesdin.[†] There he began to find out the secret intrigues of some of his

---

* He died in 1488. See note, book i. chap. 2.

† The duke arrived at Hesdin on the 2nd of August, 1470, and remained there five months and a half.

officers, and the transactions which were being managed privately in the above-mentioned towns. At first he could not be persuaded of the truth of it, so that it was some time before he would be convinced of their treachery; but at length he sent for two of the principal citizens of Amiens, whom he suspected to have a hand in those secret negotiations; yet they excused themselves so handsomely, that he suffered them to depart. Not long after this some of the duke's household revolted from him, and went over to the king, as the Bastard Baudouin*, and several others†; which made him fearful lest more should follow their example. To prevent the worst, he issued a proclamation, requiring all his people to be immediately in arms; but few obeyed it, for winter was approaching, and the duke had not been many days arrived from Holland.

Ch. II. — Of the Delivering up the Towns of St. Quentin and Amiens to the King; and upon what grounds the Constable and others fomented the War between the King and the Duke of Burgundy. — 1471.

Two days after the Duke of Burgundy's servants had deserted him (which was in December, 1470), the Constable of France entered St. Quentin ‡, and forced the inhabitants to take an oath of fidelity to the king. Then the duke began to discern the ill posture of his affairs; for he had sent all his officers to raise men in his own countries. However, with those few he could get together, and about 400 or 500 horse, he marched to Dourlans §, intending to secure Amiens,

* Baudoin, Bastard of Burgundy, knight, councillor and chamberlain of Duke Philip, was Lord of Falais, Bredain and Sommerdyk. He was a natural son of Philip the Good, by Catherine de Ticsferies. He died in 1508.

† The others were, Jean Darsson, pantler to Duke Charles, and Jean de Chassa, his chamberlain; who, with the Bastard Baudoin, were accused of entertaining designs against the duke's life.

‡ On the 10th of December, 1470. Lenglet, ii. 88.

§ He arrived at Doullens on the 17th of January, 1471, and remained there until the 3rd of February.

and keep it from revolting ; but he had not been there many days before Amiens began to treat, for the king's army being not far off, invested the town, but was refused entrance for some time, because there was still a small party left in it for the duke, who had sent his quarter-master thither, and if he had had a sufficient number of troops with him to have entered in person, that town had never been lost; but with the small brigade he had, he durst not venture himself in it, though he was much pressed by several of the townsmen.

As soon as those of the king's party perceived he was afraid, and not strong enough to trust himself in the town, they put their plans in execution, and received a garrison of the king's troops. *   Those of Abbeville intended to have done the same, but the Lord des Cordes got in for the duke, and prevented their design.   From Amiens to Dourlans is but five short leagues † ; so that upon the news that Amiens had declared for the king, the Duke of Burgundy was forced to retire with great precipitation and alarm to Arras ‡, fearing lest other places should do the like, and seeing himself surrounded by the friends and relations of the constable. Besides, the revolt of the Bastard Baudouin made him entertain a jealousy of the great Bastard of Burgundy, his natural brother.   However, by degrees, troops came in to him; and the king now thought himself master of his designs, for he believed whatever the constable and the rest had told him of their intelligences all over the Duke of Burgundy's dominions ; and had it not been in hopes it would have proved true, that enterprise had never been undertaken.

But it is now high time for me to declare what it was that moved the constable, the Duke of Guienne, and their principal ministers (notwithstanding the many good offices, the supplies, and honourable dealing which the Duke of Guienne had received from the Duke of Burgundy), and what advantage they proposed to themselves by fomenting the war

* The town of Amiens surrendered to the Count of Commartin, Grand Master of France, and lieutenant of the king, on the 31st of January, 1471.

† The distance between Amiens and Doullens is 33 kilometers, about 21 miles.

‡ He arrived at Arras on the 5th of February, and remained there until the 10th.   Lenglet, ii. 197.

between these two great princes, who were then in peace in their several provinces. I have said something of it before, that it was to secure their pensions and employments, lest the king, having no wars abroad, should either take them away, or retrench them. But this was not the chief cause. The Duke of Guienne and his party had passionately desired a match between him and the sole daughter* and heiress of the Duke of Burgundy (for the Duke of Burgundy had no sons.) The Duke of Burgundy had been often solicited in this business, and always gave them hopes, but would never suffer it to be concluded, and indeed entertained propositions from other persons.† It is worth our observation to consider what artifices these persons used to arrive at their designs, and force the duke to give his daughter to the Duke of Guienne. As soon as those two towns had revolted, and the Duke of Burgundy was returned to Arras (where he was raising what forces he could), the Duke of Guienne sent an envoy privately to him, with only three lines under his own hand (folded as close as was possible, and made up in a piece of soft wax) containing these words, "Endeavour what you can to reconcile yourself to your subjects; for other things take no care; for you will be sure to find friends enough."

The Duke of Burgundy, who at first was extremely alarmed, immediately despatched a messenger to the constable, to entreat him that he would not pursue his advantages, and do him so much mischief as he knew was in his power, since the war was begun without any proclamation. The constable was not a little pleased with this message, supposing he had the Duke of Burgundy now at his beck, and could manage him as he pleased: he returned him this answer, that he was sensible his affairs were in very great danger, and that he knew but one remedy left, which was to marry his daughter to the Duke of Guienne;

---

* Mary of Burgundy, daughter of Charles the Bold and Isabel of Bourbon, was born on the 13th of February, 1457, married the Archduke Maximilian on the 20th of August, 1477, and died on the 27th of March, 1482.

† Mary was successively promised by her father: 1. to Nicholas, Duke of Calabria; 2. to Philibert, Duke of Savoy; 3. to the Archduke Maximilian; 4. to the Duke of Berry; and 5. to the Dauphin Charles.

for by so doing he would be abundantly supplied with men,
and the Duke of Guienne and several other great lords
would declare for him, and he himself would deliver up St.
Quentin, and become of their party; but without the consummation of that marriage, nothing was to be expected; for
the king was very powerful, had his affairs well managed,
and held great intelligence in the whole territory of Burgundy.
He also made use of several other expressions to augment the
duke's fears. I never knew any man come to a good end
that took pleasure in frightening his master, or keeping him
in subjection, or indeed any other great prince whom he had
occasion to treat with, as you shall see afterwards in the example of the constable; for though the king was his master
at that time, yet his children, and the greatest part of his
estate, lay in the Duke of Burgundy's dominions. However,
it was always his method, by making them afraid of one
another, to keep both of them in awe; which at last fell
heavy upon himself. And as it is natural for all people
to endeavour to free themselves from fear and subjection,
and often hate those that keep them in that bondage, so
none do it with more eagerness and revenge than princes,
of whom I never knew any that did not pursue, with a
mortal and implacable hatred, all who attempted to use them
so.

After the delivery of the constable's answer to the Duke
of Burgundy, he found nothing of friendship was to be expected from him, but that he was the contriver and principal
manager of the war; upon which he conceived a mortal
hatred for him, which could never after be extinguished,
especially when he reflected that his remonstrances of danger
tended to no other end, but to constrain him to the marriage
of his daughter. In the meantime the Duke of Burgundy
had recollected himself in some measure, and assembled a
considerable army. By the messages which were sent, first
from the Duke of Guienne, and afterwards from the constable, it is plain the whole business was premeditated; for,
not long after, the Duke of Bretagne wrote to him in the
same, or more terrible language; and suffered the Lord of
Lescut to put himself into the king's service, with 100
of his Breton men-at-arms; so that it may be easily concluded this war was undertaken to force the Duke of Bur-

gundy to consent to that match. The king was deceived when he was put upon it; and the story of their intelligence in the Duke of Burgundy's country was utterly, or to a great extent, false. However, during this whole expedition, the king was served faithfully by the constable, who mortally hated the Duke of Burgundy, because he knew that the duke had no affection for him. The Duke of Guienne also served the king very honestly in this war, with a considerable body of troops, and the Duke of Burgundy's affairs were in a dangerous condition; yet if, in the beginning of this rupture, the duke (as I said before) would have consented to the marriage of her daughter with the Duke of Guienne, all the above-mentioned great lords would have abandoned the king, and employed all their power and interest against him; but it is in vain for man to determine in these cases, for God Almighty ever executes as he pleases.

Cн. III.— How the Duke of Burgundy took Picquigny ; and the means he found out to make a Truce with the King for a Year, to the great Dissatisfaction of the Constable of France. — 1471.

You have already been sufficiently informed of the motives of this war, and that the two princes were at first deluded, and invaded one another without understanding the true grounds of the quarrel ; which is a convincing argument of the marvellous subtilty of those that managed that affair, and confirms the old saying, That one half of the world does not know what the other is doing. But all these passages which I have mentioned happened in a very little space of time ; for, in less than a fortnight after the taking of Amiens, the Duke of Burgundy took the field near Arras (for he retired no farther), and marched afterwards towards the Somme, directly to Picquigny. As he was upon his march, a messenger (no better than a footman) came to him from the Duke of Bretagne, who told him from his master, that the king had acquainted him with much of his affairs, and among the rest, that he had considerable parties in several of his great towns, naming Antwerp, Bruges and Brussels : he gave him

notice, also, that the king designed to besiege him wherever
he should find him, though it were in Ghent itself.   I am of
opinion that this message was intended only in favour of the
Duke of Guienne, and to further the match.   But the Duke
of Burgundy was highly displeased at this information, and
told the messenger immediately, that his master was misinformed, and that it was only some bad courtiers about him
who had filled his imagination with those jealousies and apprehensions, solely with a design to deprive him of the
supplies which by his alliance he was obliged to send him ;
and that as to the town of Ghent, and the rest which he
mentioned, he was misinformed, for they were too large to be
besieged ; that he should undeceive his master, letting him
know how he found him attended, and that he was now
marching to pass the River Somme, and was resolved to fight
the King of France, if he endeavoured to interrupt the
course of his arms.   He desired him, therefore, that he would
entreat the duke his master, from him, to declare himself
immediately against the king, and that he would show himself no otherwise to the Duke of Burgundy than the Duke of
Burgundy had expressed himself towards him in the treaty
of Peronne.

The Duke of Burgundy arrived the next day with his army
near a town (strongly seated upon the Somme) called Picquigny. * His design was to lay a bridge thereabouts over the
river, and pass it with his army ; but there being by accident
at that time 400 or 500 archers, and some few of the nobility
in the town, they resolved to march out, and dispute the
passage with him.   They sallied out upon a long causeway
to engage him, and advanced so far, that, being repulsed,
their distance from the town gave the duke's men an opportunity of pursuing them ; and they did it so effectually, that
they killed a great number of them before they could recover
their works, and possessed themselves of the suburbs at the
end of the causeway.   The Duke of Burgundy immediately

---

* On the 23rd of February, 1471, the duke encamped at Winencourt,
near Picquigny, and on the 24th at Belloy : his vanguard took the town
of Picquigny, which was immediately set on fire, and in the evening the
castle surrendered on composition.   The Castle of Picquigny is now a
picturesque ruin, overlooking the town : in former times a stone stood
there to commemorate its capture by the Duke of Burgundy.

planted four or five great guns to batter the town (though the town was impregnable on that side, because of the river's running between them): however, the archers, observing that their bridge was almost finished, and expecting to be besieged as soon as the enemy had passed the river, abandoned the town, and marched away in great confusion. The castle held out two or three days, but the garrison was forced at last to surrender, and march away without their arms.

This little action revived the Duke of Burgundy's courage, so that he encamped about Amiens*, and pitched his tents in two or three several places, giving out that he kept the field, to see if the king would venture a battle with him. At length he approached so near, that his artillery fired into and over the town; and in that camp he continued for six weeks together. There were in the town 1400 of the king's men-at-arms, and 4000 frank-archers, and with them the constable, with all the great lords of France, as the grand-master, the admiral, the marshal, the seneschals, and a great number of persons of quality besides. In the meantime the king was at Beauvais, where he assembled a great army. The king was attended by his brother the Duke of Guienne, Duke Nicholas of Calabria † (eldest son of Duke John of Calabria and Lorraine, sole heir of the house of Anjou), and by the rest of the nobility of his kingdom, assembled by virtue of the arriere-ban; who, as I have been since informed, had a great curiosity at that time to find out the intrigue and mystery of this expedition, for they saw his business was far from being done, and that he was deeper engaged in war than ever he was before.

Those who were in Amiens had a design to sally out and attack the Duke of Burgundy's army, if the king would have

---

* On the 6th of March, 1471, he encamped at Mez, near Amiens; on the 10th, he advanced to the Abbey of St. Acheul; and on the 27th, he encamped in the Valley of the Cross, close to Amiens. Lenglet, ii. 198.

† Nicholas, Duke of Calabria and Lorraine, was born in 1448. He was the son of John of Calabria and Mary of Bourbon. He succeeded his father in 1470, and died, unmarried, on the 24th of July, 1473. Anne, the daughter of Louis XI., had been betrothed to him from her cradle; but, probably from the hope of espousing Mary of Burgundy, he renounced that alliance, although he had twice received the dowry of his intended bride.

advanced, and joined them with the forces which he had at Beauvais. But the king, having notice of their design, sent express orders to forbid it ; for though, in all probability, this action was likelier to turn to his advantage than other-wise, yet it could not be attempted without manifest danger, especially to those in the town, for they were obliged to sally out of the gates ; and there being but two, and one of them very near the Duke of Burgundy's army, and their whole body consisting of infantry, if they had been repulsed, it would have been difficult for them to have made their retreat, and they would have been in great danger, not only of being cut in pieces themselves, but also of losing the town. In this posture of affairs the Duke of Burgundy despatched one of his pages (called Simon de Quingy, who was afterwards Bailiff of Troyes) with a letter to the king, only of six lines, but under his own hand. The letter was very humble, and in it he complained that he had been tempted to invade him upon other people's designs, and declared that, if he had been rightly informed, he was confident he never would have attempted it.

Meanwhile the king's army in Burgundy had fought and defeated the whole force of that country, and though the number of the slain was not very considerable, yet the victory was great; many prisoners were taken, and an abundance of towns besieged and carried by storm. The news of this defeat extremely surprised the Duke of Burgundy, who immediately caused a report to be spread in his army that his forces had won the battle. The king was highly pleased at the receipt of the Duke of Burgundy's letter, for the reasons above mentioned, and because he did not love to carry on tedious enterprises; he returned him an answer, and sent a commission to empower certain persons in Amiens to enter upon a truce. At first a cessation was agreed on for some few days only ; but at length, as I remember, they had one for a year *, with which the Constable of St. Paul seemed to be highly displeased : and without doubt (whatever some people may say or think to the contrary) the constable was the Duke of Burgundy's mortal enemy. Several treaties

---

* On the 10th of April, 1471, the king and duke made a truce for three months ; at the expiration of which term, another truce was made for a year.

and conferences they had, but never the least friendship
proceeded from any of them, as the event demonstrated.
Yet they continued sending one to the other, and endeavouring a reconciliation; the duke did it in hopes by this means
to recover St. Quentin, for whenever the constable entertained the least suspicion or fear of the king, he promised to
restore that town; and sometimes it proceeded so far, that, by
the consent of the constable, the Duke of Burgundy's forces
approached within two or three leagues of the town, in expectation to be received; but when they were to be admitted,
the constable's heart always failed him, and he sent them back,
which proved afterwards highly to his disadvantage.   He
had a strong opinion that, by the strength of his position,
and the great number of his forces (which the king had to
pay), he should be able to keep the king and the duke in the
same jealousy and discord as they were in at that time; but
his design was very dangerous, for they were both of them
too powerful and too sensible to be imposed on at that rate.

Upon the breaking up of these armies, the king retired
into Touraine, the Duke of Guienne into his own country,
and the Duke of Burgundy into Flanders; and affairs continued in that posture for some time.   The Duke of Burgundy called a general assembly of the Estates * of his
country, to whom he remonstrated the damage he had
sustained by not having a good body of men-at-arms ready
as the king had; assuring them that, if he had had but 500
men-at-arms ready to secure his frontiers, the king had never
undertaken that war, and they had continued in peace.   He
laid also before them the dangers to which they were still
exposed, and pressed very hard that they would allow and
pay him for 800 lances.   At last they consented to give him
a subsidy of sixscore thousand crowns†, besides all other
duties that they yearly paid him; neither was Burgundy comprehended in this grant.   But his subjects made great scruple,
(and for several reasons), to put themselves into such a state
of subjection as the kingdom of France was in, by reason of

* The three Estates of Burgundy met at Abbeville on the 22nd of
July, 1471; and on the 12th of August following, a report of their
proceedings was made to the town-council, at Mons.   Gachard, i. 225.

† This subsidy of 120,000 crowns was not raised until towards the
close of 1471.   Gachard, i. 225.

their standing army. And to speak impartially, their unwillingness was not without cause; for when he had once got 500
or 600 horse, he hankered after more, and attempted more
boldly upon his neighbours; the sixscore thousand crowns he
multiplied to 500,000, and increased his guards to such a
number, that at last they became a great grievance to his subjects. My opinion is, that guards, or standing forces, may be
employed very usefully under a prudent and judicious prince:
but when it is otherwise, or he happens to die, and leaves his
successors, children, the service in which their governors
employ them is not always safe or advantageous for either
prince or subject.

Notwithstanding these correspondences and truces, the
hatred between the king and the Duke of Burgundy rather
increased than diminished. The Duke of Guienne, upon his
return into his own country, solicited the Duke of Burgundy
very hard to marry his daughter; which proposal the Duke
of Burgundy did willingly entertain, and indeed so he did
whoever was proposed; so that I am of opinion he had no
mind to have a son-in-law, nor that his daughter should
marry in his life-time, but chose rather to keep her as a
d coy to allure princes to his party, and bind them to his
assistance; for he had so many and so great enterprises in
his head, as could not be compassed in one man's life.
Besides, to speak the truth, they were but little better than
impossible, for one half of Europe was not sufficient to
content his insatiable desire of extending his dominions.
He had courage enough to undertake the most difficult
enterprises, his body was capable of as much pains and
fatigue as was necessary; he was powerful in men and
money; but he was defective in judgment, and in the cunning management of his affairs: and if a prince be deficient
in that point, let him be every way as complete and as
nicely qualified for heroic actions as he will, it signifies
nothing; so that I look upon sense as proceeding entirely
from the grace of God. In short, he that could have taken
part of the king's qualities, and mingled them with the duke's,
might have made a perfect prince; for certainly the king
was much superior to him in judgment and management,
and the end sufficiently demonstrated it to all the world.

CH. IV.— Of the Civil Wars between the Princes in England, during the Difference between Louis XI. and Charles, Duke of Burgundy.— 1470.

In mentioning the preceding passages, I had almost forgotten to speak of Edward, King of England; for those three great princes, King Louis XI. of France, King Edward IV., and Charles, Duke of Burgundy, were contemporaries. I shall not here observe the method and order of writing which is usual among historians, nor name the years and moments of time when every action happened; neither shall I produce any examples out of history (of which you know enough, and it would be like talking Latin to monks). I shall only give you a plain account of what I have seen, known, and heard of these three great princes above mentioned. In my judgment, you that live in the age when these affairs were transacted, have no occasion of being informed of the exact hours when everything was done.

I have formerly * mentioned the reasons that prevailed with the Duke of Burgundy to marry the sister of Edward, King of England, and it was principally to strengthen his alliance against the King of France; otherwise he would never have done it, for the love he bore to the house of Lancaster, to which he was allied by his mother, who was Infanta of Portugal, but her mother † was the Duke of Lancaster's daughter; wherefore his kindness for the house of Lancaster was as great as his hatred to that of York. At the time of this marriage, the house of Lancaster was quite depressed, and of the house of York there was no great talk; for Edward, who was both Duke of York and King, enjoyed the peaceable possession of the kingdom. In the war between these two contending houses, there had been seven or eight ‡ memorable battles in England; in

---

* See book i. chap. 5.

† Philippa of Lancaster, daughter of John of Gaunt, Duke of Lancaster, and Blanche his wife. She married John, King of Portugal; and died on the 19th of June, or 18th of July, 1415.

‡ There had been twelve, viz., at St. Albans, in 1455; at Blotheheath, in 1459; at Northampton and Wakefield, in 1460; at Mortimer's Cross, Barnetheath and Towton, in 1461; at Hexham, in 1463; at

which threescore or fourscore persons of the blood-royal of
that kingdom were cruelly slain, as is said before in these
Memoirs. Those that survived were fugitives, and lived in
the Duke of Burgundy's court; all of them young gentlemen
(whose fathers had been slain in England) whom the Duke
of Burgundy had generously entertained before this marriage,
as his relations of the house of Lancaster. Some of them
were reduced to such extremity of want and poverty before
the Duke of Burgundy received them, that no common
beggar could have been poorer. I saw one of them, who was
Duke of Exeter * (but he concealed his name), following the
Duke of Burgundy's train bare-foot and bare-legged, begging
his bread from door to door. This person was the next of
the house of Lancaster; he had married King Edward's sister,
and being afterwards known, had a small pension allowed
him for his subsistence. There were also some of the family
of the Somersets †, and several others, all of them slain
since, in the wars. The fathers and relations of these
persons had plundered and destroyed the greatest part of
France, and possessed it for several years, and afterwards
they turned their swords upon themselves, and killed one
another; those who were remaining in England, and their
children, have died as you see; and yet there are those who
affirm that God does not punish men as he did in the days
of the children of Israel, but suffers the wickedness both of
princes and people to remain unpunished. I do believe,
indeed, he does not speak and converse with mankind as he
did formerly; for he has left them examples enough in the
world to instruct them; but you may see, by the sequel of
this discourse, and by reflecting on what you know besides,
that of those bad princes, and others, who cruelly and
tyrannically employ the power that is in their hands, none,
or but few of them, die unpunished, though, perhaps, it is

Banbury and Stamford, in 1470; at Barnet, in 1471; and at Tewkesbury, in 1471.

* Henry Holland, Duke of Exeter, was the son of John, Duke of
Exeter, and Anne, daughter of Edmund, Earl of Stamford. He married
Anne, sister of Edward IV., whom he divorced on the 12th of November,
1472. He was found dead at sea between Dover and Calais, in 1475.

† The Duke of Somerset was with the Count of Charolois at the
battle of Montlhery; and again, at Ghent, in 1469.

neither in the same manner, nor at the same time, that those who are injured desire.

But to return to King Edward. The greatest support of the house of York was the Earl of Warwick ; and the greatest partisan of the house of Lancaster was the Duke of Somerset. This Earl of Warwick, in respect of the eminent services he had done him, and the care he had taken of his education, might have been well called King Edward's father ; and indeed he was a very great man ; for besides his own patrimony, he was possessed of several lordships which had been given him by the king, some of crown lands, and some that were confiscated. He was made Governor of Calais *, and had other great offices, so that I have heard he received annually in pensions and that kind of profits, 80,000 crowns, besides his inheritance. By accident the Earl of Warwick had fallen out † with his master the year before the Duke of Burgundy's expedition against Amiens.‡ The Duke of Burgundy had indeed, in some measure, been the occasion of the breach between them, as he disliked the mighty sway and authority that the earl bore in England. Besides, there was no good understanding between them, for the Earl of Warwick held constant correspondence with the King of France our master. In short, about this very time, or a little before, the Earl of Warwick was grown so exorbitant in his power, that he imprisoned his master King Edward §, put the Queen's ‖

* He received this appointment immediately after the first battle of St. Albans, which was fought on the 23rd of May, 1455.

† The Earl of Warwick, finding that his influence with Edward was on the decline, excited insurrections in the north of England, in the hope thereby to regain his power. As one of his daughters was married to the king's brother, the Duke of Clarence, he made common cause with that prince, and they both betrayed Edward's confidence by marching against him with the troops which they had received orders to levy in his name. This was in March, 1470.

‡ On the 6th of March, 1471.

§ About the beginning of 1470, the king and the earl were nearly coming to blows, when an attempt was made to reconcile them ; while the king, trusting to these negotiations of peace, had relaxed his vigilance, the Earl of Warwick fell suddenly on his camp, and took him prisoner. Edward was conveyed to Middleham Castle, but speedily made his escape from captivity.

‖ Elizabeth Woodville was married 1. to Sir John Grey of Groby,

father * (the Lord Rivers) and two of his sons to death, and the third was in great danger (though all of them were great favourites of the king.) He also caused several knights to be put to death. For some time he used the king very honourably, and put new servants about him, hoping that he would have forgotten the old, for he looked upon his master as a very weak prince. The Duke of Burgundy was extremely concerned at what had happened, and privately contrived a way for King Edward's escape, and that he might have an opportunity of speaking with him: and their plot succeeded so well, that King Edward escaped out of prison, raised men, and defeated a great body of the Earl of Warwick's troops. King Edward was very fortunate in his battles, for he fought at least nine pitched battles (always on foot), and was always conqueror. The Earl of Warwick finding himself too weak to oppose King Edward, having first given instructions to his private friends what they were to do in his absence, put to sea with the Duke of Clarence, who had married his daughter †, and was then of his faction, notwithstanding that he was brother to the king; and carrying with them their wives and children, and a great number of forces, he appeared before Calais. There were at that time several of the earl's servants in the town, and one in the quality of his lieutenant, Lord Wenlock ‡, who, instead of receiving him, fired his great guns upon him. Whilst they lay at anchor before the town, the Duchess of Clarence (who was daughter to the Earl of Warwick) was brought to

who fell in the second battle of St. Albans, on the 17th of February, 1461; and 2. to Edward IV. She had two children by her first marriage, Thomas, Marquis of Dorset, and Richard. She married King Edward in 1465; and in 1486, was confined in Bermondsey Abbey, where she died some years afterwards.

* Richard Woodville, Earl Rivers, married Jacquetta of Luxembourg, widow of the Duke of Bedford, brother of King Henry V. He was taken prisoner in 1469, with his son, John Woodville, and conducted to Northampton, where they were both beheaded.

† Isabella, daughter of the Earl of Warwick, and Anne Beauchamp, his wife, was born at Warwick Castle on the 5th of September, 1451. She was married at Calais on the 11th of July, 1469.

‡ John, Lord Wenlock, Chief Butler of England, was appointed Lieutenant of Calais in 1470, and was killed at the battle of Tewkesbury on the 4th of May, 1471.

bed of a son *, and great entreaties had to be used before Wenlock and the rest could be persuaded to send her two flagons of wine, which was great severity in a servant to use towards his master; for it is to be presumed the earl thought himself secure of that place, it being the richest treasure belonging to England, and the best captaincy in the world (or at least in Christendom); and this I know, for I was there several times during their differences, and was told by the chief officer of the staple for cloth, that he would willingly farm the government of the town from the King of England at 15,000 crowns per annum; for the Governor of Calais receives all profits on that side of the sea, and has the benefit of all convoys, and the entire disposal and management of the garrison.

The King of England was extremely pleased, and well satisfied with Lord Wenlock for refusing his captain, and sent him a patent to constitute him governor, in the Earl of Warwick's room; for he was an old experienced officer, a wise gentleman, and of the Order of the Garter. The Duke of Burgundy was also well pleased with him for this action, and being at St. Omer†, he sent me to Lord Wenlock, to assure him of a pension of 1000 crowns, and to desire him to continue that affection which he had already shown to the King of England. I found him fixed and resolved to be so, and in the Hotel de l'Etape in that town, he swore solemnly to me, that he would serve the King of England against all opposers whatsoever; and when he had done, all the garrison and townsmen took the same oath. I was near two months going and coming to and from him, to keep him steady in his allegiance: but the most part of that time I was with him, the Duke of Burgundy was come to Boulogne, and had his residence there‡, in order to the setting out a great fleet against the Earl of Warwick, who, at his departure from Calais, had taken several ships belonging to the Duke of Burgundy's subjects, which was partly the occasion of the war between the King of France and him. For the Earl of Warwick's soldiers selling all their booty in Nor-

* This child probably died very young, for Dugdale makes no mention of him.
† On the 28th of June, 1470.
‡ He had been there ever since the 26th of July.

mandy, the Duke of Burgundy, by way of reprisal, seized upon all the French merchants who came to the fair at Antwerp.

Since it is as absolutely necessary to be acquainted with the examples of the deceit and craftiness of this world, as with instances of integrity (not to make use of them, but to arm ourselves against them), I shall in this place lay open a trick, or piece of policy (but, call it what you please, it was certainly wisely managed), by which you may understand the juggling of our neighbours, as well as our own, and that there are good and bad people in all places of the world. When the Earl of Warwick came to Calais, which he looked upon as his principal refuge, and expected to be received, Lord Wenlock, being a person of great prudence, sent him word, that if he entered he was a lost man, for all England and the Duke of Burgundy would be against him; besides, the inhabitants of the town would be his enemies, as well as a great part of the garrison, as Monsieur de Duras*, who was the King of England's marshal, and several others, who had great interest in the place, were hostile to him. Wherefore he advised him, as the best thing he could do, to retire into France, and not to concern himself for Calais, for of that he would give him a fair account upon the first opportunity. He did his captain good service by giving him that counsel, but none at all to his king. Certainly no man was ever guilty of a higher piece of ingratitude than Lord Wenlock, considering the King of England had made him Governor in chief of Calais, and the Duke of Burgundy settled a large pension upon him.

* Galhard de Durfort, Lord of Duras, retired to England in 1453, was made a Knight of the Garter, and appointed Governor of Calais. He was recalled to France in 1476, by Louis XI., and was killed in that king's service in Burgundy, in 1487. He married Anne, daughter of the Duke of Suffolk.

CH. V. — How the Earl of Warwick, by the Assistance of Louis, King of France, drove King Edward IV. out of England, to the great Displeasure of the Duke of Burgundy, who received him into his Countries. — 1470.

THE Earl of Warwick, who followed Wenlock's counsel, landed in Normandy*, and was kindly received by the King of France, who furnished him with great sums of money to pay his troops.   The Duke of Burgundy had at this time a great fleet abroad, infesting the king's subjects both by land and sea; and this fleet was so powerful, that none durst oppose it.   The king ordered the Bastard of Bourbon†, Admiral of France, with a strong squadron ‡, to assist the English against any attempt that should be made upon them by the Duke of Burgundy's fleet.   All this happened the season before the surrender of St. Quentin and Amiens, which was in the year 1470.   The Duke of Burgundy was stronger at sea than the Earl of Warwick and the king together; for at Sluys he had seized upon several great ships belonging to Spain and Portugal, and two Genoese vessels, besides many hulks from Germany.

King Edward was not a man of any great management or foresight, but he was of an invincible courage, and the hand-somest prince my eyes ever beheld.   The Earl of Warwick's landing in Normandy did not so much affect him as it did the Duke of Burgundy, who presently perceiving there were great transactions in England in favour of the Earl of Warwick, gave frequent information of it to that king, but he never heeded it; which in my opinion was great weakness, considering the mighty preparations the King of France had made against him, for he fitted out all the ships he could get, and well manned and victualled them, and ordered the English fugitives to be equipped.   By his management also a marriage

---

* Between Honfleur and Harfleur, in May, 1470.

† Louis, Bastard of Bourbon, a natural son of Charles I., Duke of Bourbon, by Jeanne de Bournan, was legitimated in September, 1463; he married Jeanne, a natural daughter of Louis XI., and died on the 19th of January, 1486.

‡ According to Chastellain, it consisted of "sixty fine and powerful ships."

was concluded between the Earl of Warwick's second daughter and the Prince of Wales*, which prince was the only son to King Henry VI. (who was at that time alive, and prisoner in the tower.)   An unaccountable match! to dethrone and imprison the father, and marry his only son to the daughter of him that did it.   It was no less surprising that he should delude the Duke of Clarence, brother to the king whom he opposed, who ought in reason to have been afraid of the restoration of the house of Lancaster; but affairs of so nice a nature are not to be managed without great cunning and artifice.

During the whole time of this preparation, I stayed at Calais to keep Lord Wenlock firm to his allegiance; but I could discover nothing of his juggling, though he had been at it for three months.   My business with him then was, to desire that he would order twenty or thirty of the Earl of Warwick's servants who were there, to depart the town; for I was assured the king's fleet, in conjunction with the earl's, was ready to set sail from Normandy, and if they should land suddenly in England, it might happen that those servants of the Earl of Warwick's might raise some tumult or other in the town of Calais, that he might not be able to appease, for which reason I was very earnest for their being turned out. Before, he had always promised me he would, but then he took me aside, and told me that he would keep the town well enough, but he had something else to impart to me, and that was, that I would acquaint the Duke of Burgundy, that if he desired to show himself a friend to England, he would advise him to employ his good offices rather in mediating peace, than endeavouring to promote war; and this he said in respect of the preparations which the Duke of Burgundy had made against the Earl of Warwick.   He told me farther, that it would be no hard matter to compass an accommodation, for that very day there was a lady passed by Calais into France, with letters to the Duchess of Clarence, and in them overtures of peace from King Edward; and he said truly;

---

* Edward, son of Henry VI. and Margaret of Anjou.   He married Anne, youngest daughter of the Earl of Warwick, and was killed in the battle of Tewkesbury, on the 4th of May, 1471.   His widow afterwards married the Duke of Gloucester, who subsequently ascended the throne as Richard III.

but as he had done with others, so the lady dissembled with him; for her business was of another kind of importance, which she accomplished at last, to the prejudice of the Earl of Warwick and all his party.

You cannot be better informed by any other person of the secret contrivances and subtle collusions which happened on our side of the water, than by me, especially as to the transactions of these last twenty years.

The secret affair to be managed by this lady, was to solicit the Duke of Clarence not to contribute to the subversion of his own family, by endeavouring to restore the house of Lancaster; that he would remember their old insolences, and the hereditary hatred that was between them, and not be so infatuated as to imagine that the Earl of Warwick, who had married his daughter to the Prince of Wales, and sworn allegiance to him already, would not endeavour to place him upon the throne. This lady managed the affair that was committed to her charge, with so much cunning and dexterity, that she prevailed with the Duke of Clarence to promise to come over to the king's party as soon as he was in England.

This lady was no fool, nor loquacious; and being allowed the liberty of visiting her mistress the Duchess of Clarence, she for that reason was employed in this secret, rather than a man. Wenlock was a cunning man, and shrewd enough; yet this lady was too hard for him, wheedled him, and carried on her intrigues till she had effected the ruin of the Earl of Warwick and all his faction; for which reason it is no shame for persons in his condition to be suspicious, and keep a watchful eye over all comers and goers; but it is a great disgrace to be outwitted, and to lose anything through one's own negligence; however, our suspicions ought to be grounded on some foundation, for to be over-suspicious is as bad the other way.

You have already been informed that the Earl of Warwick's fleet, with the squadron the King of France had sent to convoy him, was ready to sail, and that the Duke of Burgundy's navy lay ready at Havre to engage them; but it pleased God to order it so, that a great storm arising that night, the Duke of Burgundy's navy was driven by stress of weather, some into Scotland, some into Holland, and all of them dispersed; after which, in a short time, the weather

coming about fair for the Earl of Warwick, he took his opportunity, and sailed safely to England. The Duke of
Burgundy had sent King Edward word of the port where the
earl designed to land, and had persons constantly about him,
to put him in mind of taking care of himself, and putting
his kingdom in a posture of defence. But he never was concerned at anything,· but still followed his hunting, and nobody was so trusted by him as the Archbishop of York * and
the Marquis of Montague†, both the Earl of Warwick's
brothers, who had sworn to be true to him against their
brother, and all opposers whatsoever; and the king put an
entire confidence in them.

Upon the Earl of Warwick's landing‡, great numbers came
in to him; and King Edward when he heard it, was much
alarmed; and (when very late) he began to look about him,
and sent to the Duke of Burgundy to desire that his fleet
might be ready at sea to intercept the Earl of Warwick on
his return to France, for on land he knew how to deal with
him. The Duke of Burgundy was not well pleased with
these words, for he looked upon it as a greater piece of policy
to have hindered the earl from landing, than to be forced to
run the hazard of a battle, to drive him out again. The
Earl of Warwick had not been landed above five or six days
before the whole country came in to him, and he encamped
within three leagues of the king, whose army was superior
to the earl's (had they·been all true to his interest), and
waited on purpose to give him battle : the king was possessed
of a fortified village or house§, to which (as he told me himself) there was no access but by one bridge, which proved of

---

* George Neville, Chancellor of the University of Oxford, was created
Bishop of Exeter on the 25th of November, 1455, before he had attained
his twentieth year. He became Lord Chancellor of England in 1460,
and Archbishop of York in 1465 ; and he died on the 8th of June,
1476.

† John Neville, Marquis of Montague, married Isabella, daughter of
Sir Edmond Ingoldsthrop of Borough Green, and was killed in the
battle of Barnet on the 30th of April, 1471.

‡ About four months after their departure from England, in August,
the Earl of Warwick, the Duke of Clarence and their retainers landed,
some at Plymouth, others at Dartmouth and Exmouth, and thence
marched towards London.

§ Rapin states that Edward was at Lynn at this time.

great service to him; the rest of his forces were quartered in the neighbouring villages. As he sate at dinner, news was suddenly brought him that the Marquis of Montague, the Earl of Warwick's brother, and several other persons of quality, were mounted on horseback, and had caused their soldiers to cry, "God bless King Henry." At first King Edward would give no credit to it, but despatched other messengers to inquire, and in the meantime armed himself, and posted guards to defend the bridge in case of any assault. There was with him at that time a very prudent gentleman called the Lord Hastings*, High Chamberlain of England, in great authority with the king; and he deserved it, for though his wife was the Earl of Warwick's sister, he continued loyal to his king, and was then in his service (as he told me afterwards) with a body of 3000 horse. There was likewise with him the Lord Scales† (brother to King Edward's queen) besides several good knights and gentlemen who began to think that all was not well, for the messengers confirmed what had been told the king before, and that the enemy was marching boldly on, with a design to surprise him in his quarters.

It happened by God's grace that King Edward's quarters were no great distance from the sea, and some ships that followed with provisions for his army, lay at anchor with two Dutch merchant vessels hard by. King Edward had but just time to get aboard one of them; his chamberlain stayed a little behind, and advised his lieutenant and the rest of the officers to go in with their men to the Earl of Warwick, but conjured them to retain their old affection and allegiance to the king and himself; and then he also went aboard the ship with the others, which were just ready to set sail. It is the custom in England, when a battle is won, to give quarter, and no man is killed, especially of the common soldiers (for they know everybody will join the strongest side), and it is

---

* William, Lord Hastings, son of Richard Hastings, and Alice, daughter of Lord Camoys. He married Catherine, daughter of Richard Neville, last Earl of Salisbury; and was beheaded by order of Richard III. on the 13th of June, 1483.

† Anthony Woodville, Lord Scales and Earl Rivers, was the son of Richard Woodville and Jacquetta of Luxembourg. He married 1. Elizabeth, daughter of Lord Scales, and 2. Mary, daughter of Henry Fitz Lewes. He was beheaded in 1483.

but seldom that they are ransomed; so that when the king had made his escape, not one of his men was put to the sword. King Edward told me, that in all the battles which he had gained, his way was, when the victory was on his side, to mount on horseback, and cry out to save the common soldiers, and put the gentlemen to the sword, by which means none, or very few of them, escaped.

And thus King Edward made his escape in the year 1470, by the assistance of a small vessel of his own and two Dutch merchantmen, attended only by 700 or 800 men, without any clothes but what they were to have fought in, no money in their pockets, and not one of them knew whither they were going. It was very surprising to see this poor king (for so he might justly be called) run away in this manner, and be pursued by his own servants. He had indulged himself in ease and pleasures for twelve or thirteen years together, and enjoyed a larger share of them than any prince in his time. His thoughts were wholly employed upon the ladies (and far more than was reasonable), hunting, and adorning his person. In his summer-hunting, his custom was to have several tents set up for the ladies, where he treated them after a magnificent manner; and indeed his person was as well turned for love-intrigues as any man I ever saw in my life: for he was young, and the most handsome man of his time; I mean when he was in this adversity, for afterwards he grew very corpulent. But see now how, on a sudden, he is fallen into the calamities of the world! He sailed directly for Holland. At that time the Easterlings * were at war both with the English and French; they had many ships at sea, and were dreaded by the English, and upon good grounds; for they were good soldiers, had done them much prejudice that year already, and had taken several of their ships. The Easterlings at a great distance descried the ships which were with the king, and about seven or eight of them began to give them chase; but being far before them, he gained the coast of Holland, or rather something lower, for he put into Friesland, not far from a little town called Alquemare †, where he came to an anchor, and,

---

* Easterlings, in French *Ostrelins*, was the name given to the merchants of the Hanseatic League.

† Alkmaar, the capital of North Holland, distant about twenty miles from Amsterdam.

it being low water, the king could not get into the har-
bour, but ran himself as near the town as he could. The
Easterlings came as near him as they could possibly make,
and dropt their anchors, intending to board him the next
tide.

Misfortune and danger never go alone : the king's success
and his courage were now strangely altered. A fortnight before that man would have been looked upon as mad, who should
have told him, "The Earl of Warwick shall drive you out
of England, and in eleven days have the supreme power and
dominion in his own hands" (for it cost him no more time
to bring the whole kingdom to obedience). Besides, he
laughed at the Duke of Burgundy for squandering his money
in the defence of the sea, giving out, that he wished his adversary were landed in England ; but what excuse could he
make for himself after such a loss, and by his own fault,
unless this, "That I did not think it possible ?" and, if a
prince be but arrived to years of discretion, he ought to
blush at such an excuse, for it will not serve his turn. So
that this is a fair example for such princes as think it
beneath them to be afraid, or have a watchful eye on their
enemies, and are fond of such courtiers as flatter and indulge them in that opinion ; and think they are the more
valued and esteemed for it, and that it is a proof of their
courage and resolution to despise and laugh at danger. I
know not what they may say to their faces, but I am sure
wise men account such expressions great folly. It is honourable to fear where there is occasion, and provide against
it with all the caution imaginable. A wise man in a prince's
court is a great treasure to his master, if the one has liberty
to speak truth, and the other discretion enough to believe
him, and follow his advice.

By chance the Lord de la Gruthuse*, the Duke of Burgundy's governor in Holland, was at that place where and
when King Edward wished to land ; who, by some persons
put on shore, was immediately informed of his miserable

---

* Louis de Bruges, Lord de la Gruthuyse, Prince of Steenhuyse,
Knight of the Golden Fleece, was the son of Jean de Bruges and
Marguerite de Steenhuyse. He was created Earl of Winchester for his
eminent services to King Edward IV. ; and he died on the 24th of
November, 1492.

O

condition, and the danger he was in by reason of the Easter-lings.   The governor sent immediately to the Easterlings to charge them to lie still, and went on board the king's ship himself, and invited him on shore; whereupon the king landed, with his brother the Duke of Gloucester (who was called afterwards King Richard III.), and about 1500 men in their train.   The king had no money about him, and gave the master of the ship a gown lined with beautiful martens, and promised to do more for him whenever he had an oppor-tunity; but sure so poor a company was never seen before; yet the Lord de la Gruthuse dealt very honourably by them, for he gave many of them clothes, and bore all their ex-penses till they came to the Hague, to which place he safely conducted them. *   He then despatched the news of his arrival to the Duke of Burgundy, who was much surprised when he heard it, and would have been much better pleased if it had been news of his death; for he was in great appre-hension of the Earl of Warwick, who was his enemy, and at that time absolute in England.   The earl, immediately after his landing, had prodigious numbers of people flock in to him†; even the king's own party, some for love, and others through fear, submitted to him wholly; so that every day his army increased, and not long after he marched to Lon-don.   A great number of good knights and squires, who were in King Edward's interest, fled to the sanctuaries in London, and did the king good service afterwards; and this did the queen his wife, who, in great want of all

---

* King Edward arrived at the Hague on the 11th of October, 1470; and the Duke of Burgundy gave him 500 golden crowns per month for his support. Lenglet, ii. 196.

† The number of Warwick's partisans was very great, especially in London. He had obtained them, according to Oliver de la Marche, by three ways, which do honour to his ability, if not to his honesty. " The first, by flatteries, and feigned humility to the people of London, by whom he was much loved. Secondly, he was master of the five ports of Eng-land, where he allowed great injury to be done; and never, in his time, was justice done in England to any foreigner who had suffered loss; wherefore he was beloved by the English freebooters, whom he thus contributed to support. And thirdly, he kept the city of London on his side by always owing 300,000 or 400.000 crowns to different citizens; and those whose debtor he was desired his life and prosperity, that they might be paid their dues." La Marche, ii. 276.

things that were necessary, was there * brought to bed of a prince.†

Cᴄ. VI.—How the Earl of Warwick released Henry VI., King of England, out of the Tower. — 1470.

Tʜᴇ Earl of Warwick, immediately upon his arrival in London, went directly to the Tower (which is the castle), and released King Henry, whom long before he had committed thither himself. When he imprisoned him, he went before him, crying "Treason, treason, and behold the traitor!" but now he proclaimed him king, attended him to his palace at Westminster, and restored him to his royal prerogative, and all in the Duke of Clarence's presence, who was not at all pleased with the sight. Immediately he despatched 300 or 400 men over to Calais to overrun the Boulonnois, which party was well received by the Lord Wenlock, whom I mentioned before, and the affection which he had always borne to his master, the Earl of Warwick, was at that time very conspicuous. That very day on which the Duke of Burgundy received the news of King Edward's being in Holland, I was come from Calais, and found him at Boulogne, having heard nothing of that, or of King Edward's defeat. The first news the Duke of Burgundy heard of him was, that he was killed, and he was not at all concerned at it, for his affection was greater for the house of Lancaster than for York, and there were at that very time in his court the Dukes of Exeter and Somerset, and several others of King Henry's party ; so that he thought by their means to be easily reconciled to that family ; but he dreaded greatly the Earl of Warwick. Besides he knew not after what manner to carry himself to King Edward (whose sister he had married); and moreover they were brethren of the same orders, for the king wore the Golden Fleece, and the duke the Garter.

---

* She went to "St. Catherine's Abbey, say some, but others say to the sanctuary at Westminster."   Chastellain, 486.

† Edward V., born on the 4th of November, 1470.

The duke despatched me presently back to Calais, and a gentleman or two with me, who were of King Henry's party. He gave me instructions how I was to proceed with this new set, and pressed me very earnestly to go, assuring me the business required good service. I went as far as Tourneghem (a castle near Guynes), but durst venture no farther; for I found the people flying from the English, who had sent out a strong party to plunder and harass the country. I sent immediately to the Lord Wenlock for a passport; though before I used to go without any such thing, and was always honourably entertained, for the English are naturally of a free and generous temper.

This was a new phase of affairs to me, for I had never seen such mutations in the world before. That night I sent the duke word of the danger which hindered me from proceeding in my journey; but not knowing what answer I should receive from Wenlock, I did not say that I had sent for a passport. He sent me a signet ring from off his finger, commanding me to go on, and if I was taken prisoner, he would ransom me. He made no scruple to expose any of his servants to danger, when he thought it for his advantage; but I had well provided for myself by sending for a passport, which I received with very gracious letters from the Lord Wenlock, assuring me that I should have the liberty of coming and going as formerly. Upon these letters I went on to Guynes; where I found the captain at the gate, who presented me with a glass of wine, yet did not invite me into the castle as he was wont, but showed me great respect, and treated the gentlemen who were with me, who were of King Henry's party, very nobly. From thence I went to Calais, but nobody came out to meet me, as formerly; all were in the Earl of Warwick's livery. At the gate of my lodgings, and the door of my chamber, the people had made more than a hundred white crosses with certain rhymes underneath, signifying that the King of France and Earl of Warwick were all one; all which I thought very surprising. I sent, however, to Gravelines (which is about five leagues from Calais), requiring them to seize all English merchants and their effects because of all the mischief done us in their incursions into the Boulonnois. The Lord Wenlock sent to me to dine with him; I found him well attended, with a ragged staff of gold

upon his bonnet, which was the cognizance of the Earl of
Warwick; all the rest had ragged staffs likewise, but they
who could not be at the expense of gold, had them of cloth.
I was informed at dinner, that within a quarter of an hour
after the arrival of an express from England with the news,
the whole town had got this livery, so hasty and sudden
was the change; and this was the first time that I had ever
seen or considered such an instance of the instability of all
human affairs.

The Lord Wenlock made me many compliments, and some
excuses in behalf of his captain the Earl of Warwick, from
whom, as he told me, he had received many favours; but for
the rest who were with him, I never heard people talk so
extravagantly. ; Those whom I had looked upon as the king's
greatest friends, were the most bitter and invective against
him; yet I am apt to think some did it for fear, though others
spoke the real sentiments of their hearts. Those whom I formerly endeavoured to have turned out of the town (as being
servants to the earl) were now in great reputation; yet
they never knew of my ever having spoken anything against
them to the Lord Wenlock. I told them upon all occasions
that King Edward was dead, and that I had certain information of it (though indeed I well knew to the contrary);
I added, likewise, that if he were not dead, it was of no great
importance, for the Duke of Burgundy's alliance was with
the king and kingdom of England, so that this accident could
not infringe it; for whomever they declared their king,
should be so to us: and in consideration of such revolutions
in times past, they had put in these very words, " with the
king and the kingdom;" and we were to have four of the
chief towns in England as a security for performance of
these articles. The merchants pressed very hard that I might
be detained, because their goods had been seized at Gravelines,
and, as they pretended, by my express command. At
length we came to this composition, that they should pay
for, or restore, all the cattle which had been plundered;
for by agreement with the house of Burgundy they had
liberty to take what cattle they wanted, for the necessary
provision of the town, out of certain grounds that were
appointed, on paying a certain price; and for prisoners,
they had taken none. Hereupon it was concluded between

us, that the alliance which we had made with the crown of England should stand good, only we were to put in Henry instead of Edward.

This accommodation was extremely welcome to the Duke of Burgundy; for the Earl of Warwick was sending 4000 men over to Calais, to make war upon him, and furiously invade his territories, and no way could be found out to pacify him. But the great merchants of London (many of whom were then at Calais) diverted him from that undertaking, because it was the staple * of their wools, and it is almost incredible what prodigious returns they make from thence twice every year; there their wool lies till the merchants come over, and their chief vent is into Flanders and Holland: for which reason, therefore, they were very solicitous to promote this accommodation, and stop the forces which the Earl of Warwick was sending over. This treaty fell out very luckily for the Duke of Burgundy; for it happened at the same time that the King of France had taken Amiens and St. Quentin, and if he had been forced to have maintained war with both these kings at a time, he had certainly been ruined. He tried all the ways imaginable to pacify the Earl of Warwick; declaring himself of the house of Lancaster, and that he would do nothing to the prejudice of King Henry; and making use of such other expressions as he thought would serve his turn best.

In the meantime King Edward arrived at the Duke of Burgundy's court at St. Pol†, and pressed very hard for supplies to enable him to recover his kingdom; for he assured him of the great interest he had in England, and entreated him, for God's sake, not to abandon him, since he had married his sister, and they were besides brethren of the same orders. The Dukes of Somerset and Exeter violently opposed it, and used all their artifice to keep him firm to King Henry's interest. The duke was in suspense, and knew not which side to favour; he was fearful of disobliging either, because

* The staple of wool at Calais was established by King Edward III. Rapin, iii. 231.

† On Wednesday, the 2nd of January, 1471, the Duke of Burgundy left Hesdin and went to Aire, where he met the King of England. He remained there on the 3rd, and returned to Hesdin, after dinner, on the 4.h. Lenglet, ii. 197.

he was engaged in a desperate war at home; but at length he struck in with the Duke of Somerset and the rest of that party, upon certain promises which they made him, against the Earl of Warwick, their ancient enemy. King Edward was present at the place, and was much dissatisfied to see how unsuccessfully his affairs went on; yet they gave him all the fair words imaginable, and told him that all was but dissimulation, to keep off a war against two kingdoms at once; for if the duke were ruined, he would not be in a capacity to assist him afterwards, if he should be ever so inclinable to do it. However, finding King Edward bent upon his return to England, and being unwilling, for several reasons, absolutely to displease him, he pretended publicly that he would give him no assistance, and issued out a proclamation forbidding any of his subjects to go along with him; but privately and underhand he sent him 50,000 florins with St. Andrew's cross*, furnished him with three or four great ships, which he ordered to be equipped for him at La Vere † in Holland, which is a free port where all persons are received; besides which, he hired secretly fourteen Easterling ships for him, which were well armed, and had promised to transport him into England, and serve him fifteen days afterwards; which supply was very great, considering those times.

CH. VII.—How King Edward returned into England, where he defeated the Earl of Warwick in Battle, and the Prince of Wales afterwards. — 1471.

KING Edward set sail for England in the year 1471‡, at the same time as the Duke of Burgundy marched towards Amiens against the King of France. The duke was of opinion that the affairs of England could not go amiss for him, since he was sure of friends on both sides. King Edward

* Equal to more than 200,000 pounds sterling.

† Now Weer, or Ter Veere, a town in the province of Zealand, on the eastern coast of the island of Walcheren.

‡ He embarked at Ter Veere on the 2nd of March, 1471, and landed at Ravenspur on the 14th of the same month.

was no sooner landed, but he marched directly for London, where he had above 2000 of his party in sanctuary; among whom were 300 or 400 knights and esquires, who were of great advantage to his affairs, for he brought over with him a small number of forces.   The Earl of Warwick was at that time in the north with a powerful army, but upon the news of King Edward's landing, he marched back again with all speed towards London, in hopes to have got thither before him.   However, he presumed the city would have been true to him, but he was mistaken; for King Edward was received into the city on Maunday Thursday*, with the universal acclamation of the citizens, contrary to the expectation of most people, for everybody looked upon him as lost : and without dispute, if the citizens had but shut their gates against him, he had been irrecoverably lost, for the Earl of Warwick was within a day's march of him.   As I have been since informed, there were three things especially, which contributed to his reception into London.   The first was, the persons who were in the sanctuaries, and the birth of a young prince, of whom the queen was there brought to bed. The next was, the great debts which he owed in the town, which obliged all the tradesmen who were his creditors to appear for him.   The third was, that the ladies of quality, and rich citizens' wives with whom he had formerly intrigued, forced their husbands and relations to declare themselves on his side.   He stayed but two days in the town, for on Easter-eve he marched with all the forces he could collect to give the Earl of Warwick battle: the next day, being Easter-day, they met†, and as they were drawn up, and stood in order of battle one against the other, the Duke of Clarence went over to his brother King Edward, and carried with him near 12,000 men, which was a great discouragement to the Earl of Warwick, and a mighty strengthening to King Edward, who before was but weak.

You have already heard how the negotiation with the Duke of Clarence was managed; yet, for all this, the battle was sharp and bloody: both sides fought on foot; and the king's vanguard suffered extremely in this action, and the

* April 11. 1471.
† The battle was fought upon a plain near Barnet, between London and St. Albans, known by the name of Gladsmore Heath.

earl's main battle advanced against his, and so near, that the
king himself was engaged in person, and behaved himself as
bravely as any man in either army.   The Earl of Warwick's
custom was never to fight on foot, but when he had once led
his men to the charge, he mounted on horseback himself, and
if he found victory inclined to his side, he charged boldly
among them; if otherwise, he took care of himself in time,
and provided for his escape.   But now at the importunity of
his brother, the Marquis of Montague (who was a person of
great courage), he fought on foot, and sent away his horses.
The conclusion of all was, that the earl, the Marquis of Montague, and many other brave officers, were killed, for the
slaughter was very great.   King Edward had resolved, at his
departure from Flanders, to call out no more to spare the
common soldiers, and kill only the gentlemen, as he had formerly done; for he had conceived a mortal hatred against the
commons of England, for having favoured the Earl of Warwick so much, and for other reasons besides, so that he spared
none of them at that time.   This battle was bravely fought,
and on the king's side there were killed 1500 men.

The very day on which this fight happened, the Duke of
Burgundy, being before Amiens, received letters from the
duchess, his wife, that the King of England was not at all
satisfied with him*; that the assistance he had given him
was not done frankly and willingly, but as if for a very
little cause he would have deserted him ; and. to speak
plainly, there was never great friendship between them afterwards ; yet the Duke of Burgundy seemed to be extremely
pleased at the news, and published it everywhere.   I had
almost forgotten to acquaint you that King Edward, finding
King Henry in London, took him along with him to the fight.
This King Henry was a very ignorant prince and almost an
idiot ; and (if what was told me be true) after the battle was
over, the Duke of Gloucester (who was King Edward's
brother, and afterwards called King Richard) slew this poor
King Henry with his own hand, or caused him to be carried
into some private place, and stood by while he was killed. †

* Edward nevertheless wrote, on the 28th of May, 1471, a letter in
which he thanked the duke for the valuable and brotherly assistance he
had given him in his distress.   See Salazard, iv. 306.

† King Henry VI., says Hume, "expired in the Tower a few days

The Prince of Wales (of whom I have spoken before) had landed in England before this battle, and had joined his forces with those of the Dukes of Exeter and Somerset, and several others of their family and party ; so that in all (as I have been informed by those who were in that army) they amounted to above 40,000 men. If the Earl of Warwick had stayed till he had been joined by those forces, in all probability they had won the day. But the fear he had of the Duke of Somerset, whose father and brother he had put to death *, and the hatred he bore to Queen Margaret, mother to the Prince of Wales, induced him to fight alone, without waiting for them. By this example we may observe how long old animosities last, how highly they are to be feared in themselves, and how destructive and dangerous they are in their consequences.

As soon as King Edward had obtained this victory, he marched against the Prince of Wales, and there he had another great battle† ; for though the Prince of Wales's army was more numerous than the king's, yet King Edward got the victory ; and the Prince of Wales‡, several other

after the battle of Tewkesbury, but whether he died a natural or violent death is uncertain. It is pretended, and was generally believed, that the Duke of Gloucester killed him with his own hands ; but the universal odium which that prince has incurred, inclined perhaps the nation to aggravate his crimes, without any sufficient authority. It is certain, however, that Henry's death was sudden ; and, though he laboured under an ill state of health, this circumstance, joined to the general manners of the age, gave a natural ground of suspicion, which was rather increased than diminished by the exposing of his body to public view."

* The Earl of Warwick was not personally the cause of their death. Edmund Beaufort, Duke of Somerset, lost his life at the battle of St. Albans, on the 23rd of May, 1455, commanding the army opposed to that of which Warwick was the leader. The two sons of this Duke of Somerset, Edmund and John, were slain in the battle of Tewkesbury.

† This battle was fought near Tewkesbury, in Gloucestershire, on the 4th of May, 1471.

‡ "Queen Margaret and her son," says Hume, "were taken prisoners, and brought to the king, who asked the prince, in an insulting manner, how he dared to invade his dominions ? The young prince, more mindful of his high birth than of his present fortune, replied that he came thither to claim his just inheritance. The ungenerous Edward, insensible to pity, struck him on the face with his gauntlet : and the Dukes of Clarence and Gloucester, Lord Hastings, and Sir Thomas

great lords, and a great number of common soldiers, were
killed upon the spot, and the Duke of Somerset, being taken.
was beheaded the next day.   In eleven days the Earl of
Warwick had gained the whole kingdom of England, or at
least reduced it to his obedience.   In twenty-one days King
Edward recovered it again, but it cost him two great and
desperate battles to regain it.   And thus you have an account
of the revolutions of England.   King Edward caused numbers of persons to be put to death in many places, especially
those that were guilty of any confederacy against him.   Of
all nations in the world, the.English are most inclined to
such battles.   After this fight, King Edward enjoyed continual peace till his death, yet not without some troubles and
afflictions of mind ; but I shall forbear saying any more
about English affairs, till I can do it more conveniently in
another place.

Ch. VIII.—How the War was renewed between King Louis and the
   Duke of Burgundy at the Solicitation of the Dukes of Guienne and
   Bretagne.—1471.

THE place where I broke off relating our affairs on this side
the water, was at the Duke of Burgundy's departing from
before Amiens*, the king's retreat into Touraine, and his.
brother the Duke of Guienne's return into his own province.
The Duke of Guienne still persisted in his solicitation for
the marriage, to which he pretended, with the Duke of Burgundy's daughter, as I have already said.   The Duke of
Burgundy seemed to entertain it very kindly, and to be
pleased with his proposals, yet never suffered it to come to
any conclusion, but admitted of every new overture that was
made ; nor could he ever forget the stratagem they had made
use of to force him to consent to this match.   The Count of
St. Paul, Constable of France, had a great desire to be the
main instrument in this marriage ; the Duke of Bretagne
had also a design to be the principal manager himself ; and

Gray, taking the blow as a signal for further violence, hurried the prince
into the next apartment, and there despatched him with their daggers."
Commines says erroneously that he fell on the field.
   * On the 10th of April, 1471.

the king's* chief business was, if possible, to break it off.
But his majesty might have spared his pains, for the two
reasons which I have mentioned before; besides, the Duke
of Burgundy had no mind to have his son-in-law so powerful, but designed to make his advantage of his daughter, and
advance his own interest by entertaining everybody; so
that the king lost his pains.   But not being able to dive into
another man's thoughts, he had good reason to be afraid, for
by this marriage his brother would have grown very considerable, and, in conjunction with the Duke of Bretagne,
might have embroiled the king's affairs, and brought his
children into very dangerous circumstances.   In the meantime several ambassadors went both publicly and privately
to negotiate this affair.

The going and coming of ambassadors in this manner
is sometimes very dangerous; for many ill things are often
transacted by them, and yet there is necessity of sending and
receiving them.   Those who read this chapter may perhaps
demand what expedient I can propose to remedy this inconvenience.   I am sensible there are many persons better
qualified to treat of this subject than myself; yet this I
shall venture to say, that ambassadors who come from true
friends, where there is no ground of suspicion, ought, in my
judgment, to be treated with abundance of freedom and
openness; and, if the quality of the persons permit, should
be often admitted to the king's presence, provided the prince
be wise and affable, for otherwise the less he is seen the
better; and whenever he gives audience he ought to be
magnificently dressed, well prepared in his answers, and not
permitted to hold any long discourse, for the friendship between princes is not of long duration.   If ambassadors are
sent in a public or private capacity between princes that are
in continual hatred and war with one another, as all those
that I have known and been conversant with in my time
have been, in my opinion they are not greatly to be trusted.
However, they are to be honourably received and civilly
entertained; for to send to meet them, to lodge them in
handsome apartments, and to appoint honest and discreet
persons to attend them, is safe as well as civil; for thereby

* See the instructions given by the king to M. du Bouchage on this
subject, in Lenglet, iii. 160.

you not only discover what persons they generally converse with, but also prevent fickle and mutinous people from resorting to them with news, and there is no court without some mal-contents. Again, I would advise that they have their audience and despatch as soon as possible, for to me it seems dangerous to keep an enemy in one's house; but to feast them, to bear their expenses, and to make them presents, is but honourable.

Moreover, though war be proclaimed, no treaty nor overture of peace ought to be interrupted, for nobody knows what occasion they may have of them hereafter, but all should be carried on smoothly, and all messengers be heard as before; yet a strict eye is to be kept upon such as have any discourse with them, or are sent to them with any message either by night or day; and this should be managed with as much secrecy as possible. Were it my case, for one ambassador or message they sent me, I would be sure to send them two; nay, though they grew weary, and desired to have no more, I would not fail to send when I had opportunity and convenience, for there is no spy so good or so safe, nor who can have such liberty to pry and inform himself; and if you send two or three ambassadors at once, it is impossible the enemy should be so cautious, but that one or other of them may secretly or otherwise pick up something to serve their turn; I mean, if they carry themselves civilly towards them, as they ought to do to ambassadors. It is also to be supposed a wise prince will make it his business to place some friend or other about his enemy, and ward him off as long as he can; for in such cases a prince cannot do always as he would. But perhaps it may be objected, that this is but the way to puff up your enemy, and make him more proud. It is no matter if it does; I shall know the more of his councils, and at the making up of our accounts, the whole profit and honour will be mine. Though the enemy should have the same designs upon me, I would not forbear sending, but listen to all propositions without rejecting any, that I might always have fresh occasion to send; for all men have not an equal share of wisdom and penetration, neither have they as much experience in such affairs, nor is there any necessity that they should have; yet in this case, the wisest is always the most fortunate, and of this I will give you a clear and undeniable proof. Never was there any treaty between the French and the English, but the French always overreached them by their sense and ability, insomuch that, as I have been told, the English have a common proverb among them, That in all, or most, of their battles and engagements with the French the English had the better, but in all their treaties of peace they were juggled and outwitted. And certainly, at least in my thoughts, I have known politicians in this kingdom as proper to manage such secret negotiations as any persons alive, especially those of King Louis's training up; for in these cases the persons employed ought to be complaisant, and men who, to compass their master's designs, can digest words and overlook neglects; and such were for King Louis's turn. I have enlarged a little on the subject of ambassadors, and the caution that is to be used towards them; but it is not without reason, for I have known so many intrigues, and so much mischief carried on under that colour, that I could not forbear laying this matter open, or speak less of it than I have done.

This marriage between the Duke of Guienne and the Duke of Burgundy's daughter proceeded so far, that promises were passed, not only by word of mouth, but by letters; but the like was done also * by Nicholas, Duke of Calabria and Lorraine, the son of John, Duke of Calabria (whom I have mentioned before); as also by Philibert, Duke of Savoy†, who died lately; and afterwards by Duke Maximilian of Austria‡, now King of the Romans, and only son to the Emperor Frederick, which last received a letter under the lady's own hand (written by her father's express command),

* By letters dated June 13. 1472.

† Philibert, Duke of Savoy, son of Amadeus IX., Duke of Savoy, and Yolande of France, daughter of Charles VII., was born on the 7th of August, 1465, and succeeded his father on the 28th of March, 1472. In January, 1474, he married Bianca Maria, daughter of Galeazzo Marie Sforza, Duke of Milan; and he died on the 22nd of April, 1482.

‡ Maximilian of Austria, son of Frederick III. and Eleanor of Portugal, was born on the 22nd of March, 1459, elected King of the Romans on the 16th of February, 1486, crowned on the 9th of April following, and succeeded his father in 1493. He married 1. Mary of Burgundy, on the 20th of August, 1477; and 2. in 1494, Bianca Maria, widow of Philibert, Duke of Savoy. In 1489, he was contracted to Anne of Bretagne, but this match was broken off. He died on the 12th of January, 1519.

and with it a rich diamond as a present. These promises were made with all these princes in less than three years' time; and sure I am none of them would ever have been accomplished while he lived, at least by his consent; but Duke Maximilian (since King of the Romans) made his advantage of that promise, as I shall declare hereafter. I do not mention this with any design to reflect upon the Duke of Burgundy, or any other person I have spoken of, but only to describe things as to my own certain knowledge they happened; for I do not suppose that blockheads and inferior persons will give themselves the trouble of reading these Memoirs, but princes and other great statesmen may do it, and find some information to reward their pains.

Whilst this marriage was in agitation, new enterprises were still contriving against the king. In the behalf of the Duke of Guienne, there were resident at the Duke of Burgundy's court, the Lord d'Urfé, Poncet de Rivière, and several other officers of less note. On the Duke of Bretagne's part, there was the Abbé de Begar * (since Bishop of Leon), who acquainted the Duke of Burgundy that the king was endeavouring to corrupt the servants of the Duke of Guienne, and was in a fair way of bringing them over to his party, either by love or force; that he had already caused a castle † belonging to Monsieur d'Estissac ‡ (one of the duke's servants) to be demolished; and that he had begun several other things against him, and inveigled several of his domestics; from whence it might be reasonably concluded, that as the king had formerly dispossessed him of Normandy, after he had given it him by way of appanage, so now he would disseize him of Guienne.

The Duke of Burgundy sent several embassies to the king about these affairs, who replied, that his brother the Duke of Guienne was in fault, who by endeavouring to

---

* Vincent de Kerleau, Abbé de Begar, Chancellor of Bretagne, and councillor of Duke Francis II., was appointed Bishop of Leon in 1473, and made his solemn entry into his church on the 10th of June in that year. He died in 1476.

† The Castle of Coulonges, between Toulouse and Lectoure.

‡ Jean, Lord of L'Esparre, Baron of Estissac, was the son of Lancelot, Lord of L'Esparre, and Jeanne, Lady of Estissac. His son Geoffroi d'Estissac, Bishop of Maillezais, was one of the patrons of the celebrated Rabelais.

extend his territories, gave occasion to all those disputes;
and without that, he would not meddle with his appanage
in the least.   But here one may observe by the by, how
great the troubles and distractions of a kingdom are, when
they happen in a time of confusion and discord, how difficult
and uneasy they are to be managed, and how far from a
conclusion, when once they are begun; for though at first
the quarrel be only between two or three princes, or persons
of lower condition, before two years be expired, the whole
neighbourhood will be concerned and invited to the feast.
However, in the beginning of an affair, every man presumes
there will be a speedy end, but it is very uncertain, as you
will plainly perceive by what follows.

At the time above mentioned, the Duke of Guienne (or
his ministers) and the Duke of Bretagne, solicited the Duke
of Burgundy not to employ the English, who were enemies
to the crown, in any of his wars upon any account whatsoever; and since their own pretences were only for the ease
and advantage of the kingdom of France, they did not
doubt but that if his forces were in readiness, they should be
strong enough of themselves, by reason of the great intelligence which they had with many officers and governors of
towns.   I was present one day when the Lord d'Urfé
pressed the Duke of Burgundy to assemble his army with
all possible diligence; the duke called me aside to a window,
and said, "Do you see this Lord d'Urfé? he presses me very
earnestly to raise what forces I can, and tells me we shall do
great matters for the advantage of the kingdom.   Do you
believe, if I enter France with my army, I shall do them any
good?" I replied (smiling) that I thought not: he answered
again in these very words, "I love the kingdom of France
better than the Lord d'Urfé believes, for whereas they have
but one king, I wish they had six."

Whilst this treaty of marriage was on foot, Edward, King
of England (being deceived as well as the King of France,
in supposing it real), used his utmost endeavours with the
Duke of Burgundy to break it off; remonstrating to him, that
as the King of France had no son*, if he died, the crown
would devolve upon the Duke of Guienne, so that all Eng-

* This is an error; for Charles VIII. was born on the 30th of June,
1470.

land would be in danger of being utterly ruined by the consummation of that marriage, which would annex so many lordships to that crown; and he took this matter marvellously to heart, and so did his whole council (though without any cause); nor could all the Duke of Burgundy's excuses induce the English to believe him. However (for all the solicitation of the agent of the Dukes of Guienne and Bretagne to the contrary), the Duke of Burgundy had a mind the English should be concerned in the war; but it was to be done privately, as if he had known nothing of it; but the English were so far from embracing this opportunity, that they would at that time rather have assisted the King of France, so fearful were they, lest by this marriage the territories of the house of Burgundy should be annexed to the crown of France.

You see here (according to my design) these great princes thoroughly employed and surrounded with men of such wisdom and foresight, that their lives were not sufficient to accomplish half what they foresaw; and it proved so afterwards, for one after another, all of them died in a short space of time, in the midst of their anxieties and hurry, every one rejoicing and triumphing at the death of his companion, as a thing which he most passionately desired. Not long after, their masters followed them, and left their successors deeply involved in wars and troubles, excepting only our present king *, who found his kingdom at peace both abroad and at home; his father having provided better for him than he ever could or would have done for himself, for in my time he was never out of war till a little before his death.

About this time the Duke of Guienne fell sick; some were of opinion he was in great danger, others said he would soon recover of his illness. His agents in the meanwhile pressed the Duke of Burgundy (seeing the season was opportune) to take the field, and open the campaign, for the King of France had already assembled his army about St. Jean d'Angely or Saintes; and they prevailed so far,

* Charles VIII., son of Louis XI. and Charlotte of Savoy, was consecrated at Rheims on the 30th of May, 1484. On the 13th of December, 1491, he married Anne of Bretagne; and he died on the 7th of April, 1498.

P

that the Duke of Burgundy ordered his forces to rendez-
vous about Arras*, and then marched towards Peronne,
Roye, and Montdidier.   His army was very numerous,
and in better order than it ever was before; for it consisted
of 1200 standing lances, who to every man-at-arms had
three archers, all of them well armed, and well mounted;
besides, in every company he had ten supernumerary
men-at-arms, without reckoning the lieutenants or cornets.
The nobles of the country were likewise in complete
order; for they were well paid (the country being at that
time very rich), and commanded by notable knights and
esquires.

CH. IX.—How the final Peace which was negotiating between the King
    and the Duke of Burgundy, was broken off by the Duke of Guienne's
    Death and how those two great Princes laboured to circumvent one
    another.— 1472.

As the Duke of Burgundy was setting out from Arras, two
couriers arrived, one of them with news, that Nicholas, Duke
of Calabria and Lorraine, heir to the house of Anjou, and
son to John, Duke of Calabria, was upon his journey to his
court, in order to marry his daughter.   The duke received
him very honourably, and gave him great hopes of success.
The next day, which (if I mistake not) was the 15th of
May†, 1472, letters arrived from Simon de Quingy (who
was the duke's ambassador at the king's court), importing
that the Duke of Guienne was dead, and the king already in
possession of great part of his country.   Not long after, we
heard the news from several parts, but all gave a different
account of his death.
    The Duke of Burgundy, being highly concerned at the
death of the Duke of Guienne, at the instigation of other
people as much concerned as himself, wrote letters‡ full of

---

    * The duke was at Arras on May 16. 1472 ; at Peronne, June 9.; at
Roye, June 14.; and on the 25th of the same month, he encamped outside Maisnil, near Montdidier.
    † The duke died on the 28th of May.
    ‡ In these letters, dated from the camp before Beauvais, July 16.
1472, the duke accuses the king of having poisoned his brother by means

bitter reflections upon the king to several of the Duke of
Guienne's towns, but to no purpose; yet I am of opinion,
that if the duke had not been dead, the king would have
found work enough, for the Bretons were up in arms, and
had a stronger party in the kingdom than ever they had
before; but his death put a stop to all. In this violent
passion the Duke of Burgundy took the field, marched
towards Nesle, in Vermandois *, and began a more cruel
and barbarous war than ever before, burning and destroying all wherever he marched. His van besieged
Nesle, in which there was a small garrison of frank-
archers, but otherwise the town was of no great strength.
The duke himself had his quarters three leagues off. A
herald, coming to them with a summons, was slain by the
inhabitants of the town. The governor† would fain have
excused it, and having obtained a passport, came out to that
purpose, but could not agree upon the matter. As he
returned into the town, the garrison stood exposed upon the
walls, but there being a truce whilst the governor was
abroad, nobody fired upon the townsmen; however, they
killed two more of the besiegers. Upon which the truce was
broken, and word was sent in to Madame de Nesle, to tell
her, that if she pleased, she and her servants might have the
liberty of coming out, and bringing all her moveables with
her; which she had no sooner done, but the town was
attacked, taken, and most of the garrison put to the sword.
Those who were taken alive were hanged, except some
few whom the common soldiers in mere compassion suffered to escape; some of them had their hands cut off,
a cruelty which gives me concern to mention; but having
been upon the spot, I thought myself obliged to give
some account of it. It must be granted that the Duke
of Burgundy was highly enraged to be guilty of so barbarous an action, or that there must have been some
extraordinary cause that provoked him to it. Two were
alleged; one was, the strange report of the manner of the

of a friar named Jourdain Favre, and of Henri de la Roche, esquire of
his kitchen.
    * On Thursday, June 11. 1472.
    † "Named Le Petit Picard, who was captain of 500 frank-archers,
from the Isle of France, who were in that town." Lenglet, ii. 94.

Duke of Guienne's death, as if the king had been concerned
in it; and the other, the indignation he conceived at the loss
of Amiens and St. Quentin, which I have mentioned before.

Whilst the Duke of Burgundy was with the above-
mentioned army, and before the Duke of Guienne's death,
the Lord of Craon, and Peter Doriole*, Chancellor of France,
came to him twice or thrice, with proposals for a final and
lasting peace, which could never be compassed before, because the duke insisted upon the restitution of Amiens and
St. Quentin, to which the king would by no means consent:
but now, seeing the duke's preparations, and hoping it might
conduce to the following design, he agreed to restore them.
The conditions of peace were, that the king should deliver
up Amiens and St. Quentin, and whatever else was in
dispute between them; that he should likewise abandon the
Count of Nevers, and the Count of St. Paul, Constable of
France, with all the lands and territories belonging to either
of them, to be disposed of as his own, if the duke could get
the possession of them. On the other side, the Duke of
Burgundy was to renounce the Dukes of Guienne and
Bretagne, as also the protection of their countries, and to
permit him to act against them as he pleased. The Duke of
Burgundy swore to these articles in my presence; and the
Lord of Craon and the Chancellor of France having taken
the same oath in behalf of the king, took their leaves of the
duke, but advised him not to disband, but rather march forward
with his army, to hasten their master's surrender of the
above-mentioned towns; and Simon de Quingy was sent
with them to see the king take his oath, and confirm what
his ambassadors had done. The king delayed the ratification
of this treaty for some days, and in the meantime his
brother the Duke of Guienne died.

Soon after Simon de Quingy returned, being sent back by
the king with mild and courteous words, but no swearing to
the peace, which the duke highly resented, as a thing done
in scorn and contempt. Whilst the war lasted, for this and

---

* Pierre d'Oriolle, Lord of Loiré in Aulnis, was the son of Jean
d'Oriolle, Burgess and Mayor of La Rochelle, and Collette du Gue-
charrox; he was appointed Chancellor of France on the 26th of June,
1472, and resigned his office in May, 1483. He died on the 14th of
September, 1485.

several other reasons you have heard before, the duke's ministers made bold with his majesty, and gave him most bitter and reproachful language, and the king's own subjects did not dissemble the matter, but were very free with his character.

Those who hereafter may read these Memoirs, may think I have spoken very disrespectfully, and with too much freedom, of these two great princes, or that else they were persons of but small honour or faith. I would not willingly speak ill of either of them; and what great obligations I have to the king my master all the world knows. But to continue my history in the same manner (as you, my good Lord Archbishop of Vienne, have desired me) I am obliged to give an impartial and true account of what I know, which way soever it happened. However, were they to be compared with the rest of the great princes that reigned in Europe at the same time, they would appear noble and conspicuous, and our king very wise, for he left his kingdom enlarged, and at peace with all his enemies. But now let us observe a little what artifices and stratagems they used to overreach and circumvent one another, that in case any young prince, who has the same game to play, should hereafter accidentally meet with this history, he may, by reading it, be prepared, and defend himself the better; for though neither enemies nor princes are always alike, yet their affairs being often the same, it is not altogether unprofitable to be informed of what is past. To give then my opinion, I am very confident these two princes had the same desire of circumventing each other, and their ends (as you shall hear afterwards) were the same.

Each of them had a numerous army in the field; the king had taken several towns, and whilst the treaty was on foot, pressed his brother very hard. There were already come over to the king, of the Duke of Guienne's party, the Lord of Curton*, Patris Foucart †, and several others. The

* Gilbert de Chabannes, Lord of Curton, Baron of Rochefort, was the son of Jacques de Chabannes and Anne de Lavieu. He was councillor and chamberlain to the Duke of Guienne, and afterwards to the king, and was made Governor of Limousin in 1473. He died in 1493.

† Patrice Foucart was captain of forty archers of the guard of the Duke of Berry and Guienne, and chamberlain to that prince.

king's army had actually invested La Rochelle, and held great
intelligence in the town, which was much increased by the
report of the peace, and the Duke of Guienne's illness; and
I believe the king's resolution was (if either he succeeded
in his enterprise there, or his brother died) not to swear to
the peace; but, if the enemy got the better of him, he would
then swear, and keep his engagements, to deliver himself
from danger. In this manner he spun out his time, managed
all his affairs with wonderful diligence, and, as you have
heard, kept Simon de Quingy eight days together in suspense, and in the meantime his brother happened to die;
for he knew the Duke of Burgundy was so intent upon the
restitution of those two towns*, that he durst not be angry,
but might securely be wheedled for a fortnight or three
weeks, till he saw what he had best do; and so it fell out.

Having already spoken of the king, and the artifice he
used to overreach and circumvent the duke, now it is necessary that we should say something of the duke's designs
upon the king, and how he would have acted if the Duke of
Guienne's death had not intervened. At the king's request,
Simon de Quingy had a commission from the Duke of Burgundy (as soon as the king had sworn to the peace, and
letters confirming what his ambassadors had done, had been
received) to signify the contents of the peace to the Duke
of Bretagne, and also to the ambassadors of the Duke of
Guienne, who were in Bretagne, to the end they might notify
it to their master, who was then at Bordeaux; and this the
king proposed as a thing that would startle the Bretons,
since they found themselves forsaken by an ally who was
the main support of all their hopes. Simon de Quingy had
by chance in his retinue one of the equerries of the Duke
of Burgundy's stable, whose name was Henry, a Parisian by
birth, and a very sensible, intelligent person, to whom the
duke had given a letter under his own hand, directed to his
ambassador Simon de Quingy, but his instructions were, not
to deliver that letter till the ambassador had left the king,
and arrived at the Duke of Bretagne's court at Nantes.
Then he was to deliver the letter to him, show him his
credentials, and let the Duke of Bretagne know, that he had

* Amiens and St. Quentin.

no occasion to fear that his master would quit his alliance
with him and the Duke of Guienne, for he would still stand
by them both with his life and fortune; that what had been
already transacted was only to avoid war for the present,
and repossess himself of Amiens and St. Quentin, which the
king had taken from him in time of peace, and contrary to
his promise. He was likewise ordered to acquaint him,
that the duke his master (as soon as he should be possessed
of what he demanded) would send notable ambassadors on
purpose to the king, to desire and entreat his majesty to
desist from his enterprises against those two dukes; and
would not adhere too strictly to the oath he had taken; for
he was resolved to keep it with no more strictness than the
king had kept his in the treaty before Paris, called the
treaty of Conflans, and the pacification at Peronne, which
for a long time he neglected to confirm and ratify. He
designed likewise to put him in mind, that he had seized the
said towns in time of peace contrary to his solemn promise,
and therefore he ought not to be surprised if the duke had
taken the same measures to recover them.

As to the Constable of France and the Count of Nevers,
whom the king had abandoned, though he had a mortal
hatred against them, and not without cause, yet the Duke of
Burgundy would pass by all their injuries and affronts, if
the king would do the same by the Dukes of Bretagne and
Guienne, and suffer all parties to live in peace according to
his oath, and the treaty of peace at Conflans, where they
were all of them assembled together; protesting that, if he
refused, he should be obliged to assist his allies with all the
forces he could raise; and that the duke was actually in the field
when this embassy was despatched. But it happened otherwise. Man proposes, and God disposes; for death (which
divides all things, and defeats the counsels of mankind)
gave them other work to do; for the king (as you have
heard) did not deliver up the two towns, and yet seized
upon the duchy of Guienne, as rightfully reverting unto him
upon the death of his brother.

Articles of a Treaty between Louis XI. and Charles, Duke of Burgundy, whereby the Treaties of Arras, Conflans, and Peronne, are confirmed.   Concluded at the Castle of Crotoy, October 3. 1472.

1. That there is a firm and lasting peace concluded between the king and his kingdom, and us and our territories; and that all hostilities shall cease for ever between them and their subjects, &c.

2. That the said peace may be the better confirmed and established, and the friendship remain inviolable, the treaty made at Arras between the late King Charles and our late most dear lord and father, as also the treaty of Conflans, together with that of Peronne, are hereby confirmed as much as if they were expressly and word for word inserted, and shall remain in their full force, so far as they concern the king and the Duke of Burgundy. And all those points and articles of the treaty of Peronne, not yet executed, shall be fully accomplished, in the same way and manner, and within the same time, as is specified in the said treaty.

3. By this present treaty the king is to surrender to us, or those authorised by us, the towns of Amiens and St. Quentin, with the provostships of Vimeux, Foulloy, and Beauvais, with all their appurtenances, and whatever has been transferred to us by the treaty of Conflans and Peronne, to be employed by us in the manner prescribed by the said treaties. In like manner the king is to give up to us the towns, provostships, and territories of Roye and Montdidier, with their appurtenances; as also what was to have been taken from the provostship of Peronne. And as to those places, towns, castles, and fortresses in the duchy, county, and country of Burgundy, Charolois, Maconnois, Auxerrois, and Liege, which the king surrenders to us, we shall enjoy them with all their appurtenances, as we did before any contests arose about them.

4. As to all moveables possessed on either side, as also all rents, revenues, and profits, no disputes or law-suits shall be made concerning them.

5. The subjects on both sides shall be fully restored to all their lands, signiories, and inheritances, and all immoveables in the condition they are; as also such moveables as

are upon the spot, and arrearages of rents, and thus be put into the possession of them without any let or molestation.

6. All disorders and injuries done and committed during the war on either side are remitted, pardoned, and abolished, in such a manner as if they had never been, and no law-suit or process shall ever be formed concerning them.

7. Seeing both the king and we have, in the beginning of the troubles, forbidden all trade and commerce between our subjects, a free trade and commerce is now restored, both by sea and land, as before the war.

8. All judgments, judicial proceedings, and sentences, given on either side during the war against the adherents of the king or us, upon the account of contumacy or otherwise, shall be null and of no effect.

9. The allies of both parties shall be comprehended in this treaty, if within a year after the conclusion of it they signify their assent in due form, which assent or declaration the king and the duke are to notify to one another within two months after the same is made; but, in case that should not be done, there shall be no breach of the peace between them. The observance of all which we do oblige ourselves unto, in the most solemn manner imaginable, upon the word of a prince, and upon the forfeiture of all we have; and in case we contravene the same, we shall subject ourselves to all censures ecclesiastical: we shall also cause these presents to be registered in all our courts by our proper officers.

Cℍ. X.—How the Duke of Burgundy having encamped before Beauais, and finding he could not take it, raised the Siege, and marched with his Army to Rouen. —1472.

But to proceed in my relation of the war, of which I was speaking before. After the Duke of Burgundy's barbarous treatment of the poor garrison of Nesle, he broke up from thence*, and marched with his whole army and invested Roye, in which place there was a garrison of 1500 frank-archers, besides a considerable number of men-at-arms of the arriere-ban. The Duke of Burgundy's army never made

* The duke left Nesle for Roye on Sunday, June 14. 1472. Lenglet, ii. 95.

so fine an appearance as at that time; whereupon the next morning the frank-archers, being struck with a sudden fear, leaped over the walls, and surrendered themselves prisoners of war. The next day the remaining part of the garrison delivered up the town upon composition, leaving behind them their horses and arms, only the men-at-arms were allowed to march away with their horses. Having left a small garrison in this town, he advanced to Montdidier, with a full design to have demolished it quite; but, finding that the people of that district had a great affection for him, he ordered it to be repaired, and put a garrison in it.

From thence his design was to have marched directly into Normandy; but as he was on his way, near to Beauvais, the Lord des Cordes, scouring the country before him with his vanguard, made some attempt upon the town; and at the first attack, the suburb, which faces the bishop's palace[*], was taken by one Jacques Montmartin[†], a covetous Burgundian, who commanded 100 of the duke's lancers and 300 of his standing archers. The Lord des Cordes made an attack in another quarter; but his ladders were too short and too few. He had two pieces of cannon with him, which were fired twice (and no more) at the gate[‡], where they made a great breach; and if he had had ammunition to have continued his attack, he had certainly taken the town; but he was ill-provided, and not furnished for so great an undertaking. Upon our first investment there were no forces in the town but Loyset de Ballaigny[§], the governor, with some few of the arriere-ban; but that would not have saved the town, had not God himself interposed, and preserved it miraculously. The Burgundians were engaged with the French

---

[*] The Burgundians arrived before Beauvais on Saturday, June 27, 1472, and attacked the town in two places, at the Porte de Bresle, and at the Porte de Limaçon, behind the bishop's palace.

[†] Jacques, Lord of Montmartin and Loulans, knight, was captain of the archers of the guard of Duke Philip the Good. On the 22nd of January, 1454, he married Guigonne, daughter of Jacques Bouton. In 1475, he was one of the chamberlains of Duke Charles of Burgundy; and he subsequently became a chamberlain and councillor of Louis XI.

[‡] The Porte de Bresle.

[§] Louis Gommel, Lord of Balagny, was an esquire, councillor and chamberlain of Louis XI., Captain of Beauvais, and captain-general of the frank-archers.

hand to hand through the breach in the gate, and the Lord des Cordes despatched several messengers to the Duke of Burgundy to acquaint him that, if he marched up presently with his army, he would take the town. Before the duke's arrival, some of the inhabitants brought kindled faggots to throw in the faces of those who were forcing the gate; and so many were thrown, that the gate was set on fire, and the Burgundians were glad to retire till the flame was extinguished.*

The duke, upon his arrival, concluded the town would be his own as soon as the fire could be quenched, which was very great; for the whole gate was in a flame. If the duke could have been persuaded to have posted part of his army on the side towards Paris, no succours could have been thrown into it, and the town could not possibly have escaped. But it pleased God that he was afraid where there was no occasion; for it was only the passing of a small rivulet that made him scruple it then; and yet afterwards, when the garrison was considerably reinforced, he would fain have attempted it, though with the hazard of his whole army; and much ado there was to dissuade him from it. In the meantime the fire, of which I was speaking, continued burning all day long (which was the 28th of June, 1472). Towards night ten of the king's standing lances, and no more, got into the town, as I have been told (for at that time I was in the Duke of Burgundy's service); but they were not perceived, because on one side everybody was busy in taking up their quarters, and, on the other, there was nobody at all. By break of day the next morning the duke's cannon came up, and some time after we saw a reinforcement of at least 200 men-at-arms enter the town together. I believe, had they not arrived as they did, the town would have capitulated. But the Duke of Burgundy was in such a violent passion, that he was for storming it immediately; and certainly, if he had taken it, he would have burned it to the ground, which would have been a great loss; and truly I am of opinion it was preserved by a miracle. From the time the recruits entered, for fifteen days together, or thereabouts, the duke's cannon fired continually on the town; and the breaches in

* " Which fire was kept up more than a week afterwards, with wood from the neighbouring houses, to prevent the enemy from entering the town." Lenglet, iii. 207.

the town-wall were wide enough and fit for a general storm. However, the ditch being full of water on one side of the gate, which was burnt, a bridge was of necessity to be made; but on the other side of the gate we could make our approaches to the walls without any danger, unless it were from one casemate, which lay too low for our cannon to batter.

It is not only dangerous but imprudent to attack a town where the garrison is so strong. Besides (if I mistake not), the constable was in or near the town, I know not which, with the Marshal Joachim, the Marshal of Loheac, the Lord of Crussol*, William de Vallée†, Mery de Cohe ‡, Sallezard, Thevenot de Vignoles §, all of them old soldiers, with at least 100 men-at-arms of the standing forces, a good body of foot, besides many brave men, who accompanied them in the nature of volunteers. For all this the Duke of Burgundy resolved to storm it; but he was singular in his opinion; for there was not one officer in the whole army that agreed with him in it. As he was in his tent that night, and laid down in his clothes, he asked some who were about him if they thought that the town expected to be stormed? They answered "Yes," and that the garrison was strong enough to defend it, though it were fortified only with a hedge. Upon which the duke laughed, and replied, "You will not find a man there in the morning."

About break of day‖ the town was bravely attacked, but better defended. Our men pressing eagerly forward over the bridge, in order to mount the breach, the Lord Despiris¶,

* Louis, Lord of Crussol and Beaudiner, Grand Pantler of France, and Seneschal of Poitou, was the son of Geraud Bastet, Lord of Crussol, and Alix de Lastic. He died in August, 1473.

† Guillaume de Valée, Esquire, Lord of La Roche-Tesson, in Normandy, was captain of 100 lances, and lieutenant of the Seneschal of Normandy. His wife was Isabeau Tesson.

‡ Mery de Coué, Esquire, Lord of Fontenailles, councillor and chamberlain of the king, was Captain of the town and Castle of Amboise. He was lieutenant of eighty lances in August, 1470, when he signed the treaty of Ancenis.

§ Estevenot de Talauresse, surnamed Vignoles, Lord of Aussemont, was Bailiff of Montferrat in 1462, councillor and chamberlain of Louis XI., and Seneschal of Carcassonne. In 1473, the king gave him the barony of St. Sulpice in the diocese of Toulouse.

‖ On the 9th of July, 1472. Lenglet, iii. 212.

¶ Amé Rabutin, Lord of Epery, and Bailiff of Charolois, had been a councillor and chamberlain of Duke Philip the Good. His wife was Claude de Travers, daughter of Pierre, Lord of La Parcheresse.

being in the middle of them, was crowded to death.   He was
an ancient knight of Burgundy, and the bravest person that
was killed that day.   On the other side of the gate several
of our men got upon the walls, but some of them never came
back again.   They were at push of pike a great while together, and the assault continued a long time.   Orders were
given for fresh troops to march up, and relieve those that
had made the first attack ; but the duke perceiving they
would lose their time, ordered them immediately to draw off.
The garrison made no sally, for they saw us drawn up in order
of battle ready to receive them.   In this attack we had about
sixscore men killed (some say more); among whom was the
Lord Despiris, who was the only officer of any note that was
lost ; and the number of the wounded was full 1000.   The
next night after this they sallied out upon us ; but the
party being small, most of them on horseback, and their
horses incommoded by the cords of our tents, they did us no
great mischief ; for they had two or three officers killed and
wounded, and we lost but one of ours, whose name was
Jacques d'Orson *, a brave soldier, and master of the duke's
ordnance, who not long after died of his wounds.

About a week after this repulse, a fancy came into the duke's
head to divide his army, and post one part of it before the gate
towards Paris ; but he found none of his officers approved of
that design.   Upon his first arrival, indeed, it was practicable ; but now the garrison was so considerably reinforced,
that it was too late to be done.   Seeing there was no remedy,
he raised the siege †, and marched off in very good order.   He
expected they would have sallied out and fallen upon his
rear, and he had taken care to have given them a warm reception ; but they were too cunning for that.   From thence
he marched with his army towards Normandy, having promised the Duke of Bretagne to meet him before Rouen ; but
upon the Duke of Guienne's death he altered his resolution,
and stirred not out of his own territories.   The Duke of
Burgundy presented himself before Eu‡; and after taking

* Jacques d'Orson was a chamberlain of the Count of Charolois, whom
he attended at the siege of Audenarde in 1452.
† On Wednesday, July 22. 1472.   Lenglet, iii. 214.
‡ The duke arrived before Eu on the 28th of July, and remained
there until the 9th of August.

that town and the town of St. Valery *, he destroyed with
fire and sword the whole country to the very walls of Dieppe.
He also took Neufchastel, and burnt it, with the whole country
of Caux, or at least the greatest part of it, to the very walls
of Rouen, to which city he marched in person. In this
expedition he lost several of his foragers, and his army
was mightily distressed for want of provisions; so that,
winter drawing on, he retired. His back was no sooner
turned, but the king's forces retook Eu and St. Valery†,
by which seven or eight of the townsmen were left prisoners
at discretion.

Ch. XI.—How the King concluded a Peace with the Duke of Bretagne, and a Truce with the Duke of Burgundy; and how the Count
of St. Paul very narrowly escaped a Plot, that was laid for him by these
two great Princes.— 1472 — 4.

ABOUT this time (which was in the year 1472), I came into
the King of France's service, who had also entertained most
of the Duke of Guienne's servants: the king was then at
Pont de Cé, having assembled all his forces against the
Duke of Bretagne, with whom he was at war. At this
place arrived certain ambassadors from the Duke of Bretagne,
and others were sent in return to his court. Among those
who came in an embassy to the king, there was Philip des
Essars ‡, a servant of the duke's, and William de Soubs-
Plainville §, a servant of the Lord of Lescut, who, when he

* On the 30th of August, 1472.
† Eu and St. Valery surrendered to the king on composition. It was
stipulated by the first town, that the knights should have liberty to
depart, "each on a little nag; and all the other Burgundians, who were
in number more than 100, departed each with a stick in his hand,
and left all their clothes, property, and horses; and payed 10,000
crowns." The second town surrendered on the same terms, and paid
6000 crowns. Lenglet, ii. 100.
‡ Philippe des Essars, Lord of Thieux, son of Antoine des Essars,
was steward to the king in 1464, and afterwards filled the same office
in the household of the Duke of Bretagne. He died in 1478.
§ Guillaume de Soupplainville was steward to Francis, Duke of
Bretagne, Vice-admiral of Guienne, Bailiff of Montargis, and Lord of
Soupplainville and Villemandeur.

saw his master, the Duke of Guienne, past all hopes of recovery, embarked at Bourdeaux for Bretagne, whither he
retired, fearing lest he might fall into the hands of the king,
wherefore he made his escape early.   And he brought with
him the Duke of Guienne's confessor, and one of the
equerries of his stable *, who were suspected to have had a
hand in the duke's death, and were kept prisoners for it in
Bretagne for several years after.   These embassies forward
and backward continued not long, before the king determined to have peace on that side, and to behave himself so
handsomely to the Lord of Lescut, as to bring him back
again into his service, and make him forget his old animosity;
for the Duke of Bretagne had neither courage nor conduct
but what he derived from him; yet so powerful a prince,
with so cunning and wise a statesman, was not to be despised.   The Bretons themselves (while he was with him)
would willingly have accepted of a peace; and certainly the
generality of them desired nothing more, for there are constantly many of them in the kingdom of France in great
posts and reputation, and not without cause, for heretofore
they have done his majesty signal service.   Some persons
(whose judgment in state affairs was not so good as the king's)
condemned this accommodation; but in my opinion I think
his majesty acted very prudently.   He had a great value for
the person of this Lord of Lescut, saying, that he could commit any affair to his management without danger, for he
knew him to be a person of honour and integrity, and one
who in all the late troubles would never hold any correspondence with the English, nor consent that any towns in Normandy should be put into their hands, but still advised to
the contrary, which was the chief reason of his preferment
afterwards.

For these reasons he desired Monsieur Soubs-Plainville to
set down in writing what the Lord of Lescut his master's
demands were, both for the Duke of Bretagne and himself.
Soubs-Plainville did so, and they were these : For the Duke
of Bretagne, a pension of 80,000 francs: for the Lord of
Lescut, a pension of 6000 francs, half of Guienne, the two

---

* Friar Jourdain Favre, surnamed De Vercors, and Henri de la Roche,
esquire of the kitchen.

seneschalships of Lannes and Bordelois, the command of one
of the castles of Bourdeaux, the captainships of Blaye, and
of the two castles of Bayonne, of Dax and St. Sever, 24,000
crowns in ready money, the king's order of St. Michael, and
the countship of Comminges. All was granted and made
good ; only the duke's pension was retrenched to half the sum,
and that paid but two years. Besides, the king gave Monsieur
Soubs-Plainville 6000 crowns; but he did not pay the
ready money which I have mentioned both for his master
and himself, till four years after the agreement. Besides
which sum, Soubs-Plainville had an annual pension of 1200
francs, the mayoralty of Bayonne, the bailiwick of Montargis, and some other little offices in Guienne ; all which were
enjoyed both by him and his master during the king's life.
Philip des Essars was made Bailiff of Meaux, and master of
the waters and forests of France, with a present of 4000
crowns and a pension of 1200 francs. From that time to the
death of our master, they enjoyed these places ; and the
Count of Comminges acquitted himself like a loyal and faithful subject.

After the king had settled his affairs in Bretagne, he
marched towards Picardy. It was always the custom of the
king and Duke of Burgundy, as soon as winter drew on, to
make a cessation of arms for six or twelve months, and
sometimes longer. According to that custom, a new one *
was proposed, and the Chancellor of Burgundy, with ambassadors, came to negotiate it. The king showed the chancellor
the final peace which had been concluded between him and the
Duke of Bretagne, by which the said duke renounced his
alliance with the English † and the Duke of Burgundy ;
wherefore the king insisted that the Duke of Burgundy's
ambassadors should not name the Duke of Bretagne among
their allies ; but the ambassadors would not agree to it, but
urged that it might be left to his own choice to declare himself for the king or their master as he pleased, provided he

* This truce was concluded on the 3rd of November, 1472 ; it was to
last for five months, from the 3rd of November to the 1st of April
following.

† The treaty of alliance between the Duke of Bretagne and the King of
England had been concluded at Chateauguion on the 11th of September,
1472

did it in the usual time.   They remonstrated, likewise, that
the duke had formerly abandoned them under letters of his
hand, and yet not departed from their amity; adding, that
they did look, indeed, upon the Duke of Bretagne as a prince
who was guided more by other men's judgments than his
own: yet, in the conclusion, they observed, he always
recollected who was most necessary to him.   And all this
happened in the year 1473.

Whilst this treaty was on foot, both sides murmured loudly
against the Count of St. Paul, Constable of France.   The
king, and those who were nearest about him, had conceived
great hatred against him, and the Duke of Burgundy a
greater, with better reason, for I have heard the true causes
on both sides.   It was impossible for him to forget that the
Count of St. Paul had been the occasion of the taking of
Amiens and St. Quentin; and he shrewdly suspected that he
was the true cause and fomenter of the war between him and
the king; for during the cessation of hostilities he gave
him the best words in the world, but as soon as war began
again, he showed himself to be his mortal enemy; besides,
the count would have forced him to have married his
daughter, as you have heard.   The duke had also another
quarrel against him, and that was, that during the time the
duke lay before Amiens, the constable made an inroad into
Hainault, and, among the rest of his actions, burned a castle
called Solre, which belonged to a certain knight called
Baudouin de Lannoy.*   At that time it was not usual to
burn any places on either side: but, to retaliate upon the
constable, the Duke of Burgundy fired all that summer
wherever he came; so that, to be revenged of the constable,
both sides began to conspire against him.   In discourse
between some of the king's party and certain of the Duke of
Burgundy's courtiers, whom they knew to be the constable's
enemies, they happened to mention him; and all of them
agreeing that he was the occasion of the war, they began to
open themselves more freely, and discover all his expressions

* Baudoin de Lannoy, surnamed the Stutterer, Lord of Molembais,
Knight of the Golden Fleece, and Governor of Lille, was the son of
Gilbert de Lannoy, and Catherine, Lady of Molembais.   He died in
1474.

Q

on both sides, and, by degrees, they unanimously resolved to contrive his ruin.

But some persons may hereafter, perhaps, demand, whether the king was not able to have ruined him alone? I answer, No; for his territories lay just between the king and the Duke of Burgundy; he had St. Quentin, a large and strong town in Vermandois; he had Han and Bohain, and other considerable places not far from St. Quentin, which he might always garrison with what troops, and of whatever country, he pleased. He had 400 of the king's men-at-arms, well paid, of whom he was commissary himself, and he made his own musters, by which means he gained much money, for he never kept up his full complement. He had likewise a salary of 45,000 francs, and exacted a crown upon every pipe of wine that passed into Hainault or Flanders through any of his dominions; and, besides all this, he had great lordships and possessions of his own, a great interest in France, and also in Burgundy, upon account of his relations.

The truce lasted a whole year, and during that time this plot was contriving against the Constable of France. The king's agents applied themselves to one of the Duke of Burgundy's knights, called the Lord of Humbercourt, who for a long time had hated the constable, but more particularly of late, upon the following occasion: In a convention at Roye, where the constable and others were met on the king's part, with the Chancellor of Burgundy, the Lord of Humbercourt, and others in behalf of the duke, in the heat of their argument, the constable in a passion gave the Lord of Humbercourt the lie. The Lord of Humbercourt made no other reply, but that he would not expect satisfaction from him, but from the king, upon whose security he was come thither, under the character of an ambassador; for the affront was not so much to him as to his master, whose person he represented, and to whom he would give an account. This single piece of insolence, which was so suddenly committed, was the occasion afterwards not only of the constable's death, but also of the ruin of his family, as the sequel of this history will inform you. For this reason, persons in great authority, and princes themselves, ought to be careful of their language, and consider to whom it is they speak; for the greater the person is, the greater is the injury, and it lies heavier upon him that is affronted, because he thinks the grandeur and authority of him that committed the outrage make it more remarkable, and more liable to be objected against him. If it be one's own king or master, it makes one despair of a further preferment from him; and generally the hope of future advancement makes courtiers serve a prince better and more faithfully than the thought of what they already possess.

But to return. The king's agents made continual applications to the Lord of Humbercourt and the chancellor (who was present when that abusive language was given at Roye, and was besides a particular friend of the Lord of Humbercourt); and so far they proceeded in that affair, that they appointed a meeting at Bouvines, which is a town not far from Namur, to consult further about it. On the king's part there were the Lord of Curton, Governor of Limousin, and Monsieur John Heberge*, afterwards Bishop of Evreux; and for the Duke of Burgundy, there were the Chancellor of Burgundy and the Lord of Humbercourt, whom I have already mentioned. This was in the year 1474.

The constable, having private information that they were contriving something against him, sent immediately to both princes to let them know that he understood their designs; and he managed the matter so cunningly, that he created a jealousy in the king that the duke intended to deceive him, and debauch the constable from his party; upon which the king, in great haste, despatched a message to his ambassadors at Bouvines, commanding them not to conclude anything against the constable, for reasons which he would tell them, but to prolong the truce according to their instructions; which was for six months or a year, I know not which. When the messenger arrived, the whole affair was concluded, and the articles sealed and exchanged the night before. But the ambassadors were so good friends, and understood one another so well, that they delivered back their writings, by which the constable, for certain reasons there mentioned, was declared criminal, and an enemy to both princes; and the princes did mutually promise and swear, that which of them soever should get him first in his power, should cause him

* Jean Heberge was appointed Bishop of Evreux in 1473, and took the oaths on the 4th of April, 1474. He died on the 28th of August, 1479.

to be executed within eight days after his apprehension, or else deliver him over to the other, to be disposed of at his pleasure ; and it was further concluded, that he should be declared an enemy to both princes by sound of trumpet, with all that served, or favoured, or assisted him. The king also promised to deliver up the town of St. Quentin, so often mentioned before, to the Duke of Burgundy, and all the money and moveables belonging to the constable which should be found in the kingdom of France, with all his signiories and lordships held of the said duke, and particularly Han and Bohain, two strong places ; in order to which it was agreed that, on a certain day, both the king's forces and the duke's troops were to meet before Han, and besiege the constable in that town.

But all this agreement was quashed*, for the reasons above mentioned, and a day and place appointed for a conference between the king and the constable (the king having first given security for his return) ; for the constable was fearful for his person, as having had intelligence of the whole business at Bouvines. The place was three leagues from Noyon, towards La Fere, upon a little river which was impassable, by reason that, on the constable's side, the fords were taken away. Upon a causeway in that place a strong barrier was erected. The constable was the first that appeared at it, attended by all, or the greatest part, of his men-at-arms ; for he had 300 gentlemen in his train, all of them well armed, and he wore his own cuirass under a loose coat. The king was attended by 600 men-at-arms, and among them the Count of Dammartin, Lord High Steward of France, who was the constable's mortal enemy. The king sent me before, to excuse him to the constable for staying so long ; but presently after his majesty's arrival they discoursed together with five or six on each side. The constable excused his coming in arms, pretending he could not otherwise secure himself against the Count of Dammartin. The conclusion was, that all things past should be buried in oblivion, and no mention be made of them for the future, upon which the constable came over to the king's side ; the Count of Dam-

---

* All the clauses of this agreement, however, recur in the truce for nine years made between the king and the Duke of Burgundy on the 13th of September, 1475.

martin and he were reconciled; he waited upon the king that night to Noyon, and the next morning returned to St. Quentin, very well satisfied, as he said. But when the king came to consider what he had done, and understood the dissatisfaction of his subjects, he began to be sensible of having committed a great oversight, in giving a meeting to his servant, suffering a barrier between them at that interview, and permitting him to come attended with such a number of men-at-arms, all his subjects, and paid out of his purse; so that if his hatred to the constable was great before, this conference mightily increased it, neither was the constable himself really much better pleased.

Cн. XII.—A Digression, not altogether improper in this place, concerning the Wisdom of the King and the Constable, with useful Remarks for those who are in authority with Princes.—1474.

He that seriously considers this action of the king's, must certainly allow, that his majesty acted with great wisdom and prudence; for it is not improbable that the constable might have made his peace with the Duke of Burgundy, by the surrender of St. Quentin, notwithstanding all his promises to the contrary. But certainly for a wise man (as the constable undoubtedly was), he took the wrongest measures in the world, or else God had strangely infatuated his understanding, to come thus in that warlike manner and disguise to converse with his king and master, under a guard of so many horse, all of them the king's subjects, and at that time in his pay; and indeed by his looks he seemed to be ashamed of the action himself, for as soon as the king came to him, though they were parted by nothing but a rail, he ordered it immediately to be opened, and in coming to the king, was in no little danger that day.

Perhaps he and some of his friends might highly value themselves upon this action, and think it glorious to have a monarch stand in awe of him, as being sensible of the king's timidity; and indeed sometimes he was fearful, but never without just cause. The king had extricated himself out of

all his troubles and wars with the great lords of his kingdom, by large presents, and larger promises, and was sensible of many false steps he had made, and for the future was
resolved to put nothing to a venture that he could gain
otherwise.   Many were of opinion it was from his fear and
cowardice that this cautious way of acting proceeded ; but
several persons, who, upon the strength of that imagination,
durst presume to provoke his anger, if they were feebly supported, found themselves strangely mistaken, as the Count
of Armagnac and others, who paid dear for that opinion ; for
he knew very well how to distinguish between the appearance and reality of danger : and this I dare boldly say in
his commendation (and if I have said it before, it is not unworthy to be repeated), that in my whole life I never knew
any man so wise in misfortunes.

But to return to the constable, who perhaps had a mind
that the king should be afraid of him—at least, I suppose he
had (for I would not accuse him wrongly, and what I say is
only for the information of such as are in the service of great
princes, and have not an equal knowledge of the affairs of
this world).—Had I a friend in that capacity, I would advise
him to carry himself so, that his master might love him, and
not dread him ; for I never saw any courtier whose authority
depended upon the awe he inspired his prince, but some time
or other he was ruined, and by his master's consent.   Many
examples of this nature have been seen in our time, or not
long before, in this kingdom, as in the case of the Lord de La
Tremouille * and others.   In England, the Earl of Warwick
and his faction were a remarkable instance; I could name
others in Spain, and elsewhere ; but perhaps those who
shall read this chapter, may know it better than I.   This
arrogance generally proceeds from some extraordinary service
that they have performed, by which they are so strangely
puffed up, that they think their merit ought to bear them out
in whatever they do, and that their masters cannot live

* George, Lord of La Trémoille, Grand Chamberlain of France, and
prime minister of Charles VII., was the son of Guy de la Trémoille and
Marie de Sully. His favour and influence with the king gained him the
hatred of many of the nobles, who arrested him and imprisoned him at
Montresor, whence he was liberated only on payment of a heavy ransom.
He died on the 6th of May, 1446.

without them. But princes, on the contrary, are of opinion, that the best service their subjects can do them, is no more than their duty : and they like to be told this by their servants, and desire nothing more than to be rid of those who are arrogant in their behaviour.

Again, in this place I must insert two things which the king, my master, told me once in a discourse about persons who had done great service (and he named the author from whom he received that information), that to have served too well is sometimes the ruin of the agent ; and that most often, great ingratitude is the reward of long and faithful services ; usually upon account of the arrogance of those who have performed them, who, presuming too much upon their good fortune, behave themselves insolently towards their master or fellow-subjects ; so that princes are not always to be blamed, if their subjects are not rewarded according to their deserts. His majesty told me further, that he thought that person more happy in his preferments at court, whom his prince had advanced beyond his desert, whereby he remained a debtor to his prince, than he who, by any signal service, had put his prince under great obligation to him ; for he himself loved those persons with a greater affection who were obliged to him, than those (whoever they were) to whom he was obliged. So that in all conditions of life, it is a difficult matter to live well in this world, and a great blessing it is to those whom God hath naturally endowed with a right understanding.

BOOK THE FOURTH.

Ch. I.—How the Duke of Burgundy, having seized upon the Duchy of
Guelders, attempted farther Inroads upon the Germans, and besieged
Nuz.—1474.

THE interview between the king and the constable occurred
in 1474, and at that time, the Duke of Burgundy seized
upon the province of Guelders *, upon a quarrel well worthy
to be related, to demonstrate the justice and power of God.
There was a young Duke of Guelders called Adolphus †, who
had married a daughter ‡ of the house of Bourbon, sister to
the present duke, Pierre. The marriage having been consummated in the Duke of Burgundy's court, he still retained
some affection for him, and continued his friend. This
young duke had committed a most execrable act, in seizing
upon his father § one night as he was going to bed, carrying
him five German leagues on foot, bare-legged, in very cold
weather, and confining him a close prisoner in a dungeon at
the bottom of a tower ||, where there was no light but what
came through a cleft in the wall; and he kept him in that

* On the 15th of June, the duke encamped near Montfoort, on the
Yssel, in the duchy of Guelders.   Lenglet, ii. 206.
   † Adolphus, son of Arnold, Duke of Guelders, and Catherine of Cleves,
married his aunt, Catherine of Bourbon, on the 18th of December, 1463,
and was killed at the siege of Tournay on the 22nd of June, 1477.
   ‡ Catherine, daughter of Charles I., Duke of Bourbon.
   § Arnold of Egmont, Duke of Guelders, was the son of John of
Egmont and Mary of Arkel.   He married Catherine, daughter of Adol-
phus, Duke of Cleves; and died on the 24th of February, 1473.
   || In the town of Thiel, on the Waal, in Guelders.   Duke Arnold was
set at liberty in December, 1470.

miserable condition for the space of six months. This barbarous action occasioned a desperate war between the Duke of Cleves (whose sister the imprisoned duke had married) and the young Duke Adolphus. The Duke of Burgundy often interposed his good offices, and would fain have accommodated their difference, but could not. At length the pope and the emperor * began to stir in the affair, and the Duke of Burgundy was commanded upon great penalty to release Duke Arnold from prison, and it was done; for the young duke, seeing so many princes concerned in the business, and fearing lest the Duke of Burgundy would otherwise have done it by force, did not dare to refuse. I saw them both several times in the Duke of Burgundy's chamber, pleading their causes before the council, and the good old man in a passion threw his son his glove, and demanded a combat. The Duke of Burgundy would fain have reconciled them, and offered to the young duke, who was his favourite, the title of governor of the province, with the whole revenue thereof, and that only a small town near Brabant, called Grave †, with a revenue of 6000 florins (one half to be received out of the profits of the said town, and the other as a pension), should be continued to his father, with the title of duke, as was but reasonable. I was deputed (with others wiser than myself) to make this proposal to the young duke, whose answer was, "That he had rather fling his father headforemost into a well, and himself after him, than consent to such an accommodation; for his father had been duke four and forty years already, and it was time now that he should have his turn; but he would willingly allow him a pension of 3000 florins, upon condition he would leave the duchy, and never come into it again;" besides several other extravagant and detestable expressions to that effect.

This happened just at the time when the king took Amiens from the Duke of Burgundy, who was then with these two dukes at Dourlens ‡, very busy in adjusting their differ-

* Pope Paul IV. and the Emperor Frederick III.
† Grave, a strong town on the Meuse, in Dutch Brabant.
‡ The Duke of Burgundy arrived at Doullens on the 17th of January, 1471, and remained there until the 3rd of February following. Lenglet, ii. 197.

ences. Upon the news of the taking of Amiens, he removed
suddenly to Hesdin, and forgot their controversy which was
before him. The young duke disguised himself like a Frenchman, and endeavoured (with only one servant) to make his
escape into his own country.* Passing a ferry not far from
Namur, he paid a florin for his passage, which being
observed by a priest that stood by, he presently suspected
him, and asked the ferry-man what it was he had given him;
then, looking earnestly upon him, he recognised him, and
caused him to be apprehended and carried to Namur†;
where he was kept a prisoner till, upon the Duke of Burgundy's death, the citizens of Ghent released him, and would
have forced the duke's daughter‡ (since Duchess of Austria)
to have married him. After which, taking him along with
them in their expedition against Tournay, he was miserably
slain, and sordidly buried, as if the vengeance of God
Almighty, for his barbarity to his father, could not have
been otherwise satisfied. The old duke dying before the
Duke of Burgundy, and during his son's imprisonment
(upon the account of his inhuman and vile treatment),
disinherited him, and left the succession of Guelders to the
Duke of Burgundy; by virtue of which title (though he
found some little resistance) the Duke of Burgundy conquered it, and enjoyed it till his death, for he was then
powerful, and at peace with the king; and his successors
enjoy it to this day, and shall do as long as God shall think
good.§ This I have related for no other reason (as I said in
the beginning) but to show that such unnatural impiety
never goes unpunished.

The Duke of Burgundy returned into his own country,
mightily puffed up by the acquisition of this duchy. He
took great pleasure in concerning himself with the affairs of

* Expresses had been sent to Maestricht and Bois-le-Duc, by Duke
Charles, on the 10th of February, to order his arrest if he made his
appearance in those towns.

† He was arrested at Namur, and sent thence, by the duke's order,
to Vilvorde, where he attempted to escape, but was recaptured, and sent
to the Castle of Courtray.

‡ Mary of Burgundy.

§ The Emperor Maximilian, husband of Mary of Burgundy, lost the
duchy of Guelders in 1492; and Charles of Egmont, the son of Duke
Adolph, was then restored to his inheritance.

the empire; for the emperor was a mean-spirited prince, and
to avoid the expense of war, would tamely suffer anything.
Besides, of himself, without the concurrence of the princes
of the empire, he could do but little. For this reason the
duke prolonged his truce with the king*, though some of
the king's courtiers were utterly against it, alleging the
danger of the duke's growing too powerful : and what they
urged was not altogether unreasonable ; but they wanted
experience and foresight, and therefore did not understand
the matter. Others† (of greater judgment and knowledge,
in respect that they had been in those countries) advised by
all means that the cessation of arms might be prolonged, and
the duke permitted to tire and exhaust himself against the
Germans (whose grandeur and strength, when united, are almost inconceivable) ; for he was of such an ambitious temper,
that the taking of one town, or the accomplishing of one
design, did but excite and hurry him on to attempt another ;
so that one war drawing a second upon him (contrary to the
king's humour), his restless desires were not to be satisfied
with any single success. Wherefore they advised the king,
as the best and easiest way to revenge himself upon him,
rather to give him some little assistance, than the least suspicion of breaking the truce ; for the greatness and puissance
of the princes of Germany would quickly confound and exhaust him, and (the emperor himself not being a warlike
prince) they would certainly unite and oppose him ; and so
it happened in the conclusion.

There were at that time two persons that pretended a
right to the bishopric of Cologne : one of them was brother
to the Landgrave of Hesse‡ ; and the other was the Count
Palatine of the Rhine.§   The Duke of Burgundy sided with

* The truce was prolonged from the 15th of June, 1474, to the 1st of
May, 1475. See Lenglet, iii. 315.

† It appears almost certain that Commines here alludes to himself.
See Meyer, Annal. Fland., 361.

‡ Herman IV., son of Louis I., Landgrave of Hesse, and Anne,
daughter of Frederick I., Elector of Saxony. He was elected Archbishop of Cologne on the 11th of August, 1480, and died in the autumn
of 1508.

§ Robert of Bavaria, Count Palatine, was the son of Louis le Barbu,
Count Palatine of the Rhine, and Matilda of Savoy. He died in
prison on the 17th of July, 1480.

the Palatine, and undertook to establish him by force in that
dignity ; and (in hopes of gaining some of the towns thereabout for himself) he besieged Nuz* (which is a town not
far from Cologne) in the year 1474. And the Landgrave
of Hesse† was there with a good number of men. The duke,
however, had so many things upon the anvil at once, and so
many enterprises and designs in his head, that he sank beneath the burden of them. He would fain have persuaded
Edward, King of England, to have brought over a great
army, which (upon his solicitation) he had raised at that
time, to favour his designs in Germany, which were as
follows : — If he took Nuz, he designed to have put a strong
garrison into it, and two or three towns more in that
neighbourhood (by which means Cologne would have been
blocked up), and then to have marched up the Rhine as far
as the county of Ferrette, which was then under his juris-
diction‡; by which means all the Rhine, as far as Holland,
would have been under his dominion; which space of
ground contains more fortified towns and castles than any
kingdom in Christendom, except France. The truce which
the Duke of Burgundy had made with the king, had been
prolonged for six months § ; and the greatest part of it being
expired, the king desired it might be renewed, that the duke
might have enough of the war in Germany ; but the duke,
because of his promise to the English‖, would not consent
to it.

I would willingly have omitted this siege of Nuz, as an
affair not absolutely necessary to my history ; and, besides,
I was not at it ; but I am obliged to mention it on account
of some matters which depend on it. The town of Nuz was
strongly fortified, and in it there were the Landgrave of

* Nuz, now called Neuss, a town in the regency of Dusseldorf, in the
Prussian States. The duke encamped before Neuss on the 30th of July,
1474. See Lenglet, ii. 214; and for details of the siege, Molinet, i. 27.
† Henry III., brother of Herman. He married Anne, daughter of
the Count of Dietz, and died on the 12th of January, 1483.
‡ He had had it in his possession since 1468. See p. 125.
§ It had been prolonged for nearly a year. See. p. 235.
‖ By the treaty of alliance and confederation made between the
King of England and the Duke of Burgundy on the 25th of July, 1474,
among other conventions, the duke pledged himself to listen to no pro-
position of truce or peace without Edward's consent. Rymer, v. 41.

Hesse, and many of his relations and friends, with a body of 1800 horse, as I was informed, all choice troops (as they proved afterwards), and as many foot as they thought needful for the defence of the place. This landgrave, as I said before, was brother to the bishop, who was chosen in opposition to that person whom the Duke of Burgundy would have advanced. Upon which, being highly disgusted, he laid siege to Nuz in the year 1474.

His army was at that time more numerous and in better order than it ever had been formerly; especially his cavalry; for, upon pretence of some designs upon Italy, he had got together about 1000 Italian men-at-arms, under the command of the Count of Campobasso, a Neapolitan, a partisan of the house of Anjou, a most perfidious and dangerous man. There was likewise James Galeot, a Neapolitan gentleman (a very brave officer), and several others, whose names, for brevity sake, I omit. Besides, he had with him 3000 English, all stout soldiers, and a vast number of his own subjects well armed, mounted, and disciplined in his wars; and a fine train of artillery. All these were prepared and in readiness to join the English (that were raising in England with all expedition) upon their first landing. But things of such importance are managed very tediously there; for the king not being able to undertake such an affair without calling together his parliament, which is in the nature of our Three Estates, and, as it consists for the most part of sober and pious men, is very serviceable and strengthening to the king. At the meeting of this parliament the king declares his intention, and desires aid of his subjects (for no money is raised in England but upon some expedition into France or Scotland, or some such extraordinary occasion); and then they supply him very liberally, especially against France; yet the Kings of England have this artifice when they want money, and have a desire to have any supplies granted, to raise men, and pretend quarrels with Scotland or France; and having encamped with their army for about three months, disband it, return home, and keep the remainder of the money for their own private use; and this trick King Edward understood very well, and often practised it.

It was a whole year before this English army could be

raised and set in order. When it was ready, towards
the beginning of the summer, notice was given to the
Duke of Burgundy, who lay then before Nuz, and was of
opinion that in a few days he should put his bishop into
possession, and have Nuz and other towns assigned him for
the purposes above mentioned.

I am of opinion this was God's own doing, in mercy to the
kingdom of France, or else the Duke of Burgundy might
have done great mischief to that nation with an army of old
troops accustomed for several years together to invade it,
without any resistance but what was made by the fortified
towns; and yet something may be attributed to the king's
wisdom and management, who would not put anything to a
venture; not so much for fear of the Duke of Burgundy,
as of tumults at home upon the loss of a battle; for he did
not believe himself safe with his servants or subjects, especially the great lords; and, if I may speak freely, he often
told me that he knew the inclination of his subjects very
well, and should find them inclinable to rebellion upon the
loss of a battle, or any such misfortune. Wherefore, whenever the Duke of Burgundy invaded any part of his dominions, his majesty's way was to put strong garrisons into
all the towns by which he was likely to march; so that (without the expense and hazard of an army in the field) the duke's
forces in a little time wasted and baffled themselves without
endangering the nation; which (in my judgment) was very
good policy. However, the duke being so strong as I have
represented him, if the English army had appeared at the
beginning of the summer (which it doubtless would have
done, if the duke had not committed the error of besieging
Nuz), certainly the kingdom of France would have been in
imminent danger; for the King of England had never invaded France with so numerous and well-disciplined an
army; all the great lords of England attended him without
any exception; and they amounted to about 1500 men-at-
arms (a great number for the English), all well accoutred
and with a great retinue; besides 14,000 archers on horseback, with their bows and arrows, and a numerous body of
camp-servants on foot, but not one page in the whole army.
Besides, the King of England was to have landed 3000 men

in Bretagne* to join the Duke of Bretagne's army. I saw
likewise two letters under the hand of the Lord of Urfé,
Master of the Horse of France, but who was then in the
Duke of Bretagne's service; one directed to the King of
England, and the other to the Lord Hastings, High Chamberlain of England, which had this among other expressions :
That the Duke of Bretagne would do more by his intrigues
in a month, than the King of England and the Duke of
Burgundy both could do in six, with all the force they
could bring. Nor do I question the truth of what he said,
if things had been managed as they might have been. But
God, who is ever careful of the preservation of this kingdom, disposed of them otherwise, as you shall understand
hereafter. These letters above mentioned were purchased
of one of the English secretaries for threescore marks of
silver by our king, whom God pardon !

CH. II.—How the Town of Nuz was relieved by the Germans and the
Emperor; and of other Enemies whom the King of France stirred up
against the Duke of Burgundy.—1474.

As I said before, the Duke of Burgundy had invested Nuz,
and met with greater difficulties in that siege than he expected. The city of Cologne (which lies four leagues higher
upon the Rhine) was forced to be at the expense of 100,000
florins of gold a month, to secure themselves against the
Duke of Burgundy, and had, in conjunction with some of
the neighbouring towns above it, upon the Rhine, put into
the field a body of 15,000 or 16,000 foot, and posted them
with a large train of artillery upon the bank of the river
opposite to the duke's camp, with a design to intercept all
his convoys of provision, which came by water out of the
country of Guelders up the river, and to sink his boats with
their cannon. The emperor and the electoral princes of the

* By letters dated June 12. 1475, King Edward entrusted to John
Audley and Galhard de Duras, Lord of Durfort, the command of the
fleet destined to succour the Duke of Bretagne. Rymer, v. 3. 64.

empire had a meeting about this affair; and it was unanimously resolved to raise an army. The king having sent
several ambassadors to them, to solicit them to that purpose,
they sent to him a Canon of Cologne (of the house of Bavaria), and another ambassador with him, with a roll or list
of the army which the emperor designed to raise, provided
the king would make a diversion on his side. They were
sure of a favourable answer from his majesty, and whatever
they demanded was granted. Besides, the king promised in
writing, both to the emperor and to several princes and
cities, that as soon as the emperor should take the field, and
advance to Cologne, he would send 20,000 men to join them
under the command of the Lords of Craon and Sallezard.

Hereupon the German army was raised, and got ready,
amounting to an almost incredible number of men; for all
the princes of Germany, both spiritual and temporal, and all
the bishops and free-towns, sent in their respective forces in
great numbers. I was informed that the Bishop of Munster *
(who is none of the greatest) led into that army 6000 foot
and 1400 horse, all clothed in green uniforms, besides 1200
waggons; but his bishopric was hard by. It was seven
months' time before this army was raised and fit to march;
and it then posted itself within half a league of the Duke of
Burgundy's camp †; and (as I have been informed by several of the duke's people) it was three times the number of
the Duke of Burgundy's army and the English army together, both in men, tents, and pavilions; and besides this
army of the emperor's, there was the army on the other side

---

* Henry, Count of Schwartzburg, was first Bishop of Bremen, and
afterwards, in 1467, Bishop of Munster. He died on the 24th of December, 1497. The valorous conduct of this prelate at the siege of
Neuss is commemorated in the following passage from his epitaph:—

Cæsareas aquilas infestaque signa, viator,
    Suspensa ad tumulum præsulis, oro, vide.
Principis hæc meruit virtus, cum Nussia dura
    Burgundi quatitur obsidione ducis.
(Witt, 564, 597.)

† "He came so near as to lodge at Zons, and, on the following day,
established his artillery at about a league from the siege. He had in
front of him a high mountain, the river Rhine on one side, and large and
deep trenches on the other, from the mountain-slope to the river."
Molinet. i. 117.

of the river, which continually annoyed the enemy, both by cannonading their camp, and intercepting their convoys.

As soon as the emperor and the princes of the empire were arrived before Nuz, they despatched a certain doctor (of great reputation among them), called Hesevare * (who was afterwards made a cardinal), to the king.   His business was to solicit his majesty to perform his promise, and to send his 20,000 men; otherwise the Germans would accommodate matters with the Duke of Burgundy.   The king promised him fair, made him a present of 400 crowns, despatched him immediately, and sent along with him to the emperor one John Tiercelin†, Lord of Brosse; but this did not satisfy the doctor, so that there were great intrigues carried on by all sides during this siege.   The king endeavoured to make peace with the Duke of Burgundy, or at least to prolong the truce, to prevent the English from landing : the King of England, on the other hand, tried to persuade the duke to raise the siege before Nuz, and (according to his engagement) to make war upon France, for the winter began to approach; on which errand the Lord Scales (nephew to the constable, and a very good knight) was sent twice, with several other ambassadors, to the duke; but the duke was perverse, as if God Almighty had infatuated his senses and understanding; for all his life long he had been labouring to get the English over to invade France, and now, when they were ready, and all things prepared to receive them, both in Bretagne and elsewhere, he obstinately persisted in an enterprise in which it was impossible for him to succeed.

There was at that time with the emperor an apostolic legate‡,

---

* George Hesler, Apostolical and Imperial Prothonotary, Canon and Archdeacon of Cologne, was a native of Wurtzburg in Bavaria.   At the solicitation of the Emperor Frederick III., Sixtus IV. created him a cardinal, on the 10th of December, 1477; and he was drowned while attempting to cross the Danube in a boat, in the month of September, 1482.

† Jean Tiercelin, Lord of Brosse, chamberlain of Louis XI., and governor of the Duke of Orleans, afterwards Louis XII., was the son of Macé Tiercelin, Lord of Brosse; and married Louise de Longchamp. His mission to the emperor was " to maintain and continue the ancient alliances between the two powers."   Lenglet. iii. 371.

‡ Alexander Nanni, appointed Bishop of Forli in 1470, Vice-Legate

R

who passed daily from one camp to the other, to negotiate
a peace. The King of Denmark also, being quartered in a
small town* not far from the two armies, endeavoured the
same; so that the Duke of Burgundy might have had
honourable terms, and marched off to the King of England,
but he would not accept of them. He excused himself as
handsomely as he could to the English, telling them that his
honour was engaged, and it would be a lessening to his reputation to raise the siege; and such like excuses. These
were not the English who had reigned in his father's days, and
had behaved themselves with so much valour and conduct
in the old wars with France; but these were all raw soldiers,
utterly unacquainted with French affairs; so that the duke
did very unwisely, if he had any design to make use of them
for the future, for he would have had to lead them on, as it
were, step by step, at least during the first campaign.

The Duke of Burgundy's perverse resolution to continue
the siege of Nuz occasioned two or three other wars to
break out upon him. The Lord of Craon, for the advantage
of the king's affairs, persuaded the Duke of Lorraine† that it
would turn highly to his advantage to quarrel with the
Duke of Burgundy in this present juncture; though he was
in perfect amity with him, and had been in treaty with
him since the death of Duke Nicholas of Calabria, yet he
sent him a defiance (by means of the Lord of Craon) as he
lay in his camp before Nuz; and immediately he took the
field, invaded the duchy of Luxembourg, committed great
ravages in the country, and razed a town called Pierre-fort‡,
in the said province, not above two leagues from Nancy.
Moreover, by the conduct and management of the king and
his ambassadors, a ten years' alliance was concluded between
the Swiss and the towns upon the Rhine (as Basle, Strasburg, and others) who had been at enmity before.

A peace was likewise made between Sigismund, Duke of

and Governor of Umbria in 1474, and Apostolic Nuncio in Germany
under the pontificate of Pius IV. He died at Rome in 1485.

* At Unterbilk, a little town on the other side of the Rhine, two
leagues from Neuss.   Molinet, i. 74.

† René II., son of Ferri II., Count of Vaudemont, and Yolande of
Anjou, succeeded Nicholas, Duke of Lorraine, in 1473, at the age of
twenty-two, and died on the 10th of December, 1508.

‡ Pierfort, in the arrondissement of Toul, and department of Meurthe.

Austria, and the Swiss, in order to facilitate his recovery of the county of Ferrette, which he had engaged to the Duke of Burgundy for 100,000 florins of the Rhine; but one thing remained in dispute between them still, for the Swiss pressed hard to have passage when they pleased (either with their arms or without) through four towns in the county of Ferrette; and it being referred to the king*, he decided in favour of the Swiss.

All things being resolved on, they were executed accordingly; for, in a fair night, Peter Archambault†, the governor of the county of Ferrette for the Duke of Burgundy, was surprised, and 800 men with him; the men were all immediately discharged, but the governor was detained and carried prisoner to Basle, where process being made against him for certain excesses and violences which he had committed in the said county of Ferrette‡, his head was struck off, and the county restored to Sigismund, Duke of Austria. Then the Swiss began to make war upon the Duke of Burgundy, and took Blasmond§, belonging to the Marshal of Burgundy, who was of the house of Neufchastel. They also besieged the castle of Hérycourt‖, belonging also to the house of Neufchastel; the Burgundians attempted to relieve it, but were beaten, and a great number of them killed; after

---

* The act in which Louis XI. declares himself favourable to the pretensions of the Swiss, is dated Senlis, June 11. 1474. See Lengler, iii. 312.

† Pierre de Hagenbach, knight, councillor and steward to Duke Charles, was High Bailiff of Ferrette, and Lord of Belmont. His name occurs in the narrative of an act of adulation and despotism so singular that we do not hesitate to mention it. Philip, Duke of Burgundy, fell ill, and his head was shaved by order of his physicians. In order not to be the only man in such a plight, he issued an edict that all his nobles should in like manner shave their heads: more than 500 noblemen, for love of the duke, did so; and Pierre de Hagenbach and others, to prove their devotedness, no sooner caught sight of an unshaven nobleman than they forcibly deprived him of his hair. Oliver de la Marche, ii. 227.

‡ The grievances of the inhabitants of the county of Ferrette are set forth in a document quoted by Lenglet, iii. 351.

§ Blamont, in the arrondissement of Montbelliard, department of Doubs.

‖ Hericourt, in the arrondissement of Vesoul, department of Haute-Saône.

which the Swiss did much mischief, ravaged the whole country, and then retired for that time.

CH. III.—How the King took from the Duke of Burgundy the Castle of Tronquoy, with the Towns of Montdidier, Roye, and Corbie, and the Endeavours he used to persuade the Emperor Frederick to seize upon such Towns as belonged to the Duke in the Empire.—1475.

THE truce between the king and the Duke of Burgundy now expired *, to the king's no small regret, for he had much rather have renewed it; but finding it was impossible to be done, he besieged a little castle called Tronquoy, in the beginning of the summer of 1475, and took it by assault in a few hours' time. The next day † the king sent me to parley with the garrison of Montdidier, who marched away with their baggage, and abandoned the town. The day after I was sent with the Admiral of France, Bastard of Bourbon, to capitulate with Roye, which, despairing of relief, surrendered to the king.‡ They would neither of them have submitted, had the Duke of Burgundy been in the country, for which reason, though contrary to our promise, both of them were burnt; from thence the king marched with his army to Corbie, where he was expected. We carried on our approaches very well, and fired from our batteries for three days successively. In the town there were the Lord of Contay §, and several other officers, who surrendered at last ‖, and marched out with their baggage; two days after, the poor town was plundered, and then burnt, as the other two had been.

---

* On the 1st of May, 1475. See above, book iv. chap. i.
† Montdidier was taken on the 4th of May.
‡ Roye surrendered on the 6th of May.
§ Louis, Lord of Contay and Forest, was the son of Guillaume de Contay and Marguerite de Sully. During his father's lifetime, he was Governor of Arras. He was also chamberlain to the Duke of Burgundy. He married Jacqueline de Nesle, and was killed at the battle of Nancy on the 5th of January, 1476.
‖ On the 11th of May; the inhabitants fled to Amiens.

The king at this time had some thoughts of retiring with his army, supposing the necessity of the Duke of Burgundy's affairs would have put him upon a new truce; but a certain lady (whom I know, but will not name, because she is still living) wrote to the king to desire his majesty to march with his army to Arras, and the country thereabouts. The king believed her, for she was a person of honour; yet I cannot commend her for it, because she was under no obligation to do it; but the king, however, sent thither the Admiral Bastard of Bourbon with a strong detachment *, who burnt a great many of their towns between Abbeville and Arras. The citizens of Arras, having enjoyed a long series of peace and prosperity, and being grown haughty and arrogant, compelled their garrison to make a sally; but being too weak for the king's party, when they came to charge, they were most of them taken or killed, especially their officers, and among the rest Monsieur Jacques de St. Paul, brother to the constable, the Lord of Contay, the Lord of Carency †, and some of the nearest relations to the lady who was the occasion of that undertaking; and indeed she herself was a great sufferer by it, but the king made her handsome reparation for the loss she had sustained.

About this time the king had sent John Tiercelin, Lord of Brosse, on an embassy to the emperor, to prevent any accommodation between him and the Duke of Burgundy, and to excuse him to the emperor for not having sent his forces according to his promise. His ambassador was to assure his imperial majesty that, for the future, he would be more punctual, and to magnify his incursions and exploits, as well against the Duke of Burgundy's own country, as against the country of Picardy. Besides which, he was to make a new proposal, that they should mutually engage and swear, one to the other, to make no peace nor truce without the knowledge and consent of both; that the emperor should

* On Wednesday, the 27th of June, the admiral came before Arras. Lenglet, ii. 117.

† Pierre de Bourbon, Lord of Carency, son of Jean de Bourbon and Jeanne de Vendôme, was born in February, 1424. Louis XI. had him tried and condemned to death for high treason; but in consideration for his family, granted him his life and restored him to liberty, but confiscated his estates, as appears by letters patent of the 20th of April, 1469.

seize and take all such lordships as belonged, or ought to
belong, to the said Duke of Burgundy, in the empire, and
declare them forfeited; upon which terms the king would possess himself of all that the duke held of the crown of France,
as Flanders, Artois, Burgundy, and the rest. The emperor
was never accounted valiant in his life, but being old he had
seen much, and had a great deal of experience; and these
treaties and contrivances between him and the king having
taken up much time, the emperor by degrees grew weary of
the war, though it had cost him nothing, for the German
princes were all at their own charges, as their custom is,
whenever the common interest of the empire is concerned.

By way of answer to the king's ambassadors, the emperor
told them the following story: Not far from a certain town
in Germany there was a great bear, that did a great deal of
mischief; two or three boon companions who used often to
drink together, came to a tavern where they had run up a
large reckoning before, and desired the landlord that he
would give them credit but for that one reckoning, and
before two days were at an end they would wipe off all
scores, for they were resolved to kill that bear which had
done so much mischief, and whose skin would yield them a
great deal of money, besides all the presents that would come
in to them for the service they had done the country in
destroying that ravenous beast. Their landlord trusted
them once more, and when they had dined, away they
marched in search of the bear. Her den happening to be
nearer than they supposed it was, they stumbled upon the
bear before they expected, and, being all three in great
consternation, they took to their heels; one ran towards
the town, the other climbed up a tree, but the third was
overtaken, and, having fallen down, the bear trampled upon
him with her feet, and ran her snout into his ear. The
poor man had thrown himself flat on the ground, and lay in
a posture as if he were dead. Now, it is the nature of that
beast to suppose that whatever prey it seizes upon, whether
man or beast, is dead when it perceives no further motion,
and it then lets it alone. Accordingly, this bear went away
to her den, without doing him any hurt. By degrees the poor
man began to look up, and finding the enemy retired, he got
upon his legs, and ran as fast as he could to the town. His

companion that had taken refuge in the tree, having seen the whole mystery, came down with all speed, ran and hallooed after him, desiring him to stop; so he turned back very civilly, and stayed till he came up. When he who had been on the tree had overtaken him, he asked his companion, upon oath, what counsel it was which the bear was so long in whispering into his ear. His comrade replied, " she charged me never for the future to sell the bear's skin till the beast was dead." And with this story the king's ambassador was despatched, for the emperor gave him no other answer in public; the meaning of which was, " That if the king came according to his promise, they would take the duke if they could; and when he was taken, they would talk of dividing his dominions."

Ch. IV.—How the Constable fell again under the Suspicion both of the King and of the Duke of Burgundy.—1475.

You have already heard that Monsieur James de St. Paul and other officers were taken prisoners in the action before Arras, which was an accident very unpleasing to the constable, for James was his favourite brother. But this misfortune came not alone; for almost at the same time* his son, the Count of Roussy (Governor of Burgundy for the duke) was taken prisoner likewise; and not long after died the constable's wife†, an excellent lady, and sister to the Queen of France, upon which account he found much favour and support; for the combination (which, as you have heard, was for some time interrupted at Bouvines) was still carried on against him; and the constable never thought himself safe afterwards, but was held in perpetual suspicion by both sides, but more especially by the king, for he was sensible

* On the 20th of June, 1475. See note, p. 150.
† Marie de Savoie, daughter of Louis, Duke of Savoy, and Anne of Cyprus, married Louis, Constable of St. Paul, on the 1st of August, 1466. She died in 1475.

his majesty repented of having withdrawn his articles at Bouvines.

The Count of Dammartin, with others, was quartered with his men-at-arms in the neighbourhood of St. Quentin; and the constable was afraid of them, as if they had been enemies, and threw 300 of his own troops into that town, and stayed amongst them himself, for he had no confidence in the king's forces, but lived in continual anxiety and disquiet of mind. The king sent several messages with orders to him to take the field and march into Hainault, and besiege Avennes at the same time that the admiral with his detachment made an incursion into Artois, which he did, but with incredible fear. He had not lain many days before the town, with a strong guard about his person, before he retired to St. Quentin again, and sent the king word (which message, by the king's order, was delivered to me) that he had raised the siege upon certain information that there were two persons in the army employed by the king to assassinate him; and he told so many circumstances to confirm it, that most people began to believe it, and one of the persons was suspected of having revealed something to him, that he ought to have kept secret. I will not name the persons, nor make any further mention of this matter.

The constable sent frequently into the Duke of Burgundy's quarters (and I think his object was to divert him from this foolish expedition); and upon the return of his agents, he always sent some news or other to the king, which he imagined would greatly please his majesty, and withal acquainted him with his design in sending so often to the duke, by which artifice he thought to amuse and cajole the king. Sometimes, also, he sent to let the king know that the Duke of Burgundy's affairs were in a very prosperous condition; but it was only to frighten him; and so fearful was he of being surprised, that he begged the Duke of Burgundy to send to him his brother James de St. Paul (before his capture), the Lord of Fiennes*, and other of his relations (who were then with the duke at the siege of Nuz), and that he would allow him to put them and their

---

* Jacques de Luxembourg, Lord of Fiennes, was the son of Thibaud de Luxembourg, and Philippa de Melun; and he died in 1487.

troops into St. Quentin (but without the cross of St. Andrew, which is the badge and cognisance of the house of Burgundy); and he promised to keep St. Quentin for the duke, and in a little time to deliver up the town entirely to him; and for better security offered to promise this under his hand. The Duke of Burgundy granted his request; but when his brother James, the Lord of Fiennes, and the rest of his relations, came twice within a league or two of St. Quentin, and were ready to enter, his fear vanished, he repented, and sent them back from whence they came; and on a third occasion he did so again; such was his desire to carry his affairs swimmingly between both parties, and preserve himself in the position he was in, for he exceedingly feared them both.

These passages I learned from several persons, and particularly from the mouth of Monsieur James de St. Paul, who, when he was prisoner, told them to the king, when nobody was present but myself, and the sincerity of his answers was very serviceable to him. The king demanded of him what number of troops he designed to have put into the town. He told his majesty that, on the third occasion, he had 3000. Then the king asked him if he had succeeded, and entered the town, for whom he would have kept it? whether for him or for the constable? Monsieur James de St. Paul replied, that on the first two occasions he came only to encourage his brother; but the third time, having observed that his brother had twice before deceived both his master and his majesty, if he had found his party the strongest, he would have kept it for his master, but without any violence or detriment to his brother; only if he had commanded him to evacuate the town, he would have disobeyed his orders. Not long after this private conference, the king released Monsieur James, gave him men-at-arms and a large estate, and employed him afterwards in several affairs as long as he lived; and all because of the freedom and sincerity of his answers.

Since I began to speak of Nuz, I have intermingled several occurrences, which, however, were coincident; for the siege continued a year*, and they happened during that time.

* The Duke of Burgundy lay before Nuz from the 30th of July, 1474, to the 27th of June, 1475.

There were two things which mightily tempted the Duke of
Burgundy to raise the siege: one was the war which the
King of France had begun against him in Picardy, in which
he had burnt three pretty little towns *, and wasted a good
part of the flat country in Artois and Ponthieu; the other
was the great army which, at his request and solicitation,
the King of England had raised; for he had been importun-
ing him all his life long to invade France, and could never
effect it till now.   The King of England and all his nobility
were highly discontented at the Duke of Burgundy's delays,
and added threats to their entreaties; as they had reason, for
they had been at a prodigious expense in raising an army,
and the best part of the season was almost spent.   The
Duke of Burgundy thought it highly for his honour that so
puissant an army as the emperor's (consisting of the forces
of so many princes, prelates, and states), which amounted to
a greater number than had been assembled together since
the memory of man, and for a long time previously, were
not able to force him to raise the siege.   But he paid dearly
for his vanity; for the man who makes profit by a war,
bears away all the honour of it.   However, the legate I
mentioned before continued his good offices on both sides so
long, that at length a peace† was concluded between the
Emperor and the Duke of Burgundy, and Nuz was delivered
into the hands of the Pope's legate, to be disposed of as his
Holiness should direct.   But to what extremity must the
Duke of Burgundy have been reduced, to see himself pressed
so hard by the French forces on one side, and the English
menaces on the other; especially at a time when Nuz was
reduced to such a miserable condition, that in fifteen days
they must have surrendered unconditionally, or starved?
Nay, I was told by a captain who was then in the town,
and whom the king afterwards took into his service, that it
could not have held out ten days longer; and yet for these
urgent reasons the Duke of Burgundy was forced to raise
the siege in 1475.

* Montdidier, Roye, and Corbie.
† This peace was confirmed on the 17th of November, 1475.

CH. V.—How the King of England passed the Sea with a powerful Army to assist his Ally, the Duke of Burgundy, against the King of France, to whom he sent a Defiance by one of his Heralds-at-arms. —1475.

BUT to proceed. The King of England, in order to embark for Calais *, had marched down to Dover with an army; the most numerous, the best disciplined, the best mounted, and the best armed, that ever any king of that nation invaded France withal. He was attended by the flower of the English nobility, consisting of 1500 men-at-arms, richly accoutred after the French fashion, well mounted, and most of them barded, and every one of them had several persons on horseback in his retinue. His archers were 15,000, on horseback, with their bows and arrows, besides a great number of foot soldiers, and others to pitch his tents and pavilions, take care of the artillery, and enclose his camp; and there was not one page in the whole army; besides which, there was a body of 3000 men who were to be landed in Bretagne. I have already mentioned this before, but however, it is not impertinent to do it again, if it were for no other reason but to show, that, if the providence of God had not, by peculiar mercy to this kingdom (which He has preserved more graciously than any other in the world), infatuated the Duke of Burgundy's understanding, no one could ever have believed that he would be so blind to his own interest as to invest, and obstinately to carry on the siege of, a town so strongly fortified and so bravely defended as Nuz was; and especially at that juncture, when he had at last prevailed upon the English, after many importunities, to pass the seas, and invade France in conjunction with him; a thing that he had been labouring at all his life-time, but could never effect till now. Besides, he knew that the troops of that nation were at present of little importance in his wars with France, and if he expected any real assistance from them afterwards, it was necessary he should have made one campaign with them at least, to have acquainted and

* "And about midsummer, in the year 1475, King Edward brought his army to Calais in great pomp and triumph. It consisted of about 22,000 men; but the archers were badly mounted, and unused to riding on horseback." Molinet, i. 139. 141.

instructed them in the method of our wars; for though no
nation is more raw and undisciplined than the English at
their first coming over, yet a little time makes them brave
soldiers, excellent officers, and wise councillors. But the
duke did just the contrary, and, among the rest of the dis-
advantages that followed, the summer was almost spent, and
his own army so diminished and fatigued, that he was ashamed
they should be seen; for he had lost before Nuz 4000 of his
standing forces, the very flower of his army; by which one
may see how God disposed him to act in this affair contrary
to his reason and interest, which he understood better than
any one else ten years before.

The King of England being at Dover, ready to embark,
the Duke of Burgundy sent him 500 Dutch boats, which
were flat and low, and very proper for the transportation of
horses (which boats, in Holland and Zealand, are called
scuts); yet, notwithstanding that vast number, and all that
the king could provide of his own, the embarking and landing his forces at Calais occupied three weeks, though the
distance between Dover and that place is but seven leagues.
From whence one may observe with what prodigious
difficulty the Kings of England transport their armies into
France; and if the King of France had understood the sea
as well as he did land affairs, King Edward could never
have landed in France, at least that year; but his majesty
had no skill in naval matters, and those to whom he gave
authority in war knew less of them than himself; yet one
of our men-of-war, belonging to Eu, took two or three of
their transports.

Before the King of England embarked from Dover, he
sent one of his heralds, named Garter, a native of Normandy, to the King of France, with a letter of defiance,
written in such an elegant style, and in such polite language,
that I can scarcely believe any Englishman * wrote it.

The contents were, that our king should surrender to the
King of England the kingdom of France as his right and
inheritance, to the end that he might restore the church, the
nobility, and the people to their ancient liberty, and relieve

---

* Our English historian, Habington, falls foul of Philip de Commines
for this passage, and casts severe censures both on him and his *Memoirs*
for this unjust reflection on our nation.

them from the great oppression and burdens they groaned under; and if he refused, he declared all the ensuing miseries and calamities would lie at his door, according to the forms usual upon such occasions. The King of France read the letter to himself, and then, wisely withdrawing into another room, commanded the herald to be called in; he then told him that he was very sensible his master had not made this descent upon any disposition of his own, but at the importunity of the Duke of Burgundy and of the Commons of England; that it was visible the summer was far spent, and the Duke of Burgundy returned from Nuz, but in such a weak and miserable condition, that he would not be in a capacity to assist him; that, as to the constable, he was satisfied he held intelligence with the King of England (for he had married his niece), but there was no confidence to be reposed in him, for he would deceive King Edward, as he had often deceived him; and having enumerated the favours which he had conferred upon him, he added, "His design is to live in eternal dissimulation, to treat with everybody, and to make his advantage of all." Besides which the king used several other arguments to induce the herald to persuade his master to an accommodation with him, gave him 300 crowns with his own hand, and promised him 1000 more upon the conclusion of the peace; and then, in public, his majesty ordered him to be presented with a fine piece of crimson velvet, thirty ells in length.

The herald replied, that, according to his capacity, he would contribute all that lay in his power towards a peace, and he believed his master would not be averse to it; but there was no making any proposals, till he was landed with his whole army in France, and then, if his majesty pleased, he might send a herald to desire a passport for his ambassadors, if he had a mind to send any to him; but withal he desired his majesty to address letters to the Lords Howard * or Stanley †, and also to himself, that he might introduce his herald.

* John Howard, created Duke of Norfolk and Earl Marshal of England on the 28th of June, 1483, was the son of Robert Howard and Margaret, daughter of Thomas de Mowbray, Duke of Norfolk. He was killed at the battle of Bosworth Field on the 22nd of August, 1485.

† Thomas Stanley, afterwards Earl of Derby and Lord High Constable of England. He died on the 9th of November, 1504.

There were abundance of people attending without, during the king's private discourse with the herald, all of them impatient to hear what the king would say, and to see how his majesty looked when he came forth. When he had done, he called me, and charged me to entertain the herald, till he ordered him an escort, that I might keep him from talking privately with anybody; he commanded me like-wise to give him a piece of crimson velvet of thirty ells, which I did. After which the king addressed himself to the rest of the company, gave them an account of his letters of defiance, and calling seven or eight of them apart, he ordered the letters to be read aloud, showing himself very cheerful and valiant, without the least sign of fear in the world; for indeed he was much revived by what he had learned from the herald.

Ch. VI.—Of the Trouble and Perplexity of the Constable, and of certain Letters he wrote to the King of England and the Duke of Burgundy, which afterwards were partly the Cause of his Death.—1475.

I here must say a word or two concerning the constable, who was in great perplexity for the trick which he had played the Duke of Burgundy about St. Quentin; and he now looked upon himself as quite ruined in the king's favour, who had already drawn away from him the Lords of Genly* and of Moüy (two of his principal servants), though the Lord of Moüy went to visit him sometimes. The king very earnestly desired the constable to come to him, and offered him certain recompenses which he demanded for the county of Guise, and which the king had formerly promised him; the constable was willing to come, but required that the king should swear upon the cross of St. Lou of Angers † neither to do, nor con-

---

* Jean de Hangest, Lord of Geulis, was the son of Jean de Hangest and Marie de Sarrbruck. After having served the Duke of Burgundy until the death of that prince, he became a councillor and chamberlain of Louis XI., and was appointed Captain of Rouen. He died in 1490.

† The cross of Saint Lo or Saint Loup at Angers, was very celebrated during the reign of Louis XI.; it was a piece of the true cross preserved in the collegiate Church of Saint Lô, in the suburbs of Angers.

sent that any mischief should be done to his person ; insist-
ing, that his majesty might as well take this oath to him now,
as he had formerly done to the Lord of Lescut.*   The king
replied, that he would never take that oath again for any
man whatever ; but let him propose any other, and he would
take it.   You must understand that both constable and king
were in great uneasiness and perplexity of mind ; so that for
a good while together there was not a day passed, but somebody or other went between them to settle this oath.   And
to a thoughtful man it is a great instance of the misery and .
infelicity of human life, that we should speak and write so
many things contrary to our minds, as if it were done on purpose to shorten it.   But if these two I have mentioned were
full of cares and anxieties, the King of England and the Duke
of Burgundy had their share of trouble also.

The King of England's landing at Calais, and the Duke of
Burgundy's raising the siege of Nuz, occurred much about
the same time.   The duke, with long journeys (but a small
retinue), came directly to wait on the King of England † at
Calais, having sent his army (shattered and fatigued, as you
have heard) into the countries of Barrois and Lorraine to
plunder, and refresh themselves : for you have already heard
that the Duke of Lorraine had begun war upon him, and
defied him before Nuz.   This was a great oversight (among
the rest) of which he was guilty in respect to the English,
who expected him to have joined them at their landing with
at least 2500 men-at-arms, well provided, and a considerable
body of horse and foot (as the duke had promised) ‡ ; and
that he should have opened the campaign in France three
months before their descent, that they might have found the
king either tired of the war, or in great distress : but, as you

* That Louis XI. respected this oath, is evident from a letter which
he wrote to Tanneguy Duchastel on the 13th of November, 1472.   "I
have sworn to M. de Lescun on the true cross of Saint Lô that he may
come to me in safety ; wherefore I beseech you to set no ambushes, for
I would not wish to be in danger on account of breaking that oath."
Morice, iii. 250.

† He arrived at Calais on the 14th of July.   Lenglet, ii. 217.

‡ By the treaty concluded between the two princes on the 27th of
July, 1475, it was stipulated that the succour to be given by the Duke of
Burgundy to King Edward should consist of not less than 10,000 men,
or more than 20,000 men.   Rymer, v. 3. 43.

have heard before, God Almighty prevented it. The King of England, accompanied by the Duke of Burgundy, went from Calais to Boulogne, and from thence to Peronne, where the duke entertained the English but coldly; for he ordered the gates to be shut, and suffered very few to come into the town, and the rest had to encamp in the fields, which they were the better able to endure, because they had tents, and were well provided with all things necessary upon such an occasion.

They were no sooner arrived at Peronne, but the constable despatched one of his servants (called Louis de Creville) to make his excuse to the Duke of Burgundy for not having delivered St. Quentin, pretending that if he had done so, he would have been for ever disabled from serving him any further in the kingdom of France, for he would have thereby lost all his credit and influence in that nation. But now the King of England was come, he would act hereafter according to the Duke of Burgundy's directions; and for greater assurance, the messenger delivered him a letter to the King of England, in which the constable seemed to refer the character of his integrity to the Duke of Burgundy's testimony. Besides this, the Duke of Burgundy received another sealed up and addressed to himself, in which the constable made strong professions of friendship and service to the duke, and that he would assist him and his allies (and particularly the King of England) against all persons and princes whatever. The Duke of Burgundy gave the letter to the King of England, and acquainted him with the contents of his own, exaggerating a little, and assuring the king that the constable would receive him into St. Quentin, and all the rest of the towns; and the king really believed it, because he had married the constable's niece, and he thought him so terribly afraid of the King of France, that he would not venture to break his promise to the duke and himself. Nor was the Duke of Burgundy less credulous than King Edward. But neither the perplexities of the constable, nor his dread of the King of France, had as yet carried him so far; his design was only to wheedle and amuse them (according to his custom), and lay before them such plausible reasons as might prevail upon them not to force him to declare himself openly. The King of England

and his nobility were not so well skilled in artifice and subtlety as the lords of this kingdom, but went more bluntly and ingenuously about their affairs; so that they were not so sharp at discovering the intrigues and deceptions common on this side the water. The English that have never travelled are naturally passionate, as the people are generally in all cold countries. Our kingdom (as you see) is neither pierced with cold, nor scorched with the sun, being bounded on the east by Italy, Spain, and Catalonia; on the west, by Flanders and Holland; and by Germany on the south, all along the country of Champagne; so that part of our country being hot, and part of it cold, our people are of two complexions; but in my judgment, there is no country in the whole universe better situated than France.

The King of England (who perhaps had had some promises made him before, but not to so great an extent as now) being overjoyed at the news he received from the constable, set out with the Duke of Burgundy and his small retinue (for the main body of his army had marched into Barrois and Lorraine, as I have said) from Peronne towards St. Quentin. A party of English (not having patience to march with the army) had gone forward, expecting (as I was told some few days after) that the citizens would have ordered the bells to be rung for joy at their approach, and that they would have met them with the usual ceremony of the cross and holy water. But they were mightily mistaken; for they no sooner came in sight of the town, than the great guns were fired upon them, and a strong body of horse and foot sallied out to engage them; in which action two or three English were killed, and some few taken prisoners. It happened to be a terrible rainy day, yet they were forced to march through it, and retire to their army, much out of humour with the constable, and calling him a traitor. The Duke of Burgundy was resolved to take his leave the next morning of the King of England (which was a strange thing, considering it was upon his importunity that he had undertaken this expedition), and return to his forces in Barrois, pretending he would do great feats for the English; but the English being naturally of a jealous temper, novices on this side of the water, and astonished at this kind of proceeding, began to entertain an ill opinion of their ally, and

s

could not believe he had any army at all; besides, the Duke
of Burgundy could not satisfy them as to the constable's
manner of receiving them, though he endeavoured to persuade them all was well, and that what was done would turn
to their advantage; but all the Duke of Burgundy's arguments could not pacify them, and being disheartened at the
approach of winter, they seemed by their expressions to be
more inclinable to peace than war.

CH. VII.—How the King of France disguised one of his menial Servants in
a Herald's Coat, and sent him with a Message to the King of England,
who gave him a favourable Answer.—1475.

IN the meantime, even at the very moment of the duke's
taking his leave, the English took a gentleman's servant
belonging to the King of France's court, named James de
Grassé.*   This servant was brought immediately before the
King of England and the Duke of Burgundy; and being
ordered into a tent, after some slight examination of him,
the Duke of Burgundy took his leave, and set out by the
way of Brabant for Mazières†, where part of his army lay.
The King of England ordered the servant to be released, as
being the first prisoner they had taken.   Upon his departure,
the Lords Howard and Stanley gave him a noble, and desired him "to present their most humble service to the
king his master, when he had an opportunity of speaking to
him."   The servant came with all speed to Compiègne
(where the court was at that time) to give the king an account of their message; but his majesty was afraid of him,
and suspected him to be a spy, because his master's brother
Gilbert de Grassé‡, was then in Bretagne, and a great

* Jacques de Grassay, Esquire, Lord of Yors and Estrée in Bourbonnois, was the son of Regnault Grassay, Lord of Savigny-sur-Brais. He
was one of the gentlemen of the king's body-guard at this period; and
he afterwards became esquire-carver to King Charles VIII.
† Mezières, in the department of Ardennes.
‡ Gilbert de Grassay, Knight, Lord of Champciroux, was an equerry
to the Duke of Bretagne in 1465. He was taken prisoner at the sur-

favourite of that duke.   The servant had irons clapped upon him immediately, and a guard was set to watch him that night; yet several courtiers talked with him by the king's orders, and told his majesty that by his discourse he seemed a very honest fellow, and that he might venture to see him without any manner of danger.

Upon these assurances, the next morning the king spoke with him himself; and, after he had discoursed with him a little while, he ordered his irons to be knocked off, but kept him still in custody: from thence the king went to dinner, full of thought and consultation, whether he had best send to the King of England or not.   Before he sat down to the table he spoke something of it to me, for his way was (as you know, my Lord of Vienne) to speak privately and familiarly with those who were about him, as I was then, and others have been since; and he had a strange fancy to whisper into people's ears.   He was thinking upon what the King of England's herald had told him, that he should send to the King of England for a passport for his ambassadors, as soon as that prince had landed, and that his negotiation should be addressed to the Lords Howard and Stanley.   As soon as he was sat down, and had considered a little, according to his custom (which to those who were unacquainted with his fancy seemed strange, and might induce them to believe he was a prince of no great wisdom, but that his actions declared the contrary), he whispered me in the ear, and bade me rise and go dine in my chamber, and send for a servant* belonging to the Lord des Halles†, who was son to Merichon‡ of Rochelle, and ask him whether he would venture with a message into the King of England's army, in the habit of a herald.   I obeyed his orders, and was much astonished at the sight of the servant, for he seemed to me neither of a stature nor aspect fit for such an undertaking; yet his judgment was good (as I found afterwards), and his manner of expressing himself tolerable

render of Vannes in 1488 ; and soon afterwards he entered the service of France, and became one of the king's councillors and chamberlains.

* According to Lenglet, this servant's name was Merindot.

† Olivier Merichon, Knight, Lord des Halles de Poitiers, was cup-bearer to King Louis XI. in 1472.

‡ Jean Merichon, councillor of King Louis XI., was Lord of Uré and La Gort, near La Rochelle ; he married Marie de Parthenay-Soubise.

enough; but the king had never talked with him but once. The poor man was confounded at the proposal, and fell down upon his knees before me, as one that thought himself ruined and undone. I did all I could to encourage him, and told him he should have money for his pains, and a place in the Isle of Ré; and for his greater assurance, I persuaded him that the English had made the first overture themselves. I made him dine with me, and (there being nobody but he and I, and one servant that waited) by degrees I gave him instructions what he was to do, and how he was to behave himself in this affair.

Not long after, the king sent for me, and I gave him a relation of what had passed, and recommended others to him, who, in my opinion, were more proper for his design; but he would employ no other, and went and talked with him himself, and animated him more with one word than I could do with a hundred. There came along with the king into my chamber only the Lord de Villiers*, at that time Master of the Horse, and now Bailiff of Caen. When the king had sufficiently prepared and encouraged his man, he sent the Master of the Horse for the banner of a trumpeter to make his herald a coat of arms, for the king was not so stately or vain as to have either herald or trumpeter in his train, as other princes have; wherefore the master of the horse and one of my servants made up the coat of arms as well as they could; and having fetched a scutcheon from a little herald (called Plein Chemin, in the service of the Admiral of France), they fastened it about him, sent for his boots and his cloak privately, and his horse being got ready, he mounted, and nobody perceived him, with a bag or budget at the bow of his saddle, in which his coat of arms was put; and having been well instructed what he was to say, away he went directly to the English army.

Upon his arrival in his herald's coat, he was immediately stopped, and carried to the King of England's tent; being asked his business, he told them he was come with a message from the King of France to the King of England, and

* Alain Goyon de Villiers, councillor and chamberlain of Louis XI., Captain and Bailiff of Caen, and Master of the Horse of France, was the son of Jean Goyon, Lord of Matignon, and Marguerite de Mauny. He died in 1490.

had orders to address himself to the Lords Howard and
Stanley. He was carried into a tent to dinner, and very
civilly entertained. After the King of England had dined,
he sent for the herald, who told him that his errand was to
acquaint his majesty, that the King of France for a long
time had had a desire to be at amity with him, that both
their kingdoms might be at ease, and enjoy the blessing of
peace; that since his accession to the crown of France, he
never had made war, or attempted anything against him or
his kingdom; and as for having entertained the Earl of
Warwick formerly, he said he had done that more in opposition to the Duke of Burgundy than out of any quarrel
with King Edward. Then he went on to state that the
Duke of Burgundy had invited him over, only in order to
make his own terms the better with the King of France;
and if others had joined with him, it was only to secure
themselves against their former offences, or to advance their
own private affairs; which when they had once compassed,
they would not regard the interest of the King of England,
provided they had attained their own ends. He represented
likewise the lateness of the season, that winter was approaching, that his master was sensible of the great charge
the King of England had been at, and that he knew there
were in England many, both of the nobility and merchants,
who were desirous of a war on this side the water; yet if
the King of England should be inclined to a treaty, his
master would not refuse to come to such terms as should be
agreeable both to himself and to his subjects; and if the
King of England had a mind to be more particularly informed of these matters, if he would give him a passport for
100 horse, his master would send ambassadors to him with
full instructions : or if the king should think it more proper
to depute certain commissioners, and let them have a conference together in some village between the two armies, he
would willingly consent, and send them a passport.

The King of England and part of his nobility were extremely pleased with these proposals; a passport was given
to the herald according to his desire, and having been presented with four nobles in money, he was attended by a herald
from the King of England to obtain the King of France's
passport in the same form as the other ; which being given,

the next morning the commissioners met in a village near
Amiens.   On the part of the King of France, there were the
Bastard of Bourbon, Admiral of France, the Lord of St.
Pierre *, and the Bishop of Evreux, called Heberge.   On
the King of England's side †, there were the Lord Howard,
one Chalanger ‡, and one Doctor Morton §, who is at present
Chancellor of England and Archbishop of Canterbury.

Some people (I believe) will think this too great a condescension in our king; but the wiser sort may see, by what
I have said before, that his kingdom was in great danger,
had not God himself supported it by disposing the king to
so fortunate a resolution, and infatuating the Duke of Burgundy's understanding so as to make him commit so many
irreparable errors, and lose that by his own obstinacy which
he had been endeavouring so long to obtain.   We had,
besides, many private intrigues and secret cabals among us,
which would have produced great and speedy troubles to
this nation, as well in the direction of Bretagne, as of other
places, had not the king consented to this peace : so that
what I have often said before, I must once again repeat and
confirm, that I do certainly believe, by what I have seen in
my time, that God has a particular and more than ordinary
care of the preservation of this kingdom.

* Jean Blosset, Lord of Saint Pierre, was councillor and chamberlain
of the king, Seneschal of Normandy, and Captain of Avranches. He died
about 1507.

† The ambassadors of the King of England were four in number: the
three mentioned by Commines, and William Dudley, dean of the royal
chapel.

‡ Thomas Saint Leger, one of the king's body-guard; he was created
a Knight of the Bath on the 5th of July, 1483, by Richard III.; and
subsequently beheaded by order of that same prince, for having joined
the party of the Earl of Richmond.

§ John Morton, born at Bere, near Blandford, in Dorsetshire, was
originally Rector of St. Dunstan's Church in London.   He was appointed
Bishop of Ely on the 8th of August, 1478, translated to the see of
Canterbury on the 9th of October, 1486, and created Lord Chancellor
on the 8th of August, 1487.   Pope Alexander VI. made him a cardinal
in 1493; and he died at Knole on the 21st of September, 1500.

CH. VIII.— How a Truce for nine Years was negotiated between the Kings of France and England, notwithstanding the Difficulties and Impediments interposed by the Constable and the Duke of Burgundy. —1475.

As you have heard, our ambassadors met on the day after the return of our herald, for we were within four leagues of one another, or even less. Our herald was well treated, and had his money, and the office in the Isle of Ré, where he was born. Many overtures passed between our ambassadors. The English at first demanded, according to their custom, the crown of France, and by degrees they fell to Normandy and Guienne; our commissioners replied as became them: so that the demand was well urged on the one side, and well refused on the other: yet, from the very first day of the treaty, there was great prospect of an accommodation, for both parties seemed very inclinable to hearken to reasonable proposals: our commissioners came back, and the others returned to their camp. The king was informed of their demands, and the final resolution* was, to have 72,000 crowns paid them down before they left the kingdom; a marriage was to be concluded between our present king and the eldest daughter† of King Edward, who is now Queen of England, and for her maintenance either the duchy of Guienne was to be assigned‡, or a pension of 50,000 crowns,

* The terms finally agreed upon by the Kings of France and England are contained in four distinct acts, reported in Rymer (vol. v. part 3. pp. 65—68), and all dated on the 29th of August, 1475. Their provisions may be thus briefly stated: 1. King Edward engages to return to England with his army as soon as Louis XI. has paid him the sum of 75,000 crowns. 2. A truce of *seven* years, commencing at the date of the treaty, and finishing at sunset on the 29th of August, 1482, is concluded between the two sovereigns. 3. The Kings of France and England undertake to mutually assist each other in case either prince should be attacked by his enemies or by his rebellious subjects; and to make this alliance still closer, Prince Charles, son of Louis XI., is to wed the Princess Elizabeth, daughter of Edward IV., as soon as they are both of marriageable age. 4. The King of France engages to pay annually to the King of England, in two instalments, the sum of 50,000 crowns; such payment to continue only during the life-time of either prince.

† Elizabeth, born in 1466, married Henry VII., King of England, on the 18th of January, 1486, and died on the 11th of February, 1503.

‡ It will be seen by the previous note, that no reference was made to this demand in the final treaty.

to be paid annually during nine years, in the Tower of London; at the end of which term, the present king and his queen were to enjoy quietly the whole revenue of Guienne, and our king was to be discharged from paying the pension for the future. There were several other articles; but, as they were of no great weight or importance, I shall pass them over; only this I shall add that in this peace, which was to continue nine* years between the two crowns, the allies on both sides were to be comprehended if they pleased, and the Dukes of Burgundy and Bretagne were named expressly by the English. The King of England offered (which was strange) to make a discovery of some persons who (as he said) were traitors to our king and his crown, and to produce proofs of their treason under their own hands.

King Louis was extremely pleased with the progress that our commissioners had made in this affair. He held a council to consult what measures to take, and I was present at it: some were of opinion all this was but a trick and artifice in the English: but the king was of another mind, and he inferred it from the time of the year (it being pretty near winter), and their being unprovided with any place for a secure quarter; as also from the delays and disappointments which they had suffered from the Duke of Burgundy, who had (as it were) forsaken them already; and as for the Constable, he was well assured he would not deliver up any of his towns, for the king sent every hour to entertain and wheedle him, and prevent him from doing any harm. Besides, our king was perfectly acquainted with the King of England's temper, and that he loved to indulge himself in ease and pleasures: so that, by consequence, it plainly appeared that his majesty spoke more wisely, and had a better judgment of these affairs, than any of his council. Whereupon he resolved to raise the money with all expedition, and after debating the means of raising it, it was resolved it should be done by a loan, and that every one should advance something for greater despatch. The king declared he would do anything in the world to get the King of England out of France, except putting any of his towns into his possession; for rather than do that, he would hazard all.

* This is a mistake: the truce was to last *seven* years.

The Constable began to perceive these intrigues, to fear he had offended all parties, and to be jealous of the designs which he knew had been concluded against him at Bouvines; for which reason he sent very frequently to the king. At this very hour there arrived at court a servant of the Constable's, named Louis de Creville, and one of his secretaries, named John Richer, who are both still alive, who were ordered by the king to deliver their message to the Lord du Bouchage and to me. The message which they brought to the king pleased his majesty extremely; for he resolved to make his advantage of it, as you shall hear. The Lord of Contay, who (as I have already mentioned) was a servant to the Duke of Burgundy, had not long since been taken prisoner before Arras; and he travelled upon his parole between the duke and the king, who had promised him not only his liberty, but a considerable sum of money, if he could dispose his master to a peace. It happened that he was just returned from waiting on the Duke of Burgundy the very day the two gentlemen above mentioned arrived from the Constable. The king caused the Lord of Contay and myself to hide ourselves behind a great old screen that stood in his chamber, that the Lord of Contay might hear and report to the Duke of Burgundy the language with which the Constable and his creatures treated him. The king seated himself upon a stool near the screen, that we might more distinctly hear what the said Louis de Creville (with whom none of the king's servants except the Lord du Bouchage were admitted) had to say; and he and his colleague began their discourse, telling the king that their master had sent them lately to wait on the Duke of Burgundy, and that they had used many arguments to induce him to a rupture with the English, and that they had found him in so great a passion against the King of England, that they were in a fair way to prevail upon him, not only to abandon, but also to fall upon and destroy his army, in their retreat; and to please the king the more, as he thought, when he spoke those words, Louis de Creville, in imitation of the Duke of Burgundy, stamped with his foot, swore by St. George, called the King of England Blancborgne, the son of an archer who bore his name, with as many invectives besides, as could possibly be used against any man.

The king pretended to be highly pleased at the relation, and desired him to tell him it over again, and to raise his voice, for of late he was grown a little deaf; De Creville was not backward, but began again, and acted it to the life.

The Lord of Contay, who was with me behind the screen, was the most surprised person in the world, and all the arguments that could have been used could never have made him believe it, had he not overheard it himself. In the conclusion, they advised his majesty, in order to prevent the imminent danger that threatened his affairs, to make a truce; and promised that the Constable should do all that lay in his power to forward the negotiation; and, to satisfy the English in some measure, they proposed that the king should give them a small town or two for their winter quarters, which could not be so bad but they would be glad of them; yet, naming no towns, it was presumed they intended St. Valery and Eu. By this means the Constable thought to reconcile himself to the English, and expiate the affront which he had put upon them by refusing to admit them into his towns. The king, having sufficiently acted his part, and made the Lord of Contay hear every word that was spoken, gave them no uncivil answer, but only told them that he would send to his brother, and give him an account of his affairs; and then they took their leave, and withdrew.

One of them swore to the king, that whatever secret he might be intrusted with that concerned his majesty's affairs, he would certainly discover it to him. The king could scarce dissemble his resentment at their advising him to give the English the towns; but, fearing lest it might provoke the Constable to do worse, he would not make such a reply as might lead them to suspect that he disliked the proposition; but he sent a messenger of his own to the Constable, for the way was but short, and it took up no great time to go thither and return. When the ambassadors were gone out, the Lord of Contay and I came from behind the screen, and found the king very pleasant, and laughing heartily; but the Lord of Contay was out of all patience to hear such fellows speak so disrespectfully of his master the Duke of Burgundy, especially considering the great transactions which were at that time pending between the Constable and him. The Lord of Contay was impatient to be on horseback, and to make a relation of it to his master; and he therefore was immediately despatched, with a copy of instructions written with his own hand, and a letter of credence under the king's hand.

Our negotiation with the English was already concluded, as you have heard, and all these intrigues were carried on at one time. The King of France's commissioners, who had had a conference with the English, reported their proposals, and the King of England's envoys returned to their camp. At last it was agreed upon by the ambassadors on both sides, that the two kings should have an interview, and swear mutually to the performance of the articles; after which the King of England should return into his own country, upon the receipt of 72,000 crowns, and that the Lord Howard and Sir John Chene *, his Master of the Horse, should be left as hostages till he was arrived in England. Lastly, a pension of 16,000 crowns a year was promised to the privy councillors of the King of England — viz., to the Lord Hastings, 2000 crowns a year, who would never give an acquittance for it †; to the Chancellor ‡, 2000; and the rest to the Lord Howard, the Master of the Horse, Chalanger, Sir Thomas Montgomery §, and several others; besides a great deal of ready money and plate that was distributed among the rest of the King of England's retinue.

The Duke of Burgundy, who was then at Luxemburg, having notice of these proceedings, came in mighty haste ‖ to the King of England, attended only with sixteen horse in his retinue. The King of England was extremely surprised

* Sir John Cheyne was, at the period of his visit to France, Master of the Horse. He was created a Knight of the Bath by Richard III. on the 5th of July, 1483. He afterwards joined the party of the Earl of Richmond, and was wounded at the battle of Bosworth Field on the 22nd of August, 1485.

† Lord Hastings was not always so scrupulous, for he gave receipts for a pension granted him by the Duke of Burgundy in 1471. Lenglet, iii. 617.

‡ See note, p. 276.

§ Sir Thomas Montgomery was a Knight of the Garter, and one of King Edward's council. He was created a Knight of the Bath by Richard III. on the 5th of July, 1483.

‖ On the 18th of August, he slept at Peronne, and proceeded on the following day to King Edward's camp near Saint Christ, on the Somme. Lenglet, ii. 217.

at his unexpected arrival, and demanded what it was that brought him thither, for he saw by his countenance that he was angry. The duke told him he was come to discourse with him. The King of England asked whether it should be in public or private? Then the duke asked him if he had made a peace; the king told him, he had made a truce for nine years, in which the Duke of Bretagne and himself were comprehended, and he desired they would accept of that comprehension. The duke fell into a violent passion, and in English, a language that he spoke very well, began to commemorate the glorious achievements of his predecessors on the throne of England, who had formerly invaded France, and how they had spared no pains, nor declined any danger, that might render them famous, and gain them immortal honour and renown abroad. Then he inveighed against the truce, and told the king he had not invited the English over into France out of any necessity he had of their assistance, but only to put them in a way of recovering their own right and inheritance; and to convince them he could subsist without their alliance, he was resolved not to make use of the truce till the king had been three months in England *; and having delivered himself after this manner, he took his leave of the king, and returned to Luxemburg. The King of England and his council were extremely displeased with his language, but others who were adverse to the peace highly extolled it.   *

CH. IX.—How the King entertained the English in Amiens, and of the Place appointed for the Interview of the two Kings.—1475.

IN order to bring the peace to a conclusion, the King of England advanced within half a league of Amiens, and the King of France being upon one of the gates †, saw his army marching at a great distance. To speak impartially, his

* He nevertheless made a proposal for a truce of nine years with the king, on the 13th of September following. See Lenglet, iii. 409.

† Louis XI. arrived at Amiens on the 22nd of August. See Dupont, i. 362.

troops seemed but raw and unused to action in the field; for they were in very ill order, and observed no manner of discipline. Our king sent the King of England 300 cart-loads of the best wines in France as a present; and I think the carts made as great an appearance as the whole English army. Upon the strength of the truce, numbers of the English came into the town, where they behaved themselves very imprudently, and without the least regard to their prince's honour; for they entered the town all armed, and in great companies, so that if the King of France could have dispensed with his oath, never was there so handsome an opportunity of cutting off a considerable number of them; but his majesty's design was only to entertain them nobly, and to settle a firm and lasting peace, that might continue during his reign. The king had ordered two large tables to be placed on each side of the street, at the entrance of the town gate, which were covered with a variety of good dishes of all sorts of food most proper to relish their wine, of which there was great plenty, and of the richest that France could produce; and abundance of servants to wait on them, but not a drop of water was drunk. At each of the tables the king had placed five or six boon companions, persons of rank and condition, to entertain those that had a mind to take a hearty glass; amongst these were the Lord of Craon, the Lord of Briquebec *, the Lord of Bressure †, the Lord de Villiers, and several others. Those English who were within sight of the gate, saw the entertainment, and there were persons appointed on purpose to take their horses by the bridles, and lead them to the tables, where every man was treated handsomely as he came, in his turn, to their very great satisfaction. When they had once entered the town, wher-ever they went, or whatever they called for, nothing was to be paid; there were nine or ten taverns liberally furnished with all that they wanted, where they had whatever they had a mind to call for, without paying for it, according to

* Jean d'Estouteville, Knight, was Lord of Briquebec, Hambie, Gaseé, and Mesnil-Seran, and Castellan of Gavre.

† Jacques de Beaumont, Lord of Bressuire and La Motte-Sainte-Heraye, and Seneschal of Poitou, was the son of André de Beaumont and Jeanne de Torsay. He married Jeanne de Rochechouart. He was one of the chamberlains of Louis XI.

the King of France's orders, who bore all the expense of
that entertainment, which lasted three or four days.

You have already heard how dissatisfied the Duke of Burgundy was with the truce, but the Constable was much more
so ; for having deceived all parties, he could expect nothing
but inevitable ruin.   He sent therefore his confessor to the
King of England with letters of credence to this purpose,
to desire him for God's sake not to depend on the oaths and
promises of the King of France, but for the present to accept
of Eu and St. Valery for his winter quarters, for in two months
time he would manage affairs so as that his troops should be
better accommodated ; but he said nothing about security,
he only gave him great hopes: and lest the want of money
should have forced the king to consent to this truce, he
offered to lend him 50,000 crowns, and made him several
other fair proposals besides.   By this time the King of
France had ordered the two towns of Eu and St. Valery to be
burnt, because the Constable had proposed to deliver them
up to the English, and the English were informed of it.
However, the King of England returned this answer to the
Constable, that the truce was already concluded, and could
not be altered ; but if he had performed his promise, it had
never been made.   Which answer stung the Constable to the
very soul, and made him desperate on all sides.

I have already given you an account of the king's noble
entertainment of the English at Amiens.   One night the
Lord of Torcy * came to the king, and told him their numbers in the town were so considerable, that he apprehended
there might be some danger in it; but his majesty was
angry with him for it, so everybody else was silent.   The next
day was Childermas-day, on which the king neither spoke
himself, nor permitted any one else to apply to him about
business, but took it as an ill omen, and would be very
pettish when any such thing was proposed, especially by
those who waited on him, and knew his temper.   However,
on the morning I speak of, when the king was dressed, and
had gone in to his devotions, one came to me with news that

* Jean d'Estouteville, Lord of Torcy, Blainville and Ondeauville, and
grand master of the cross-bow-men of France, was the son of Guillaume
de Torcy and Jeanne d'Ondeauville; he married Françoise de la Roche-
foucauld, and died on the 11th of September, 1494.

there were at least 9,000 English in the town. I resolved
to risk his displeasure, and acquaint him with this fact;
whereupon, entering into his closet, I said, " Sir, though it
be Childermas-day, I think myself bound in duty to inform
your majesty of what I have heard." Then I gave him an
account of the number of troops already in the town, and
that more were coming in every moment; that they were
all armed, and that nobody durst shut the gate upon them
for fear of provoking them. The king was not offended, but
left his prayers, and told me, that for once he would put off
the devotions of that day. He commanded me immediately
to get on horseback, and endeavour to speak with some of
the English officers of note, to desire them to order their
troops to retire ; and if I met any of his captains, to send
them to him, for he would be at the gate as soon as I.

I met three or four English commanders of my acquaintance, and spoke to them according to the king's
directions; but for one that they commanded to leave the
town, there were twenty came in. After me, the king sent
the Lord of Gié * (now Marshal of France), and having
found me, we went together into a tavern, where, though it
was not nine o'clock, there had already been 111 reckonings
to pay that morning. The house was filled with company,
some were singing, some were asleep, and all were drunk ;
upon seeing which, I concluded there was no danger, and
sent to inform the king of it; who came immediately to the
gate, well attended, and ordered 200 or 300 men-at-arms to
be armed privately in their captains' houses, and some of
them he posted at the gate by which the English entered.
The king ordered his dinner to be brought to the porter's
lodgings at the gate, where his majesty dined, and did
several English officers the honour of admitting them to
dinner with him. The King of England had been informed
of this disorder, and was much ashamed of it, and sent to the
King of France to desire his majesty to admit no more of
his troops into the town. The King of France sent him
word back, he would not do that, but if he pleased to send a

* Pierre de Rohan, Knight, Count of Marle and Porcien, and Lord
of Gié, was the son of Louis de Rohan and Marie de Montauban. He
was created Marshal of France in 1475, and died on the 22nd of April,
1513.

party of his own guards thither, the gate should be delivered up to them, and they might let in or shut out whomever they pleased. In short, so they did, and several of the English, by their king's express command, were ordered to evacuate the town.

And then, in order to bring the whole affair to a conclusion, they consulted what place would be most convenient for the interview of the two kings, and persons were appointed to survey it; the Lord du Bouchage and I were chosen to represent our master; and the Lord Howard, one Chalanger, and a herald, represented the King of England. Upon our taking a view of the river, we agreed the best and securest place was Picquigny, a strong castle some three leagues from Amiens, belonging to the Vidame * of Amiens, which had been burnt not long before by the Duke of Burgundy; the town lies low, the River Somme runs through it, and is not fordable or wide near it. On the one side, by which our king was to come, was a fine champaign country; and on the other side it was the same, only when the King of England came to the river, he was obliged to pass a causeway about two bow-shots in length, with marshes on both sides, which might have produced very dangerous consequences to the English, if our intentions had not been honourable. And certainly, as I have said before, the English do not manage their treaties and capitulations with so much cunning and policy as the French do, let people say what they will, but proceed more ingenuously, and with greater straightforwardness in their affairs; yet a man must be cautious, and have a care not to affront them, for it is dangerous meddling with them.

After we had fixed upon the place, our next consultation was about a bridge which was ordered to be built, large and strong, for which purpose we furnished our carpenters with materials. In the midst of the bridge there was contrived a strong wooden lattice, such as the lions' cages are made with, the hole between every bar being no wider than to thrust in

* The Vidame of Amiens, at this time, was Jean d'Ailly, Knight, Baron of Picquigny, Raineval, La Broye, Merancourt, and Poissy, and councillor and chamberlain of King Louis XI. He married Yolande de Bourgogne, a natural daughter of Duke Philip the Good; and died in 1492.

a man's arm; the top was covered only with boards to keep off the rain, and the body of it was big enough to contain ten or twelve men of a side, with the bars running across to both sides of the bridge, to hinder any person from passing over it either to the one side or the other; and in the river there was only one little boat rowed by two men, to convey over such as had a mind to cross it.

I will now relate the reason that induced the king to have the place of their interview contrived after such a fashion, that there should be no passage from one side to the other; and perhaps the time may come, when this may be useful to some persons, who may have the same occasion. During the minority of Charles VII. the kingdom of France was much infested by the English. Henry V. lay before Rouen*, and had straitened it very much, and the greatest part of those in the town were either subjects, or partisans of John, Duke of Burgundy, who was then reigning.

There had been a long and great difference† between John, Duke of Burgundy, and the Duke of Orleans, and the whole kingdom, or most of it, was engaged in their quarrel, to the prejudice of the king's affairs; for faction never begins in any country, but it is difficult to extinguish, and dangerous in the end. In this quarrel that I speak of, the Duke of Orleans had been killed in Paris one year before.‡ Duke John had a powerful army, and advanced to raise the siege of Rouen; that he might do it with more ease, and assure himself of the king's friendship, it was agreed that the king§ and he should have an interview at Montereau-Fault-Yonne, where a bridge was erected, with a barrier in the midst, and

* This was in the year 1418.

† The frequent attacks of insanity to which King Charles VI. was subject, rendered it impossible for him to govern alone, and the administration of the affairs of the kingdom was therefore entrusted to his brother the Duke of Orleans, and to his cousin the Duke of Burgundy. Neither of these princes was, however, satisfied with a mere share in the royal power; and on the 23rd of November, 1407, the Duke of Orleans was assassinated by order of the Duke of Burgundy. Hence arose a civil war, which lasted until 1435.

‡ This should be *eleven* years — (1407—1418).

§ Charles VII. was at this time Dauphin only, as his father did not die until 1422. It was not until after the capture of Rouen by Henry V. that the dauphin and the Duke of Burgundy became reconciled, and signed a peace at Arras on the 11th of July, 1419.

T

in the middle of the barrier a little wicket, which was bolted on both sides; by which means, and by the consent of both parties, they might pass to either side.   The king came on one side, and Duke John on the other, both attended with a strong party of their guards, but especially Duke John; they met, and had a long conference upon the bridge, and about the duke's person there were not above three or four at the most.   In the height of their discourse, the duke (either by the persuasion of others, or out of a desire to pay a more than ordinary respect to his majesty) unbolted the wicket on his side, and it being opened by the others, he passed through it to the king, and was immediately slain *, himself and all those who attended him; which was the occasion of abundance of mischief that ensued afterwards, as everybody knows: but this is not material to my design, so I shall speak of it no farther, only let me tell you, you have the story just as the king told it me himself, when he sent me to choose a place, commanding expressly that there should be no door; for said he, if that had not been, there had been no means of inviting the duke to the other side, and then that misfortune had been prevented,—the principal contrivers and executors of which were some of the murdered Duke of Orleans' servants, who were present at that time, and had great authority with King Charles VII.

Ch. X.—Of the Interview between the two Kings, and of their swearing to the Truce which had been concluded before; and how some fancied the Holy Ghost descended upon the King of England's Tent in the Shape of a White Pigeon.—1475.

THE barrier being finished, and the place fitted for the interview, as you have already heard, on the next day, which was the 29th of August, 1475, the two kings appeared.   The King of France came first, attended by about 800 men-at-arms: on the King of England's side, his whole army was drawn up in order of battle; and though we could not discover their whole force, yet we saw such a vast number

---

* On the 10th of September, 1419.

both of horse and foot, that the body of troops that were
with us seemed very inconsiderable in comparison with
them; but indeed the fourth part of our army was not there.
It was given out that twelve men of a side were to be with
each of the kings at the interview, and that they were already
chosen from among their greatest and most trusty courtiers.
With us we had four of the King of England's party to view
what was done among us, and they had as many of ours, on their
side, to have an eye over their actions. As I said before,
our king came first to the barrier, attended by twelve persons;
among whom were John, Duke of Bourbon, and the Cardinal
his brother. It was the king's royal pleasure (according to
an old and common custom that he had), that I should be
dressed like him on that day.

The King of England advanced along the causeway (which
I mentioned before) very nobly attended, with the air and
presence of a king : there were in his train his brother the
Duke of Clarence, the Earl of Northumberland*, his chamberlain the Lord Hastings, his Chancellor, and other peers of
the realm ; among whom there were not above three or four
dressed in cloth of gold like himself. The King of England
wore a black velvet cap upon his head, with a large fleur de
lys made of precious stones upon it : he was a prince of a
noble and majestic presence, but a little inclining to corpulence.
I had seen him before when the Earl of Warwick drove him
out of his kingdom; then I thought him much handsomer,
and to the best of my remembrance, my eyes had never
beheld a more handsome person. When he came within a
little distance of the barrier, he pulled off his cap, and bowed
himself within half a foot of the ground ; and the King of
France, who was then leaning against the barrier, received him
with abundance of reverence and respect. They embraced
through the holes of the grate, and the King of England
making him another low bow, the King of France saluted
him thus :—"Cousin, you are heartily welcome ; there is no
person living I was so ambitious of seeing, and God be
thanked that this interview is upon so good an occasion.'

* Henry Percy, Earl of Northumberland, was the son of Henry Percy
and Eleanor Poynings. He married Maud, daughter of William Herbert,
first Earl of Pembroke. He was killed in a popular riot, during the fourth
year of the reign of King Henry VII.

The King of England returned the compliment in very good French.

Then the Chancellor of England (who was a prelate, and Bishop of Lisle *) began his speech with a prophecy (with which the English are always provided) that at Picquigny a memorable peace was to be concluded between the English and French. After he had finished his harangue, the instrument was produced which contained the articles the King of France had sent to the King of England. The Chancellor demanded of our king, whether he had dictated the said articles? and whether he agreed to them? The king replied, Yes: and King Edward's letters being produced on our side, he made the same answer. The missal being then brought and opened, both the kings laid one of their hands upon the book, and the other upon the holy true cross, and both of them swore religiously to observe the contents of the truce, which was, that it should stand firm and good for nine years complete; that the allies on both sides should be comprehended; and that the marriage between their children should be consummated, as was stipulated by the said treaty. After the two kings had sworn to observe the treaty, our king (who had always words at command) told the King of England in a jocular way, he should be glad to see his majesty at Paris; and that if he would come and divert himself with the ladies, he would assign him the Cardinal of Bourbon for his confessor, who he knew would willingly absolve him, if he should commit any sin by way of love and gallantry. The King of England was extremely pleased with his raillery, and made his majesty several good repartees, for he knew the cardinal was a jolly companion.

After some discourse to this purpose, our king, to show his authority, commanded us who attended him to withdraw, for he had a mind to have a little private discourse with the King of England. We obeyed, and those who were with

* The personage here alluded to by Commines, is Thomas of Rotherham, who was born on the 24th of August, 1423, and became Keeper of the Great Seal, Bishop of Rochester in 1468, Bishop of Lincoln in 1471, and Archbishop of York in 1480. He was appointed Lord High Chancellor of England in 1474, and with an interval of two years, occupied that post until his death, on the 29th of May, 1500. Commines here mistakes *Lisle* for *Lincoln*.

the King of England, seeing us retire, did the same, without waiting to be commanded. After the two kings had been alone together for some time, our master called me to him, and asked the King of England if he knew me? The King of England replied he did, and named the places where he had seen me, and told the king that formerly I had endeavoured to serve him at Calais*, when I was in the Duke of Burgundy's service. The King of France demanded, if the Duke of Burgundy refused to be comprehended in the treaty (as might be expected from his obstinate answer), what the King of England would have him do? The King of England replied, he would offer it him again, and if he refused it then, he would not concern himself any farther, but leave it entirely to themselves. By degrees the king came to mention the Duke of Bretagne (who indeed was the person he aimed at in the question), and made the same demand about him. The King of England desired he would not attempt anything against the Duke of Bretagne, for in his necessity he had never found so true and faithful a friend.† The king pressed him no farther, but recalling his retinue, took his leave of the King of England in the handsomest and most civil terms imaginable, and saluted all his attendants in a most particular manner : and both the kings at a time (or very near it) retired from the barrier, and mounting on horseback, the King of France returned to Amiens, and the King of England to his army. The King of England was accommodated by the King of France with whatever he wanted, even to the very torches and candles. The Duke of Gloucester, the King of England's brother, and some other persons of quality, were not present at this interview, as being averse to the treaty ; but they recollected themselves afterwards, and the Duke of Gloucester waited on the king our master at Amiens, where he was splendidly entertained, and nobly presented both with plate and fine horses. ‡

---

* See above, p. 188.

† Our historian Habington states this reply of King Edward somewhat differently, and says he answered resolutely, "That he would never forsake the care of a confederate who had maintained his faith so constantly."

‡ The other English lords who took presents, or rather pensions from the French king, were, the Lord Hastings, lord chamberlain ; the Lord

As the king returned from this interview, he spoke to me by the way upon two points: one was, that the King of England had been so easily persuaded to come to Paris. His majesty was not at all pleased with it, and he told me, "He is a very handsome prince, a great admirer of the ladies, and who knows but some of them may appear to him so charming, as may give him a desire of making us a second visit. His predecessors have been too often in Paris and Normandy already; and I do not care for his company so near, though on the other side of the water, I shall gladly esteem him as my friend and brother." Besides, the king was displeased to find him so obstinate in relation to the Duke of Bretagne, on whom he would fain have made war, and to that purpose made another overture to him by the Lord du Bouchage and the Lord of St. Pierre. But when the King of England saw himself pressed, he gave them this short but generous answer, "That if any prince invaded the Duke of Bretagne's dominions, he would cross the seas once more in his defence." Upon which they importuned him no farther.

When the king had arrived at Amiens, and was ready to go to supper, three or four of the English lords, who had attended upon the King of England at the interview, came to sup with his majesty; and the Lord Howard being of the number, he told the king in his ear, that if he desired it, he would find a way to bring his master to him to Amiens, and to Paris too, to be merry with him for some time. Though this offer and proposition were not in the least agreeable to the king, yet his majesty dissembled the matter pretty well, and fell a washing his hands, without giving a direct answer; but he whispered me in the ear, that what he suspected was at last come really to pass. After supper they fell upon the subject again; but the king put it off with the greatest wisdom imaginable, pretending that his expedition against the Duke of Burgundy would require his departure immediately. Though these affairs were of very great importance, and great prudence was used on both sides to manage them discreetly; yet there were some

Howard; Sir John Cheyne, master of the horse; Sir Anthony St. Leger, and Sir Thomas Montgomery.

pleasant occurrences among them, worthy to be transmitted to posterity. Nor ought any man to wonder (considering the great mischiefs which the English have brought upon this kingdom, and the recentness of their date), that the King of France should be at so much labour and expense to send them home in a friendly manner, that he might make them his friends for the future, or at least divert them from making war against him.

The next day, a great number of English came to Amiens, some of whom reported that the Holy Ghost had made that peace, and prophecies were produced to confirm it; but their greatest argument to support this opinion was that, during the time of their interview, a white pigeon came and sate upon the King of England's tent, and could not be frightened away by any noise they could make in the camp. But some gave another reason, and that was, that a small shower of rain having fallen that day, and soon after the sun shining out very warmly, the poor pigeon, finding that tent higher than the rest, came thither only to dry herself. And this reason was given me by a Gascon gentleman, called Louis de Breteilles *, who was in the King of England's service. He was very much displeased at this peace; and having been an old acquaintance of mine, he told me privately, that we did but laugh at the King of England. Among the rest of our discourse, I asked him how many battles the King of England had won. He told me nine, and that he had been in every one of them in person. I demanded next how many he had lost? He replied, never but one, and that was the one in which we had outwitted him now; for he was of opinion that the ignominy of his returning so soon, after such vast preparations, would be a greater disgrace and stain to his arms than all the honour he had gained in the nine former victories. I acquainted the king with this smart answer, and the king replied, "He is a shrewd fellow, I warrant him, and we must have a care of his tongue." The next day he sent for him, and had him to dinner at his own table, and made him very advantageous proposals, if he would quit his master's service, and

---

* According to Oliver de la Marche, ii. 266, he was a Gascon squire in the service of Lord Scales.

T 4

live in France; but finding he was not to be prevailed on, he presented him with 1000 crowns, and promised that he would do great things for his brothers in France. Upon his going away, I whispered him in the ear, and desired him to employ his good offices to continue and propagate the love and good understanding which had now begun between the two kings.

The king was in the greatest concern imaginable, for fear he should drop some word or other, that might make the English suspect he had imposed upon them, and laughed at them. The next morning after the interview, his majesty being in his closet, with only three or four of us with him, he began to droll and jest about the wines and presents which he had sent to the English camp; but, turning suddenly round, he perceived a merchant of Gascony, who lived in England, and had come to court to beg leave to export a certain quantity of Bordeaux wines, without paying the duties; the obtaining of which privilege would have been very advantageous to him. The king was much surprised at the sight of him, and wondered how he came thither. The king asked him of what town in Guienne he was; and whether he had married in England? The merchant replied, yes, he had a wife in England, but the estate he had there was but small. Before he went out, the king appointed a person to go with him to Bordeaux, and I had also some discourse with him by his majesty's express command. The king gave him a considerable employment in the town where he was born, granted him the exemption of the duties upon his wines, and gave him 1000 francs to bring over his wife; but he was to send his brother into England for her, and not go thither to fetch her himself; and this penalty the king imposed upon himself for having used his tongue too freely.

CH. XI.—How the Constable endeavoured to excuse himself to the King of France, upon the Conclusion of the Peace with the English; and how a Truce was likewise made for Nine Years between the Duke of Burgundy and the King of France.—1475.

THE next day after the interview, the Constable despatched one of his servants, called Rapine, with letters to the king, who preferred him afterwards for having been faithful to his master; the king ordered the Lord du Lude* and myself to receive his message. At the same time the Lord of Contay, whom I have mentioned so often, had returned from the Duke of Burgundy's court with his head full of designs against the Constable; so that the Constable looked upon himself as ruined and undone, and knew not to which of the saints he should address his devotions. Rapine's message was very submissive; he told us that his master was very sensible that many accusations and charges had been brought against him to the king, but his majesty would know from experience, that he had no traitorous intentions. However, to give the king greater evidence of his loyalty, he made some proposals to his majesty, that if he pleased to order matters so, he would persuade the Duke of Burgundy to join his forces with the king's, and destroy the King of England and his whole army on their return; and by his manner of speaking, it seemed to us that his master was in the height of despair. We told him that peace was already concluded with the English, and that we were not desirous of beginning a new war. The Lord du Lude proceeded so far as to ask Rapine if he did not know how his master had disposed of his ready money? I was amazed that this question (for Rapine had the character of being a good servant) did not give him a hint of his master's impending ruin, discover the designs that were forming against him, and make the Constable fly, especially when he reflected on the danger he had escaped only the year before. But I have seen but very few people in my time, that knew how to fly from danger in time. Some have not profited by the experience they might have had of their neighbours' misfortunes; others never travelled into foreign countries, which is certainly a great fault in a man of quality, for to have seen the world gives a man great wisdom and presence of mind; others are too passionately fond of their wives, their children, or their estates; and one or other of these reasons has been the ruin of many a brave man.

After we had given his majesty an account of Rapine's

* Jean Daillon, Lord du Lude, knight, councillor and chamberlain to Louis XI., and Governor of Dauphiny. He was a *compère* of the king, who nicknamed him *Maistre Jehan des habiletez.*

message, he called for one of his secretaries. There were
then in his presence only the Lord Howard *, an English
courtier, who knew nothing of our intrigue with the Constable, the Lord of Contay, who was newly returned from
the Duke of Burgundy, and we two who had been in discourse with Rapine. The king dictated a letter to the
Constable, in which his majesty acquainted him with what
had been transacted the day before in relation to the truce.
He told him, that at that instant he had many weighty
affairs upon his hands, and wanted such a head as his to
finish them; and then turning to the English nobleman and
the Lord of Contay, he told them, "I do not mean his body
— I would have his head with me, and his body where it is."
After the letter was read, it was delivered to Rapine, who
was mightily pleased with it, and took it as a great compliment in the king to say, that he wanted such a head as
his master's, for he did not understand the ambiguity of the
phrase. The King of England sent two letters, which the
Constable had written to him†, to the King of France, and
acquainted his majesty with all the proposals he had ever
made him, by which it may easily be discerned into what a
miserable condition he had brought himself, when every one
of these three great princes desired his destruction.

As soon as the King of England had received his money,
and delivered the Lord Howard and Sir John Cheyne, his
master of the horse, as hostages, as he had promised till he
was landed in England, he retreated towards Calais by long
and hasty marches; for he was apprehensive of the Duke of
Burgundy's anger, and of the hatred of the peasants; and
indeed if any of his soldiers straggled, some of them were
sure to be knocked on the head.

At the beginning of our affairs with the English, you may
remember that the King of England had no great inclination

* This was that John, Lord Howard, who, in consideration of his
descent from the Lady Margaret, daughter of Thomas, first Duke of
Norfolk, was, by Richard III., created Duke of Norfolk, and lost his life
with him at Bosworth Field. From him are descended the Duke of
Norfolk, and all the noble families of the Howards now in being.

† In these letters he told him that "he was a cowardly, dishonoured
and poor king, for having made such a treaty with the King of France, on
account of the promises he had made him, none of which he intended to
keep." Lenglet, ii. 120.

to make this descent; and as soon as he came to Dover, and before his embarkation there, he entered into a sort of a treaty with us. But that which prevailed with him to transport his army to Calais, was, first, the solicitation of the Duke of Burgundy, and the natural animosity of the English against the French, which has existed in all ages; and next, to reserve to himself a great part of the money which had been liberally granted him for that expedition; for, as you have already heard, the kings of England live upon their own demesne revenue, and can raise no taxes but under the pretence of invading France. Besides, the king had another stratagem by which to content his subjects, for he had brought along with him ten or twelve of the chief citizens of London, and other towns in England, all fat and jolly, the leaders of the English commons, of great power in their country, such as had promoted the war, and had been very serviceable in raising that powerful army. The king ordered very fine tents to be made for them, in which they lay; but, that not being the way of living they had been used to, they soon began to grow weary of the campaign, for they expected they should come to an engagement within three days after their landing, and the king multiplied their fears and exaggerated the dangers of a war, on purpose that they might be better satisfied with a peace, and aid him to pacify the murmurs of the people upon his return into England; for since Arthur's days, never King of England invaded France with so great a number of the nobility and such a formidable army. But, as you have heard, he returned immediately into England upon the conclusion of the peace, and reserved the greatest part of the money that had been raised to pay the army for his own private use; so that in reality, he accomplished most of the designs he had in view.* The King of England was not of a complexion or turn of mind to endure much hardship and labour, and those any King of England who designs to make any considerable conquest in France, must expect to suffer. Besides our king was in a tolerable posture of defence, though in all places he was not so well prepared as he ought to have been, by reason of the variety

* The city of London, however, seemed well pleased with this expedition, and the lord mayor and aldermen received the king on Blackheath with great formalities, and conducted him in great pomp to Westminster.

and multitude of his enemies. Another great design the King
of England had in view, which was the accomplishment of
the marriage between our present King Charles VIII. and
his daughter *, and this wedding, causing him to wink at
several things, was a great advantage to our master's affairs.

After all the English, except their hostages, were landed
in England, the King of France retired towards Laon, to a
little town called Vervins, bordering upon the marshes of
Hainault ; for the Chancellor of Burgundy and other ambassadors were at Avesnes in Hainault with the Lord of Contay,
with a commission from the Duke of Burgundy to treat of
an accommodation ; and the king himself had a great desire
to obtain a general peace. The vast numbers of the English
had put him into great alarm; he had seen enough of their
exploits in his time in his kingdom, and had no mind to see
any more of them. The Chancellor, who was one of the
Duke of Burgundy's plenipotentiaries, as you have heard,
sent news to the king, that if he pleased to send his ambassadors to a bridge half way between Avesnes and Vervins,
he and his colleagues would certainly meet them there. The
king sent them word he would come thither himself; and
though some persons whom he consulted endeavoured to
dissuade his majesty from it, yet he went, and took the
English hostages along with him ; and they were present
when the king gave audience to the ambassadors, who had a
strong guard of archers and other soldiers ; but no business
was despatched then, only the king took them to dinner with
him.

One of the English that was there began to repent of the
peace, and told me at the window, that had they seen many
such men of the Duke of Burgundy's before, perhaps the
peace had not been concluded so soon. The Viscount of
Narbonne† (now called the Lord of Fouez) overhearing him,
replied, "Could you be so weak as to believe the Duke of

* King Edward upon his return from France, caused his eldest
daughter Elizabeth to be styled Dauphiness.

† Jean de Foix, Viscount of Narbonne, was the son of Gaston IV.,
Count of Foix, and Eleanor of Arragon, afterwards Queen of Navarre.
He married Marie de France, sister of King Louis XII; and died in
November, 1500. He assumed the title of Count of Foix in 1483, on
the death of his nephew, François Phœbus, Count of Foix and King of
Navarre.

Burgundy had not great numbers of such soldiers? he had only sent them into quarters of refreshment, but you were in such haste to be at home again, that six hundred pipes of wine and a pension from our king sent you quickly back into England." The Englishman was in a passion, and answered with much warmth, "I plainly see, as everybody said, that you have done nothing but cheat us. Do you call the money your king has given us a pension? It is a tribute, and, by St. George, you may prate so much as will bring us back again to prove it." I interrupted their discourse, and turned it into a jest; but the Englishman would not understand it so, and I informed the king of it, and his majesty was highly offended with the Viscount of Narbonne.

The King of France had but a short conference with the Chancellor and the rest of the plenipotentiaries at that time; for it was agreed they should wait on his majesty at Vervins, and so they did. When they were at Vervins, the king appointed Tanneguy du Chastel, and Pierre Doriole, Chancellor of France, to negotiate with them, and committed the whole management of the affair to them. Great representations were made, and both sides were very zealous for the advantage of their masters. The king's ambassadors made their report and acquainted his majesty that the Duke of Burgundy's commissioners had been haughty in their language, but they had given them as good as they brought, and then repeated their answers. The king was not pleased with them, and told them there had been too many of those smart answers already; and that as the debate was only about a truce, not a final peace, he would have no more such expressions used, and therefore he would treat with them himself. Whereupon his majesty requested the Chancellor and the rest of the Duke of Burgundy's plenipotentiaries to attend him in his chamber, where none of his court being present but the Lord Admiral, the late Bastard of Bourbon, the Lord du Bouchage, and myself, he concluded a truce with them for nine years to come*, whereby all things were to be restored that had

---

* This treaty is dated on the 13th of September, 1475, and was to continue from that date until the 12th of September, 1484. Commines does not mention that, by one of the articles, four gentlemen, one of

been taken: but the ambassadors desired the king that it might not yet be proclaimed by sound of trumpet, as the usual manner was, in order to save the duke's oath to the King of England (when he swore in his passion he would not accept of the benefit of the truce till the king had been in England three months), lest he should think their master had spoken otherwise than he designed.

The King of England being highly disgusted at the Duke of Burgundy's rejection of his truce, and present endeavour to make a separate peace with the king, despatched a great favourite of his, called Sir Thomas Montgomery, to the king at Vervins, and he happened to arrive there at the very time the king was negotiating with the Duke of Burgundy's envoys. Sir Thomas desired, on behalf of the King of England, his master, that the King of France would not consent to any other truce with the duke than what was already made. He also pressed his majesty not to deliver St. Quentin into the duke's hands; and, as farther encouragement, he offered to pass the seas next spring with a powerful army to assist him, provided his majesty would continue the war against the Duke of Burgundy, and compensate him for the prejudice he should sustain in his duties upon wool at Calais, which would be worth little or nothing in war time (though at other times they were valued at 50,000 crowns a year). He proposed, likewise, that the King of France should pay one half of his army, and he would pay the other himself. The King of France returned the King of England abundance of thanks, and made Sir Thomas a present of plate; but as to the continuation of the war, he begged to be excused, for the truce was already concluded, and upon the same terms as that which had been agreed to between them; only the Duke of Burgundy pressed mightily to have a separate truce by himself*; which he excused as well as he could, to please and satisfy the English ambassador, who with this answer returned into England, and the hostages with him. The king was extremely surprised at the King

whom was himself, were excluded from all share in the treaty. Lenglet, iii. 409.

* This was the main point King Edward endeavoured to prevent, since, by articling apart, the duke showed his independence, and that the English, by their arms, had in no way advanced his affairs.

of England's offers, which were delivered only before me : he conceived it would be very dangerous to bring the King of England into France again, for between those two nations (when together) any trifling accident might raise some new quarrel, and they might easily make friends again with the Duke of Burgundy,—which consideration greatly forwarded the conclusion of the treaty with the Burgundians.

A Treaty or Truce of Commerce made for Nine Years between Louis XI. and Charles, the last Duke of Burgundy, at Vervins, September 13. 1475.

1. That there shall be a good and firm truce concluded ; and all hostilities cease, both by sea and land and on fresh waters, between the king and the duke, their heirs, successors, territories, and subjects, from the 13th day of September, for nine years — *viz.*, to 1484, without any manner of contravention on either side, under the pretence of letters of mark, countermark, reprisals, debts, or otherwise whatsoever; and supposing anything done contrary hereunto, restitution shall be made without delay, that is, within eight days after the imparting of the fact by one party to the other ; and if that be not done, the party aggrieved shall by force of arms recover such places as have been voluntarily given, or taken from him, and the other shall make no resistance ; and yet the truce shall not be violated thereby ; and the party that shall not make the said restitution, shall bear all the other's charge.

2. All the subjects and servants on either side, of what quality, condition, or nation soever they be, shall follow their occupations peaceably, and quietly, and without any molestation whatsoever, as in time of peace.

3. No manner of hostilities shall be committed during the truce, but all persons whatsoever, without distinction, shall go, sojourn, converse, or trade in the dominions of each other without any safe-conduct, and without any molestation or injury whatsoever ; only armed soldiers shall not enter into each other's territories in a greater number than fourscore or a hundred horse.

4. All persons of all ranks and vocations, during the truce, shall return to the enjoyment and possession of their benefices, places, lands, signiories, and other estates, in the con-

dition wherein they shall find them; and shall be admitted without any molestation or delay, without being obliged to do homage anew, but either in person or by their substitutes making oath before the proper officer that they will do nothing in prejudice to the party to whom they belong; and upon the expiration of the truce they shall be left in full obedience to the party whose they are at present: nevertheless, the king is content to give up Rambures entirely to the lord of it, without putting any guard into it, upon condition he swears and signs before the person who shall make that restitution, that during the truce, and after the expiration of it, he shall do nothing that is prejudicial to the king and his dominions, nor to the Duke of Burgundy and his territories, nor put any garrison into the place, that shall endamage either party.

5. As to the fortresses of Beaulieu and Vervins, the duke consents, that upon the actual restitution of the town and bailiwick of St. Quentin, and the places concerning which treaties have been made between the king and himself, they shall be demolished, and the revenue and lordships remain in the possession of the lords of them.

6. The lands and signiories of La Fere, and Chastellez, Vandeul, and St. Lambert, depending on the Count of Marle, shall remain under the king's obedience; but the signiory and revenue thereof are to be the count's.

7. The castles, towns, territories, and chastellanies of Marle, Jassy, Montcornet, St. Goubain, and Assy, shall be under the duke's obedience; but the revenue shall belong to the said count.

8. As to this truce, so far as it concerns persons returning to their possessions on either side, the Bastard of Burgundy, the Sieur de Renty, Jean de Chassa, and Philip de Commines, are wholly excepted.

9. All infractions made on either side of this truce, shall be severely punished according to the demerits of them, and reparation shall be made, within six days after they come to be known, by the conservators of the truce on either side.

10. The conservators are on the king's part: for the county of Eu, St. Valery, and the adjacent places, the Marshal de Gamaches; for Amiens, Beauvoisis, and the neighbouring marches, Monsieur de Torcy; for Compiegne, Noyon, and

those marches, the Bailiff of Vermandois; for the county of Guyse, La Tierache, and Rathelois, the Sieur de Villiers; for the chastellany of La Fere and Laon, the Provost of the city of Laon; for all Champagne, the governor thereof; for the countries of the king about the marches of Burgundy, Monsieur de Beaujeu; for the bailiwick of Lyonnois, the Bailiff of Lyon; for all the sea-coast of France, the lord admiral.

11. On the part of the Duke of Burgundy: for the country of Ponthieu and Vimeux, Monsieur Philip de Crevecœur, Lord des Cordes; for Corbie and the provostship of Feüilloy and Beauquesne, the Lord of Contay; for Peronne, and the provostship of Peronne, the Lord of Clary, and in his absence the Lord de la Hargerie, and likewise for the provostships and towns of Montdidier, Roye, and the adjacent countries ; for Artois, Cambresis, and Beaurevoir, John de Longueval, Lord of Vaux ; for the country of Marle, the Lord of Humbercourt; for the country of Hainault, the Lord of Aimeries, Grand Bailiff of Hainault; for the country of Liege and Namur, the Lord of Humbercourt; for the country of Luxembourg, the governor of the said country of Luxembourg, the Marquis of Rothelin ; for the country of Burgundy, duchy and county, &c., subject to the duke, the Marshal of Burgundy ; for the country of Mâconnois and adjacent places, Monsieur de Clessy, Governor of Mâconnois; for the country of Auxerre and places adjacent, Monsieur Tristan de Toulonjon, Governor of Auxerre ; for the town and chastellany of Bar-sur-Seine, the Sieur d'Eschauez; for the sea of Flanders, Monsieur de Lalain, admiral; for the sea of Holland, Zealand, Artois, and Boulonnois, the Count of Boukam, admiral of those parts.

12. If any of the conservators of the truce on either side shall contravene the same, the king and the duke shall appoint others well instructed in the premises, in the room of them.

13. The conservators, or their deputies in their lawful absence, shall meet once a week alternately, on the borders of the territories of each prince, to hear complaints and to redress them ; and if great difficulty should arise, they are to refer the same to the superior councils, who shall determine them.

VOL. I.   U

14. The decisions of the conservators are to be obeyed, without any appeals whatsoever.

15. The allies on both sides are comprehended in this truce, if they have a mind to it, and if they intimate the same in due time; but if any of the king's allies shall, for themselves, or in favour of him, make war on the said Duke of Burgundy, he is free to oppose them with his arms, and the king is to give them no manner of assistance, without making an infraction of the truce: and the king is in the same position in respect to the allies of the Duke of Burgundy.

16. The king shall declare himself in favour of the Duke of Burgundy against the Emperor of the Romans, the citizens of Cologne, and all that shall assist them; and he promises to give them no manner of aid against the duke and his territories.

17. Seeing this treaty has been on foot since the month of May, 1474, all the places the king has taken since that time from the duke shall be restored.

18. Narcy and Gerondenelles shall be demolished, if that be not already done, and the lands remain in the possession of the rightful owners.

19. The king, in consideration of this truce, and in order to a perpetual peace, will deliver up the town and bailiwick of St. Quentin to the duke or his commissaries, only the king is to take away the artillery he brought thither, but not to meddle with the artillery of the town, nor any other that was in it before the Duke of Burgundy lost the possession of it; and the duke may appoint persons to make an inspection hereof; but is obliged to maintain the inhabitants in their rights and privileges, and to treat them as good subjects.

20. As to all other things and places, not expressly mentioned, they are to remain in their present state during the truce.

21. Lastly, if the king does not deliver up St. Quentin as aforesaid, the duke is not obliged to the observance of the nine years' truce any longer than to the 1st of May, 1476.

Ch. XII.—How the King of France and the Duke of Burgundy swore the Death of the Constable, who, retiring into the Duke's Country, was, by his Command, delivered to the King, and publicly executed.—1475.

IMMEDIATELY upon the conclusion of the truce, they proceeded in their designs against the constable; and, to shorten the process, they began where they left off at Bouvines, and the agreement in writing was renewed on both sides. For the duke's concurrence in this affair, it was stipulated that he should enjoy St. Quentin, Ham, Bohain, and whatever else the constable held under the said duke, besides all the constable's moveable goods, wherever they could be found.* In the next place, they arranged how he was to be besieged in Ham, where at that time he was ; and it was resolved, that whoever of the two should have the fortune to take him first, should see justice executed upon him within eight days, or surrender him to the other. Everybody began immediately to have some suspicion of this confederacy, and the constable's chief servants began to forsake him, as for instance, Monsieur de Genly, and several others of his principal companions. The constable having received information that the King of England had delivered his letters, and discovered all his secret practices, and knowing they were his enemies who had promoted the truce, grew extremely fearful about his condition, and sent a message to the Duke of Burgundy that, if he would please to give him a safe-conduct, he would wait on his highness, and impart several things to him of great importance concerning his own affairs. The duke hesitated at first, but at last he sent him one.

In the meantime, this great man was irresolute and wavering in his mind, and could not tell whither he should fly for security : for he had received information from all hands of his intended ruin, and had seen copies of the agreement signed against him at Bouvines. Sometimes he consulted his Lorraine servants, and then he resolved to go with them into Germany, and (there being no danger of travelling that

* This arrangement was made by letters dated September 13. 1475. " The king said that his cousin of Burgundy had treated the constable as huntsmen treat a fox ; for like a wise man, he had taken the skin, and left him only the carcase, which was worth nothing." Molinet, i. 181.

way) to carry such a sum of money with him as would purchase some place upon the Rhine, where he might live securely till he could make his peace either with the king or the
Duke of Burgundy.   Another time, he was for staying in
the fine Castle of Ham, which he had been at vast expense in
fortifying, on purpose to defend himself in such a case of necessity; and indeed it was as well provided with ammunition
and provision as any castle that I ever knew; but he had no
soldiers that he could depend on, for all his garrison were
subjects either of the king or of the Duke of Burgundy; and
perhaps his fear was so great, he durst not discover his condition to them; for I verily believe if he had, he would
have been deserted only by a very few; nor would it have
been so dangerous for him to have been besieged by both
princes at once as by one, for it would have been impossible
for their two armies to have agreed.   At last he resolved to
put himself into the Duke of Burgundy's hands, upon the
strength of his safe-conduct; and accordingly, attended only
by fifteen or twenty horse, he went * directly to Mons, in
Hainault, of which the Lord of Aimeries, who was his particular friend, was governor.   He stayed with him till he could
hear further from the Duke of Burgundy, who had begun a
war against the Duke of Lorraine, for sending him a defiance
as he lay in his trenches before Nuz, and for the ravages and
devastations he had committed in the province of Luxembourg.

The king having received information of the constable's
departure, resolved to attempt some action that might prevent his reconciliation with the Duke of Burgundy; wherefore he marched with all expedition towards St. Quentin †,

* It was currently believed in the Netherlands that the constable went
to Mons by order of the king.   The registers of Ypres state : "The
king and the duke agreed on an expedient to obtain possession of the
constable's person.   The king proposed to him to go on an embassy to
the duke, who was then at Luxembourg about certain matters ; which he
undertook.   The duke sent orders at the same time that his person
should be secured as soon as he appeared in any town in his dominions.
Accordingly, when the constable arrived at Mons, the gates of the town
were shut upon him, and he was kept there a month, after which he was
conducted, under a strong escort, to Peronne, and delivered to the officers
of the King of France."   Gachard, i. 277.

† "The King of France, being informed that the constable was treating

with a detachment of 700 or 800 men-at-arms, whom he
had assembled on a sudden, being privately advised of what
number of troops the garrison consisted. Upon the king's
approach, some of the citizens came out to meet his majesty, and submitted themselves to him. The king commanded me to enter the town, and order the garrison to
evacuate their quarters, which I did; and our men-at-arms
having entered, the king himself followed, and was well
received by the inhabitants; upon which some of the constable's party fled after him into Hainault. As soon as the
king was in possession of St. Quentin, he immediately despatched a courier with the news of it to the Duke of Burgundy, to let him understand that all hope of recovering it
by the constable's interest was now entirely lost. Upon
receiving this news, the Duke of Burgundy sent his commands to the Lord of Aimeries (his grand bailiff in Hainault)
to keep such guards in Mons that the constable might not
escape, and in the meantime to confine him to his house.
The bailiff durst not disobey the duke's orders, yet his guards
were not so strict but the constable might have escaped if
he had pleased.

What account can we give of Fortune in this place? This
person was seated between the territories of these rival
princes; he was possessed of several strong castles, had
400 men-at-arms well paid, and all his own creatures, under
his control, and had had the command of them a dozen
years: he was a person of great wisdom and valour, was
very rich, and had great experience; and yet none of all
these powerful advantages could, in the time of danger and
distress, either afford him relief, or inspire him with courage
enough to attempt his escape. One may say (and not without reason) that deceitful Fortune had assumed another
air, and begun to regard him with a frowning aspect: but
alas! Fortune is nothing but a poetical fiction; such surprising mysteries as these are far above her power to effect;
and, when I reflect upon what has already been said, and
what may farther be urged, I cannot help thinking but that

for the surrender of St. Quentin to the Duke of Burgundy, marched with
20,000 men to prevent it, and entered the town at about six o'clock in the
evening of the 14th September." Molinet, i. 179.

God had forsaken him; and if it were no offence in any man to judge (which it would be, and especially for me), I should maintain that the most probable cause of all his misfortunes, was his restless endeavours and designs to foment and continue the war between the king and the Duke of Burgundy, upon which alone his authority and power depended; nor indeed was this very difficult to accomplish, upon account of their humours and dispositions, which were naturally in themselves so vastly different.

That person would indeed be guilty of the greatest ignorance, who should believe Fortune or Chance had such an influence over human affairs as to force a man of his experience in the world, to incur the simultaneous displeasure of two such mighty princes, who in their lives never agreed in any one point but his ruin and destruction; and it would be more astonishing still, that she should have created an enmity between him and the King of England, who had married his niece *, and had a great value and respect for all his wife's relations, and particularly for those of the house of St. Paul. To speak impartially (neither can it be otherwise), God had withdrawn His grace from him, or else he would never have incensed these three powerful princes, and have managed his affairs so ill as not to have one friend left that would give him a night's entertainment in his distress; so that God Himself was the Fortune that did this: and as it has happened formerly, so it will happen to many hereafter, who, after a long continuance of ease and prosperity, must expect to fall into great misfortunes and adversity.

As soon as the king was informed of the constable's being arrested in Hainault by the Duke of Burgundy's order, he sent to require the duke either to deliver him up to him, or perform their agreement. The duke promised he would, and accordingly he caused the constable to be removed to Peronne, and placed a strong guard upon him. The Duke of Burgundy had made himself master of several places in Lorraine and Barrois, and had formally invested Nancy†, which made a

---

* Queen Elizabeth Woodville's mother was Jacquetta of Luxembourg, daughter of Pierre de Luxembourg, the constable's father.

† He encamped before that town on the 24th of October, 1475. Lenglet, ii. 218.

vigorous defence. The king had a considerable army in Champagne, of which the duke was extremely afraid ; for by the truce he had no liberty to invade the Duke of Lorraine's territories, who had put himself under the king's protection. The Lord du Bouchage and the other ambassadors strongly pressed the Duke of Burgundy to perform his agreement. The duke told them always he would, and yet the eight days (by which time the constable was to be either executed or delivered to the king) were expired a month since. At last, finding himself hard pressed, and fearing the king might put a stop to his conquests in Lorraine, which he extremely desired to complete, in order to open a passage through Luxembourg into Burgundy, and join all his territories together (for if this little duchy were once subdued, he might go from Holland almost as far as Lyons, without leaving his own dominions); for these reasons he wrote to his chancellor and to the Lord of Humbercourt (both of them the constable's inveterate enemies) immediately to repair to Peronne, and on a certain day to deliver the constable* to such ambassadors as the king should send to receive him (for in the duke's absence, they two had the administration of all his affairs); and he sent the Lord of Aimeries orders to deliver him to them.

In the meantime the Duke of Burgundy vigorously pushed the siege of Nancy, in which town there was a strong garrison that made a brave defence. One of the Duke of Burgundy's captains, called the Count of Campobasso (born in Naples, but banished that kingdom upon account of his having espoused the interest of the house of Anjou), had lately entered into a correspondence† with the Duke of Lor-

---

* The duke did not consent to deliver the constable into the hands of the king until the latter had assured to him the complete and entire confiscation of the property of the prisoner, only a portion of which had been assigned to him by the treaty of the 13th of September, 1475. Louis XI. therefore issued new letters, dated 12th November, 1475, by which he not only ratified his former engagements, but left the duke his choice between all the property of the constable, or those towns in Lorraine of which Charles the Bold had taken possession. The duke chose the towns, as is proved by the king's letters, dated 18th December, 1475, in which he promises not to quarrel with the Duke of Burgundy for his choice. Lenglet, iii. 444—448.

† Molinet thus states the reasons which induced the Count of Campobasso to betray his master. That nobleman, he says, "was captain of

raine (a near relation and next heir to the house of Anjou, after the death of King René*, his maternal grandfather), and promised to prolong the siege by not providing the army with ammunition, and other things that were necessary for the taking of the town by force. It was indeed in his power, for he was then a person of the greatest influence in the army, and therefore his villany and perfidiousness to his master were the greater, as you shall hear hereafter; and this was a kind of earnest of all the misfortunes that happened afterwards to the duke. I really believe the duke expected he would have been master of the town before the day came on which he would be obliged to deliver up the constable, and then he would not have done it. Besides, if the king had had him sooner, his majesty would have attempted something more in favour of the Duke of Lorraine than he did; for the king was informed of his intrigue with Campobasso. But the king would not engage in the quarrel between them, though he was not bound by treaty to stand still, and let the Duke of Burgundy overrun Lorraine. Besides, he had a considerable army upon the frontiers, but, for several reasons of state, he thought it better to stand neutral.

The Duke of Burgundy not being able to take Nancy† before the day on which the constable was to be delivered up, and that day being come, those who were commissioned to deliver him (being the constable's mortal enemies), delivered him willingly at the gates of Peronne into the hands of the Bastard of Bourbon, Admiral of France, and the Lord of St. Pierre, who conducted him to Paris. I have been since informed by several persons, that within three hours messengers came post from the duke with orders to the Lord of Aimeries not to deliver up the constable till after the taking of Nancy; but they arrived too late. Imme-

400 lances, which he had brought from Italy; but on New Year's Day, Duke Charles gave 100 of the lances to Signor Angelo, the count's son, to command, and as many to the count's younger son, at which the said Campobasso was greatly displeased." Molinet, i. 77. Oliver de la Marche (ii. 420) says it was because the duke owed him money.

* René, surnamed the Good, Duke of Anjou, and King of Sicily, was the son of Louis II., Duke of Anjou, and Yolande of Arragon. He died on the 10th of July, 1480.

† Nancy surrendered to the duke on Thursday, November 30. 1475.

diately upon his arrival at Paris his trial began *, and the duke sent all his papers and whatever he thought might be brought in evidence against him.   The king pressed the court to despatch, and persons were appointed to manage his trial: so that upon the proofs that the King of England had before given in against him, and those that the Duke of Burgundy now furnished, the constable was found guilty, condemned, executed, and all his estates confiscated.

Ch. XIII. — A Digression concerning the Duke of Burgundy's Error in delivering up the Constable to the King, contrary to the Safe-conduct which he had given him; and what happened to him afterwards.—1475.

THE whole management of this affair was very strange.   I do not speak it either to excuse the constable's faults, or to upbraid the duke or the king, for both of them had been sufficiently injured by him: but there was no necessity for the Duke of Burgundy, who was so potent a prince and of such an illustrious and honourable family, to have given him his protection in order to imprison him; and without dispute, it was the highest act of injustice and severity imaginable to deliver him up to a person who, he was sure, would put him to death, especially upon the account of avarice.   After this dishonourable action the duke's good fortune was strangely altered ; so that by reflecting upon what God has done in our time, and does still every day, it is evident He will not let injustice go long unpunished, and that all these strange dispensations proceed solely from Him ; for these sudden chastisements are beyond the power of nature, especially when they are inflicted on such as commit violence or cruelty, who are commonly great persons, as kings, princes, or potentates.   The house of Burgundy had been in a very prosperous and flourishing condition for a long time, and for a hundred years, or thereabouts, four of that family had reigned in as great splendour and reputation

* The trial began on the 27th November, and the constable was executed on the 19th December, 1475.

as any house in Christendom.   Others, perhaps, were more
potent, but they were involved in wars and afflictions, whilst
this family enjoyed an uninterrupted career of peace and
plenty.

The first great person of this family was Philip the
Bold *, brother to Charles V., King of France †, who married
the daughter and heiress of the Earl of Flanders, countess of
that country, Artois, Burgundy, Nevers, and Rethel.   The
second was John.   The third was Philip the Good, who
annexed to his hereditary territories the duchies of Brabant,
Luxembourg, Limbourg, Holland, Zealand, Hainault, and
Namur.   The last was Charles, who after his father's death
was reputed to be one of the richest and most powerful
princes in Christendom, and possessed, in jewels, plate,
household stuff, and books, more than any other three houses
of Europe could boast of.   Of ready money I have seen
more elsewhere (for Duke Philip the Good had levied no
taxes for a long time), and yet he left his son above
300,000 crowns in ready cash, and at peace with all his
neighbours; but that was of no long continuance.   Yet
I will not lay the beginning of the wars solely to his
charge, for there were other persons as deeply concerned in
that affair as himself.

Immediately upon the death of his father, his subjects,
upon very little importunity, willingly granted him a
supply for ten years, each country by itself; which could
not amount to less than 350,000 crowns per annum,
besides the revenue of Burgundy; and at the time of the
constable's being delivered up to the king, he had raised
an additional 300,000 crowns, and had by him in his coffers
300,000 more.   All the goods he could obtain of the
constable's were not worth 80,000 crowns (for in money
he had but 76,000), and yet for so poor and inconsiderable
an advantage, he committed so base and dishonourable an
act.   But he paid dearly for it; for God stirred up a new

* Philip the Bold, Duke of Burgundy, born on the 15th of January,
1341, was the son of John, King of France, and Bonne de Luxembourg.
He married Marguerite, Countess of Flanders, and died on the 27th of
April, 1404.

† Charles V., born on the 21st of January, 1337, married Jeanne de
Bourbon, and died on the 16th September, 1380.

enemy* against him, who was impotent and inconsiderable both in power, years, and experience ; and made him jealous of his subjects, and suspicious of his best servants, and place his greatest confidence in another†, who constantly betrayed him.   And are not these the same steps and methods in which God Almighty proceeded in the Old Testament with those whose fortunes he intended to change from better to worse, from prosperity to adversity ?   Yet the duke's heart never relented : but to the end he imputed all his success to his own wisdom and sagacity, and before his death was more potent and in greater renown than any of his predecessors.

Yet before the surrendering of the constable, he was grown very diffident and distrustful of his best subjects, and seemed to hate and despise them; for he had sent for 1000 Italian lances, and had numbers of them in his army before Nuz.   The Count of Campobasso had 400 Italian men-at-arms under his command, but no revenue of his own ; for, as I said before, being a partisan of the house of Anjou, upon account of the wars which they had raised in the kingdom of Naples, he was banished, and having lost all his estate, he had served ever since either in Provence or Lorraine under René, King of Sicily, or Nicholas the son of John, Duke of Calabria ; after whose death the Duke of Burgundy entertained most of his servants, and particularly all the Italians, and among the rest this count, and one James Galeot, a gentleman of great courage, honour, and loyalty.

When this Count of Campobasso went into Italy to raise his men, he received from the duke 40,000 crowns by way of advance.   Passing by Lyons, he accidentally fell into the acquaintance of a certain physician called Simon of Pavia, by whom he signified to the king that, if his majesty would comply with his demands, at his return he would betray the Duke of Burgundy into his hands; and he made the same proposals to the Lord of St. Priest ‡, the king's ambassador at that time in Piedmont.   When he came back,

---

* René II., Duke of Lorraine, who was at that time twenty-five years of age.
† The Count of Campobasso.
‡ Louis, Lord of St. Priest, knight, chamberlain of the king, was sent

and was quartered with his forces in the county of Marle, he offered the king, upon his arrival at the duke's camp, either to kill him, or make him prisoner, which he designed to execute thus : —The duke was accustomed to ride about the camp upon a little ambling nag, attended but by few of his guards, which, as he said truly, would be a fair opportunity of effecting his purpose. If this was disapproved of, he had another offer to make, which was, that when the king and the Duke of Burgundy should be drawn up in order of battle, and ready to engage, he would come over to the king's side with his whole battalion, upon certain conditions which he stated. But the king utterly abhorred his treachery*, and sent the Lord of Contay very generously to acquaint the duke of his intentions to betray him; but the duke was so far from believing it, that he looked upon it as an artifice of the king's, and showed the count greater favour than before. From whence it is evident, that God Almighty had infatuated his understanding, in not suffering him to believe the clear proof given by the king. But though Campobasso was treacherous and disloyal, James Galeot was quite of another stamp ; and having acquired great reputation in the world, died at last with as much honour as he had lived.

by that prince as his ambassador to Berne on the 2nd of August, 1474. Lenglet, iii. 337.

* Louis XI. had nevertheless attempted to induce Campobasso to desert the Duke of Burgundy, and enter his service. See Dupont, i. 405.

BOOK THE FIFTH.

CH. I.—How the Duke of Burgundy, making War upon the Swiss, was defeated by them at the Foot of the Mountains, near Granson.—1476.

AFTER the Duke of Burgundy had conquered all Lorraine, and received of the king St. Quentin, Ham, and Bohain, with all the constable's goods which could be found, he agreed to meet the king at Auxerre. The king and he were to have an interview upon a river, with a bridge built over it after the same manner as that at Picquigny for King Louis and the King of England; and several messengers passed and repassed continually about this affair. And the Duke of Burgundy resolved to put the greatest part of his army, that had been much fatigued and harassed in the siege of Nuz and their expedition into Lorraine, into quarters of refreshment, and to canton the rest in such towns as belonged to the Count of Romont and others near to Berne and Friburg; upon which towns he had resolved to make war for their insolent behaviour during the siege of Nuz, for their having assisted the enemy in taking from him the county of Ferrette, and for their usurpation of some part of the Count of Romont's territories. The king was extremely desirous of this interview, and earnestly entreated the duke to let his army lie still in their quarters of refreshment, and not to attempt anything against the poor Swiss. Upon the approach of this army, the Swiss sent ambassadors to the duke, and offered to restore whatever they had taken from the Count of Romont. On the other hand, the Count of Romont pressed him to come in person to his assistance; and, contrary to sober counsel and what all declared would be the best, considering the season and the shattered state of his army, the duke resolved to march against them himself; it being agreed between the king and him, under both their hands, that as to the affair of Lorraine, there should be no dispute between them.

With this shattered and fatigued army the duke marched out of Lorraine into Burgundy, where the ambassadors of the old German leagues, called Swiss, came to him, and offered, besides the restitution before mentioned, to abandon all alliances that were contrary to his interest (and particularly that with the King of France), to enter into alliance with him, and (for a small sum of money) to serve him against the king with 6000 men, whenever he should require their assistance. But the duke would hearken to no overtures, for his ruin was decreed. The new allies (as they term them in those parts), namely, Basle, Strasburg, and other imperial towns situated near the head of the Rhine, had heretofore joined with Sigismund, Duke of Austria, at the time when he was at war with the Swiss; but now a confederacy was made between them and the Swiss for ten years, at the solicitation and expense of the King of France, at the time that the county of Ferrette was taken from the Duke of Burgundy, and his Governor Pierre d'Archambault (who was the cause of all his misfortunes afterwards) put to death at Basle. A prince ought narrowly to observe and watch the conduct of those persons he appoints as governors over his new conquests; for, instead of easing his subjects, administering justice, and treating them with more gentleness than before, this Archambault proceeded quite otherwise and oppressed them with all manner of violence and extortion, and was the occasion of great mischief both to himself, his prince, and abundance of brave men besides. This alliance (which, as I said before, was to be ascribed wholly to the king's management) proved afterwards very advantageous to his majesty's interest, and more so than most people were able to foresee, for I esteem it as one of the wisest and most important actions of his reign, and the most prejudicial to his enemies; for if the Duke of Burgundy's affairs were once in a low condition, there would be none left to cope with the king, or oppose him in any of his designs — I mean of his subjects, and in his own kingdom, for all the rest

sailed under his wind.   For this reason, it was of great importance to combine Duke Sigismund and these new confederates in an alliance with the Swiss, between whom there
had been great enmity for a long time; but it put his
majesty to the expense of several embassies and a vast sum
of money.

All hopes of an accommodation being entirely vanished, the
Swiss ambassadors returned to acquaint their masters with the
Duke of Burgundy's absolute refusal of their propositions, and
to make preparations for their defence.   The duke marched
with his army into the Pays de Vaud (in Savoy), which the
Swiss had taken from the Count of Romont, and he took
three or four towns belonging to Monsieur de Chasteau-
Guyon, which the Swiss had seized upon but defended very
ill.   From thence he advanced to besiege a place called
Granson * (which also belonged to Monsieur de Chasteau-
Guyon), into which they had thrown 700 or 800 of their
best troops; and because it was near them, they had resolved to defend it to the last extremity.   The duke's army
was mightily increased, for he daily received considerable
reinforcements out of Lombardy and Savoy; and he entertained strangers rather than his own subjects, of whom he
might have formed a sufficient army that would have been
more faithful and valiant: but the death of the constable
had filled him with strange jealousies of them, and various
other imaginations.   He had a fine train of artillery, and he
lived in great pomp and magnificence in the camp, to show
his grandeur and riches to the Italian and German ambassadors who were sent to him; and he had all his valuable
jewels, plate, and rich furniture with him: besides, he had
great designs upon the duchy of Milan, where he expected
to find a considerable party.   It was not many days after the
duke's investing Granson, before the garrison being terrified
with his continual battering it with cannon, surrendered at

---

* "The duke encamped before Granson on the 19th of February, 1476,
with an army of 50,000 men or more, of all languages and countries, with a quantity of cannon and other engines of novel construction,
and tents and accoutrements all glittering with gold, and a great host of
servants, merchants, and courtezans."   Chronique du Chapitre de Neuchastel, p. 386.

discretion, and were all put to the sword.* The Swiss were
assembled, but they were not very numerous†, as several of
them have told me (for that country produced not so many
soldiers as was imagined, and still fewer than at present,
because of late many of them have left their husbandry, and
followed the wars), and of their confederate troops there
were not many, because they were obliged to hasten at short
notice to the relief of their friends in Granson ; and when
their army was ready to march, they received advice that the
garrison had all been put to the sword.

The Duke of Burgundy, contrary to the opinion of his
officers, resolved to advance and meet the enemy at the
foot of the mountains, to his great disadvantage ; for he
was already posted in a place much more proper for an
engagement, being fortified on one side with his artillery,
and on the other by a lake, so that in all appearance there was
no fear of his being injured by the enemy.   He had detached
a hundred of his archers to secure a certain pass at the
entrance of the mountains‡, and was advancing forward himself, when the Swiss attacked him, while the greatest part of
his army was still in the plain.   The foremost troops
designed to fall back ; but the infantry that were behind,
supposing they were running away, retreated towards their
camp, and some of them behaved themselves handsomely
enough ; but, in the end, when they arrived in their camp,
they wanted courage to make a stand and defend themselves,
and they all fled, and the Swiss possessed themselves of their
camp, in which were all their artillery, a vast number
of tents and pavilions, besides a great deal of valuable
plunder, for they saved nothing but their lives. §   The duke
lost all his finest rings, but of men, not above seven men-

---

* " All the garrison were given over to the provost-marshal, who, without pity or mercy, caused them to be hanged on the nearest trees by
three executioners, to the number of 400 or thereabout, and the rest were
drowned in the lake." Molinet, i. 191.

† Three hundred men of Berne and a hundred of Neufchatel assembled to march to the relief of Granson, but finding it impossible to pene-
trate the Burgundian lines, they " returned home groaning." Chronique
de Neuchastel, p. 387.

‡ The Castle of Bomacourt, by which he received supplies of provisions for his army. Molinet, i. 191.

§ This rout took place on the evening of the 3rd of March, 1476.

at-arms ; the rest fled, and the duke with them. It may more properly be said of him, " That he lost his honour and his wealth in one day," than it was of King John of France, who, after a brave defence, was taken prisoner at the battle of Poictiers.

This was the first misfortune that ever happened to the Duke of Burgundy in his whole life : for by the rest of his enterprises he always acquired either honour or advantage. But what a mighty loss did he sustain that day by his perverseness and scorn of good advice! How greatly did his family suffer! in what a miserable condition it is at present! and how like to continue so! How many great princes and states became his enemies, and openly declared against him, who but the day before the battle were his friends, or at least pretended to be so! And what was the cause of this war? A miserable cart-load of sheep-skins that the Count of Romont had taken from a Swiss, in his passage through his estates. If God Almighty had not forsaken the Duke of Burgundy, it is scarce conceivable he would have exposed himself to such great dangers upon so small and trivial an occasion; especially considering the offers the Swiss had made him, and that his conquest of such enemies would yield him neither profit nor honour; for at that time the Swiss were not in such esteem as now, and no people in the world could be poorer. A gentleman, who had been one of their first ambassadors to the Duke of Burgundy, told me, that one of his chief arguments to dissuade the duke from invading them was, that there was nothing for him to gain from them; for their country was barren and poor, and he believed that, if all his countrymen were taken prisoners, all the money they could raise for their ransom would not buy spurs and bridles for his army.

But to return to the battle; the king had many spies and scouts abroad about the country (most of them despatched by my orders), and it was not long before he received an account of this defeat, at which he was extremely pleased, and if he was grieved at anything, it was because so few of the enemy had been slain. The king, for his better intelligence, and to countermine the duke's designs, had removed to Lyons; and being a prince of great wisdom and penetration, he was afraid lest the duke should, by force of arms, annex Switzerland to his own dominions. The house of Savoy was at the Duke of Burgundy's absolute disposal. The Duke of Milan was his ally.* King René of Sicily intended to deliver Provence into his hands; so that if his affairs had been crowned with success, he would have been lord of all the countries from the western to the eastern sea, and the people of France could not have stirred out of the kingdom by land without the duke's permission, if he had possessed Savoy, Provence, and Lorraine. To every one of these princes the king now sent ambassadors. The Duchess of Savoy was his sister†, but in the duke's interest; the King of Sicily was his uncle‡, yet he was exceedingly cautious of receiving his ambassadors, and when he did, he referred all to the Duke of Burgundy. The king also sent to the German confederates, but with some difficulty; for the roads being blocked up, he was forced to employ mendicants, pilgrims, and such kind of people. The confederate towns replied somewhat haughtily, "Tell your king (said they), if he does not declare for us, we will patch up a peace with the duke, and declare against him!" and the king was afraid they would have done so. § However, as yet he had no inclination to declare war against the duke, and was very fearful he might hear of his secret negotiations with these countries.

---

* A treaty between the Duke of Burgundy and the Duke of Milan had been concluded at Moncalier on the 30th of January, 1475.

† Yolande de France, sister of Louis XI., was born on the 23rd of September, 1434, married Amadeus IX., Duke of Savoy, in 1452, became a widow on the 28th of March, 1472, and died on the 29th of August, 1478.

‡ He was brother of Marie of Anjou, the mother of Louis XI.

§ Louis XI. had made a treaty of alliance with the emperor and the electors in December, 1475. He confirmed it on the 17th of April, 1476. This confirmation is probably what the confederate towns now demanded.

Ch. II.—How, after the Defeat near Granson, the Duke of Milan, René, King of Sicily, the Duchess of Savoy, and others, abandoned their Alliance with the Duke of Burgundy.—1476.

BUT let us now take a view of the sudden alteration of affairs after this battle, how negotiations were set on foot, and with what prudence and judgment our king managed his affairs; for it may serve as a fair example to such young princes who foolishly undertake enterprises, without any foresight, without any experience, or without consulting such persons as are capable of advising them. The first step the Duke of Burgundy made, was to despatch the Lord of Contay to the king, with many submissive and friendly expressions, contrary both to his temper and custom. See what a change one hour had made in him! He entreated the king not to break the truce, excused himself for not having met his majesty at Auxerre according to the agreement between them, and assured the king that in a little time he would attend him there, or at any other place that his majesty might be pleased to name. The king received his envoy very kindly, and promised to comply with his demands; for he thought it not convenient to do otherwise at that juncture of time; as his majesty was aware of the loyalty and affection of the duke's subjects towards their prince, and that by their assistance he would quickly be recruited*; and therefore he had a mind to see the end of the war, without giving any occasion to either party of making a peace. But how kindly soever the Lord of Contay

---

* His subjects were, however, beginning to reject his demands. He assembled the Estates of Franche-Comté at Salins, and stated his inten- tion to levy an army of 40,000 men, and to impose a tax of one- fourth of their property on his subjects. In answer, the Estates declared that all they could offer him was a force of 3000 men, "to guard the country." The Estates of Burgundy declared at Dijon that the war was utterly useless, and that they would not involve themselves in a ground- less quarrel, in which they could have no hope of success. And to crown all, the Flemings wrote to him that, if he were surrounded by the Swiss and Germans, and had not men enough to extricate himself, they would come to his relief. See Michelet's *Louis XI., et Charles le Temeraire*, pp. 129, 130.

was entertained by the king, the people treated him with nothing but libels and lampoons; and ballads were publicly sung in the streets, to extol the courage of the conquerors and to jeer at the conquered.

As soon as Galeas, who was Duke of Milan at that time, had received an account of this defeat, he was extremely pleased, notwithstanding his alliance with the duke; which alliance indeed was only the effect of fear, upon account of the great favour and interest which the Duke of Burgundy had in Italy. The Duke of Milan immediately sent a citizen of Milan to the king (a person of no promising aspect), who by the mediation of others, was directed to me, and brought me letters from his master. I informed the king of his arrival, and his majesty commanded me to receive his instructions; for he was not yet reconciled to the Duke of Milan, who had forsaken his alliance, and made a new one with the Duke of Burgundy, though he and the king had married two sisters.* The design of his embassy was, to signify to the king that his master the Duke of Milan was informed that the king and the Duke of Burgundy had agreed upon an interview, in order to a final peace and alliance between them, which would be much to the prejudice of the duke his master; and he urged several arguments (but of no great force) against it: but at last, in the conclusion of his speech, he told the king that, if he would promise to make no such truce or treaty with the Duke of Burgundy, the Duke of Milan would pay him immediately 100,000 ducats. After the king had heard the substance of his embassy, he ordered him to be brought into his presence, and (there being nobody there but myself) his majesty spoke thus to him in short: "Here is Monsieur d'Argenton, who has told me so and so; pray tell your master I will have none of his money, and that my yearly revenue is thrice as much as his. As for war or peace, I will act as I please. However, if he repents having left me to enter into a league with the Duke of Burgundy, I am content our old alliance shall be renewed and confirmed." The

---

* The Duchess of Milan, Bona of Savoy, was sister of Charlotte of Savoy, the second wife of Louis XI. She married Galeas Sforza, on the 9th of May, 1468, and died in 1485, after a widowhood of nine years.

ambassador returned the king most humble thanks; and concluded by his answer that he was no covetous prince; and entreated his majesty that he would cause the said alliance to be published in the same form as before, for he was sufficiently empowered to promise that his master would do the same. The king consented, and after dinner it was proclaimed*, and an ambassador was immediately despatched from the king to Milan, where it was proclaimed with great pomp and solemnity. This was one of the Duke of Burgundy's first strokes of misfortune : and this was the first great man that abandoned his interest, who but three weeks before had sent a magnificent and solemn embassy to him to desire his alliance.

René, King of Sicily, had a design to make the Duke of Burgundy his heir, and to put Provence into his hand; and accordingly the Lord of Chasteau-Guyon† (who is now in Piedmont), and several other of the Duke of Burgundy's officers, were sent with 20,000 crowns to raise soldiers to take possession of Provence. But upon the news of this defeat, they had much ado to escape themselves, and the Count of Bresse seized upon their money. The Duchess of Savoy had received information of it also, and sent immediately to the King of Sicily to extenuate the loss, and strengthen him in his alliance. But the messengers, who were natives of Provence, were apprehended, and by that means the treaty between the King of Sicily and the Duke of Burgundy was discovered. The king our master immediately sent a good body of troops towards Provence, and despatched ambassadors to the King of Sicily, to invite him to come to him, and to assure him he should be heartily welcome; or otherwise his majesty would be obliged to provide for his own safety by force of arms. The King of Sicily was persuaded to visit the king at Lyons, and was received

---

* This treaty between Louis XI. and the Duke of Milan was concluded on the 9th of August, 1476.

† Hugues de Chalon, Lord of Chasteau-Guyon and Nozeroy, was the son of Louis de Chalon, Prince of Orange, and Leonore d'Armagnac. He was a man of distinguished bravery. At the battle of Granson, he twice dashed amidst the enemy's ranks and nearly succeeded in taking their standard ; but his charge was unsupported, and therefore unavailing.

with great honour and civility.   I happened to be present at
his arrival, and after their first compliments of salutation,
John Cossé *, Seneschal of Provence (a person of honour,
and of a noble family in the kingdom of Naples), addressed
himself to the king in the following manner: "Be not
surprised, sire, if the king, my master and your uncle, has
offered to make the Duke of Burgundy his heir; for it was
the advice of his council (and particularly mine), upon
this ground, that notwithstanding you were his nephew and
sister's son, yet you had injuriously taken from him the
castles of Bar and Angers, and used him unhandsomely in
all his other affairs.   We therefore promoted this treaty with
the Duke of Burgundy, that your majesty being informed of
it, might thereby be the better inclined to do us justice, and
be put in mind that my master is your uncle.   But we never
intended to bring that treaty to a conclusion."

The king took his speech very wisely and well; and he
knew it was true, for Monsieur Cossé was the person that
managed the whole affair.   In a few days after, all their
differences were adjusted; the King of Sicily and all his
retinue were largely presented with money †; and the king
entertained him among the ladies, and treated him in every
respect as he loved to be treated; so that a perfect reconciliation took place between them, and no mention was made
of the Duke of Burgundy, for not only King René but all his
allies had abandoned him; and this was another misfortune
occasioned by his defeat.   The Duchess of Savoy‡, who for a
long time had been suspected to be her brother's enemy,
sent a private messenger (called the Lord of Montaigny),
who addressed himself to me, to endeavour her reconciliation,
and to represent the reasons which had induced her to
abandon the interest of the king her brother, and to state her
doubts of the king.   However, to speak impartially, she was
a lady of great wisdom, and my master's true sister.   She
was unwilling to proceed to an open rupture with the Duke

---

* Jean, Lord of Cossé in Anjou, was one of the councillors and chamberlains of King René, and Seneschal of Provence.

† Louis XI. undertook to pay René a pension of 60,000 francs yearly
during the remainder of his life.   Lenglet, iii. 392.

‡ Yolande of France, Duchess of Savoy, and sister to Louis XI.

of Burgundy, but seemed desirous to temporise and to renew her friendship with the king. And she continued to send him news of the duke's adventures, that the king might treat her more favourably; and he ordered me to despatch her envoy with all expedition, to give her good encouragement, and to invite her into France. Thus another of the Duke of Burgundy's confederates fell off from him, and endeavoured to abandon his alliance. In Germany they began universally to declare against the duke; and several towns of the empire, as Nuremberg, Frankfort, and others, joined in a confederacy with the new and old allies of Switzerland against him; and it seemed that whatever mischief could be done to him, was quite pardonable.

The poor Swiss were mightily enriched by the plunder of his camp.* At first they did not understand the value of the treasure they were masters of, especially the common soldiers. One of the richest and most magnificent tents in the world was cut into pieces. There were some of them that sold quantities of dishes and plates of silver for about two sous of

---

* The following is a list of the spoil taken by the Swiss at Granson, from Peignot's Amusemens Philologiques :—

"1. Five hundred pieces of heavy artillery, with a quantity of ammunition, and abundance of provisions.

"2. Four hundred tents of great richness, fitted with silk and velvet, and with the duke's arms embroidered thereon in gold and pearls. Most of these were spoiled by the Swiss, who made them into clothes.

"3. Six hundred banners and standards; 300 helmets; 300 cwt. of gunpowder; 3000 sacks of barley; 2000 baggage wagons; 2000 barrels of herrings, and a quantity of other dried fish, and salted meat, geese and fowls; and abundance of sugar, raisins, figs, almonds, and other things innumerable; and 8000 spiked clubs.

"4. Four hundred lbs. weight of silver plate, which was taken to Lucerne, and divided among the Swiss, to say nothing of that which was carried off by the soldiers.

"5. Three hundred complete services of magnificent silver plate; and so great a quantity of coined money that it was distributed by handfulls; four wagon-loads of crossbows and strings; and three wagon-loads of bed-linen.

"6. The coffer containing the duke's archives, and his great diamond.

"7. The duke's rosary, with the apostles in massive gold.

"8. The duke's sword, adorned with seven large diamonds and as many rubies, with fifteen pearls of the size of a bean, and of the finest water; 160 pieces of cloth of gold and silk; with innumerable relics

our money, supposing they had been pewter. His great
diamond (perhaps the largest and finest jewel in Christendom), with a large pearl fixed to it, was taken up by a
Swiss, put up again into the case, thrown under a wagon,
taken up again by the same soldier, and after all offered to a
priest for a florin, who bought it, and sent it to the magistrates of that country, who returned him three francs as a
sufficient reward.* They took also three very rich jewels,
called the Three Brothers, another large ruby called La
Hatte, and another called the Ball of Flanders, which were
the fairest and richest in the world; besides a prodigious
quantity of other goods, which has since taught them what
fine things may be purchased for money; for their victories,
the esteem the king had of their service afterwards, and
the presents he made them, have enriched them prodigiously.

The king made every one of their ambassadors that was
sent in the first embassy to his majesty very considerable
presents in plate or money, by which means he pacified them
for not openly declaring and entering into an alliance with
them; and they returned with their purses well filled,
and their persons clothed in silk, besides a promise of
a pension of 40,000 florins of the Rhine (which he paid
afterwards, but he saw the event of a second battle first),
20,000 to the towns, and 20,000 to the governors of
them.† Nor should I tell an untruth in saying, that from
the battle of Granson to the death of our master, their
towns and magistrates received of his majesty above a
million of Rhine florins; and by the towns I mean only four,
Berne, Lucerne, Friburg, Zurich, and their cantons, or

in rich shrines; the duke's gilded chair, and his gold ring, and the ring
of his brother Antony, and two large pearls set in gold, each as large as
a nut.

* This famous diamond, called the *Sancy* diamond, was sold by the
last-mentioned purchasers to M. de Diesbach, for 5400 Rhine florins;
he sold it to a Genevese jeweller for 7000 Rhine florins; it was next sold
to the Duke of Milan for 11,000 ducats; then to Pope Julius for 20,000
ducats; and in 1835, it was purchased by Prince Demidoff for 20,000*l.*
It is said to weigh 53½ grains.

† Of this sum, 9000 francs were given to certain private individuals,
and the remainder was thus divided: 6000 francs to Berne, 3000 to
Lucerne, and 2000 to Zurich. Lenglet, iii. 379.

mountains. Schwytz also is another of their cantons, though but a small village; yet I have seen an ambassador of that village, who, though he was in a mean dress, yet gave his opinion with the others. The other cantons are Glaris and Underwald.

CH. III.—How the Duke of Burgundy was again defeated by the Swiss, near the Town of Morat.—1476.

BUT to return to the Duke of Burgundy's affairs. He assembled forces on all sides, and, in three weeks' time, he had as many as he had had in the late battle. His quarters were at Losanne, in Savoy *, where you, my Lord of Vienne, attended him with your counsels in an illness, which melancholy and vexation for the dishonour he had sustained, had occasioned; and truly I am of opinion, that from the very day of his defeat, his understanding was never so good as it had been before. The account I give you of the great army he had assembled again, I received from the Prince of Tarento†, who in my presence made the same relation to the king. This prince had come to the duke's court about a year before, with a very splendid equipage, in the hope of marrying his daughter, the heiress of Flanders. And, indeed, he appeared to be a king's son by the gracefulness of his person, and the splendour of his appearance and retinue; for his father, the King of Naples‡, had spared no cost to set him off. The Duke of Burgundy did but dissemble with him; for, at the same time, he was in treaty with the Duchess of Savoy for her son, besides others elsewhere. The Prince of Tarento (called

* The duke reached Lausanne on the 29th of April, 1476, and remained there until the 27th of May.

† The principality of Tarentum was not actually conferred on Don Frederic of Arragon until 1485, but he appears to have enjoyed the titular dignity for some time previously. He became King of Naples in 1496, and died on the 9th of November, 1504.

‡ Ferdinand I., natural son of Alphonso, King of Naples, succeeded his father in 1458, and died on the 25th of January, 1494.

Don Frederic of Arragon) and his council, growing weary
of his delays, sent a herald, who was a clever person, to our
king, to desire his majesty to grant the prince a passport to
return safely through his dominions into his own country,
for his father had sent for him.   The king granted it very
willingly, because he believed it would redound to the Duke
of Burgundy's dishonour, and would lessen his interest
abroad.   However, before the return of the messenger, the
German confederates had taken the field, and lay encamped
not far from the Duke of Burgundy.

The prince took his leave of the duke the night before the
battle*, in obedience to his father's command ; for in the
first engagement he had given signal proofs of his valour.
There are some (my Lord of Vienne) who affirm, that he
left the army by your advice; and I heard him say, upon
his arrival at court, to the Duke of Astoly†, called the Count
Julio, and to several others, that your lordship transmitted
an account into Italy of all that happened both in the first
and second battles, several days before they were fought.‡

At the prince's departure, the confederates (as I said
before) were encamped near the Duke of Burgundy, with a
design to give him battle, and raise the siege of Morat. a
small town near Berne, belonging to the Count of Romont.
The confederates (as I was informed by those who were
present in that action) might be about 30,000 foot, all
choice troops and well armed: that is to say, 11,000
picked men, 10,000 halberdiers, and 10,000 musketeers, besides
a body of 4000 horse.   The confederate forces were not
all arrived; so that only those mentioned above were in
the engagement, and they were more than was necessary.
The Duke of Lorraine arrived at their camp also with a

* On the 21st of June, 1476.

† According to some commentators, the person here referred to is the
Duke of Ascoli, but as the name of that nobleman was Orso Orsino, it
is impossible that he can be identical with "Count Julio," who, as Commines tell us, possessed the dukedom in question.   It is more probable
that our author alludes to Giulio Antonio Aquaviva, Duke of Atri, a
distinguished statesman and warrior, known in Neapolitan history as
"Count Giulio."   The Duke of Atri, moreover, had been chosen by
King Ferdinand to accompany Prince Frederic of Arragon on his visit
to the Court of Burgundy.

‡ Angelo Catto was celebrated as a physician and astrologer.

small reinforcement, which was of great advantage to him afterwards, for the Duke of Burgundy was in possession of his whole dukedom. Nor was it to his prejudice that our court began to grow weary of him, though I believe he was never conscious of it himself. But when a great person has lost all, those that support and maintain him soon grow weary of him. The king gave him a small sum of money, and sent a strong party of troops with him through the duchy of Lorraine, to conduct him safely into Germany, and then to return. The Duke of Lorraine had not only lost that country, but also the country of Vaudemont, and most part of Barrois (the rest being secured by the king, so that all was gone); and, which was worse, all his subjects, and even his domestics, had sworn allegiance to the Duke of Burgundy, and that voluntarily, without any compulsion, ; so that his condition seemed past recovery. However, in such cases God always remains judge and arbitrator, and decides such affairs according to His own pleasure.

When the Duke of Lorraine had passed through his own dominions, after several days' march, he arrived at the camp of the confederates not many hours before the engagement. Though he brought but few men, yet his arrival was much to his honour and advantage, for otherwise he would have had a poor reception. Just as he arrived, both armies were advancing to engage; for the allies had lain three days or more strongly encamped at a small distance from the Duke of Burgundy, whose army, after some small resistance, was entirely defeated and put to flight.* Nor did he escape so well as in the first engagement: for the Swiss not having then a body of horse, he lost not above seven men-at-arms; but at this battle of Morat they had 4000 good horse, who pursued the Burgundians a great way, and cut off a considerable number of them. Besides, their whole body of infantry was engaged with the duke's foot, who were very numerous; for, besides his own subjects, and a considerable

* Four years after the battle a chapel was erected on the field with this inscription : " *Deo Optimo Maximo. Inclyti et fortissimi Burgundiæ Ducis Exercitus, Moratum obsidens, ab Helvetiis cæsus, hoc sui Monumentum reliquit.*" In 1822 a handsome stone obelisk was set up, in a commanding position overlooking the lake, also in commemoration of this victory.

body of English, who were in his pay, he had great reinforcements out of Piedmont and Milan, as I said before. And when the Prince of Tarento was with the king, he told me he had never seen a finer army in his life; for, as they marched over a bridge, he caused them to be numbered, and they amounted to 23,000 men in pay, besides those that belonged to the train of artillery, and followed the camp. To me this seems a very great number, yet there are some who make it much greater, and upon very slight grounds will multiply armies prodigiously.

The Lord of Contay arrived at our court not long after the battle, and owned in my presence, that the Duke of Burgundy lost in that battle 8000 of his standing forces, besides those that followed the camp; and, by the best information I could get, I presume that the number of the slain in all, might amount to near 18,000 men; which is not at all improbable, if we consider the great bodies of horse that the princes of Germany had there, and the vast number of those that were slain in the duke's camp before Morat. The duke fled himself as far as Burgundy, in great disconsolateness, and not without reason; he stopped at a place called La Riviere *, where he rallied what forces he could. The Germans pursued only that night, and then gave over the chase, without following him any farther.

CH. IV.—How, after the Battle of Morat, the Duke of Burgundy seized upon the Duchess of Savoy, and how she was delivered by our King, and sent back into her own Country.—1476.

THIS defeat drove the Duke of Burgundy almost to despair; for by what he had observed since his first loss at Granson, he perceived all his friends and allies were resolved to aban-

---

* La Rivière is a small town in the arrondissement of Pontarlier, in the department of Doubs. The duke arrived there on the 22nd of July. Lenglet, ii. 220.

don him; and his defeat at Granson happened not above three weeks previously.* In this apprehension, by the advice of some people, he caused the Duchess of Savoy and one of her sons, who is now Duke of Savoy †, to be brought into Burgundy by force. Her eldest son at that time was saved by some of the servants belonging to the family; for those who committed this act of violence did it in fear, and were obliged to use more haste than was convenient. That which moved the duke to this exploit, was a suspicion lest she should retire to the king her brother, though, as he pretended, all this misfortune was caused him by his great affection to the house of Savoy. The duke ordered her to be conducted to the Castle of Rouvre ‡, near Dijon, and placed some small guard about her, but whoever had a mind had liberty to visit her. Among the rest, the Lord of Chasteau-Guyon and the Marquis of Rotelin came to wait on her highness, between whom and two of her daughters the duke had treated of marriage, though at that time neither of them had been concluded, but both have been since. Her eldest son Philibert, at that time Duke of Savoy, was conveyed to Chambery by those who contrived his escape §, at which place he found the Bishop of Geneva, who was a son of the house of Savoy, but a very headstrong man, and governed wholly by a Commander de Ranvers. ‖ With this bishop and his governor, the Commander de Ranvers, the king managed affairs so artfully, that the Duke of Savoy and a younger

* This is a mistake; the battle of Granson occurred three months and nineteen days before that of Morat. The former was fought on the 3rd of March, and the latter on the 22nd of June, 1476.

† Charles I., born on the 29th of March, 1408, succeeded his brother Philibert in 1482. He married Blanche of Montferrat, and died on the 13th of March, 1489.

‡ In the department of the Cote-d'Or. This expedition was entrusted to Oliver de la Marche, who had to answer for its performance with his head. See his Memoirs, ii. 417, 418.

§ "Geoffroi, Lord of Riverol, a Piedmontese gentleman, rescued the duke from the hands of those who had seized him. Louis de Villette, a gentleman of Savoy, saved his brother." Guichenon, ii. 142.

‖ Jean de Montchenu, Commander of St. Antoine de Ranvers, became Bishop of Agen in 1477, and was translated to the see of Vivier in 1478. In previous editions, he has been erroneously termed a Commander of *Rhodes*.

brother of his *, called the Prothonotary, with the Castles of Chambery and Montmeillan †, were delivered into his majesty's hands; and he already had another castle in his possession, in which were all the jewels belonging to the duchess.

As soon as the duchess found, upon her arrival at Rouvre, that she was attended by her whole train of maids of honour and a host of other servants, as I said before; and observed the Duke of Burgundy wholly intent upon raising men, and that her guards did not retain that dread and awe of their master which they formerly had, she resolved to send to her brother the king, to propose a peace and beg his assistance; yet she would have been unwilling to have put herself into his power, had she been in any other place but where she was, for there had been a great long-standing quarrel between them. The duchess sent a gentleman of Piedmont, named Riverol ‡, who was steward of her house, and had instructions to apply to me. As soon as I had received his message, and communicated it to the king, his majesty ordered him to be introduced into his presence; and after he had given him audience, he told him that he would not abandon his sister in this extremity, notwithstanding the differences that had been between them; and if she would trust to him, he would send the Governor of Champagne, who was then Charles d'Amboise, Lord of Chaumont, to fetch her.

Monsieur Riverol took his leave of the king, and posted with all speed to his mistress with the news. The duchess was overjoyed to hear it, yet she immediately sent another agent to the king, to desire his majesty would give his word that she should have liberty to return into Savoy whenever she pleased, and that he would restore to her not only the duke her son and his young brother, but the castles and places which he had seized upon, and would defend and

* Jacques Louis de Savoie, Count of Geneva and Marquis de Gex. He died at Turin on the 27th of July, 1485, without issue.

† "The Bishop of Geneva forced the Governor of Montmeillan to surrender the place, wherein were all the treasures and jewels of the Regent." Guichenon, ii. 143. This must, therefore, be the castle to which Commines refers in the succeeding paragraph.

‡ Geoffroi de Riverol, mentioned in a preceding note. The duchess had previously sent her secretary Cavorret to the king; but Louis XI. had put him in arrest because he was dressed in the Burgundian fashion.

maintain her authority in Savoy; and then she would renounce all other alliances, and keep herself entirely in his interest. The king promised to grant all she desired, and immediately despatched an express to the Lord of Chaumont to go and deliver her; which was well attempted, and as well performed; for the Lord of Chaumont, with a strong detachment*, went to Rouvre, without the least disorder or damage to the country through which he marched, and brought away the Duchess of Savoy and her whole train to the next garrison belonging to the king. When the king despatched this last message to the Duchess of Savoy, his majesty had left Lyons, where he had sojourned full six months, on purpose to defeat and countermine the designs of the Duke of Burgundy, without violating the truce; and if we seriously consider the posture of the duke's affairs, we shall see that the king was a greater enemy to him in not opposing him openly, but creating him new enemies underhand, than if he had declared open war against him; for upon such a declaration, the duke would have abandoned his rash enterprises and designs, and that would not have occurred which happened to him afterwards.

The king having left Lyons, continued his journey directly to Rouanne, from whence he came down the River Loire to Tours. Upon his arrival there, his majesty received the news of his sister's deliverance, at which he was extremely pleased, and sent an express immediately to direct her to come to him, and ordered a sum of money to be remitted to defray the expense of her journey. When the king was informed of her approach, he sent several persons of quality to meet her, and went himself as far as the gate of Plessis-du-Parc, where he received her with abundance of tenderness and civility, and saluted her thus, "My Lady of Burgundy, you are heartily welcome." She knew well by his countenance that he was in a merry humour, and replied very prudently, "that she was no Burgundian, but a true French woman, and ready to obey him in whatever he might command." The king conducted her to her apartment, and entertained her with great splendour; but the truth is he

---

* Oliver de la Marche says that the Lord of Chaumont took with him 200 lances.

was very desirous to be rid of her, and she being a cunning woman, and understanding his temper perfectly well, was even more desirous to be gone than he was to have her go.   The management of this whole affair was committed to me, and the king ordered me to supply her with money during her stay at court, to provide for her return, to furnish her wardrobe with silks, and to draw up the form of their alliance for the time to come.   The king used his utmost endeavours to break off the matches that I mentioned before, but she excused herself, and pretended that the affections of her daughters were so far engaged, that it would be impossible to break them off; and when the king found that, he pressed it no farther.

After the duchess had been at Plessis about seven or eight days, the king and her highness entered into a mutual oath of amity for the future, and instruments to that purpose were interchangeably delivered *: after which she took her leave, and the king ordered her to be conducted safely into her own country; and her children, castles, jewels, and whatever belonged to her besides, were punctually restored to her.   Both were extremely pleased to be rid of one another upon such handsome terms; and ever after they continued very good friends, as a brother and sister ought to do.

CH. V.—How the Duke of Burgundy lived in a solitary manner for some weeks at La Riviere, and how the Duke of Lorraine retook Nancy in the meantime.—1476.

BUT to continue the chief subject of these Memoirs, we are obliged to return to the Duke of Burgundy, who, after his defeat at Morat (in the year 1476), had fled to a town called La Riviere, at the entrance into Burgundy, where he lay six weeks, under pretence of raising men to recruit his army;

* These papers are dated on the 2nd of November, 1476.   The king thereby pledged his word to defend and support his sister and her son against the attacks and pretensions of Charles of Burgundy.

but he proceeded very slowly in that affair, and instead of being active and vigorous, he lived like a hermit, and all his actions seemed rather the effect of sullenness and obstinacy than anything else, as will appear by what follows.

His concern and grief for his first defeat at Granson was so great, and made such a deep impression on his spirits, that it threw him into a violent and dangerous fit of sickness ; for whereas before, his choler and natural heat were so great that he drank no wine, but only in a morning took a little tisane, and ate conserve of roses, to refresh himself ; this sudden melancholy had so altered his constitution, that he now drank the strongest wine that could be got, without any water at all ; and to reduce the rush of blood to his heart, his physicians were obliged to apply cupping-glasses with burning tow to his side. But this (my Lord of Vienne) you know better than I, for your lordship attended on him during the whole course of his illness, and it was by your persuasion that the duke was prevailed upon to cut his beard, which was of a prodigious length.   In my opinion his understanding was never so perfect, nor his senses so sedate and complete, after this fit of sickness, as before.   So violent are the passions of men unacquainted with adversity, who never seek the true remedy for their misfortunes, especially princes, who are naturally haughty : for in such cases our best method is to have recourse to God, to reflect on the many vile transgressions by which we have offended His Divine goodness, to humble ourselves before Him, and to make an acknowledgment of our faults : for He determines all things as it seems best to His heavenly wisdom, and who dare question the justness of His dispensations, or impute any error to Him ? It is also well to unbosom ourselves freely to some intimate friends, not to keep our sorrows concealed, but to expatiate on every circumstance of them, without being ashamed or reserved ; for this mitigates the rigour of our misfortunes, revives the heart, and restores their usual vigour and activity to our dejected spirits.   There is another remedy also, and that is labour and exercise (for as we are but men, these sorrows cannot be dissipated without great pains and application, both in public and private), which is a much better course than that which the duke took in hiding

himself, and retiring from all manner of company; for by
that means he grew so terrible to his own servants, that none
of them durst venture to come near him to give him either
counsel or comfort, but suffered him to go on in that melancholy state of life, fearing lest their advising him to the
contrary, might have turned to their destruction.

During these six weeks (or thereabouts) that he lay at La
Riviere with very few troops (nor was it to be wondered at,
after the loss of two such great battles as you have heard
before), many declared themselves openly against him, his
friends were grown cold, his subjects were defeated and
rebellious, and began (as is usual) to murmur and contemn
their master on account of his misfortunes. He lost several
little towns in Lorraine, as Vaudemont, Espinal, and others.
All the neighbouring states began to make preparations to
invade him; and the vilest and most insignificant of them
were now the most forward in doing him mischief. The
Duke of Lorraine (upon this report) assembled a small
body of forces, and besieged Nancy *; the small towns about
it were most of them in his possession already; but the Duke
of Burgundy was master of Pont-à-Mousson, about four
leagues off. Amongst those that were besieged in Nancy,
there was a gentleman of the house of Croy, called the Lord of
Bievres†, a good officer, and a person of honour, whose forces
were made up out of several countries. There was also an
Englishman called Colpin, a brave soldier (though of no
great birth), who with other officers belonging to the garrison of Guynes, had entered the service of the Duke of
Burgundy. This Colpin had the command of about 300
English in the town, and though they were not pressed
either by approaches or batteries ‡, they began to be uneasy at

---

* The garrison of Nancy consisted of about 1000 or 1200 Burgundian troops. Duke René laid siege to the town on the 15th of September,
1476.

† Jean de Rubempré, Lord of Bievre, was appointed Bailiff of Hainault
in 1473, and created a Knight of the Golden Fleece in 1475. He was
killed in the battle of Nancy.

‡ Molinet (i. 208.) says: "The besieged ran so short of provisions that
they were glad to eat horse-flesh. The townspeople were so false and
disloyal to them, that if the captains had made a sortie, they would not
have been admitted again into the town. And furthermore, two bom-

the duke's slowness in marching to their relief *: and indeed he was highly to blame; for the quarters where he lay were at so great a distance from Lorraine, that he could do them no service, and certainly it would have been better for him to have defended what was left, than to have meditated revenge on the Swiss for what he had lost. But his perverseness in following no counsel but his own, turned greatly to his disadvantage; for notwithstanding that he was daily pressed to relieve that place, yet he continued (without any necessity) at La Riviere full six weeks; whereas if he had done otherwise, he might easily have raised the siege of Nancy, for the Duke of Lorraine's forces were not numerous †, and so long as the country of Lorraine was in his possession, he had free communication between his other territories (through Luxembourg and Lorraine) into Burgundy; so that if his intellects had been as right and his judgment as sound as they were formerly, he would certainly have marched with greater expedition to their relief.

Whilst the garrison of Nancy lay in continual expectation of being relieved, it happened that the above-mentioned Colpin, who commanded the English troops in the town, was killed by a cannon ball; his death was a vast prejudice to the Duke of Burgundy's concerns, for a prince very often is preserved from great inconveniences by the management of one single person, provided he has wisdom and valour, although his extraction be mean; and in this particular I knew no man more careful than our master, for certainly never prince was more fearful of losing his men than his

bards, one culverin, and several serpentines, were continually firing on them, as many as twenty-one shots a day, by which means a gate was broken through, and the dilapidated wall was razed to the ground."

* The Lord of Fay, Lieutenant of Luxembourg, collected a body of forces, and marched with the Count of Campobasso to the relief of Nancy. But instead of proceeding thither at once, they spent a considerable time in deciding on the route they should take, and in waiting for reinforcements. This delay arose chiefly from their expectation that they would get but little booty in Lorraine; and their allegiance to Duke Charles had been greatly shaken by his defeats at Granson and Morat, so that, says Molinet, "their succour, which should have been prompt and zealous, was very tardy and unwillingly given."

† According to Molinet (i. 207.) the duke had 10,000 Swiss, horse and foot.

majesty.   Upon the death of Colpin, the English under his
command began to murmur and despair of relief.   They
were not aware of the Duke of Lorraine's weakness, and that
the Duke of Burgundy had many ways of reinforcing his
army; and besides, the English, not having been abroad for
a long time, had but little experience in foreign wars, and
were wholly ignorant in regard to a siege.   In short, they
mutinied for a composition, and plainly told the governor,
Monsieur de Bievres, that if he would not consent to a
capitulation, they would make one without him.   Though
Bievres was a good knight, yet he wanted courage and resolution.   He remonstrated, entreated, and begged of them to
have a little patience; whereas, in my opinion, if he had
hectored, and carried matters with an air of greater authority and resolution, he had succeeded better; but God
had ordered it otherwise: for had they held out but three
days longer, the Duke of Burgundy would have certainly
raised the siege.   But, in short, the governor complied with
the English, and the town was surrendered* to the Duke of
Lorraine, upon condition of saving their goods and sparing
their persons.

The next day, or at furthest two days after the surrender,
the Duke of Burgundy appeared with a very good army,
considering his condition, for several of his own subjects had
marched up through the province of Luxembourg to join
him.   The Duke of Lorraine and he faced one another†, but
no action of importance happened between them, the Duke
of Lorraine being too weak to attempt anything.   The Duke
of Burgundy, in his old obstinate way, was resolved to besiege Nancy again‡, though it had been much wiser in him
not to have undertaken it at that time; but when God is
pleased to change the fortune of princes, he puts these obstinate inclinations into them.   Had the Duke of Burgundy
been persuaded to have garrisoned the little places about
the town, as he was advised, he would quickly have reduced
it to great straits, and would have forced it to surrender in
a short time, for it was but ill provided with provisions, and

* On the 6th of October, 1476.
† On the 10th of October the Duke of Burgundy came up with Duke
René at Pont-à-Mousson.   Lenglet, ii. 220.
‡ On the 22nd of October, 1476.

the multitude in the town would have presently distressed it; while he would have had time to recruit his army, and put them into quarters of refreshment; but he took quite another course.

Ch. VI.—Of the Count of Campobasso's great Treachery, and how he prevented the Duke of Burgundy from hearing a Gentleman who would have revealed it to him before his Execution, and how the Duke also rejected the Information that was sent him by the King.—1476.

Whilst the Duke of Burgundy was pushing on the siege of Nancy (so unfortunately for himself, his subjects, and many others who were not at all concerned in his quarrel), many of his own party began to enter into a conspiracy against him, and new enemies, as you have heard, surrounded and invaded him on all sides. Among the rest there was the Count Nicolo Campobasso, of the kingdom of Naples, who had been banished from thence for espousing the interest of the house of Anjou*, and whom, after the death of Nicholas, Duke of Calabria, the Duke of Burgundy had entertained in his service, with several other of the Duke of Calabria's servants. This count was very poor, both in money and lands; at his first coming to him, the Duke of Burgundy gave him 40,000 ducats in ready money, to raise a troop in Italy, which was to consist of 400 lances, and to be commanded and paid by himself. From that very moment, as I said before, he began to form designs against the life of his master, and continued to carry on his secret practices to the time of which I am now speaking; for, finding his master's power declining, he began to practise underhand with the Duke of Lorraine, and such of the king's officers and servants in Champagne as were not far from the Duke of Burgundy's army. His first proposal to the Duke of

---

* The pretensions of the house of Anjou to the kingdom of Naples date from the will of Joan I., Queen of Naples, made on the 23rd of June, 1380, in favour of Louis I., Duke of Anjou, and brother of King Charles VI. of France.

Lorraine was, to delay the siege of Nancy, by not taking care to provide a sufficient quantity of provisions and ammunition, so that the army would be unable to carry it on for want of necessaries ; and, indeed, it was no hard matter for him to do this, for he was entrusted with this charge, and had the greatest influence with the duke his master. With our officers he dealt more freely, and promised to take or kill the Duke of Burgundy, provided he were continued in the command of his 400 lances upon the same footing as before, and had 20,000 crowns and a good county in France besides.

Whilst he was driving his bargains after this manner, several of the Duke of Lorraine's officers attempted to throw themselves into the town ; some of them got in, but others were taken, and among the rest one Cifron*, a gentleman of Provence, who had managed the whole affair between Campobasso and the Duke of Lorraine. The Duke of Burgundy immediately commanded this Cifron to be hanged, affirming that when a prince had once invested a town, and erected batteries to play upon it, if any endeavoured to reinforce and strengthen the garrison, they were condemned to death by the laws of war. However, this was not practised in our wars, which, in other respects, are much more cruel than those of Italy or Spain, where that custom prevails. But, right or wrong, this gentleman was to die by the Duke of Burgundy's express order. The gentleman, finding that his death was inevitable, sent to acquaint the duke that, if he pleased but to admit him to his presence, he would make a discovery of something that nearly concerned his person. Some gentlemen who heard his proposal, brought the news of it to the duke at a time when the Count of Campobasso was with him, either by accident, or else on purpose, having intelligence that Cifron was taken, and fearing he would discover all he knew ; for he knew the whole intrigue from one end to the other, and that was the secret he would have discovered to the duke.

The duke answered those that brought him this message, that it was only an artifice to gain time, and that if he had anything to discover, he might tell it to them. The Count

---

* Suffron de Bachier, councillor and steward to King René.

of Campobasso highly applauded this answer, there being
only himself, who was the chief commander in the army,
and a secretary that was writing, then present. The prisoner
sent word again, that he could discover it to nobody but the
duke himself; upon which the duke ordered him to be carried to execution immediately, and his orders were obeyed.
As he was going to the place of execution, Cifron entreated
several to intercede with the duke to save his life, and he would
discover a secret that was of greater importance to him than the
best province in his dominions. Several of his acquaintance had
compassion on him, and went to desire the duke that, for their
sake, he would vouchsafe to admit him into his presence; but this
treacherous count stood at the door of the wooden house in
which the duke lodged, refused them entrance, and told them,
"The duke commands that he be immediately executed," *
and sent messengers on purpose to hasten the provost; so
that finally poor Cifron was hanged, to the unspeakable prejudice of the Duke of Burgundy. for whom it had been
much better to have treated this unfortunate gentleman
with more humanity, and heard what he had to say; for
then, perhaps, he might have been alive to this day, and
his house in a more flourishing condition, considering what
occurrences have happened since in this kingdom.

But we have reason to believe that God had otherwise
ordained it, as a punishment for his late disloyalty to the
Count of St. Paul, Constable of France, of which you have
heard elsewhere in these Memoirs; how he seized upon his
person, contrary to his solemn promise and engagement,
delivered him to the king to be put to death, and sent all his
letters and contracts to serve as an evidence against him at
his trial. And though the duke had just reason to bear a
mortal hatred against the constable, and to pursue him even to
death, yet he should have done it without breaking his faith;
nor can all the reasons that could be alleged in this case
extenuate the crime, or cover the dishonour that will always
be a stain and blot on the duke's character; for notwith-

* According to the Chronicle of Lorraine, Campobasso acted in just
the opposite way. He undertook the defence of Suffron so strenuously
that the duke, "who was armed, and had his gauntlets on, raised his
hand, and knocked the count down." Calmet, vii. 118.

Y 4

standing the safe-conduct and protection that he granted the
constable, he yet seized upon him afterwards, and sold him
for covetousness, not only to obtain the town of St. Quentin
and other fortresses, inheritances and moveables belonging to
the constable, but also in the hope of taking Nancy the first
time he besieged it; for after many excuses and dissimula-
tions he delivered up the constable, for fear that the king's
army in Champagne might interrupt his enterprise; his
majesty having threatened to do so by his ambassadors,
unless he should perform his articles, by which the first that
took the constable was obliged to deliver him up within
eight days, or to see him executed himself. But the duke
had deferred his surrender for several days longer than was
agreed upon between them; and the fear of being called to
account for this, and of being interrupted in the siege of
Nancy, prevailed with him to deliver up the constable, as
you have heard.

And it is worthy of our observation, that as, in his first
siege of Nancy, he was guilty of that dishonourable action
towards the constable; and in his second, he ordered Cifron
to be hanged (for he would not hear him, like a person
whose understanding was infatuated, and his ears stopped to
his own ruin) — so, in the same place he was deceived and
betrayed himself by the very person in whom he reposed
most confidence (and not altogether unjustly, if we reflect
upon what has been said before), both in regard to the constable and Nancy. But the determination of such events
depends only upon God; and I have given my opinion only
to illustrate my proposition, that a good prince ought never
to consent to such a base and ignominious action, whatsoever plausible reasons may be urged in vindication of it;
for it often happens that those who give their advice in such
an affair do it either out of flattery, or fear of contradicting
their prince, though, when the thing is done, they are
heartily sorry for it, knowing how liable they are to be
punished in this world and the next; however, such counsellors as these are better far off, than near any prince.

Thus you have seen how God, the sole Governor of human
affairs, raised up the Count of Campobasso to be the instrument of His vengeance in the case of the constable, in the
same place, and after the same manner, but with more cir-

cumstances of cruelty ; for he betrayed the very person who
had entertained him in his service when he was old, poor,
and friendless, and had given him an annual sum of
10,000 ducats, with which to pay his soldiers, besides
other posts of great advantage. And, when he first
began his conspiracy he was on his journey into Italy with
40,000 ducats to raise his regiment ; and yet, in that very
journey, he made overtures in two several places, first,
to a physician at Lyons, called Simon of Pavia, next, to
another person in Savoy, as you have already heard ; and at
his return with his regiment, being quartered in certain
small towns in the county of Marle in Lannois, he fell to his
old practices, and offered to deliver up all the towns he held ;
or, if that were not sufficient, if the king would but face his
master, and pretend to give him battle, when they were
drawn up, and ready to engage, upon a signal to be agreed
on between the king and him, he would come over to him
and join his majesty's army with the troops under his command ; but the king was not pleased with this last overture
by any means.   He offered, likewise, the first time his master
lay in the field, either to take him prisoner, or kill him, as
he was reviewing his army ; and indeed he might easily have
done it ; for the duke's custom was, as soon as he was alighted
from his horse, at the place where his army was to
encamp, to pull off the rest of his armour, and with his
cuirass only, to mount upon a little palfrey, and, attended
only by eight or ten archers on foot, or two or three gentlemen of his bedchamber, to ride about the army, and see that
it was strongly enclosed ; so that with a small party of ten
horse, the count might have performed this execrable action
without much difficulty.   The king, observing the restless
malice of this man against his master, and that he was con-
spiring against him even during the time of the truce
between them, and being not well informed of the object of
these overtures, resolved upon showing a singular piece
of friendship and generosity to the Duke of Burgundy, and
sent him in writing, by the Lord of Contay (whom I have so
often mentioned in these Memoirs), the whole progress of
the count's conspiracy. I was present at the delivery of the
letters, and I am sure the Lord of Contay acquitted himself
faithfully to his master ; but the duke would give no credit

to his information, and said, that if there was any truth in it, the king would never have communicated it. This was long before the duke's arrival before Nancy, and I verily believe he never took any notice of it to the count, for he continued his old practices afterwards.

CH. VII.—How the Duke of Lorraine with a powerful Army of Germans took the field, and encamped at St. Nicholas, whilst the Duke of Burgundy lay before Nancy ; and how the King of Portugal, who was in France at that time, paid a visit to the Duke in his Camp before that Town.—1477.

BUT now to proceed with our principal subject. You must know that the Duke of Burgundy besieged Nancy in the depth of winter, with a small army which was ill provided and ill paid. Several of his officers had entered into a conspiracy against him, and there was a general mutiny among the common soldiers, who censured and despised all his enterprises; which, as I have observed at large before, is the common fate in times of adversity ; but nobody practised against his person and dominions except the Count of Campobasso, for his subjects were all loyal to him. The Duke of Burgundy being in this miserable condition, the Duke of Lorraine treated with the old and new allies* (whom I have mentioned before) for a supply of troops to enable him to give the duke battle, and raise the siege of Nancy. They all readily consented, and every town furnished him with a body of troops, so that now his only want was money for their subsistence. The king by his ambassadors in Switzerland encouraged him extremely in this enterprise, and remitted him 400,000 francs to pay his Swiss : and the Lord of Craon, the king's lieu-

---

* Oliver de la Marche (ii. 420.) also states that "the Duke of Lorraine intrigued with the Swiss to induce them to come to Nancy; and the King of France secretly furnished him with money to obtain their assistance, that they might do to the Duke of Burgundy that which he did not dare to undertake himself."

tenant in Champagne, was quartered in Barrois with
a body of 700 or 800 lances and frank-archers, commanded by experienced officers. The Duke of Lorraine,
by help of the king's favour and money, assembled a good
body of Swiss, both horse and foot ; for, besides the troops
that were in his own pay, they furnished him with some at
their own expense. He had also many French volunteers,
and the king's army (as you have already heard) was
quartered in Barrois, not with a design to commit any act of
hostility, but only to wait the issue of a battle, which was
every day expected ; for the Duke of Lorraine had marched
with his Germans to St. Nicholas*, not far from Nancy.

The King of Portugal† had now been in France for nine
months or thereabouts ; for our king, being in an alliance
with him against the King of Castile‡, the King of Portugal
flattered himself that he would assist him with a powerful
army to make war upon his adversary on the side of Biscay
or Navarre, for he had several towns in Castile, upon the
frontiers of Portugal, and some upon our borders, as the
Castle of Burgos, and others ; so that I am of opinion, if our
king had assisted him, as he was sometimes inclined to do,
the King of Portugal might have succeeded in his designs ;
but, by degrees, the king's mind changed, and the King of
Portugal was amused with fair words, and fed with hopes,
for a year or more.

In the meantime the King of Portugal's affairs in Castile
began to decline : for, when he came into France, almost all
the nobility of Castile were in his interest ; but his long
stay in France tired their patience, and they began to grow
weary, and made their peace with Ferdinand and Isabella,

* "On Saturday, the 4th of January, the Duke of Lorraine arrived at
St. Nicholas with 10,500 Swiss."   Molinet, i. 231.

† Alphonso V., surnamed the African, was the son of Duarte I., King
of Portugal, and Eleanor of Arragon. He was born in 1432, and succeeded his father in 1438. He married his cousin Isabella, the daughter
of Don Pedro ; and he died on the 28th of August, 1481. He was the
first King of Portugal who possessed a private library.

‡ Ferdinand V., surnamed the Catholic, was the son of John, King of
Navarre and Arragon, and Juana Henriquez. He was born on the 10th
of March, 1452, and ascended the throne of Spain in 1474. His first
wife was the celebrated Isabella of Castile. He died on the 23rd of
January, 1516.

who now reign. The King of France indeed had promised to assist him, but he excused himself afterwards upon account of the war in Lorraine, pretending that if the Duke of Burgundy prevailed, he feared that he would afterwards invade his dominions. The King of Portugal, who was a very good and just prince, took a fancy to pay a visit to the Duke of Burgundy, who was his cousin-german*, and to try whether his good offices could effect a pacification between the king and the duke, supposing that when this obstacle was removed, the king would certainly assist him ; for he was ashamed to return into Portugal or Castile without having been successful in his solicitations at our court, especially after coming thither in so imprudent a manner, and contrary to the opinion of the greatest part of his council.

With this design the King of Portugal began his journey towards the latter end of the winter, and being arrived at the Duke of Burgundy's camp before Nancy †, he began to discourse with him about what the king had told him in relation to a peace : but he found it would be no easy matter to accommodate things between them, their demands ran so high ; and therefore he stayed but two days, before he took his leave of his cousin, and returned to Paris. The Duke of Burgundy pressed him to stay, and command the body of troops that were to defend the pass at Pont-à-Mousson, near Nancy, for he had received intelligence that the German army was posted at St. Nicholas. The King of Portugal excused himself, by saying that he was neither armed nor provided for such an enterprise ; and upon this he returned to Paris, where he had resided so long already. At last the King of Portugal grew suspicious of the King of France, and fancied his majesty had a design to seize on him, and deliver him up to his enemy the King of Castile. Upon the strength of this imagination he put himself into a disguise, and with two more in his company, resolved to go to Rome, and enter some religious house : but he was taken in that

* The mother of Duke Charles, Isabella of Portugal, was aunt to King Alphonso V.

† He arrived at the camp before Nancy on the 29th of December. Lenglet, ii. 221.

disguise by a Norman called Robinet le Beuf *; at which our king was extremely concerned, and being ashamed of what had passed, ordered several ships to be equipped on the coast of Normandy, and gave the command of them to Master George le Grec†, with orders to conduct him safe into Portugal, which he performed accordingly.

The occasion of his war against the King of Castile was in favour of his sister's daughter ‡, which sister was wife to Don Henry, late King of Castile §, and had a beautiful daughter still living (but unmarried), in Portugal : but Queen Isabella ‖, who was sister to the said King Henry, disputed the young lady's right of succession to the crown of Castile, pretending she was illegitimate, and born in adultery.   Many others were of the same opinion, objecting impotence in King Henry, and proving it by arguments, which for certain reasons I shall here omit.   However this may be, and though the young lady was born in wedlock, and under the veil of marriage, yet the crown of Castile was enjoyed by Queen Isabella of Castile, and her husband the King of Arragon and Sicily, who now reigns.   The King of Portugal was very ambitious of making a match between his niece and our King Charles VIII., who is now reigning; and indeed that was the great design of his journey into

* Robinet le Beuf, a Norman knight, from the neighbourhood of Evreux, was valet de chambre to Louis XI. in 1466.   In 1471 he was appointed one of the gentlemen of the king's household, and held that office until 1488, when he was killed in the battle of Saint-Aubin-du-Cormier.

† In the letters of naturalization granted to this person by Louis XI. in 1477, he is designated as "George de Bicipat, surnamed the Greek, Knight, native of Greece, Captain of our great ship and of our town and Castle of Touque, and our well-beloved and trusty councillor and chamberlain."   Pierre de Lailly mentions him as George Paleologo de Bicipat.   In previous editions of Commines he is erroneously called George Leger.

‡ Juana, daughter of Henry IV., King of Castile, and Juana, Infanta of Portugal, was born in 1462.   She was twice betrothed, first to the Duke of Guienne, and afterwards to her uncle, Alphonso V.   On the 15th of November, 1480, she took the vows in the convent of Santa Clara at Santarem, and she died at Alcacova in 1530.

§ He died in 1474.

‖ Isabella of Castile, daughter of Juan II , and Isabella of Portugal, was born on the 23rd of April, 1451.   In 1469, she married Ferdinand the Catholic, King of Arragon, and she died on the 20th of November, 1504.

France, which turned so much to his disadvantage, for not long after his return into Portugal he died.   Wherefore (as I have already observed in the beginning of these Memoirs), it highly concerns a prince to be very careful in the choice of persons qualified to be sent on embassies to foreign courts; for if those ambassadors that came to our king from the King of Portugal upon the above-mentioned proposal (at which I was present by deputation from our king), had been as wise as they ought, they would have informed themselves better of our affairs before they advised their master to undertake a journey which proved so disadvantageous and dishonourable to him.

Cʜ. VIII.—How the Duke of Burgundy, by rejecting the Counsel of several of his Officers, was defeated and slain in a Battle between him and the Duke of Lorraine, not far from Nancy.—1477.

I ᴄᴏᴜʟᴅ willingly have omitted this relation of the King of Portugal's affairs, had it not been to show, that one prince ought not rashly to put himself into the power of another, nor go in person to solicit his own supplies.   But to proceed with my history:—The King of Portugal had not left the Duke of Burgundy's camp above a day, before the Duke of Lorraine and his army of Germans broke up from St. Nicholas, and advanced towards the Duke of Burgundy, with a resolution to give him battle.   The Count of Campobasso joined them that very day, and carried off with him about eight score men-at-arms; and it grieved him much that he could do his master no greater mischief.   The garrison of Nancy had intelligence of his design, which in some measure encouraged them to hold out; besides, another person* had got over the works, and assured them of relief, otherwise they were just upon surrendering, and would have capitulated in a little time, had it not been for the treachery of this count; but God had determined to finish this mystery.

* His name was Thierry, a draper in the town of Mirecourt.   Calmet, vii. 122.

The Duke of Burgundy, having intelligence of the approach of the Duke of Lorraine's army, called a kind of council, contrary to his custom, for generally he followed his own will. It was the opinion of most of his officers that his best way would be to retire to Pont-à-Mousson, which was not far off, and dispose his army in the towns about Nancy ; affirming, that as soon as the Germans had thrown a supply of men and provisions into Nancy, they would march off again ; and the Duke of Lorraine being in great want of money, it would be a great while before he would be able to assemble such an army again; and that their supplies of provisions could not be so great but before half the winter was over, they would be in the same straits as they were now ; and that in the meantime the duke might raise more forces, and recruit himself : for I have been told by those who ought to know best, that the Duke of Burgundy's army did not then consist of full 4000 men [*], and of that number not above 1200 were in a condition to fight. Money he did not want; for in the Castle of Luxembourg (which was not far off), there were in ready cash 450,000 crowns, which would have raised men enough. But God was not so merciful to him as to permit him to take this wise counsel, or discern the vast multitude of enemies who on every side surrounded him. Therefore he chose the worst plan, and like a rash and inconsiderate madman, resolved to try his fortune, and engage the enemy with his weak and shattered army [†], notwithstanding the Duke of Lorraine had a numerous force of Germans, and the king's army was not far off.

---

[*] Oliver de La Marche (ii. 420.) says he had not 2000 fighting men.

[†] Before the battle, says Molinet (i. 229.) he inquired how many men there were in his army. " The Count of Chimay, a very eloquent, wise, and discreet man, told him in gentle and amiable language, that the captains had made inquiries, and that there were not more than 3000 men in a condition to fight. 'I deny what you say,' replied the duke, in great anger ; ' but if I were to fight alone I would fight all the same. You are what you are, and show clearly that you are sprung from the house of Vaudemont.' The count prudently and gently replied, that his deeds should show that he was sprung from an honourable line, and that, although he saw no chance of overcoming the enemy, he would remain faithful to the duke."

As soon as the Count of Campobasso arrived in the Duke of Lorraine's army, the Germans sent him word to leave the camp immediately, for they would not entertain such traitors among them. Upon which message he retired with his party to Condé*, a castle and pass† not far off, where he fortified himself with carts and other things as well as he could, in hopes, that if the Duke of Burgundy were routed, he might have an opportunity of coming in for a share of the plunder, as he did afterwards. Nor was this practice with the Duke of Lorraine the most execrable action that Campobasso was guilty of; but, before he left the army, he conspired with several other officers (finding it was impracticable to attempt anything against the Duke of Burgundy's person) to leave him just as they came to the charge; for, at that time, he supposed it would put the army into the greatest terror and consternation; and if the duke fled, he was sure he could not escape alive, for he had ordered thirteen or fourteen sure men, some to run as soon as the Germans came up to charge them, and others to watch the Duke of Burgundy, and kill him in the rout; which was well enough contrived, for I myself have seen two or three of those who were thus employed to kill the duke. Having thus settled his conspiracy at home, he went over to the Duke of Lorraine upon the approach of the German army; but, finding they would not entertain him, he retired to Condé, as I said before.

The German army marched forward, and with them a considerable body of French horse, whom the king had given leave to be present in that action. Several parties lay in ambush not far off, that if the Duke of Burgundy were routed, they might surprise some person of quality, or take some considerable booty. By this every one may see into what a deplorable condition this poor duke had brought himself, by his contempt of good counsel. Both armies being joined, the Duke of Burgundy's forces, which had been twice beaten before, and were weak and ill-provided besides, were quickly broken and entirely defeated. Many saved

---

* Conde-Northen, or Contghen, in the arrondissement of Metz, and department of Moselle.

† At the Pont de la Bussiere, half a league from Nancy.   Molinet, i. 233.

themselves by flight; the rest were either taken or killed *;
and among them the Duke of Burgundy himself was killed
on the spot.† Not having been in the battle myself, I will
say nothing of the manner of his death; but I was told by
some, that they saw him beaten down but, being prisoners
themselves, were not able to assist him; yet, whilst they
were in sight, he was not killed, but a great body of
men coming that way afterwards, they killed and stripped
him in the throng, not knowing who he was. This battle
was fought on the 5th of January, 1476, upon the eve of
Twelfth-day.

---

*The Epitaph of Charles, the last Duke of Burgundy, who
was killed before Nancy, in Lorraine, in the year 1476,
on Twelfth-eve.*

CAROLUS hoc busto Burgundæ gloria gentis
 Conditur, Europæ qui fuit ante timor.
Ganda rebellatrix hoc plebs domitore, cremata
 Post patriæ leges perpete pressa jugo est.
Nec minùs hunc sensit tellus Leodina cruentum,
 Cùm ferro et flammis urbs populata fuit.
Monte sub heritio Francas cum rege cohortes,
 In pavidam valido truserat ense fugam.
Hostibus expulsis Eduardum in regna locavit
 Anglica, primævo restituens solio.
Bella ducum, regumque, et Cæsaris omnia spernens
 Totus in effuso sanguine lætus erat.

---

* "In that battle were slain, among others, the Lord of Bièvre, the
Lord of Verun, and the Lord of Contay; and among the prisoners
were the Lord Anthony, Bastard of Burgundy, and his brother Baldwin;
Philip de Croy, Count of Chimay; the Count of Nassau, and the Count
of Challane; the Lord Josse de Lalain, Sir Oliver de la Marche, the
Lord of Croy, the eldest son of the Lord of Contay, the eldest son of the
Lord of Montagu, and other noblemen." Molinet, i. 236.

† "The Duke of Burgundy was knocked off his black horse, and fell
into a ditch near St. Jean." Lenglet, iii. 493. "A knight named
Claude de Bausemont, came up with the Duke of Burgundy, and gave
him a lance thrust; others then charged him suddenly, and he was put to
death in a meadow near St. Jean." Calmet, vii. 133. "A page came

Denique dum solitis fidit temerarius armis,
  Atque Lotharingo cum duce bella movet,
Sanguineam vomuit media inter prælia vitam,
  Aureaque hostili vellera liquit humo.
Ergò triumphator longæva in sæcla renatus,
  Palmam de tanto principe victor habet.
O tibi qui terras quæsisti (Carole) cœlum
  Det Deus, et spretas anteà pacis opes.
Nunc die Nanceios cernens ex æthere muros,
  A clemente ferox hoste sepulchror ibi.
Discite terrenis quid sit confidere rebus,
  Ilic toties victor denique victus adest.

At the foot of the tomb are engraven the following verses:

Dux jacet hîc Carolus Belgarum illa ignea virtus
  Cui Mavors dederat bella gerenda pater:
Quem timuit subditis animosus Gallus in armis,
  Cuique Alemannorum terga dedêre duces,
Quique animum Hesperias bellis agitabat in urbes,
  Sed subitò invertit sors temulenta viam:
Nam cùm Ranerium bello sibi provocat hostem,
  Occubuit fuso milite stratus humi:
Et ne tanta viri laus intestata jaceret,
  Hoc victor victi condidit ossa loco.

ECCE LEO CECIDIT, IAM PAX
QUÆSITA VIGEBIT.
NOCTE REGUM SUCCUBUIT
CAROLUS.

to the Duke of Lorraine, and being interrogated, declared plainly that he had seen the Duke of Burgundy thrown from his horse, and killed in a certain place which he was ready to point out. On the following morning the page, with many notable personages, went to the field, and found the body of the Duke of Burgundy quite naked, lying on the ground among other corpses; and he had received three mortal wounds, one in the head from a halberd, which clove his skull in two, another with a pike in the groin, and a third in the buttock." Molinet, i. 234. By order of the Duke of Lorraine, the body was buried with great magnificence in St George's Church at Nancy.

CH. IX.—A Digression concerning the Virtues of the Duke of Burgundy, and the Time of his House's Prosperity.

I SAW a seal-ring of his, after his death, at Milan, with his
arms cut curiously upon a sardonyx that I have often seen
him wear in a riband at his breast, which was sold at Milan
for two ducats, and had been stolen from him by a varlet
that waited on him in his chamber.   I have often seen the
duke dressed and undressed in great state and formality, and
by very great persons ; but, at his last hour, all this pomp
and magnificence ceased, and both he and his family perished
(as you have heard already) on the very spot where he had
delivered up the constable not long before, out of a base and
avaricious motive; but may God forgive him!   I have
known him a powerful and honourable prince, in as great
esteem and as much courted by his neighbours (when his
affairs were in a prosperous condition), as any prince in
Europe, and perhaps more so; and I cannot conceive what
should have provoked God Almighty's displeasure so highly
against him, unless it was his self-love and arrogance, in
attributing all the success of his enterprises, and all the
renown he ever acquired, to his own wisdom and conduct,
without ascribing anything to God : yet, to speak truth, he
was endowed with many good qualities.   No prince ever
had a greater desire to entertain young noblemen than he ;
or was more careful of their education.   His presents and
bounty were never profuse and extravagant, because he gave
to many, and wished everybody should taste of his generosity.
No prince was ever more easy of access to his servants and
subjects.   Whilst I was in his service he was never cruel,
but a little before his death he became so, which was an
infallible sign of the shortness of his life.   He was very
splendid and pompous in his dress, and in everything else,
and, indeed, a little too much.   He paid great honours to
all ambassadors and foreigners, and entertained them nobly.
His ambitious desire of glory was insatiable, and it was that
which more than any other motive induced him to engage
eternally in wars.   He earnestly desired to imitate the old
kings and heroes of antiquity, who are still so much talked

of in the world, and his courage was equal to that of any prince of his time.

But all his designs and imaginations were vain, and turned afterwards to his own dishonour and confusion, for it is the conquerors and not the conquered that win renown.   I cannot easily determine towards whom God Almighty showed his anger most, whether towards him who died suddenly, without pain or sickness in the field of battle, or towards his subjects, who never enjoyed peace after his death, but were continually involved in wars against which they were not able to maintain themselves, upon account of the civil dissensions and cruel animosities that arose among them; and that which was the most insupportable was, that the very people to whom they were now indebted for their defence and preservation, were the Germans, who were strangers, and not long since had been their enemies. In short, after the duke's death, there was not a man who wished them to prosper, whoever defended them.   And by the management of their affairs, their understanding seemed to be as much infatuated as their master's was just before his death; for they rejected all good counsel, and pursued such methods as directly tended to their destruction; and they are still in great danger of a relapse into calamity, and it will be well if it turn not in the end to their utter ruin.

I am partly of the opinion of those who maintain that God gives princes, as He in His wisdom thinks fit, to punish or chastise their subjects: and He disposes the affections of subjects to their princes, as He has determined to exalt or depress them.   Just so it has pleased Him to deal with the house of Burgundy; for after a long series of riches and prosperity, and six-score years'* peace under three illustrious princes, predecessors to Duke Charles (all of them of great prudence and discretion), it pleased God to send this Duke Charles, who continually involved them in bloody wars, as well winter as summer, to their great affliction and expense, in which most of their richest and stoutest men were either killed or taken prisoners.   Their misfortunes began at the siege of Nuz, and continued for three or four battles successively, to

* A hundred and four years only, as Philip the Bold was created Duke of Burgundy in 1363, and Philip the Good died in 1467.

the very hour of his death ; so much so, that at the last, the
whole strength of the country was destroyed, and all were
killed or taken prisoners who had any zeal or affection for
the house of Burgundy, or power to defend the state and
dignity of that family; so that in a manner their losses
equalled, if they did not overbalance, their former prosperity;
for as I had seen these princes puissant, rich and honourable,
so it fared with their subjects : for I think I have seen and
known the greatest part of Europe, yet I never knew any
province or country, though of a larger extent, so abounding
in money *, so extravagantly fine in their furniture, so sumptuous in their buildings, so profuse in their expenses, so luxurious in their feasts and entertainments, and so prodigal in
all respects, as the subjects of these princes in my time ; and
if any think I have exaggerated, others who lived in my time,
will be of opinion that I have rather said too little.

But it pleased God, at one blow, to subvert this great and
sumptuous edifice, and ruin this powerful and illustrious
family, which had maintained and bred up so many brave
men, and had acquired such mighty honour and renown far
and near, by so many victories and successful enterprises,
as none of all its neighbouring states could pretend to boast
of. A hundred and twenty years it continued in this
flourishing condition, by the grace of God ; all its neighbours
having, in the meantime, been involved in troubles and
commotions, and all of them applying to it for succour or
protection : to wit, France, England, and Spain, as you
have seen by experience of our master the King of France,
who in his minority, and during the reign of Charles VII.,
his father, retired to this court, where he lived six years, and
was nobly entertained all that time by Duke Philip the
Good. Out of England I saw there also two of King Edward's brothers, the Dukes of Clarence and Gloucester (the
last of whom was afterwards called King Richard the Third);
and of the house of Lancaster, the whole family or very
near, with all their party. In short, I have seen this family

* " Philip the Good left his son 400,000 crowns of gold in cash, 72,000
marks of silver in plate, not to mention rich tapestries, splendid jewels,
gold plate adorned with precious stones, and his large and valuable
library ; besides which, he died worth 2,000,000 gold pieces in furniture
alone." Oliver de la Marche, ii. 267.

z 3

in all respects the most flourishing and celebrated of any in Christendom : and then, in a short space of time, it was quite ruined and turned upside down, and left the most desolate and miserable of any house in Europe, as regards both prince and subjects.   Such changes and revolutions of states and kingdoms, God in His providence has wrought before we were born, and will do again when we are dead ; for this is a certain maxim, that the prosperity or adversity of princes depends wholly on His Divine disposal.

———————

CH. X.—How the King of France received intelligence of the Duke of Burgundy's last Defeat, and managed his Affairs after the Duke's Death.—1477.

BUT to proceed with my history.   The king having established posts * in all parts of his kingdom (which before never had been done), it was not long ere he received the news of the Duke of Burgundy's defeat ; and he was in hourly expectation of the report, for letters of advice had reached him before, importing, that the German army was advancing towards the Duke of Burgundy's, and that a battle was expected between them.   Upon which many persons kept their ears open for the news, in order to carry it to the king.   For his custom was to reward liberally any person who brought him the first tidings of any news of importance, and to remember the messenger besides.   His majesty also took great delight in talking of it before it arrived, and would say, "I will give so much to any man who first brings me such and such news."   The Lord du Bouchage and I being together, happened to receive the first news of the battle of Morat, and we went with it to the king, who gave each of us 200 marks of silver. The Lord du Lude, who lay without the Plessis, had the first news of the arrival of the courier, with the letters

———

* The ordinance instituting this postal service is dated at Luxies (now Lucheux) near Doullens, on the 19th day of June, 1464. Duclos, v. 220.

concerning the battle of Nancy; he commanded the courier
to deliver him the packet, and as he was a great favourite of
the king's, he durst not refuse him. By break of day the
next morning, the Lord du Lude knocked at the door next
to the king's chamber, and it being opened, he delivered in
the packet from the Lord of Craon and other officers. But
none of the first letters gave any certainty of the duke's
death; they only stated that he was seen to run away, and
that it was supposed he had made his escape.

The king was at first so transported with joy at the news,
he scarce knew how to behave himself: however, his majesty
was still in some perplexity. On one hand, he was afraid
that if the duke should be taken prisoner by the Germans,
by means of his money, of which he had great store, he
would make some composition with them. On the other, he
was doubtful, if the duke had made his escape, though defeated
for the third time, whether he should seize upon his towns in
Burgundy or not*; which he judged not very difficult to
do, since most of the brave men of that country had been
slain in those three battles. As to this last point, he came
to this resolution (which I believe few were acquainted with
but myself,) that if the duke were alive and well, he would
command the army which lay ready in Champagne and
Barrois to march immediately into Burgundy, and seize
upon the whole country whilst it was in that state of terror
and consternation; and when he was in possession of it, he

* The king's first design was to seize them, as is proved by the subjoined letter, addressed to the Lord of Craon : — " My Lord Count, my
Friend—I have received your letters, and heard the good news which you
tell me, for which I thank you as much as I am able. Now it is time to
employ all your five senses so as to get the duchy and county of Burgundy into my hands; and with that view, with your band and the
Governor of Champagne (if the Duke of Burgundy is really dead) throw
yourself into that country, and as you love me, take care that your men
of war keep as good order as if you were in Paris, and tell them that I wish
to treat them and keep them better than any of my own kingdom ; and
that with regard to our god-daughter, I intend to complete the marriage
which I have already negotiated between the dauphin and her. My
lord count, I do not intend that you should enter the country or mention
what I have stated above, unless the Duke of Burgundy is dead; and in
that case, I beg you to serve me according to the confidence I have in
you. Farewell. Written at Plessis du Parc, on the 9th of January.
Signed Louis, and countersigned De Chaumont." Molinet, ii. 2.

would inform the duke, that the seizure he had made was only to preserve it for him, and secure it against the Germans, because it was held under the sovereignty of the crown of France, and therefore he was unwilling it should fall into their hands ; and whatever he had taken should be faithfully restored: and truly, I am of opinion his majesty would have done it, though many people who are ignorant of the motives that guided the king, will not easily believe it.   But this resolution was altered as soon as he was certain of the Duke of Burgundy's death.

Upon the king's receiving the above-mentioned first letter, (which gave no account of the duke's death), he immediately sent to Tours, to summon all his captains and other great personages to attend him.   Upon their arrival, he communicated his letters to them.   They all pretended great joy; but to such as more narrowly observed their behaviour, it was easy to be discerned that most of them did but feign it ; and, notwithstanding all their outward dissimulation, they had been better pleased if the Duke of Burgundy had been successful.   The reason of this might be, because the king was greatly feared, and now if he should find himself clear and secure from his enemies, they were afraid they would be reduced, or at least their offices and pensions retrenched ; for there were several present who had been engaged against him with his brother the Duke of Guienne, in the confederacy called the Public Good.   After his majesty had discoursed with them for some time, he went to mass, and then ordered dinner to be laid in his chamber, and made them all dine with him ; there being with him his chancellor*, and some other lords of his council.   The king's discourse at dinner-time was about this affair, and I well remember that myself and others took particular notice how those who were present dined ; but to speak truth (whether for joy or sorrow, I cannot tell), there was not one of them that half filled his belly; and certainly it could not have been from modesty or bashfulness before the king, for there was not one amongst them but had dined with his majesty many times before.

As soon as the king rose from table, he retired, and

* Pierre d'Oriolle. See a previous note.

distributed to some persons certain lands belonging to the Duke of Burgundy, as though he had been dead. He despatched the Bastard of Bourbon, Admiral of France, and myself, into those parts, with full power to receive the homage of all such as were willing to submit and become his subjects. He ordered us to set out immediately, and gave us commission to open all his letters and packets which we might meet by the way, that thereby we might ascertain whether the duke was dead or alive. We departed with all speed, though it was the coldest weather I ever felt in my life. We had not ridden above half a day's journey, when we met a courier, and commanding him to deliver his letters, we learned by them that the Duke of Burgundy was slain, and that his body had been found among the dead, and recognised by an Italian page that attended him, and by one Monsieur Louppe*, a Portuguese*, who was his physician, and who assured the Lord of Craon that it was the duke his master, and the Lord of Craon notified the same at once to the king.

CH. XI.—How the King of France seized upon Abbeville after the Death of the Duke of Burgundy, and the Answer he received from the Inhabitants of Arras.—1477.

Upon receiving this news we rode directly to the suburbs of Abbeville, and were the first that announced the intelligence to the duke's adherents in those parts. We found the inhabitants of the town in treaty with the Lord of Torcy, for whom they had held a great affection for a long time. The soldiers and officers of the Duke of Burgundy negotiated with us, by means of a messenger whom we had sent to them beforehand ; and in confidence of success, they dismissed 400 Flemings who were then quartered in the town. The citizens, laying hold of this opportunity, opened the gates

* In the list of the duke's household, this physician is named Master Lope de la Garde. With reference to the page, one of the manuscripts of these Memoirs speaks of him as "a Spaniard, named Don Diego ;" other authorities state that he was an Italian, of the house of Colonna.

immediately to the Lord of Torcy, to the great prejudice and disadvantage of the captains and officers of the garrison, —for there were seven or eight of them to whom, by virtue of the king's authority, we had promised money, and pensions for life ; but they never enjoyed the benefit of that promise, because the town was not surrendered by them. Abbeville was one of the towns that Charles VII. delivered up by the treaty of Arras in the year 1435, which towns were to return to the crown of France upon default of issue male ; so that their admitting us so easily is not so much to be wondered at.

From thence we marched to Dourlans, and sent a summons to Arras, the chief town in Artois, and formerly part of the patrimony of the Earls of Flanders, which for want of heirs male always descended to the daughters. The Lord of Ravestein and the Lord des Cordes, who were in the town of Arras, offered to enter into a treaty with us at Mount St. Eloy*, and to bring some of the chief citizens with them. It was concluded that I and some others should meet them in the king's behalf ; but the admiral refused to go himself, because he presumed they would not consent to grant all our demands. I had not been long at the place of appointment, when the two above-mentioned Lords of Ravestein and Des Cordes arrived, attended by several persons of quality, and by certain commissioners on the part of the city ; one of whom was their pensionary, named Monsieur John de la Vaquerie†, whom they appointed to be their spokesman, and who since that time has been made first president of the Parliament of Paris. We demanded in the king's name to have the gates immediately opened, and to be received into the town, for both the town and the whole country belonged to the king by right of confiscation ; and if they refused to obey this summons, they would be in danger of being besieged, and compelled to submit by force, since their duke was defeated, and his dominions utterly unprovided with

---

* An abbey of regular canons of the Augustinian order, at about five miles to the north-west of Arras.

† Jean de la Vacquerie, a native of Picardy, was admitted a councillor of the Parliament of Paris on the 12th of November, 1479 ; he became fourth president of that body on the 30th of May, 1480, and first president on the 27th of February, 1481. He died in July, 1497.

means of defence, upon account of their irrecoverable losses
in the three late battles. The lords returned answer by
their speaker Monsieur John de la Vaquerie, that the county
of Artois belonged to the Lady of Burgundy, daughter of
Duke Charles, and descended to her in a right line from
Margaret, Countess of Flanders*, Artois, Burgundy, Nevers,
and Rethel, who was married to Philip I., Duke of Burgundy,
son of King John of France†, and younger brother to King
Charles V. ; wherefore they humbly entreated the king, that
he would observe and continue the truce that had existed
between him and the late Duke of Burgundy her father.
Our conference was but short, for we expected to receive
this answer ; but the chief design of my going thither was to
have a private conference with some persons that were there,
to try if I could bring them over to the king's interest.
I made overtures to some of them, who soon afterwards did
his majesty signal service. We found the whole country in
a state of very great consternation, and not without cause ;
for in eight days' time they would scarce have been able to
raise eight men-at-arms, and for other soldiers there were
not in the whole country above 1500 (reckoning horse and
foot together) that had escaped from the battle in which the
Duke of Burgundy was slain ; and they were quartered
about Namur and Hainault. Their former haughty language was much altered now, and they spoke with more
submission and humility ; not that I would upbraid them
with excessive arrogance in times past, but to speak impartially, in my time they thought themselves so powerful, that
they spoke neither of nor to the king with the same respect
as they have done since; and if people were wise, they
would always use such moderate language in their days of
prosperity, that in the time of adversity they would not need
to change it.

I returned to the admiral, to give him an account of our
conference; and there I was informed that the king was

* Margaret of Flanders, daughter of Louis II., Count of Flanders, and
Margaret of Brabant, was born in April, 1350, and married Philip the
Bold, Duke of Burgundy, on the 12th of April, 1369. She died on the
16th of March, 1405.

† John, surnamed the Good, was son of Philip VI. of France, and
Joan of Burgundy. He died on the 8th of April, 1364.

coming towards us, and that upon receiving the news of the duke's death, he immediately set out, having despatched several letters in his own and his officers' names, to send after him what forces could presently be assembled, with which he hoped to reduce the provinces I have just mentioned to his obedience.

CH. XII.—A Digression (not altogether foreign to my principal Design) concerning the King's Joy at being delivered from most of his Enemies, and of the Error his Majesty committed in the Reduction of the Duke of Burgundy's Countries.—1477.

THE king was overjoyed to see himself rid of all those whom he hated, and who were his chief enemies; on some of them he had been personally revenged, as on the constable of France, the Duke of Nemours, and several others. His brother, the Duke of Guienne, was dead, and his majesty came to the succession of the duchy. The whole house of Anjou was extinct; both René, King of Sicily, John and Nicholas, Dukes of Calabria, and since them their cousin, the Count du Maine, afterwards made Count of Provence.* The Count d'Armagnac had been killed at Lestore, and the king had got the estates and moveables of all of them. But the house of Burgundy, being greater and more powerful than the rest, having maintained war with Charles VII., our master's father, for two and thirty years together without any cessation, by the assistance of the English; and having their dominions bordering upon the king's, and their subjects always inclinable to invade his kingdom; the king had reason to be more than ordinarily pleased at the death of that duke, and he triumphed more in his ruin than in that of all the rest of his enemies, as he thought that nobody, for the

* Charles of Anjou, King of Naples, Count of Maine, Guise and Provence, was the son of Charles of Anjou and Isabella of Luxembourg. In 1480, he succeeded to all the estates and dominions of René, Count of Provence and King of Naples and Sicily. He appointed Louis XI. his heir by a will dated on the 10th of December, 1481, and he died on the day following. Anselme, i. 236.

future, either of his own subjects, or his neighbours, would
be able to oppose him, or disturb the tranquillity of his reign.
He was at peace with England*, as you have heard, and
made it his chief business to continue so : yet, though he
was freed in this manner from all his apprehensions, God
did not permit him to take such courses in the management of his affairs as were most proper to promote his own
interests and designs.   And certainly although God Almighty
has shown, and does still show, that His determination is to
punish the family of Burgundy severely, not only in the
person of the duke, but in their subjects and estates ; yet I
think the king our master did not take right measures to
gain his end.   For, if he had acted prudently, instead of pretending to conquer them, he should rather have endeavoured
to annex all those large territories, to which he had no just
title, to the crown of France by some treaty of marriage ;
or to have gained the hearts and affections of the people, and
so have brought them over to his interest, which he might,
without any great difficulty, have effected, considering how their
late afflictions had impoverished and dejected them.   If he had
acted after that manner, he would not only have prevented
their ruin and destruction, but extended and strengthened
his own kingdom, and established them all in a firm and lasting
peace.   He might by this means have eased his own country
of its intolerable grievances, and particularly of the marches
and countermarches of his troops, which are commanded
continually up and down from one end of the kingdom to the
other, sometimes upon very slight occasions.

In the Duke of Burgundy's life-time the king often talked
with me about this affair, and told me what he would do if
he should outlive the duke, and his discourse at that time
was very rational and wise : he told me he would propose a
match between his son (our present king) and the Duke of
Burgundy's daughter (who has since become Duchess of
Austria), and if she would not consent to that, on the ground
that the dauphin was too young, he would then endeavour to
marry her to some young prince† of his kingdom, by which

* By a treaty concluded on the 29th of August, 1475. See book iv.
chap. viii. of these Memoirs.

† In the third chapter of his sixth book, Commines especially mentions the Count of Angouleme.

means he might keep her and her subjects in amity, and
obtain, without war, what he intended to lay claim to for
himself; and this was his resolution not more than a week
before he heard of the Duke of Burgundy's death; but the
very day he received that news, his mind began to change,
and this wise counsel was laid aside when the admiral and I
were despatched into those provinces: however, the king
spoke little of what he intended to do, — only to some few
that were about him, he promised sundry of the duke's lordships and possessions.

Cu. XIII.—Of the Delivery of Han, Bohain, St. Quentin, and Peronne,
to the King, and how he sent his Barber, Monsieur Oliver, to treat
with the Citizens of Ghent.—1477.

As the king was upon the road towards us, he received from
all parts the welcome news of the delivering up the castles of
Han and Bohain, and that the inhabitants of St. Quentin had
secured that town for him themselves, and opened their
gates to their neighbour, the Lord of Mouy.   He was certain
of Peronne, which was commanded by Master William Bische,
and, by the overtures that we and several other persons had
made him, he was in great hopes that the Lord des Cordes
would strike in with his interest.   To Ghent he sent his
barber, Master Oliver*, born in a small village† not far off;
and other agents he sent to other places, with great expec-
tations from all of them; and most of them promised him
very fair, but performed nothing.   Upon the king's arrival

---

* This personage will be familiar to all who have read Sir Walter
Scott's novel of Quentin Durward.   Oliver le Mauvais was valet de
chambre and chief barber to Louis XI.; in October, 1474, he received
letters of nobility from that prince, authorizing him to change his name
of Mauvais to that of Le Dain.   On the 19th of November, 1477, the king
conferred the estates of the deceased Count of Meulant on Oliver le
Dain and his heirs; and to this gift he added the Forest of Senart in
October, 1482.   On the 21st of May, 1484, Oliver was hanged "for
various great crimes, offences, and malefactions."
† The village of Thielt.

near Peronne, I went to wait on his majesty, and at the same time William Bische and others brought him the surrender of the town of Peronne, with which he was extremely pleased. The king stayed there that day, and I dined with him, according to my usual custom, for it was his humour to have seven or eight always with him at table, and sometimes many more. After dinner he withdrew, and seemed not to be at all pleased with the admiral's little exploit and mine; he told us he had sent his barber, Master Oliver, to Ghent, and he doubted not but he would persuade that town to submit to him; and Robinet Dodenfort* to St. Omer, as he had great interest there; and these his majesty extolled as fit persons to manage such affairs, to receive the keys of great towns, and to put garrisons of his troops into them. He also mentioned others whom he had employed in the same negotiation in other places; and with this he upbraided me, by the Lord du Lude and others. It was contrary to my duty to argue or expostulate with him; only I told his majesty I had great reason to fear that Master Oliver, and the others whom he had named, would not be able to reduce those towns to his obedience so easily as they proposed.

That which occasioned the king to speak to me after this manner was, that he had changed his mind, and the success which had crowned the beginning of his affairs, flattered him with the hopes of a speedy surrender of all the towns in the Duke of Burgundy's territories: and his majesty was advised by some persons (who found his inclinations lean that way) to root out and destroy that family quite, and make a distribution of their territories among his servants. Upon which he began to declare openly for whom he designed them. Namur and Hainault, which border upon the frontiers of his kingdom, he bestowed on his own subjects; Brabant and Holland, being larger and at a greater distance, he intended for certain princes of Germany, who, by that means, would be obliged to espouse his interest, and to assist him in all his enterprises. He was pleased to impart all his designs to me, because I had formerly recommended another method, and his majesty was desirous that

---

* The name of Robinet d'Edinfort or De Dampfort occurs in the list of gentlemen of the king's household for the years 1471 and 1474.

1 should be thoroughly informed of all the reasons that induced him to the contrary, and endeavoured to convince me that his design was far more advantageous for the interest of his kingdom, which had formerly suffered great troubles on account of the exorbitant power of the house of Burgundy, and the vast extent of their territories. And certainly, in respect to this world, there was great plausibility in what he said; but, as to matter of conscience, I thought it quite otherwise. However the king's policy and penetration were such, that neither I nor any of his council, could see so far into his affairs as himself; for, without dispute, he was one of the wisest and most subtle princes of his age; but the hearts of kings being in the hands of God Almighty alone, He disposes them in such important affairs as is most proper for the events which He, in His heavenly wisdom, has determined to bring to pass. For, certainly, had it been His Divine pleasure that our king should have continued in the resolution which he had formed before the Duke of Burgundy's death, the wars which have since occurred, and still continue, would never have happened. But we were not worthy on either side to receive so lasting a peace as was prepared to our hands; and that was the true cause of the great oversight of which our king was guilty, and not any defect in his judgment or understanding; for, as I said before, he was a prince of consummate wisdom and experience. I have dwelt the longer upon this subject, to show how necessary it is, at the beginning of any action of importance, to debate and deliberate seriously upon its consequences, in order that the most proper way of effecting it may be chosen, but especially that the whole affair be recommended to God, and that in our prayers He be solemnly entreated to direct us, for from Him all events proceed, as is evident, both by Scripture and experience.

My design is not to upbraid or reflect the least upon the king, when I say he was mistaken in this business; for, perhaps, others of a greater judgment than myself were, and still are, of his opinion. However, this affair was not debated either with us, or anywhere else. Chroniclers commonly write nothing but what redounds to the praise and honour of those princes whose actions they record, and they omit, and often ignore many occurrences that are absolutely necessary to the illustration of the truth; but, for my part, I am resolved to state nothing but what I can prove to be matter of fact, either upon my own knowledge, or the testimony of such persons whose veracity and honour are unquestionable, without the least regard to the praises of any man; for it is not to be thought there is any prince so wise, but he must sometimes err, and, if he lives long, often; and so it will be found perpetually, if one may be allowed to speak the truth. The greatest senates, and the greatest governments in the world, have erred, and will err, as is known by daily experience.

The king having sojourned for some time in a village near Peronne, resolved the next morning to make his entry into that town, which (as I said before) had surrendered to him. As all things were ready for his departure, the king took me aside, and despatched me into Poictou and the frontiers of Bretagne, whispering me in my ear, that if Master Oliver failed in his design, and the Lord des Cordes did not come over to him, he was resolved to destroy with fire and sword all that part of Artois which borders upon the Lys, and is called La Levée *, and afterwards retire to Touraine. I recommended some persons who, by my means, had already come over to his party, upon promise of pensions and other advantages from him; he set down their names in writing, and honourably performed the promises I had made them; and so I took my leave of him for that time.

As I was just taking horse, the Lord du Lude happened to be near; he was a person in some things very acceptable to the king, but he was too much addicted to covetousness, and scrupled not to abuse or delude any man, and, being easy and credulous himself, he was often imposed upon. He had been educated with the king in his youth, and knew very well how to humour his majesty, for he was a jocose man; he said to me, in a jesting manner (though the counsel was solid enough), "How now, sir, are you leaving the court, when you should now make your fortune, or never? Do not you see what great things fall daily into the king's hands, which

* Allouagne, in the arrondissement of Bethune and department of the Pas de Calais. The Lys rises near Bethune, and falls into the Scheldt, at Ghent.

will enable him to advance and recompense his favourites? As for my part, I expect to be Governor of Flanders, and to be made up of nothing but gold." He laughed all the while he was speaking to me, but I had no such inclination, for I was afraid it had come from the king : I replied, " That I should be very glad of any good fortune that befell him, and hoped the king would not forget me ;" and so I departed.

Not above half an hour before my departure, a person of some quality came to me out of Hainault, and brought me news from several to whom I had written to persuade them to enter into the king's service. This gentleman and I are nearly related ; but he is still living, and therefore I shall not mention his name, nor the names of any of the rest. He immediately made offers to surrender all the chief towns and fortresses in Hainault ; I waited at once on the king, and acquainted him with this overture : his majesty ordered the gentleman to be admitted to his presence, but told me, that neither he nor those he came from, were persons whom he had occasion to make use of. One he did not like upon one account, and another, upon another ; all their offers appeared to him inconsiderable, and he was of opinion he should gain greater advantages without their assistance ; so I left him, and he ordered the gentleman to confer farther with the Lord du Lude. The gentleman highly resented it, and left the court immediately, without any farther treaty, for the Lord du Lude and he would never have agreed : for he had undertaken the journey in hopes of advancing himself, and raising his own fortune, and the first question that the Lord du Lude asked him when he came in, was, " What the towns would give him to intercede with the king in their behalf?" Wherefore I am of opinion, that the king's refusing to hearken to the overtures that were made him by these gentlemen, was God's own doing ; for I have since known that he would have refused no honour or employment to have gained them over to his side ; but perhaps, God would not suffer him to be successful in all places, for the reasons above mentioned ; or else He did not think fit to permit him to usurp the country of Hainault (which is a fief of the Empire), both because his title was not just, and by reason of the ancient oaths and alliances between the emperors and the kings of France. And he seemed afterwards to acknowledge as much ; for when he had possessed himself of Cambray, Quesnoy, and Bouchain, in Hainault, he delivered up Bouchain*, and restored Cambray to a condition of neutrality†, as it is an imperial town. It is true, I was not upon the spot, yet I was well informed of all that occurred, and could easily understand it by my acquaintance and education in both countries, and I have since been assured of all this by those very persons who were chiefly employed in the affair.

CH. XIV.—How Master Oliver, the King's Barber, not succeeding in his Designs upon Ghent, found out a way to secure Tournay for the King. —1477.

MASTER OLIVER (as you have already heard) was despatched by the king's orders to Ghent, with letters to the Lady of Burgundy, Duke Charles's daughter, and full power to make certain secret overtures to her, if she would put herself under the king's protection. This was not the main design of his errand, for he knew it would be a difficult thing to have a private conference with the young lady alone; and, if he had one, it would be no less difficult to persuade her to do what he wanted. His chief business was to bring about some innovation in the city of Ghent, knowing it had been always inclinable to change, and had been kept in subjection under Dukes Philip and Charles by means of fear, for the citizens had lost many of their privileges in

---

* Bouchain was surrendered about the 29th of May.

† On his first visit to Cambray, Louis XI. had effaced the imperial arms from the public buildings of the town, and substituted the arms of France in their stead ; but he afterwards directed the authorities to restore the holy imperial eagle, saying, " We wish you to be neutral, and to continue in your former condition. We are viscount of your city, and intend to maintain our jurisdiction and rights over it. But in regard to our arms, you may take them down some evening, and put up your bird again, and you may say it had flown away for a time, but returned to its place just like the swallows which return with the spring." Molinet, ii. 154.

their wars with Duke Philip*, by the articles of peace;
besides, another of their privileges was taken from them by
Duke Charles (and that was about the election of their
magistrates), upon occasion of an offence they committed on
the first day of his entrance into their town as duke.   As I
have mentioned this already, I shall say no more about it
in this place.   These passages added much confidence to
Master Oliver the barber, who, following his instructions,
tampered with some persons whom he judged most tractable,
and offered them not only that all their old privileges should
be restored, but that new ones should be added.   These
overtures were not made in their Town-hall, nor publicly,
but in private, as I said before, for he had a mind to try
first what he could do with the young princess; but they
guessed his design.

After Master Oliver had been some days in Ghent, he
was conducted to his audience in the best garb he could
possibly procure; and he delivered his credentials.   The
Lady of Burgundy was in her chair of state, the Duke of
Cleves on one hand, the Bishop of Liege on the other, and
several other persons of quality attending her.   After the
lady had read his credentials, she bade him deliver his message; his answer was, that his instructions were to deliver
it only in private.   They replied, that was a custom never
practised among them, and certainly could not be introduced
now with a young lady that was fit for marriage.   He persisted in saying, that by his orders he could communicate
his business to nobody else.   Upon which they threatened to
compel him by force, and put him into a terrible consternation.   I fancy when he delivered his letters, he had not
provided himself with a speech, for, indeed (as you have
heard) that business was only secondary; however it may
be, Master Oliver left the assembly without any farther conference.   Some of the council had a very contemptible
opinion of him, both in respect of the meanness of his pro-
fession, and the uncomeliness of his demeanour and language; but more especially the citizens of Ghent (because he
was born in a pitiful village near that city), put many

---

* First of all by the treaty of Gavre in 1453, and afterwards in 1467.
See book ii. chap. iv.

affronts upon him, in consequence of which he took to flight suddenly; for he was informed that if he had stayed a little longer, they would have thrown him into the river: and truly I am of opinion that would have been his destiny.

This Master Oliver assumed the title of Count de Meulant, which is a small town near Paris, of which he was captain. When he had made his escape out of Ghent, he fled to Tournay, which town, though neutral, bore a great affection to the king, for it had formerly belonged to his predecessors, and paid him 6000 Parisian livres a year: in all other respects it was free, entertaining all comers, and it is a fair and strong town, as everybody in those countries knows very well. All the revenues of both their clergy and townsmen lie in Hainault and Flanders, for it borders upon those two countries; and upon that account in the wars between Charles VII. and Duke Philip of Burgundy, they paid constantly 10,000 livres per annum to the said duke, and I have known them give an equal sum to Duke Charles; but at this time, when Master Oliver came to them, they paid nothing, but enjoyed great quiet and repose.

Though the management of the affair which was committed to Master Oliver's discretion was far beyond his capacity, yet certainly he was not so much to be blamed as those who employed him in it; for though his success was such as might have been easily presaged, yet he gave proof both of courage and conduct in what he did; for knowing that the town of Tournay lay so nearly, as I said, between those two provinces that it would be easy to make inroads into either, if he could contrive to put a French garrison into it (to which the townsmen were always averse, having all along preserved their neutrality, and connected themselves neither with the one nor the other), he sent privately to Monsieur de Mouy (whose son* was bailiff of the town, but not resident there) to come to him at a certain hour with what forces he could draw out of St. Quentin, and whatever other troops he could assemble. Monsieur de Mouy came to the gate at the appointed hour, where he found thirty or

---

* Jacques, Lord and Baron of Mouy, councillor and chamberlain of the king, Master of the Waters and Forests of Normandy and Picardy, and Captain of St. Quentin and Ribemont.

forty men, and Master Oliver at the head of them, who boldly commanded the barrier to be opened, and partly for love, and partly for fear, they obeyed him. Monsieur de Mouy marched with his detachment into the town, with which the people were well enough satisfied; but the magistrates were not pleased with it, of whom seven or eight were immediately sent to Paris, and never dared to return during our king's reign.*

As soon as these forces had made themselves masters of Tournay, a more considerable body was sent to reinforce the garrison, and many barbarous incursions were made into Hainault and Flanders, in which many fine houses and villages were plundered and burnt, more to the prejudice of the inhabitants of Tournay than of anybody else; and these cruelties they continued so long, that at last the Flemings rose up in arms, released the Duke of Guelders out of prison, where he had been confined by Duke Charles, made him their captain, and invested Tournay†; but they did not continue the siege long, for they retired suddenly in great disorder and confusion, and the Duke of Guelders undertaking to secure the rear, and not being timely supported, was defeated, many of his men slain, and he among the rest, of which I shall give you a more particular account in another place.‡ And thus far the king's affairs were crowned with success, and his enemies over-reached by Master Oliver's management; and perhaps a man of greater rank and penetration could not have managed them with so much success. But I have said enough already of so politic a prince's employing so inconsiderable a person to conduct

* This is a mistake. At the end of May, 1483, three months before the death of Louis XI., the Governor of the Bastille, in obedience to the king's orders, sent the prisoners home, after having required them to swear that they would do nothing to the prejudice of his majesty. Gachard's Analectes Belgiques, i. 472.

† With 700 or 800 horse.

‡ "François de la Sauvagière, a very valiant man-at-arms, charged the Duke of Guelders so roughly with a lance, as he was drawing off his men, that he bore him to the ground. Notwithstanding this, he defended himself as best he could, like a bold and valiant knight, full of virtuous courage; but it was of no avail. He received two wounds in his head, and another in his throat, and finally his death blow. Then he shouted, 'Guelders!' and spoke never a word more." Molinet, ii. 68. This was in June or July, 1477.

so important an affair; and certainly God had infatuated his understanding at that time; for, as I said before, had he not looked upon everything as likely to be easily executed, and given too great a loose to his passion and vindictiveness against the Duke of Burgundy's family, there is no question but all, or the greater part, of their dominions had been at this day under his power and government.

CH. XV.—Of the Ambassadors whom the Lady of Burgundy, Duke Charles's Daughter, sent to the King, and of the Delivering up of Arras, Hesdin, Boulogne, and the City of Arras, to the King by the Assistance of the Lord des Cordes.—1477.

THE king being in possession of Peronne, which was surrendered to him by Master William Bisches (a person of obscure parentage, born in Molins-Engilbert, in Nivernois, but enriched and advanced afterwards by Charles Duke of Burgundy, who had given him the command of that town, because it was near a house called Clery, which the said Bisches had purchased, and fortified very strongly); the king, I say, in this very town received an embassy from the Lady of Burgundy, consisting of the principal personages of her court. In my opinion, it was not prudently done to employ so many, and send them all together; but their terror and consternation were so great, they knew not what they did. The chief of the ambassadors were one Messire William Hugonet*, the chancellor (a wise and notable man, who had gained a considerable fortune and vast reputation under Duke Charles), and the Lord of Humbercourt, whom we have frequently mentioned in these Memoirs, a person of such consummate prudence and dexterity in the management of great affairs, that I do not remember any man who exceeded him. There were likewise the Lord de la Vere†

---

* William Hugonet, Lord of Saillans, Epoisses, and Lys, and Viscount of Ypres, was beheaded at Ghent on the 3rd of April, 1477. He had been appointed Chancellor of Burgundy on the 22nd of May, 1471.

† Wolfert de Borselen, Lord of La Weer, in Holland, Count of Grand-Pré, chamberlain of Louis XI., and Knight of the Golden Fleece. He

a great man in Zealand, the Lord of Gruthuse, and several
other noblemen, besides ecclesiastics and burgesses of great
towns. *   Before they were admitted to an audience, either
public or private, the king tampered with them, and tried all
manner of ways to bring them over to his party. They all of
them returned him very humble and respectful answers, as
became people under affliction ; but those whose estates were
remote, and out of danger from the king, refused to gratify him
in anything, unless a marriage were first concluded between
the Dauphin and the Lady of Burgundy. The chancellor and
the Lord of Humbercourt having been long in authority,
and desiring to continue to possess it, and having their
estates near the king's dominions (one in the duchy of
Burgundy and the other in Picardy, near Amiens) were
inclined to accept the king's offers, upon condition the
said marriage proceeded, which they would endeavour to
promote with all their power and interest, and, when it was
consummated, would engage themselves entirely in his
service.   Though this was certainly the better method for
the king, yet he was mightily dissatisfied, because they did
not join themselves immediately to his party ; but he dissembled this feeling as much as he could, intending to make
use of them in other affairs. The king already held a
correspondence with the Lord des Cordes, who advised his
majesty to press the ambassadors to send orders to him
as Governor of Arras, to deliver up that which they called
the city of Arras, between which and the town there were
walls, ditches, and gates, which were formerly kept shut
against the city ; but now the case was altered, and the city
shut out the town. After many arguments and difficulties
had been started by the ambassadors, being at last convinced
it would be for the best, and contribute much to the hastening
of a peace, they consented, especially the chancellor and the
Lord of Humbercourt ; and letters were immediately des-

married 1. Mary of Scotland ; and 2. Charlotte of Bourbon ; and he died
in 1487.
  * To those mentioned by Commines, we may add the Bishop of Tournay,
the Bishop of Arras, the chief Echevin of Ghent, the High Bailiff of
Ypres, and the son of the Burgomaster of Bruges. The ambassadors set
out at the beginning of February, and returned towards the end of the
month.

patched to the Lord des Cordes to discharge him of his trust and command him to deliver up the city to the king. As soon as the king had got possession of it*, he threw up works before the gate of the town, and such other places as he thought would be convenient; upon which the Lord des Cordes marched with his garrison out of town, and every man went whither he pleased, and took what side he liked best.

The Lord des Cordes looking upon himself to be free from the service of his mistress, by virtue of the discharge which the ambassadors had sent him, resolved to swear allegiance to the king, and enter into his service for the future, since his name and arms were taken from a place on this side of the Somme, not far from Beauvais; for his name was Philip de Crevecœur, second brother to the Lord of Crevecœur; and indeed the territories which the house of Burgundy had possessed upon the Somme in the time of Dukes Philip and Charles returned, of course, to the king in pursuance of the treaty of Arras, by which they were then entailed upon the said dukes and their heirs male only, and Duke Charles had left only this daughter. By that means the Lord des Cordes became the king's subject immediately, and would not have been to blame in putting himself and all that belonged to him into the king's service, had he not taken a new oath to be true to the young Lady of Burgundy.† I know there are various reports of this affair, and it is a matter of contest to this very day, and therefore I will say no more about it; only this I can affirm, that he was educated, advanced, and put into places of great trust and power by Duke Charles: his mother‡ had some share in the education of the young Lady of Burgundy; and he was Governor of Picardy, Seneschal of Ponthieu, Captain of Crotoy, Governor of Peronne, Montdidier, and Roye, and Captain of Boulogne

* He entered the city on Tuesday, the 4th of March, 1477; and the town capitulated on the 4th of May. Lenglet, ii. 141.

† The young duchess had confirmed him in all his estates and offices, and furthermore bestowed on him the captaincy of Hesdin. But at a chapter of the order of the Golden Fleece, held at Bois-le-Duc on the 8th of May, 1481, he was expelled the order, " on account of his crimes, demerits, falsity, treason, and disloyalty."

‡ Margaret de la Tremouille.

and Hesdin for the duke when he died; and at this present time he holds the same governments for the king, in the same manner and form as our master confirmed them to him.

After the king had added some new fortifications to the city of Arras, he marched to besiege Hesdin, carrying the Lord des Cordes with him, who had been the governor of it but three days before, and the garrison consisted of none but his own soldiers. At first, they declared they would keep it for the young princess, alleging that they were bound to do so by their oath of allegiance, and they fired their guns upon us for several days; but at last they were prevailed upon by their old master (for to speak plainly, there was a very good understanding between them), and the town was delivered to the king, who marched from thence to Boulogne, where his success was the same, though, perhaps, it did not surrender so soon by a day. However, this had been a very dangerous way of proceeding, had those that held the towns for the young princess been able to have assembled any forces in the country (and the king, in the relation he afterwards gave me of this affair, admitted as much himself); for there were some in Boulogne who, perceiving the juggle, endeavoured to throw a body of troops into the town, and if they had succeeded in their design, they would have defended it in earnest.

Whilst the king lay before Boulogne (which was about five or six days), the townsmen of Arras, finding they were deceived, and enclosed on all sides with great numbers of soldiers and abundance of artillery, laboured to procure forces if possible, that might garrison the town; to which purpose they wrote letters to Lisle and Douay. At Douay there were some few horse commanded by the Lord of Vergy*, and others, whom I have forgotten, who had escaped from the battle of Nancy, and were returned thither. These gentlemen resolved to throw themselves into Arras, and in

---

* Guillaume de Vergy, Baron of Bourbon-Lancy. Louis XI. appointed him his councillor and chamberlain, and gave him the Castle of Vergy and the estate of St. Dizier. He held the commission of captain of fifty lances in the standing army of Charles VIII. After the death of that monarch, he entered the service of the Emperor Maximilian, who appointed him Marshal of Burgundy in 1498. Philip of Spain made him lieutenant and captain-general of Guelders and Zutphen in 1504, and he died in 1520.

order to effect it, assembled a body of about 200 or 300 horse, good and bad, and about 500 or 600 foot. The inhabitants of Douay, having at that time more pride than sense, forced this party to march at noon-day, in spite of their unwillingness, and all that could be urged to the contrary: which certainly was a great piece of folly and indiscretion, and the design failed accordingly; for the country between Douay and Arras is as flat as one's hand, and not above five leagues, so that if they had deferred their march till night, they had certainly effected their design. When they were in the midst of their march, those who were left in the city (to wit, the Lord du Lude, John du Fou*, and the troops of the Marshal de Lohenc), having intelligence of their motion, resolved to sally out, and rather venture an engagement, than suffer them to get into the town; for they knew that if once this reinforcement got into the town, they would never be able to defend the city. Their enterprise was bold and perilous, but they performed it bravely, and the whole party from Douay was defeated, most of them killed, or taken prisoners†, and the Lord of Vergy was among the latter.

The next day the king arrived at Arras in person, and was highly pleased with their victory; he took the prisoners into his own custody, and caused several of the footmen to be put to death as a terror to the rest, who he knew were not numerous in those parts. The Lord of Vergy was kept prisoner a long time, as he could not be induced to swear allegiance to the king, though he was kept in irons, and confined very closely; at length, at the importunity of his mother, after he had been a prisoner a year or more, he submitted to the king's good pleasure, and I think he acted very prudently, for the king restored to him all his own lands, and all that he had any pretensions to, gave him a revenue of above 10,000 livres a year, and other considerable employments besides. Those few that escaped in this action, got into the town. The king caused his artillery (of which he had a very fine and large train) to be brought, with which he fired briskly upon the town; and

* Jean du Fou, councillor and chamberlain of the King of France, Captain of Cherbourg, and chief cup-bearer to Louis XI.

† Molinet (ii. 25.) says there were 400 or 500 prisoners, including several men of rank.

the walls and fortifications being very weak, and scarce any soldiers in garrison, his batteries did the town considerable damage, and threw the inhabitants into terrible consternation. The Lord des Cordes had a party in the town, and after the delivering up of the city, it was impossible to think of defending the town any longer. Upon this consideration they capitulated, and surrendered upon terms*, but their articles were not performed, for which the Lord du Lude was partly to blame; for several citizens and other persons of quality were put to death† in the presence of the Lord du Lude and of Monsieur William de Cerisay‡ (which was much to their private advantage); for the Lord du Lude told me himself he got at that time 20,000 crowns, besides rich furniture and furs, and the poor town was fined 60,000 crowns more to the king, which was an excessive tax; but I suppose this was remitted, for the citizens of Cambray lent the king 40,000, which was repaid punctually afterwards; wherefore I presume all these taxes were restored or remitted.

Ch. XVI.—How the Citizens of Ghent, having usurped Authority over their Princess upon the Death of the Duke of Burgundy her Father, sent Ambassadors to the King of France in the Name of the Three Estates of their Country.—1477.

During the siege of Arras, the Princess of Burgundy was at

---

* It surrendered on the 4th of May. The king entered Arras on horseback, not by the gate, but by the breach in the wall. He rode to the market-place, where he thus addressed the citizens: "You have been very uncourteous to me, but I pardon you. If you are good subjects to me, I will be a good lord to you." Molinet, ii. 26.

† Three days after his arrival, the king inquired who had been most hostile to him in Arras during the siege. Some envious person named Pierchon du Chastel, who was thereupon beheaded, together with an archer who had taken aim at the king, and would have shot him, had not a butcher prevented him. Molinet, ii. 26. The king changed the name of the town from Arras to Franchise, and colonised it with artificers from other towns. See Vaissette, v. 53.

‡ Guillaume de Cerisay was, in 1475, prothonotary and secretary to the king, and clerk of his court of Parliament. In 1479, he was appointed Mayor of Angers.

Ghent, in the power of a rash and inconsiderate people, which proved much to her disadvantage, but greatly advanced the king's interest ; for there is no losing without somebody being the gainer. As soon as the Gantois were informed of the death of Duke Charles, they thought themselves fairly delivered from their subjection, and seizing upon their magistrates* (who were in all twenty-six), they put most of them to death, under pretence of revenging the death of a person whom the day before the magistrates had caused to be beheaded : not but that the person deserved it, if they had had power to have done it; but the duke being dead, who gave them their power, their authority, of course, expired with him. They also put to death several substantial citizens besides, and others who had been friends or favourers of the duke's interest, of which number there were some in my time, who, in my presence, used their utmost endeavours to dissuade Duke Charles from destroying a great part of Ghent, which the duke otherwise would have done. These tumultuous citizens forced the young princess to restore and confirm their ancient privileges†, which Duke Philip had taken away in the peace of Gavre, and also those that Duke Charles had deprived them of afterwards. They made no other use of their privileges, but as a cause of quarrel with their prince, and their chief inclination was to

---

* A short time after the death of Duke Charles, the citizens of Ghent rose in arms, and seized several notable burghers, to wit, Roland Van Wedergract, who had been chief echevin of the city; John Serssanders, who had been second echevin; Peter Hurribloc, one of the lords of the council-chamber of Flanders, Peter Boudins, Oliver de Grave, and John Vander Poucke; which six persons were condemned and beheaded. The reason of this was, that they had been connected with the government of the city during the year 1468, when peace was made with Duke Charles, on occasion of the excesses committed by the Gantois against the duke on the day on which he made his joyful entry into their city . . . "and had granted letters under the great seal of Ghent, that if in future any persons should attempt to excite any sedition or tumult in the town, they should be mulcted of life and fortune, and their children be deprived, in perpetuity, of the freedom of the guild to which they had belonged." See the Bulletins de l'Académie Royale de Bruxelles, vol. vi. part ii. p. 227.

† The letters-patent by which the Princess Mary restored their privileges to the Flemings are dated at Ghent on the 11th of February, 1477.

encroach upon and weaken him. During the minority of
their princes, and before they are fit to manage affairs of
state, they are extremely fond of them; but when once they
are in possession of the government, they hate them as
mortally. Thus it happened to this young princess, whom
they guarded very carefully, and loved very tenderly, till she
came to the government. Had not the citizens of Ghent preferred their own seditious designs before the public interest,
it may be easily presumed they would have bethought themselves of defending their country, and put a strong garrison
immediately into Arras, and perhaps into Peronne, upon the
death of their master; but they could think of nothing but
contriving tumults and innovations at home. However, as
the king lay before Arras, ambassadors* came to him in the
name of the three Estates of the provinces belonging to the
said princess, for there were certain deputies of the three
Estates at Ghent; but the citizens, having the young princess
in their power, managed matters as they pleased. The king
admitted them to an audience; and among other things, they
told his majesty that the overtures which they made tended to
a peace, and proceeded from the sincere desire of the princess
herself, who was resolved to be entirely guided by the advice
and consent of the three Estates of her country; and they
desired that the king would desist from his hostilities in
both Burgundy and Artois: that a day might be appointed, on
which they might meet to treat about an accommodation;
and that, in the meantime, all warfare might cease on both
sides.

The king now thought he had entirely gained his point,
and supposed his affairs would have taken a much better
turn than they did. He had certain information that a great
part of their best soldiers were killed or dispersed, and many
others had revolted from the princess, and in particular the
Lord des Cordes, for whom his majesty had a great esteem,

* These ambassadors were, for Brabant, the Lord de Berssele, the
Mayor of Louvain, and the Pensionary of Brussels; for Flanders, the
Abbot of St. Peter's at Ghent, the Lord of Moldeghem, M. de Dudzeele,
and the Pensionary of Ghent; for Artois, the Abbot of St. Bertin, Jean
de Beaumont, and Louis Lemire; for Hainault, the Lord of Ligne, and
the Pensionary of Mons. They set out on their mission towards the end
of February, 1477.

and not without reason, for he would not have been able by
force to have got that in a long time which, as you have
heard, he got in a few days, by holding correspondence with
him.   Upon this account he did not much regard the requests and demands of the ambassadors; besides, he was
informed, and well knew himself, that the Gantois were a
people of so turbulent and seditious a temper, that they would
so trouble and confound their rulers that no orders or direction could be given for carrying on the war against him;
for no man of sense, or any that had borne authority under
their former princes, was consulted in anything, but rather
persecuted, and in danger of being killed.   But their hatred
was most bitter against the Burgundians, on account of the
great power they had exercised in former times.   Besides,
it was not unknown to the king (whose foresight in state-
affairs was as great as any man's in his kingdom) what the
custom of the Gantois had been in all ages, and how desirous
they are to lessen the power of their princes, provided it
brings no inconvenience upon themselves ; for these reasons,
the king resolved to foment and encourage the divisions
which existed amongst them already; for the persons with
whom he had now to deal were brutes, and townsmen for the
most part, who had not the least acquaintance or knowledge
of state-affairs.   Our king knew well enough how to take
advantage of their ignorance, and did whatever was proper to
advance his own object, and destroy his enemies.

The king took hold of that expression of the ambassadors,
where they said, "That the young princess was resolved to
do nothing without the advice and approbation of the three
Estates of her country;" and told them that they were misinformed, not only of her resolution, but of that of other
people; for he was assured she intended to manage her affairs
by means of certain persons, who had no inclination to peace,
and that what they proposed, he knew would be disowned by
the princess.   The ambassadors were extremely concerned at
this, and as persons not used to manage such important
affairs, replied with some warmth, that they were certain of
what they said, and if it were necessary, would produce their
instructions.   It was answered, that if the king pleased,
letters could be produced under such a hand as they would
not dispute, importing that the princess would commit the

administration of her affairs to no more than four persons; they persisted in stating the contrary. Upon which the king caused a letter to be produced (which the Chancellor of Burgundy and the Lord of Humbercourt had brought to him when he was at Peronne), part of it written by the hand of the young princess, part by the Duchess Dowager of Burgundy* (widow of Duke Charles, and sister to Edward, King of England), and part by the hand of the Lord of Ravestain, brother to the Duke of Cleves, and nearly related to the said princess. Though this letter was under three several hands, yet it ran only in the name of the young princess, and had been so contrived, to give it greater weight. The contents of the letter were to recommend the chancellor and the Lord of Humbercourt, and their whole negotiation, to the king; to let him know that the intention of the princess was to have her affairs wholly governed by four persons only—to wit, the duchess dowager her mother-in-law, the Lord of Ravestain, the chancellor, and the Lord of Humbercourt; and to desire the king that what affairs soever he should be pleased to communicate to her, might pass through their hands, and be addressed to nobody else.

When the Gantois and the rest of the ambassadors had seen this letter, they were highly incensed, and the king's commissioners well understood how to improve and take advantage of their passion. Finally, the letter was given into their hands, and they were despatched without any other material answer; nor did they indeed desire any other, for their thoughts were so wholly fixed upon their domestic divisions, and the reconstruction of their whole system, that they had no leisure to think of anything so foreign as the loss of Arras, though that, in my opinion, ought to have concerned them more nearly. But they were for the most part citizens, as I observed before, and unacquainted with public affairs. They returned immediately to Ghent, where they found the young princess, and with her the Duke of Cleves, her near kinsman by the mother's side. He was very old, and had been educated in the Duke of Burgundy's court, and for a long time had enjoyed a pension of 6000 Rhine florins, so that he as often waited on the princess to

* Margaret of York.

receive his annual allowance, as out of cousinly affection. The Bishop of Liege and several other great persons were with her at the same time, to advance their particular affairs.   The Bishop of Liege's business was to get off the payment of a tribute of 30,000 florins, or thereabouts, which his subjects had to pay to Duke Charles by agreement between them after the wars, which I have mentioned before; all which wars having been undertaken in the behalf and quarrel of the said bishop, there was no necessity that he, whose interest doubtless it was to keep the Liegeois poor and humble, should solicit that favour for them ; for though his country was rich and extensive, he had nothing but some little demesnes of his own and his ecclesiastical revenue to maintain him.   This bishop (who was brother to the two reigning Dukes of Bourbon, John II. and Peter II.) being a man addicted wholly to pleasure and a luxurious way of living, and scarce able to distinguish good from bad, took into his councils Master William de la Marck*, a noble gentleman and a brave soldier, but a man of a cruel and malicious temper, who favoured the citizens of Liege †, and had been always an enemy to the Duke of Burgundy's family, and to the bishop himself.   The Princess of Burgundy gave this De la Marck 15,000 Rhine florins, partly on the bishop's account, and partly to induce him to

---

* William de la Marck, surnamed William with the Beard and the Wild Boar of Ardennes, was Count of Aremberg, Lord of Aigremont and Seraing, sovereign mayor of Liege, and prime minister of the Bishop of Liege, Louis de Bourbon. He obtained his surnames from peculiarities in his personal appearance; for he endeavoured, by the length and growth of his beard, to conceal the circumstance that had originally procured him the denomination of the Wild Boar. This was an unusual thickness and projection of the mouth and upper jaw, which, with the huge projecting side-teeth, gave that resemblance to the brute creation which, joined to the delight that De la Marck had in haunting the forest so called, originally earned him the title of the Boar of Ardennes. He affected to delight in this surname, and endeavoured to deserve it by the unvarying cruelty and ferocity of his life; and to complete the resemblance, he usually wore over his shoulders a strong surcoat of dressed boar-skin. He was beheaded on the 18th of June, 1485. Readers of "Quentin Durward" will remember Sir Walter Scott's admirable description of this monster and his crimes.

† He had excited the Liegeois to revolt against Duke Charles of Burgundy and the Bishop of Liege in 1468.

espouse her interest; but it was not long before he openly declared both against her and his master the bishop, and by the assistance and favour of our king would have made his own son* Bishop of Liege; after which he encountered, defeated, and with his own hands slew the bishop in battle†, and ordered his body to be thrown into the river, where it was found three days after.

The Duke of Cleves also was at Ghent, soliciting a marriage between his son ‡ and the young princess, which he thought might be convenient for many reasons; and truly I think it might have succeeded, had the young gentleman found favour in his person with the young princess and her ministers; for he was of her own family, held his duchy of the Dukes of Burgundy, and had been educated in their

---

* John de la Marck, Lord of Luman. After the death of Louis de Bourbon, three candidates were nominated to the vacant bishopric of Liege by the electors. One of these candidates was John de la Marck. Pope Sextus IV. decided against him, but directed that the successful candidate should allow him a pension of 1800 golden crowns a year.

† The bishop's murder took place in 1482. In the months of August and September of that year, La Marck entered into a conspiracy with the discontented citizens of Liege against him, and was aided therein with considerable sums of money by the King of France. By this means, and by the assistance of many murderers and banditti, who thronged to him as to a leader befitting them, La Marck assembled a body of troops, whom he dressed in scarlet uniform, with a boar's head on the left sleeve. With this little army he approached the city of Liege. Upon this the citizens, who were engaged in the conspiracy, came to their bishop, and, offering to stand by him to the death, exhorted him to march out against these robbers. The bishop, therefore, put himself at the head of a few troops of his own, trusting to the assistance of the people of Liege. But as soon as they came in sight of the enemy, the citizens, as before agreed, fled from the bishop's banner, and he was left with his own handful of adherents. At this moment, La Marck charged at the head of his banditti with the expected success. The bishop was brought before the profligate knight, who first cut him over the face, saying, " Louis de Bourbon, I strove long to obtain your favour, but you would not receive me; now I have found you;" then murdered him with his own hand, and caused his body to be exposed naked in the great square of Liege, in front of St. Lambert's Cathedral.

‡ John II., surnamed the Clement, born on the 23rd April, 1458; married Matilda, daughter of Henry III., Landgrave of Hesse; and died on the 15th May, 1521. He is said to have had sixty-three illegitimate children; an enormous number even in those licentious times!

court; but perhaps the knowledge and character they had received of him caused his rejection.

CH. XVII.—How the People of Ghent, upon the Return of their Ambas-dors, put the Chancellor Hugonet and the Lord of Humbercourt to Death, against their Princess's Consent; after which they, in con-junction with some other Flemish Troops, were defeated before Tournay, and the Duke of Guelders, who commanded them, was slain; and the Duchy of Burgundy was placed in the hands of the King of France.—1477.

As soon as the commissioners returned to Ghent, a council was called, the Princess of Burgundy was placed in her chair of state, with her servants attending her, to receive their report. They began with repeating their instructions from her highness, and insisted chiefly upon what they thought would serve their own turns best. They told her that, as they were giving his majesty an account of her highness's resolution to be wholly advised and directed by the counsel of the three Estates, the king had made answer that he was positively assured of the contrary, and offered to show letters from her to that purpose. The princess was extremely surprised and angry; and, presuming her letter had not been seen, strenuously denied it; upon which the person that spoke (who was the Pensionary either of Ghent or Brussels) put his hand into his bosom, produced the letter publicly, and delivered it to the council, by which he showed himself to be a person of no honour or conscience, to have treated a lady of her rank and quality in such a rude and disrespectful manner; for, granting she had committed an error, she ought not to have been vilified or confronted with it in a public assembly. It is not to be supposed but she was strangely confounded, for she had professed the con-trary to everybody. There were present at the same time the duchess dowager, the Lord of Ravestain, the Lord of Humbercourt, and the chancellor.

The Duke of Cleves and others had been hitherto enter-tained and amused with hopes of marriage, but, upon this discovery, all of them were highly incensed, and dissensions began now to break out and discover themselves. The Duke of Cleves had all along taken the Lord of Humbercourt to be his friend, and believed him willing to promote his marriage with the princess; but this letter convinced him to the contrary, and made him entirely become his enemy. The Bishop of Liege had a quarrel with him before, for what he had done against him at Liege (where the Lord of Humbercourt had been governor), and William de la Marck was his adversary also. The young Count of St. Paul*, son to the Constable of France, mortally hated both him and the chancellor, upon account of their having delivered his father into the king's hands at Peronne, as you have already been informed. The Gantois had a spite against them, not that they had ever injured them in the least, but merely on account of the great authority which they had borne; and certainly they were as deserving of the power they exercised as any ministers of state that ever had the administration of affairs in their time, having always discharged their trust faithfully and honestly, as good and loyal servants to their master.

In short, the letter having been shown in the morning, the very same night† the chancellor and the Lord of Humbercourt were arrested by the people of Ghent; and although they had been informed of their design, they had no power to attempt making their escape, as it often happens in such cases. I question not but the Duke of Cleves and their other enemies, whom I mentioned before, were very active and instrumental in seizing them. With them they also secured Monsieur William de Clugny‡, Bishop of Theroüenne (who died afterwards Bishop of Poictiers), and put them all three together into custody. The people of Ghent, contrary to their old method of revenge, proceeded legally, as they pretended, against them, and appointed lawyers to interrogate them, one of whom was of the house

---

* Pierre de Luxembourg, Count of St. Paul, Marle, and Soissons, was created a Knight of the Golden Fleece in 1478, and died on the 25th of October, 1482.

† On the 19th of March, 1477.

‡ William de Clugny was at this time suffragan to Henry of Lorraine, Bishop of Terouenne.

of La Marck*, a mortal enemy to the Lord of Humbercourt.
Their first question was, why they had commanded the Lord
des Cordes to deliver up Arras?† but that they did not
much insist on, though indeed they had committed no other
action that was criminal ; but their rage did not stop here,
for the citizens were not in the least concerned to see their
prince divested of such a town, nor were their prudence and
penetration so great as to foresee the ill consequences that
would attend the loss of so important a place. They insisted
more particularly upon two points ; the one was, certain
bribes, which it was urged they had lately taken in a certain
cause between a private person and the city of Ghent, upon
account of which the chancellor had given judgment for the
city ; but to that charge of bribery they made a good defence,
by alleging that their cause was good, and their judgment
was fair and just: and as for money, they had never demanded it, or ordered it to be demanded, but the townsmen
had offered it of their own accord, and they had accepted it.
The second article of their charge was, that during their
tenure of authority under their late master Duke Charles,
they had done many things contrary to the privileges and
statutes of the town of Ghent, and whoever did so, was condemned to die by their charter. But this charge was of no
force nor validity against them, for they being neither subjects nor natives of that city‡, were not bound by their privileges ; and if Duke Charles or his father had infringed or
encroached upon those said privileges, it was by their own

* Everard de la Marck, Lord of Aremberg and Neufchatel, a younger
brother of the Wild Boar of Ardennes.

† The convention in pursuance of which Louis XI. occupied Arras
was not the work of Hugonet and Humbercourt only, but of the embassy
of which they were members; and their conduct had been not only
justified, but highly praised by the States-General, who, on hearing their
report, sent other envoys to thank Louis XI. for the suspension of
hostilities which the said ambassadors had obtained by means of the said
convention. It is not surprising, therefore, that the Gantois should have
laid little stress on this charge. See some valuable remarks on this
subject by M. Gachard, in the sixth volume of the Bulletins de l'Académie Royale de Bruxelles.

‡ The chancellor was a Burgundian, and Humbercourt a native of
Picardy. They were, therefore, quite beyond the jurisdiction of the
Gantois.

act and deed, and they had consented to it by articles of
agreement that had been drawn up between them, after
numerous wars and dissensions ; and the remaining privileges which were confirmed to them (which, indeed, were
greater than was necessary for their advantage) were still
preserved inviolably, without the least diminution. Notwithstanding the defence of these two worthy and eminent
persons to the two charges that were brought against them
(for the chief one, which I have mentioned before, was not
insisted on), they were both condemned to death by the magistrates of the city of Ghent, assembled in their Town-hall,
for infringement of their civic privileges and receiving
bribes. After judgment was given, the two lords were
astonished at their cruel sentence, and not without reason,
for being in their enemies' hands, there was no possibility of
escaping. However, they thought fit to appeal to the King
of France in his court of Parliament at Paris, hoping at least
it would defer their execution for some time, and, in the
meanwhile, give their friends an opportunity of exerting
themselves to save their lives. Before sentence was passed,
they had been put upon the rack, contrary to all law and
justice. In six days' time their whole process was finished,
and when sentence was given, in spite of their appeal, they
allowed them but three hours for confession and the settle-
ment of their temporal affairs, upon expiration of which
they were brought upon the scaffold*, which had been erected
in the market-place.

As soon as the Princess of Burgundy (since Duchess of
Austria) had received the news of their condemnation, she
came herself in person to the Town-hall to beg their lives ;
but, finding she could not prevail, she ran into the market-
place, where all the people were assembled together in arms,
and saw the two prisoners upon the scaffold. The young
princess was in mourning, with her head dressed merely with
a simple kerchief, on purpose to move pity and compassion,
and, in this posture, with tears in her eyes, and her hair
dishevelled, she begged and entreated the people to have pity
upon her two servants, and restore them to her again. A
great part of the people would fain have complied with her

* They were beheaded on the 3rd of April, 1477.

request, and were willing they should be saved, but others
violently opposed it, and they were at push of pike one with
another.   At last, those who were for the execution, being
the stronger party, called out to the executioners to do their
office, and immediately both their heads were struck off, and
the poor princess returned to her palace very sad and disconsolate for the loss of the two persons in whom she chiefly
confided.

After the Gantois had committed this exploit, they removed from about the Princess the Lord of Ravestain and
the duchess dowager, Duke Charles's widow, because both
of them were mentioned in the letter which the chancellor
and the Lord of Humbercourt had delivered to the king, as
you have heard; so that the citizens had now the sole authority and management of the poor young princess; and well
may she be called poor, not only in respect of her great loss
of the important towns which had been taken from her, which
were irrecoverable by force, by reason of the great power
and strength of the king, who was now in possession of them
(though by favour, friendship, or composition, she might still
hope to have them restored); but her greatest misfortune was
that she was in the power of the mortal and inveterate
enemies of her family.   Their actions, however, in the main
proceeded rather from folly than cunning, the generality of
them being stupid and heavy mechanics, who have the sole
power and administration of affairs among the Gantois, though
they be persons of no experience in politics, and no knowledge in the government of a state.   Their cunning consists
chiefly in two points; one is always to desire and endeavour
to weaken and retrench the power of their prince; the other
is, that when they have been guilty of the least false step,
and find themselves not able to defend it, never any persons
seek peace with so much humility and submission as they do,
nor give more liberally to purchase it; for this I will say
of them, never any people understood better how to make
their applications, and where to place their bribes, than the
Gantois.

Whilst the king was busy in subduing the towns and
places above mentioned in the marches of Picardy, his army
was in Burgundy, under the command, apparently, of the

Prince of Orange* (who is still reigning), a native and subject of the county of Burgundy, but one who had recently, for the second time, become an enemy of Duke Charles, so that the king made use of him, because he was a powerful noble in both the county and duchy of Burgundy, and was likewise well connected and greatly beloved. But the Lord of Craon was the king's lieutenant, and had the real charge of the army, and was the person in whom the king reposed most confidence; for he was a man of great wisdom, and thoroughly devoted to his master, though somewhat too fond of gain. This Lord of Craon, when he drew near Burgundy, sent forward the Prince of Orange and others to Dijon, to use persuasion, and require the people to render obedience to the king; and they managed the matter so adroitly, principally by means of the Prince of Orange, that the city of Dijon and all the other towns in the duchy of Burgundy, together with many in the county, gave their allegiance to the king. But Aussonne and some other strongholds held out for the Princess Mary.

Large estates were promised to the Prince of Orange for that service, and furthermore, that all the towns in the county of Burgundy should be placed in his hands, which came to him in succession from the Prince of Orange his grandfather†, and concerning which he was in litigation with his uncles, the Lords of Chasteau-guyon‡, who he said had been favoured by the late Duke Charles. For their cause had been solemnly argued before him for several days §, and the duke, by advice of many learned clerks, gave judgment

* John II., Prince of Orange, son of William VII., Prince of Orange, and Catherine, daughter of Richard de Bretagne, Count of Etampes. He succeeded his father in 1475. Having abandoned the cause of Louis XI., and joined the Duchess of Burgundy, the King of France issued a decree against him, on the 7th of September, 1477, by which he was declared guilty of high treason, and banished the realm. He died on the 25th of April, 1502.

† Louis de Chalon, Prince of Orange, son of Jean de Chalon, Baron of Arlay, and Marie de Baux. He died on the 13th of December, 1463, aged seventy-five.

‡ Louis and Hugh de Chalon, Lords of Chasteau-guyon, were children of the above-mentioned Louis de Chalon, by Eleanor of Armagnac.

§ This cause had already been argued by his father, William VII. of Orange, before Duke Philip the Good.

against the prince, at least so he stated ; for which cause
he left the duke's service, and joined the king. But notwithstanding his promises, when the Lord of Craon found himself
in possession of the places above mentioned, and had in his
hands all the towns and estates to which the prince laid claim
as part of his grandfather's succession, he would not give them
up to the Prince of Orange for all the solicitation he could
make. Wherefore the king wrote to him on several occasions
without any dissimulation, for he knew well that the Lord of
Craon was on bad terms with the Prince of Orange ; but the
king was afraid of displeasing the Lord of Craon, for he
had all the country under his control ; and his majesty did
not think the Prince of Orange would have courage to stir
up Burgundy to revolt, as he afterwards did to a very great
extent. But for the present, I will leave this subject till a
more convenient place.*

After the Gantois had taken the government of the young
princess into their hands, and caused her two favourites to be
beheaded, and removed such persons from the court as they
thought obnoxious to them, they began to assume the power
of appointing and displacing all officers, both civil and military ; and they plundered and banished all such as had
served the house of Burgundy in any remarkable way,
without any respect to their merit or character ; and their
malice being more particularly aimed at the Burgundians,
they banished them all, as if they had laboured and studied as
much to force them into the king's service as his majesty did
to allure them ; and he used all the ways of fair words, great
presents, and large promises, besides the terror of his forces,
which were very numerous in their country, to gain them
over to his interest. To begin their authority with a piece
of novelty, they released the Duke of Guelders out of
prison, who had been committed by Duke Charles, and
endured a long confinement for reasons previously mentioned.
The towns of Bruges, Ghent, and Ypres, having assembled
an army among themselves, they made the Duke of Guelders
general of it, and sent him with orders to burn and demolish

* In previous editions, the two preceding paragraphs have been
placed at the beginning of the sixth book. They are here restored to
the position they occupy in the manuscripts and in the original French
editions of these Memoirs.

the suburbs of Tournay; but that enterprise proved little to his advantage. It had been better for him and themselves, too, if they had sent a body of 200 men to have reinforced the besieged garrison of Arras, or 10,000 francs to have paid those troops that were there already (provided they had arrived in time), than ten such armies, though it consisted of 12,000 or 14,000 well-paid men; because, all they could hope for by this expedition, was to burn a few pitiful houses of no importance to the king, as they paid him no tax; but their knowledge in state affairs was not deep.

The Duke of Guelders having invested Tournay, ordered the suburbs to be set on fire. There were in the town about 300 or 400 men-at-arms, who sallied out and fell upon the rear of the besiegers, and they at once began to fly. The Duke of Guelders, being a valiant prince, thought to restore the fight and give his men opportunity to retreat; but, not being vigorously sustained, he was knocked off his horse, and himself, with a good number of his men, slain, though in the action there were not many of the king's soldiers engaged; and therefore with this loss the rest of the Flemish army retreated. The Princess of Burgundy (according to report) was very well pleased with their misfortune, and so were all those who had any kindness for her; for she was credibly informed, that the Gantois had resolved to force her to a marriage with the Duke of Guelders; being assured, that by fair means they could never have prevailed with her, for the reasons mentioned in a previous part of these Memoirs.

CH. XVIII.—A Digression, serving to demonstrate that Wars and Divisions are permitted by God for the Punishment of wicked Princes and People, with various Arguments and Instances which happened in the Author's Life-time, chiefly intended for the Instruction of Princes.

I CANNOT understand why God has preserved the city of Ghent so long, which has occasioned so much mischief, and which is no good either to the public, or the country wherein it is seated, and much less to its prince. It is not like Bruges, which indeed is a place of trade, and of great resort

for foreigners of all nations, in which more commodities and
merchandise are disposed of than in any other town in
Europe, so that to have had that town destroyed, would
have been an irreparable loss; but it seems to me, that
God has not made any created being in this world, neither
man nor beast, nor anything else, but He has set up some
other thing in opposition to it, to keep it within just bounds
of fear and humility.   In this respect Ghent is admirably
well situated, for certainly the countries round about it are
the most luxurious, the most splendid, and the most addicted
to those pleasures to which man is inclined, of any country
in Christendom; yet they are good Christians, and to outward appearance God is religiously honoured and served.
But it is not the house of Burgundy alone that has a thorn
in its side; France has England as a check: England has
Scotland; and Spain, Portugal (I will not mention Granada*,
for they are enemies to the true faith, though otherwise
Granada has given the kingdom of Castile much trouble to
this very day.)   The princes of Italy, who generally have
no other title to their territories but what they derive from
Heaven (and of that we can have no certain knowledge),
and who rule their subjects with cruelty, violence, and
oppression in respect to their taxes, are curbed and kept in
check by the commonwealths and free states in Italy,
namely, Venice, Florence, Genoa, Bologna, Sienna, Pisa,
Lucca, and others; which are in a great many respects dia-
metrically opposite, they to the princes, and the princes to
them; and all keep a watchful eye over one another, that
neither of them may grow too powerful for his neighbour.
But to come to particulars in relation to the state of Italy.
The house of Arragon has that of Anjou to curb it; the
Visconti Dukes of Milan have the house of Orleans, and
though they be feeble abroad, their subjects hold them in
great dread.   The Venetians (as I said before) have the
princes of Italy, but more especially the Florentines, in
opposition against them; and the Florentines, the neigh-

---

* Granada was at this time a Moorish kingdom.   At the beginning of
the eighth century, the Saracens invaded Spain, and maintained their
footing there until 1492, when they were finally expelled by Ferdinand
and Isabella.

bouring commonwealths of Sienna and Genoa. The Genoese are sufficiently plagued with their own bad government and treachery towards each other, not to mention their factions and parties, the Fregosi, the Adorni, the Dorias, and others; but this everybody knows so well, that I shall insist no longer on it.

In Germany you are well acquainted with the animosity that rages between the houses of Austria and Bavaria, and how the house of Bavaria is subdivided within itself. The house of Austria again has the Swiss for its enemy, upon the account only of a small village called Switz (not able to raise 600 men), but now the whole country takes its denomination from it, and is so increased in power and riches that two of the best towns belonging to the house of Austria are Zurich and Fribourg, both of which are in Switzerland. Besides, they have won several memorable battles, and slain several of the Dukes of Austria in the field. There are also many other factions and private animosities in Germany; the house of Cleves against the house of Guelders, and the Dukes of Guelders against the Dukes of Juliers. The Easterlings (that remote people in the north) withstand the Kings of Denmark; and, to speak in general of all Germany, there are so many fortified places, and so many people in them ready for all manner of mischief (as plundering, robbing, and killing) upon every trivial occasion, that it is a wonder to think of it. A private person, with only one servant to wait on him, will defy a whole city, and declare war against a duke, that he may have a pretence to rob and plunder him; especially if he has a little castle, perched upon a rock, to retreat to, where he can keep twenty or thirty horse, to scour the country, and plunder according to his directions. Robbers of this kind are seldom punished by the German princes, who employ them upon all occasions; but the towns and free states punish them severely whenever they catch any of them, and have often besieged and blown up their castles, for which purpose they have generally a certain number of forces in pay, who are always in readiness to defend them. So that these princes and towns in Germany are placed in this opposition and discord, that no one may encroach upon his neighbour — which is absolutely necessary, not only in Germany, but all the world over.

I have spoken only of Europe, for of the affairs of Asia and Africa I am not sufficiently informed, though I have heard they are not exempted from factions and wars, which are carried on even more mechanically than ours; for I myself have known, that in some places in Africa they have sold one another to the Christians; as Portugal can witness, which has had, and still has, abundance of slaves of that nature. But I think, we have little reason to object on this account against the Saracens, for there are some places in Christendom where Christians practise the same thing, but they are either situated under the Turk's dominion, or else bordering upon it, as in some parts of Greece.

It may seem, therefore, that these factions and parties which prevail everywhere, are necessary for the world, and that these contradictions and oppositions which God has set up against all states, and almost against every private person, are so many pricks and spurs to enforce them to be just. For my own part, it seems so to me (who am a person but of indifferent learning, and will not hold any opinion that is not obvious to every one's capacity), and that chiefly upon account of the brutishness of some princes, and the wickedness of others, who have judgment and experience enough, but choose to pervert it; for a prince, or any man else, who has power and authority over those with whom he resides, and has seen or read more than other people, must of necessity be greatly improved, or rendered worse by his conversation with men and books; for wicked men grow the worse for their knowledge, but the good improve extremely. However, it is probable that learning does more good than harm to the persons that are possessed of it, for being conscious within themselves when they act contrary to their reason, it deters them from doing wrong, or at least from doing it so often as perhaps they otherwise would; and though they be not really good, it makes them unwilling to appear bad, or be thought to do injustice to any one. Of this I have seen many instances among great persons, where learning has restrained them from putting in practice their mischievous intentions; and sometimes men are deterred by the prospect and dread of God's judgments, of which they have a greater idea than the ignorant, who have neither observed nor read anything. This, therefore, I will venture to say, that those princes who do not know themselves, and for want of a right education, or perhaps through some defect in their constitution, are indiscreet and rash, cannot have any true knowledge how far God has extended the power and dominion which He has given them over their subjects: for they have neither read nor learned it themselves, nor conversed with any but fawning sycophants, who know nothing of the matter, and if they did, would be afraid to instruct and admonish them, for fear they should incur their royal displeasure : and if any bold-spirited men venture to remonstrate, they are so far from being encouraged in it, that they are at best looked upon as fools, and many times their good intentions are misinterpreted.

It is therefore to be concluded, that neither natural reason, nor our own knowledge, nor the fear of God, nor love of our neighbour, nor anything else, is always sufficient to restrain us from doing violence to one another, or to withhold us from retaining what we have got already, or to hinder us from usurping the possessions of other people by all possible ways. For if great princes once get possession of any towns or castles, though they belong to their nearest relations or neighbours, all the reasons above mentioned will not prevail with them to restore them ; and after they have once published some artful reasons or specious pretence for keeping them, everybody applauds their reasons, especially those who are nearest about them, and desirous of being in their favour. I am not speaking here of disputes between inferior persons, for they have superiors above them who sometimes do them justice ; at least, if a man's cause be at all good, his pockets full, and he willing to part with his money, and unless the court (that is the prince under whose authority he lives) opposes him. So that it would seem probable that God is as it were constrained to show many signs, and to chastise us with many rods for our indolence and perverseness ; but the brutishness and ignorance of princes are very dangerous and dreadful, because the happiness or misery of their subjects depends wholly upon them. Wherefore, if a prince who is powerful and has a large standing army, by the help of which he can raise money to pay his troops, or to spend in a luxurious way of living, or in anything that does not directly tend to the advancement of the common

good, and if he will not retrench his outrageous extrava-
gances himself, and those courtiers that are about him
rather endeavour to flatter and applaud him in everything
he does, than to dissuade him from doing ill (for fear of
incurring his displeasure), who can apply any remedy in
this case but God alone?

God indeed does not now converse with mankind after the
same manner as He did of old, nor are there any prophets
to declare His pleasure, but His word is sufficiently known
and declared, and clear enough to any that are willing to
understand it; so that there will be none excused for ignorance, especially if they have had time and natural sense to
consider these matters. How, then, shall those great princes
escape who keep their people in such subjection, that they
raise what taxes they please by force, by which they compel
their subjects to obedience, and enforce the least of their
commands with penalty of life? Some of them punish under
pretence of justice and have those about them who are
always ready to comply with their wishes, and make a capital
crime of what in itself is a venial offence. If they want
sufficient evidence to condemn a man, they have ways of
multiplying interrogatories, and falsifying the examinations
of the witnesses, to weary the defendant, and destroy him
with expenses, delaying his trial, and by that means giving
encouragement to any that will bring a fresh information
against him. If that will not do, and answers not their
intentions, they have a shorter method, by stating the case
as they please themselves, and giving out it was necessary
the culprit should be made an example of. To others that
are of a higher quality, and depend upon them, they say,
" You have disobeyed and done contrary to the duty and
allegiance you owe me:" and upon that bare pretence and
allegation they proceed, if they can, to seize upon their
estates by force, and reduce them to extreme poverty and
distress. If they have a neighbour that is of a martial temper, they will be sure not to disturb him: but if his kingdom
is in a poor weak condition, he will never be left at rest:
they will assert he has assisted their enemies, or levied con-
tributions on their countries; or else they will excite quarrels to give them occasion to ruin him. If that will not do,
they will support their enemies secretly against him, and

will supply them with troops.   They think their own subjects live too long, though they have served their predecessors never so faithfully, and will displace* them to make
room for new creatures of their own.   They will molest and
quarrel with the clergy upon the score of their benefices, in
order to extort compositions for the enriching of some
person recommended to them by such as are subservient to
their looser pleasures, and who often have great influence upon them. They exhaust their nobility in preparations
for war, which they undertake at their pleasure, without
consulting their council, or such as they ought to advise
with before they enter upon action, though they have employed both their persons and estates to enable them to undertake it.   To the common people they leave little or
nothing, though their taxes be greater than they ought ; nor
do they take any care to restrain the licentiousness of their
soldiers, who are constantly quartered throughout the country
without paying anything ; and commit all manner of excesses
and insolencies, as everybody knows ; for not contented with
the ordinary provisions for which they are paid, they beat
and abuse the poor country people, and force them to buy
bread, wine, and other dainties, on purpose for their eating ;
and if the good man's wife or daughter happens to be handsome, his wisest course is to keep them out of their sight.
And yet, where money is plenty, it would be no hard matter
to prevent this disorder and confusion, by paying them every
two months at farthest, which would obviate their pretence
of want of pay, and leave them without excuse, and
cause no inconvenience to the prince, because his money is
raised punctually every year.   I speak this in compassion
to this kingdom, which certainly is more oppressed and
harassed in quartering soldiers than any in all Europe ; nor
can anything but the wisdom of a king redress these injuries.
But neighbouring countries have other modes of punishment.

* As Louis XI. did after the death of his father, Charles VII.

Cn. XIX.—On the Character of the French People, and the Government of their Kings, with Reflections on the Misfortunes which occur to both great and small.

But to proceed in my design.   Is there any king or prince upon earth who has power to raise one penny of money, except on his own demesnes, without the consent of the poor subject who is to pay it, unless it be by tyranny and violence? It may be objected, that there are some times in which the assembling of great councils cannot be waited for, and that their debates would be too tedious.   The preparations and beginnings of war are never so sudden but kings have time enough to consider of it ; and when it is begun with the consent and concurrence of his subjects, the prince is always more strong and formidable to his enemy.   If it be a defensive war, the storm is seen afar off, especially if it be an invasion, and then the good subject cannot complain, or refuse anything that is demanded : nor can any case happen so suddenly, but some important persons may be called together, to show the necessity of the war, which is much better than to commence hostilities arbitrarily and feignedly, with a design only to raise money.   Money, I am sensible, is necessary at all times to secure the frontiers, in times of peace as well as war, that they may not be surprised ; but all should be done with moderation, and depends much upon the wisdom of the prince; for if he be a good man he knows what God is, what the world is, what he ought to do, and what he ought to avoid.   In my opinion, of all the countries in the world with which I was ever acquainted, the government is no where so well managed, the people no where less obnoxious to violence and oppression, nor their houses less liable to be destroyed and demolished by war than in England, for there the calamities fall only upon the authors of them.

Of all the kings in the world our sovereign has the least reason to use this expression, " I have the privilege to raise what money I please upon my subjects ; " for that is a power neither he nor any prince else has ; and they do him no honour who say so in order to make him appear greater, for they make him only more terrible and odious to his neighbours, who would never consent to live under his government. But, if our king or his courtiers, who are desirous of augmenting his reputation and grandeur, were to say thus: " My subjects are so good and loyal, that they refuse me nothing I ask them; I am the most feared, best obeyed, and best served by my subjects of any prince in the world; my subjects are the most patient under injury and affliction, and most forgetful of all past sufferings;" this, in my judgment, is more honourable (and I am sure it is true) than to say, "I take what I will; I have privilege to do it, and I will keep it." Our late King Charles V. used no such expression ; nor indeed did I ever hear it from any king; but I have heard it from their servants, who thought they had done their masters great service thereby; but they either mistook the interest of their master, or spoke thus to show their devotion to his power; if otherwise, they did not know what they said.

As an instance of the affections of the French to their prince, we need look no further back than our own times. At the meeting of the three Estates at Tours*, upon the death of our good master Louis XI. (whom God pardon!), who died in 1483, that assembly in such a juncture might be thought dangerous ; and some there were (but considerable neither for their quality nor virtue) who said then, and have often repeated it since, that it was a diminution of the king's prerogative, and no less than treason against him to talk of assembling the Estates ; but it is such as these who commit treason against God, the king, and their country ; and those who use these expressions are in undeserved authority and reputation, and are wholly unfit for anything but flattery, whispering lies and stories into the ears of their masters, which make them afraid of these assemblies, lest they should take notice of them and their manners, and call them to an account for their villanous practices. This kingdom was at that time accounted very weak by all people, having endured for twenty years and upwards, such great and hor-rible taxes as exceeded all precedent by above 3,000,000 of

---

* The first session of the Estates, at their meeting at Tours in 1483, was held on the 14th of January ; their last occurred on the 14th of March following.

francs per annum.   For Charles VII. never in any one year
raised above 1,800,000 francs; and his son, Louis XI., in the
very year of his death, raised 4,700,000 francs, besides what
was raised for the artillery and ammunition ; and certainly
it was a sad thing to see and hear of the poverty of the
people.   But one thing was very commendable in our master ;
he hoarded up none, but employed all he raised in building
citadels, castles, or fortifications for the defence of his kingdom; which he performed with more judgment and profusion
than any of his predecessors.   He was likewise very liberal
to the church, and in some respects more than was necessary;
for he robbed the poor to give to the rich : but in this world
no one can arrive at perfection.

   And yet, in this weak, oppressed, and impoverished kingdom, upon the death of our king, was there any sedition
among the people against the prince who now reigns ?   Did
either nobles or commons take arms to oppose him?   Was
there any one else whom they desired to place on the
throne ?   Did they endeavour either to deprive, or so much
as to restrain him in his authority, that he should not have
the power of a king?   Not at all ! and indeed if any had
been so conceited as to say yes, they would have had none to
help them, for his subjects acted quite contrary ; and all the
nobility. gentry, commons, and citizens, obeyed his summons,
made their personal appearance before him, recognised his
power, and swore allegiance to him.   The princes and nobles
delivered in their petitions humbly upon their knees, and a
council of twelve were appointed to take them into consideration, and according to the advice of that council, the
king (being then but thirteen years old) did either grant or
refuse them.   In the assembly of the Estates, the king and his
council being present, some requests and remonstrances were
made for the good of the kingdom, with all possible humility
and deference to the good pleasure of the king and his
council.   Whatever was desired they granted ; and whatever
was made appear by written calculation to be necessary for
the king's expense, they complied with without the least
opposition.   The sum was 2,500,000 francs (enough in all
conscience, and rather too much, unless some new occasion of
expense happened); but, lest that should not be sufficient
the Estates entreated, that at the end of two years they

might be convened again, and in case he should be in want of money, they would furnish him with as much as he pleased; and if he were invaded, or in any way affronted, they would be ready with their lives, as well as fortunes, to support him, and would refuse nothing that he should demand.

Is it to such obedient subjects as these that the king should insist upon his prerogative, and take at his pleasure what they are so ready and liberal to give? Would it not be more just, both towards God and the world, to raise money this way, than by violence and disorder? For there is no prince who can raise money any other way, unless it be by tyranny, and contrary to the laws of the church; but many are so stupid as not to know what rights they have in this respect. On the other hand, there are people in the world who affront and provoke their princes, neither obeying their commands, nor supplying their wants, but mutinying, rebelling, and contemning their authority, wherein they act contrary to both their allegiance and their duty.

When I say kings and princes, I mean themselves or their deputies; when subjects, I mean such as are magistrates and bear any rule or authority under them.

The greatest misfortunes proceed from the most powerful; for those who are weak are patiently contented. When I speak of great powers, I mean women * as well as men; for sometimes they are placed in authority, either by the over-fondness of their husbands, or for the administration of their own or their children's affairs, or when any territory accrues by them on their marriage. If I should treat of the inferior states and conditions of human life, I should be too tedious, and therefore I shall confine myself to the greater, since by those the power and justice of God are more visibly made known; for if calamities befall a poor man, they are imputed to his poverty and imprudence, and nobody cares about him; if he breaks his neck, or is drowned, it was because he had nobody with him, and none will give themselves any farther trouble about it. But when an accident happens to any great city it is otherwise; yet even that is not so much

---

* The author in this reflection on the exorbitant power of women, seems to point at the Princess Anne, Countess of Beaujeu, sister of Charles VIII., and Regent of France during his minority.

spoken of as anything which happens to princes. The reason therefore why the power of God is more conspicuous against princes and great men, is, because the poor and such as are in distress have enough to punish them whenever they offend; and are frequently chastised when they are innocent, either as a terror to other people, or for the forfeiture of their estates, or not improbably by the wickedness of the judge. But if the offenders are great, as princes, princesses, governors, or counsellors of any rebellious town or state, let their exorbitance be never so enormous, who will dare to inquire into their faults? who will inform against them? who will question them? who will punish them? I speak of the bad, not the good; for of good there are but few to be met with. And what are the motives that induce great persons to commit these enormities, and many more (which for brevity's sake I have not mentioned) without the least regard or consideration of God's divine power and justice? In men of learning it is want of faith, in ignorant persons, it is want of knowledge and faith also; but principally of faith, from whence (in my opinion) all the mischiefs that are incident to mankind do spring, and more especially the mischiefs of those who complain of being injured and oppressed by such as are powerful and strong; for whether a man be rich or poor, if he puts his trust in God, and is firmly convinced that the pains of hell are such as they really are; if he is conscious of any injury that he has done to his neighbour, or that his grandfather or father came wrongfully by anything that he now enjoys (let it be what it will, whether a duchy, a county, a town, a castle, moveable goods, a meadow, a pool, a mill, or anything else); and if he firmly believes, as we all ought to believe, "I shall never enter into Paradise, if I do not do what I ought, and restore all that I hold wrongfully from other people," it is not to be supposed that any prince or princess, or in short, any person of what condition soever, would detain anything from his subject or neighbour, or condemn any innocent person to death, keep him in prison, or impoverish one to enrich another, or do anything dishonourable to their parents and relations, to gratify themselves in their pleasures with women or otherwise. Certainly not: it is incredible. If, therefore, men had firm faith, and believed what God and the church have commanded under pain of damnation, knowing that our life is but short, and the horrible pains of hell eternal and without intermission, they would never act as they do. We may safely conclude therefore, that the want of faith is the source of all mischiefs and villany.

But to illustrate this idea by an example :—When a king or prince happens to be taken prisoner, and is apprehensive of continuing so all the days of his life, is there anything so dear to him in the world that he would not give to purchase his liberty? He will part not only with his own property, but that of his subjects too, for his redemption ; as you may remember in the case of King John of France, who was taken prisoner by the Prince of Wales* at the battle of Poictiers. This King John paid 3,000,000 of francs, gave away all Aquitaine (at least all that he held of it), besides other territories and towns, to the extent of a third part of his dominions (by which means he so impoverished the kingdom, that for a long time after, the current coin of it was nothing but round bits of leather with a silver nail in

* Edward the Black Prince, son of Edward III., King of England. The battle of Poictiers was fought on the 19th of September, 1356 ; it was one of the most glorious achievements in English history, and one of the most splendid exploits in the life of its illustrious hero. The Black Prince was a man of whom his country was justly proud, and his early death has only served to add additional lustre to the brilliancy of his life. His character is thus eloquently summed up by an old writer : "And thus fell this victorious prince, in whose fall the hopes of all England seemed to be cast down ; while he lived, they feared no invasion, they doubted no warlike encounter. He never marched against any whom he overcame not, never besieged any city which he took not. All nations, both heathen and Christian, dreaded his fortune and conduct in war, as of another Hector ; nor did his wisdom any way come short of his courage, both which were equalled by his exemplary justice, clemency, liberality, piety, and moderation—virtues but seldom sincerely embraced by persons of high condition. He was a prince of whom we never heard any ill, nor received any other note than of goodness, and the noblest performances that magnanimity, generosity, courage, and wisdom could ever show, insomuch as what praise can be given unto virtue is due unto him. He was of so obliging a character that he won the hearts of all mankind, especially of those who delighted in martial performances ; and in general he was a prince of such excellent demeanour, so valiant, wise, and politic in his doings, that the very perfect image of knighthood appeared most lively in his person." Barnes's History of Edward III., pp. 883, 884.

the middle*); all which was given by King John and by his
son Charles the Wise for the ransom of his father; though
the English would not have put him to death if they had
given nothing, but at worst would only have made his confinement more severe; but even if they had put him to death,
the pains of the execution would not have been any way equal
to the torments of hell.   Why then did he yield what he did,
to the ruin and impoverishment both of his children and subjects, unless because he believed what he saw, and imagined
there was no other way of obtaining his liberty?   But perhaps when he committed that sin which brought down this
judgment upon himself, his children and subjects, he had no
steadfast belief that the doing of it was an offence against
God's will and commandments.   Now, though King John
gave all these territories and towns to his enemies, to redeem
himself from captivity; yet there is not one prince (or at
least very few princes), who, having any town or province
that belongs to their neighbours in their possession, will
restore it upon consideration of God's justice, or to avoid the
torments of hell.   I say, therefore, that it is want of faith.

I accordingly asked the question before, Who would inform
against great persons? who would accuse them to the judge?
and where would a judge be found to punish them?   The
information that will be brought against them shall be the
cries and clamours of the people whom they have in so many
ways injured and oppressed, without the least pity or compassion; and the mournful complaints of widows and or-
phans, whose husbands and parents they have unjustly put
to death to their utter ruin and destruction: and in short,
the lamentations of all those whom they have tortured or
persecuted either in their persons or estates.   These with
their sighs, their piteous tears, and their groans, shall be an
information against them before our Saviour, the true Judge

---

* " The statement of Commines with regard to the leather money current in France after the payment of the king's ransom appears to me
very erroneous; as it is certain that the king, on his return from England, coined so much gold and silver money that the silver mark was
worth only five livres, and the gold mark sixty livres; which would have
been impossible if there had been so great a dearth of those two metals
in France as Commines would have us believe."   Leblanc's Traité des
Monnaies, p. 277.

of the world, who perhaps will not defer their punishment
till the next world, but do them justice in this ; which
punishment, as I said before, will proceed from their want
of faith, and a firm trust and belief in God's commandments.

It must be acknowledged, therefore, that God is forced to
show tokens and examples, that princes and the rest of the
world may be convinced, that the enormity of their actions
and the weakness of their faith have drawn those heavy
judgments upon them ; and that they may understand that it
is God who exercises His power and justice to punish them,
because their offences are above any other cognizance but
His.   But the judgments of God, at first, seldom produce
any amendment, how great or how lasting soever they may
be.   However, they never fall upon any prince, minister of
state, or magistrate, but the consequences are very dangerous
and dreadful for the subject.   When I speak of misfortunes,
I mean only such as are detrimental to the subject ; for, if a
prince falls from his horse, breaks his leg, or falls into a
violent fever, he is cured again, and it makes him wiser for
the future.   I call them misfortunes, when God is so highly
provoked that He can endure no longer, but will manifest His
Divine justice and power, and then His method is first to infatuate their understanding (which is a great punishment
where it is inflicted), then He visits their family, and suffers
murmurs and dissensions to arise in it ; then the prince himself is so far abandoned and given over by God that, in the
height of his indignation and folly, he shuns and despises the
counsels and conversation of wise men, and consults none
but irrational fiery upstarts without either merit, virtue, or
estate, but who will flatter him and comply with whatever
he says.   If he proposes to raise one penny, they say two :
if the prince threatens a man, they advise him to hang him ;
and so in everything else, spurring him still on to make
himself feared, and behaving themselves in the meantime
proudly and insolently, in hopes to strike awe and terror into
the people, as if authority had been their inheritance.   Those
whom such princes, by the advice of such evil counsellors,
have deprived of their posts and employments, after having
served in them a long time, and contracted friendship and
acquaintance in their dominions, are very much disgusted,
and all their relations and well-wishers are equally dis-

satisfied; and perhaps they are pressed so far as to stand
upon their defence, or else enter into the service of some
neighbouring prince, who possibly may be at enmity with
him that discarded them, by which means the dissatisfaction
within the country may give opportunity to bring in a
foreign army. Is there any plague or persecution so horrible
as war between friends that are provoked? or is any
hatred so mortal and pitiless? Foreign enemies are easily
repelled when a nation is unanimous at home, because the
invaders want intelligence and correspondence. Can you
imagine that an imprudent prince, surrounded with such
silly advisers, can foresee calamities that are remote, when
he cannot discern domestic divisions, nor comprehend how
they can hurt him, nor conceive they proceed from God?
His table is as well served, he sleeps as well as ever in his
bed, his stables and his wardrobe are the same, and the pomp
and splendour of his court is much increased; for he attracts
persons by promises, divides among them the spoils and
estates of those whom he has banished, and lavishes away
abundance of his own to increase his renown. But, when
he thinks least of it, God will raise him up an enemy whom
perhaps he never heard of: then melancholy thoughts will
arise, and suspicions of those whom he has offended, and he
will be afraid even of his very friends; yet will he not make
God his refuge, but will have recourse to arms.

Ch. XX.—Examples of Misfortunes that have happened to Princes, and
Revolutions that have been brought to pass in States by the Judgment
of God.

HAVE we not seen in our own days such examples among
our neighbours? Have we not seen King Edward IV.
of England, the head of the house of York, supplant the
house of Lancaster, under which his father and he had
lived a long time; and though he had actually sworn allegiance to Henry VI., who was of the Lancastrian line, yet
afterwards this Edward kept King Henry a prisoner for
many years in the Tower of London (the metropolis of that
kingdom), and at last put him to death?

Have we not seen the Earl of Warwick, the chief manager of all King Edward's affairs (after having put all his adversaries to death, and particularly the Dukes of Somerset), at length turn rebel against his master King Edward, marry his daughter to the Prince of Wales, son to King Henry VI.; endeavour to restore the house of Lancaster; and return into England, where he was defeated, and slain in battle himself, his brothers, and relations; besides many others of the nobility of England, who not long before had vanquished and put to death their adversaries? Afterwards, times changed, and the children revenged the destruction of their parents. It is not to be imagined that such judgments proceeded from anything but the Divine justice. But (as I observed before) England enjoyed this peculiar mercy above all other kingdoms, that neither the country, nor the people, nor the houses, were wasted, destroyed, or demolished; but the calamities and misfortunes of the war fell only upon the soldiers, and especially on the nobility, of whom they are more than ordinarily jealous; for nothing is perfect in this world.

As soon as King Edward had settled his affairs in this kingdom, he received of our master 50,000 crowns a year*, constantly paid him in the Tower of London, and was grown as rich as his ambition could desire, on a sudden he died† (and as was supposed) of melancholy for our present king's‡ marriage with Margaret§, the Duke of Austria's daughter* (his distemper seizing him upon the news of it), for then he

---

* By the terms of the treaty of the 29th of August, 1475. See note, book iv. chap. viii.

† On the 9th of April, 1483, "he died of apoplexy, say some; but others say that he was poisoned by drinking some good wine of Challuau, which Louis XI. had given him." Lenglet, ii. 169.

‡ Charles VIII. of France.

§ Margaret of Austria, daughter of the Emperor Maximilian and Mary of Burgundy, was born at Brussels on the 10th of January, 1470. In July, 1483, she was married to the Dauphin, afterwards Charles VIII. at Amboise. After having been considered Queen of France for ten years, she was sent back to her father on the 12th of June, 1493. She afterwards married John, Infante of Castile, in 1497, and Philibert, Duke of Savoy, in 1501. She died on the 1st of December, 1530, after a widowhood of twenty-six years.

found himself outwitted as to his own daughter*, to whom he had given the title of Dauphiness. Upon this marriage the pension, which he called tribute, was stopped, though indeed it was neither pension nor tribute, as I have declared before. King Edward left his wife with two sons (one called the Prince of Wales, and the other the Duke of York) and two daughters. The Duke of Gloucester, King Edward's brother, took upon him the protectorship of his nephew, the Prince of Wales (who was then about ten years old), swore allegiance to him as his sovereign, and brought him to London, pretending to crown him; but his design was only to entice the Duke of York out of the sanctuary†, where he was at that time with his mother, who had conceived some suspicion of his intentions. In short, the conclusion was this; by the assistance of the Bishop of Bath‡, (who had been formely King Edward's chancellor, but falling afterwards into disgrace, had been removed from his place, thrown into prison, and paid a round sum for his ransom), he executed his designs, as you shall hear by and by.

This bishop discovered to the Duke of Gloucester that his brother King Edward had been formerly in love with a beautiful young lady§, and had promised her marriage, upon

---

* The Princess Elizabeth.

† Westminster Abbey.

‡ Robert Stillington was appointed chancellor on the 20th of June, 1467. He appears to have been of humble origin, but he gained a great name at Oxford, where with much applause he took the degree of Doctor of Laws. He was a zealous legitimist, and on the succession of Edward IV. he was a special favourite with that prince, who successively made him Archdeacon of Taunton, Bishop of Bath and Wells, Keeper of the Privy Seal, and finally Lord Chancellor. He held this last office for six years, with the exception of the few months when Edward was obliged to fly the kingdom, and the sceptre was again put into the feeble hands of Henry VI. He resigned the chancellorship from ill health on the 8th of June, 1473. After the coronation of Henry VII., Stillington showed his never-dying enmity to the house of Lancaster, by taking up the cause of Lambert Simnel; but being detected in this conspiracy, and expecting no mercy from the king, he fled for refuge to Oxford. The university consented to deliver him up on condition that his life should be spared; and he was conducted to Windsor, where he remained a prisoner till his death, in June, 1491. See Lord Campbell's Lives of the Chancellors, vol. i. pp. 385—391.

§ Habington mentions two ladies whom public rumour indicated as aving been seduced by the king, Lady Elizabeth Lucy and Lady

condition he might lie with her ; the lady consented, and, as the bishop affirmed, he married them when nobody was present but they two and himself. His fortune depending upon the court, he did not discover it, and persuaded the lady likewise to conceal it, which she did, and the matter remained a secret. After this King Edward married the daughter of an English gentleman, called the Lord Rivers ; this lady was a widow, and had two sons. The Bishop of Bath, as I said before, discovered this matter to the Duke of Gloucester, and gave his assistance in the execution of the barbarous designs of the duke, who murdered his two nephews, and made himself king, by the name of Richard III.* He caused the two daughters to be declared illegitimate by parliament†, took their coats of arms from them, and put all his brother's faithful servants to death, at least all he could get into his power. But his cruel reign did not last long ; for, being at the height of his pride, in greater pomp and authority than any King of England for a hundred years before, when he had beheaded the Duke of Buckingham‡, and assembled a numerous army under his own command, God Almighty raised him up an enemy that destroyed him, and that was the Earl of Richmond, a person of no power, and one who had been long prisoner in Bretagne ; but he is now King of England, and is of the house of Lancaster, though, as I am informed, not the next heir to the crown.

This Earl of Richmond told me, not long before his departure from this kingdom, that from the time he was five

Eleanor Butler. Lord Campbell indignantly denies the charge brought against Stillington by Commines, but has adduced no evidence in support of his denial.

* Richard III. was proclaimed king on the 22nd of June, 1483.

† The English parliament, at a meeting held at Westminster, on the 23rd of January, 1484, declared that the marriage of Edward IV. with Elizabeth Woodville had been effected in contravention of the customs of the Anglican Church, seeing that, by a previous contract, the King had plighted his troth to Lady Eleanor Butler, and that consequently, Edward and Elizabeth had lived in adultery, and their children were evidently bastards, and as such unable to inherit the crown.

‡ Henry, Duke of Buckingham, was son of Humphry, Earl of Stafford, and Margaret, daughter of Edmund, Duke of Somerset. He married Catharine, daughter of Richard Woodville, Earl of Rivers. Being

years old he had been always a fugitive or a prisoner.   He
had endured an imprisonment of fifteen years or thereabouts
in Bretagne, by the command of the late Duke Francis, into
whose hands he fell by extremity of weather, as he was
escaping out of France with his uncle the Earl of Pembroke.*
I was at Duke Francis's court at the time when they were
seized ; the duke treated them very handsomely for prisoners,
and at King Edward's death, supplied the Earl of Richmond liberally both with men and ships; and having intelligence with the Duke of Buckingham (who died for it
afterwards) he sent him to land his forces in England; but,
meeting with foul weather and contrary winds, he was
driven into Dieppe, and from thence went back by land
into Bretagne.   Being returned into Bretagne, he was
afraid, having 500 English in his train, of becoming burden-
some to the duke, and feared he might thereby induce him
to make some agreement with King Richard†, to his prejudice and disadvantage, for he had some intimation that there
were secret practices on foot to that purpose ; and therefore,
he and his whole retinue went away privately, without
taking leave of the duke.   Not long after, our present king
paid for the passage of 3000 or 4000 men, gave him and
his companions a considerable sum of money, and some
pieces of artillery, and sent him out of Normandy to land in
some part of Wales, where he was born.   King Richard
marched immediately to fight him, but an English gentleman,
called the Lord Stanley, who had married the Earl of Richmond's mother, joined the earl with 26,000 men.   They came
to a battle‡, and the issue was, King Richard was slain, and
the Earl of Richmond crowned King of England on the field
of battle, with the crown that King Richard had brought
along with him.   Will you say this is fortune?   Certainly

detected in a conspiracy against Richard III., he was beheaded at Salisbury on All Saints' Day, 1483.
    * Jasper, Earl of Pembroke, afterwards Duke of Bedford, was the son
of Owen Tudor, and Catharine of France, widow of Henry V., King of
England.   He married Catharine, the widow of the Duke of Buckingham, and died on the 21st of December, 1495.
    † Pierre Landais, the treasurer and favourite of the Duke of Bretagne,
had made overtures to Richard III. for the surrender of the Earl of
Richmond.
    ‡ The Battle of Bosworth Field, fought on the 22nd of August, 1485.

it is the just judgment of God. But, to make it the more evident, not long after the murder of his nephews, as you have heard, he lost his wife*, (some say he made her away); he had but one son, and he died presently after. This would have come in more properly hereafter when I shall have to speak of King Edward's death (for he was alive at the time of the occurrences of this chapter), yet I thought it not unseasonable here, as being pertinent to my discourse.

In like manner, it is not many years since we have seen as strange revolutions in Spain, upon the death of the late King Henry of that kingdom, who was married to the late King of Portugal's sister, and by her had a beautiful daughter; yet that daughter was not suffered to succeed to the throne, but was deprived of the crown under pretence of illegitimacy. But this business did not pass over without controversy and blood; for the King of Portugal, assisted by several of the nobility of Castile, took part with his niece: but King Henry's sister carried the kingdom in spite of all their opposition, and enjoys it to this very day, having married the son of John, King of Arragon; so that this judgment and decree was made in heaven, where many of the same nature are undoubtedly made.

You have seen likewise, not many years since, the King of Scotland† at war with his son‡, who was not above thirteen or fourteen years of age.. The son won the battle, and the king was killed upon the spot. This king was accused of having caused the death of his brother and several other

* Anne Neville, daughter of the great Earl of Warwick.

† James III., son of James II., King of Scotland, and Mary of Guelders, ascended the throne of Scotland in 1460, at the age of seven years. He married Margaret, daughter of Christian I., King of Denmark. He surrounded himself by ministers sprung from the lower ranks of the people, and the Scottish barons, in indignation, hanged the unworthy favourites upon the bridge of Lauder, in 1482. In 1488, they rebelled again, gave the king battle at Sauchie, and slew him in his flight on the 11th of June, 1488.

‡ James IV. succeeded his father, at fifteen years of age. He made terms with the Scottish nobles, and married Margaret, daughter of Henry VII., King of England. He thereby secured peace and tranquillity for his country for many years; but Henry VIII. forced him into an alliance with France, war was renewed between England and Scotland, and James IV. fell on the battle-field of Flodden on the 9th of September, 1515

persons of quality. You see also the duchy of Guelders out of the right line, and you have heard of the late duke's unnatural usage of his father. I could instance many other cases of the like nature, that might easily be known to be Divine chastisements, which are the sources of war, and from whence proceed mortality and famine; and all evils arise from want of faith. It must therefore be acknowledged (considering the wickedness of mankind, and especially of great persons, who neither know themselves, nor believe there is a God) that there is a necessity that every prince or great lord should have an adversary to restrain and keep him in humility and fear, or else there would be no living under them, nor near them.

END OF THE FIRST VOLUME.

LONDON:

PRINTED BY WILLIAM CLOWES AND SONS,

STAMFORD STREET AND CHARING CROSS.

LIST OF

BOHN'S VARIOUS LIBRARIES.

A Complete Set, in 653 Volumes, Price £135 9s.

SEPARATE LIBRARIES.

	No. of Volumes.	Price. £	s.	d.
STANDARD LIBRARY (including the Atlas to Coxe's Marlborough)	202	36	1	6
HISTORICAL LIBRARY	21	5	5	0
LIBRARY OF FRENCH MEMOIRS	6	1	1	0
SCHOOL AND COLLEGE SERIES	6	1	5	6
PHILOSOPHICAL LIBRARY	11	2	9	0
BRITISH CLASSICS	29	5	1	6
ECCLESIASTICAL LIBRARY	14	3	8	0
ANTIQUARIAN LIBRARY	33	8	5	0
ILLUSTRATED LIBRARY	83	21	0	0
CLASSICAL LIBRARY (including the Atlas)	92	22	11	0
SCIENTIFIC LIBRARY	60	15	13	6
REFERENCE LIBRARY	31	7	7	6
NOVELISTS' LIBRARY	5	0	19	0
ARTIST'S LIBRARY	2	0	10	0
CHEAP SERIES	58	5	1	6

LONDON:

GEORGE BELL AND SONS, YORK STREET,
COVENT GARDEN.

A CATALOGUE OF
BOHN'S VARIOUS LIBRARIES.
PUBLISHED BY
GEORGE BELL AND SONS,
4 & 5, YORK STREET, COVENT GARDEN,
LONDON.
1877.

N.B.—The Classification of the Books has lately been improved by the rearrangement of some of the Libraries.

I.

STANDARD LIBRARY.

A SERIES OF THE BEST ENGLISH AND FOREIGN AUTHORS, PRINTED IN POST 8VO.

3s. 6d. per Volume, excepting those marked otherwise.

Alfieri's Tragedies, including those published posthumously. Translated into English Verse, and edited with Notes and Introduction, by EDGAR A. BOWRING, C.B. 2 vols.

Bacon's Essays, Apophthegms, Wisdom of the Ancients, New Atlantis, and Henry VII., with Introduction and Notes *Portrait.*

Beaumont and Fletcher, a popular Selection from. By LEIGH HUNT.

Beckmann's History of Inventions, Discoveries, and Origins. Revised and enlarged. *Portraits.* In 2 vols

Bremer's (Miss) Works. Translated by MARY HOWITT. *Portrait.* In 4 vols.
Vol. 1. The Neighbours and other Tales
Vol. 2. The President's Daughter.
Vol. 3. The Home, and Strife and Peace.
Vol. 4. A Diary, the H --- Family, &c.

British Poets, from Milton to Kirke WHITE. Cabinet Edition. In 4 vols

Browne's (Sir Thomas) Works. Edited by SIMON WILKIN. In 3 vols.

Butler's (Bp.) Analogy of Religion, and Sermons, with Notes. *Portrait*

Camoens' Lusiad, Mickle's Translation. Edited by E. R. HODGES,
[*In the Press.*]

Cary's Translation of Dante's Heaven. Hell, and Purgatory Copyright edition, being the only one containing Cary's last corrections and additions.

Carafas (The) of Maddaloni: and Naples under Spanish Dominion. Translated from the German of Alfred de Reumont.

Carrel's Counter Revolution in England. Fox's History and Lonsdale's Memoir of James II. *Portrait.*

Cellini (Benvenuto), Memoirs of Translated by ROSCOE. *Portrait.*

Cervantes' Galatea. Translated by GORDON GYLL.

Coleridge's (S. T.) Friend. A Series of Essays on Morals, Politics, and Religion.

——— **(S. T.) Biographia Literaria,** and two Lay Sermons.

Condé's Dominion of the Arabs in Spain. Translated by Mrs. FOSTER. In 3 vols.

Cowper's Complete Works. Edited, with Memoir of the Author, by SOUTHEY. *Illustrated with 50 Engravings* In 8 vols.
Vols. 1 to 4. Memoir and Correspondence.
Vols. 5 and 6. Poetical Works *Plates.*
Vol. 7. Homer's Iliad. *Plates.*
Vol. 8. Homer's Odyssey. *Plates.*

Coxe's Memoirs of the Duke of Marlborough. *Portraits.* In 3 vols.
. An Atlas of the plans of Marlborough's campaigns. 4to. 10s. 6d.

——— **History of the House of** Austria. *Portraits.* In 4 vols.

De Lolme on the Constitution of England. Edited, with Notes, by JOHN MACGREGOR.

Emerson's Works. 2 vols.

Foster's (John) Life and Correspondence. Edited by J. E. RYLAND. In 2 vols.

——— Lectures at Broadmead Chapel. Edited by J. E. RYLAND. In 2 vols.

18

Foster's (John) Critical Essays. Edited by J. E. RYLAND. In 2 vols.

———— Essays—On Decision of Character, &c. &c.

———— Essays—On the Evils of Popular Ignorance, &c.

———— Fosteriana: Thoughts, Reflections, and Criticisms of the late JOHN FOSTER, selected from periodical papers, and Edited by HENRY G. BOHN (nearly 600 pages). 5s.

Fuller's (Andrew) Principal Works. With Memoir. Portrait.

Goethe's Works, Translated into English. In 7 vols.
Vols. 1. and 2. Autobiography,20 Books; and Travels in Italy, France, and Switzerland. Portrait.
Vol. 3. Faust, Iphigenia, Torquato Tasso, Egmont, &c., by Miss SWANWICK; and Götz von Berlichingen, by Sir WALTER SCOTT. Frontispiece.
Vol. 4. Novels and Tales.
Vol. 5. Wilhelm Meister's Apprenticeship.
Vol. 6. Conversations with Eckermann and Soret. Translated by JOHN OXENFORD.
Vol. 7. Poems and Ballads, including Hermann and Dorothea. Translated by E. A. BOWRING, C.B.

Greene, Marlowe, and Ben Jonson, Poems of. Edited by ROBERT BELL. With Biographies. In 1 vol.

Gregory's (Dr.) Evidences, Doctrines, and Duties of the Christian Religion.

Guizot's Representative Government. Translated by A. R. SCOBLE.

———— History of the English Revolution of 1640. Translated by WILLIAM HAZLITT. Portrait.

———— History of Civilization. Translated by WILLIAM HAZLITT. In 3 vols. Portrait.

Hazlitt's Table Talk. A New Edition in one volume.

———— Lectures on the Comic Writers, and on the English Poets.

———— Lectures on the Literature of the Age of Elizabeth, and on Characters of Shakespear's Plays.

———— Plain Speaker. 5s.

———— Round Table; the Conversations of JAMES NORTHCOTE, R.A.; Characteristics, &c. 5s.

———— Sketches and Essays, and Winterslow (Essays Written there). New Edition.

Hall's (Rev. Robert) Miscellaneous Works and Remains, with Memoir by Dr. GREGORY, and an Essay on his Character by JOHN FOSTER. Portrait.

Hawthorne's Tales. In 2 vols.
Vol. 1. Twice Told Tales, and the Snow Image.
Vol. 2. Scarlet Letter, and the House with the seven Gables.

Heine's Poems, complete, from the German, by E. A. BOWRING, C.B. 5s.

Hungary: its History and Revolutions; with a Memoir of Kossuth from new and authentic sources. Portrait.

Hutchinson (Colonel), Memoirs of, with the Siege of Latham House.

Irving's (Washington) Life and Letters. By his Nephew, PIERRE E. IRVING. In 2 vols.

———— Life of Washington. Portrait. In 4 vols.

———— Complete Works. In 11 vols.
Vol. 1. Salmagundi and Knickerbocker Portrait of the Author.
Vol. 2. Sketch Book and Life of Goldsmith.
Vol. 3. Bracebridge Hall and Abbotsford and Newstead.
Vol. 4. Tales of a Traveller and the Alhambra.
Vol. 5. Conquest of Granada and Conquest of Spain.
Vols. 6 and 7. Life of Columbus and Companions of Columbus, with a new Index. Fine Portrait.
Vol. 8. Astoria and Tour in the Prairies.
Vol. 9. Mahomet and his Successors.
Vol. 10. Conquest of Florida and Adventures of Captain Bonneville.
Vol. 11. Biographies and Miscellanies.
For separate Works, see Cheap Series.

James's (G. P. R.) Richard Cœur-de-Lion, King of England. Portraits. 2 vols.

———— Louis XIV. Portraits. 2 vols

Junius's Letters, with Notes, Additions, and an Index. In 2 vols.

Lamartine's History of the Girondists. Portraits. In 3 vols.

———— Restoration of the Monarchy, with Index. Portraits. In 4 vols.

———— French Revolution of 1848, with a fine Frontispiece.

Lamb's (Charles) Elia and Eliana. Complete Edition.

———— Dramatic Poets of the Time of Elizabeth; including his Selections from the Garrick Plays.

19

Lanzi's History of Painting. Translated by Roscoe. *Portraits.* In 3 vols.

Locke's Philosophical Works, containing an Essay on the Human Understanding, &c., with Notes and Index by J. A. St. John. *Portrait.* In 2 vols.

————— **Life and Letters, with Extracts from his Common-Place Books, by Lord King.

Luther's Table Talk. Translated by William Hazlitt. *Portrait.*

Machiavelli's History of Florence, The Prince, and other Works. *Portrait.*

Menzel's History of Germany. *Portraits.* In 3 vols.

Michelet's Life of Luther. Translated by William Hazlitt.

————— **Roman Republic.** Translated by William Hazlitt.

————— **French Revolution,** with Index. *Frontispiece.*

Mignet's French Revolution from 1789 to 1814. *Portrait.*

Milton's Prose Works, with Index. *Portraits.* In 5 vols.

Mitford's (Mary R.) Our Village. Improved Ed., complete. *Illustrated.* 2 vols

Molière's Plays. Translated by C. H. Wall. In 3 vols. [Vol. 3 *in the Press.*

Neander's Church History. Translated: with General Index. In 10 vols.

————— **Life of Christ.** Translated.

————— **First Planting of Christianity, and Antignostikus.** Translated. In 2 vols.

————— **History of Christian Dogmas.** Translated. In 2 vols.

————— **Christian Life in the Early** and Middle Ages, including his 'Light in Dark Places.' Translated.

Ockley's History of the Saracens. Revised and completed. *Portrait.*

Percy's Reliques of Ancient English Poetry. Reprinted from the Original Edition, and Edited by J. V. Prichard. In 2 vols.

Ranke's History of the Popes, Translated by E. Foster. In 3 vols.

————— **Servia and the Servian Revolution.**

Reynolds' (Sir Joshua) Literary Works. *Portrait.* In 2 vols.

20

Richter (Jean Paul Fr.) Autobio-graphy and Levana. With Memoir.

————— **Flower, Fruit, and Thorn** Pieces. [*In the Press.*

Roscoe's Life and Pontificate of Leo X., with the Copyright Notes, and an Index. *Portraits.* In 2 vols.

————— **Life of Lorenzo de Medici,** with the Copyright Notes, &c. *Portrait.*

Russia, History of, by Walter K. Kelly. *Portraits.* In 2 vols.

Schiller's Works. Translated into English. In 6 vols.

> Vol. 1. Thirty Years' War, and Revolt of the Netherlands.
> Vol. 2. *Continuation of* the Revolt of the Netherlands; Wallenstein's Camp; the Piccolomini; the Death of Wallenstein; and William Tell.
> Vol. 3. Don Carlos, Mary Stuart, Maid of Orleans, and Bride of Messina.
> Vol. 4. The Robbers, Fiesco, Love and Intrigue, and the Ghost-Seer.
> Vol. 5. Poems. Translated by Edgar Bowring, C.B.
> Vol. 6. Philosophical Letters and Æsthetical Essays.

Schlegel's Philosophy of Life and of Language, translated by A. J. W. Morrison.

————— **History of Literature,** Ancient and Modern. Now first completely translated, with General Index.

————— **Philosophy of History.** Translated by J. B. Robertson. *Portrait.*

————— **Dramatic Literature.** Translated. *Portrait.*

————— **Modern History.**

————— **Æsthetic and Miscellaneous** Works.

Sheridan's Dramatic Works and Life. *Portrait.*

Sismondi's Literature of the South of Europe. Translated by Roscoe. *Portraits.* In 2 vols.

Smith's (Adam) Theory of the Moral Sentiments; with his Essay on the First Formation of Languages.

Smyth's (Professor) Lectures on Modern History. In 2 vols.

————— **Lectures on the French Re-**volution. In 2 vols.

Sturm's Morning Communings with God, or Devotional Meditations for Every Day in the Year.

Taylor's (Bishop Jeremy) Holy Living and Dying. *Portrait.*

Thierry's Conquest of England by the Normans. Translated by WILLIAM HAZLITT. *Portrait.* In 2 vols.

Ulrici (Dr.) Shakespeare's Dramatic Art. Translated by L. D. Schmitz. 2 vols.

Vasari's Lives of the Painters, Sculptors, and Architects. Translated by Mrs. FOSTER. 5 vols.

Wesley's (John) Life By ROBERT SOUTHEY. New and Complete Edition. Double volume. *With Portrait.* 5s.

Wheatley on the Book of Common Prayer. *Frontispiece.*

II.

HISTORICAL LIBRARY.

5s. per Volume.

Evelyn's Diary and Correspondence. *Illustrated with numerous Portraits, &c.* In 4 vols.

Pepys' Diary and Correspondence. Edited by Lord Braybrooke. With Notes, important Additions, including numerous Letters. *Illustrated with many Portraits.* In 4 vols.

Jesse's Memoirs of the Reign of the Stuarts, including the Protectorate. With General Index. *Upwards of 40 Portraits.* In 3 vols.

Jesse's Memoirs of the Pretenders and their Adherents. *6 Portraits.*

Nugent's (Lord) Memorials of Hampden, his Party, and Times. 12 *Portraits.*

Strickland's (Agnes) Lives of the Queens of England, from the Norman Conquest. From official records and authentic documents, private and public. Revised Edition. In 6 vols.

——— **Life of Mary Queen of Scots.** 2 vols.

III.

LIBRARY OF FRENCH MEMOIRS.

3s. 6d. per Volume.

Memoirs of Philip de Commines, containing the Histories of Louis XI. and Charles VIII., and of Charles the Bold, Duke of Burgundy. To which is added, The Scandalous Chronicle, or Secret History of Louis XI. *Portraits.* In 2 vols.

Memoirs of the Duke of Sully, Prime Minister to Henry the Great. *Portraits* In 4 vols.

IV.

SCHOOL AND COLLEGE SERIES.

5s. per Volume, excepting those marked otherwise.

Bass's Greek and English Lexicon to the New Testament. 2s.

Donaldson's Theatre of the Greeks. Illustrated with Lithographs and numerous Woodcuts.

Herodotus, Turner's (Dawson W.) Notes to. With Map, &c.

——— **Wheeler's Analysis and Summary of.**

New Testament (The) in Greek. Griesbach's Text, with the various readings of Mill and Scholz at foot of page, and Parallel References in the margin; also a Critical Introduction and Chronological Tables. *Two fac-similes of Greek Manuscripts.* (650 pages.) 3s. 6d.; or with the Lexicon, 5s.

Thucydides, Wheeler's Analysis of.

21

V.

PHILOSOPHICAL LIBRARY.

5s. per Volume, excepting those marked otherwise.

Comte's Philosophy of the Sciences. By G. H. LEWES.

Draper (J. W.) A History of the Intellectual Development of Europe. By JOHN WILLIAM DRAPER, M.D., LL.D. A New Edition, thoroughly Revised by the Author. In 2 vols.

Hegel's Lectures on the Philosophy of History. Translated by J. SIBREE, M.A.

Kant's Critique of Pure Reason. Translated by J. M. D. MEIKLEJOHN.

Logic; or, the Science of Inference. A Popular Manual. By J. DEVEY.

Miller's (Professor) History Philoso-phically considered. In 4 vols. 3s. 6d. each.

Tennemann's Manual of the History of Philosophy. Continued by J. R. MORELL.

VI.

BRITISH CLASSICS.

3s. 6d. per Volume.

Addison's Works. With the Notes of Bishop HURD, much additional matter, and upwards of 100 Unpublished Letters. Edited by H. G. BOHN. *Portrait and 8 Engravings on Steel.* In 6 vols.

Burke's Works. In 6 Volumes.
  Vol. 1. Vindication of Natural Society. On the Sublime and Beautiful, and Political Miscellanies.
  Vol. 2. French Revolution, &c.
  Vol. 3. Appeal from the New to the Old Whigs; the Catholic Claims, &c.
  Vol. 4. On the Affairs of India, and Charge against Warren Hastings.
  Vol. 5. Conclusion of Charge against Hastings; on a Regicide Peace, &c.
  Vol. 6. Miscellaneous Speeches, &c. With a General Index.

Burke's Speeches on Warren Hast-ings; and Letters. With Index. In 2 vols. (forming vols. 7 and 8 of the works).

—— **Life.** By PRIOR. New and revised Edition. *Portrait.*

Defoe's Works. Edited by Sir WALTER SCOTT. In 7 vols.

Gibbon's Roman Empire. Complete and Unabridged, with Notes; including, in addition to the Author's own, those of Guizot, Wenck, Niebuhr, Hugo, Neander, and other foreign scholars; and an elaborate Index. Edited by an English Churchman. In 7 vols.

VII.

ECCLESIASTICAL AND THEOLOGICAL LIBRARY.

5s. per Volume, excepting those marked otherwise.

Bleek (F.) An Introduction to the Old Testament, by FRIEDRICH BLEEK. Edited by JOHANN BLEEK and ADOLF KAMPHAUSEN. Translated from the German by G. H. VENABLES, under the supervision of the Rev. E. VENABLES, Canon of Lincoln. New Edition. In 2 vols.

Chillingworth's Religion of Protestants. 3s. 6d.

Eusebius' Ecclesiastical History. With Notes.

Hardwick's History of the Articles of Religion. To which is added a Series of Documents from A.D. 1536 to A.D. 1615. Together with Illustrations from Contemporary Sources. By the late C. HARDWICK Archdeacon of Ely. 5s.

Henry's (Matthew) Commentary on the Psalms. *Numerous Illustrations*

Pearson on the Creed. New Edition. With Analysis and Notes.

Philo Judæus, Works of; the contemporary of Josephus. Translated by C. D. Yonge. In 4 vols.

Socrates' Ecclesiastical History, in continuation of Eusebius. With the Notes of Valesius.

Sozomen's Ecclesiastical History, from A.D. 324–440; and the Ecclesiastical History of Philostorgius.

Theodoret and Evagrius. Ecclesiastical Histories, from A.D. 332 to A.D. 427 and from A.D. 431 to A.D. 544.

VIII.
ANTIQUARIAN LIBRARY.
5s. per Volume.

Bede's Ecclesiastical History, and the Anglo-Saxon Chronicle.

Boethius's Consolation of Philosophy. In Anglo-Saxon, with the A. S. Metres, and an English Translation, by the Rev. S. Fox.

Brand's Popular Antiquities of England, Scotland, and Ireland. By Sir HENRY ELLIS. In 3 vols.

Chronicles of the Crusaders. Richard of Devizes, Geoffrey de Vinsauf, Lord de Joinville.

Early Travels in Palestine. Willibald, Sæwulf, Benjamin of Tudela, Mandeville, La Brocquière, and Maundrell; all unabridged. Edited by THOMAS WRIGHT.

Ellis's Early English Metrical Romances. Revised by J. O. HALLIWELL.

Florence of Worcester's Chronicle, with the Two Continuations: comprising Annals of English History to the Reign of Edward I.

Gesta Romanorum. Edited by WYNNARD HOOPER, B.A. [In the Press.

Giraldus Cambrensis' Historical Works: Topography of Ireland; History of the Conquest of Ireland; Itinerary through Wales; and Description of Wales. With Index. Edited by THOS. WRIGHT.

Henry of Huntingdon's History of the English, from the Roman Invasion to Henry II.; with the Acts of King Stephen, &c.

Ingulph's Chronicle of the Abbey of Croyland, with the Continuations by Peter of Blois and other Writers. By H. T. RILEY.

Keightley's Fairy Mythology. *Frontispiece by Cruikshank.*

Lepsius's Letters from Egypt, Ethiopia, and the Peninsula of Sinai.

Mallet's Northern Antiquities. By Bishop PERCY. With an Abstract of the Eyrbiggia Saga, by Sir WALTER SCOTT. Edited by J. A. BLACKWELL.

Marco Polo's Travels. The Translation of Marsden. Edited by THOMAS WRIGHT.

Matthew Paris's Chronicle. In 5 vols.
FIRST SECTION: Roger of Wendover's Flowers of English History, from the Descent of the Saxons to A.D. 1235. Translated by Dr. GILES. In 2 vols.
SECOND SECTION: From 1235 to 1273. With Index to the entire Work. In 3 vols.

Matthew of Westminster's Flowers of History, especially such as relate to the affairs of Britain; to A.D. 1307. Translated by C. D. YONGE. In 2 vols.

Ordericus Vitalis' Ecclesiastical History of England and Normandy. Translated with Notes, by T. FORESTER, M.A. In 4 vols.

Pauli's (Dr. R.) Life of Alfred the Great. Translated from the German. To which is appended Alfred's Anglo-Saxon version of Orosius, with a literal Translation, and an Anglo-Saxon Grammar and Glossary.

Roger De Hoveden's Annals of English History; from A.D. 732 to A.D. 1201. Edited by H. T. RILEY. In 2 vols.

Six Old English Chronicles, viz.:— Asser's Life of Alfred, and the Chronicles of Ethelwerd, Gildas, Nennius, Geoffrey of Monmouth, and Richard of Cirencester.

William of Malmesbury's Chronicle of the Kings of England. Translated by SHARPE.

Yule-Tide Stories. A Collection of Scandinavian Tales and Traditions. Edited by B. THORPE.

IX.
ILLUSTRATED LIBRARY.
5s. per Volume, excepting those marked otherwise.

Allen's Battles of the British Navy. Revised and enlarged. *Numerous fine Portraits.* In 2 vols.

Andersen's Danish Legends and Fairy Tales. With many Tales not in any other edition. Translated by CAROLINE PEACHEY. 120 Wood Engravings.

Ariosto's Orlando Furioso. In English Verse. By W. S. ROSE. Twelve fine Engravings. In 2 vols.

Bechstein's Cage and Chamber Birds. Including Sweet's Warblers. Enlarged edition. *Numerous plates.*
. All other editions are abridged.
With the plates coloured. 7s. 6d.

23

Bonomi's Nineveh and its Palaces. New Edition, revised and considerably enlarged, both in matter and Plates, including a Full Account of the Assyrian Sculptures recently added to the National Collection. *Upwards of 300 Engravings.*

Butler's Hudibras. With Variorum Notes, a Biography, and a General Index. Edited by HENRY G. BOHN. *Thirty beautiful Illustrations.*

————; or, *further illustrated with 62 Outline Portraits.* In 2 vols. 10s.

Cattermole's Evenings at Haddon Hall. 24 *exquisite Engravings on Steel, from designs by himself* the Letterpress by the BARONESS DE CARABELLA.

China, Pictorial, Descriptive, and Historical, with some Account of Ava and the Burmese, Siam, and Anam. *Nearly 100 Illustrations.*

Craik's (G. L.) Pursuit of Knowledge under Difficulties, illustrated by Anecdotes and Memoirs. Revised Edition. *With numerous Portraits.*

Cruikshank's Three Courses and a Dessert. A Series of Tales, *with 50 humorous Illustrations by Cruikshank.*

Dante. Translated by I. C. WRIGHT, M.A. New Edition, carefully revised. *Portrait and 34 Illustrations on Steel, after Flaxman.*

Didron's History of Christian Art in the Middle Ages. From the French. *Upwards of 150 outline Engravings.*

Dyer (T. H.) The History of Pompeii; its Buildings and Antiquities. An account of the City, with a full description of the Remains and the Recent Excavations, and also an Itinerary for Visitors. Edited by T. H. DYER, LL.D. *Illustrated with nearly 300 Wood Engravings a large Map, and a Plan of the Forum.* A New Edition, revised and brought down to 1874. 7s. 6d.

Flaxman's Lectures on Sculpture. *Numerous Illustrations.* 6s.

Gil Blas, The Adventures of. 24 *Engravings on Steel, after Smirke, and 10 Etchings by George Cruikshank.* 6s.

Grimm's Gammer Grethel; or, Ger- man Fairy Tales and Popular Stories. Translated by EDGAR TAYLOR. *Numerous Woodcuts by Cruikshank.* 3s. 6d.

Holbein's Dance of Death, and Bible Cuts. *Upwards of 150 subjects, beautifully engraved in fac-simile,* with Introduction and Descriptions by the late FRANCIS DOUCE and Dr. T. F. DIBDIN. 2 vols. in 1. 7s. 6d.

24

Howitt's (Mary) Pictorial Calendar of the Seasons. Embodying the whole of Aiken's Calendar of Nature. *Upwards of 100 Engravings.*

———— (Mary and William) Stories of English and Foreign Life. *Twenty beautiful Engravings.*

India, Pictorial, Descriptive, and Historical, from the Earliest Times to the Present. *Upwards of 100 fine Engravings on Wood, and a Map.*

Jesse's Anecdotes of Dogs. New Edition, with large additions. *Numerous fine Woodcuts after Harvey, Bewick, and others.*

————; or, *with the addition of 34 highly-finished Steel Engravings.* 7s. 6d.

King's Natural History of Precious Stones, and of the Precious Metals. *With numerous Illustrations.* Price 6s.

———— **Natural History of Gems** or Decorative Stones. *Finely Illustrated.* 6s.

———— **Handbook of Engraved Gems.** *Finely Illustrated.* 6s.

Kitto's Scripture Lands and Biblical Atlas. 24 *Maps, beautifully engraved on Steel,* with a Consulting Index.

————; *with the maps coloured,* 7s. 6d.

Krummacher's Parables. Translated from the German. *Forty Illustrations by Clayton, engraved by Dalziel.*

Lindsay's (Lord) Letters on Egypt, Edom, and the Holy Land. New Edition, enlarged. *Thirty-six beautiful Engravings, and 2 Maps.*

Lodge's Portraits of Illustrious Per- sonages of Great Britain, with Memoirs. *Two Hundred and Forty Portraits, engraved on Steel.* 8 vols.

Longfellow's Poetical Works. *Twenty-four page Engravings, by Birket Foster and others, and a Portrait.*

————; or, *without illustrations,* 3s. 6d.

———— **Prose Works,** complete. 16 *page Engravings by Birket Foster, &c.*

Loudon's (Mrs.) Entertaining Natur- alist. Revised by W. S. DALLAS, F.L.S. *With nearly 500 Woodcuts.*

Marryat's Masterman Ready; or, The Wreck of the Pacific. 93 *Woodcuts.* 3s. 6d.

———— **Poor Jack.** *With 16 Illustrations, after Designs by C. Stanfield, R.A.* 3s. 6d.

———— **Mission; or, Scenes in Af-** rica. (Written for Young People.) *Illustrated by Gilbert and Dalziel.* 3s. 6d.

Marryat's Pirate; and Three Cutters
New Edition, with a Memoir of the
Author. *With 8 Steel Engravings, from
Drawings by C. Stanfield, R.A.* 3s. 6d.

—— **Privateers-Man One Hun-**
dred Years Ago. *Eight Engravings on
Steel, after Stothard.* 3s. 6d.

—— **Settlers in Canada.** New
Edition. *Ten fine Engravings by Gilbert
and Dalziel.* 3s. 6d.

Maxwell's Victories of Wellington
and the British Armies. *Steel Engravings.*

Michael Angelo and Raphael, their
Lives and Works. By DUPPA and QUA-
TREMÈRE DE QUINCY. *With 13 Engravings
on Steel.*

Miller's History of the Anglo-Sax-
ons. Written in a popular style, on the
basis of Sharon Turner. *Portrait of
Alfred, Map of Saxon Britain, and 12
elaborate Engravings on Steel.*

Milton's Poetical Works. With a
Memoir by JAMES MONTGOMERY, TODD'S
Verbal Index to all the Poems, and Ex-
planatory Notes. *With 120 Engravings
by Thompson and others, from Drawings
by W. Harvey.* 2 vols.
Vol. 1. Paradise Lost, complete, with
Memoir, Notes, and Index.
Vol. 2. Paradise Regained, and other
Poems, with Verbal Index to all the
Poems.

Mudie's British Birds. Revised by
W. C. L. MARTIN *Fifty-two Figures and
7 Plates of Eggs* In 2 vols.

—— ; or, *with the plates coloured,*
7s. 6d. per vol.

Naval and Military Heroes of Great
Britain; or, Calendar of Victory. Being a
Record of British Valour and Conquest
by Sea and Land, on every day in the
year, from the time of William the
Conqueror to the Battle of Inkermann.
By Major JOHNS, R.M., and Lieutenant
P. H. NICOLAS, R.M. *Twenty-four Por-
traits.* 6s.

Nicolini's History of the Jesuits:
their Origin, Progress, Doctrines, and De
signs. *Fine Portraits of Loyola, Lainès
Xavier, Borgia, Acquaviva, Père la Chaise,
and Pope Ganganelli.*

Petrarch's Sonnets, and other Poems.
Translated into English Verse. By various
hands With a Life of the Poet, by
THOMAS CAMPBELL. *With 16 Engravings.*

Pickering's History of the Races of
Man, with an Analytical Synopsis of the
Natural History of Man. By Dr. HALL.
Illustrated by numerous Portraits.

—— ; or, *with the plates colou ed* 7s.6d.
. An excellent Edition of a work ori-
ginally published at 3l. 3s. by the
American Government.

Pictorial Handbook of Modern Geo-
graphy, on a Popular Plan. 3s. 6d. *Illus
trated by* 150 *Engravings and* 51 *Maps.* 6s.

—— ; or, *with the maps coloured*,
7s. 6d.

Pope's Poetical Works. Edited by
ROBERT CARRUTHERS. *Numerous Engravings.* 2 vols.

—— **Homer's Iliad.** With Introduction and Notes by J. S. WATSON, M.A.
*Illustrated by the entire Series of Flax-
man's Designs, beautifully engraved by
Moses (in the full 8vo. size).*

—— **Homer's Odyssey, Hymns,**
&c., by other translators, including Chapman, and Introduction and Notes by J. S.
WATSON, M.A. *Flaxman's Designs beautifully engraved by Moses.*

—— **Life.** Including many of his
Letters. By ROBERT CARRUTHERS. New
Edition, revised and enlarged. *Illustrations.
The preceding 5 vols. make a complete
and elegant edition of Pope's Poetical
Works and Translations for 25s.*

Pottery and Porcelain, and other Ob-
jects of Vertu (a Guide to the Knowledge
of). To which is added an Engraved List
of Marks and Monograms. By HENRY
G. BOHN. *Numerous Engravings.*

—— ; or, *coloured.* 10s. 6d.

Prout's (Father) Reliques. New
Edition, revised and largely augmented.
Twenty-one spirited Etchings by Maclise.
Two volumes in one. 7s. 6d.

Recreations in Shooting. By
"CRAVEN." New Edition, revised and
enlarged. 62 *Engravings on Wood, after
Harvey, and* 9 *Engravings on Steel, chiefly
after A. Cooper, R.A.*

Redding's History and Descriptions
of Wines. Ancient and Modern. *Twenty
beautiful Woodcuts.*

Rennie's Insect Architecture. New
Edition. Revised by the Rev. J. G.
WOOD, M.A.

Robinson Crusoe. With Illustrations
by STOTHARD and HARVEY. *Twelve beautiful Engravings on Steel. and* 74 *on Wood.*

—— ; or, *without the Steel illustrations,* 3s. 6d.

Rome in the Nineteenth Century.
New Edition Revised by the Author.
Illustrated by 34 *Steel Engravings.*
2 vols.

Sharpe's History of Egypt, from the
Earliest Times till the Conquest by the
Arabs, A.D. 640. By SAMUEL SHARPE.
With 2 Maps and upwards of 400 Illus-
trative Woodcuts. Sixth and Cheaper
Edition. 2 vols.

Southey's Life of Nelson. With
Additional Notes. *Illustrated with* 64
Engravings.

25

Starling's (Miss) Noble Deeds of Women; or, Examples of Female Courage, Fortitude, and Virtue. *Fourteen Illustrations.*

Stuart and Revett's Antiquities of Athens, and other Monuments of Greece *Illustrated in 71 Steel Plates, and numerous Woodcuts.*

Tales of the Genii; or, the Delightful Lessons of Horam. *Numerous Woodcuts, and 8 Steel Engravings, after Stothard.*

Tasso's Jerusalem Delivered. Translated into English Spenserian Verse, with a Life of the Author. By J. H. WIFFEN. *Eight Engravings on Steel, and 24 on Wood, by Thurston.*

Walker's Manly Exercises. Containing Skating, Riding, Driving, Hunting, Shooting, Sailing, Rowing, Swimming, &c. New Edition, revised by "CRAVEN." *Forty-four Steel Plates, and numerous Woodcuts.*

Walton's Complete Angler. Edited by EDWARD JESSE, Esq. *Upwards of 203 Engravings.*

——; or, *with 26 additional page Illustrations on Steel,* 7s. 6d.

Wellington, Life of. From the materials of Maxwell. *Eighteen Engravings.*

White's Natural History of Selborne. With Notes by Sir WILLIAM JARDINE and EDWARD JESSE, Esq. *Illustrated by 40 Engravings.*

——; or, *with the plates coloured*, 7s. 6d.

Young, The, Lady's Book. A Manual of Elegant Recreations, Arts, Sciences, and Accomplishments; including Geology, Mineralogy, Conchology, Botany, Entomology, Ornithology, Costume, Embroidery, the Escritoire, Archery, Riding, Music (instrumental and vocal), Dancing, Exercises, Painting, Photography, &c., &c. Edited by distinguished Professors. *Twelve Hundred Woodcut Illustrations, and several Engravings on Steel.* 7s. 6d.

——; or, *cloth gilt, gilt edges,* 9s.

Y.

CLASSICAL LIBRARY.

5s. per Volume, excepting those marked otherwise.

Æschylus. Literally Translated into English Prose by an Oxonian. 3s. 6d.

——, **Appendix to.** Containing the New Readings given in Hermann's posthumous Edition of Æschylus. By GEORGE BURGES, M.A. 3s. 6d.

Ammianus Marcellinus. History of Rome from Constantius to Valens. Translated by C. D. YONGE, B.A. Dble. vol. 7s. 6d.

Antoninus. The Thoughts of the Emperor Marcus Aurelius. Translated by GEO. LONG, M.A. 3s. 6d.

Apuleius, the Golden Ass; Death of Socrates; Florida; and Discourse on Magic. To which is added a Metrical Version of Cupid and Psyche; and Mrs. Tighe's Psyche. *Frontispiece.*

Aristophanes' Comedies. Literally Translated, with Notes and Extracts from Frere's and other Metrical Versions, by W. J. HICKIE. 2 vols.
   Vol. 1. Acharnians, Knights, Clouds, Wasps, Peace, and Birds.
   Vol. 2. Lysistrata, Thesmophoriazusæ, Frogs, Ecclesiazusæ, and Plutus.

Aristotle's Ethics. Literally Translated by Archdeacon BROWNE, late Classical Professor of King's College.

Aristotle's Politics and Economics. Translated by E. WALFORD, M.A.

—— **Metaphysics.** Literally Translated, with Notes, Analysis, Examination Questions, and Index, by the Rev. JOHN H. M'MAHON, M.A., and Gold Medallist in Metaphysics, T.C.D.

—— **History of Animals.** In Ten Books. Translated, with Notes and Index, by RICHARD CRESSWELL, M.A.

—— **Organon; or, Logical Treatises.** With Notes, &c. By O. F. OWEN, M.A. 2 vols. 3s. 6d. each.

—— **Rhetoric and Poetics.** Literally Translated, with Examination Questions and Notes, by an Oxonian.

Athenæus. The Deipnosophists; or, the Banquet of the Learned. Translated by C. D. YONGE, B.A. 3 vols.

Cæsar. Complete, with the Alexandrian, African, and Spanish Wars. Literally Translated, with Notes.

Catullus, Tibullus, and the Vigil of Venus. A Literal Prose Translation. To which are added Metrical Versions by LAMB, GRAINGER, and others. *Frontispiece.*

Cicero's Orations. Literally Translated by C. D. Yonge, B.A. In 4 vols.

Vol. 1. Contains the Orations against Verres, &c. *Portrait.*

Vol. 2. Catiline, Archias, Agrarian Law, Rabirius, Murena, Sylla, &c.

Vol. 3. Orations for his House, Plancius, Sextius, Coelius, Milo, Ligarius, &c.

Vol. 4. Miscellaneous Orations, and Rhetorical Works; with General Index to the four volumes.

———— **on the Nature of the Gods,** Divination, Fate, Laws, a Republic, &c. Translated by C. D. Yonge, B.A., and F. Barham.

———— **Academics, De Finibus, and** Tusculan Questions. By C. D. Yonge, B.A. With Sketch of the Greek Philosophy.

———— **Offices, Old Age, Friendship,** Scipio's Dream, Paradoxes, &c. Literally Translated, by R. Edmonds. 3s. 6d.

———— **on Oratory and Orators.** By J. S. Watson, M.A.

Demosthenes' Orations. Translated, with Notes, by C. Rann Kennedy. In 5 volumes.

Vol. 1. The Olynthiac, Philippic, and other Public Orations. 3s. 6d.

Vol. 2. On the Crown and on the Embassy.

Vol. 3. Against Leptines, Midias, Androtion, and Aristocrates.

Vol. 4. Private and other Orations.

Vol. 5. Miscellaneous Orations.

Dictionary of Latin Quotations. Including Proverbs, Maxims, Mottoes, Law Terms, and Phrases; and a Collection of above 500 Greek Quotations. With all the quantities marked, & English Translations.

————, **with Index Verborum.** 6s. Index Verborum only. 1s.

Diogenes Laertius. Lives and Opinions of the Ancient Philosophers. Translated, with Notes, by C. D. Yonge.

Epictetus. Discourses with Encheiridion and Fragments. Translated with Notes, by George Long, M.A.

Euripides. Literally Translated. 2 vols.

Vol. 1. Hecuba, Orestes, Medea, Hippolytus, Alcestis, Bacchae, Heraclidae, Iphigenia in Aulide, and Iphigenia in Tauris.

Vol. 2. Hercules Furens, Troades, Ion, Andromache, Suppliants, Helen, Electra, Cyclops, Rhesus.

Greek Anthology. Literally Translated. With Metrical Versions by various Authors.

———— **Romances of Heliodorus.** Longus, and Achilles Tatius.

Herodotus. A New and Literal Translation, by Henry Cary, M.A., of Worcester College, Oxford.

Hesiod, Callimachus, and Theognis. Literally Translated, with Notes, by J. Banks, M.A.

Homer's Iliad. Literally Translated,

———— **Odyssey, Hymns, &c.** Literally Translated.

Horace. Literally Translated, by Smart. Carefully revised by an Oxonian. 3s. 6d.

Justin, Cornelius Nepos, and Eutropius. Literally Translated, with Notes and Index, by J. S. Watson, M.A.

Juvenal, Persius, Sulpicia, and Lucilius. By L. Evans, M.A. With the Metrical Version by Gifford. *Frontispiece.*

Livy. A new and Literal Translation. By Dr. Spillan and others. In 4 vols.

Vol. 1. Contains Books 1—8.

Vol. 2. Books 9—26.

Vol. 3. Books 27—36.

Vol. 4. Books 37 to the end; and Index.

Lucan's Pharsalia. Translated, with Notes, by H. T. Riley.

Lucretius. Literally Translated, with Notes, by the Rev. J. S. Watson, M.A. And the Metrical Version by J. M. Good.

Martial's Epigrams, complete. Literally Translated. Each accompanied by one or more Verse Translations selected from the Works of English Poets, and other sources. With a copious Index. Double volume (660 pages). 7s. 6d.

Ovid's Works, complete. Literally Translated. 3 vols.

Vol. 1. Fasti, Tristia, Epistles, &c.

Vol. 2. Metamorphoses.

Vol. 3. Heroides, Art of Love, &c.

Pindar. Literally Translated, by Dawson W. Turner, and the Metrical Version by Abraham Moore.

Plato's Works. Translated by the Rev. H. Cary and others. In 6 vols.

Vol. 1. The Apology of Socrates, Crito Phaedo, Gorgias, Protagoras, Phaedrus, Theaetetus, Euthyphron, Lysis.

Vol. 2. The Republic, Timaeus, & Critias.

Vol. 3. Meno, Euthydemus, The Sophist, Statesman, Cratylus, Parmenides, and the Banquet.

Vol. 4. Philebus, Charmides, Laches, The Two Alcibiades, and Ten other Dialogues.

Vol. 5. The Laws.

Vol. 6. The Doubtful Works. With General Index.

Plato's Dialogues, an Analysis and Index to. With References to the Translation in Bohn's Classical Library. By Dr. DAY.

Plautus's Comedies. Literally Translated, with Notes, by H. T. RILEY, B.A. In 2 vols.

Pliny's Natural History. Translated, with Copious Notes, by the late JOHN BOSTOCK, M.D., F.R.S., and H. T. RILEY, B.A. In 6 vols.

Propertius, Petronius, and Johannes Secundus. Literally Translated, and accompanied by Poetical Versions, from various sources.

Quintilian's Institutes of Oratory. Literally Translated. with Notes, &c., by J. S. WATSON, M.A. In 2 vols.

Sallust, Florus, and Velleius Paterculus. With Copious Notes, Biographical Notices, and Index, by J. S. WATSON.

Sophocles. The Oxford Translation revised.

Standard Library Atlas of Classical Geography. *Twenty-two large coloured Maps according to the latest authorities.* With a complete Index (accentuated), giving the latitude and longitude of every place named in the Maps. Imp. 8vo. 7s. 6d.

Strabo's Geography. Translated, with Copious Notes, by W. FALCONER, M.A., and H. C. HAMILTON, Esq. With Index, giving the Ancient and Modern Names. In 3 vols.

Suetonius' Lives of the Twelve Cæsars, and other Works. Thomson's Translation, revised, with Notes, by T. FORESTER.

Tacitus. Literally Translated, with Notes. In 2 vols.
 Vol. 1. The Annals.
 Vol. 2. The History, Germania, Agricola, &c. With Index.

Terence and Phædrus. By H. T. RILEY, B.A.

Theocritus, Bion, Moschus, and Tyrtæus. By J. BANKS, M.A. With the Metrical Versions of Chapman.

Thucydides. Literally Translated by Rev. H. DALE. In 2 vols. 3s. 6d. each.

Virgil. Literally Translated by DAVIDSON. New Edition, carefully revised. 3s. 6d.

Xenophon's Works. In 3 Vols.
 Vol. 1. The Anabasis and Memorabilia. Translated, with Notes, by J. S. WATSON, M.A. And a Geographical Commentary, by W. F. AINSWORTH, F.S.A., F.R.G.S., &c.
 Vol. 2. Cyropædia and Hellenics. By J. S. WATSON, M.A., and the Rev. H. DALE.
 Vol. 3. The Minor Works. By J. S. WATSON, M.A.

XI.

SCIENTIFIC LIBRARY.

5s. per Volume, excepting those marked otherwise.

Agassiz and Gould's Comparative Physiology. Enlarged by Dr. WRIGHT. *Upwards of 400 Engravings.*

Bacon's Novum Organum and Advancement of Learning. Complete, with Notes, by J. DEVEY. M.A.

Bolley's Manual of Technical Analysis. A Guide for the Testing of Natural and Artificial Substances. By B. H. PAUL. 100 *Wood Engravings.*

BRIDGEWATER TREATISES. —
—— Bell on the Hand Its Mechanism and Vital Endowments as evincing Design. *Seventh Edition Revised*
—— Kirby on the History, Habits, and Instincts of Animals. Edited, with Notes, by T. RYMER JONES. *Numerous Engravings, many of which are additional.* In 2 vols.

BRIDGEWATER TREATISES—*cont.*
—— Kidd on the Adaptation of External Nature to the Physical Condition of Man. 3s. 6d.
—— Whewell's Astronomy and General Physics, considered with reference to Natural Theology. 3s. 6d.
—— Chalmers on the Adaptation of External Nature to the Moral and Intellectual Constitution of Man.
—— Prout's Treatise on Chemistry, Meteorology, and Digestion. Edited by Dr. J. W. GRIFFITH.
—— Buckland's Geology and Mineralogy. 2 vols. 15s.
—— Roget's Animal and Vegetable Physiology. *Illustrated.* In 2 vols. 6s. each.

Carpenter's (Dr. W. B.) Zoology. A Systematic View of the Structure, Habits, Instincts, and Uses, of the principal Families of the Animal Kingdom, and of the chief forms of Fossil Remains. Revised by W. S. DALLAS, F.L.S. *Illustrated with many hundred Wood Engravings.* In 2 vols, 6s. each.

———— **Mechanical Philosophy, Astronomy,** and Horology. A Popular Exposition. 183 *Illustrations.*

———— **Vegetable Physiology and** Systematic Botany. A complete Introduction to the Knowledge of Plants. Revised, under arrangement with the Author, by E. LANKESTER, M.D., &c. *Several hundred Illustrations on Wood.* 6s.

———— **Animal Physiology.** In part re-written by the Author. *Upwards of* 300 *capital Illustrations.* 6s.

Chevreul on Colour. Containing the Principles of Harmony and Contrast of Colours, and their application to the Arts. Translated from the French by CHARLES MARTEL. Only complete Edition. *Several Plates.* Or, with an additional series of 16 Plates in Colours. 7s. 6d.

Ennemoser's History of Magic. Translated by WILLIAM HOWITT. With an Appendix of the most remarkable and best authenticated Stories of Apparitions Dreams, Table-Turning, and Spirit-Rapping, &c. In 2 vols.

Hogg's (Jabez) Elements of Experimental and Natural Philosophy. Containing Mechanics, Pneumatics, Hydrostatics, Hydraulics, Acoustics, Optics, Caloric, Electricity, Voltaism, and Magnetism. New Edition, enlarged. *Upwards of* 400 *Woodcuts.*

Hind's Introduction to Astronomy. With a Vocabulary, containing an Explanation of all the Terms in present use New Edition, enlarged. *Numerous Engravings.* 3s. 6d.

Humboldt's Cosmos; or, Sketch of a Physical Description of the Universe. Translated by E. C. OTTÉ and W. S. DALLAS, F.L.S. *Fine Portrait.* In five vols. 3s. 6d. each; excepting Vol. V., 5s
. In this edition the notes are placed beneath the text, Humboldt's analytical Summaries and the passages hitherto suppressed are included, and new and comprehensive Indices are added.

———— **Travels in America.** In 3 vols.

———— **Views of Nature;** or, Contemplations of the Sublime Phenomena of Creation. Translated by E. C. OTTÉ and H. G. BOHN. With a complete Index.

Hunt's (Robert) Poetry of Science; or, Studies of the Physical Phenomena of Nature. By Professor HUNT. New Edition, enlarged.

Joyce's Scientific Dialogues. Completed to the present state of Knowledge, by Dr. GRIFFITH. *Numerous Woodcuts.*

———— **Introduction to the Arts and** Sciences. With Examination Questions. 3s. 6d.

Knight's (Chas.) Knowledge is Power. A Popular Manual of Political Economy.

Lectures on Painting. By the Royal Academicians. With Introductory Essay, and Notes by R. WORNUM, Esq. *Portraits.*

Lawrence's Lectures on Comparative Anatomy, Physiology, Zoology, and the Natural History of Man. *Illustrated.*

Lilly's Introduction to Astrology. With numerous Emendations, by ZADKIEL.

Mantell's (Dr.) Geological Excursions through the Isle of Wight and Dorsetshire. New Edition, by T. RUPERT JONES, Esq. *Numerous beautifully executed Woodcuts, and a Geological Map.*

———— **Medals of Creation;** or, First Lessons in Geology and the Study of Organic Remains; including Geological Excursions. New Edition, revised. *Coloured Plates, and several hundred beautiful Woodcuts.* In 2 vols., 7s. 6d. each.

———— **Petrifactions** and their Teachings. An Illustrated Handbook to the Organic Remains in the British Museum. *Numerous Engravings.* 8s.

———— **Wonders of Geology;** or, a Familiar Exposition of Geological Phenomena. New Edition, augmented by T. RUPERT JONES, F.G.S. *Coloured Geological Map of England, Plates, and nearly 200 beautiful Woodcuts.* In 2 vols., 7s. 6d. each.

Morphy's Games of Chess. Being the Matches and best Games played by the American Champion, with Explanatory and Analytical Notes, by J. LÖWENTHAL. *Portrait* and Memoir.

It contains by far the largest collection of games played by Mr. Morphy extant in any form, and has received his endorsement and co-operation.

Richardson's Geology, including Mineralogy and Palæontology. Revised and enlarged, by Dr. T. WRIGHT. *Upwards of* 400 *Illustrations.*

Schouw's Earth, Plants, and Man; and Kobell's Sketches from the Mineral Kingdom. Translated by A. HENFREY, F.R.S. *Coloured Map of the Geography of Plants.*

Smith's (Pye) Geology and Scripture; or, The Relation between the Holy Scriptures and Geological Science.

Stanley's Classified Synopsis of the Principal Painters of the Dutch and Flemish Schools.

Staunton's Chess-player's Handbook. *Numerous Diagrams.*

———— Chess Praxis. A Supplement to the Chess-player's Handbook. Containing all the most important modern improvements in the Openings, illustrated by actual Games; a revised Code of Chess Laws; and a Selection of Mr. Morphy's Games in England and France. 6s.

———— Chess-player's Companion. Comprising a new Treatise on Odds, Collection of Match Games, and a Selection of Original Problems.

Staunton's Chess Tournament of 1851. *Numerous Illustrations.*

Stockhardt's Principles of Chemistry, exemplified in a series of simple experiments. Based upon the German work of Professor STOCKHARDT, and Edited by C. W. HEATON, Professor of Chemistry at Charing Cross Hospital. *Upwards of 270 Illustrations.*

Ure's (Dr. A.) Cotton Manufacture of Great Britain, systematically investigated; with an introductory view of its comparative state in Foreign Countries. New Edition, revised and completed to the present time, by P. L. SIMMONDS. *One hundred and fifty Illustrations.* In 2 vols.

———— Philosophy of Manufactures; or, An Exposition of the Factory System of Great Britain. Continued by P. L. SIMMONDS. 7s. 6d.

XII.
REFERENCE LIBRARY.

Blair's Chronological Tables, Revised and Enlarged. Comprehending the Chronology and History of the World, from the earliest times. By J. WILLOUGHBY ROSSE. Double Volume. 10s.; or, half bound. 10s. 6d.

Clark's (Hugh) Introduction to Heraldry. *With nearly 1000 Illustrations.* 18th *Edition.* Revised and enlarged by J. R. PLANCHÉ, Rouge Croix. 5s. Or, with all the Illustrations coloured. 15s.

Chronicles of the Tombs. A Collection of Remarkable Epitaphs. By T. J. PETTIGREW, F.R.S., F.S.A. 5s.

Handbook of Domestic Medicine. Popularly arranged. By Dr. HENRY DAVIES. 700 pages. With complete Index. 5s.

———— Games. By various Amateurs and Professors. Comprising treatises on all the principal Games of chance, skill, and manual dexterity. In all, above 40 games (the Whist, Draughts, and Billiards being especially comprehensive). Edited by H. G. BOHN. *Illustrated by numerous Diagrams.* 5s.

———— Proverbs. Comprising all Ray's English Proverbs, with additions; his Foreign Proverbs; and an Alphabetical Index. 5s.

Hofland's British Angler's Manual. Improved and enlarged, by EDWARD JESSE, Esq. *Illustrated with 60 Engravings.* 7s. 6d.

Humphrey's Coin Collector's Manual. A popular Introduction to the Study of Coins. *Highly finished Engravings.* In 2 vols. 10s.

Index of Dates. Comprehending the principal Facts in the Chronology and History of the World, from the earliest to the present time, alphabetically arranged. By J. W. ROSSE. Double volume, 10s.; or, half-bound, 10s. 6d.

Lowndes' Bibliographer's Manual of English Literature. New Edition, enlarged, by H. G. BOHN. Parts I. to X. (A to Z). 3s. 6d. each. Part XI. (the Appendix Volume). 5s. Or the 11 parts in 4 vols. half morocco, 2l. 2s.

Polyglot of Foreign Proverbs. With English Translations, and a General Index bringing the whole into parallels, by H. G. BOHN. 5s.

Political Cyclopædia. In 4 vols. 3s. 6d. each.

———— Also in 2 vols. bound. 15s.

Smith's (Archdeacon) Complete Collection of Synonyms and Antonyms. 5s.

The Epigrammatists. Selections from the Epigrammatic Literature of Ancient, Mediæval, and Modern Times. With Notes, Observations, Illustrations, and an Introduction. By the Rev. HENRY PHILIP DODD, M.A., of Pembroke College, Oxford. Second Edition, revised and considerably enlarged; containing many new Epigrams, principally of an amusing character. 6s.

Wheeler's (W. A., M.A.) Dictionary of Names of Fictitious Persons and Places. 5s.

Wright's (T.) Dictionary of Obsolete and Provincial English. In 2 vols. 5s. each; or half-bound in 1 vol., 10s. 6d.

XIII.

NOVELISTS' LIBRARY.

Manzoni (Alessandro) **The Betrothed** (I promessi Sposi). The only complete English translation. With numerous Woodcuts. **5s.**

Uncle Tom's Cabin. With Introductory Remarks by the Rev. J. SHERMAN. *Printed in a large clear type. Illustrations.* 3s. 6d.

Tom Jones; the History of a Foundling. By HENRY FIELDING. With *Illustrations by George Cruikshank.* In 2 vols. **7s.**

Joseph Andrews. By HENRY FIELDING. With *Illustrations by George Cruikshank.* In 1 vol. 3s. 6d.

Amelia. By HENRY FIELDING. With Cruikshank's Illustrations. In 1 vol. 5s.

XIV.

ARTIST'S LIBRARY.

Leonardo da Vinci's Treatise on Painting. *New Edition, revised.*
[*In the Press.*
Planché's History of British Costume. Third Edition. *With numerous Woodcuts.* 5s.

The Anatomy and Philosophy of Expression as connected with the Fine Arts. By Sir CHARLES BELL, K.H. *Seventh Edition, revised. With numerous Woodcuts and 20 Plates.* 5s.

XV.

CHEAP SERIES.

Boswell's Life of Johnson, and Johnsoniana. Including his Tour to the Hebrides, Tour in Wales, &c. Edited, with large additions and Notes, by the Right Hon. JOHN WILSON CROKER. The second and most complete Copyright Edition, rearranged and revised according to the suggestions of Lord Macaulay, by the late JOHN WRIGHT, Esq., with further additions by Mr. CROKER. *Upwards of 50 fine Engravings on Steel.* In 5 vols. cloth. 20s.

Carpenter's (Dr. W. B.) Physiology of Temperance and Total Abstinence. 1s.

Dibdin's Sea Songs (Admiralty Edition). *Illustrations by Cruikshank.* 2s. 6d.

Franklin's (Benjamin) Genuine Autobiography. From the Original Manuscript. By JARED SPARKS. 1s.

Hawthorne's (Nathaniel) Twice Told Tales. First and Second Series. 2 vols in one. 2s. **Snow Image** and other Tales. 1s. **Scarlet Letter.** 1s. 6d. **House with the Seven Gables.** A Romance. 1s. 6d.

Hazlitt's Table Talk. Parts 1, 2, and 3. 1s. each. **Plain Speaker.** Parts 1, 2, and 3. 1s. 6d. each. **Lectures on the English Comic Writers.** 1s. 6d. Lectures on the English Poets. 1s. 6d. Lectures on the Literature of the Age of Elizabeth. 1s. 6d. **Lectures on the Characters of Shakespeare's Plays.** 1s. 6d.

Emerson's Twenty Essays. 1s. 6d. **English Characteristics.** 1s. **Orations and Lectures.** 1s. **Representative Men.** Complete. 1s. 6d.

Irving's (Washington) Life of Mohammed. *Portrait.* 1s. 6d. **Successors of Mohammed.** 1s. 6d. **Life of Goldsmith.** 1s. 6d. **Sketch Book.** 1s. 6d. **Tales of a Traveller.** 1s. 6d. **Tour on the Prairies.** 1s. **Conquests of Granada and Spain.** 2 vols. 1s. 6d. each. **Life of Columbus.** 2 vols. 1s. 6d. each. **Companions of Columbus.** 1s. 6d. **Adventures of Captain Bonneville.** 1s. 6d. **Knickerbocker's New York.** 1s. 6d. **Tales of the Alhambra.** 1s. 6d. **Conquest of Florida.** 1s. 6d. **Abbotsford and Newstead.** 1s. **Salmagundi.** 1s. 6d. **Bracebridge Hall.** 1s. 6d. **Astoria.** 2s. **Wolfert's Roost, and other Tales.** 1s.; fine paper, 1s. 6d. **Life of Washington.** Authorized Edition (uniform with the Works). *Fine Portrait, &c.* 5 parts, with General Index. 2s. 6d. each. **Life and Letters.** By his Nephew, PIERRE E. IRVING. *Portrait.* In 4 parts. 2s. each.

₊ For Washington Irving's Collected Works, see STANDARD LIBRARY.

Lamb's (Charles) Essays of Elia. 1s. Last Essays of Elia. 1s. **Eliana,** with Biographical Sketch. 1s.

31

www.ingramcontent.com/pod-product-compliance
Lightning Source LLC
Chambersburg PA
CBHW052337110726
47901CB00005B/1262